Morty Spence 1999

ECLIPSE OF THE SUN

A Novel

MICHAEL D. O'BRIEN

Eclipse of the Sun

A Novel

For the end of the world was long ago—
And all we who dwell today
As children of some second birth,
Like strange people left on earth
After a judgement day.

G. K. CHESTERTON, *The Ballad of the White Horse*

IGNATIUS PRESS   SAN FRANCISCO

Cover art by Michael D. O'Brien
Arrow and Nick

Cover design by Roxanne Mei Lum

© 1998 Ignatius Press, San Francisco
All rights reserved
ISBN 0–89870–687–4 (HB)
Library of Congress catalogue number 97–76852
Printed in the United States of America ∞

Contents

Preface

The shape of things to come is uncertain. Yet many elements of the totalitarian state dramatized in *Eclipse of the Sun* are already with us and growing. This novel is an imaginative reflection on what might come to pass if we do not recognize the gravity of social and spiritual disorders at work in the Western world and respond accordingly.

I have situated the events of the story in British Columbia, not because I believe that it is especially vulnerable to totalitarian developments, but because I lived there for fifteen years and know the texture of its geography and people better than those of other places. The characters depicted here are not intentionally based on real individuals; any similarity to persons living or dead is coincidental. The town of Fort George is fictional, as are Jackfish Reserve and Swiftcreek. The other communities in the novel are real, and I hope that the people who live in these places will forgive my "artistic license" in adapting their hometowns to the needs of the plot. I am especially grateful to the Catholic people and the archbishop of Vancouver for their forbearance, as I have "borrowed" their archdiocese in the interests of giving to a highly speculative piece of fiction a sense of realism, character, and place.

This novel is dedicated to my family, to Sheila and our children: John, Joseph, Mary-Theresa, Elizabeth, Benjamin, and Angela.

My name is Aaron, though in the beginning I was called Arrow. My father's face I cannot remember, for I was taken far away from him when I was born. Once he sent a word of promise that he would find me, that he would know me and love me as a father should love his child. He did not return from a last journey into the shadow, and thus was he unable to keep his word, though he held that word in his heart, even as his flesh passed into death. He was but one of the nameless who disappeared during that time.

Many people were lost, and many stories will not be told. How can I speak of them? How can I break my long silence? Silence is a form of respect for the wisdom of Time, for it too is a servant of God. If I were like the old ones who gather around the fire on summer evenings when the stars are sharp in the sky and hearts are full of ache for the missing, I would tell my story. But I am not an elder, scorched and twisted, gathering a tribe with my eloquent gestures and art of tongue to hearken back to an evil era. Memory is not so sweet to me; the making of the world afresh is my proper aim. I watch them, these burned ones, and I see that they still carry in their eyes the shadows of the vanished days. Their hands are raised, and eye-whites loom large out of the night. They frighten the children with warnings, for they are the guardians; they have seen too much; they tell us of what once was and may be again if we forget.

I know they are right, of course. I too was a child when the darkness took a form that tested everything. I too was changed by it. But now I turn toward the balm of the cooling earth, the return of the seasons, and a blessed unremembering.

Even so, I am growing old. Soon, my small memories will be submerged. Is there a word or two that I can give to those who are being born? Is there a promise I can leave to those who have not yet come into being?

The little ones pull at my fingers and stroke my hair. They kiss my face until I admit defeat.

"Tell us a story, Aaron!" they cry. "Tell us a story of how it was!"

I am not very good at this. But I shall try. It is only a small thing, children. Be still, be still, and I shall tell you a little story about the end of the world.

I

Flight

I will try to reconstruct it from the fragments Father Andrei told me and from other details I learned later.

In my mind I see an old man, older than I am now. I was a child when I first met him, and still a child when he died, and so my perception of him is of a life completely rounded with age. I see him standing on a hill of snow, so white that the eyes are dazzled. His white, white hair juts from under a ragged gray tuque. He watches my father go away into the forest, pushing a sled on which lies a dying boy—someone I did not know.

It is a strange feeling to think that my own father was more a father to a stranger than to me. He died attempting to save this other one's life. He had little or no part in mine.

Yet he sent Father Andrei to me.

I did not see this scene with my own eyes. It was told to me. It was a story. But my mind has replayed it as a memory, remembered a thousand times over. It occupies a place within me that should have been inhabited by a man. I see it. Yes, as if I were there that day.

There he stood on the hill of snow watching my father go into the shadow. He gazed toward the northeast, his eyes closed, his lips moving occasionally, a pillar, a staff, an old priest in a patched felt greatcoat. All day long he was in and out of the cabin, mostly out, watching the forest. When the sun had moved across the mountain faces and the valley had slipped into the blue shadows of the winter afternoon, he turned toward the window where my great-grandfather Thaddaeus Tobac had lit a kerosene lantern. The light threw a cruciform onto the violet snow, and Andrei looked at it for a time.

"Father," said Thaddaeus from the door, "Tanny said we should wait six, maybe seven, hours. He's pretty bad late. It's eight hours he didn't come."

"We must presume that he has been captured", the priest replied.

"I think so, too", said Thaddaeus, choking on his words. "If it's true, we're in lotsa danger here. We gotta go. Just like we promised him."

"Where are the children?"

"The boy's makin' tea, and the girl's readin'."

"Please ask them to pack everything that will be needed for the journey."

The priest waited outside, watching the sun drop behind the mountains, and then he went in. He found the two children stuffing their meager belongings into knapsacks. Thaddaeus was packing a cardboard box. Sleeping bags and dried food were stacked by the door.

Father Andrei put his hands on the children's shoulders.

"Your father may be delayed for a time. It will be safer if you go over the mountains to the valleys in the west. There you can live, and the government will soon forget about you. Your father knows where to find you."

Thaddaeus caught Andrei's eye. "I told Tanny the way to find my cabin over in the Cariboo country. He got a map in his head."

The children forced a laugh out of their worried faces.

"Children, pray for your father", Andrei said. "And pray for me, please. I am going in another direction."

"Aren't you coming with us?" they cried.

"You will be safe with our good Thaddaeus." He smiled and patted their shoulders. "But I have another task. I made a promise to your father. I must keep it."

"What is it? Where are you going?"

"I am going to find your brother."

"Our brother?"

They barely remembered their small brother, the baby who left with their mother, years ago—most of their short lives ago.

"You mean Arrow?" the boy asked.

The priest nodded.

"And Mum?" whispered the girl.

He nodded again.

Within moments they had loaded the long wicker dogsled. Thaddaeus no longer owned dogs, but the push-pull basket was still practical, for its runners glided over the snow with little effort.

The priest embraced his friend and blessed the children. They hugged him. They cried. Then, he watched my brother and sister and my great-grandfather go up the mountain in the nightfall, seeking sanctuary in the west.

* * *

Father Andrei went down the footpath through the snow. It was a mile's walk to the highway. The wind blew colder, and the stars began to appear. He stood by the side of the pavement for hours with his thumb out. Many of the passing vehicles were startled by the gaunt figure dressed in black, a shape looming out of the falling night. They did not stop.

By late evening he was shivering uncontrollably. He watched the satellites crossing the sky and the running lights of search aircraft tearing up and down the valley, and he prayed. He prayed that my father and the boy he was trying to save would be protected from the police. He prayed that the three other fugitives struggling up the mountainside behind him would encamp safely for the night and find a permanent refuge on the other side of the range. He prayed also for the woman and child he was seeking.

13

Close to ten in the evening, a transport truck ground to a slow halt down the road and flashed its signal lights back at him. Breathing sighs of thanksgiving, he limped toward it.

"Up y'come, old-timer", said the driver, reaching down a hand. Father Andrei felt himself being pulled into the warm cocoon of the truck's cab. He sank with relief into the upholstered cushions. Soft country music played on the cassette deck. Tiny purple lights surrounded the windshield.

"Thank you. Thank you for stopping", he said to the man, who was inspecting him with curiosity.

"No problem."

The brakes hissed, and they were rolling down the grade, gathering speed. The electronic singer wailed. The guitar twanged and sobbed. The driver turned down the volume.

"What you doin' out there miles from noplace?"

"I was visiting a friend. He has a cabin back in the mountains."

The driver reached over and offered the old man a chocolate bar. He accepted and ate it hungrily. The driver flashed short glances toward his passenger every now and then.

"Bad time of night to be hitchhiking—winter too."

"The rides were not good."

"I almost didn't see you. I almost didn't stop."

"I am grateful that you did."

"Funny thing me stopping like that. I never stop for hitchhikers."

"Why did you stop?"

"I dunno", he shrugged. "It ain't legal. I'm not covered by insurance if there's an accident and a hiker's in here with me. I do three thousand miles and more a week. I make good money, but you get too much of your own company after a while. Sometimes my wife comes along. Not strictly legal, but that's okay. She's good company. Am I boring you?"

"No, not in the least."

"How far you goin'?"

"To a place near the coast."

"You want me to let you out in Chilliwack or Vancouver?"

"Near Fort George."

"You live there?"

"Yes."

"Well, I guess I can take you all the way."

"You are very kind. I thank you, my friend."

"You're welcome, *my friend.*"

Even as the driver's unspoken curiosity grew louder, Father Andrei felt himself sliding into half-sleep. A blanket of warmth swept over his body, and his head nodded forward onto his chest. He realized that he was exhausted. He had not slept properly for many nights. Not a great problem for an old man, he reminded himself. Yes, there would be more hours to stay awake and watch for the dawn, to think, to pray for the conversion of the world as it slid toward its blind burning—blind, so blind— most blind because it was convinced of its superior vision. Night was falling on the world. Like the times in prison during the war when night fell absolutely upon his soul, and all memory was eclipsed and all hints of the future shut off by the universal victory of dread. The torturers experimented with new methods—degradation worse than physical pain. The physical pain was a help because it knocked him into unconsciousness for a short while, until they threw buckets of ice water upon his naked body. For a few minutes he was released into blessed unawareness, then awakened to torment.

"You from Europe someplace?"

Startled awake, he looked at the face of the driver in the purple glow. A nice face, but heavy and unintelligent. The eyes were troubled. Not a happy man.

"Yes."

"What are ya? Ukrainian? Polish? My wife's family's Czech. I got a soft spot for you people who went through all that."

"Many of us did not come through it."

"Yeah. Long time ago, though. My kids don't even think it happened. They don't think nothin' happened before the sixties."

"It happened."

"So where you come from?"

"I was born in Germany. Then I spent much time in Poland and escaped to Canada during the war."

"So you're a German."

"Polish-German." He refrained from telling the man that his mother was a Jew from Lodz, a convert to Catholicism, who had married a professor from Dresden.

"Polish-German, huh? Same thing, really."

"A very great difference."

"Where did your family stand on Hitler and all that? You look like you were about the right age for the Nazi army."

"Nothing could be farther from the truth, in my case", he said. "My family suffered greatly under the National Socialists. I too . . ."

"Y'know, every German I meet says the same thing", said the driver coldly. "Seems like there never was a Nazi in Germany except a handful of gangsters."

"There were many. I was not one. I fought them."

The driver turned his head for a long look. The old man recognized suspicion and disbelief.

He tried to push the faces of the torturers from his mind. Worse, worse than the pain was the look in their eyes: the calm, inquiring expression of a human being observing the anguish of a rat he has skewered.

In the eyes of this man beside him he beheld a different kind of barbarism, not cruelty, merely ignorance. But had not the ignorance of the decent masses, manipulated by Hitler's propaganda, placed total power into the hands of the absolutely cruel?

"It was a confused time", he said to the driver. "People became confused by all the speeches. There were dozens of political parties. They wanted relief from the depression, from shame. They chose evil to save themselves from evil. It was very foolish."

"Evil?"

"Yes. May we use that word?"

"You religious?"

The old man nodded and turned his eyes within himself.

The driver turned up the volume on the cassette player and stared straight ahead for close to a hundred miles as the pavement wound around peaks and canyons in his headlights.

"News time", said the driver. He switched to a radio station, and they listened to the stream of events that the editors decided was news: global conferences, ecological catastrophes, interviews with experts, the "voice of the people", wars and rumors of wars. It sounded all too familiar. No jackboots stamping in the streets. No ranting by monster-tyrants. The tone sounded impersonal, emotionally detached, as if to reassure the listener that the reporting was objective. But Father Andrei listened with some indefinable inner faculty and recognized the selectivity and, beneath it, an undercurrent of deception.

"Now for the regional news. Today, police continue a massive manhunt in the interior of British Columbia, where, despite a concerted effort on the part of several law enforcement agencies, two missing children have yet to be located. Cynthia Connor reports:

"'The crisis began four days ago with the brutal murder of a school employee in the village of Swiftcreek. Nathaniel Delaney, the owner and editor of a local newspaper, abducted two children from their school late Tuesday afternoon, and the following morning the school's custodian was found bludgeoned to death. Delaney had gained prominence during the past year for his dissent against the hate-literature laws. He escaped arrest on Friday morning by firing upon and seriously damaging a police helicopter. He was apprehended near

Swiftcreek this afternoon, and there was another exchange of gunfire. Delaney died during the attempted arrest.'—Cynthia Connor reporting for Eyewitness News."

The priest closed his eyes.

"There are sure a lot of wackos in the world, eh?" said the driver.

"Yes, so many."

"Why would a guy do stuff like that? It's crazy!"

"Yes, it's crazy."

The radio droned on:

"Delaney had won awards for essays that appeared in periodicals around the world, but in his native land he was regarded as an enigma and a throwback to a less democratic era. Dr. Alan Thorold, dean of the Department of Political Science at Simon Fraser University:

"'The career of Nathaniel Delaney is a strange one. He was considered by many of his colleagues to be a wild card, although he had a brilliant mind. I thought of him as someone with a talent for writing but afflicted by the limitations of his Judeo-Christian background. He was an unstable personality, and I think this eventually pushed him in the direction of fascism. A liberal during the sixties and seventies, he had become increasingly conservative during the past decade, and I think some of this has to be attributed to mental unbalance. Clearly, the violent events that took place at Swiftcreek this week are tragic evidence of his basic instability.'

"Police continue to search for the two missing children. At the time of his flight from justice, Delaney was under investigation for abuse on a number of counts—sexual, psychological, and physical violence against children."

The driver turned off the radio.

"That's sick!" he growled.

"It is not true."

"Are you nuts? That's the national news talkin', guy."

The old man sighed and remembered a comment that Nathaniel's grandmother had once made to him. She too had been a journalist. *Father, if Dante were alive today, he would consign the news people to the lowest circle of hell.* She said it in that sardonic English tone of voice that was peculiarly her own. A fierce woman.

"Things are not always as the government wishes us to think", he said at last.

The driver glanced at him with an angry brow and looked back at the road.

"He was not a fascist", Andrei added.

"You knew this guy?"

Andrei hesitated. Then, because of fatigue or a failure of prudence, he replied, "Yes."

"Okay, so you knew him. But don't tell me a dead guy and two missing kids is a figment of the government's imagination."

"The dead man was not killed by him. And the two children are his own children. They are not missing."

The driver chewed on what he had been told.

"It was around Swiftcreek I picked you up, wasn't it?"

"Yes, it was."

"You say you know this killer?"

"I knew his family."

"You seen those missing kids?"

The priest hesitated, for he was not in the habit of lying. The silence went on too long.

"You know where those kids are?"

"No. I do not", said the priest, knowing that the children and their great-grandfather might now be anywhere.

An hour of strained silence passed until the truck emerged from the mountain pass and rumbled to a halt by an all-night restaurant.

"You want a coffee? Hamburger? It's on me."

"Yes, please. Thank you very much."

"You stay here, and I'll get it."

Andrei sat and waited and was nearly asleep again when, for some unknown reason, he sprang instantly awake. He heard a faint inner warning bell and listened to it. He opened the door and got out. He looked over at the window of the restaurant and saw the driver inside, talking into a pay phone, his back to the truck.

The priest turned and walked down the highway and into the night.

2

Dreamfields

Arrow rolled over in his blankets. The yurt was full of gray cloud, the ashen remains of the night's fire smoldering and the haze of dream smoke lingering around the vent hole in the roof. Light came in. It was morning. He jumped up and quickly dressed in his pants and moccasins.

"Maya!"

His mother groaned under the fur blanket and waved an arm at him.

"Shuttup, Arrow."

"Maya, I'm hungry", he said.

"There's bread and yogurt in the icebox. Fix yourself some breakfast."

He was scooping yogurt out of a bowl and gulping it down when the other lump under the robe snored, turned over, and revealed his face.

It was the shaman.

Arrow took a step backward. Men often came to sleep with his mother, but never had the shaman come. The shaman cured people of sickness, and he cursed people, too, if he did not like them. He had a medicine bag that was very powerful, and amulets tied in his long blond hair, and when he went into a trance you could see the spirit lines as streaks of color in the air around him. Arrow was not permitted to be in the shaking tent or to see the serpent dance, but the older boys, the big teenagers who were almost men, told him about it.

A screeching owl came out of the shaman's mouth, they said.

They saw it. They heard it. Once, these same stupid boys crept into the shaman's tent on a dare and found him drunk or stoned on dream smoke. Smirking and giggling, they pulled back his robes to see his nakedness and found him lying with the bones of a dead medicine man, as if the skeleton were his woman. They ran out fast with their hair standing on end and their hands clamped over their mouths, and Arrow had to give the oldest boy his favorite red miniature racing car in exchange for the story of what they had seen.

Later that day, still shaken, they were shooting fish in the stream with bows and arrows when the shaman came upon them. He pointed one by one to the three who had stolen into his tent.

"You boys want to die? No one comes into my tent without permission. You think I can't see with the eyes of the spirit even when I'm travelling out of my body?" Then the three big teenagers began to shake and cry, and they begged the shaman not to kill them.

"This time you are spared. I will not make the spirits strangle you. But never again. No second chance."

"Yes sir, thank you, sir", they cried and kissed his hand. He slapped the three of them hard in the face, looked at Arrow without expression, and stalked away.

The shaman brought a woman into his tent almost every night—now this one and now that one. Sometimes he took a young boy, but not so often. It was considered a great honor to be chosen. Arrow heard stories about the things the shaman did with the chosen ones, though he did not understand the things that were described. There were bits and pieces that did not fit together. They were not good, though how he knew they were not good was beyond him. The words made pictures in his mind, and the pictures made him sick when he thought about them, and he did not like to feel sick. He tried never to think of them. He tried never to cross paths with the shaman or the elders who were disciples of his art. The village was large, maybe thirty or forty tents and cabins, and a small, quick boy could easily remain unseen.

Now this man had come into his home. He had come into his mother's bed. It made the sickness come into his heart, worse than it had ever come before. He grabbed his stuffed monkey, flipped back the leather sheet of the door, and scrambled into the forest.

* * *

Arrow ran. If the shaman could see in his sleep, maybe he could see the feelings that Arrow had against him. Many times Arrow had wished that the shaman would fall into a deep hole and die there. Or that a bear might come out of the trees and fight with him and kill him—but he remembered the shaman's power over beasts. Maybe his tent would burn down and destroy him, he thought. Maybe his boat would turn over when he was netting salmon, and the river would sweep him away.

So he ran with the wind, hoping that he was not being chased by a *windigo*, a crazed, man-eating ogre roaming the forest in search of food, wailing, *Arrow, Arrow, come to me, Arrow!* The arms of the trees lashed in gusts that were blowing down the creek, and the fingers ripping through his scalp were *windigo*'s spirit-hands pulling him back, back, back toward the tent where the shaman would drag him under the bear-hide robes. Then he would be inside the picture, and he would *become* the picture, and the shaman would suck him into his mouth like sick, sweet, blue dream smoke and blow him out again as a shadow.

He screamed.

He felt better after the scream. He ran over rocks and the rotting corpses of the spawned salmon and the driftwood and the split clams and the condoms and broken beer bottles, and he screamed again. He ran far upstream. Then he stopped by a pool of deep water that bubbled out of a gash in the cliff. He wanted to leap in and wash himself clean, clean of the shadows that were smeared across his mind by the fingers of the shaman.

He screamed again.

Then he saw a man standing on the other side of the pool. The scream died in his throat. The man was very old and bent, he saw, and white hair stuck out from under his tuque. He was dressed in a long brown robe with a white cord knotted around his waist. Maybe he was a man. Maybe he was a spirit.

"Why are you crying?" said the man.

Arrow did not answer. Was the old man a clown? Was he a werewolf in disguise? He was dressed strangely. Many strange people came and went from this valley where The People lived. Maya warned him to stay away from them, especially the ones who came in vans to buy the plastic garbage bags full of dream-plant. Whenever he looked at them, their eyes and mouths melted, and he saw the forms of pigs and sometimes a werewolf. He tried never to look at them—which is not hard to do if you are fast and small.

"Why are you crying?" the man asked again.

Arrow could not answer. But he did not wish to run away. He waited for the man's face to melt into an animal or into a spirit face, but it did not. It remained a face that looked kindly at him, and the eyes were as clear and deep as the pool.

"Ah, I think I understand", he said. "In your world, many things are not what they appear to be."

Arrow did not understand the words, but he sensed that the meaning was true, for the eyes were true.

"Do not be afraid. Tell me, what is your name?"

"Arrow."

And then an amazing thing happened. The old face looked for a moment as if it were a child's, and his mouth opened.

"How merciful is the All Holy One!" said the man. But Arrow did not know these words.

"May I come across? May I visit with you?"

The boy nodded, and the old man hiked up his robes to his knees and sloshed across the creek at the ford of green pebbles below the pool. He came around and sat on a log a few feet away from Arrow. He removed his sandals and shook the water out of them.

"I am Father Andrei."

"Father? Andrei?"

"That is correct."

"You are a father?"

"Yes."

"You have children?"

"Oh, yes, in a sense I have many children."

"Where is your woman?"

"My woman?"

"The one who sleeps with you."

"I have no woman. I sleep alone."

"Then you are not a father."

"I am a different kind of father. I know your father."

"I don't have a father", the boy said with emphasis.

"Everyone has a father. But some fathers cannot be with their children. The man who is your father sent me to find you. You are a part of his family."

"The People are my family", the boy said woodenly, but the memorized response fell like sawdust from his tongue.

"Ah", sighed the old man, and his face became very sad. "Did you know, Arrow, that you have a real father, a man-father? He loves you."

"He loves me?"

"He does. He asked me to visit you and your mother. Can you tell her that you have met me and that I would like to speak with her?"

Arrow stared at him without replying.

Love? Father? The words felt good from the old man's lips, but he did not understand why it should be so, because the *love* word was for things that crawled under the bear hide, which made you sick and afraid, and it also meant the crushing embraces from Maya when she was drinking or smoking and stroked your face and cried on you and made you sad. He did not want the love of a man-father, if there really was a man-father. It was a tale told by the fire at night. It was mind-pictures when you slept. Love was sadness. He did not want more sadness.

"Flesh of his flesh. Bone of his bone, heart of his heart, little boy", said the man, and his eyes seemed very old.

Heart of his heart? How strange that in these words there was sadness yet also goodness. Was there a good sadness? It felt sweet and clean. Tears began to run down the boy's face, but he did not know why. Then, in his mind, he saw a baby wrapped in a blanket lying on a car seat. And the baby was happy, watching the windshield wipers sweeping the wet glass in the night. And there was Maya, crying. Why was she crying, and why was she yelling at the darkness? That was the beginning of the sadness, the bad sadness.

"Bad sad", he said.

Not knowing why he did it, Arrow slid along the log and stopped two feet from the old man. Feeling both drawn and cautious, he put Curious George between himself and the man as a buffer, lowered his head, and closed his eyes. A bubble of something down inside himself swelled up large, larger than the whole world, and it hurt bad and sad. It burst and poured out of his throat, a wailing so deep, a sobbing so fathomless it had no sound at first, for it could never empty the ocean of deepest sad. The old man held him and patted his shoulders, which heaved with the immense burden of his short life.

Then the bigger sound came. Waves of it. It did not take long. A few minutes. But Arrow felt as if he had cried forever. When the inner sea was poured out at last, its beds lay empty and waiting.

"There, there. Is the storm passed?"

Arrow nodded.

"Good. I see that you are a good boy."

Arrow looked at him.

"You are good", the old man repeated. "We must part now, my friend. I will come here to visit you in a few days, if I can. Please tell your mother about me."

"Yes", the boy nodded.

"We will see each other soon."

"Where do you live?" Arrow asked, drying his eyes on a sleeve.

"I live everywhere and anywhere. Usually I live near my sisters." He pointed to a white tower on a crest of the southern hills.

"They're crazy", the boy said with a worried look.

Andrei smiled. "They are holy."

"What is holy?"

"I will teach you about that another day. It is time for me to go."

The old man put both his hands on the child's head, and his lips moved in a whisper. When he was finished, he walked away into the trees and disappeared.

I am good? Arrow said to himself.

For a while he watched the red slices of fish play in the jade light at the bottom of the pool.

"I am good?" he said aloud.

"Arrow! Arrow! Where is that kid?" Maya's voice shouting though the trees. His fingers clenched, his eyes swung around searching the wall of green leaves for an escape. The screeches came closer. Arrow got up and walked back toward the angry voice.

"Arrow!" cried the voice falling like the breath of *windigo*, "Where the hell are you? Little bastard's been nothing but trouble since the day he was born."

* * *

It was long past Arrow's bedtime. Ordinarily he would have been asleep by now, but he lay awake savoring the warm imprint of the old man's hands upon his head and the quiet space within himself where once there had been an ocean. Maya was singing to herself, thwacking the hand loom. A kettle hissed on the wood burner. Arrow could see stars through the vent at the peak of the yurt.

He had a father. It was good.

The shaman threw open the door, stooped through the entrance, and walked in. Maya looked up sharply.

"You might have knocked."

"After last night I should knock?"

"Last night was real nice, Ricki, but it wasn't permanent. Don't presume we're going to make it a habit."

Peeping through a fold of his blankets, Arrow watched the man smirk and saunter to a chair by the loom. His mother continued to work the shuttle.

"You're still a city girl, aren't you?"

She gave him a look over her glasses.

"You know," he went on, "the very first time I saw you, when you came here with your kid to visit Tara and Crysta, I knew you were going to be mine."

"People don't own other people, Ricki."

"Don't call me Ricki."

"Okay, Standing Elk."

"That's my name. Don't forget it."

"How could I? It's . . . unique. A bit tough to get the tongue around."

"I have other names. You should respect me."

"Believe me, I respect you. You're a big man in the village."

"I have powers beyond this village."

She gave him another look.

"You've seen them", he said. "Don't pretend you haven't."

"Seen what? The devas? The fairies?"

"My powers."

"I've seen a lot of things since I came here. Some of it's great, like it was in the beginning. Some of the new stuff worries me."

"You should trust the elders more."

"I trust them."

"No, you don't. I can see it in your eyes."

"Okay. So maybe I've got a few doubts about the direction the community's been taking. Like this whole business of reverting entirely to primitive ways. Now that the electricity's gone, there's no more water pump. Back to packing water from the creek in buckets. The women carry the buckets, right? No more electric potting wheel. No more electric kiln. The women get the firewood for it, right? No more walk-in freezer at the center, eh? Now it's back to dry meat and fish and a lot of spoilage. Waste. The twentieth century got a few things right, you know."

"It's more pure this way. The guardian spirits are pleased."

"Well, what can I say? There's no arguing with that."

"You should be more careful. I see your resentment. It can land you in trouble."

"With whom? Hey, aren't we a community of free spirits here?"

"We are."

"Are we?"

"You see, there it is again. The questioning."

"Let's drop it. You want some tea?"

She served him, and they sat together on cushions by the wood stove.

"It's too hot in here", he said.

He took off his hat, and a rope of blond braid fell down his back. He took off his jacket and opened his shirt.

"When I first saw you, eight years ago, I said to myself, that woman is mine."

"Did you indeed?"

"I said to myself, I can take whatever I want. But this one is special. This one will give herself to me."

Maya shot a look toward Arrow's sleeping alcove.

"Are you asleep, Arrow?"

But his eyes were hidden in blankets, and he did not answer.

"The kid's asleep. Let's go."

"Not so fast. Don't the spirits teach you manners?"

"Be careful", he said coldly. "You don't understand them. You don't know them."

"I've never had the pleasure."

"You will. I promise. So what d'you say? Let's go, eh?" he said pulling his shirt over his head.

"I want to talk."

"She wants to talk", he groaned and looked at the ceiling.

"You could be a nice guy if you didn't treat women like residents of a brothel."

"You'd be a happier lady if you didn't always try to sound like a university professor."

"You'd even be a handsome guy, Ricki, if you took about forty pounds of amulets off your body and cut your hair."

He laughed at that.

"Hey, why don't you wake the kid up, and he can watch."

"You know, Standing Elk, you're a little bit warped sometimes."

He laughed again.

"C'mon, relax. What's all this prude stuff? It's good for kids to see it. It's earthy. It's primitive."

"No thanks."

"You're still a member in good standing of the bourgeoisie, Maya."

"Don't be insulting."

"No, seriously, you are."

"Okay, so I am. What about it?"

"You live on the surface. You need to go deeper."

"Into what?"

"The mysteries."

"I don't go for the medicine man routine. It's too far out. It's irrational. I don't like what it's been doing to the community."

"What's wrong with the community?"

"Look at us. Look, dammit. When I first came here, there was art and literature and theater. I came just for a weekend, remember? And it was the high level of culture that kept me here. It was only going to be temporary, I told myself. Just long enough to have a good visit with Crysta and Tara and to get a break from my uptight workaholic hubbie. I fell in love with this place and these people. The gentle ways. The circle dances. The fantastic music. The crafts. The love that everybody seemed to have for each other. Nobody laying guilt trips on anybody else. It was so mellow."

"Nothing's changed."

"It has. It's changed a lot in eight years. Gradually it's become something else. The theater group disintegrated last year. Nobody has poetry readings any more. The dulcimer workshop burned down because somebody got drunk and left a damper open. We used to make our money by arts and crafts. Now we make it selling . . ."

"You eat because of the crop."

"I admit it. But there're other things that are more serious. We seem to be living in a hierarchy now. You, the elders, your disciples. The bankers who handle the dope money. The field guards who carry pistols and get to play Gunslinger. They've all got little pieces of the power pie. I didn't see it in the beginning, but I've been watching it closely for some time now. And it's getting worse. Power gives you guys a handle on everyone else. You've given yourself permission to use some of us underlings as if we were things. I don't like it. I don't like the way you're trying it out on me tonight."

"It seemed okay to you last night."

"Last night we had the dance and the chanting and the wine and the smoke, and it was all a dream. And you *asked*, Ricki. You asked. Tonight you decided to take."

He murmured and took her hand. She pulled it back.

"I brought you something", he said in a soothing voice.

He pulled a bottle and two little glasses out of his jacket pocket.

"It's *absinthe*, the wine of the gods."

"Ambrosia is the drink of the gods", she corrected.

"Whatever. C'mon, try it."

"Wormwood and anise? No thanks."

"Trust me."

She shook her head and said in a voice loaded with irony, "Drink, Psyche, and be immortal, nor shall Cupid ever break away from the knot in which he is tied."

"What's that supposed to mean?"

"Nothing. Just a quote from an old story."

"Drink this, professor," he smirked, taking her hand, "and be immortal."

"Such a charming fellow you are", she said, letting her hand be taken.

Arrow listened to them talk for a long time. He saw the bottle go empty. He saw the dream smoke go up. He was afraid, and his heart beat like a drum at the circle dance, slow and hard, yet he could not keep his eyes open. Even so, his mind did not sleep. All the words spoken that night came to him and entered into the quiet place, and the sickness came with it.

"Tell me your other names, Ricki Standing Elk. It's hard to think of you as a medicine man with that Bronx accent."

She giggled, and he smiled at her.

"Torture me, and I'll give you my name, rank, and serial number. But give me a little love, and I'll tell you everything. Even my real name."

"Your real name? I've seen it at mail time. Your grandma

sends you money from New York every month, and your name is Richard Schwartz. Right?"

"That's no big deal. Most people here know my old name."

"And you've got your ever so romantic counterculture name, Standing Elk—though it seems to me that this particular elk does more lying around than standing."

"Don't get smart. You wouldn't be so smart if you knew my real name."

"So let the other moccasin fall. Tell me, which culture did you adopt this week? Sioux, Cree, Haida?"

"Don't sneer at me!"

"I studied anthropology at Simon Fraser, Ricki," she replied patiently, "and I can assure you that your interesting blend of aboriginal infatuations is totally eclectic. *Windigo* is Algonquian, *Manito* is Ojibwa, and the Raven Spirit is West Coast, not to mention whatever spirituality you picked up in some dirty basement in Manhattan."

"My name is *Dragonstongue*."

"Dragon's Tongue?"

"That's right."

"Where does that come from? Your mother give you that at your christening?"

"Don't joke about what you don't understand."

"I'm all ears."

"It was given in blood ritual."

"What blood ritual?" she said slowly.

"Last year. At the solstice."

"I was there at the harvest party. There was no blood ritual, or whatever you call it. A lot of baying at the moon and prancing. I thought you looked rather dashing in your loin cloth, leaping around the fire with a cougar head strapped to your skull."

"You are a stupid woman!" he barked.

She stared at him, astonished.

"It was later. In the middle of the night. We had other rituals after the people were all asleep. We have an altar up on the mountain. We go there sometimes."

"Who's we?"

"Some of the elders, but not all of them. My disciples. Sometimes a Master comes from another community and joins us."

"What exactly do you do up there?"

"We have a ritual and a sacrifice."

"What kind of sacrifice?"

"We began with animals a few years ago. And every time we did one, our power grew. Then last year the ascended Masters told us—each of us—in a vision—that it was time to move deeper into the mysteries. It was around then the narcs were getting wind of us. Remember? They always prowl around at solstices, because they know we're up to stuff that's against the law. The community was in danger. Our whole work could have gone under. So we had a special sacrifice. We took a step farther."

He pulled another bottle from his jacket pocket and drank from it. Maya stared at him hard, and Arrow saw her hand go to her throat.

"So we did that kid Stupid Tania was pregnant with."

"She miscarried the night of the harvest party. I heard the baby was born dead. Somebody buried it."

"Most people here don't know which way is up. They think they got the spirit life, and they've just been sucking on candy. They're just playing with toys. If they knew what we're into, they'd fall on their faces and worship when we walk by."

"Look, Rick, it's late", said Maya, standing up fast. "I gotta finish this weaving for the craft fair by Saturday. I gotta get some sleep. So you just prance off home, okay, and tuck yourself into your little trundle bed. I know this was all absinthe and dope talking. I don't want to hear any more about it. Let's forget it. And you come by tomorrow, and we'll have a good time. And . . ."

He grabbed her wrist and said, "Shut up." He yanked her back down onto the cushion. "You wanted to know, so I'm telling you."

"I don't want to know", Maya said with a shaking voice.

"We made Stupid Tania's baby come a few weeks early. It came out alive. Tania was stoned out of her mind. She doesn't know. We took it and sacrificed it. The narcs backed off and haven't returned. The crop this year looks like the best we've ever had. The second one we did guarantees that."

"The second one?"

"Yeah. At the spring solstice."

"Whose . . . ?"

"Some kid came in off the highway who couldn't get a ride. She was seven or eight months along. Perfect."

"Perfect . . ." Maya's voice broke, and she just sat there staring at him in disbelief. Then she shot the shaman with a short burst of piercing hatred.

"Don't look at me that way. You and all your friends let doctors do it so many times you lost count. So what's the problem? What's the difference?"

"There's a difference. Those girls didn't decide. You took their babies."

"Both of them hated being pregnant. They were pregnant because their pills failed. This was just a back-up. Besides, they were the sentimental types. Too mush-brained to get it done right. We solved it for them."

She stared at him.

"There's a big thing going on over our heads, Maya, and you're just the kind of smart lady who's so stupid in all the wrong places that you're going to get whacked."

"What do you mean?" she shrilled. "Are you going to do me in too?"

"No chance", he smiled. "All I'm saying is if you shed your bourgeois taboos, maybe you'd be a happier girl."

35

He pointed to the ceiling.

"There are giants in the world, Maya. Spiritual giants. I've met them. I talk with them. They have power. They can kill or give life. Some are ascended high Masters. They're on the brink of cleansing this planet. There are others—middle-level Masters hovering in spacecraft above the earth, waiting for us to win as many as we can to our side before the final battle. There are the native spirits too, the juniors in the big league. And there're animal and bird spirits, very bottom rung. They're all on the side of the planetary new age. If you step outside the harmonic convergence, girl, you'll hate what happens to you. You'll be left out in the cold forever. Or worse."

Maya rubbed her face with her hands and shook her long hair violently.

"Look. I'm really worn out", she pleaded. "I've got to get some sleep. Please go."

He pulled her down beside him and said, "You're mine."

Maya did not say anything.

Arrow covered his ears and turned away toward the wall. To keep from screaming, he looked inside of himself until he found the eyes of the old man in brown robes, gazing at him across the pool of water.

* * *

"Is he going to eat me, Maya?"

She looked at him over the rim of a cup of tea. Her eyes had black pouches.

"What did you say, Arrow?"

"Is the man who came last night going to do me too, Maya?"

"*Do you*? What do you mean, *do you*?"

"Is he going to kill me and eat me?"

She stared at him, swallowed, and said, "No. He's not going to eat you."

Her fingers were trembling.

"I want to go away, Maya."

"Yes. We're going to go away. We're not staying here any more."

"Can we bring our house with us?"

"It's a Tibetan yurt, Arrow, not a tent. It's too heavy. We'll go away, just you and me. Okay?" She ruffled his hair.

"Can we bring my teddies and my Babar books?"

"Yes. Everything like that."

"Can we go *now*?"

"No. I'm waiting for some money in the mail. We'll go soon. As soon as we can."

"Can the old man in the brown dress come with us?"

"What old man? What brown dress?"

"The one in the woods. At the creek. Where the water's blue and there are round stones. By the dead fish."

"Arrow. Was it an old man in your mind? Like a picture? Or was he real?"

He wondered what she meant.

"Answer me. Were you talking to somebody in the woods?"

"Yes. He was nice. He wants to see you. He said I should ask you if he could visit us."

"He did? Who is he?"

"He lives on the hill with the crazy ladies."

She thought about that and sipped her tea.

"I don't want you talking with strangers in the woods. There really are crazy people in the world. They might hurt you."

"He wouldn't hurt me."

"You're sure about that, are you?"

"He was nice."

"The world has been ruined by the nicest people."

He cocked a puzzled head at her. She frowned at him, then went to get more raisins to sprinkle on his porridge.

"C'mon, Arrow, eat up."

37

"Maya, I don't like that man who came to our house last night."

"Me neither."

"I want to go away from him."

"Me too."

"I'm scared of him."

"The shaman? Don't worry. He can't hurt you. I won't let him."

"What if he's stronger than us?"

"We're going. I promise you. Soon."

"But the man in the woods is nice."

"I don't want you talking to strangers. You got lost yesterday down by the creek. You have to tell me where you go. You're lucky I found you. What if I couldn't find you?"

"You yelled at me."

"I know. I'm sorry, Arrow. You made me so worried."

"The man in the woods washed the bad sad out of my mind." She glanced at her loom.

"Bad sad", she murmured.

"Are there giants in the world?"

"No. There aren't any giants in the world."

"The shaman said there were."

"How much did you hear last night?"

"I heard about giants."

"He says lots of things that aren't true. You don't have to worry."

"He said he talks with the giants and the people in the space-ships in the sky."

"He doesn't. It's just a story. No more daydreams now, Arrow. Go bring in some firewood."

"Okay, Maya."

"And no talking to strangers. No running off without telling me. Promise?"

"I promise, Maya."

Sometimes he forgot promises. He didn't mean to. It was not as if he disobeyed Maya on purpose. And one morning he forgot. He was walking toward the river to watch minnows when he passed the mouth of the path that snaked out of the woods beyond the shaking tent circle. A gust of wind whispered to him, *Come up the mountain, and then you will know.* He was afraid but not *very* afraid. In his mind he held out his right hand to the memory of the old man in the brown dress, and the warm raccoon paw of the old man took his and guided him upward. He knew that the old man was only in his mind this day. By the creek he had been there. You could touch him that day. Now he was here, but you could only pretend to feel his hand.

He climbed for a long time on deer trails. When he reached a plateau on the side of the mountain, he came out onto a clearing that overlooked the valley. To the west lay the ocean, a line of silver on the horizon. To the south was the mountain of the crazy ladies, and to the east the black coastal range. To the north, more mountains, brooding like the hump of monsters crawling into the interior of the land. Below him the river and the creek. Beyond them, the village, with smoke rising from many cookstoves. The sun was creeping higher.

At the edge of the cliff there was a flat stone raised on smaller stones. He had to stand on tiptoe to look at the surface. It smelled bad. It smelled like dead things. Worse than the fish by the creek. It was a black rock with spouts carved like dragons at the corners. Little stone dragons that vomited brown water from their mouths. He saw it in his mind even though the table and the mouths of the dragons were dry. It looked like rusty water, rivers of red water dribbling out of the dragon throats onto the earth.

Then he stepped back because now he was more afraid. He reached out for the warm raccoon paw but could not find it.

Then he looked up, and he saw a little man of bones on a tree beyond the table. A very little man. Its ribs and arms and legs were all apart in pieces, but the pieces were nailed together on the tree. The tiny skull was just like the pirate's flag in the storybook, but it was red. A black starling pecked in the holes.

Then a spirit voice spoke to him.

"The Giants' victory is the great surprise of the season . . ."

Arrow crouched down behind the stone table to hide from the high thin voice that came from nowhere. He looked all around at the sky. He searched the treetops. The voice went on chanting strange names and spells. Where was the voice coming from? It got louder and louder, and then the leaves rustled by the trail, and the shaman came up out of the bearberry bushes.

He did not see Arrow. He was carrying a small silver box, and the voices were coming from it. It had sorcery in it. The giants talked through this box. They spoke to the shaman. The man sat down in the grass under the tree on which the little bones were nailed. He put the silver box by his feet and leaned against the base of the tree and stared at the box. Then the boy saw that many pictures were in the box. There were roars and screams coming from it. Arrow froze in terror.

"Third down, dummy, four yards to go!" the shaman shouted at the box, and then the boy knew that the shaman had much power if he could talk to giants that way.

Arrow crawled into the trees and made a wide, silent circle around the clearing. When at last he stumbled across the deer path, he broke into a headlong run down the mountain.

* * *

He screamed.

Then her voice came through the dark seeking him.

A match flared, and the lamp swelled golden.

"What's the matter, Arrow?"

"I had dreams."

40

"What kind of dreams?"

"Bad dreams."

She pulled him onto her lap, and the sick bad sad faded slowly.

"Hush, hush. It was just a nightmare."

"It scared me."

"Tell me about it. Tell Maya."

"Big black birds came through the sky and went over the village. They came all over the sky. Then they turned into giant beetles with wings. They had tails that stung us. They spit fire at us. We were burning, and I ran away and jumped into the pool by the dead fish."

"Just a dream . . .", she whispered, rocking him.

"Then the man in the brown dress took my hand, and we ran away."

"Who the hell is this man in the brown dress?" she said fiercely. "Whoever he is, he really frightened you. Arrow, promise me you won't go into the woods alone again. Never, never go anywhere without telling me. Promise?"

"I promise." He began to cry. "Please let's go away from here, Maya. I'm scared."

"Stop that crying! You're a big boy. Just wait a few days longer."

"I'm scared, I'm scared!"

"I know. We'll go soon. I promise."

* * *

Arrow came out and looked at the sky. It was just after dawn. The sun was warm, melting the skiff of frost. Spring was still far away, but the mild coastal winter had been unusually warm, and there were days when it played tricks and made you think it was summer.

Most villagers were still sleeping. A few of the little children crept out from under tent flaps. They rolled around in the dust and scavenged from plates of food left over from last night's feast. Over by the fire pit, dogs lifted themselves up on front paws and gave their funny stretching *rowls*.

He smiled. It was always easier to smile in the morning. He was happy because he and Maya were going away soon and because the sky was very blue and the birds were talking to each other about something. The sun was just above the peaks.

Then he was not so happy because he smelled his clothes and knew that he had wet his bed again. Maya always scowled when he wet the bed. Big boys did not wet the bed. In his mind he saw the pool of round stones by the creek. He wanted to go there. The water would be good to drink, and it would clean him. The bugs would make singing music, and the frogs and turtles would jump and swim under to escape. He could watch them as they lashed their legs in silent frenzy below the surface of the water.

He remembered that Maya had said he mustn't go away from the village without asking her. Then he remembered her scowl. If he woke her and asked her, she would be mad. If he went and got lost, she would be mad.

What should he do? How could you know the right thing?

Maybe mad about *pee* was worse than mad about *not telling*. If she woke up and smelled him, there would be one mad. If he went to the water and she found him gone, it would be a different mad. If he went to the water and came back before she woke up, there would be no mads. Maya would be happy. They would both be happy. And soon they would go away.

He crawled back into the yurt and gathered his teddies together. He told them with his eyes that they smelled bad and would have to have a bath. He stuffed Curious George, Freddy-the-Teddy, and Leo into a knapsack. He tried to push Rampa in after them, but the panda was too big. Rampa did not smell as bad as the others, so he left him.

The pool of water was steaming when he broke through the

bush. An eagle that had been feasting on last autumn's dead fish took off with heavy wings. Arrow ran toward the water with a cry of glee, then splashed in fully clothed. When the shock of the numbingly cold water registered, he hooted and cried, oh, oh, oh! After a few minutes he no longer felt it. He smiled secretly to himself, diving and sputtering in the shallows. He looked for frogs and turtles, but they were still sleeping.

When the sun had climbed a part of the sky, he got out of the water, shivering uncontrollably, wrung his clothes almost dry, and put them on again. He sloshed the teddies about in the pool and swung them around until the beads of water stopped flying off their feet. He put them back into the knapsack. Then he lay down on the beach of smooth gray pebbles to let the sun dry his clothing a little more.

He put the knapsack under his head.

"You are heavy", said Leo.

"But we don't mind", said George.

"You are our father", said Freddy-the-Teddy.

He tried to make a picture in his mind of a man standing on a mountaintop looking at him. It was a father. But the man-shape was only that—a shape, far away, looking.

Then the birds stopped singing.

Arrow opened his eyes and glanced up. A big black bird went straight overhead. The noise it made was not a bird noise. It was like a hum, and when it had passed, there was a faint sound like a zing, and the surface of the pool quivered. The black bird disappeared over the tops of the trees, going in the direction of the village. Then, as he watched, two, three, four more birds followed. As they went over, they changed into scorpions; they swerved and became black beetles. Then Arrow's heart began to pound. He cried out and jumped to his feet. His hands clenched and unclenched.

"Maya?" he screamed.

Then he heard the big thumps and the *bam-bam-bam*s just like the tinsmith making pails with his mallet. Then more thumps. Smoke rose up over the crest of the trees.

Screams. Shouts. Many, many screams and shouts.

He saw a wall of flames through the trees in the direction of the dreamfields. There were more tappings on metal from the heart of the fire and more thumps.

He turned toward the village and was about to run to it when he heard someone call his name.

"Arrow!"

The old man in the brown dress was waving his arms and calling to him. Arrow did not move. He wanted to run to Maya to help her. But he also wanted to go to the old man. He could not make his legs do what he wanted them to do. Then the old man waded across the ford and came to him.

"Those are bad men", he said, pointing in the direction of the bangs. "We must run."

"Are the beetles going to spit fire at us?"

"Come with me, little boy. Please, come."

"They're going to spit fire at Maya! I have to help her!"

"Your mother would want you to come with me."

"She told me not to go without asking."

"Yes," he said urgently, "that is for most of the time. But today is different. She does not want you to be burned. She wants you to run away."

"Did she tell you?"

"I cannot explain it to you. It is hard for you to understand. But, I believe she wants this. You cannot help her right now. Maybe later, when the bad men are gone, we can help her."

"Okay."

"Do you remember my name?"

"Andrei."

He reached up and took the old raccoon paw, and it was warm.

"Quickly, let us go", Andrei said.

44

"Where are we going?"

"Across the valley. To the hills where my sisters live."

They were just turning to go when a man ran out of the woods from the direction of the village. Arrow jumped and cried out.

"The shaman!" he shrieked. "The *windigo*!"

The shaman stopped ten feet away, stared at Arrow, then at Andrei, and suddenly bolted in another direction.

They ran. Arrow was faster. Still shrieking, his hand slipped out of Andrei's, and he raced ahead through a swath of thimble-berry bushes, tearing his clothing, scratching his hands and face. Andrei panted heavily, trying to catch up. He struck his chest with the flat of his palm.

"Do not fail me now, my old heart!"

Arrow was pulling ahead too quickly, and Andrei lost sight of him. He stumbled along, following the line of smashed under-growth and the airborne trail of the boy's cries. He found him thrashing, twisting and turning and wailing, trying to extract himself from an impenetrable wall of blackberry thorns. Trickles of blood ran down his hands and across his forehead. The priest wrapped his arms around him and pulled him out. He took the boy's hand and led him along the hedge of blackberries until they came to an opening that led down to the gravel embankment beside the creek.

They crossed over on the railroad bridge, and beyond it they found a beaten path that snaked southeast in the direction of the big mountains. The path led them to a highway. Transport trucks roared past. A few cars. Billboards advertised vacations in Hawaii, television stars, electronic toys. Arrow understood none of it. On the far side of the highway they found a farm field grown over with tall weeds and saplings. They forged ahead, steadily making their way toward the hills upon which the tower stood. Arrow looked back once but could hear no sounds from where they had come. He saw smoke rising.

Eventually they arrived at a big river and walked along its banks until Andrei stopped by a cedar tree that hung over the water. A blue rowboat floated beneath the tree, its bow tethered to the trunk by a rope. Andrei untied the rope, climbed in, and dipped the oars into the water. He signalled to Arrow to enter also, and the boy did, seating himself on the floor boards, clutching his knapsack to his chest. On the far side of the river, he saw the white tower rising from the crest of a high hill.

They beached the boat on a stony spit and crossed another field overgrown with weeds. They were in the shadow of the southern range now and beyond the reach of the sun's direct glare. The shadow had turned everything blue and green. The air was cool. They entered a copse of young poplars. Grasshoppers sang, and Arrow watched them leap left and right to avoid the two humans plunging through the brown knee-high grass. Last year's leaves whispered *shaman, shaman, shaman, shaman, shaman . . .* beneath his feet. He laughed. His laughter was high and uncontrolled and laced with fright.

Just then Andrei fell to the ground and pulled the boy down beside him.

"Do not move!"

A big black beetle went humming over the trees, leaving the topmost leaves rippling, though there was not a breath of wind. Four more shapes streaked across the valley, following the first.

"Where are they going?" Arrow asked.

"I think they are going to the convent", Andrei said. His eyes were greatly worried. "Why there?"

They were on the first slope of the foothills now, and the tower seemed much closer. But there was still a long way to go. Andrei bustled up over stones and around fallen fir trees as fast as he could. His breath came in gasps. He held his chest constantly. Prayers and suppressed cries came from his throat. Now it was he who went too fast, and the boy lagged behind. Arrow's legs hurt. He let go of Andrei's hand for a moment to stop a fall, righted himself, and scrambled to catch up. Arrow grabbed a fistful of brown robe and held on. He felt himself being jerked up the hill by fits and starts.

They were halfway when the *thump, thump, thump* began, and the banging on tin pails, and the tapping on wood. As they approached the summit of the hill, the tower disappeared from view, hidden by the thick forest of birch and pine. Through breaks in the branches they could see wisps of smoke rising over the edge.

They stumbled through bushes at the top, and suddenly before them was the white tower. A castle, the boy thought, a castle without knights. A big garden lying in neat rows of dark earth. On the far side of the rows a small barn was burning, and an animal was crying inside. All the beetles were going up into the sky. Then they turned and flew away into the sun.

The wind blew through the grass of the lawn and rustled the dead leaves of rose bushes. The animal stopped bawling, and a sound like a cracked bell banged in the tower.

The old man looked like death. His mouth hung open, and his eyes were like pools that had no bottom. Arrow tugged on his robes.

"Andrei?"

"Yes?"

"Bad men hurt people here?"

"Yes, I think so."

"They hurt your sisters?"

"Perhaps they are unharmed. I must go see."

Andrei looked into the west where the beetles had gone. "With this blow against us, you bring destruction upon yourself", he said.

"Who are you talking to, Andrei?"

"To the men in the black helicopters."

"The big black birds that turned into beetles?"

47

He nodded. "Stay here. Sit on this stone."

Arrow sat down.

"Do not move from it", Andrei said firmly.

"Where are you going? Can I come too?"

"I am going to look through the monastery. There may be things you should not see. You will wait here."

The old man walked slowly across the garden and went into the castle.

The boy sat on the stone for a very long time and watched the sky change colors with the passage of the sun. The barn burned to the ground. A rooster crowed. Then, he lay down on the grass and fell asleep.

* * *

The portress lay in a pool of blood in the office, beside the splintered door to the enclosure. Andrei found the other bodies in several places, all lying at their stations, as obedient in death as they had been in life. They had all been shot. Beside each was a yellow leaflet. Sister Matilda was slumped over her sewing machine in the annex behind the grille. Five other sisters were in the chapel. The tabernacle had been punctured by three bullet holes, but the Sacrament was undamaged. Andrei consumed it hastily and went to search throughout the rest of the building. In the hallways of the enclosure he found only a loudly complaining cat padding up and down the waxed floors and a canary singing in its cage. There were more yellow leaflets scattered everywhere. In the infirmary he discovered Mother Agatha, the abbess, in her hospital bed, a rosary in her fingers, and the nursing sister sprawled on the floor beside her, a broken cane locked in one hand. There were two sisters in the kitchen—a kettle was melting on a bright red stove element—and one more sister in the basement laundry room.

She was still alive, bleeding heavily, unconscious. Her pulse was fluttering and her face pale blue. He tried to staunch the flow of blood from a wound in her chest and another that had grazed her forehead.

He raced upstairs to the office and searched unsuccessfully for the telephone book. There was no ambulance number on the bulletin board. He tapped 911 into the machine, and a woman's voice answered.

"You have reached emergency assistance. Can I help you?"

"Something terrible has happened", he stammered. His voice sounded far away. "Please call an ambulance."

"Can you give me your address?"

He tried to tell her, but his voice failed.

"I'm at . . . I'm at . . ."

"That's all right, sir, your location just came up on our screen. Stay on the line."

"Please, hurry! A woman is dying."

He picked a leaflet from the floor and stared at it, but his eyes would not focus on the letters. He put it into his pocket.

Then a male voice cut in:

"This is Response Division."

"There has been a murder", Andrei said. "Several murders . . . but one is still alive."

"All right, sir. Try to stay calm. Tell me where you are."

He told him.

There were more clicks and buzzes, and another male voice come on line.

"Where are you?"

"At the office of the convent."

"Who is this?"

"I'm the chaplain."

"We'll have a response team to you in a few minutes. What is your name, sir?"

Andrei told him.

There was a pause, and then the voice said, "Have you informed anyone else of the situation?"

"No. Please, please come quickly."

"We're on our way. Don't move. Don't touch anything."

"I won't. With whom am I speaking? Are you a doctor?"

"You're talking to the police. Don't make any phone calls. Leave the line free until we get there."

"All right."

Andrei hung up. He looked away from the portress' body and shook uncontrollably. When the nerve reaction was over, he retraced his steps and anointed the bodies quickly, making the sign of the cross over each. He moved as if he were a ghost in a bad dream, shocked beyond any capacity for emotion, aware only of the need to perform his priestly duties. When he returned to the laundry room, he found that the sister was dead. He anointed her also and returned to the visitors' foyer. While he was splashing cold water on his face in the visitors' washroom, he suddenly remembered Arrow and went outside. He found the boy curled up beside the stone and woke him.

Arrow sat up and yawned.

"I'm hungry", he said.

"Yes, little one. But right now we must wait for the police."

Andrei put his head in his hands while Arrow rummaged in his knapsack, talking nonsense into it.

Five minutes later Arrow said in a small voice: "Beetles."

Andrei looked up. Coming toward them from the west was a tiny black helicopter, growing at a rapid rate. Behind it, a second, then a third.

"They are coming back!" Andrei cried. He grabbed the boy's arm and threw himself over the edge of the lawn into the bushes. They rolled downhill for a few feet and came to a stop against the trunk of a giant fir tree. Above them they could see the helicopters, swift and soundless, descending onto the lawn.

"Run, Arrow."

But Arrow was already running, crashing downhill through the undergrowth. Andrei careened after him, scratching himself on thorns and dead twigs, falling, scrambling on all fours, standing, loping too fast, tumbling, bruising an arm, stubbing his toes repeatedly against stones and roots. A sandal strap broke, and he tripped. He tore the sandals off, got up, and ran onward, barefoot. Halfway down the hill, he crashed into Arrow, the boy crouching beside a tree, gasping and wild-eyed. Ahead of them a gravel road cut an oblique slash through the forest.

"This is the main entrance to the convent", Andrei said. "We will wait here. The police should arrive in a few minutes."

They sat down and leaned their backs against the trunk, panting. Gradually the boy's chest ceased heaving, but his cheeks and ears were flaming, his eyes still terrified. Andrei's breathing slowed little by little, but his chest felt as if the point of an iron bar pressed into it without mercy.

"They'll be here soon", he said. "A few minutes at the most."

He looked up and down the road, straining to hear the sound of motor vehicles. He glanced at his wristwatch. It was now twenty minutes since the phone call. The police should have arrived. He looked back and saw small black insects swarming over the hilltop, visible in the shards of blue between the branches, zigzagging above the canopy of the forest, searching.

Andrei waited another five minutes. Then he understood. The knowledge came like the unfolding of a camera shutter that is so designed it lets in sufficient light for a single image: The police had already come.

They had landed in the black helicopters, and their voices were now speaking into radios and calling in every direction. Andrei heard a voice, then two voices. They were still distant, but it was obvious that they would soon begin searching beyond the perimeter of the convent grounds.

He pulled the boy to his feet and dragged him downhill onto the road, crossed it in frantic haste, and disappeared into the bush on the far side. Hidden by a thick screen of Douglas fir trees, they climbed parallel to the road until at last, reaching a footpath that cut through the forest on the right, they slipped into the deepening shadows.

"This is the way to my cabin", whispered Andrei, pointing along the trail. "Quickly, now, we must get away."

The path wound along the side of the hills, going steadily upward. The dusk came on quickly, and before long it was difficult to see the path in front of them. But Andrei seemed to know his way in the dark. The stars were brilliant in the sky when they arrived at a cabin perched on the edge of a ravine hidden by an overhang of rock. They went in. A spark of crimson came from a light in a corner of the one-room shelter.

"This is my home."

Andrei lit a kerosene lantern, and the dwelling was filled with soft gold. Arrow looked about with fascination. In the corner of the room there was a shelf covered with a white cloth, and on it a metal box; beside it the flickering flame of a red lamp. Andrei knelt before the gold box. He laid his forehead against it, and Arrow could see his shoulders heaving, hear the harsh whistle of his breathing.

On the walls were pictures of men and woman with gold circles around their heads. They stared at Arrow. He averted his eyes.

Andrei got up slowly and set a bowl and plate on the crude plank table. There was a bench beside it. A sleeping pallet on the far wall. A shelf of books. A cupboard containing several gallon jars of dried food.

"I'm hungry."

"Of course you are hungry. For the world to keep going, we must eat."

Andrei found bread and cheese. Arrow ate it.

"Yes," said the priest, "it is good that you eat and drink."

He poured milk from a gallon jar into a cup. Arrow gulped it down and asked for another. Andrei refilled the cup. Then, distracted by his grief, he sat down on a chair by the plank table and covered his face with his hands. Arrow, sipping the milk, swinging his legs, twitching his fingers, watched him for a few minutes until he grew bored. He opened his knapsack and extracted a monkey in a red jacket and yellow cap. He began to talk to it, making soundless words.

"George is hungry", he said to the priest.

"Are you still hungry, Arrow?"

The boy nodded.

"Of course. Little bodies must grow. Bread and cheese is not enough. I will make you some supper."

He lit a fire in the wood stove and set a pot of rice to boil. He put two eggs into another pot and set it to boil as well.

"When can I go back and find Maya?"

"You cannot go back just now."

"Why?"

"Because it is very dangerous."

"What if she needs me?"

"We cannot help her now. Please believe me. She would want you to be safe with me."

Arrow thought about that and then began to eat what the old man had made for him.

"We will stay here tonight until it is clear what we should do", Andrei said.

"Then what will we do?"

"I think we will go away."

At this Arrow's face lit up.

"Maybe Maya wants me to find my father."

The priest opened his mouth but could not formulate a reply. He merely watched as the boy ate steadily, his eyes focused inward, distracted by a hunger of another kind.

3

Winnebago Country

Arrow passed the night on the bed, and Andrei on a foam pallet on the floor. The boy slept fitfully, the man not at all. He lay in agony throughout the darkest hours, trying to pray, haunted by the scenes of death he had seen at the convent, feeling a lump of sick dread growing steadily within him and around him. He tried to make sense of the dual crimes, but no matter how he looked at it, he could not. The drug commune had nothing in common with the convent. Nothing whatsoever. Their beliefs were diametrically opposed. The counterculture people mistrusted the Christians and avoided them at all costs. Immersed in their culture of paranoia, many of their fears imaginary or blown out of proportion, they considered the nuns to be part of the establishment and thus a danger to The People. If the sisters had known this, they would have been puzzled. Although they worried over the occult practices and the drug habits of their neighbors, they did not feel any hostility toward the people at Salmon Creek; they had prayed for them and loved them silently for many years. But there had never been any communication between the two communities.

Before dawn he stoked the fire, prayed his office, and said Mass. When Arrow woke, Andrei made a breakfast of oatmeal and the last of the eggs—scrambled, served on bread. The simplest tasks were difficult to accomplish. His hands shook from time to time, but he tried with some success to quell his emotions, arguing that he would be useless to the boy, and to himself, if he succumbed to grief. He would grieve later, he decided.

While Arrow ate, Andrei dressed himself in farmer's overalls, work boots, a plaid shirt, and a worn coat. Into a knapsack he placed his breviary, a portable Mass kit, vestments, bread, and a toilet kit. He went to the shelf below the tabernacle and picked up a stone carving that Nathaniel had given to him at their last meeting.

"Tell Arrow I love him, Father. Tell him I'm going to try to find him someday. Tell him how sorry I am that I wasn't a good father for him. Give him this. It belonged to my great-grandfather."

Andrei now put the stone cross into the sack, resolving to give it to the boy at a better time.

They walked all morning across the valley's grid of back roads. Andrei watched the sky, but no black helicopters appeared in it. *Hellcops*, Nathaniel had called them. Occasionally a car passed, but no one stopped. Andrei hoped they assumed that he and Arrow were just another old man and a boy out for a walk.

They reached the on-ramp of the bridge over the Fraser River shortly before noon. The traffic was heavy going in both directions, but none of the northbound vehicles stopped to offer them a ride. The crest of the big arc of concrete lost itself in low clouds that hovered above the river, and Andrei thanked God for them. When the walkway began to slope down toward the north shore, they emerged into thinner fog. The water below the guardrails was gray and choppy. The wind was cold and blew occasional snowflakes horizontal into their faces. A seine trawler passed under their feet, heading downriver to the open sea. The hustle and bustle of the town of Fort George appeared out of the mist ahead.

At the bottom of the bridge a car pulled over to the curb, and a young face popped out of the passenger window, a teenage boy, oriental. He waved them toward the car.

"Want a ride?" he said. His voice was high, musical, heavily accented.

"Yes, please", said Andrei. The boy hopped out and opened the back door. He wore jeans, a checkered shirt, and a high-school jacket emblazoned with the letters of a sports team: *Mission Angels*. The driver, a diminutive middle-aged woman, nodded and smiled emphatically. Dressed in blue silk pajamas, she wore a silver crucifix on a chain around her neck.

Andrei and Arrow got into the back seat.

"My mum says we should stop for you. It too cold to walk on water this day."

"It is cold, indeed", said Andrei. "Thank you, Madam."

"My mum she doesn't speak English."

"Please tell her I am grateful for her kindness."

The boy fired a rocket of unintelligible words at his mother, who responded with many smiles and nods and made the car lurch back onto the highway. The oriental boy sat sideways on the front seat, facing the rear.

"Where you going? Where you want us take you?"

"We would like to go up the mountain above town, close to Eighteenth Avenue."

"No trouble. We take you. My family live on Fourteenth."

"Excellent. Thank you."

"No trouble", the boy said again. "My name is Théophane Nguyen." He extended his hand. Andrei shook it.

"How do you do, Théophane. My name is Andrei. This is Arrow."

Théophane shook Arrow's hand. Arrow dropped the hand and watched the proceedings as if he were a deaf mute. Andrei, assuming they were immigrants from Hong Kong, said, "Are you from China?"

The boy laughed, translated for his mother, and replied, "No. We from Vietnam. Ten years ago we come here, work in fields of fruit farms. We are—you know—boat people."

Andrei thought about Anthony Thu, about his horrible wounds, and about Nathaniel Delaney, who only a few weeks ago had pushed the boy on a dog sled into the forest of the northern wilderness, searching for a doctor.

"I know a family from your country", he offered. "Perhaps you know them. Their name is Hoàng Van Thu."

"We know some Thu family in Vancouver."

"My friends are in Swiftcreek, many hundreds of miles north of here."

Théophane spoke to his mother, and she shook her head.

"No. My mum says she doesn't know them. Different people. Are they Buddhist or Catholic?"

"Catholic."

"We Catholic too", he said proudly. He reached into his shirt and pulled out a brown cloth scapular on a string from which dangled many religious medals. *Not exactly a typical teenager*, Andrei observed to himself.

As the car left Main Street and climbed slowly past Second and Third, the woman said something to her son. The boy looked embarrassed.

"My mum says you are Catholic too."

"Yes. That is true. How did she know that?"

"Mum can tell", he smiled. "God give her many gifts."

The woman pulled into a self-service gas station on Seventh, and while Théophane was filling the tank, she turned around and bowed to Andrei.

"Faddah," she said reverently, "Faddah."

It was difficult to know her meaning. The boy jumped back into the front, and they drove on. The woman spoke to her son in Vietnamese for several blocks, and the boy began to look more and more somber, staring straight ahead, saying nothing. On Eleventh he turned around.

"My mum says you're a priest. Are you a priest?"

Andrei, feeling a jab of fear, hesitated. Then he nodded.

On Fourteenth they pulled over to the curb.

"You want us to take you see Father Ron at Saint George's?"

57

Andrei considered. Who was Father Ron? Their parish priest? What was Father Ron's position on political questions? Was he sufficiently awake to understand what was happening? Would he believe Andrei if he tried to tell him what had happened? Had Arrow's face surfaced in the media? Would Father Ron make a discreet telephone call to the police, uncertain about who was telling the truth, feeling regret for failing to trust a brother priest, but confident that the authorities would sort it all out? Was he that kind of cleric?

"No, thank you. Another time, perhaps. We must go visit some friends."

"Okay."

They drove the rest of the way in silence. They parked on the corner of Eighteenth and Wapiti, and Andrei opened the door.

"Thank you again", he said.

The woman spoke to her son in rapid-fire Vietnamese. The boy turned around slowly and started to say something, then held it back, looking uneasy.

"Don't think my mum's crazy, okay? She says God tell her you in trouble. You in trouble?"

Andrei didn't reply.

"My mum want you bless us."

Andrei made the sign of the cross over them and prayed a blessing in Latin.

The woman bowed and kissed his hand.

"My dad and my mum they was in prison in Vietnam", Théophane explained. "We know. We know."

"What do you know?"

"Police, radio, paper, they talk one thing—do another thing."

"Oh, I see."

"You in bad trouble, Father?"

"Yes. Have you heard about it on the radio or television?"

"No. Nothing. But my mum knows in her heart."

The woman's anxious eyes were fixed on Andrei's face.

"Please ask her to pray for me and for this boy. And ask her to pray for the Thu family in the place where I have come from. Pray that the eyes of the government do not see them."

"Okay. We pray."

Andrei and Arrow got out and were a half block up the hill when Théophane jumped out of the car and ran after them. He fumbled in his pockets and forced a ten-dollar bill into Andrei's hand.

"We not see you. You forget see us, we forget see you." He tapped his chest. "But we remember you here."

* * *

Bill and Irene Wannamaker lived on a dirt road three blocks off Wapiti, near a minimum security prison. Andrei and Arrow drew little attention as they walked past the prison golf course. On the other side of a low chain link fence, three prisoners looked up from the green where they were knocking balls into a hole and looked back down, resuming their game. Andrei wondered if he would soon be incarcerated there. The rock music blaring from a transistor radio on a park bench was not inviting, nor were the three satellite dishes on the roof of the main building in any way reassuring. Still, he thought that if he were apprehended it would be possible to climb this fence and slip into the forest across the road. But what would happen to Arrow?

He had visited Bill and Irene several times during the past decade. A wedding supper, a baptism party. They were friends of the nuns, financial benefactors of the convent, friendly work-ing-class people who liked to do charitable acts without draw-ing too much attention. One of their daughters, Julie, had entered the convent as a postulant in the 1980s. A sensitive, creative girl, she had longed to be a contemplative nun but discovered that she didn't have a vocation to the religious life and had left the community after six months. Andrei was the chaplain at the time, a spiritual director to several of the sisters. He had felt a special affection for Julie, who was guileless, artistic, and devout but had *Motherhood* engraved deeply in her personality. He had helped her through the crisis, and they had corresponded ever since. A daughter in the spirit. She was married now and lived at the Fort George marina on a sailboat she and her husband had built. Bill and Irene sent Christmas and Easter cards to Andrei every year, with a steady stream of prayer intentions and photos of their trips to California, Julie's children and their other grandchildren, and the boat.

A quarter of a mile past the prison, Andrei and Arrow turned onto a dead-end lane, and five minutes later they saw the roof of the Wannamakers' house appear through a wall of holly trees and ornamental shrubs. In the driveway stood a large Winnebago mobile home. Its axles were up on cement blocks, and a bright orange tarpaulin covered its top half. Parked beyond it in the long driveway was the cab of a transport truck, missing its box. Bill had been an owner-operator of a small trucking firm. He was retired. He and Irene hoped to travel through the southern U.S. in their Winnebago come spring.

The afternoon was heavily overcast. A fine drizzle had replaced the scattered snowflakes. The lights were on in the house, radiating sanctuary. The doorbell went *bing-bong*, *bing-bong*, and a minute later a tall, heavy man in his seventies opened the door.

"Bill."

The florid face looked stunned. When he saw Andrei, he went redder and rubbed his eyes with a very large hand. Arrow stepped behind Andrei.

"Good Lord, it's you! C'mon in, Padre."

Bill patted Andrei's shoulder as he drew him into the vestibule. He whipped a cap off his head. *Vancouver Canucks*, it said. He didn't seem to notice Arrow.

"Thanks for coming. We just heard. Irene's in the kitchen. She's all broke up."

The man seemed to choke on his words. Rubbing his close-cropped white hair, he led Andrei and Arrow up a short staircase and through a plush living room upholstered in blues and greens. A television set flashed brightly colored images across the furniture, the volume turned down to almost nothing. Arrow stopped in front of it and stared. Andrei took his hand and drew him away. When they entered the kitchen, they found a small, silver-haired woman seated at the kitchen table with her head in one hand, a dish towel in the other.

When she saw Andrei she cried out, got up, and ran over to embrace him. She sobbed hysterically, burying her face in his chest. Andrei put his arms around her and tried to collect his thoughts. Bill plugged in the kettle and stood watching—a helpless ox of a man.

"Who could do such a thing?" Irene cried. "Why would anyone hurt our dear sisters! They never did a stitch of harm to anyone in their whole lives!"

Andrei made her sit down. Bill sat down across from her.

"We just heard", he said, pointing to a portable television on the counter beside the stove. "It's insane! Why?"

"I'm not sure."

"Have you just come from there?"

"Yes."

"Have the police found anything?"

"Nothing is clear."

"Do they have any clues who these madmen are?"

"I don't know. The situation is very confused."

"Monsters! Killers!" Irene fumed.

"The bulletin said the police believe it's some kind of hate group", said Bill. "They left messages all over the place."

Andrei took a yellow leaflet out of his pocket. "This is one of the messages."

"My God!" Irene said, clutching her throat.

"Can I see that?" Bill asked.

He and Irene read it silently. Bill's face went red again.

"Bastards! It says here that the sisters and all their kind are servants of Satan. The true Messiah, some guy they claim lives in Montana, calls on all true servants of God to liquidate the enemies of God. This is crap!" he said, throwing the leaflet down on the table. "God, when is it going to end?"

"Religious nuts!" Irene said in disgust. "Psychotics!"

"I don't think religious fanatics did this", said Andrei quietly. Bill and Irene looked at him as if they hadn't heard him right.

"You don't?"

"No, I don't. It's difficult to understand. I'm not even sure I understand."

"Were you there?" said Bill. "Did you see some of it?"

"I saw it from a distance."

"Did they kill everyone?"

"Yes, I'm afraid so."

Irene resumed sobbing, holding her face in the dish towel. Bill got up and made three cups of instant coffee. He seemed to notice Arrow at last. The boy was standing, leaning against a wall, clutching his knapsack to his chest, looking at the shiny appliances, the Sacred Heart calendar, the plastic water font by the door, the holy card magnets on the fridge.

"Uh, would you like a Coke?"

"No, thank you", said Arrow.

"Milk?"

"Yes, please."

"Who is this?" Irene asked, drying her eyes.

"This is Arrow."

"Hello", she said absentmindedly. "Would you like a sandwich?"

"Yes, please."

She bustled about the kitchen and brought him a cheese sandwich. He ate it in three large bites. Bill, Irene, and Andrei watched him.

"First that drug commune yesterday, and now this", said Irene eventually. "What is happening to this country? It used to be a decent place to bring up children."

Andrei rubbed his forehead.

"Bill, Irene, I have something to tell you. It will be difficult for you to believe. Perhaps even harder for you to understand."

"What?" they said simultaneously.

"Something terrible has happened. Something bigger than the deaths of our friends."

"Something bigger?" said Bill, screwing up his face. "What could be bigger than this?"

"I will tell you when we are alone."

Irene, taking the cue, said to Arrow, "Would you like to watch cartoons?"

The boy looked at her vacantly.

"He has never seen television before, I think", the priest explained.

"Never seen a television?" said Bill. "You're joking!"

They stared at Andrei, then at Arrow.

"We've got some children's books", said Irene. "Milly and Todd left a bundle here last visit." She left the room and came back a minute later. "Arrow, why don't you come with me to the rec room and look at some books for a while?" She led him out and returned shortly.

"What's going on?" said Bill. "You said you don't think it was a right-wing group did it?"

"That is correct."

"The police think it was."

"The police may be part of the problem."

"Well, who did it, then?"

"I am not absolutely positive, but I think it was our government."

They both sat back abruptly and looked at him in disbelief.

"Oh, no. That's crazy!" said Irene. "That can't be."

"Maybe it was a nut", said Bill.

"No", said Andrei. "I don't think it was."

"You don't?" They looked angry—angry at Andrei. Confusion wrestled across their faces. They looked at each other, and Andrei read the unspoken suspicions that flashed wordlessly between the couple.

"There are many things going on beneath the surface of the nation", he said. "Things you don't know about."

"What sort of things?" Bill demanded.

"And how do you know about it?" said Irene, folding her arms across her chest.

Andrei said nothing until they calmed down.

"I'm sorry", said Irene. "I didn't mean it to sound that way. It's just, I'm so upset. When I think that Julie could have been one of them . . ." She began to cry again.

"I think you'd better tell us", said Bill. "Right from the beginning. Take it slow, and don't leave anything out."

They listened without interrupting. From time to time they shook their heads, wondering if what Andrei was telling them was true or not. When he was finished, they shook their heads again. Bill pushed his cap back onto his head and let out a long sigh.

"It's crazy", he said.

"Tell us again about the helicopters", Irene prompted.

"I saw five very fast black helicopters, with no markings, attack the drug commune. I took the boy from there, and we ran away. We saw—"

"The news said the police are investigating that one too", Bill interrupted. "They say it's drug related—a war between the drug gangs."

"It happens in South America all the time", said Irene. "And with this new wave of immigrants from Hong Kong there are all kinds of criminals coming into the country. Vancouver's getting to be like New York City."

"If it weren't for what has happened to me during the past week, I too would have accepted the police statement. It seems to make sense, doesn't it? But crime gangs do not have fleets of high-tech helicopters. At least not here."

"The news didn't say anything about helicopters."

"They were there. I saw them. There were automatic weapons and small rockets."

"Bombs? So who were they?"

"The same people who killed our friends. Those helicopters flew straight across the valley, even as the boy and I ran toward the convent. The sisters were dead when we arrived."

Irene got up and walked back and forth, wringing her hands.

"It's just so hard to believe, Father. Maybe the drug cartels do have helicopters. Maybe they came from across the border from the U.S. Maybe there was some kind of aircraft carrier out on the Pacific from another country. Maybe . . ."

He let her run through the scenarios until she had exhausted the possibilities.

"You say you saw these same choppers fly across the valley to the sisters?" Bill interjected.

"Yes. It all happened within an hour."

"Are you sure? The news said the drug commune thing was yesterday. The sisters were attacked this morning."

"No. Everything happened yesterday."

They shook their heads again.

"Why would the police and the media say it was two different days and two different sets of criminals? Why would they say that, eh?"

"It could be they want to make a separation between the two in the mind of the public."

"But why? Why would they lie? Maybe they just made a mistake."

"A strange mistake, don't you think? I saw it happen with my own eyes. They are lying. That is certainly strong evidence of their involvement."

"The police don't have black choppers", Bill protested.

"Do we know that? Within the past few months they have acquired a fleet of jet helicopters. They are called 'gray and greens'. I have seen them. They apprehended Arrow's father in the North Thompson. At Swiftcreek."

"Your old stomping grounds", said Bill. "Did you see that, too?"

"I did. I also saw a boy who had been machine-gunned by one of them."

They stared at him silently, their faces saying, "Oh, no, that can't be. That's too bizarre. Not here. Not in this country."

Andrei, who was beginning to realize the futility of any attempt to modify their comfortable view of the world, sighed and said nothing. Irene, surprisingly, was the first to reconsider.

"Now that you mention it I *have* seen those helicopters going up and down the valley. They're gray and green. We just thought they were a branch of Forestry."

"I don't think they are."

"But gray and green isn't black!" said Bill.

"It wouldn't take long to spray paint them", Andrei replied.

Bill shrugged. "But you're just guessing. The Mounties aren't allowed to have secret agencies."

"As a matter of fact, under the new laws, they are. But I do not think the people in the helicopters are R.C.M.P."

"Who are they, then?"

"I'm not sure. They could be some other kind of police agency, or perhaps a government paramilitary service."

He told them about the 911 call and the return of the black helicopters.

"Something like that couldn't happen here", Bill said shaking his head. "Not in Canada."

"As strange as it may sound, the government does seem to have paramilitary services, and they seem to be active."

"Ah, come on, Father", Bill growled, throwing his cap onto the table. "That sounds like paranoia to me!"

"If it is paranoia, then so be it. There are worse things than paranoia."

"Like what?"

"A country in which civil rights are quietly destroyed without comment or protest."

"Is that happening? I don't see that happening!"

"It is so subtle, and so protected by disinformation, that you will not suspect any change in the life of the country until you are personally hit."

"I haven't been hit. And I haven't seen anybody else hit, either."

"Bill," said Andrei firmly, "we have just been hit. And hit very hard."

Bill and Irene looked dubious, avoiding Andrei's eye.

"If, in the end, the situation is exactly as the government says it is, then the worst that will happen is that a paranoid like me looks a little foolish. But if I am right, and we do nothing, then worse evils will follow. We will all pay a terrible price."

"Even if what you're saying is true, what can we do? This is the government you're talking about!"

"Please hear yourself, Bill. Has the government become so all-powerful that it has forgotten it is our employee, our servant?"

"Hell, none of those guys ever thinks of himself as a servant. They never have; they never will. So what's unusual about that?"

"It's just a bad attitude", Irene suggested.

"There is a great difference between an attitude and a policy", Andrei replied. "I think we may be dealing with a policy of deception. In a democracy that is degenerating into totalitarianism, the State's first task would be to ensure that few people, if any, recognize what is happening."

They remained silent.

"Tell me this: Are you afraid of our government?" Andrei asked.

"Hell, no!" Bill growled.

"I think you are. I think we have all become afraid of our government."

"Maybe", said Irene. "Maybe there's a smidgen of truth in that. Nobody wants trouble. We all want a quiet life. At least I do. And they've been passing so many laws lately you can't keep track of them all. You just can't tell when you're going to break the next one. But you're still guessing, Father. We don't know for sure."

Arrow came back at that moment and sat down on a chair by the door. He took a stuffed animal out of his knapsack and began to button and unbutton its little red jacket. A button popped off and rolled across the floor.

Irene jumped to get it and asked Arrow if he wanted her to sew it back on. He nodded. Relieved by the promise of a definite chore, she put on reading glasses, rummaged in an ample sewing basket, and got out needle and thread. Arrow watched her closely.

Bill stood and said, "Reenie, these folks must be hungry. How about I get that casserole out of the freezer and pop it in the microwave?"

"All right, Bill. Get the leftover salad too. I'll make some garlic bread after I fix Curious George here."

Arrow brightened up, wondering how she knew George's name.

* * *

Bill didn't know how to play chess, but Irene did. She played three games with Arrow on the living room rug and let him win two of them. Bill and Andrei stayed talking in the kitchen. She wanted to hear what they were saying but felt that the boy

68

needed her attention. Bill would tell her everything later, after lights out. He always did. At eight o'clock she ruffled Arrow's hair and told him he was pretty good at chess, better than her grandchildren. He didn't smile. He didn't say a word. That worried her.

Andrei asked Bill and Irene if he and the boy could sleep at their place and try to go north into the interior after breakfast tomorrow. They had no objections. Irene showed Arrow to the guest room, which had two bunk beds, overspilling bookshelves, and toy boxes. She found some boy's pajamas for him and went out to find an extra blanket. He scrambled into the pajamas, fast. Then he snuggled deep beneath a Star Wars quilt on one of the bottom bunks, dragging his teddies in too.

When she returned, she asked if he would like her to say prayers with him.

He didn't answer.

"Do you know any prayers?"

He shook his head.

"Would you like me to teach you some?"

He gave her a half nod, half shrug.

She sat on the edge of the mattress, closed her eyes, made the sign of the cross, and said aloud the Our Father, Hail Mary, and a prayer to his guardian angel. She concluded with: "God bless Arrow and his mum and dad and all his family. Keep him safe, dear Lord, and bring him to heaven one day."

Then she produced a teary smile, kissed his forehead, and messed up his hair again.

"There, that wasn't hard, was it?"

He shook his head. She went out, leaving a night light glowing in a plug beside the door. On the wall beside the bed, the pale green plastic face of a man with a thorny crown on his head watched him for a few minutes, then faded. He felt quiet inside, like a calm ocean. He closed his eyes and floated on a tide of dreams.

When they were sure Arrow was asleep, Bill opened a can of beer, poured Andrei a glass of sherry, and fixed Irene a tumbler of Mary Poppins, which was her version of a Shirley Temple. While he was doing that, Irene made a long distance call to the chancery office in the city and, when she hung up, informed the men that the sisters' funeral would be at the cathedral two days from then. Internment would be at the motherhouse of the Order following the Mass.

She sat beside Bill on the sofa, took a sip of her drink, and began to cry again. Bill held her, and they stared silently out the living room window, watching the rain fall down like brass streamers from the dome of light above the prison. Andrei suggested that they pray. They said a rosary for the souls of the sisters. Then Bill said they should say another one for the police to bring the killers to justice. After that Irene asked if they could pray another for Arrow's family. When they finished, Bill tapped the remote control, and the television flashed on. Commercials galore. He flicked quickly through the channels, surfing over car ads, teenagers fornicating, political commentators, gum ads, canned laughter, cartoons, talk shows, a police drama, a rerun of *Walton's Mountain*, a beer commercial, adults fornicating, a religious channel discussing the power of crystals, followed by a nature show about the rain forest and ozone layer, another sitcom, and finally a news channel. They stayed with that.

A documentary on gun control. The murder of the nuns was central to the thesis of the producers. The increase of violent crime in recent weeks had forced the federal Parliament to re-examine the lenient measures in the new Civilian Firearms Control Act. An Order in Council had just been passed prohibiting the possession of firearms other than low-caliber rifles, which would remain legal only in certain restricted areas where farmers and ranchers depended on them for protection of livestock from predators.

"What?" said Bill, leaning forward.

The two-year grace period for registration of all legal fire-arms had shrunk to three weeks. All weapons, even those owned by citizens in agricultural and frontier regions, must now be registered or turned over to police. Any citizen in possession of an unregistered weapon would be subject to a sentence of up to ten years in prison. Police were granted wide-ranging powers of seizure. Search warrants were no longer required whenever po-lice had reasonable grounds to believe unauthorized weapons were concealed in the homes or on the property of citizens.

Bill whistled. "Well, now," he said, "isn't that interesting." He seemed more fascinated than angry.

"Bill", said Irene in a placating tone. "We've been through this a million times."

"Don't worry, Irene, I'm not going to hit the roof."

Irene looked at Andrei apologetically. "It makes his blood boil", she said. "He's been fighting it for years. He doesn't see why there should be gun registration. Decent law-abiding people register guns. Criminals don't. He thinks it's ridiculous, all that red tape for something that won't stop crime. It's his pet hate." She patted his arm. "Now don't blow a fuse in front of Father."

"I'm not, I'm not", he said quietly, listening to her with one ear, trying to hear the program with the other.

"Last summer he shot a black bear in the backyard", she went on. "It was going through our garbage cans. The thing is, four of the grandchildren were tenting beside the patio that night. I hate to think what could have happened. We're not agricultural here on the hill. Bill, do you think maybe we'll qualify for fron-tier?"

"Not bloody likely", he murmured.

"I hate guns", she informed Andrei.

"I am not fond of them either", he replied. "I have seen too many of them in my life."

"Shush, shush, you two", Bill waved them into silence.

The commentary was interlaced with footage from police seizures of large gun caches in raids on right-wing paramilitary compounds discovered in the southern regions of the prairie provinces and in the interior of British Columbia. American connections. Citizens' Militia. K.K.K. Neo-Nazis. Assassinations of rival groups. Archive shots of the Oklahoma City bombing. Then a reference to an obscure religious cult in the B.C. interior, connected to a right-wing newspaper, *The Swiftcreek Echo*, now closed down under the hate-literature laws.

"There is our first verifiable lie", said Andrei. "*The Echo* never, in the many years I knew and read it, *ever* said a word to encourage acts of hatred. Its editor was Arrow's father."

Bill and Irene looked at Andrei with amazement.

"Then why would they say such a thing?"

"Because in his editorials Nathaniel continued to refer to abortion and euthanasia as murder, long after the law declared the term to be a defamation of character and an incitement to violence."

There was the editor's face on the screen. Nathaniel Delaney, said the commentator, had abducted two children, wards of the State, still missing. He had bludgeoned a school employee to death during the abduction. There was another victim, a teenager dead of gun-shot wounds. Delaney had been killed in a shoot-out with the police. Cut to an interview with an agent in a gray and green pilot's jumpsuit. Behind him a gray and green helicopter. No markings.

Bill and Irene, confused and upset, looked back at Andrei questioningly.

"There are our second and third lies", said Andrei "The two children were his own children. They were not wards of the State, although they were close to being abducted by one of the provincial ministries, probably at the urging of the federal agency that orchestrated all of this. The man who was bludgeoned to death was in fact a friend of Nathaniel's and helped him and his children to escape. Someone else killed him—perhaps these new police. And regarding the dead teenager, he was a friend of the Delaneys who travelled with them when they fled—I know for certain that an agent in a gray and green helicopter fired upon and mortally wounded that boy. I heard his last confession. I saw Nathaniel risk his life to try to save him."

Bill and Irene stared at Andrei with open mouths. It was too much to take in all at once, but Andrei hoped they were big enough to accept it.

"You mean to tell us", said Irene, "that Arrow's father has been killed, and he doesn't even know?"

"That is correct. I ask you not to mention it to him. His world has been turned upside down, totally. He is emotionally fragile. Tomorrow I will try to take him into the interior to his great-grandfather, Thaddaeus Tobac. His brother and sister are there too. That is a better place to inform him of this horrible news."

The Wannamakers didn't know what to think. Bill got up and returned with another beer.

More footage crossed the screen. Waco, Texas, burning. Scenes from several other police actions, gun seizures—some of it political, some of it pure criminal, some of it the outer limits of the lunatic fringe, if there was an outer limit. Then scenes from yesterday's mayhem at the drug commune near Fort George. Yellow police tape. Squad cars, cherry lights flashing, corpses in body bags being loaded into ambulances. Plastic garbage bags split open revealing marijuana.

Bill harrumphed. "Loco-weed", he snorted. "The whole thing's loco."

All residents dead except for one man and an eight-year-old boy, last seen running from the scene of the crime. Interview with the lone adult survivor, a long-haired druggie in an Indian costume. Richard Schwartz, under arrest for possession of illegal substances. Quick cut to the same man, cleaned up, seated at a desk in front of a microphone, dressed in a prison uniform. Behind him a law enforcement agent in a gray and green uniform. The prisoner looked straight at the camera and said in a sullen voice that the destruction of his community was an act of vengeance committed by a rival organization. Hong Kong drug lords, he said.

The shaman! Andrei thought.

"Another lie", he said.

By now Bill and Irene were not paying much attention to Andrei. They bent forward, absorbing every word from the television.

"His mother is dead", said Andrei, barely audible. Bill and Irene did not reply.

Next, a women's rights organization condemned male violence. Then an articulate spokesman for a coalition of citizens' groups urged the government to get tough with crime. Followed by a short interview with a gun-rights spokesman who massacred English grammar and made not a single coherent point, though he made several that were obviously inflammatory. Then an interview with a provincial party leader, who said that the voters in the province were increasingly concerned about the growth of religious cults and their use of lethal weapons to defend their communities from intervention by ministries of the government. He cited child neglect and abuse statistics taken from studies of the cults.

The program reached a climax with a brilliant summation of the "massing configuration of violence in the country" and an appeal to the government to reintroduce effective measures for the maintenance of law and order. Finally, an interview with the federal Minister of Justice, who assured a journalist that the government was especially sensitive to the need for preservation of human rights in emergency situations and that it would never resort to the War Measures Act. However, he said that the ministry would do everything in its power under the existing statutes, assisted by a temporary extension of emergency measures, to bring the guilty to justice. End of program.

"Whew", said Bill, shaking his head. "When I got up this morning, I thought it was going to be another boring day."

Bill put the broadcast on mute. They waited silently through five commercials. Then the late night news came on.

North Korea saber rattling at the South. More free trade negotiations. U.N. commanders asking for more powers in Africa and the Balkans. The President of the Europarliament negotiating a dispute in Africa. Russia asking for bigger loans from the U.S. The Pope's health failing. Illegal Mexican refugees shot near San Diego.

Then the local news: "This morning's" massacre of the nuns. (Irene began to cry again. Bill put his arm around her.) Police investigation. No black helicopters in sight, but a ten-second shot of a gray one scanning the woods around the convent. Positive clues linking the murder to a secret religious cult. The nuns' missing chaplain wanted for questioning. A photo of Father Andrei. (Bill and Irene froze and didn't look across the room at him.) Interview with the Ministry of Human Resources on the need for the severest possible sentencing against abductors. Three missing children. (Bill and Irene still wouldn't look at him.) Police had uncovered a link between last week's abduction case in the interior to the child missing from the drug commune near Fort George, British Columbia. The missing children were all Delaneys. Three photos. More gun control interviews, followed by the Minister of Justice. Five commercials, executed with stunning computer graphics, then an announcement urging viewers to stay tuned for the special report on violence (which Bill, Irene, and Andrei had just watched), to be rebroadcast after sports and weather.

The phone rang. Irene went to answer it. Bill muted the television and stared at the commercials without blinking. Irene's voice carried from the kitchen, a weave of silences and comments:

75

"I know. It's terrible. How could this happen?"

Sobbing. Blowing of nose.

"It's breaking my heart too. Yes, at the cathedral on Friday. Ten in the morning. Uh-huh. I know."

Long silence.

"I know, honey. We just saw the news. No, he's all right. He's here."

More silence.

"I don't think you should come up right now."

Pause.

"It's complicated. I'll explain tomorrow."

Irene called from the kitchen, "Bill, it's Julie. Can you talk to her?"

Bill groaned and maneuvered himself off the sofa. Andrei listened to his deep bass rumbling to his daughter.

"Yeah, sweetie. It's a mess. The police don't know for sure. Just a sec. I wanna talk on the extension. Don't hang up."

Bill went down the hall to the bedroom and shut the door. Irene hung up the wall phone in the kitchen and returned to the living room. She sat on the edge of the sofa, dabbing her eyes with a handkerchief.

"Is she all right?" said Andrei.

Irene nodded but said nothing. She kept staring at the television screen. Andrei prayed silently.

Bill opened the bedroom door and called, "Father, can you talk to Julie?"

Andrei went to the bedroom. Bill handed him the receiver and went out, closing the door behind him.

"Hello, Julie."

"Father." Her voice was weak but steady.

"Words are impossible", he said.

"I know. Don't try."

"Pray."

"I've been praying ever since we heard it on the ten o'clock

76

news. Colin is really upset. The kids don't know. They're asleep."

"Did your mother and father explain what I've been trying to tell them?"

"Dad told me some of what you said. Mum's just hurting."

"It's very hard for them to understand."

"They're in shock. Give them a little time."

"They are struggling with it. They are not sure if they should believe me."

"Don't worry. They love you. This thing has scrambled everyone's brains. It'll settle out in the morning."

"I hope so. It's too much to explain over the phone, but I am in danger."

"What kind of danger?"

"I'm not exactly sure. But I think it's a web of deception created by the government. It wants me in custody, and it wants the child who is with me."

"The missing boy?"

"Yes. And if what I suspect is true, we are in danger because both of us are witnesses to the government's involvement in the death of our friends and the attack on the commune."

"Dad said that much. Are you sure?"

"I'm sure. I saw it with my own eyes. I beg you, do not believe anything the media or police say from now on."

She sighed.

"Don't worry, Father. I figured that out a long time ago. Why do you think we're going sailing around the world?"

"I'm glad you understand."

"Can I see you? I could drive up now."

"Better wait until morning. I hope to find a ride to the Cariboo mountains tomorrow sometime."

"I'll drive you."

"No, I don't think that would be wise."

"Why not?"

"Because if the situation is as bad as I suspect, you would be putting yourself into danger."

"What, for giving a guy a lift?"

"Things are not normal, Julie. The laws have changed radically, and hardly anyone knows it yet. You can be perfectly innocent, and yet they would arrest you if they suspect I've told you about their involvement in the massacres. If we were stopped by police, it would mean imprisonment for all of us. You could be held indefinitely without legal representation, without trial, under the emergency measures law."

"That's scary", she breathed. "What's going on?"

"There have been deaths. More than you know about. I suspect the media is permitted to reveal only enough to help engineer the government's objectives."

"I'm a bit worried about Mum and Dad. They're glued to that idiot box day and night, ever since Dad's retirement. They used to have a lot of wisdom. Lately, I don't know, they seem to have lost some of it. They say stuff that I know came right out of the tube."

"I sense it too. They have invested considerable trust in the media."

"Colin and I stopped watching TV years ago. You know, like the song says, *movin' to the country, gonna eat peaches, throw away my tee-vee!* The kids have never had it, thank God. I can't pry Cub out of a book with a crowbar."

"More to your credit."

"So what are your plans?"

"I'm staying with your parents tonight. I hope to say Mass for them early tomorrow. If you can join us, please do. Then we'll discuss ways of reuniting this boy with his family."

"Okay. What time?"

"About eight?"

"I'll be there."

"Thank you, Julie. Your trust in me means a great deal."

"Not to worry. And don't worry about Mum and Dad, either. They'll come around."

After she hung up, he sat in the darkened bedroom. A wave of exhaustion hit him, and his heart began to palpitate. When it steadied, he went back to the living room. Bill and Irene were sitting close together on the sofa, whispering, holding hands.

"She's coming here at eight in the morning", said Andrei. "Would you like me to say Mass then?"

They nodded.

Irene stood and kissed Andrei on the cheek.

"You can sleep in the den, Father. I just took a Prozac. I'm going to lie down. Don't be long, Bill."

"Okay, Reenie."

When she was gone, Bill flicked off the television and stared at the floor.

"Try to believe me", Andrei said.

"I believe you. It's a lot to take in at once."

"I know."

"You want some more sherry?"

"No, thank you."

"Well, I'm gonna have another beer."

Bill settled into his armchair, drank half a can, and said, "Julie says she'll disown us if we don't listen to you."

"She always was prone to exaggeration."

"I'll say. Feisty gal. More guts than a slaughterhouse."

He got up and closed the curtains.

"Don't want anyone peeking", he said. "You got a famous face now. A real celebrity. Like what's-his-name—you know, that actor in *The Fugitive*—Harrison Ford."

Bill rambled, describing a number of his favorite videos and television dramas.

"What bothers me", he said, musing, "is if the sisters got killed this morning, how come that fancy program on violence had a big section about them, eh?"

79

"Supposedly only a few hours after the crime."

"Yeah. That's uncanny."

"It is, isn't it?"

"Pretty fast work, I'd say."

"They are fast", said Andrei.

"Damn fast."

Bill opened another beer.

"Did I ever tell you about the war, Father?"

"No."

"I landed in Normandy four days after D-Day. Drove Sherman tanks across Europe. I had three shot out from under me. I could show you my scars. I survived three crews killed. I held my best friend in my arms as he died. I still dream about Nazis chasing me. Almost every night I dream about them."

"I dream about them sometimes too. When I was in prison as a young priest, I met several."

"Really? Nazis?"

"Gestapo."

"No kidding!" said Bill, looking impressed.

"I have scars too."

"Yeah, I always meant to ask you about that thing on your cheek."

"A souvenir from an interrogation." Andrei did not mention the fact that the worst of his scars were lodged in his memory.

"So what did we fight the war for? If what you say is true, how come all those guys died, if we end up being ruled by a bunch of Nazis anyway?"

"The problem is, these are very discreet Nazis. They continually declare their hatred of Nazism. They don't look like tyrants, do they?"

"If it talks like a lamb but walks like a wolf and kills like a wolf, maybe it's a wolf."

"I would say it *is* a wolf. But there is a transition period during which the wolf does not reveal his true nature."

"And you're saying this is that time?"

"I believe it is."

Bill groaned.

"Terrific! Just what I needed. Reenie and me have been planning this trip in the Winnebago for years. We're due to leave next month, after Julie and the gang sail off on their trip around the world."

"You can still go."

"Yeah, I guess. But I'd rather stick around for a while and keep an eye on things. We got six kids in this province and a flock of grandkids. What's gonna happen to *them*, eh?"

"Probably nothing. The government relies on the majority of the population remaining undisturbed."

"Sure, everybody keep nice and quiet while they bend our kids' heads. Right?" Bill was beginning to slur his words. An irritable note was growing sentence by sentence.

"Right?" Bill demanded.

"Absolutely correct."

"So what do we do, eh?"

"Each man must decide that for himself. You must pray and ask God for wisdom. Ask for the protection of the holy angels for every member of your family."

Bill sucked his can dry and said, "Where were the angels when the sisters got whacked?"

"Where were they when Christ was crucified?" the priest replied.

"I dunno. You tell me."

"Some of God's children are called to martyrdom. God permits it in order for a greater good to come about."

"That's nice, Father. Hope you don't mind if we go for the lesser good."

The phone rang.

"Who the hell's that? It's after midnight!"

Bill went to the kitchen and grumbled into the phone for ten minutes. When he came back he said, "That was Eddie Coglin. He wants me to chair a meeting at the Legion tomorrow night. The valley vets are hopping mad about the new gun law. He's got other stuff he wants to talk with me about. Says it's secret. Thinks something real bad is shaping up. It's just a theory of his, but he needs to bounce it off someone. He's coming over tomorrow."

"Is that wise? I should not be seen."

Bill thought about that. "What time are you leaving?"

"I'm not sure. Is there a car rental agency in Fort George?"

"Yeah. But I don't think you wanna go down and rent one, not with your mug on the TV. I can arrange it. I got friends."

"Thank you, Bill."

"No problem. I can do it for you. But look—no offense—I think renting a car is a real dumb idea."

"How so?"

"You and the kid drive up north, and sure enough somebody's gonna spot you on the highway, even if there are no cops checking cars. You'll need to stop for gas, won't you? What if you have engine trouble? Probably three million people in this province saw your face on TV tonight."

"You have a point."

"I'm gonna drive you."

"No. That would be foolish. If we are stopped by police, we will all be arrested."

Once again, Andrei tried to explain the situation. After a while it became obvious that Bill wasn't listening.

"So what if they arrest me? What can they do? They'll just make jackasses of themselves if they try. I'm the head of the Royal Canadian Legion post here. I'm bowling champion of the Lower Fraser. I'm a respectable businessman, good church-going guy, property owner —"

"Bill, Bill, you simply do not understand. Everything has changed. The State, the police, the law. It has all been trans-

formed, practically overnight, and only a handful of people realize it."

Bill fell asleep in his armchair, and Andrei went to bed.

* * *

He was up, washed, and dressed before the rest of the household was awake. The overcast had broken, and the dawn sky was
a broad, clean blue. According to the thermometer on the back
porch, the temperature was a degree above freezing. He prayed
his office in the den and then set up the altar vessels on the
dining room table. The portable Mass kit smelled musty, but the
tiny chalice and paten were untarnished, the linens and the hosts
still fresh inside a plastic bag. Bill's electric razor buzzed down
the hall, and Irene puttered in the kitchen, setting up the coffee
maker. He vested and sat down at the head of the dining room
table, preparing the day's Scripture readings. Irene passed
through the room in her pink chenille bathrobe, gave him a pat
on the shoulder, and said, "Seven forty-five. Julie should be here
in a few minutes. Can you let her in? I'll get myself decent."

"Fine, we'll begin when she arrives."

"Do you want me to wake up the boy?"

"Let him sleep."

Shortly after, a yellow Honda purred into the driveway, and
Andrei went to the front door to answer the *bing-bong*.

Julie hustled in, carrying a paper bag, and closed the door
quickly. She hugged Andrei, looked him over to see if he was all
right, and gave him a brave smile.

"Sleep okay?"

"I rested", he said.

"Where's Mum?"

"She's getting dressed. Your Dad is shaving."

"I've brought breakfast. You like Eggo waffles?"

Andrei had never heard of them.

She put the bag on the counter by the toaster, rattled the

coffee maker to get it going, and sat down at the end of the dining room table. She opened an old Bible and flipped through it.

"I don't know for sure what this means, Father", she said as Andrei took his seat. "Last night after we talked, I was reading Scripture, and I really felt the Holy Spirit speaking to me through one passage in particular. It just seemed to be meant for you."

"What passage?"

"Revelation. Chapter twelve."

"Yes, I know it well."

"Let me read it to you: 'And a great sign appeared in the heavens, a woman clothed with the sun, with the moon under her feet, and on her head a crown of twelve stars. She was with child, and she cried out in her birth pangs, in anguish, for delivery. And another portent appeared in the heavens; behold a great red dragon, with seven heads and ten horns, and seven crowns upon his heads. His tail swept down a third of the stars from heaven, and cast them to the earth. And the dragon stood before the woman who was about to bear a child, that he might devour her child when she brought it forth.' "

She looked up. "Mean anything to you?"

"Yes, I think so. Read on, Julie."

" 'But her child was caught up to God and to his throne, and the woman fled into the wilderness.' "

She read the rest silently until her mother appeared, kissed her, and sat down beside her. Bill arrived a moment later and said, "Morning, everyone."

The Mass was brief. There was no homily. The Lenten epistle was apocalyptic. The day's Gospel was the Lord's foretelling of his Passion. The apostles didn't seem to believe him. The recollection after Communion was long. No one wished to break the flow of interior peace. After the final blessing and dismissal, everyone sat in his place, eyes closed, wanting it to go on.

Eventually Irene said, "Well, someone has to be responsible here." She got up and went out to the kitchen to fix breakfast.

"Did you bring these, Julie?" she called.

"I did, Mum. There's real maple syrup too."

"Found it. Give me a hand, will you?"

The phone rang, and Bill took it.

He talked into it cryptically, grunted and uh-huhed repeatedly, and said he'd phone back later.

"That was Eddie Coglin, Reenie. He's really got a burr under his saddle about the gun thing. Wants me to chair a meeting at the Legion tonight. I said I'd phone him back."

"Dear Eddie", said Irene. "I suppose he'll want you to drink with him after."

"I suppose", Bill drawled.

"Guns and war stories. That's all you think about."

"Well, a bit more than that. He's all fired up about another conspiracy theory."

"Oh, no, not again!"

"You have to know this friend of mine", Bill said, turning to Andrei. "Eddie's still slightly shell-shocked, fifty-five years after D-Day. He's got more conspiracy theories than spots on a leopard. He's got one about a leopard too. Anyway, that's another story."

"Don't let him drag you into anything, Bill. We have a funeral the day after tomorrow."

She choked up. Julie hugged Irene and held her.

The waffles popped. The coffee maker burbled. Arrow walked into the room looking dazed, rubbing his eyes. His pajamas were wet. Irene bustled him down the hallway toward the bathroom.

Bill turned to Andrei and grimaced. "Eddie says he thinks the cops killed the hippies. And he's pretty sure a secret army unit run by Masons killed the sisters. He saw a black helicopter heading upriver yesterday afternoon. Wants to know if I've ever noticed them before."

Irene came back, shaking her head.

"You'd think that child had never seen a tub. He's sitting in it splashing hot water on himself as if it were a seven-day wonder!"

"Eddie thinks we should discuss the murders and the chopper with the members tonight. The Calgary thing too."

Irene rolled her eyes. "Groan", she said.

"What's this about Calgary, Dad?"

"Don't you remember, Julie? Oh, maybe you were in the convent then."

"Eddie dragged Dad off to Calgary", said Irene. "When was it? Sometime in the late eighties, I think. Eddie said if we didn't go we'd all be in concentration camps within a year."

"Yup. Eddie's crazy, but he hits the nail on the head sometimes."

"So what happened in Calgary, Dad?"

"This judge took out a full-page ad in the *Calgary Herald*. He said the Prime Minister and the Cabinet just passed a whole bunch of Orders in Council with provisions for suspension of civil rights in emergency situations, for national security. One of the items was for the construction of civilian internment camps."

"Civilian internment camps? What's that?" said Julie, munching an Eggo, brows arched.

"Don't ask me. That's what the judge called it. I guess it's what Ottawa called it too. So this ad announced a public meeting to talk the whole thing over. The judge said that no members of Parliament had voted for it, no media were saying a word about it, and why should we accept it as law without discussion, when such a law would've been squashed like a bug if it had ever come to the House and Senate. There were several fishy elements to the new law, he said. Citizens had better act now, or they could say so long to civil rights within a few years."

"Are you serious? I never heard anything about that", said Julie.

"Yeah. Most people haven't. But it happened. Eddie and me drove to Calgary for the meeting. Only about two hundred people turned out for it. It was in a high-school gym. The judge chaired it. He explained the powers of the Prime Minister and his Council under the Constitution. It's legal. They can do it. The only solution, he said, was to kick up such a fuss that the whole country turfed those guys out of office fast."

"What happened?"

"A big fat zero. Not a word about that meeting in the press. Not a word on TV. The judge was retired a few months later."

"Was there any solid information at the meeting?" Andrei asked. "Any proof that these camps have been built?"

"Nothing for sure. But a funny thing happened during the question period. This guy—a regular-looking guy—stands up and says he hopes the audience won't think he's crazy, but something just happened to him, and it might be related. He says he's a truck driver, an eighteen-wheeler man out of Edmonton. He says he's just delivered a transport load of handcuffs to some place in northern Alberta. It was a federal shipment, insulation, according to the bill of lading. But he said he knew it was too heavy for insulation and checked it out.

"He said the place isn't even on the map. Some kind of government installation. High security, warning signs, guards, fences. It was huge, a lot of square miles inside those fences. He said he didn't see any buildings, just a warehouse near the gate where he dropped the load. That's all he saw, but it struck him as pretty strange at the time.

"That got Eddie excited, but I was trying to stay cool. I told him it could be a coincidence; it could be anything. Told him not to get paranoid. Then another guy stands up on the other side of the room. He says, 'People, you're probably not going to believe me, but I'm a transport driver too, and I just delivered a load to the same kind of place in northern B.C.'

"Someone in the crowd asked him if he knew what the contents of the shipment were. He said he had a minor accident on the road. A blowout and a dented trailer. For insurance purposes he had to check for damage in the box. The bill of lading said it was plastic pipe. It wasn't. It was handcuffs and riot equipment.

"By this time some folks in the crowd were getting worked up. Lots of others were making noises like they thought it was all a big deal over nothing. I would have thought so too, except that the second driver was a guy I know. He does contract work for our company sometimes. He's as down to earth as you can get and honest as the day is long. These people weren't telling fairy stories. The meeting broke up into a hundred arguments. The judge looked disgusted and walked out. I haven't heard a word about it since."

"Okay, Bill, but that doesn't mean anything's going on in those places", Irene objected. "It could be Ottawa just wants the right to build them in case of war or . . ."

"Or what?" said Bill.

"Well, I don't know what. But it's the last thing we need to be concerned about right now."

"Maybe, maybe not", Bill grunted.

Arrow sat down at the table, fully dressed. Irene introduced him to Julie and loaded his plate. She poured syrup, and he tore into the waffles.

Bill drank three cups of coffee while the women washed dishes. He was thinking hard about something.

"Look, Father. I know a way we can get you up to wherever it is you want to go. We'll take the Winnebago. You can sit pretty in the back, have a great ride, sleep if you want, and no one'll see your faces."

Irene stopped chattering and listened.

"It might work", Andrei said.

Bill looked at Irene, and Irene looked at Bill, until some kind of soundless negotiation was hammered out between them. When Irene's permission was granted, with a few anxious looks, Bill went out to the driveway to jack up the Winnebago and get the blocks out from under it.

Half an hour later he was back, looking cheerful.

"Hey, this feels great. It's just what we've been needing. I've been turning into a couch potato lately."

He got Eddie on the phone and told him he couldn't make it to the Legion that night, but maybe after the funeral on Friday they could have a meeting. The faint metallic voice on the other end of the line sounded upset. Bill grumbled, placated, and teased.

"Friday's poker night. The world won't fall apart till then. We can talk about the conspiracy with the over-the-hill gang, have a pizza'n'beer, chew the rag. Yah, yah, of course I'll be there. Wouldn't miss it for the world. My only chance to get back that forty bucks you gypped me out of, you card shark! Ha, ha! You too, Ed, have a good one!"

Bill hung up, muttering to himself, rubbing frustration off his face.

"Have a good one, have a good one! Sheesh! Why do I put up with that guy?"

* * *

There were no other houses at the end of the Wannamakers' lane. But Bill went outside first to check for observers. He started up the motor, filled the water tanks from the garden hose, and turned on the propane heater in the back.

Making sure the coast was clear, he signalled to the living room window, and everyone came out. Julie asked for Andrei's blessing. She and Irene knelt down on the wet tarmac, while Bill stood, looking uncomfortable. All three made the sign of the cross. Julie hugged the priest and tried to look positive.

"Happy trails", she said breezily.

"Until we meet again", said her father. Andrei and Arrow climbed into the back and sat on the soft cushions of the side seats.

Irene jumped up beside them with a big wicker basket.

"Lunch", she said.

Arrow gazed around, entranced.

"Do you like the Winnebago, Arrow?" said Julie, poking her head through the open back door.

He nodded.

Irene closed the back door, locked it, and went out through the other door at front left. Bill closed the sliding doors between the cockpit and the back, and put the gear into reverse. He slammed on the brakes suddenly, as Irene jumped into the passenger seat beside him.

"Not so fast, Bud."

"Where you think you're going, Reenie?"

"With you."

"No, you aren't."

"Yes, I am."

"Out. Right now. I'm not joking."

"Me neither."

"Reenie", he pleaded. "Don't be stubborn. There could be problems."

"Exactly. That's why you need someone level-headed to fly navigator."

He bowed his head over the wheel and muttered. "All my life I've fought this woman, and all my life she's beat me. Why should I start winning now?"

She whipped out a large rosary of green plastic beads and grinned at him.

"Okay, couch potato, let's go!"

"Mum, are you sure about this?" Julie yelled through the window.

"As sure as I'll ever be. Somebody has to look after him."

Julie threw up her hands.

Fifteen minutes later they were cruising into the east on the north side of the Fraser River.

Irene pulled open the sliding doors, and Bill called into the back:

"Okay, directions, please, Father. Where are we going?"

"First we have to go to Williams Lake. From there we turn east into the Cariboo. I'll tell you the rest when we arrive at Horsefly."

"The teeming metropolis of Horsefly it is!"

Andrei went forward and put the ten dollars Théophane Nguyen had given him onto Bill's lap. "This is for gas. It's not much, but I hope it helps."

Irene took the money and handed it back with a scold in her eyes.

"You just keep that, Father. You'll be needing it, no doubt. And here . . ." She dug around in her purse. "Oh, dear, I wanted to give you something, but it looks like I'm fresh out. If we pass a bank machine, Bill, just pull over, will you? I need to get some cash."

Bill grunted, "You bet!" Andrei thanked them and went back to sit beside Arrow, who was pressing his face to the glass.

"Arrow, I think you had better keep away from the window."

"Why, Andrei?"

How to tell him? How to explain that practically everyone in the province was looking for him, and if he were caught, he would be turned over to men who would . . . He tried not to think about it.

"Just for now, we should be private. Your great-grandfather wants to meet you very much. If we are stopped, you might not be able to see him for a long time."

Arrow pondered that and slid away from the window.

"We'll gas up at Hope", Bill said. "Forty-five minutes from here. You and the boy should keep out of sight at the station.

There's a sleeping alcove you can tuck yourselves into when we stop. Or the john."

The valley narrowed toward its eastern end. Climbing steadily along the flanks of the ridges, the vehicle slowed to thirty miles an hour. It crept around the more precipitous curves and descended from time to time into small, hanging valleys, only to rise again on steeper inclines. The forest crowded the road, tall firs and spruce, pine and cedar. Bald eagles soared above the valley floor, while below their serene flight the river broadened out and washed ice-blue over shallow flats. The sun crested the southern range and filled the cab with a sweet light. It was warmer now, and Andrei turned down the heater.

Three miles before Hope, where 7 east joined 1 north, the Winnebago rounded a bend. Bill instinctively pumped the brakes and decelerated.

"Uh-oh! Cops!"

"Good Lord!" Irene said, hand on her heart.

Two white cars with flashing cherries on top were parked across from each other on the shoulders of the highway. A road-block across the northbound lane. An officer standing on the yellow line waving an orange fluorescent baton.

Bill slowed to a stop beside him and rolled down his window.

"Morning, officer."

"Good morning, sir. Where are you travelling today?"

"Wife and I are going up number 1 to Williams Lake."

"May I see your driver's license and insurance, please."

Bill handed them over, smiled at him, and tilted his Legion hat down a little so the constable could notice—big maple leaf, upstanding citizen, patriot, loyal.

"That's fine, sir. Everything seems in order. May I ask the reason for your journey?"

"Sure. We're giving old Bessie a trial run. We're taking her to California come May."

"Just the two of you in the vehicle?"

Irene leaned over and gave the constable her most ingratiating smile—grandmother, sweet as pineapple upside-down cake.

"We're spending our kids' inheritance", she quipped. "Just like the bumper sticker says."

He smiled back at her.

"Just the two of you in the vehicle?" he repeated.

"Uh-huh", Bill said.

"Would you open up the back, please, sir."

"Uh, no problem. But is that really necessary? I mean, Reenie and me are—"

"Open the back, please."

"Just a moment, officer", Bill said, looking grumpy. "Is that legal? Don't you have to have a search warrant?"

The constable looked across the road to the other white car and made a gesture. A constable got out of it and stood watching.

"It's perfectly legal. We're searching for missing persons. Now, if you'll just get out, please, and open it up."

"I got a bad back."

"I understand, sir. Then you'll have to give me your keys. I'll open it from the outside. It's just a formality."

"I'm going to write to my M.P. about this. I'm a vet. I drove a tank in the war, and I got wounded keeping this country safe for democracy. Before you were born, young man."

"Well, that's fine, sir. Give me the keys, please."

Bill handed him the keys and prepared to die. His face turned beet red. His fingers gripped the wheel until they turned white. Irene's eyes were terrified, and her lips turned blue. She whispered prayers frantically.

"Jesus, Mary, and Joseph, don't let him find them! Jesus, Mary, and Joseph, make them invisible!"

They didn't breathe when the back door opened on its rusty hinges. They stared straight ahead through the windshield as the constable thumped and bumped in the back. Then the hinges squealed again, and he was by the passenger window, handing Bill the keys.

"Thanks. Sorry for the inconvenience. We have to check everything leaving the lower Fraser Valley."

"No problem", Bill exhaled.

"Have a nice trip."

"Thanks. I won't write to my M.P."

The constable looked amused.

"That's okay. You can write to him."

"Who you looking for?"

"Missing persons."

"Oh, you mean those kids?"

"Yep."

"That's a real tragedy. Some people are crazy, abducting kids."

"Yep, they sure are crazy."

"It's sick", Bill said, indignant. Irene tugged his arm. Cars were lining up behind them.

"Please move on now, sir."

The officer tipped his cap, and Bill drove on.

They didn't look at each other until the exit for the town of Hope. Bill pulled into the first gas station and unclamped his fingers. Irene patted her heart.

"That was not funny", she murmured.

"I agree. Not funny in the least."

While the attendant was filling the tanks, Irene slid open the folding doors and peeked into the back.

"Father?" she whispered.

No reply.

"Not a sign of them."

"Leave it be, Irene. We'll check outside of town."

They paid for the gas and drove back toward number 1 north.

"That was a close call", she said.

"Too close for comfort."

"Bill, I'm not sure about this. Maybe we should go home."

"No. We just got through their checkpoint. We'll be fine from now on."

"What if there are other roadblocks?"

"There probably won't be."

"But what if there *are*?"

"We got through one", he said fiercely. "We'll get through another."

"The Lord saved us this time. But it could be his way of warning us. Let's turn around."

"No."

"Bill", she pleaded.

"I said no!"

Hurt, she looked out the passenger window.

Half an hour later they were still coasting high above the Fraser canyon. The river roiled through the canyon below the road. A large sign flashed by: *You are now entering Spuzzum*. Three seconds later they had passed through a cluster of houses and a store. Another sign: *You are now leaving Spuzzum*.

"At least someone has a sense of humor", Bill said.

"Let's turn around. Please!"

"Forget it. I went through the Battle of the Bulge. I'm not letting some twerp of a cop stop us."

At Hell's Gate, where the river tore through a narrow gorge, they pulled off onto a public siding overlooking the river. A sign by the trash barrels said: *Scenic view*. Irene went into the back and called nervously, "Father? Arrow?"

Andrei and Arrow appeared suddenly, rising up from under the hinged seats of the kitchenette benches.

"Thank God!" she gasped. "Thank God!"

"Yes, thank God! These are quite good priest holes."

"Were you hiding in there all this time?"

"Yes. It was comfortable."

"Arrow, are you all right? Could you breath okay in there?"
The boy nodded.

"Were you frightened?"
He shook his head.

She fed them lunch from the basket, fussing over them.

Bill came back and ate a sandwich with them and drank the coffee Irene poured for him from the thermos. He described the roadblock to Andrei.

"We should have expected that", Andrei said. "Nevertheless, we have survived. Do you want to go on?"

"Not much", said Irene.

"Sure do", said Bill.

At that moment a police car drove up beside them and parked. The driver gazed up at the kitchenette window with a bored expression. Bill and Irene smiled down at him. He looked away without acknowledging.

"Quick," Bill said, "you two, under the seats!"

Bill and Irene continued to finish their lunch without hurry, glancing down at the police car every so often. The driver ate a sandwich and drank coffee from a styrofoam cup. When he was finished, he got out, put the trash in the barrel, and drove away. Bill went forward to the cockpit and watched him. The police car went a hundred yards down the pavement and pulled over to the shoulder. A few minutes later a second car pulled up on the opposite side. Both drivers got out, talked, and removed road-block equipment from their trunks.

"Uh-oh", said Bill.

"There's no telling how many of those we'll meet going north", Irene said anxiously. "One of them is bound to search us with a fine-tooth comb."

"We don't know that for sure."

"Should we risk it?"

"I'm willing. Come on, Reenie, what have we got to lose? A few years in front of the boob tube? Let's go out in style."

She pondered it, squinting at him. Then she said emphatically, "You're right. Let's go for broke."

When Andrei came up out of his hiding place, they told him their plan. He asked for a few minutes to think about it. He put his head in his hands. They could tell he was praying. When he looked up, he said, "I am not at peace. We must turn back."

Irene and Bill exchanged a look and shrugged.

"Just when Reenie was finally ready to play Joan of Arc!" grumbled Bill.

"That's not funny", Irene said, sliding into the copilot's seat. "Couch potato", she added.

The Winnebago circled slowly through the parking lot and eased back onto the highway. At Hope they took the branch to the south side of the river and followed the Trans-Canada Highway west, arriving at Fort George just before suppertime. While Bill shut the Winnebago down, turned off its heater, and drained the water tanks, the others went into the house, fighting a heavy feeling of defeat. Irene told Andrei to fix himself and the boy a meal from the leftovers in the fridge. She went into the bedroom and lay on her back with the lights off, staring at the ceiling. When Bill came in later and lay down beside her, she rolled away and faced the wall. He gave her half an hour like that. Then he took her hand and held it.

4

Arion Empiricorum

"That settles it", Bill said. "We're leaving right after the funeral."

He and Irene sat alone at the kitchen table in the early morning light, drinking their second pot of coffee.

"Are you sure we aren't being a little hasty?"

"Not at all", Bill said in a reasonable tone. "I've been going crazy ticking off days on the calendar. Why wait till May? It's warm in Oregon and California right now. We can be there in twelve hours."

"If you're sure. Maybe we're just running away."

"Reenie," he said, fixing her with a patient look, "that's exactly what it is. You want to sit around here for another six weeks brooding about the sisters, counting the days till we leave? What are we waiting for?"

"Well, we can't go till Father and the boy are safely on their way."

"He'll be awake soon. We'll talk it over with him."

"Don't get any ideas about taking them with us."

"I'm not that stupid."

"We'd all be arrested at the border, lickety-split. I'm sure of it."

She sighed. She put on her glasses, opened her sewing basket, and began crocheting a half-finished house slipper from a skein of rainbow-colored wool.

"If we go on Saturday, that means we won't see the children again until we meet up in Los Angeles", she murmured.

"I know."

"It could be months before we see them again."

"Yep", he said moodily.

"I'm not even finished with Julie's slippers. I'm still waiting for that order of pale green for Cub's sweater too. The craft store's all out of the right color. Kathy's is done, and Tessa's, but that's all. Do you think Colin will be hurt if I don't have his sweater finished on time?"

"I don't think so. I gave him my army binoculars."

"Oh, but that's so . . . so *male*. I mean, shouldn't we give him something from us that's warm and comfy?"

"I don't think Colin will miss it."

"Julie says he thinks you don't like him."

"I like him well enough. He's okay. He shouldn't be so sensitive."

"Well, he is sensitive. And smart. And he's so far from home."

"She shouldn't have married a guy from Australia."

"Well, there's no accounting for love, is there, dear?" She reached out and patted the back of his hand affectionately.

"And what about the kids?" Bill grumbled. "Taking them out of school like that! They're going to be ignorant and uneducated."

"No, they won't. Think of all those university degrees Colin's got. Julie's stuffed the boat with books and correspondence courses for the children."

"Books!" Bill said. "Some ballast!"

"Don't worry, they'll be fine."

"Why couldn't they have just stayed in Vancouver? He made a real success of that computer business. They could be rich. But oh, no, what does he do with it? Sells the business and builds a leaky barge so he can take my daughter and my grandchildren around the world. Great!"

"Now, now, Bill. It's an adventure. The children will thank their parents for it some day."

"I hope so."

"Still, it doesn't seem reasonable."

"What doesn't?"

"For us to leave so suddenly. Without their gifts being ready."

Bill was an old hand at negotiations with Irene. He wisely chose to keep silent.

"Sometimes I lie awake at night," she continued, "and I can see them, just *see* them, on the North Atlantic. The *Osprey* sinking, and Cub, Tessa, and Kathy bobbing on the surface in their life vests, freezing cold, in the dark, crying, 'Grandma, Grandma!' "

Bill laughed.

"Oh, yes, go ahead and laugh. When I said that to Julie, she laughed too."

"Don't forget the pirates."

Irene grimaced. "That's no joke either. There are lots of them in the Caribbean. They race up to these little sailing boats, shoot everyone on board, strip off the electronic equipment, and sink them."

Irene bent over a dropped stitch, and her face looked suddenly cruel. Her eyes filled with tears. Bill could tell she was thinking about the sisters. He slid his chair next to hers and put his arm around her shoulders.

"They didn't suffer long, honey. Father says it was instant."

"I know. I know. It's just . . . Mother Agatha was like a mother to me. Sister Immaculata was like my sister."

"I know."

"It's too much, Bill. It's too hard."

Her sobbing was muted and dark, the kind Bill knew he had no power to fix. He let her cry for a while until she was able to talk again.

"Saturday's too soon to leave", she said. "I think we should get the tribe together on Sunday. Have a good-bye dinner for everybody." She went over to the freezer, opened the lid, and perused its contents uncertainly.

"That's fifteen adults and twenty-nine children", she mused. She took out a turkey and a beef roast.

"Maybe we should have those candied yams, too", Bill suggested.

"Perfect. Garlic and onion stuffing?"

"Uh-huh. Reenie, we shouldn't say anything about Father and the boy to the others."

"You're right. And they'll be gone by then."

"We'll need Monday to pack a few things. Go to the bank. Bessie needs a tune up. I'll call the real estate agent after breakfast and get him to list the house."

Surprisingly, she had no objections.

"All right, we'll leave on Tuesday", she said. "What will we do when we come back?"

"*If* we come back."

"We have to live somewhere. What about the furniture? We have tons of other stuff too. . . ."

"We'll talk about that on the road. We'll pray about it. We'll know what to do and where to go when the time comes."

"All right", she said meekly, drying her eyes, sniffing. "That sounds reasonable."

The front door rattled and opened. Julie and Colin came up the front stairs into the living room. Bill and Colin shook hands, and Julie hugged her mother.

"Well, how did it go?" she said.

"It didn't go", said Bill.

"What happened?"

They went into the kitchen and poured coffee all around. Bill described the previous day's journey in detail, while Irene stood behind him with her hands on his shoulders.

"Dad was very brave", she said. "I was so proud of him."

"Nah, it was your Ma who was brave. Cool as a cucumber. Joan of Arc."

"Couch potato", she whispered, kissing him on the ear.

"So, what's this priest going to do?" Colin asked in a thoughtful voice.

"We don't know", said Irene. "He's still sleeping. The poor man hasn't had any rest since—"

"Mum, you want me to help make breakfast?" Julie interrupted.

"Would you, dear?"

While the two women busied themselves at the stove, Colin probed his father-in-law for more details. A lean, fine-featured man in his late thirties, he radiated intelligence and a no-nonsense attitude, his few words liberally seasoned with accent. Bill was accustomed to asking Colin to repeat practically everything he said. Usually he didn't say much.

"Julie tells me he's got a brumby with him."

"Brumby?"

"Sorry, that's Aussie for a wild colt. An outlaw."

"Yeah, well, he's another story. It's messy, Colin. Real messy."

Over toast, bacon, and fried eggs Bill and Irene filled in the missing blanks for Julie and Colin. Colin ate without comment, listening carefully, his brow furrowed. Bill began to worry that his son-in-law was finding the whole thing too farfetched. *Well*, he said to himself, *it is farfetched, dammit!*

"So you're saying you buy it?" Colin asked.

"That's right, I buy it", Bill answered.

"You too, Mum?"

"Yes, I believe him. Father Andrei is a saint."

"A saint he may be", said Colin. "But has he read the situation correctly? Maybe he's jumped to a whole lot of conclusions."

Julie was also entertaining some second thoughts: "Colin's got a point, Dad", she said. "How do we know if what Father says about the police is true? I believe he *thinks* it's true, but he might have misunderstood what happened."

"I'm not saying it isn't true", Colin went on. "I'm just asking if our perceptions are a little screwed up here. If what he says is accurate, then we're talking about a massive breakdown of society. Take a walkabout. Everything looks fairly normal, doesn't it?"

"I suppose it does, really", said Irene uncertainly. "Maybe we've got ourselves all worked up in the wrong direction."

She showed the yellow leaflet to Colin and Julie. They read it carefully. Colin's mouth soured. Julie groaned.

"This is so evil!" she exclaimed. "Who are these people?"

"Nobody knows", said Bill. "Nobody knows for sure."

They sat together in uneasy silence, until Bill broke it by saying, "I'm the last person in this family you'd expect it from, but I think Father Andrei's got it right."

He described the anomalies of the evening news and the television special on violence. He explained how the scraps of evidence, insignificant as they were, pointed to the possibility that the media might be feeding them disinformation. Irene added the things Arrow had said.

"Black beetles?" said Colin, thinking hard.

"What is it?" Julie said to her husband.

"Two days ago, around the time of the murders, I was on deck teaching Cub to tie bowline knots. I happened to be looking south and noticed a flock of crows acting strange. They were flying straight east along the valley in perfect unison, like bullets. I thought nothing of it at first, but then it struck me that crows never do that, and moreover, they must have been going three, four hundred miles an hour. I realized they were aircraft, flying low, almost no sound. I wondered if maybe they were a new aircraft of some kind, from the Armed Forces base at Chilliwack. I assumed they'd been out over the ocean doing exercises and were heading home. The thing is, an hour later I saw them fly west again."

"How many?" said Bill.

"Five. Then about twenty minutes after that I saw them going like hell back east again."

"Five of them?"

"This time there were just three. I didn't give it any more thought."

"Five and three", said Bill, whistling, pushing his cap far back on his head. "Just like Father described it."

"Suppose Father Andrei's scenario is right on", said Colin. "I'm not saying it is, but let's not rule it out. If he's right, then every single detail of what you've described and what I saw lines up perfectly. We've got triangulation."

Bill and Irene didn't understand that.

Julie flipped an arch look in Colin's direction. "Okay, Mister Logic, skip the technical talk. Say it in plain English."

"All I'm saying is we've got a confirmation of observations here. Different eyes, different positions, each observing a small piece of the puzzle from a different vantage point. In this scenario we've got consistency. In the official account we've got contradictions."

"Pretty small ones, I'd say", Irene inserted, trying to be objective.

"Yes, fairly small. But large enough to raise a doubt."

"Add this to the equation", said Julie. "I've known Father a long, long time, and I've never seen a hint of alarmism in him. He's the essence of moderation and charity, leaving aside the whole question of falsehood, which in his case is pretty absurd. On the other hand, how often have we caught the media doctoring the news, leaving important things out, blowing other things out of proportion?"

"Not to mention the way police cover their asses every time they break the law", said Bill. "I've been watching it and excusing it for decades, thinking, oh, well, they risk their lives, they keep the peace, nobody's perfect."

"Let's get back to your walkabout, Colin", said Julie. "Maybe it's not quite as normal as we think it is. Maybe only the surface looks normal."

"Cosmetics?" said Irene.

Bill contributed another word for it and made them laugh.

"Yeah, well that's one of the reasons we're going on this cruise", said Colin. "Normal isn't necessarily healthy, is it?"

The others shook their heads.

"I sold the business because I want our kids to see a bigger picture."

Bill and Irene nodded emphatically.

"Oh, yes, you're doing the right thing", said Irene.

"It's an adventure", Bill added. "They'll thank you for it someday."

Colin and Julie traded a barely perceptible smile.

* * *

Arrow appeared in the doorway shortly after, looking dishevelled, rubbing his eyes. Irene scanned his pajamas, trilled and chirped over him, and led him away to the bathroom. She returned a minute later with the pajamas and the boy's other clothes and threw them into the washing machine.

"I left him in the tub with the water running. Do you know I had to teach him how to turn off the taps."

"That's our brumby, is it?" said Colin.

"That's him", said Bill. "The brumby could use a haircut too."

"I'll ask him if he wants a trim", Irene said, and disappeared again.

Andrei came into the kitchen a few minutes later. He shook hands with Colin, said good morning to the others, and sat down. As he ate breakfast, Bill replayed the morning's discussion. The priest nodded from time to time but said little.

"I want to thank you for your kindness", he said when Bill had finished.

"Nah, it's nothin'."

"I know how difficult it must be for all of you."

"Not to worry, Father. Not to worry", said Bill. "We were dying of boredom until you and Arrow came along. I was shaping up for a retirement heart attack."

"You've just added years to Dad's life", said Julie.

"Father," Colin interjected, "what are your plans?"

"I must take the boy to his great-grandfather in the Cariboo."

"Great-grandfather? That sounds pretty old to me", Julie objected. "Maybe he should stay with us."

"Despite his age, Thaddaeus Tobac is a robust man, quite capable of looking after the children. And I think a child who has lost what this boy has lost will be needing his own family."

"But how are you going to get there without being arrested?" Julie said.

"I'm not sure."

"We could give it another try in Bessie", said Bill. "Maybe in a few weeks from now. You could hang out here till the manhunt cools down. They're not going to have roadblocks forever."

"That would be a possibility. However, I think my presence is a danger to you and Irene. No, I must go, and soon."

"You can't walk there."

"The Lord will provide a way."

"Maybe he already has", said Julie. Everyone looked at her.

"Colin," she said, turning to her husband, "we've been planning to sail up the coast for a trial run before we hit the open sea in late spring. We're just twiddling our thumbs and polishing brass until then. Why don't we take Father north as far as we can?"

Colin looked doubtful. "We're not ready", he said curtly.

"But we've been up and down the river several times, and we've had those jaunts out on the straits to get our sea legs. I think we're ready."

Colin stared at the tabletop. "It'd be risky."

"Not half as risky as another trip in Bessie", Julie replied.

"The coast guard won't be looking inside every dinghy along a thousand miles of coastline. We could drop him wherever he wants."

"It might work, Colin", said Bill.

Colin began to look very tense.

"It's a great idea, hon", Julie urged. "We could get away with it."

She linked arms with him and looked into his eyes imploringly.

"Will you consider it?"

Colin pursed his lips, avoiding everyone's eyes, running through complicated equations in his brain.

"I want to think about it."

At that moment Irene came in looking nonplussed, clacking scissors in her right hand, a comb in her left.

"Well, I did what I could to that head of his. He wasn't happy about it, but he let me clean him up a little. Poor tyke. Every one of his ribs is showing. What *do* they eat in those communes?"

"Lotus blossoms", said Bill. "And funny mushrooms."

"Now, now, Mister Redneck."

"Hippies!" said Bill, disgusted.

"He's a very nice little boy", said Irene. "Someone has taught him manners. Though I must say he hasn't seen a shampoo bottle in a long time. He has the most lovely, shiny, sandy-colored hair. He just needs a little fattening up, I think."

Irene asked Andrei if he would say Mass, and he agreed. Colin excused himself and said he was going out for a long walk.

Julie went with him to the door, hugging his arm, talking in a low voice. She began to do up the toggles on his navy-blue duffle coat. Lost in thought, he watched her abstractedly.

"I don't know about this", he said unhappily. "You sprang it on me too fast, girl."

"Please think about it", she said, tying a scarf snugly around his neck.

"Do you really want to put the kids into that kind of danger?"

"But, hon, if Father's wrong, then there's no real danger. If he's right, then we're already in a lot of danger—everyone, maybe the whole world. Don't we owe it to the kids to do what we can to help a friend?"

She flipped the hood of his coat up over his ears. Colin, realizing that she was fussing, grabbed her wrists.

"Next you'll be pinning little mittens to my cuffs."

They kissed each other, and Colin left. Julie locked up behind him.

* * *

The Wannamakers lived at the end of a lane that curved around the midriff of a hill covered by shining holly trees and cedars. The sun was high over Mount Baker to the south, the sky scraped clean, a few low cumulus clouds lingering in the west. The air was chilly but not unpleasant. Colin thrust his hands into the pockets of his coat and strode briskly along the lane until it hit the corner where the pavement began.

As always, when irrational elements intruded into the blueprint of his life, he felt uneasy and mildly resentful. His wife was proposing, in one swift move, something quite impulsive (which included him as an essential factor) and engaging in a religious event (from which he had excluded himself). His respect for Julie was absolute; his promise to allow her to raise the children as Catholics had never been broken. He did not attend Mass with her and the children, but he was the one who got them up early on Sunday mornings, cooked breakfast, made sure Cub was dressed in a semi-civilized fashion, and scooted them all out the door on time for church. He never questioned the faith in front of the children, and he scolded Julie when she indulged in rare moments of melancholic doubt. He was an honorable man. But he knew that her desire to help the priest and the boy had sprung from spiritual, emotional, intuitive faculties of her personality, and he did not trust that. It was illogical.

The matrix of his past was complicated. Casting his mind back to the station by Gum Creek in the Gulf country of Australia, he now recalled with a certain fondness the red soil, the wet and the dry, the stock and the boongs and the solitude. There had been a spotted heeler named Booligal (Gal for short) and several generations of needle-toothed yellow pups, the offspring she threw whenever she took off into the outback and dated a dingo. He remembered the radio school, the mangoes and stringybarks, the poddy calves, and the dead alligators hanging from the barn beams. His Mum wrote novels for young adults, occult adventure stories about Ouija boards, mediums, and séances, which didn't sell very well but well enough. Some of her books were still in print. His Dad had chucked religion fairly early on and didn't like the things his wife wrote, but the royalties had helped to pay for a secondhand truck and a new water pump. Colin read three of her books and didn't enjoy them. He never did get around to reading the rest. He preferred *Treasure Island*, *Kidnapped,* and *Robinson Crusoe*—things like that—his favorite was Jules Verne's *The Mysterious Island*, which had a lot of useful information in it.

His father gave him a telescope for Christmas when he was fourteen, and Colin fell in love with the stars. Dad was gone a fair part of the year, chasing cattle across their range land, leased from the government, a relatively small place measuring only a few hundred square miles. Every Christmas they made the summer jaunt to Cairns so Mum and Dad and the girls could kick up their heels at the Stockmen's Ball and Concert. Dad (whom Colin had taken to calling "Pa" in a stilted attempt at closeness) was one of the shining lights of the concert. Dad, an artful poddy dodger, had a medal from fighting the Japs with the Anzacs and was good at step-dancing. His repertoire was limited—he knew only a clog and a jig—and for this reason was known locally as Covey Two Step, which was a compliment. Every Christmas Colin was encouraged to get up onto the stage and prove himself his father's son, and every year Colin refused. Public scrutiny filled him with horror, for the force of it came close to breaking through a seal that protected the secret refuge within himself, an inland sea of liquid, inarticulate forms that shaped and reshaped themselves into an eloquence of vast solitudes, deserts, hills, and horizons—a language both shocking and beloved for its sere beauty. Each year when he refused to dance, he endured the sort of teasing that came just short of mockery. The other station hands called him Covey No Step, or Joey, depending on their moods.

He read a lot of *National Geographic*s, collected postage stamps, captured insects and mounted them in glass cases. Most of all he recalled the loneliness, the longing to know a pretty girl that surged up from somewhere inside of himself when he was twelve, a feeling that just grew and grew until it became the dominant feature of his life. Any pretty girl would have been fine; just to walk with her in the red hills, watch sunsets, and talk about station life would have been paradise. He did not meet one until he went to the university in Sydney.

When he first saw her, she was standing in front of the campus library, selling flowers. He bought one just for the chance to speak with her. She smiled at him and asked him about himself. He replied diffidently. She sent a burst of sweetness in his direction, and he returned her attention without a word. She was very beautiful, though her eyes looked as if she hadn't slept for days. She invited him to a banquet. He went with her to a mansion on a hill above the bay. Inside, a hundred young people were packed into a bare room, seated cross-legged on the floor, listening to a man in a white tuxedo give a talk about the war between good and evil on the planet. The speaker mentioned Satan several times and someone named the Lord of the Second Advent, a man who would defeat Satan by raising armies of the young across the world—a children's crusade. Later he would learn that this man was from the Orient, an ardent anti-Communist, the savior of the world. Young people everywhere were flocking to his side, learning to live by The Principle, making an astonishing number of converts among their peers.

Colin recalled the long and dreary years after he became a member of the cult. They called it The Family, and it felt like a family. It was a clan, a singing, praying tribe that gathered around a savage messiah who threw temper tantrums and amassed a fortune on the backs of thousands of fervent, exhausted, ill-fed, and ill-clad disciples, most of them young, almost all of them idealistic, all of them looking for salvation of one kind or another.

He was intoxicated with the drug of high purpose and by the profound reassurance of belonging, of warmth in a mercilessly cold, disjointed universe. Eventually they moved him to the Berkeley House near San Francisco, where he became a Center Man. He "love-bombed" hundreds of other young people and felt genuine affection for them, though it was a cosmic affection, dissociated from their personhood. It was technique, pure technique, done for the highest motives, and it worked. But gradually the campfires, the arm-in-arm group dances, and the sweet companionship gave way to relentless exhaustion, hunger, squabbles, ambition, and the chronic desperation to please those who were above him in the divine ascent. There were endless trips in white vans to the cities of America, selling flowers, proselytizing, seeking a newer world within the crumbling ruins of the old, never finding it. He watched personalities of all kinds succumb to the technique, the broken psyches and the normal ones—it didn't seem to make much difference. Something big had happened to the world that was driving people of all backgrounds to exchange their autonomy for a sense of identity and a home.

The boy who watched stars and insects was crammed into

the back of a dark closet of his interior, bound and trussed, increasingly mute as the years went on. Gradually his awe of the stars faded; then he gave up watching them altogether. He worked hard at convincing himself of the tenets of the new faith, the necessity of devotion to the founder, the value of endless privations and the crushing negation of diversity in temperament and human character. He excused it all. The elders instructed him to continue his university education, because in the future The Family would need educated people in the front lines of public relations. He lived at the Berkeley House for three years and completed his degree in mathematics. During that period he attempted to write a treatise that would integrate the founder's spiritual doctrines with what he was learning from universal mathematical principles. No one, not even the elders, could understand it. And sometimes even he wondered if much of it was sheer myth and romance disguised as science.

From time to time he fell in love, a curious dissociated sort of love, in which there was never a feeling of permanence or union or any exchange of passion, physical or otherwise. He watched these young women grow pasty-skinned, exhausted, and empty, mouthing The Principle, selling wilting flowers and rehashed karma year after year, as if they believed it. They did believe it.

He knew that the Catholic Church was in the camp of the enemy. He had heard a lot about that, though he had never been in a Catholic church. His mother had told him about Catholicism too, how she had abandoned it when she left home, because it was stifling the evolution of mankind into the god-self. During his childhood, many others had discussed the Church, fundamentalist stock boys and pentecostal ringers, all saying the same thing: The Catholic Church was the Whore of Babylon.

One day, prompted by a remaining scrap of curiosity, he went into a Catholic church in downtown Chicago. There was an enormous stone carving of the crucified Christ on the outer wall, facing the street, squeezed between two giant steel and glass towers. The old building was packed for a noon Mass. He sat in the back pew and observed. At the time, he believed the Catholic Church was an enormous cult. He believed that The Principle was the divine means God had chosen to liberate man from primitive religions such as this. He looked around at the worshippers, expecting to see vacant looks, fixed expressions, and glassy eyes, the symptoms of a robotic existence. He was surprised to find none of that. There was a gentle fervor (he was acquainted with fervor), but it did not seem exhausted and driven. Most astonishing was the variety of human types in that single room—old and young, street people and businessmen, women and children, intelligent and not so intelligent, extroverts and introverts, haggard, life-scarred faces and the exquisitely groomed. He saw half a dozen priests that day, one at the altar, others talking to parishioners in the lobby, another going into a box in a wall. Unlike the masters of The Principle, they seemed to be men of varying dispositions, their eyes kind or reflective, or both, some of them tense, some of them radiant and relaxed, but all of them in possession of their lives. It seemed a very strange contradiction. These Catholics were in possession of their lives, but they had given away their lives. Then Colin entertained an unwelcome thought—the masters of his religion had given up their wills to a higher cause as well, but, unlike the Catholic priests, they were no longer in possession of their lives. The difference lay in the fact that his masters had not given their lives freely. At least not as a perfect giving of the self. All members of The Family had been recruited through the promise of love, drawn by the yearning for tribal belonging, by the magnetism of relief from personal responsibility, and by "holy deception". They had let their lives be taken by technique, in the name of salvation. It was willingness of a sort, but was it freedom?

The question disturbed him. Was salvation something one should purchase at *any* price, even that of destroying one's unique individuality, one's gifts, one's power to choose? He knew that this kind of thinking was from Satan, that doubts and individualism were rays of diabolic "negativity". The doctrine of the master quickly flooded in to quell the revolt in his soul.

Yet he lingered for a while. He looked up at the crucifix over the altar and felt an instant of longing. The moment did not last, nor was it focused on any consideration of the outmoded doctrines connected to it. He felt only a sense of pity for this crowd of deluded people worshipping an ancient myth, bowing before a messiah of a bygone age. Not a single person in that crowd made an attempt to recruit him, which he thought was strange behavior for a cult. He got up and left.

From then on, for no reason that he could discern, the Family lectures and disciplines began to ring hollow. He began to dislike the inconsistencies and the lies, the fabulous material wealth of the ones directly above him on the scale of authority, the wretchedness of the mass of underlings who toiled to produce the wealth. He caught himself looking up at the stars from time to time, and once, in Denver, Colorado, he sneaked away from the team, bought a hamburger and ate it, drank a glass of beer in a pub, and smoked three cigarettes in a row. It was satanic, but he survived.

The small infidelities grew into larger ones. The doubts increased. He found himself listening to the technique of the Jesus Freaks with whom he debated on the streets of Berkeley. They seemed every bit as driven and intense as members of his own community, though there were some differences. Finding himself alone with them (an extremely rare event), he accepted an invitation to visit their house in a warehouse district of San Francisco. It was in a dilapidated tenement situated between a bar and a landing pad for alien spaceships, both of which possessed sound amplifiers. The music on each side was annihilating. The bar belted out an endless cycle of live country-and-western music, robotic heartbreak songs in twanging accents and jingling spurs, a mixture of lust and self-pity that Colin decided was low-grade satanic in the key of despair. On the other side, there was a live rock band, one of the new subsects of the youth culture that was then fragmenting into hundreds of variants. They practiced for hours every day and throughout most of the night—a long, sustained screech of rage and disgust, a paeon to cosmic negativity. It too was satanic (the Jesus Freaks were agreed on that), but there was nothing robotic about it as far as Colin could tell. It was at the opposite end of the spectrum—anarchic, savage, a scorpion feast in a ruined garden.

He stayed with the Jesus Freaks for three months, long enough to find out that they had their own lock-step formulas, wildly irrational interpretations of Scripture, "love-bombing", and "holy deceptions". They were crazy, but their technique was not nearly so masterful or so absolutely depersonalizing as that of his former masters. The trade in human souls was brisk, and at times it was a spiritual shark-feeding frenzy. When the Jesus Freaks converted one of the street cowboys and one of the Jesus Freaks backslid and joined the heavy metal band, Colin decided it was time to clear out.

Shaken, mistrusting everything—above all, his own perceptions—and terrorized by the thought that he was now completely in the claws of Satan, he bought a bus ticket for someplace that was as far away as his money could buy. The bus deposited him in downtown Vancouver at the end of June 1975.

He wired home for help and learned that Dad had died. Mum had sold her share in the station at Gum Creek to the manager and moved to Melbourne. His sisters, she lamented in a letter, were living in Sydney and were into drugs and sleeping around. She couldn't understand why. There was a check for three thousand Australian dollars in the envelope—his inheritance, Mum said.

Sick at heart, totally adrift in the cosmos, he walked toward Lion's Gate Bridge, preparing to throw himself off. He thought he would tear up the check first, as a final gesture. But as he passed the gates of Stanley Park, a poor old native woman walked by, pulling a rusty Red Flyer wagon in which sat a statue of a woman. The statue was white with a gold crown on its head. Strings of long black beads were draped over the Indian woman's shoulder, and she carried a basket in her free arm. She tried to give him a string of beads, but when he saw the aluminum crucifix on the end of it, he refused. She pushed a medallion into his hand, closed her eyes, and chanted something in a high-pitched wail. Then she smiled at him and went on down the sidewalk toward the center of the city, accosting every passerby with her gifts.

He looked at the medal in his hand. It was a small, oval thing, with the picture of a woman on it. A woman in a long robe, arms spread, hands open, rivers of water coming from her palms. He didn't know what to make of it and almost threw it onto the sidewalk, but then he reconsidered and thrust it into the back pocket of his jeans. He kept walking toward the bridge, convinced that his life was over. For no reason, he thought that before he ended it all he would like to find a bank and cash the check. After that he would track down the old woman and give her the money. Then he would kill himself. He cashed the check and went searching for her in the streets. He wandered around the downtown core for hours, and when he finally gave up looking, the urge to self-destruction had subsided into almost nothing. He never found her. He never saw her again.

The weeks that followed were a blur. There was a construction job, carpentry, gardening, and nights in a small barren apartment on Howe Street. In August he applied for graduate studies in mathematics at the University of British Columbia and was accepted. In 1979 he was an assistant professor, working on a degree in computer science. By 1983 he was a full professor of mathematics, working on an astrophysics degree in his spare time.

His needs were simple, his possessions few. On Sundays he

took long walks in the cathedral of pines in the park, sat on benches watching cargo ships creep along Burrard Inlet, scoured the public library, observed the endlessly complex behavior of the masses of urban humanity, or else read alone in his apartment. He had little difficulty turning away the overtures of interested women. He had no difficulty whatsoever declining the invitations of the transvestites on Davie Street. Nor did he feel the mildest tug of attraction to the invitations of the Moonies, the Divine Light Missionaries, the Hare Krishna people, and devotees of the satanic cults who were crowding into the downtown streets. Even the Jesus Freaks arrived. For the lonely women he felt regret. For the transvestites he felt pity. For the recruiters he felt loathing. He did, however, succumb to the cults of hang gliding, scuba fishing, and sky diving—the latter his favorite, for he loved the sensations of free fall, pulling the chute cord only at the last possible moment.

In the ensuing years he met many different kinds of women: bubbling, romantic women looking for a husband; cool, ambitious women looking for a career; and lost, broken women looking for any man willing to become their private devotion. With none of them was he able to form a relationship that lasted beyond the first explorations of physical sensation and complicated emotion. They found him distant, cold, numbingly abstract. He dismissed all emotion as variations on "love-bombing" and all forms of religion (there were a few religious women) as "holy deception". Science alone was objective, though as the decade of the eighties gathered momentum, he was more and more disgusted as he discovered evidence of mythological thinking in every faculty at the university. Eco-feminism, eco-spirituality, and old-fashioned cutthroat academic ambition were spreading like growths in a petri dish. Everywhere, large omnivores ate smaller omnivores while spinning a nice metaphysic around their appetites. Eventually he gave up women and tried to concentrate on pure science.

It was an operation of natural law, or perhaps the principle of probability, that engineered his meeting with Julie. He was crossing the quad by the bell tower one rainy afternoon in October, not looking where he was going, thinking intently about a problem of quantum mechanics, trying to develop an equation for the relationship between molecular structures and the structure of the universe, microcosm and macrocosm, when he crashed into her. No, he literally knocked her down. No, she crashed into him and fell down. With clinical objectivity, his mind instantly analyzed the difference in their respective weights, considered two of Newton's laws, the relative speed of the two bodies in question, and concluded that she was responsible for the unfortunate accident, but being the lighter and swifter had experienced the collision somewhat differently than he had—that is, subjectively. Entirely subjectively.

She lay sprawled in a puddle, glaring at him, a large black vinyl valise beside her in the water, a wooden box broken open at the hinges, tubes of artists' colors scattered along the sidewalk.

"You big goof!" she muttered. "Why don't you watch where you're going?"

Absentmindedly, he helped her up by the arm. "I'm sorry", he said.

"You're sorry!" she fumed.

He picked up her things. He turned her vinyl case upside down, and water spilled out of the flap.

"Oh, no!" she cried. "O God, my drawings!" She opened the flap, looked inside, and burst into tears.

The whole scene was so utterly wretched he wanted to flee.

"Look, Miss, my office is just over there. Let me take these and dry them out for you. You look like you could use some drying out too."

"No, thank you", she said primly, trying to dry her eyes on a sodden sleeve.

"Please. I have a fan heater. Maybe we can save some of these. If you leave them to soak like this, they'll be ruined."

She huffed and deliberated. It was a long way to the parking lot, longer still to her home in Fort George.

Reluctantly, she agreed. She followed him grimly across the quad, under an arch, and into the math building. On the third floor he unlocked his office door and invited her in. She thought it a strikingly neat office for a young professor. None of the usual tumble of books and test papers, cute Marxist posters and superior bric-a-brac. The wall-to-wall books were arranged flawlessly. His desk was a paradigm of order, and she had no doubt it reflected a mind that was efficient, controlled, and sterile. An over-large conference table along one wall was the only break in this hideous display of perfection.

He quickly opened her case and withdrew the sheets of paper, laid them along the table, and rummaged in a closet for his heater. Within a minute it was blowing warm air over the pieces of art.

"I feel terrible", he said. "These must mean a lot to you."

"Yes. They do", she replied in a clipped tone, laying more papers on the rug.

"It looks like the colored ones are okay. Unfortunately, the charcoal ones are running."

"Unfortunately", she said.

He offered her a cup of coffee from a machine in the corner. She accepted. They stood watching the drying process without further comment.

"I'm going to get some paper towels", he murmured, and left. While he was gone, she looked curiously about the room. There wasn't much decoration. A single framed watercolor of white trees against a background of barren, rusty-looking countryside. A half-completed model of a racing schooner on a shelf. Beside it, a small medallion of some kind. And a sea shell—a *chambered nautilus*, she thought. A dwarf lemon tree in a terra cotta pot.

The miniature fruit were the only strokes of vibrant color in the room. A jade plant in the window box looked well cared for—watered, pruned, the branches artfully cultivated. *What an odd duck,* she thought. *And what's that accent?*

He came back, apologizing again, got down on his knees, and gently tamped the charcoal drawings, not rubbing, soaking up the water.

"Are you English?" she asked.

"Aussie", he said.

"Oh."

He took off his owlish glasses. Underneath the disguise he was a fine-looking fellow, stuffed shirt that he was.

He sat down in a swivel chair behind his desk and offered her the students' hot seat. She took it.

"Are you an art student, Miss?"

Very perceptive, she was tempted to say. *How did you guess?*

"I used to be one until about ten minutes ago", she shot back. She was surprised to see his face fall so drastically. She had expected him to take the bait, to engage her in witty dialogue for the sole purpose of alleviating his guilt. He didn't look as if he felt guilty. He just looked sad. Very sad.

That's unusual, she thought.

"I can't tell you how sorry I am", he said. "I hope we can save most of these. But I'll speak with your professors. I'll explain what happened. These were a submission for marks, weren't they? I'm not sure how things work over there in Fine Arts, but I expect our accident didn't help."

"Good guess", she said. "I was on my way to make my term presentation, when I happened to meet an immovable object."

"Irresistible force", he countered. She detected a faint, very faint, hint of humor around his eyes. A young face, trim body, button-down shirt, dumb tie, a tweed jacket, khaki pants, and oxfords. Typical.

Typical but withdrawn, she thought. *Some kind of sad past.*

Probably a trail of broken hearts behind this lad. Watch your step, girl.

"Well, if you would do that for me, I'd appreciate it. My prof doesn't like me, and this is going to cinch it."

"Why doesn't he like you?"

"Because he's into post-abstractionist abstraction. Brain-death art. I'm totally flat-earth society in his books. I'm into realism. You may have noticed."

He got up and went to the table, bending over the drawings.

"These are really fine", he said. "They're . . . beautiful."

"That's a forbidden word you just used. Bourgeois."

He didn't respond.

"The charcoals were high realism ten minutes ago", she said. "Now they're impressionist."

"I'm sorry. They must have been wonderful before. But they're interesting even now."

"You think so?"

He nodded.

The oil pastels were magnificent, he thought. Mountains and Indian villages. Seascapes. The tangled undergrowth of the Pacific rain forest. Birds in flight. A lot of vivid movement, exhilaration, enthusiasm for life. A deep-looking tenderness for live things, a sensitivity to the nuances of hue and texture. She really had talent.

"Don't admire them too much. They're derivative. Emily Carr's my guru."

He gave her a grave, inquiring look.

Guru? he wondered.

By then the first set of pictures was dry, and they went to work on the remaining ones. Ships plying the coast. A few still lifes (rather wooden). A Madonna and Child (rather alive). He blinked twice at that one and passed on quickly.

She took off her purple anorak jacket and hung it on the back of a chair by the heater. He offered her another cup of coffee. She said thanks, and her expression thawed some more. She sat facing him in the hot seat, regarding him thoughtfully, a thoroughly self-possessed young woman. He realized in a glance that a hundred undergraduates were madly in love with her and that probably she wasn't even aware of it. He tried not to stare obsessively, kept his eyes above the collar as best he could, admired her flaxen shoulder-length hair, the understated pink dots of earrings, the beautiful facial features, fresh complexion, perched on a slender neck. She wore a rumpled turquoise shirt that was very becoming, despite the streaks of paint that adorned it. Other details gradually swam into focus: baggy, olive green corduroys and sockless sandals, long expressive hands and delicate fingers, without rings. The mouth ready to smile, though it hadn't yet done so. Crinkles around the eyes that were striving not to seem amused. It was the eyes most of all. Very sweet and gentle green eyes, which would have been childlike were they not also impelled by that quality another generation would have called character.

All alarm bells were suddenly ringing loudly. Warning lights flashed: Subjectivity! Subjectivity! Subjectivity! The critical faculty cut in, and not a moment too soon.

Analysis:

Was she a bubbling romantic looking for a husband? No, she didn't exactly bubble, except perhaps with lava, which was not exactly the best way to entice a husband. She'd called him a goof. Not very romantic for a first encounter. She didn't seem overly eager to retract the comment.

Was she the cool, ambitious type, looking for a career or a live-in faculty partner? No, not a whiff of ambition. In fact just the opposite, considering that she seemed determined to be a reactionary in the art department, the faculty most notorious on campus for freedom of expression but which in fact fostered a merciless peer pressure and enforced a conformism that would have been the envy of a Stalinist commissar. Obviously she didn't give a damn about a career, nor about clawing her way to the top of the cultural ant heap. She cared about painting.

Final option: Was she a lost, broken woman looking for any man willing to become her private cult? Hardly.

What was she, then? He knew only this: she was the sort of beauty who wasn't vain, which made her twice as beautiful in his eyes. She was intelligent, creative, humorous, knew how to forgive without holding onto price tags, and she had that elusive thing he had vaguely identified as character. He wouldn't want to call it virtue, because that was an old-fashioned word tainted by religious associations. Nor did he want to call it a healthy ego, self-esteem, or self-image, because those terms had been tainted by psychology, which he believed was a pseudo-science, dominated by theory, myth, and subjectivism.

So began a tentative friendship, stitched together by an occasional walk, a cup of coffee here and there, a phone call to see how she had done on her term grades. In the second month after their accident, one of Colin's students gave him two free tickets to *The Tree of Wooden Clogs,* by the Italian filmmaker Ermanno Olmi. Not knowing what it was about, he asked Julie to accompany him. It was about familial love among a group of humble nineteenth-century peasants. It was also about faith, and that made Colin uneasy. When the lights came on in the theater, Julie sobbed loudly and had to bury her face in the shoulder of his coat. A week later she invited him to Henryk Górecki's *Symphony Number Three*, performed by the Vancouver Philharmonic. It was a cycle of sorrowful songs memorializing the sufferings of man, a meditation on the Holocaust. It left her solemn and awed, not wanting to move, needing only to remain in the silent moment of *attention* before the mystery of iniquity and the triumph of the human spirit over evil. Though he tried valiantly to hide his emotions, she recognized the flicker of pain, of loss, of longing in his eyes.

The following Sunday he invited her to go hang gliding with

him. She said, "No thanks, Buster!" and laughed at him. He laughed back. His first laugh.

She knew early on it was going to be one of those long, slow relationships that push their roots too deep into the soul and are terribly difficult to leave. She didn't try. Eventually she didn't want to try. Gradually it changed into something else. Right from the beginning she knew that he found her attractive, that he was wrestling with a lot of conflicting feelings, powerful feelings that he hadn't wanted and that he probably hadn't suspected he was capable of. She respected his privacy, didn't probe, didn't pour on the charm. It was rather refreshing to meet a man who treated her with respect. He wasn't a wolf on the make, but neither was he immune to her. She couldn't figure him out and rather surprised herself by not wanting to.

Round about month three he took her hand in the cathedral of pines during a walk through Stanley Park. They both realized that a line was being crossed but said nothing about it. They fed the Canada geese in the pond with the remains of a loaf of French bread she had brought along. He told her about a native woman with a wagon. At month four she gave him a birthday gift (she had to work hard to get the date out of him), an oil pastel of a brilliantly colored ship, Chinese red and glacier green, steaming up Howe Sound against a background of black mountains and a sky full of writhing cobalt clouds.

In the fifth month her mother, who had antennae, asked her if she had met someone. Yes, she had, she replied. Nothing too serious. Mum asked her if it was getting, ah, um, you know . . . *passionate*.

"No," she replied, "that sort of thing is there, all right, but on the back burner. It's deeper than that."

"Oh", said Mum. And after a judicious pause, "Just remember, Julie, men are men. Don't forget to pray every day. You don't want to get serious too fast." She said some more about chastity and prudence, tactfully, as only Mum knew how.

The following summer she and Colin were married in the sisters' chapel by Father Andrei. Colin told her he loved the sisters, had never met people so joyful. They loved him too and assured Julie (privately) that they would pray for his conversion. It wouldn't be long, they told her. They just knew. He was such a good man.

Colin found the religious ceremony practically painless. Afterward there was a whopping great party at Mum and Dad's place, with a live band, a cast of thousands, stampeding herds of nieces and nephews, guests spilling all over the house and out into the big party tents that Dad put up on the back lawn. Colin seemed to love it all. He danced and joked and laughed. He kissed her every five minutes. He wrestled her across the patio flagstones a few times, to the tune of a waltz, saying sweet things in her ear, stepping on her toes—he wasn't much of a dancer. He drank too much of Aunt Zélie's homemade blackberry wine, not to mention Uncle Pete's peach schnapps, and made a fool of himself—Julie was delighted to see him make a fool of himself. Standing on a table, he made an announcement.

"Ladies and gentlemen," he cried in a loud, theatrical voice, "kinfolk and company, wayfarers and exiles, from this time henceforth and forever more, let it be known that Colin of Gum Creek doth swear to abide by the laws of this tribe that has drawn him to its bosom. For yea, though you have recruited me through thy most comely daughter, the recruitment was fair! And yea, though I retain certain philosophical reservations about the tribe's collective notion of the transcendent, I am yours, fully yours! And you are mine! We are one People and one Family!"

Hardly anyone got the meaning of it, but they thought young Colin was funny, his heart in the right place, and his sentiments in order, as much as could be expected from a groom who had succumbed to the allure of Aunt Zélie's art. They applauded him loudly. Then, holding up his hands for silence, he announced that henceforth and forever he resigned from the Loyal Order of Abstract Fools (L.O.A.F.) and was applying for permanent membership in the Loyal Order of Voluptuous Embraces (L.O.V.E.)—Nuptial Branch! Which was greeted by delirious laughter from the aunties and roars of appreciation by the uncles and brothers-in-law. More cheers, confetti, and plastic wine glasses were tossed into the air. "God bless us, body and soul", Dad cried, pitching his Legion hat into the warm summer sky. "God bless us, everyone!" Mum said in her quietest, happiest voice.

Yes, those were the nights, unequalled and unrepeatable. Fleeting in all aspects but memory. Evenings superabundant with fireflies and larks, children singing around a campfire, roasting spiced sausages and reducing marshmallows to flaming coals. The incense of burnt sugar, dark rosy ale, children playing Mother May I and Red Rover in the dark. Hollies swaying in the breeze with sharp spikes defending their fertile berries. The men discussing serious things over beer in the garage, bottles held just so, for emphasis. The women officiating over mysterious rites in the kitchen, discussing the men. Crickets bursting with good news and galaxies burning with passion. Nights of sweet, hushed talk, of dreams, of the end of past things, and the beginning of new ones. Nights of shooting stars! Nights of consummation. Nights of nuptial love.

Cub was born when they lived in the apartment on Howe Street; Kathy, after they moved to the house on 95th; Tessa, just after they rented the old farmhouse near the convent outside of Fort George, during the years they were building the boat. Their fourth child, Francis, had died of crib death the summer they were painting the hull. It had taken Julie a long time to get over it.

Colin, remembering it all, now turned north onto the trunk road that cut across the hills toward Stave Lake. He was feeling frustrated by the situation that had arisen, for it seemed extremely disordered, teeming with unknowables. It contained a potential for collapse into chaos, not to mention the threat of destruction of all he and Julie had worked for. He assessed the dangers, not least of which was the pull toward irrational conclusions, projection, and, yes—even paranoid thinking. But he could not dismiss the triangulation of observation, as he called it, solid facts that lodged in the precise center of his consciousness, demanding an explanation. In order to find one, he knew that he must expand the grasp of his mind, work out several complicated configurations, nearly mathematical in their precision, none of them quite adding up to a perfect equation. Something vital was missing, but he didn't know what.

He was struck by the sudden realization that only two days had passed since the murder in their midst—a catastrophic blow—the annihilation of close friends, the most innocent and loving kind of friends. It was incredible that he and Julie, and Mum and Dad, were carrying on more or less as if nothing much had happened. Oh, yes, sometimes they stared into space and their eyes filled with tears, the pain fountaining up like an artesian well. But feeble attempts at humor were surfacing through the agonized grief, trying to reestablish a semblance of order, as were the rituals of meals and coffee-making, nightcaps, and, at least for the others, their religious consolations. Life went on. You couldn't let yourself succumb to the mad impulse to scream, to smash something, to sink into a bottomless pool of anguish, to have a self-indulgent breakdown. As Mum said, it was too much, it was too hard. The best thing you could do was knit a slipper or learn to tie a bowline knot.

For the past few years there had seemed to be less and less time for such small acts. Teaching at the university, building up the business, then selling it, moving, building the dream boat. It had taken most of his time. He was a perfectionist at everything except human relationships, which he left to the much better equipped Julie. But on the level of empirical data and practical responsibility, nothing, simply nothing, was ever done without long-range planning, thorough research, and a jeweler's dedication to measurement. Why, then, was he entertaining the thought of this mad escapade into the north? Why had he so impulsively agreed to consider ferrying a Catholic priest and a brumby across the uncharted waters of the abyss, to a spurious sanctuary? How could he be so rash?

For the first time in many years he thought about his father. He remembered the telescope Dad had given him on his fourteenth birthday. The telescope had been a window into a larger universe, and he realized now that it might have been his father's inarticulate way of trying to communicate, the only language of which he had been capable. It had been a solid word, a commerce of the heart devoid of womanish emotionalism. A vocabulary limited by generations of privation and neglect, long absences in prisons and wars, and the need to scratch a living from the inhospitable soil.

So many men no longer knew how to live because the chain of communication between fathers and sons had been broken, a chain that once, a long time ago, might have been connected to some ultimate meaning but which now dangled anchorless, surrounded by the sea of an indifferent cosmos. He wondered if he and his father had really known each other. How many times had he thought about the man since he had left the homestead at Gum Creek twenty years ago? Not often. He felt a sudden and almost irresistible urge to fill in the gap he had helped to make. He desired to write to his father, but of course he was dead. Then he tried to imagine the man as he might have appeared riding down the road toward him, seated ramrod straight on their old horse, a sorrel named Golliwog, a swayback with good legs and a high horn saddle. Pa pushing back his sweaty ringer's hat, revealing the band of white between his sunburned face and black hair.

"Speak to me, Colin", said Pa. "Tell me about your life."

"You wouldn't be interested."

"Sure I would, joey-joey", Pa drawled, spitting chewing tobacco into the amber dust. "I bet you've had a bonza life."

"Oh, yeah. Bonza."

"Did you ever learn to dance?"

"Covey No Step learn to dance? Not me."

"What? Never learned to dance! I could have taught you."

"You were busy. You were always too busy."

"I was too busy trying to feed you", said Pa. "But I got time now."

Then Pa and the sorrel disappeared in a gust of cold air, and sparrows twittering about their sharp nests in the hollies brought him back to the present. It was too late to tell Pa about his bonza life. It had always been too late.

Then he thought that he might write a story for him, a story about the grandchildren he had never met and the son he had never really known. A tale the real Pa would not have liked but that he might have understood eventually, if he had been permitted enough time to digest the events of his own life. But memory was a coded book for which one needed a key. He hoped his father had the key now—had found it or been given it.

Perhaps a tale could supply the missing memory. It was a tale written in the mind, the sort of thing that would dissolve almost before it materialized. If you tried to write it down, it would evaporate. It was about the nature of time, about *kronos*, not as the physicists know it, but as the poets know it, and as those who sail on the high seas know it, gripped in the transience of physical waves, dependent on the constancy of eternal stars. He composed it in the form of a letter to a dead man, half a globe away, a quarter of a century beyond his reach.

Dear Pa,

You really shouldn't read this. You're too busy. I know. I'm too busy myself! So to save you the trouble of reading it, I'll just tell you that it's about a little girl and a snail. That's all, nothing else. You have the information now. Read no more! Of course, it's also about what the girl and snail taught a father on a certain day in spring not so long ago, but that's the longer version, and you would have to read it for yourself. But I warn you, the story is rather dull and very, very slow-moving.

You have never seen the homes Julie and I lived in or the boat we built together as a family. You have never seen your grandchildren. They weren't able to teach you the things the very young teach the very old. Let me describe something our youngest daughter taught me one day when I was neither young nor old.

The road that went past the house and wound through the trees toward the sisters' mountain was seldom used. Fallen into anonymity, it was replaced many years ago by the highway, which was the source of a muffled roar a mile away. Occasionally, the farmers who lived along the way rattled past on ancient tractors, pulling creaking hay wagons or bins full of firewood, bouncing on balloon tires. Or, if surprised walking under the golden trees in the autumn, they might lift a hat and glance shyly away into the woods. Julie and I were newcomers, though perhaps in a few more generations we would belong.

Upon this road was the apparent stillness of a place that had missed its time, that had begun to fall relentlessly through sunshafted afternoons into the bottomless pool of time, accompanied by the drone of bees and the hysteria of the distant highway. Ancient cottonwoods arched overhead to form a canopy of dappled green light. It was not a landscape where one expected to meet an event of cosmic significance.

The little girl was of an age to go walking with her father. But her father was a very, very busy man. He had his work, and then some extra work, and then household repairs, the endless repairs. And of course there were the upkeep and the animals, and driving here and there, to school, from school, to friends and family, from friends and family, and stories and diapers and trips to the garbage dump, and lots and lots of listening. Lots and lots of dreaming and planning, blueprints of the future, diagrams of the universe.

Life had become increasingly full with each passing year, each new child. They were beautiful, these children. He and Julie marvelled at how each of them was unique. He would hold the latest newborn in his hands and gaze down for a long time, simply wondering at the mysteriousness of being itself. "Who are you?" he would ask each one. "Whom will you become?" But he did not linger long over such philosophical questions. There was little time for pondering. Each addition to the family whittled away the time and the energy. The babies had colic, which meant months of sleep-deprivation, exhaustion, and inner stress. He had to function in this state through his many responsibilities and projects. In addition, there were roles to fill at work; there were commuting, friendships, discussions, and decisions to be made with his wife during their all-too-brief moments of late-night quiet. And sometimes there was a moment with his children. Not for an instant did he suspect that he was a "workaholic", for he did not especially like this state of things, nor did he really want to have so little time with his children. They held first place in his heart, of course, but they had somehow (he didn't really understand how) got nudged to the bottom of the list. He hadn't even detected the downward slide. Oh, yes, all those good and worthy activities were for them, above all for them. He worked hard, six days a week, eight to ten hours a day (and sometimes sixteen hours), year in, year out, with few holidays, so that they would have a decent life, read good books, have creative toys, interesting experiences, and all the other things he thought they should have. He was planning an adventure, a great adventure, for when they were older. They would see the sea and feel the largeness of life.

Sometimes, not very often, but sometimes it just all seemed too much. Take for instance that week when the basement flooded and the septic tank leaked, flowing in to join the general deluge, and the local rats had decided to parade around the house after lights-out (he had trapped twelve within a few days, and the infestation was getting on everyone's nerves). More than this, he had spotted a corner of the foundation that looked ready to crumble. It was an old house, built in the 1890s as a country church, then sold to a homesteader. Generations of families had added on bits and pieces until it had reached its present condition. Julie fondly called it "the patchwork house". He, privately, called it a disaster zone, because it was falling into ruins, and if he wanted it to survive just a bit longer, he would have to invest a great deal of nonexistent money. Thus, he was hard at work on the computer that Saturday morning in spring when his daughter Tessa burst into his workroom. His thoughts and his fingers were racing, and his mind was connected to the world around him only by a string. The little girl gave a ferocious yank on it with her voice.

"Daddy, I need you!" The voice was urgent but under control. In a split second of assessment, he decided there was no calamity to which he need attend. There was no blood, no cries of anguish, no psychological trauma.

"Where's Mum", he muttered vaguely, as his fingers and his thoughts continued to race.

"Nursing the baby!"

Tessa was two and a half years old and articulate for her age.

"Go ask her to give you a hand", he said.

"Daddy, I need *you*!"

He turned in his chair. He looked at her face. *How can I ever get any work done?* he said to himself. But to her he said, "Honey, I'm just too busy."

"But I need you to come with me!"

Perhaps he had a moment of insight or felt an extra hard

nudge in the conscience. He was momentarily speechless. He had been about to say many ridiculous things to his daughter, such as, "I need to concentrate", or "I'm doing this for you!" or, worst of all, in a fierce voice, "Please do not interrupt me one more time! I'm just too busy!!!"

He loved this little girl very, very much. But he was also a rather harassed creature, trying to live a productive life. He was a reflective person by nature, but the pace of his world had driven him to press his foot down fraction by fraction on the accelerator. Rush, rush, rush, all to keep the whole complex system of North American-style, comfortable family life rolling along smoothly. But things were actually not all that smooth. There was a hidden cost. The cost was time. And peace. He saw also that beyond the obvious price there was a greater and more ominous price to pay. Eventually, in order to keep on top of everything, to remain in control, and to make a success of his life, he might be tempted to consider doing something about . . . well, about those equations that seemed to have been written into his heart and flesh. Take fertility, for instance. In order to survive in the modern world, the "real" world, some of his friends had indeed done something drastic about this fertility business. They had eliminated the chance of more children. They had done it, he knew—they had explained it carefully to him—in order to make a better life for the children they already had. To give them, well, . . . time. And to give them . . . the good things. Not the evil things of our society. The good things. Right?

Well, there it was. He had wondered when the doubt and the temptation would come to him. The noonday devil, the seduction that slides in sideways when you are tired and besieged and vulnerable, suggesting that there might be a better way. An invisible, love-bombing recruiter, selling roses going black on the edges, said to him compassionately, "You've got it tough, and we really don't want that, do we?" He sat staring at the question for a long time, until at last a thought sprang unbidden into his mind: "Are children a problem?" he asked. "Maybe our world's the problem!" Instantly, the love-bomber fell silent.

He thought about his friends who had solved their problem. He liked some of these people very much. He had observed carefully the long-term effects of the decision in their lives. He would never consider it his place to criticize them, but he knew instinctively there was something wrong about the whole business, and he wanted this heart knowledge to meet the head knowledge. Were children a mistake? Wasn't it the state of the society that was wrong? Gobbling down things and experiences, more and more, faster, faster, faster. It wasn't the evil things that were killing us. It was the good things! True enough, after their operations these friends now seemed able to keep up with the pace of the traffic around them. Most of them surged ahead, built bigger and better things, houses that did not fall apart, for instance, and boats that took shape like mystic dreams in the space of a year, while his boat took form with agonizing slowness, five years of labor and longing for the tide, waiting for its mast and its name.

He took a big financial risk when he resigned from the university. They hadn't saved much money, and the computer business was bringing in only a modest profit. There were some tense years there, when he began to wonder if the *Osprey* was a mistake. While he slaved away, his friends began interesting projects and hobbies, spent "quality time" with their children, who were also now involved in bigger and better things. You can travel far and fast when you travel light. Fewer kids, more distance covered. And sure enough, they so often looked less harassed. Nice orderly lives. Successful. Nothing wrong with that.

Now in his situation, there just didn't seem to be time enough for everything that needed to be done. He wasn't thinking of the luxury things but the basic things. When was it he had stopped enjoying the mere doing of things and got into the habit of just trying to get them done? He had a business to take care of, employees for whom he was responsible, a dream to build! He suddenly admitted to himself that he was extremely tired. And it was not a good tired, such as one might feel after a day steadily splitting firewood or digging up the garden as an act of meditation.

All of the above passed through his mind in the seconds that he sat staring at the hopeful face of his daughter. Tessa stood blinking, her eyebrows pleading. He opened his mouth and left it hanging there because not a single word would come out. Then the girl took his fingers in hers and implored, "I need you to take me for a walk!"

He looked at his desk heaped with things to do. He thought of the basement flooded with other things to do. He sighed, knowing that he had been defeated by a conspiracy of sunlight and youth. She gripped his fingers tightly, and then they went outside to encounter the great chain of being, though neither father nor daughter would ruin the day by calling it that.

The little girl led the man down to the end of the lane, and they turned onto the road. As I said, the girl was of an age to go walking with her father. A walk is a kind of art form, a certain school of contemplation. But a father who set out on such a walk for the first time in ages could not immediately remember this. His motors were still racing, though he had slowed his body with an enormous effort of the will in order to match her pace. She was interested in everything: colored pebbles (you can fill a pocket), the smell of a cottonwood bud unfurling (crush the leaves and smear the wine-colored gum across your face), watch a bug whirl and twirl insanely (Why does it do that? Why? Why?). Everything is new when you see it again with someone. This child who had come from his body and that of his wife was not yet old enough to understand her origins. It was unnecessary. It was enough only to see the miraculous world step by step, to wonder at the incredible richness and variety heaped upon each other. When had he stopped seeing it; when had he stopped looking? His adrenaline slowed, as did his heart and his thoughts and the twitching in his muscles. It was a rather lovely day, he noticed.

They were not far into their journey when the event occurred. She saw it first, pointed, and ran ahead. And he, musing, having seen it all before, brought up the rear. When he caught up with her, she was squatting in the middle of the road, forming with her body a human barricade. The snail had just noticed and screeched to a halt.

"What is it?" she whispered.

"A snail. A very big snail."

It was actually a slug, but he did not want to use the ugly word. He had never seen such a big one. Five inches long by one inch high! It was shining and black as an old steam engine. They had surprised it in the act of charging down the road under full steam.

"It's got no shell!" she said.

"No, this kind doesn't."

The black punctuation mark on the gray pavement could have led to many other questions. But she was unusually quiet. She had never seen anything quite like this before, and she was just watching it be. He, foolish man, had had enough of this and wished to get on with the walk. Before long it might even be done. Then he would be able to get back to doing those other things that kept the family rolling. He looked at his watch, and the adrenaline pump started up again. Tessa, however, was not ready to move. This in turn forced father to look more closely.

A bull snail, no doubt, he thought. Masculine, independent, a loner. One big muscle flexing and unflexing its way at top speed toward who knows what end. Searching for a home perhaps. Are houseless snails condemned to wander aimlessly in search of a security that forever eludes them? Do they occasionally attempt to escape their drifter's world of lush bogs and rotting stumps to tear along this long, hard expressway? Is their lot made any simpler that way?

The snail did not move, but its horns were erect and twisting around.

"It's got antlers!" said the girl.

That caught his attention. Yes, I suppose they are a bit like antlers, he said to himself. Antlers with eyes attached to the ends of them, or feelers or sensors or some such invention. Amazing thing, this creation, thought the father, with a sudden small jolt of awe. He looked more closely.

"Who are you?" he almost asked it. It was called "slug" or "snail", but what was its essential being really all about? It was a shape that formed and reformed itself as if in answer. It was certainly repulsive, but at least it had integrity. Maybe it had a purpose. That is what the ravens thought too. They sat up in the high, dead branches just ahead along the road, and they were watching. He was not very fond of them. These were fat, fast, clever, and industrious carnivores, cracking their voices in dispute. They would make a short meal of this mystery. For the time being they were content to drop horse chestnuts on the pavement and swoop down to devour the white nut meat. They could wait for mobile nourishment. Time was on their side.

The snail was clearly at a disadvantage. Doubtless from a distance it was only a slow-moving black speck in the eye and brain of a raven. Of little interest. But it would eventually creep directly beneath their gaze and become more interesting, and woe to the snail if the ravens were hungry. In the meantime, this girl had seen through the disguise. It was no speck. It was alive! And life is the great mystery.

Tessa reached out a finger and gently touched the tip of an antler. Instantly it retracted. She touched the other antler. The snail recoiled in shock, became a ball of protoplasm. She watched it, concentrating. And her father, that great omnivore of knowledge, watched them both. Her eyes were fixed on what it would do. First a black bud appeared tentatively on the surface, like a periscope examining the surrounding territory. Then it became a stump. Beside it, like a shy mate, the other horn made its appearance. They grew and grew until the entire body had once again assumed its own true form.

"You must touch gently", she said, full of secret understanding. And touched again.

Instant recoil! All defense systems were being brought into play. This snail was no sluggard, for it was equipped with a battle array of tactics. What determined the amount of time it would remain in the primordial fetal position? When would its confidence return? When would it forget its terror? When did it dare to hope again, unseeing? Because it did not see; it could not know. Yet, within this bundle of cells there was a complex decision-making process flashing at that very moment through the inner codes. *Yes*, came the command, now extend the brave folly of your horns into space. Push back the liquid air; not only reshape your own form, but alter a little the balance of the universe.

The girl looked up at the man, and a knowledge like light had come upon her.

"It wants to go", she said intensely. "We mustn't step on it", she added. She duck-walked aside to let it pass. Maybe the shifting of her shadow informed the snail, because it began to move.

"Ah," she said, "Ah!" and it was a moment of immense importance to her.

If they waited for twenty minutes, it would move possibly a foot or two. Already it was leaving a silver trail. Even snails, if given enough time, would perform astounding feats. They would circle the world, leaving frail traces as a memorial of their quest, of their greatness.

By snail-reckoning, this girl was hundreds of years old. She was immeasurably wise, an ancient. She moved closer to the speed of light than he. And the man, with his staggering knowledge, was unthinkably transcendent. But he was growing impatient—twenty minutes is an awfully long time to watch a snail and a little girl's wonder. He reached down to pull her back to human standard time. She evaded his hand. He called her name. She did not hear. Instead, still squatting, she shifted her body a step or two to see better the great passing of the snail.

"Time to go, Tessa", he said.

No answer. Immobile, her antlers retracted. He saw that it was already too far gone. The snail had told her its secret: far better to see a few things closely and well than to consume a whole universe and not see it, not love it.

All very well for her and the snail, he observed, *but what if a car comes?* He could feel the old adrenaline pump snap into action. Time instantly sped up, and he was running out of *kronos* again, too fast, too fast, too fast. He looked nervously up and down the road. What if a car did come, and he couldn't get her off to the side fast enough? There were speeders on this road, he knew, people who travelled faster even than he did. He pulled her upright by the arm. He made foolish adult noises of command and dragged her toward home. All the while she looked backward over her shoulder with clear, firm concentration, long after the note of black was too small to be seen.

Later, following an incredible avalanche of activity that completed this quite ordinary day, he found a moment of quiet. Julie had gone with the baby for an early sleep. The older children were also abed. Tessa was breathing deeply when he looked into her room to give her a final good-night kiss. The crickets chorused wildly, and a cool breeze came in from the field, where grass was sprouting again after the long winter.

He placed his hand on her head.

"I'm sorry, little dove", he whispered. "I didn't have much time for you today. I'll try to do better tomorrow."

She sighed in her dreams, and he went out, quietly closing

the door. He was tired, but his mind was awake. He buried himself in the encyclopaedia under the entry titled "Mollusc". Their slow-moving friend was *Arion Empiricorum*, a princely name for the common slug. It was first-cousin to the chambered nautilus and the garden snail. He read about an occurrence at the Natural History Museum in London, where a desert snail was brought from Egypt. It had been glued to a display exhibit for many years, where it had remained immobile and supposedly long dead. Examined by chance, the snail was found to be peering out of its cave. Placed in tepid water, it revived and began at once to rebuild the damaged shell.

He went outside to look at the night sky for a few moments before bed. He thought about his own little shell that he called home, which appeared to have sustained some damage. Then, not wanting to go in, he climbed the hill behind the house. They were far out in the country, and no lights from other houses could be seen. The sky was black glass reflecting nothing, but dazzling with billions of stars. At the crest of the hill, he lay in the damp grass. He was still. He gazed deeply into the infinite pool that bears the stars into being. Above him was a tiny smudge of light that was the closest galaxy. It was spinning, spinning, but so far away was it that one could look for a whole lifetime and not see it alter. There were galaxies out there, he knew, that whirled into each other like discs, blending in space without colliding. They passed through each other, those billions of worlds, at thousands of miles per second, yet they did not appear to move at all.

He understood suddenly what his little dove knew, what the sailors and the poets knew, what the sparrows in the holly knew. He understood, despite his blindness, blinder than the eyeless snail:

Time is an illusion of the mind. Only love remains.

Your son,

Colin

When Colin came in the front door, he frowned at Julie and said, "Okay. We'll take him."

She hugged him and gave him a long look in the eyes. "Thanks."

"I don't feel good about this, Jules, but I'm doing it for you."

"I know", she said.

"We'll take him up the coast and drop him wherever he likes. But from then on it'll have to be good luck, cobber, and don't look back."

They went arm-in-arm into the kitchen and told the others.

"Colin, Julie", said Andrei. "Your offer is kind. But I must refuse."

"Sorry, Father," Julie shrugged, "it's too late to refuse. Colin has made up his mind."

Andrei shook his head. "No. I couldn't let you do it. You would be harboring a fugitive from the law. You could find yourself in a great deal of trouble."

"No bloody fear", said Colin. "Trouble's my middle name. Where I come from, you're nobody if you don't have a criminal background. My great-granddad on one side was sent to Australia for stealing a loaf of bread. Another granddad was sent there for bona fide forgery. Good crooks and bad on both sides. It's in the blood!"

"Wish you'd told me that before we got married", said Julie.

"Good thing I didn't", Colin shot back.

"Really, Father, aren't you being just a bit overcautious?" Julie argued. "The chance of anyone stopping us on the water is almost nil. On the road you'd be nailed for sure."

"Right", said Bill, taking his cue. "Right. And I guess I'm gonna have to withdraw my offer about you staying here. We took a chance yesterday. We didn't get caught because

Somebody was working overtime trying to keep you from taking a ride in a beetle. There's probably a whole bunch of exhausted angels here in the room with us, right now, just begging you to say yes."

Andrei considered it silently.

"Besides, Reenie and me are leaving for California on Tuesday." Bill folded his arms and made himself look immovable.

"Then I have no choice?"

The others folded their arms too. "No choice", said Julie.

"None whatsoever", said Colin.

"It's settled", said Bill.

"All right", Andrei said quietly.

"Good-oh!" Julie cheered. "Good-good-oh!!!"

"Now we should decide where we're going to drop you", said Colin. "Julie says you have to get to the Cariboo."

"That's correct. First Williams Lake. After that we'll find our way."

"Williams Lake is a long way from the coast. We could take you as far as Ocean Falls. It's approximately the same latitude as Williams Lake."

"I have a friend at Bella Coola. It's at the head of the Burke Inlet, about sixty kilometers from the sea. It's a deep channel, so I think your boat could reach it without much trouble. There is a road from Bella Coola to Williams Lake, about four or five hundred kilometers."

"Can your friend be trusted?" Colin asked.

"Potempko? Almost certainly he can be trusted. He will have heard about our troubles on the news. He is blessed with a naturally suspicious mind, does not trust governments of any kind, and he knows me well. He may be willing to help."

"Why don't you call him right now?" said Bill. He took the receiver off the wall phone and handed it to Andrei.

Andrei hesitated for a moment, then tapped the number from memory.

"Allo! Glory be to God!" a voice answered, a high-pitched electric babble.

Andrei said something in Latin. Then, "Potempko, it's me."

Everyone in the kitchen could hear the burst of noise coming back over the wire.

"Yes, it's true, Potempko. A horrible tragedy."

Pause.

"They died instantly. I anointed them."————"The funeral Mass is Friday at the cathedral."————"No, I cannot be there. Haven't you heard about my situation?"————"You have? You understand? I knew you would. Nothing is as it appears. Remember the past, my friend. Remember what we went through when the beast was unmasked for a time."————"Yes, the Liar is working very hard. He has let his mask slip, but few people have eyes to see."————"Thank you. Thank you from the bottom of my heart. I was sure you would."————"No, I do not need money. I need something more important . . . your prayers."————"I also need sanctuary."————"For your sake, and for the sake of others, I cannot tell you how I am coming to Bella Coola. It will be within a few days."

"Tell him we'll call him when we get close to Bella Coola", said Colin.

Andrei passed on the message.

More Latin.

"Yes. Bless you too, Father. Until we meet, my friend."

He hung up.

"You called him *Father*", said Julie.

"Potempko is a priest."

"Potempko? Is that his first name or his last?" she said.

"His last", Andrei smiled. "No one except his parents has ever attempted to call him by his first name, which is extremely difficult to pronounce. He prefers Potempko. That is what he calls himself."

"You think he really understands the situation?" said Julie.

"He is considered by many to be a fool. But he is a man of much experience and insight. We can trust him."

"So, when do we leave?" Julie said, looking at Colin.

"It'll take me a few hours to get things ready", he answered. "Also, I think it would be better if they come on board after dark. There'll be fewer wowsers loafing about the quay."

"Wowsers?" said Bill.

"People hanging around staring, looking for something to criticize."

"Righto", said Julie. "How about I come back after dark and pick up Arrow. No one will look twice at me. Just another mum bringing her boy home from Scouts. Dad, do you think you could drive Father down in your car?"

"Sure, no problem."

"We'll space it half an hour apart, so as not to arouse suspicion. There are other people living on boats in the marina, and we wouldn't want them *wowsing*."

"We'll up anchor at dawn tomorrow and be off. Any objections?" said Colin.

No one had any.

5

A Dance upon Fair Waters

After sunset, Irene bestowed supper, advice, prayers, care packages, gifts, and an anxious good-bye. Bill took Andrei to the wharf in his old Pontiac. Half an hour later Julie followed in the Honda. Arrow sat in the back clutching his knapsack, staring out the window at the passing lights of Fort George, alternately nodding or shaking his head in response to Julie's questions.

The wharf was deserted when she parked, and they went down the ramp and along the dock without being seen. There were a few lights burning in the larger boats where people lived, but no one came out. Her heart thumping, she held tightly to Arrow's hand, turned left at the end of the L, and came to the *Osprey*, which was rising and falling gently beside pylons and a light post. An arc lamp flooded that section of the dock. Arrow had only a second or two to take in the impression of a large white sloop before Julie hurriedly lifted him up onto the boards and plunked him unceremoniously into the cockpit.

"Knock-knock", she said, opening the door into the cabin.

Colin pulled them inside and closed the door behind them.

"Righto", he said. "Anyone see you?"

"Not a soul. I think we're fine."

Bill was standing in the chart room drinking beer from a can. Andrei was seated on the left at the galley table, listening with attentiveness to a twelve-year-old boy who was apparently explaining the intricacies of celestial navigation. The boy's red hair stuck out in all directions. His face was Colin's, but his eyes were his mother's. The eyes were slightly idiosyncratic—green, bold, and disturbingly intelligent. He wore a dark blue jogging suit, and his socks did not match. He stopped talking and stared directly at Arrow.

An eruption of giggles from across the room drew Arrow's attention. Two blond, blue-eyed, neatly groomed girls, ages eight and six, were seated on a berth in pink pajamas and bathrobes, dangling their long skinny legs, at the end of which were two sets of battered ballet shoes. They were, if anything, more beautiful than their mother but were at that stage of growth when the knees of girls who are destined to be graceful and devastating seem as large as their feet. Arrow thought they looked like great blue herons, though pink. When he stared back at them, they giggled again and tried to bury their heads in their arm pits.

"Kathy and Tessa are really excited to meet you, Arrow. They've been practicing their ballet steps. Would you like them to show you?"

Arrow shook his head.

"Okay, maybe later. Now come on over here and meet Thomas—we call him Cub. Actually, his real name is Horatio Hornblower."

Everyone laughed, except Arrow. Cub put out his hand, and Arrow shook it reluctantly.

"Do you play chess?" Cub asked.

Arrow shrugged.

"Grandma says you play very well", Julie interjected. "She says you beat her two games out of three."

Arrow looked away, searching for something inanimate to fix his eyes upon.

Colin recognized the boy's condition and drew everyone's attention in another direction.

"Father, we're going to put you and Arrow in these two galley berths, if you don't mind. It's not very private, but it's comfortable."

"That's just fine, Colin."

"These seats do double duty as beds. The girls have the forward bunks in the bow. Julie and I are in the double berth up to the left. Across from our cabin is the head, just aft of the cubhole."

"He could squeeze in with me", Cub offered.

"I don't think so, honey", said his mother. "You can barely get yourself in there. I think Arrow probably wants to stay with Father Andrei tonight."

"Mum, he could come in with us", Kathy suggested.

"It's pretty tight in there too, girls. Besides, you'd drive him crazy with your chatter, and none of you would get any sleep. Speaking of sleep, have you two brushed your teeth?"

They scampered off to the head, leaving a trail of giggles and swirls of gossamer that Arrow saw hanging in the air long after they had disappeared.

A voice from outside made them suddenly jump.

"Houston calling Apollo! Houston calling Apollo. Do you read me, Apollo?"

"Oh, my word," said Colin, looking worried, "it's Captain Cook. I'll go up and talk with him. Julie, take Father and Arrow forward, would you, and park them in the honeymoon suite. I don't want him seeing them if he barges in."

"I'll go chew the fat with him", said Bill, grabbing two beers from the fridge. He and Colin went up through the cockpit door and closed it firmly behind them.

Julie took Andrei and Arrow forward, warning them to duck their heads, and directed them into a cabin just past the galley on the port side. A little sign on the door informed them that the room belonged to Colin and Julie—"Honeymoon Suite". Andrei and Arrow sat down on the double bed.

"That's Reggie Cook", Julie explained. "An Englishman who lives in the boat next door. Nice guy, but a trifle nosy. He drops in all the time, usually just before suppertime. Lonely, I think."

Five minutes later Colin came back inside, laughing.

"Your Dad! What a con artist! He's up there talking to Reggie like an old salt, when I know for a fact that he hates getting his feet wet."

"Do you think Reggie's going to want to come in? Won't it look suspicious if we keep him out?"

"I told him the kids have to get an early sleep, and it's not a good time for company. I said we might weigh anchor tonight."

"Oh-oh, I told him this afternoon that we're going for a test run up the coast after daybreak tomorrow."

"Well, he'll just have to think we changed our minds."

"Have we changed our minds?"

"I think we should. We might have other uninvited guests, especially if word's got around that we're shipping out tomorrow. Every wharf rat in Fort George will come dropping by to wish us the best, and it could get tricky."

"All right", she said uneasily. "But we've never sailed at night before."

"The channel's well marked. We'll have the floodlights too. We won't use sails—go by motor downriver as far as Georgia Strait. We'll be in open water by dawn."

"If you're sure. But I won't sleep a wink."

"Don't worry."

He turned to Andrei. "How are you doing, Father?"

"I'm fine, Colin. Our situation is looking better now that we're in good hands."

"Thanks. But let's not count our blessings before they're hatched."

Julie laughed and punched him softly on the arm.

"Speaking of hatches, are they battened down?" she said.

"Yeah. I'll go check and give the motor a warm-up. Maybe your Dad has Cap'n Cook squared away. Back in a minute."

Shortly after, the girls tumbled down the gangway, and Julie tucked them into their berths. She read to them for awhile, said prayers with them, kissed them good-night, and turned off the light. The motor was rumbling, and the hull gently vibrating when she went out to see if there were any developments.

Colin and Bill were just coming in the cockpit door.

"Coast clear?" she said.

"All clear", said Bill. "I asked him to show me his boat. What a beaut! He's sure proud of that thing. Thirty-four-foot launch, built in New Zealand in 1907, wraparound windows, teak woodwork, stereo, large-screen TV, and a mahogany bar. Lots of Scotch and rye for ballast."

"Yeah, that's our Reggie", said Colin. "I told him we're getting an early start and not to mind our engine. He says to tell you so long, Julie."

"Good. No suspicious questions?"

"None at all."

Bill laughed wickedly. "I shut the party down by praising the Knights of Columbus to high heavens and asking him if he'd like to join."

"Reggie sputtered and reversed engines fair fast", Colin grinned. "Said he liked the nautical theme, was a great admirer of Christopher Columbus and all that, but the religious motif wasn't exactly his style. No offense, thanks anyway, he said."

"Right. Well, maybe we should make a start", Julie suggested.

Bill went forward to say good-bye to the girls. He came back a few minutes later, dragged a reluctant Cub out of *Wooden Boat* magazine, and hugged him. Cub, mouth hanging open like a zombie, barely acknowledged his grandfather's parting jests and plunged back into his magazine as quickly as he could.

Bill went to Julie and Colin's cabin to say good-bye to Andrei and Arrow. He stood in the doorway, took off his Legion cap, and handed it to the boy.

"Here, this is for you, lad."

Arrow looked at it and said, "No, thank you."

"What! My grandson's begged me for this hundreds of times.

Sure you don't want it? Genuine redneck cap. It can get you into any place and out of it fast."

Arrow shook his head.

Bill shook his head too, more amazed than insulted. He thumped Colin on the back, hugged him awkwardly, and said, "Good luck." Then he scooped Julie in a bear hug, looked as if he were going to say something, and swallowed it.

"See you in a week, Dad", she said jauntily.

Bill turned away.

"Dad, can you give me a hand casting off?" Colin asked.

The two men went up to the cockpit, and Bill stepped onto the dock. Colin revved the engine and spun the wheel over. Bill threw the bow line onto the foredeck and pushed the boat's prow away from the pylon.

"Take care of them", he called.

"No fear", Colin yelled back.

Down in the cabin Julie brought Andrei and Arrow back to the galley seats. She could feel the deck tremble as the *Osprey* nosed away from the marina and slipped forward into the river. By the time she found sheets, sleeping bags, blankets, and pillows in the seat lockers and set up beds on either side of the table, the boat was in midchannel, accelerating nicely. The rumble of the baffles became a purr, and the lap of water against the bulkheads increased steadily until it levelled off to a soft background noise that did not distract but rather calmed and reassured the senses.

Julie found an extra pair of Cub's pajamas and offered them to Arrow. Andrei told him to change in the head. When he came back, he untied his knapsack, snuggled with his stuffed animals under the sleeping bag on the starboard berth, and turned his head to the wall.

"Good night, Arrow", said Julie.

"God bless you", said Andrei.

There was no reply.

150

Andrei sat down on the port berth by the table and opened his breviary. Julie warmed a pot of milk on the propane stove. While it was simmering, she came and sat across the table from him, observing him, absorbing his presence, wondering where everything would lead. She felt reassured that whatever happened, it would be in the company of a saint, an old friend, a spiritual father who knew her soul better than her own father did. She wanted to reach out and touch his gnarled, liver-spotted hands, hands that had held the Body of Christ thousands of times, that had blessed and healed more souls than she could begin to guess. Hands that had been scarred and broken. She knew that he had endured many things in his life, especially during the war, and that he had been in prison. She suspected that he had been tortured, but she had never dared to ask him about it.

Though she was worried about the outcome of the voyage, it suddenly did not seem to her a great danger or a burden. She was struck with a feeling of gratitude for this old priest and was happy for the opportunity to help him. As he prayed his office, oblivious to her presence, her eyes lingered on his thinning white hair, the stoop of his shoulders, the thick glasses perched on a tired, dignified face that had seen far too much of the fallen human condition and yet remained an icon of charity. She thanked God for him and prayed silently for an extraordinary gift of divine protection for him and the boy.

When he had completed his office, she put a mug of warm milk in front of him and sipped from her own. Andrei removed his glasses. He looked across the room toward Arrow's inert form, now emitting quiet snores, and made the sign of the cross over him with his right hand.

"That is one troubled boy", Julie said in a low voice.

"Yes", said Andrei. "He has seen more than is right for a child to see."

"He hardly ever speaks, does he?"

"Very little", said Andrei. "Only what is sufficient to keep strangers from intruding into his private world."

"We must all seem like strangers to him."

"That is true. But when this darkness is over, when he is returned to his family, he will begin to recover."

"I hope so. What family does he have left? I mean, if his mother and father . . ."

"His great-grandfather is a unique man. He is a person of few words, like his great-grandson, but in time he will draw this child out of himself. Not with words. With presences, and with the knowledge of wildlife and woodcraft, which are the delight of small boys everywhere."

"He has a brother and sister too, I hear."

"Yes, but Arrow has never met them."

Julie sighed. "Well, that's a sad commentary on our times, I'd say."

"Indeed it is."

"Colin and I are lucky."

"There is much love between you. Your children are very happy."

"You know, Father, when we were first married, I thought it would be only a matter of time before he became a Catholic. Now I'm not so sure. I've tried everything."

Andrei smiled. "Perhaps you are trying too hard. It is precisely your pressure that Colin resists. He has something to teach you."

"What?"

"That love is possible only if there is a free gift of the self."

She thought about that.

"He and I have tried to live that way from the beginning. We have a great love on the human level. But I can't help wanting it all for him."

"Love is the foundation, isn't it?"

"Uh-huh. I know it is."

"Do you see any changes in all these years?"

"Oh, sure, lots of changes. But the Great Barrier Reef is still there. Colin veers away from it whenever he gets too close. Then he just sails away."

"Does he believe in nothing then?"

"He believes in me and the children. We're his religion. He's sacrificed a lot for us."

Andrei thought for a bit, then said, "Why is he taking this risk?"

"He said he's not sure if what you've been telling us is a correct reading of things. If you're wrong, then this trip won't cost us anything. No harm done. But if you're right, then we have to do it."

"Have to? That sounds like faith to me."

"No. It's his sense of honor, you see. He says that if the government is becoming what you think it is, then it's just a cult. A giant cult. He despises cults."

"I see."

"He admires you, Father. Of course he can't accept a lot of the things you believe in, but he respects you very much."

"Then you mustn't worry. His nature dwells in the realm of justice. Give him time. Pray."

"Remember the talks you used to give us at the convent? You said once that grace builds on nature. Of all the things you said, that's the one I remember most."

"Aquinas said it first. When you have time, one day, I would like to introduce you to some of the other things he wrote. There are several volumes worth—the *Summa*."

She laughed. "Can you lend me a set? The *Osprey*'s still low on ballast."

"When our present difficulties are over, I will bring you a set."

"It's a deal. Maybe I can even get Colin to read it."

"Don't use pressure."

"All right, I won't use any of my tricks. It wouldn't work anyway. He got my number long ago. Nothing works."

"Never discount grace."

"That's true", she admitted wistfully. "You know, I always figured a guy as intelligent as he is would need some kind of super-intellectual Catholic to argue him into the faith. He's talked with a few. It didn't work."

"It never could."

"Why do you say that?"

"Because the way to faith leading through the intellect is the eye of a needle. Intellectual conversions are rare. The way through the heart is a wider door. But the way that leads directly to the soul, in the unfathomable depths of mystery and providence, is an open gate."

"You mean the imagination?"

"Not quite. The imagination may be baptized, but it is fraught with danger and easily misled. I mean, rather, the faculty of the soul that perceives the hidden shape of reality itself."

"That's a bit over my head."

"Suffice it to say that Colin is a man who sincerely seeks the truth, at least in his soul. He has suspended any thought of finding the transcendent truth through the mind, because he believes only in empirical data. He accepts the life of the heart, because you have taught him to, but he retains a certain caution about the illusory elements of emotion, especially where spiritual matters are concerned."

"And yet he's always supported my right to my beliefs, my thoughts and feelings about religion."

"I suspect that your husband is a man who guards your freedom carefully. You see, having been in bondage during his youth, he now values freedom above all things, freedom in its most overarching and profound meaning, though perhaps he would not express it that way. He is a philosopher and doesn't yet know it."

"A philosopher? Hmmm, maybe."

"But a philosopher can spend a lifetime examining the minutiae of being and never look beyond them to the source. And so, the way to lead him to the source is directly through the soul. Do you see?"

"Uh, I think so. You mean prayer?"

"Yes."

"I've been praying for fourteen years."

"The ground of the soil is being tilled and planted. The harvest will come."

"I don't know, Father. He's so proud."

"Yes, he is that too. His is the pride of excellent men who have been forced to struggle against the annihilation of the self, and have done so alone. By long labors and much agony he has arrived at a state of equilibrium. He believes he has achieved it by the sole effort of his will. Thus, it is inevitable that he would be proud."

"That worries me. Especially since he's ten times better than most of the Christians I know. He's certainly a better person than I am."

"That is his great danger", said Andrei. "He truly is better than most of us. But he will learn some day that Christianity is not a code of ethics for improving the behavior of humanity. Our faith is much more than that. It is light breaking into darkness. It is salvation. It is fire."

He lapsed into silence. Julie patted the back of his scarred hand, drank the dregs of her cup, and said, "Well, I'm going to take a thermos of coffee up top. We wouldn't want the philosopher to fall asleep at the wheel and drown us all."

* * *

Julie's favorite moment was dawn at sea. She woke to see a gray light in the porthole, rolled over, and gave herself another fifteen minutes of dozing until the alarm clock built into the bulkhead at the foot of the bed beeped seven o'clock. By then the porthole was letting in beams of silver, and she became aware of the boat pitching forward in a steady roll that was gentle but definite. She dressed herself in slacks, bulky blue sweater, and tan windbreaker and went to the galley, noting that the children and Andrei were still asleep. She turned up the heater, got the porridge bubbling, then turned it down to simmer, made a pot of coffee and took two cups up top. Colin smiled at her, but his eyes continued to scan the horizon off the bow. He looked peaceful but bleary eyed, his skin flushed from the night in the open air and his hair whipping about his head in a fresh breeze. This was the way she loved him best, strong, calm, and in command, balancing sea and sky and land by the arc of the wheel, as if he were personally oriented at last, as if he had found the true pole of the north.

"How did it go?" she asked, handing him a cup.

"Fine. Not a hitch. We passed the Tsawwassen lighthouse half an hour back. There's the city off to starboard."

She looked behind to her right and saw the towers of Vancouver strewn like a child's sand castle against the base of the mountains. Small red and white lights twinkled throughout, not yet conscious of the morning.

"We're in salt water now", he said. The sea was gray with a light chop, the bow tipping over it, up and down. The sky was lightly overcast with a veil of high altostratus cloud.

"Rain?" she said.

"Hard to say. Barometer's dropped a point in the last two hours. We could be in for some dirty weather."

"Good cross breeze. Should we put up the sails?"

"Let's wait until we're out on Georgia Strait a bit farther."

"I hardly heard the engine all night."

"Yeah, she's a bonza motor. Purring like a cat."

"I can't wait to get the sails up. The kids will help when they're awake."

"How's the brumby? He sleep all right?"

156

"I think so. He didn't twitch when I was getting breakfast started. It'd be good for him to see the sails going up. Ask him to help, would you, Colin? He's so waifey and withdrawn. He needs someone to pull him out of himself."

"Sure, I'll have a go at him."

"Thank you, Captain."

"Don't mention it, Ma'am. However, there is a price?"

"What price?"

"Captain needs a kiss."

"Captain gets one. Maybe two."

She gave him three.

"I'm going to roust out the crew", she said, "and stow some salt pork and hardtack into their bellies. I'll be back after breakfast. You'll need some sleep."

"Right. Maybe after we change over to wind I'll go below for a couple of hours."

"You look tired."

"I'm not, really. It was great along the river. Peaceful. The current was strong. I had a nervous moment or two bending round the islands near Albion, but I enjoyed the challenge, and she turned on a dime."

Arrow was awake, sitting up in bed, mouthing words to a monkey. Andrei was washing in the head, and the girls were giggling in their berths. Cub had to be dragged from his lair—she discovered a rumpled magazine and a flashlight burning down on exhausted batteries under his blankets. He staggered to the galley and slumped at the table, staring into midspace as if he had been drugged.

She served everyone porridge with milk, bananas sliced on top. Andrei said grace. The girls finished breakfast first and tied on their ballet shoes. They practiced stretches for a few minutes, with poised feminine gestures, watching Arrow's reaction out of the corners of their eyes. When it was certain that he wasn't interested, they scampered down the gangway to their cabin to dress themselves. They emerged wearing jeans and pastel-colored sweaters, one lavender, the other jasmine.

"My, aren't we looking lovely this morning", said their mother, raising her eyebrows.

"Mummy, we simply *must* wear our Samoyed sweaters! It's so cold!" Kathy stated.

"Can we, can we, can we?" Tessa pleaded, jumping up and down on her tiptoes.

"Those are your very best sweaters. It took Auntie Meg's dog a long, long time to grow that fur. Special events only, girls. Church and socials. They're not for swabbing the decks."

"Oh Mummy, just this once, *pleeease!*" said Tessa.

"Isn't it special having Father Andrei with us?" Kathy argued. "Besides, it's our biggest trip ever. It's practically our maiden voyage!"

"Just this once, then. You can go on deck for a while. Say good morning to Daddy. Maybe he'll let you take the wheel. But I want you back down here in two shakes, because we're going to put up the sails soon. You'll need work clothes for that."

"Oh, thank you, thank you, thank you!" they squealed. After the girls had gone topside, Julie ordered Cub back to his lair to get dressed. Arrow, who needed no instructions, went to the head and returned a minute later fully dressed, with a bundle of pajamas rolled tightly in his hands. He stood by the sink looking tormented. As she finished washing dishes she noticed the smell. She tousled his hair and said quietly, "Here, I'll take those, Arrow."

She washed the pajamas in the sink with a bar of soap, rinsed them three times, wrung them out, hung them over the curtain pole in the miniature shower room of the head, and turned on the heater. Arrow followed her every move.

"They'll be dry in an hour or so", she reassured him. "It's our secret, just between you and me. Okay?"

He nodded, the torment gone, eyes relieved.

"Now, how about that bed roll?"

Fortunately, the mattress was vinyl and easily sponged. His sleeping bag had a synthetic cover, which contained most of the smell. She took it topside and draped it over the cabin roof, hoping that exposure to fresh air would help.

"Ahoy, Mate", Colin shouted. "What's going on? This isn't laundry day!"

"That's the royal pennant, Captain! Prince is aboard, but indisposed. Have large mercies on small guest!"

She jumped down from the cabin roof into the cockpit.

"Translation, please?" Colin asked with a puzzled smile.

"Our young passenger suffers from urinary incontinence", Julie explained in a low voice. "And he's rather mortified about it."

"Ah", Colin nodded understandingly.

The girls were seated on either side of their father, with red noses and ears, enjoying the sensation of their hair blowing about their heads. They were accustomed to their parents speaking in cryptic language and ignored it. Colin said nothing more. Julie could tell he felt sympathy for the boy, which pleased her.

Later in the morning, shearings of pale blue edged into the sky, and the wind began to stiffen. Julie called the rest of the crew and passengers on deck. Arrow came out last, his expression blank but his eyes glancing around curiously, taking in every detail. He tilted his head to the sky, opened his eyes wide, and sucked a gust of salt air into his lungs. He seemed to be dancing as he tried to keep his balance on the now lunging deck. With an enigmatic smile and a quickening of the blood, he fumbled for a stern seat in the cockpit beside Andrei.

Julie took the wheel and headed into the wind, while Colin began cranking the halyards. The standing rigging hummed as the mainsail went up, and the *Osprey* surged forward like an eager racehorse, cutting into the waves. Cub already knew a great deal about rigging. After preparing the jib and foresail for hoisting, he returned to the cockpit to winch in the sheets. Kathy and Tessa flew about the deck in bright orange life vests, twirling in a free-form ballet.

Colin took the wheel. He cut the engine and eased off to starboard to begin tacking up the strait. Off to the right they saw a large black boat steaming away from the coast, trailing a ribbon of diesel exhaust.

"There's the Vancouver-Nanaimo ferry", said Colin.

"Will we hit her, Daddy?" Kathy cried.

"Not a chance. She's heading southwest, and we'll be crossing her lane before she's anywhere near."

"Distances are misleading at sea", Andrei said.

"Right", said Colin. "A sailor should get his sea eyes before he gets sea legs."

He stood, legs braced apart, chin jutted forward, eyes bright, adjusting the wheel from time to time with both hands. Eventually Julie noticed the girls traipsing along the side boards, taking chances, and ordered them below to change out of their special sweaters and to clean up their berths. Andrei went below with them, explaining that he had not yet prayed his office. Julie said she had something to talk over with Cub—disobedience for one thing, sloppiness for another—and shanghaied him without too much difficulty.

Colin was left alone with Arrow. The boy leaned against the side of the pit and stared at the horizon. Colin, glancing at him from time to time, thought that the boy's face had hunger in it, but not the physical kind. He knew the feeling well.

"First time on a boat?"

"Yes."

"Nothing in the world like it, is there?"

No reply.

"Would you like to take the wheel?"

"No, thank you." Perfect politeness. Impenetrable.

"Are you sure? I could hold it with you."

A shake of the head. Eyes swerved away to avoid contact.

That's all right, brumby, Colin thought. *You can stay as private as you like. I was once a kid like you.*

About ten-thirty Julie brought them sandwiches and a thermos of mushroom soup. She was surprised to see Arrow still standing where she had left him.

"You must be wiped out", she said to Colin. "Want me to take over?"

"No, thank you", he said in perfect imitation of the brumby. Numbingly polite. Impenetrable.

She got it and winked at him. "You're the Captain, Captain. I'll make myself scarce."

Every so often various members of the crew would surface, watch the sea for a time, and go back below. Cub was most in evidence, but about eleven o'clock his mother put her head out the cabin door and called, "Thomas! Thomas! Where is that boy? He hasn't done his geography yet. Send him below, would you, Colin?"

Arrow stayed put, though he had now settled himself on the stern seat behind Colin's back. The massive heights of Vancouver Island were closer, and the wind held steady from the northwest. Large and small vessels passed slowly by, going in all directions.

"This is a fine boat, isn't she?" Colin said.

"Yes."

"She's a sloop, forty-two feet long, all wood, no fiber glass."

"Oh."

"It took me a lot of research and five years to build her."

"Oh."

"I never saw the ocean till I was eighteen. And I never sailed till we built this boat. I was a long time waiting."

No reply.

"This the first time you've seen the ocean?"

"Yes."

"When I was a boy, I lived on the edge of the dry. That means near a desert. We had cows and sheep. It was hot most of the time, in a country called Australia. You ever hear of it?"

Arrow nodded. "Kangaroos", he said in a small voice. "And koalas."

"That's right. I had me a baby roo once. A joey."

No reply.

"He was about two foot high and loved to jump all over. They're good jumpers, joeys."

"Was he your pet?"

"That's right, he was my pet. When he got older, he went wild again. Here, take a look at this."

Colin rolled up the sleeve of his jacket and sweater and held out an arm. Arrow took a step toward him. He examined two white scars on Colin's forearm.

"One day he just kicked me and took off. He left this as a souvenir."

"Did he run away?"

"Too true. Ran away and never looked back."

"Where did he go?"

"Into the outback. That's our word for wilderness."

"Was he alone?"

"Yeah. He lived alone out there for a time. Then he found his family."

"Oh."

"Do you know why I always wanted to go to sea?"

"No."

"When I lived in the outback, and later when I lived in cities, I couldn't stop thinking about it. I always wanted to live by the water and sail on it. But I never could until now."

"Why not?"

"That part's hard to explain. It took me a long time, but eventually I figured out why I fell in love with the sea."

He let that sit for a bit until Arrow said finally, "Why did you?"

"At home on the station we were surrounded by thousands of square miles of sand and brush. The only water I ever saw was the kind that fell out of the sky once a year or sat in the swamp by Gum Creek. But there in the middle of our parlor was a picture my Dad had framed from a calendar. It was a three-masted schooner tossing on heavy seas. I looked at that painting all my life till I left home."

This monologue was too much for Arrow. He sat back down. Colin flashed a look at the boy and chuckled.

"When I was eight or nine I found a book of photos about America. There was this black and white one of San Francisco Bay, full of clipper ships abandoned by their crews. They'd all run off to the gold fields of California. I was convinced I could just go and get me one of those ships, pick one up for sixpence. I was dreamin' big in those years. I wanted to sail my very own boat to a secret island. Alone." Colin laughed again. "I should have checked the date on that photo. 1849!"

No response. Ten more minutes passed.

"What was his name?" Arrow piped.

"Who?"

"The baby kangaroo."

"The joey? I called him Jumper."

"Oh. Jumper."

"Not very original. But he was always Jumper to me. I loved him."

"Even after he scratched you?"

"Oh, yes, even then. I love him more every year, even though I'll never see him again."

Arrow gave that some serious consideration.

"When you name somebody," said Colin, "he's yours forever. You can't ever forget him."

"Can you give him away?"

"You can give him away, or he can run away, but he always carries your name inside him. And he leaves his name inside you."

"Even if he gets lost?"

"Especially if he gets lost."

"Oh."

"I named this boat the *Osprey*. That's a bird."

"I know."

Colin pointed to the sky. "If you were a bird flying way up there and looked down on this boat, you'd think she was a snail. A sea snail. You'd think she was crawling so slow she wouldn't ever get anyplace."

Arrow looked up at the sky. "But she's fast!" he said.

"It's all relative", Colin said. "The earth's orbital velocity around the sun is 18.5 miles per second; it spins on its axis at more than a thousand miles per hour. And here we are just inching over its skin, so slow you'd think we weren't moving at all."

This was too technical for Arrow. He stared back blankly, and Colin suddenly realized the boy did not know this particular language, had no experience in the barter of facts that is customary between men and boys. *Orbital velocity?* he admonished himself. *You should know better, Covey No Step!*

Colin wondered why it was proving so difficult to capture Arrow on the hook of dreams. He recalled the several stages of his own developing dream, beginning with the calendar, then the old photograph, and eventually a habit of drooling over wooden-boat magazines, followed by that later period (in the post-cult years) when the surge of marine romance arose again like a salvaged wreck and began to mix with the cool exaltation of a more mature logic. That was the story of his life, he reminded himself—reason and romance ever courting each other until, in the end, reason had to dominate if romance was to survive in any form whatsoever.

164

Colin would have preferred to build a many-masted schooner. He was in love with the complexity of their sails and rigging, their snapping pennants, the spears of their bowsprits, and headsails in the Grand Banks tradition, the way they danced upon the fair waters, plying the undulating waves. But that dream had to take second place to reality if he was to sail at all. He needed a simpler boat, one that could be handled single-handedly if necessary. Julie was trainable, but she was a limited crew. Moreover, she was an artist.

And so, reason and romance courted, and married, and when that happened neither was ever quite the same again.

"Did you name the little boat?" Arrow asked, pointing.

"The dinghy? She's called *Peppermint*. Cub named her."

Arrow examined the dinghy that hung on bent arms over the stern. It was enamelled white with parallel green stripes down its sides.

"Did you ever give something a name, Arrow?"

"I named my teddies."

"That's a grand thing to do. What did you name them?"

"Curious George, Freddy-the-Teddy, and Leo."

"Oh, my word, those are fine names."

No reply. Another long silence.

"Feel like taking the wheel for a bit? I won't let go of it if you don't want me to, but you can do the turning."

Arrow came up beside the wheel and touched a spoke with one hand. He turned it clockwise a degree, timidly. Colin pushed it farther. The *Osprey* heeled slightly, and the forward horizon line altered.

"Go ahead. I'm right here if you need me. Turn it a bit more."

Arrow curled his hand around the pin and turned it a few degrees. Then a bit more. When the bow swung, his eyes widened.

"Here, stand in the middle and take it in both hands."

Arrow tried it. His eyes began to look excited. The wind hit the left side of his face.

"Try it by yourself now, lad."

The boy braced his legs and spread his arms to take the pins. He gripped them firmly, moved the wheel slowly to starboard, and watched the ship respond; then revolved it back to port. His mouth fell open. He panted, his nostrils flaring. He swallowed hard.

"Did you feel how she moved under your feet?"

"Yes."

"You can do it again if you like."

He did it again.

"Oh!" he said, "Oh!"

His mouth uttered a single cry of elation. The *Osprey* was alive! She was flying! The sensations of awe, of mastery, of commanding an impossibly large and swiftly moving vessel, were so alien to Arrow's experience, so mystic and frightening and beautiful, that the words that might have burst forth from sheer joy refused to take shape on his lips. The man standing solid behind him, the liquid heaving of the sea, and the waves of hot light that now broke through the last of the overcast and beat upon his back conspired a silence within him that was different from any absence of sound he had ever known. It was no longer the muteness of introversion. It was worship.

After lunch Julie took the wheel and sent Colin and Arrow to the galley to eat. Afterward Colin crawled into their bunk and fell asleep. The girls practiced knitting in their berth. Cub closed his textbooks, set up a magnetic chessboard on the table and began to play a game with himself, while Arrow watched.

When he had defeated himself, he set the pieces up and invited Arrow to play. Cub beat him easily, twice, and Arrow lost interest. Andrei went topside and sat beside Julie for a while, neither of them speaking. By midafternoon the sun was falling toward the western hump of Vancouver Island. They saw several seals and the spray of a killer whale, its ebony fin curving out of the water and sliding back into it. A fleet of whistling water ducks flew in formation across their bow, going east, low over the waves. When it came time for them to come about, Julie instructed Andrei in the art of loosing the sheets on one side of the boat and hauling them in on the other.

"How far have we come?" Andrei asked.

"I'm not sure exactly. Colin will take the readings from the Loran when he gets up. I expect we've covered a good bit of Georgia Strait."

"Will we sail through the night?"

"Colin thinks we shouldn't risk it. The strait ends where the upper half of Vancouver Island bulges in toward the coast. The mainland juts out farther west at that point too, so the passage gets pretty narrow. There are islands in the channel and riptides. It would be tricky even for experienced sailors."

"What will we do?"

Leaving Andrei at the wheel, Julie went to the chart room and returned a moment later with a plastic tube. She extracted a chart and unrolled it.

"See this cove just north of Campbell River? We'll anchor there and get under way at first light. Tomorrow we'll spend most of the day cruising up the channel. We should be into clear water on Charlotte Strait, north of the Island, by nightfall. The day after that we should reach Fitz Hugh Sound, and maybe even as far as Burke Channel, which cuts east into the mainland a fair piece." She looked up. "With good winds, and depending on the tides, we could be at Bella Coola by evening, the day after tomorrow, but Colin thinks we should take our time and get into port on the morning of the fourth day."

"Yes, I agree, we should take our time and arrive safely."

"As Dad says, *I'd rather be late at the Golden Gate than arrive in hell on time.*"

"Your father is a unique theologian."

"Isn't he!"

* * *

Twilight was falling when they dropped anchor thirty yards off-shore in a bay north of Campbell River. In the lee of the great island there was little wind, but a chilly breeze rippled the surface of the water. The cry of eagles soaring over the forest pierced the silence after the motor died. The anchor chain rattled down into the depths; the boat rocked, then steadied.

Colin flicked the switch of the wind generator, which whirred softly on its bracket halfway up the main mast. After a final check of the anchor lights, left burning to warn off other vessels, he went below. Julie called everyone for supper, and they ate quietly around the galley table, a hearty meal of steaming rice with clams, baked yams, string beans, and halibut sautéed in mushroom sauce.

"How'd you whip up a meal like this, Jules?"

"It's an art", she smiled.

The girls yawned throughout the meal, and Cub could hardly keep his eyes open. Clearly, everyone was ready for an early sleep. After coffee, Colin put the girls to bed, Julie went in to read to Cub in his lair, and Andrei set up the galley berths for himself and Arrow. Arrow lay down beneath the sleeping bag and was asleep within minutes. Colin rubbed his eyes, made small talk with Andrei for a while, and soon left for the honeymoon suite.

Julie switched off Cub's light and the light in the gangway and returned to the galley. She sat with Andrei and prayed the office with him, saying the alternate verses of the psalms in a low voice. Then she said good night and left to join her husband.

Andrei shut off the galley light, undressed in the dark, and lay down under the blankets of his berth. He prayed a rosary, made an examination of conscience, and tried to sleep. But he knew he was suffering that state of overexhaustion in which it becomes difficult to slip into unconsciousness. With a stab of pain he recalled that the sisters' funeral had been that morning. He had prayed for their souls during that hour, and throughout the day they had never been far from his thoughts. Now that all distractions and physical motion had subsided, their faces rose in his mind with particular intensity. He prayed for their souls, as he had done numerous times since their death, but now he also asked for their prayers for him. He had no doubt that they were in heaven and could intercede for the Church in a new way. They had died martyrs' deaths, and whatever sins they were capable of, or had committed, had been washed in the Blood of the Lamb. Now the power of the sisters, which had seemed during their lives to be the quintessence of powerlessness, was multiplied a thousandfold—rather, beyond measure.

He asked them to beg a great gift from the Lord: that Arrow, this child reared in darkness, marked by it, and still burdened by it, might somehow be spared, might even—O miracle of miracles—be brought through the fire to a new heaven and a new earth. He offered his life for this, a tangible sacrifice joined to his formal request, and yet, as always, subject to the will of God. He raised his arms in supplication, and tears streamed from the corners of his eyes. He pleaded again and again, like a child tugging on the hand of a father, begging the extraordinary favor, the extravagant treat. Then, with some shame, he realized that his request was no less than what the Father himself desired for all of his children, each and every one, from the greatest saint to the most abject criminal, the persecutor and the persecuted alike.

He prayed that the blood of the sisters, united to that of the Lamb, would merit the conversion of countless souls and speed the end of the time of darkness. One by one he brought each of their faces before the eyes of his heart. Then, at last, he grieved.

* * *

The second day was uneventful. The *Osprey* motored at six knots through the channel, passing from time to time small fishing craft and pleasure boats and a single coast guard cutter. There were a few nervous minutes when a police cruiser roared across their bow, but it was merely in transit between Beaver Cove on the island and Minstrel on the mainland side.

When its wake had flattened out, Colin wheeled the boat to starboard, made a turn around some large channel islands, and entered Queen Charlotte Strait. By late afternoon the gash in the continent was wide enough for sailing. There was some light swell, and the sea was running higher, but so far the crests of the waves were not threatening undue violence.

Arrow spent most of the day sitting on the stern seats in the cockpit. Colin let him take the wheel a few times, and the boy's exultation seemed in no way diminished by a growing familiarity. Rather, experience worked like a stimulant with addictive side effects, for each encounter with the wheel left him more intoxicated, needing a bigger dose.

There was little spoken exchange between the captain and the boy, but whenever Julie emerged from the cabin with cups of cocoa or sandwiches, she noticed a gradual shifting of body language in both of them. She observed Colin, who was not blessed with outstanding talent for expressing affection, clap the boy on the shoulder, muttering obscure Australian words. Arrow, on his part, no longer seemed to be a compressed gravity, waiting to implode. His eyes looked . . . *happy*, she thought. His glance flashed from island to mainland repeatedly, anchored on the man at the wheel occasionally, then played all over the boat, the sky, the dwindling shores. His hair whipped about his forehead, and his face was flushed, slightly burned from the sporadic sun. She wiped some lotion on his nose and cheeks, and he did not resist. He actually smiled at her when she came on deck for the third time—a shy smile, fleeting, swiftly gone—and yet, she knew it was a message hurled across a vast distance.

"How is Arrow?" Andrei asked her when she went back down to the galley.

"Lots of male bonding going on up there, Father. Deaf-mute variety."

"This voyage is good for all of us", he replied.

"How so?"

"The sensation of motion speaks to the soul. We are no longer bound by the limitations of our flesh. We fly on the wind and the water, toward a destination that promises sanctuary. A living metaphor. A glimmer of transcendence."

"I think of it as a mother rocking her babies", she mused. "The sea is a mother, isn't it?"

"You could say that. Like the waters of the womb."

"Yes." She sipped her coffee, remembering the feel of Francis in her arms.

After supper Colin called everyone up on deck to watch the fabulous display of the sunset.

"It looks like somebody tipped over a whole bunch of paint buckets up there", said Cub.

"Whoever he is, he's quite an artist, I'd say", Julie agreed.

When the west was dark green and the hot colors gone, the girls asked their mother if she would come below and read to them.

"First, into your pajamas, girls. Arrow, maybe you should get ready for bed too. You too, Cub."

"Aw, Mum!"

"No sass, now. If you want me to begin that Arthur Ransome story tonight, you'd better show me how fast you can do what you're told."

The children went below, with Julie riding herd. When they were all ready, they arranged themselves comfortably on cushions around the galley settees, wrapped in bathrobes and blankets. The girls cuddled their dolls. Cub opened a cardboard box on the table and began to remove electronic components from it.

"This is an old Loran", he said to Arrow. "Long Range Aid to Navigation. Captain Cook gave it to me for painting his dinghy.

It's busted and he got a new one. I'm gonna take it apart and make it work. Someday I'll have my own ship."

"Oh", said Arrow.

"I'll have a sextant too, for the stars. But I won't get a satellite instrument. No radar either. I don't believe in them."

"Oh", Arrow said again.

"I'm Sally", said the doll on Tessa's lap.

"I'm Violet", said the doll on Kathy's.

"Their real names are Sullen and Violent", snickered Cub.

The girls shot him a sullen and violent look.

Smiling wryly, Julie said, "Why don't you go get Jocko, Cub?"

"That's babyish", he said.

Kathy ran to the lair and returned with her brother's battered little stuffed monkey and propped it up on the seat beside Cub. He looked disgusted but let the monkey stay.

Arrow watched it all, then removed his three stuffed animals from his knapsack. He set them up beside him.

"What are their names, Arrow?" Kathy asked.

"Curious George, Freddy-the-Teddy, and Leo the Lion."

The two dolls bowed and waved to the newcomers.

"Okay, let's get started", Julie interjected. "Do you want me to read *Swallows and Amazons* or *We Didn't Mean to Go to Sea*?

"*We Didn't Mean to Go to Sea! We Didn't Mean to Go to Sea!*" shouted the girls.

"*Swallows and Amazons*", Cub said.

"You're outvoted, guy", said his mother. "Sorry."

Julie sat down beside Arrow, tucked her legs under her, and began to read aloud from a dog-eared paperback, one of the many dozens of children's books that lined the walls of the cabin. She read to them for an hour. The two girls and Arrow paid close attention; Cub pretended not to as he bent over his project. It was a gripping tale, the adventure of four children who sailed a schooner unaided across the English Channel to Holland.

When she ended the third chapter, her children pleaded for more, but she told them it was now after eight o'clock and time for prayers. Then she led them in a rosary. The children said their responses distractedly, the girls fidgeted with their dolls' hair, braiding the wool tresses. Cub, surprisingly, closed his eyes and prayed with a semblance of interior recollection that gratified his mother. Arrow kept his eyes wide open, expressionless, his mouth firmly closed, and listened.

After the remaining prayers, Julie opened a Bible and read from the fifth chapter of Matthew's Gospel.

" 'Blessed are the poor in spirit, for theirs is the kingdom of heaven. Blessed are those who mourn, for they shall be comforted. Blessed are the meek, for they shall inherit the earth. Blessed are those who hunger and thirst for righteousness, for they shall be satisfied. Blessed are the merciful, for they shall obtain mercy. Blessed are the pure in heart, for they shall see God. Blessed are the peacemakers, for they shall be called sons of God. Blessed are those who are persecuted for righteousness' sake, for theirs is the kingdom of heaven. Blessed are you when men revile you and persecute you and utter all kinds of evil against you falsely on my account. Rejoice and be glad, for your reward is great in heaven, for so men persecuted the prophets before you.' "

The children were quiet after that and went off to their berths thinking about the passage. She settled them without too much trouble and shortly after heard the anchor chains rattling. Colin and Andrei came down to the galley and sat with her, drinking hot chocolate.

"Where are we?" Julie asked.

"About forty kilometers from the north tip of the island", Colin said. "It's not the greatest spot to anchor. We're by the mainland, in a bend. Not exactly a cove, but it's breaking the swell, and the wind shouldn't blow too hard on us here."

"Did we make good time?" Andrei asked.

"Not bad. I'd say an average of seven knots. We covered about a hundred miles today."

"Will we reach Bella Coola tomorrow?"

"It would take a miracle. In the best of circumstances, we'd have to cover about 120 nautical miles. Even if we weigh anchor before dawn, we couldn't reach the village until long after nightfall."

"You say the best of circumstances", said Julie. "What if conditions aren't so good? Is there rough weather coming?"

"Nothing unusual. We've had it fairly calm in the channel, but once we're beyond the north end of the island we're in open sea, and those Pacific swells will start to hit us hard around Cape Caution. It's famous for its strong currents too. We'll be lucky if we make it into Burke Channel by dark. After that, I don't want to risk it."

"Couldn't we use floodlights?" said Julie.

"Well, we could. But that's odd behavior for a sailboat, and we shouldn't attract undue attention. Also, I'm getting flagged out. We don't need to wear ourselves down; there's the return voyage to think about, and we'll be one man and one boy short of a crew."

"So, you think we'll reach Bella Coola by the following morning", Julie said.

"I hope so. Probably before noon the day after tomorrow."

"That is good", said Andrei. "There is no need to rush. The longer we wait before trying to reach the Cariboo, the less the police will be searching."

"I hope you're right", said Colin.

Julie looked worried. "But if your thesis is correct—you know, about the government having Big Brother plans—then they're not going to give up looking for you."

"That may be so," said Andrei, "but I think each day gives us a little more time, more distance. There must be many fugitives, many crimes, in a country as large as this. They cannot hunt forever."

"Father, here's a thought", Colin said. "We know that something is brewing. Martial law? Police state? Maybe a long-range dictatorship of some kind? But we're not really sure, are we?"

"There are signs . . ." Andrei began.

"Yes. There are signs of *something*. But up there on deck today it struck me that everything looks so normal, so beautiful really, that our scenario may be kind of, well, blown out of proportion. I'm not saying they aren't after you, and I'm not doubting for a moment that they're capable of all sorts of nasty stuff. But, consider this: Don't they already have the whole thing in the bag? Politics, media, culture, law enforcement, military—you name it, they've got it, all sealed up tight as a drum. They're totally confident. They don't need concentration camps. The whole thing is becoming one big camp."

"Er, just a moment, professor", Julie argued. "Can you really call it a prison if the prisoners don't even realize they're caught?"

"Good point. But isn't the definition of a prison the restriction of freedom?"

"Okay, Colin. But look at us! Here we are sailing off around the world. Are we prisoners?"

"How much longer do you think we'll be able to do this? Isn't the most effective prison the one in which the authorities have absolute control but are saved the trouble of dealing with prison riots because the convicts are all tranquillized? They're so drugged they don't even know where they are."

"Hey, Mister Logic, you're sounding more and more like me by the minute."

"I know", he grinned. "Consider it my little exercise in creative thinking. Call it an intuition."

"Colin," said Andrei, "if your intuition is correct, my troubles, the deaths of the sisters and the people at the commune, would then be simply bizarre incidents. Aberrations. Excesses caused by individuals exceeding their authority."

"Maybe they were."

"Possibly. But consider well the gravity of these crimes. Consider also that, because of the media collaboration with the State, we have little chance of finding out if they are part of a larger pattern. There may be similar incidents happening throughout the country."

"All right. We have no way of knowing. But doesn't that underline my point? Maybe we shouldn't assume that the worst is happening. It looks bad, no doubt about it. But it may stabilize soon."

"At least you'll agree that we're in a prison?" Julie said.

"Depends on what you mean by prison. But I'd say we're definitely in the middle of some kind of institutionalizing of restricted freedom."

"Sounds like a prison to me. Maybe what we really have to figure out here is whether we're in a maximum security, medium security, or minimum security prison?"

"Yeah, something like that."

"Are you suggesting that if it's just minimum security, we can adapt? Have a nice life despite everything?"

"No! Look, Julie, you're not hearing me. I'm not making statements. I'm just thinking out loud, just trying to get my mind around a situation that has a whole lot of unknowables."

"We can speculate as much as we wish", Andrei cut in. "We can call it minimum or maximum, soft or hard, but the important thing is to grasp the total effect upon souls, not so much the size or number of prison camps. In the end a global prison without out fences may be the worst of all, for the destruction would then proceed without alarming the populace. This is the most dangerous form of totalitarianism, impossible to throw off, because it never appears to be what in fact it is."

Julie and Colin digested that.

"Are you saying a monster-type tyrant is preferable?" Julie asked doubtfully.

"A monster tyrant is a great evil", Andrei replied. "But all recognize him for what he is. Resistance becomes possible."

"But . . ."

"The important thing is to see the form of it", said Andrei.

"I think I get what you're saying", Colin nodded. "Seeing the form is the key."

No one said much after that. Eventually Colin yawned and stretched. "I'm beat. I'm turning in. Set the alarm for 5 A.M., would you, Julie?"

"Okay, love. See you in a few minutes."

When he had gone, Julie sighed. "I guess he's right. We do need to get a reading on how bad it is, then adjust our course."

"If it is maximum," Andrei replied, "then I suspect that the entire West is in the grip of the same menace."

"So traipsing around the world may not be such a hot idea?"

"Perhaps not."

"We were planning to go through the Panama Canal and sail to England. We wanted to spend a year cruising the coast, see the Channel Islands, go up the Thames as far as we can. But maybe it's going to be the same over there."

"I suspect so."

"Maybe we'll go to France. *Liberté, Egalité, Fraternité.*"

"The question is, how large is this form we're trying to see? It may be everywhere."

"You think it's apocalypse to the max, Father?"

"These are the birth pangs."

"Then we still have time."

"I do not know if it can be stopped now. But we can mitigate the intensity of it and shorten the time."

"How?"

"By prayer. By sacrifice."

"The old medicine."

"Yes. It is still quite effective."

"I hope Colin will come to believe that."

"It was interesting to see how your two minds grappled with the problem."

She laughed. "Mr. Left Brain meets Mrs. Right Brain? Uh-huh, I guess between the two of us we have a single human mind."

"More like a woman seeing things from the inside out, and a man trying to see from the outside in. It's not a bad combination, you know."

She smiled at him, touched his shoulder, and went to bed.

* * *

The following morning, the passengers and crew woke to feel the boat heeling and plunging forward. Bright sun poured in through the portholes. Andrei went on deck, greeted Colin at the wheel, and saw that the water stretched ahead like a rolling sheet of hammered aluminum. Sea gulls were screeching, and all sails were tight in a light crosswind.

"Pretty heavy swell", Colin explained. "I'm taking it on the quarter, which will slow us down a little, but she's doing about six knots."

"What time did you start?"

"Shortly after five. It's eight-thirty now. There's the last of the out-islands off to port, that hump behind us. Good-bye, duck pond; hello, big deep."

"And that ship?" he said, pointing to a large black liner in the northwest.

"That's the Prince Rupert ferry. Miles away."

"It should be a fine day."

"There's no predicting. Barometer's high but falling steadily. See that ridge of clouds on the horizon? A storm is coming in, and this may be the fringe of it. With luck we'll outrun it, but I wouldn't want to bet on it. It can turn crook without much warning."

The children spent most of the early part of the day on the cabin roof, alternately reading their textbooks and watching the horizon. Because of the rising sea, Colin made them keep their safety harnesses on, over sweaters and life jackets. As usual, Arrow stationed himself behind Colin and took the wheel eagerly whenever the man offered it to him. His joy was palpable, and Andrei delighted in watching it. He thought to himself that all children should be given the chance to feel such things. It need not be the sea. A mountain, a forest, a river would do. Children needed something to dream on, something that reminded them that existence was not a complex of geometrical warrens set in concrete. He remembered his childhood passion for the River Elbe, for the long yellow and green barges that plied its waters, the rows of elderly anglers hoping for golden scaled carp, the summer when he leaped over the bonfire on Saint John's Night, and white German Christmas, with straw stars and red ribbons, the smells of baking strudel, sizzling sausage, foaming cherry liqueur, and the boy's choir at Midnight Mass singing *Jesu Joy of Man's Desiring*. Dresden, Dresden, the most beautiful city in the world.

His last glimpse of her was from the back of a Gestapo van in 1936, on the way to Sachsenhausen, and he, a young priest, memorizing the view through a small square of bulletproof glass, saw a city-as-art-form, a crenelated jewel, a monument of medieval splendor, a witness to the timeless principles of civilization—eternal, until the massive Allied fire-bombing destroyed it during the war.

Fire! Like water, like the sea, it was a friend or an enemy, according to how one understood its form and purpose. Seeing the form, as Colin said, was the key.

At ten o'clock the *Osprey* passed the outer point of Cape Caution. The sky was darkening quickly, and a black squall was spotted moving over the surface on the horizon.

"On with your foulies, crew!" Julie shouted to the children. They went below and returned shortly, wearing foul-weather coats, leggings, and caps. The impending storm excited them; they clung to rigging and stays, letting the spray sting their faces. Whitecaps began to crest dangerously. The temperature dropped, and a harsh polar wind began to blow. When the swells were about seventy feet apart and the troughs about eight feet deep, slosh began to pelt the length of the deck, and Colin sent the children below.

The remainder of the morning and into the afternoon he progressively shortened sails and wrestled with the wheel. Though Andrei's strength was limited, he was able to help bring in the main sail and the jib. From then on they proceeded by motor power alone. By three o'clock they had passed Cape Calvert on the port and were making good way into the lee of the islands of Fitz Hugh Sound. The swell subsided and the wind dropped steadily, sufficient to warrant putting up some canvas. They were cold and exhausted but relieved that the worst seemed to be over. Julie took the wheel for an hour while Colin went below for a bite to eat and a break.

After supper the wind shifted abeam and the overcast broke up. The *Osprey* began to make good time from then on, logging about eight and a half knots, and just after sunset the old cannery at Namu, on the mainland, appeared ahead, its lights twinkling like a Christmas tree in its terminal stage. Julie suggested that they drop anchor there for the night, but Colin was possessed by a determined Aussie ringer look. He said he wanted to press on to make up for lost time; the channel was well marked, and they could run for a while with lights.

Andrei reminded Julie and the children that it was Sunday and that he had not yet said Mass. While he vested in the galley, Julie set up the portable Mass kit on the table. Throughout the Mass, Arrow sat in a corner, his hands on his knees, observing everything with solemn interest.

Later, while Julie was putting the children to bed, Andrei went topside to keep company with Colin. The sea was relatively calm, and there was not much wind. The sky had cleared entirely, and a big sulky moon was rising. They were well into Burke Channel by then, and the shores on either side were clearly visible. After securing all sails, they motored east into the mainland for another hour, until about ten o'clock Colin threw on the floodlights and searched along the south shore for a cove. The chart did not lie, and within minutes they dropped anchor just inside the mouth of a cove fed by the Kwatna River.

Colin went below.

"You look pretty haggard, joey", Julie said. "Have a hot shower and go get some sleep."

"It's been sixteen hours straight, love. I think I'll skip the shower. I'd better crash."

He went directly to bed, and Julie followed him shortly after.

Andrei sat at the galley table reading his breviary, listening to the sounds of gentle breathing and children murmuring in dreams. He lay down on the bed and closed his eyes but was unable to sleep. A few minutes later he heard a motor approaching and the squawk of a loud hailer.

"Ahoy! Anyone aboard?"

Julie came flying out of the honeymoon suite, wrapping herself in a housecoat, and went up top. Andrei stayed below by the open cockpit door.

The boat idled in alongside the *Osprey* and stood off about ten yards.

"Hello there!" Julie shouted. "Is it okay if we anchor here tonight?"

"Should be no problem", the hailer replied. "Not much traffic up the Kwatna, but there's no guarantee. I suggest you keep a light on, Miss. Sometimes speedboats tear around these bays—

you know—kids. Weekends are party time at Fort Whoop-up. If they've been drinking, they could collide with you before they see you."

"Okay, will do! Thanks!"

"Where's your home port?"

"We're the *Osprey* out of Fort George, B.C."

"Long way from home!"

"Yup. Trial voyage. Ran through that storm this afternoon. I'd invite you in for a coffee and debriefing, but I've got one tired Captain below and a pack of sleeping kids."

"Okay, Ma'am. Just keep a light on. Take care, now."

"Take care, fellows", she called cheerily. The motor revved and pulled away, leaving the *Osprey* rolling gently in the wake.

Julie switched on the running lights and the mast light, and left them on battery power. When she came below, she rolled her eyes.

"That was close", she exhaled loudly. "Police cruiser."

"I wonder if they will return?"

"I don't think so. And frankly, I'm too tired to worry about it."

She hugged him and said good night. Andrei lay down again and gradually drifted into a sleep that was fitful and troubled by dreams.

* * *

After breakfast the next morning, Colin came growling down from the cockpit.

"Blast!"

"Blast?" Julie inquired with raised eyebrows.

"Double blast!"

"What's up?"

"The batteries are dead. It'll take hours to recharge them with the wind generator. But there's no wind. Dead calm."

"Oh, no! What'll we do?"

"I guess we'll have to sit it out here until we can put up some sail, or at least until we can get the motor started. But it's crook too. I opened up the bilge and found the engine sitting up to its hips in sea water. Looks like we sprang a leak in the storm. Nothing serious, but it may have thrown a spanner in the works for today. I'll hand-pump the bilge and see if we can't dry out the motor. If I find the crack we should have no problem sealing it. But I doubt we'll see Bella Coola till tomorrow. Sorry, Father."

"That's all right. Can I help, Colin?"

"Maybe you and Julie could take the kids on shore in the dinghy. It's a beaut day. Clear sky, warm."

"Right, Colin", said Julie. "I'll pack a lunch, and we'll have a picnic on the rocks."

"Take the rods. Maybe there's salmon here. Oh, my word, how about a cohoe grilled over a bonfire?"

"Well worth the price of a day, wouldn't you say?"

After breakfast, they lowered the *Peppermint,* and everyone except Colin went down the ladder and crowded into it. Julie took the oars and pulled toward a rocky shelf thirty yards away. Beyond it, a clearing in the forest promised a perfect picnic site.

"Bye, Daddy! Sorry you can't come."

"Me too, little dove. Cub, I'm counting on you to bring me back a forty pounder."

"Okay, Dad!"

They waved, threw him kisses, and flailed their fishing rods and caps.

Colin opened the engine room hatch and let himself down into the crawl space. He pumped hard for an hour, and gradually the water line went down until he found the leak. The packing around the propeller shaft was dribbling in a slow, steady stream of brine. He repacked it and pumped out the remaining water. From time to time he heard the excited cries of the children, happy and faint, and around lunchtime he smelled wood smoke drifting off shore. He went up top to check on them and called to Julie, who was guarding a small bonfire on the rocks. She waved, and he waved back.

After lunch a gentle breeze came in over the forest and riffled the surface of the water. Both the anemometer and the wind generator began to revolve slowly. Every hour or so he tried the ignition, but the diesel engine refused to respond. Late in the afternoon a fishing boat went past the mouth of the cove. He tried to hail it, hoping for a jump-start with cables or a tow into Bella Coola, but its crew didn't see him.

The sun was behind the trees when the dinghy returned, bearing a cargo of flushed, deliriously happy children. They smelled of sun and sweat and wood smoke. Even Arrow was smiling steadily. They scampered on board, followed by Andrei, who despite his years seemed rejuvenated by the excursion.

"Surprise, Cap'n!" said Julie, pulling two small salmon out of the bottom of the dinghy and throwing them up on deck.

"Wow! Well done, girl. Looks like a three pounder and maybe a five pounder!"

"Cub caught the three, and Father caught the big one", said Julie.

"You've earned your passage for sure, Father. Many thanks."

"How is the engine, Colin?" the priest asked.

"Well, we'll see in a moment. I've let the battery charge for the past few hours and dried the motor as much as I can. I found the leak and fixed it temporarily. The fuel line seems water-tight."

He turned the ignition key; a low rumble and a cough came from below, then a chug-chug. Finally, it caught, and clouds of black smoke burst out the exhaust pipe. Everyone cheered.

Julie gutted the fish on the stern. "Colin, I'm going to get these cooking", she said. "Do you think we should weigh anchor?"

"Maybe. But that would put us into Bella Coola long after dark, and I don't know if we should travel blind so close to the end of the sound. What do you think, Father?"

"Would you mind if we stayed here for the night? It's such a lovely evening, and perhaps we need a good rest after yesterday."

"You're right. Let's have a fish fry and turn in early. What say, Julie?"

"Sounds good to me."

Julie served broiled salmon with lemon slices and tartar sauce, canned corn, and brown rice topped with butter and a sprinkling of parsley. After coffee and chocolate cake (store-bought "fossil-cake", Julie apologized), Colin went topside and shut off the engine, then restarted it again. It fired without hesitation.

"Working good", he called down into the galley. "Barring unforeseen events, we'll have you at your friend's place tomorrow morning."

"Bless you", said Andrei.

Julie and the children were yawning by the time they had completed two more chapters of *We Didn't Mean to Go to Sea*. Cub fell asleep sitting up, his mouth hanging open. Colin dragged the inert form of his son to the lair and threw him onto the mattress. He came back laughing and scooped up the girls. When they were safely tucked away in the forward berth, Julie and Colin said good night and went to their suite, leaving Andrei and Arrow alone.

"Are you tired?" Andrei asked.

Arrow shook his head. He smiled.

"You've had a wonderful day, haven't you?"

The boy nodded.

"There will be many wonderful days in your life, Arrow. Life is good. Your life will be different from now on."

To which Arrow made no reply. He merely stretched out on his berth, opened his knapsack, and removed the stuffed animals. Andrei realized that Arrow had now concluded his foray into the treacherous shoals of communication and was retiring to his private world. He said good night to the boy and went up to the cockpit, where he sat on the stern seat, contemplating the dusk as it settled over the cove and the mountains.

The *Osprey* floated on a plate of black glass. The pennant drooped, the cups on the anemometer stopped revolving, and the tall firs on the rocky shore ceased whispering to each other about the presence of the ship. When occasionally a bald eagle beat its way toward a high nest on the shore, the sound of its huge wings was like silk being lifted and dropped and folded. Against the sheet of salmon-colored sunset, Andrei watched the silhouette of a peregrine falcon overtake a smaller speck of a bird and strike a killing blow with its taloned feet, then drop down and swing away into the shadow of the forest.

The sky bled into indigo blue, leaving a last streak of vermilion to gash the horizon in the southwest, then it fell asleep beneath a blanket across which the first stars were being strewn. As he watched the night become absolute, he meditated on his long life. He remembered his parents and the beauty of Dresden, and the day he was beaten by schoolmates on the steps of the cathedral for being a half-Jew. Later, the dark night of Sachsenhausen, where the Mother of God had appeared to him in his cell and offered him the two crowns, one of obedience and the other of martyrdom. His escape still struck him as miraculous more than sixty years later. Then the years in Poland, in Warsaw, and Czestochowa. Later, the missions of Canada.

So many faces surged up from the reservoir of memory, the hidden saints and the great sinners, the children and the old. For no reason that he could discern he recalled one face in particular, a young bookseller whose confession he had heard at Jasna Gora in 1937. He did not remember the man's sins; in fact, he was rarely able to recall anyone's sins after the completion of the sacrament. But he had kept a permanent place for Pawel Tarnowski in the sanctuary of his heart. He had known a few dozen people like him, those whose names he recalled, others who remained anonymous. Although he prayed daily for all souls, and also for the large number of particular souls he had known, this smaller group was an invisible family scattered across the century and the world, the adopted children of his heart.

He wondered if Pawel had survived the war. If so, he would be an elderly man now, for they were both young in the 1930s. Was he dead of old age, having learned to resist the impulse to self-destruction? Had he married, had a family, done good or evil? Had he touched many lives for the better, or for ill? Andrei did not know, but he sensed that this man had done a singular good, for that is what the voice of the Lord had told him he would do:

Here is my little son who has been broken. Give him the words of hope, for he will do a singular good in the world.

Millions upon millions of words had been woven into the fabric of his life, countless sermons and counsels, conversations, inspirations and meditations, letters, essays, and even on occasion homilies preached to the birds and to the wind, when no man would listen. Words, so many, many words: spoken and textual, intuitive and rational—a surging sea of messages, crashing like waves in the tide of affairs both human and divine. Few actual words could be recalled, though he had no doubt they slept in the reservoir of memory. How strange that this interior locution uttered by the Lord during a confession more than half a century ago should rise with such disturbing vividness. Why?

Perhaps it was necessary to carry some people in your heart to the very end, to pray without ceasing for their salvation. Perhaps some souls needed the grace invoked by the offering of his, Andrei's, life—the martyrdom that had been promised and that had continually eluded him—united across time to the Sacrifice of Christ on his Cross.

If time was a dimension wholly within the boundaries of material creation, and if God was beyond time, then he could, if he so wished, accept the prayer of a man who lived at the end of the second millennium and apply it to the needs of those who had gone before. Were not the death and Resurrection of Christ still active and effective, not simply as a linear chain of cause and effect, but as a living thing whose generative power is undiminished? The Mass itself was a mysterious suspension of time, a reaching through impossible barriers into the eternal Present, a moment of union with the Sacrifice on the Cross of Calvary. History, therefore, was a limited dimension, a compression of an unspeakably vast and beautiful dance into a solid icon, an incarnate Logos, a terrarium of fertile gardens in the cup of a Hand. The metaphors mixed and agitated in his mind, each reflecting a facet of the light of understanding, none of them complete, none of them a summation of the entire problem.

As Andrei gazed at the burning phosphorus stars, it struck him, as it had so often in his life, that it was unnecessary to know *how* creation worked; the essential thing was to know that it *worked*, and that one's place in the dance was irreplaceable. He felt that Pawel had done something (in his weakness, despite his weakness, rather *through* his weakness) that no other could have done. Andrei did not know what it was or how it had affected the balance of the world. He sensed only that it had been accomplished and that it was good. He did not know if Pawel had died in difficult circumstances, but if so, he hoped to offer his own life for him and for the other children of his heart. What shape the offering would take was still unclear. He disliked pain but no longer feared it. He had lived with the pain of his body, which was an inheritance from Sachsenhausen, for six decades, and though it made him suffer he had become detached from it. If death came in the form of a falcon seizing him suddenly, fiercely, finally, in a swift moment, he would be grateful. If it came slowly, with torment, he would try to thank God for that too, begging that the greater sacrifice would merit an increase of grace to countless souls unknown to him. He would ask, above all, that his tormenters be forgiven, and more—that the executioner would come to the narrow gate that leads into the Kingdom of God.

He heard a sharp intake of breath and realized that someone else was on deck with him. He could see the silhouette of a boy standing on the cabin roof by the mast, his head tilted toward the night sky, his mouth open. It was Arrow.

"What is it? What did you see?"

"I saw stars falling from the sky", the boy said.

"Did you? What did they look like?"

"First, an orange ball fell slowly, over there by the big island, above the mountain. Then another star fell after it, a blue one, that left a long trail, and it burned up too."

"Did they strike the earth?"

"No. They burned in space."

"Ah."

Arrow climbed down through the rigging and sat beside Andrei on the stern seat. They watched the sky together without speaking. They remained like that for close to an hour. One by one the lights of the cabin shut off, leaving only a single warning light burning on the bow. The brilliance of the stars increased, the wash of the galaxy's spiral extended over them, and the water of the cove reflected it flawlessly.

Eventually Arrow broke the silence. "There's water under us and water on top of us", he said.

"There is?"

"Yes. Under us the fish are swimming." He pointed. "Up there the stars are swimming like little fish."

"Yes, I think it is so."

"They are happy."

"Yes, Arrow, I think they are happy."

"Why do they eat each other?" Arrow asked.

"Who, the fish?"

"No, the giants."

"There aren't any giants."

"Not any?"

"There may have been, long ago, but they are all gone."

"Where did they go?"

"They died."

"Did bigger giants kill them and eat them?"

"No", Andrei replied, disturbed.

"Where did they go?"

"Our Savior defeated them."

"Who is our Savior?"

Andrei sighed. It was a big story, too big for a little mind.

"Our Savior is the Son of God, who came down to earth a long time ago to defeat the invisible giants."

"What was his name?"

"Jesus."

After a thoughtful pause, Arrow said, "I don't think he did. There are still giants."

He told Andrei about the dragon table and the shaman, about how the giants talked to the shaman through a little box.

Andrei puzzled over that.

"The little box, did it have pictures in it?"

"Yes."

"Did many sounds come out of it?"

"Yes. Talking and yelling."

"Arrow, do you remember the big box at Bill and Irene's house? That was a television. The shaman had a small television by the table of the dragons."

"But he talked to it!"

"Yes, people do. But it's not real. The stories inside of it are pretend."

"Like fairy tales? Like plays?"

"Exactly like that. There are no real giants."

"But the shaman *said* there are giants."

"He believes a lie in his mind."

"Oh. Is Jesus pretend?"

190

"He is real."

"Is he in the water above us?"

"He is there, and he is here."

"I don't see him."

"We see him with the eyes of the soul, we hear him with the ears of the heart."

"I don't."

"Perhaps some day you will."

"If giants came back here, would he kill them?"

"He would do what is best."

"Will we ever go there, up to the star water?"

"Some day we will. Do you like water, Arrow?"

"Yes, it's good."

"Does it make you happy?"

He nodded.

"Tell me, what kind of water do you like best?"

"I liked the water by the pool of the red fish. But now I like the ocean best of all."

"You held the wheel of the *Osprey* yesterday, didn't you? You made her sail."

"Yes."

"Would you like to sail her again?"

"Oh, yes. I could sail up to the stars. Where the water above touches the water below."

"That is no longer possible."

"Why not?"

"Because God made a gap between the above and below."

"Why did he do that?"

"Because men would spread their darkness into the universe, if that were possible."

"Why would they do that?"

"It is a long story."

"Can you tell me?"

Andrei collected his thoughts. Such a long, long story,

containing so many elements that sounded mythological, as if they were merely symbols or a seascape of dreams. Could the boy grasp the solid material of history filtered through millennia of art, metaphors, icons, beams of light and dark, refracting in the prism of time? Could he comprehend the shattering reality of it all?

A tale is the form through which the true story is passed on, he thought. *Who better to understand it than a child?*

"In the beginning," Andrei said, "there was the Father. He loved with an everlasting love. Into his hand he placed a thought, the most beautiful thought he could imagine. It was a sphere of swirling stars, of radiant colors and warmth, which was the heat of his heart. He touched the sphere, and a star was born from it, and he touched the star, and a planet was born from it. He touched the earth, and a garden was formed in it. He touched the garden, and a man and a woman were formed in it. And it was good."

"Who were the man and the woman?"

"They were a mother and a father. Adam and Eve were their names."

Andrei sighed. Now the difficult part: the fall, the rupture of the perfect sphere, the fissure in the garden wall, the lie, the corruption, the mystery of iniquity.

"Were they happy?"

"Yes, for a time. But a serpent came into the garden and tried to destroy it."

"Where did the serpent come from?"

"From beyond the stars. He was from the spirit world, like a giant, though he too was only a creature."

"Was he pretend?"

"He was real, though invisible. He hated what the Father had made."

"Why did he hate it?" said Arrow puzzled.

"Because the Father had done a marvel in the garden that

amazed all the spirits whom he had made. He told them that he planned to go down into the garden and walk with the first mother and the first father, and that he would be their friends."

"Why didn't the serpent like it?"

"Because he was very great, and he thought the Father had made a mistake. If the Father became like the creatures made of flesh and blood, then the serpent would have to bow before him in the form of mud. He didn't like that. He was very proud."

"What did he do?"

"He coiled about the heart of the mother and father and whispered a lie into their ears. They believed him and ran away into the forest. They hid themselves from the Father."

"Did they have children?"

"Yes, they had two sons."

"What were their names?"

"Their names were Cain and Abel."

"Did they listen to the serpent too?"

"One did, the other didn't. The one who listened to the lie killed his brother."

"That is bad."

"Yes, it is."

"What happened next?"

"A long time after, there were many people in the world. They became very bad. Only a few did not believe the lie. These ones built a ship and went into it."

"Then what?"

"The waters of the heavens fell down from the sky and flooded the earth. The bad people died."

"What happened to the people in the boat?"

"The boat floated on the top of the waters, and they were saved."

Arrow thought about it. He looked up at the stars.

"There was a lot of water up there?"

"Some people believe that once, a long time ago, the earth

was covered by thick clouds, like other planets. The world was very warm, and the soil was rich. People were as tall as giants. Then something happened to make the clouds empty their waters."

"What happened?"

"No one is sure."

"Is it pretend?"

"It is real. It happened. Do you know, Arrow, I have climbed to the top of these mountains, and to the top of other mountains in Europe, the land where I came from, and do you know what I found there?"

"No."

"Sea shells. Also, I have travelled on boats in other parts of the world and looked down into the water of the ocean and seen the ruins of cities many fathoms below."

"Is water not always good?" Arrow asked uncertainly.

"It is good in its rightful place. When you cook food, it does a good work, but you mustn't put your hand into the pot. When you sail on it, it is good, but you mustn't fall into it and drown."

"Oh. Like the pool of red fish."

"What do you mean?"

"The pool where the red fish are happy, and sometimes we eat them. But in the middle it's deep and the water's fast. You mustn't swim there."

"That's right. Like that."

"That's where you touched my head, and the bad sad came out."

"Bad sad?"

"When I saw you near the place where I live."

"You mean your village?"

"Yes, where Maya lives. Where the blue pebbles roll. Where the eagles come."

"Do you mean the day we first met by the stream? We sat together on a log, didn't we, and you were sad?"

He nodded. "You told me about my father. He's standing on a mountain looking at me."

"Your father loves you. He is sad that he can't come for you."

"Will he come to me?"

"I think he wants you to come to him."

"Oh."

"Does it make you sad?"

"Good sad. Not bad sad."

"What is bad sad?"

"The shaman's things. Pictures in my mind. The dragons and the *windigo*."

"Is the bad sad gone now?"

"When you put your hand on my head and made words, the words came into me like water, and they washed out the dream smoke. Then the *windigo* ran away."

"I see."

"But the pictures came back."

"Do the pictures frighten you?"

"Yes."

"You can make them go away, too, Arrow, if you wish."

"I tried, but they don't go away."

"Would you like me to make the words to tell them to go away?"

"Yes. And make the water come inside again."

Andrei put his hands on the crown of the boy's head. Arrow bent over, put his hands between his knees, and long sighs came from his lips. The sighs became groans, then the muted sobbing of an ordinary child.

After a time, when his crying had subsided, Andrei said, "Do you feel better?"

"Yes. It was like warm water."

"Jesus gave me this water for you."

"He did?"

"Yes, he did. He loves you."

"But you can't see it."

"Usually you can't. But it's very powerful. So powerful that most of the time we can't even feel it."

"Oh. Doesn't he have real water?"

Andrei thought about that. He was not sure how he should answer. Jesus did indeed have water to give, water that you could touch and taste. God's intention was to restore every aspect of human nature, not only the spiritual integrity of his creatures, but their minds and flesh as well. But how could this child possibly understand the theology of baptism? In the end he decided to answer simply and see how Arrow responded.

"Yes, he also has water you can touch."

"Can you give that too?"

"Yes, when the time is right, if a person is ready to receive it."

"Can you give it to me?"

Andrei hesitated. The child was in no way prepared for a sacrament. He understood nothing beyond the sketch of Genesis he had just heard. No proper formation, no catechesis.

"Yes, I can give it to you. Jesus longs to give it to you, through my hand. But I think he wants you to understand it more before he gives it."

"Why?"

Andrei wasn't sure why. He fumbled for explanations and ran them through his mind.

"When you meet your great-grandfather, he will tell you more about this water. Your brother and sister, they too are followers of Jesus. They will tell you about him."

"You could tell me about him now."

"There is far too much to tell, and you are tired."

"I'm not tired."

"In any event, you need to know much more."

Then it came to Andrei that infants knew far less than this boy did. He pointed out to himself that in the baptism of a newborn it was assumed that parents and godparents would ensure proper instruction as the child grew in understanding. The actions of divine grace upon the soul were not limited by the faculties of the mind or dependent on emotion. The child desired it. Was that not enough?

He saw also that the time in which they were living, the configuration of its sinister struggle for souls, its frantic pace, the acceleration of events, and the predicament in which he and the boy found themselves were extraordinary. Who could tell if they would be apprehended by the State, whether or not this was the only opportunity Arrow would ever have to receive the sacrament? What if the police boat returned and the police demanded to come aboard? Tomorrow or the next day, or in a week from now, the adversary might sweep Arrow into its net and destroy him with one swift, killing blow. Or worse—a slower eradication of light within his soul.

The boy looked up at him, his eyes yearning, helpless, confused by the priest's reticence.

"Please", he pleaded, taking the old man's right hand and squeezing it tightly. "Give me this water."

It was so guileless and fervent, so very much a movement of the spirit, that Andrei said at last, "Yes. I will."

He thought he should go below and call Julie and Thomas, who would be willing to stand as godparents. But the lights in the cabin were off, and he felt a wave of pity for their exhaustion. They needed sleep. In the morning there would be time for a baptism. Then he wondered if there was as much time as he supposed. It was highly unlikely, but there was always the possibility of arrest by the coast guard or marine police in the middle of the night. What if the moment of grace was now, and only now? Surely, in this situation, love impelled him to focus on the essence of the gift.

"Did you know, Arrow, that when Jesus washes you clean, inside and out, and makes you his own forever, he also gives you a new name?"

"A new name? He names us?"

"Yes, he names us."

"Even if we get lost he carries our names inside of him?"

"Yes, like that."

"What is my new name?"

"That is for you to decide."

"I don't know a new name."

Andrei pondered it. *Arrow* was hardly a Christian name. On the other hand, most human names had been pagan until God reached down and baptized them.

"Would you like to have a name that some of God's best friends have borne?"

"Yes."

"I know one that is very old. A brave man's name. He helped to bring God's children out of slavery a long time ago. His name was Aaron."

"Aaron." He rolled the syllables around on his tongue, tasting its alien flavor. "Aaron."

"And you may choose a second name as well. Does one come to mind?"

"What is my father's name?"

"Nathaniel."

He tasted it also. "I like it."

"That is good. And so, when you are washed in the water of Jesus, you will become Aaron Nathaniel."

"Won't I be Arrow any more?"

"Do you want to be Arrow?"

"I *am* Arrow, but a different Arrow."

"Very well, let us keep the name Arrow, though it will become a different Arrow. You will be Arrow-in-the Bow-of-the-Lord."

"Arrow-in-the-Bow-of-the-Lord!" The boy half-smiled, overcome by awe.

"That will be your hidden name, your third name before the

throne of God. Your first and second names will be Aaron Nathaniel."

Arrow bounced up and down on the seat. A wave of delight emanated from him.

"Do you like it?"

"I like it. It's good."

"From this time forward you will belong to God completely. You are his son. He is your father."

"Oh", the boy breathed. "Oh!"

It was like holding the wheel of the *Osprey*. It was like wind. It was like worship.

The sacrament took its simplest form. Andrei prayed over the boy, explained the death and Resurrection of Jesus in terms he could understand. He told him that baptism would cleanse him from original sin and the power of death. It would help him to resist the whisperings of the serpent. It would make him grow strong and true like a straight arrow. It would help him to hear God, to love him, and to serve him. Then he anointed the boy and laid a white stole on his shoulders.

He bent over the gunnels and scooped a handful of salt water. He poured it over the boy's head, saying, "I baptize you, Aaron Nathaniel, in the name of the Father, and of the Son, and of the Holy Spirit."

When it was done, Aaron sat back in the seat, resting against the cushions. He closed his eyes, a smile playing on his lips. Andrei prayed silently, and when he was finished he saw that the boy was asleep. Despite his age and the child's weight, he lifted him and carried him below. Aaron sighed once when he was placed on the galley berth. The old priest covered him with the sleeping bag, blessed him, and went back on deck, where he watched the stars until the sky in the east attested that the planet had completed another revolution.

6

The Superstitious General and Many Other Adventures

Colin was awake before everyone else. He went out on deck to check the sky, which was turning slate gray above the coastal mountains. In the west the stars were still bright in the deep black. The water was calm. He sparked the engine and made it rumble until it purred. He shivered in the chilly breeze and went inside to get the coffee perking. He checked the chart for the third time, read the satellite locator, though he didn't need to do either, and sat waiting for the gulls and the kids.

By six-thirty Julie was awake, puttering in the galley, and soon after the others stirred and got up, yawning and stretching.

Aaron rolled over, rubbing sleep from his eyes.

My name is Aaron, he thought.

Cub shook his shoulder and said, "No pirates on the horizon. Dad says it's a couple of hours to the end of the inlet. We can get in a few games."

Cub set up the chessboard on the blankets. Aaron made the first move; Cub flashed out his hand and made an instant riposte. Ten minutes later he said "checkmate". They set up the pieces again and were well into the next game when Tessa and Kathy squeezed in beside them to watch. Then Aaron put Cub in check, more by fluke than by skill. The ballerinas giggled. Cub moved his king. Aaron moved his queen and, to everyone's surprise, had won his first checkmate.

"Wow!" Cub grinned. "Awesome!"

Backslapping and laughter all around. Aaron beamed. Julie tousled the boys' hair, making *tsk-tsk* sounds over her son's mop of red spikes.

"Go comb that mess, carrot-top!" she commanded. She made the others clear the table for breakfast, and presently they all sat down to toast and jam, fried eggs, bacon, and orange juice. Aaron ignored the bacon. Andrei and Colin went up on deck to talk. Everyone else stayed in pajamas, eating more than they needed to, trying to prolong the last meal. No one mentioned that they would be parting soon. Cub began a long dissertation on nautical instruments, Kathy got out her embroidery, and Julie (unabashedly eavesdropping) scrubbed the frying pan. Tessa kept looking glumly at Aaron. Eventually her eyes filled up with tears.

"Why can't we keep him?" she blurted.

Aaron looked down at his empty plate, his face expressionless, his eyes turned inward. Julie slid into the seat beside him and put an arm around his shoulders.

"There's nothing I'd like better in the world", she said to her children. "But I think Arrow wants to find his own family."

No one replied to that.

"All right, you bilge rats," she growled, "get into your sailor suits and swab those decks." Her three children groaned and went off to their berths to get dressed.

"I meant that, Arrow", she said quietly when the others had disappeared. "I'd like nothing better. You can stay with us if you want to."

He shook his head, his mouth tight.

"Think of poor Cub. He's outnumbered. He hates girl germs. He needs another guy on board."

He shook his head again.

"And we need a cabin boy. Ever thought of sailing around the world?"

"No."

"Tropical islands? Seven Seas? Adventures?"

He didn't bother to shake his head a third time.

She hugged him. "I know. You want to find your mum, don't you?"

He nodded.

"And your dad", she said slowly.

He nodded again and stared out the porthole.

Up in the cockpit, Andrei told Colin and Julie about Aaron's baptism. Julie was moved.

"That's wonderful", she beamed. "Just wonderful!"

Colin said nothing. He handed Andrei a cellular phone.

"We're about fifteen minutes from the dock. Why don't you call your friend and let him know we're coming in. The less time we spend waiting around, the less chance anyone will see you."

Andrei punched in the numbers. When Potempko answered, he said, "We're coming by sea. We'll be at the dock in a few minutes."

"Deo gratias!" said Potempko, and hung up.

Aaron came up on deck then and stood beside Colin. He touched the wheel gently and watched the approaching shore with concentration.

Eventually Colin cleared his throat and reached into his pocket. He withdrew a small medallion and put it into the palm of Aaron's hand.

"This is from me to you", he said.

Aaron stared at it.

"Will you keep it?"

Aaron nodded.

"I've had it a long time. It saved my life once."

Julie emerged from the cabin at that moment and saw the medallion in the boy's hand. She looked back and forth between him and Colin, then went inside and returned a moment later with a thin chain dangling from her hand.

"Here, why don't you wear it around your neck, like I do?" she said. "The kids wear these, and so does Father Andrei."

Aaron nodded. She clamped the medallion and a tiny crucifix onto the chain and hung it over his neck.

"Do you know who she is, the lady on the medal?"

"No."

"She's the Mother of Jesus. She'll look after you."

"Oh", Aaron said. But there was no more conversation because the Bella Coola marina was only a hundred yards off the bow.

Potempko was standing at the end of the wharf, a short, plump man in a dirty green parka. His rumpled black slacks were stuffed into knee-high rubber boots that looked several sizes too large for him. The crown of his head was bald; two great wings of silver hair swept back from his temples. Scowling, puffing fiercely on a pipe that jutted from the corner of his mouth, he waved at Andrei, who returned the greeting.

Colin cut the motor; the *Osprey* glided in and thumped softly against the rubber tires hanging from the pylons. Cub jumped off the bow onto the dock and tied her to a post. Sea gulls rose up screaming.

When everyone was off the boat, clustered around the little priest, no one knew quite what to say. Potempko shook Andrei's hand and searched his eyes. Then he looked at Aaron as if he knew him.

"Trouble, trouble", he muttered, shaking his head. He kept looking over his shoulder.

"We should make our good-byes quickly", said Andrei.

"Yes", said Potempko, shooting sparks from the bowl of his pipe. "Nobody must see you."

Colin shook hands with Aaron. "So long, pal. It's been a great trip. Wish you could come along with us. Maybe another time. Good luck, Father."

"How can I thank you? How can I thank you?" said Andrei.

"Don't mention it."

Cub turned his back to them and forced himself to look bored. The girls were solemn, straining to suppress their tears. Julie hugged Aaron, who did not resist. She held him for a minute, not speaking, communicating at some unfathomable depth the current of meaning that only mothers know. Eventually Aaron put his arms around her waist, squeezed timidly, and let them drop.

Julie kissed him, hugged the priest, and tried to say something. Her face convulsed suddenly; she jumped back onto the *Osprey* and went below.

"Okay, kids", said Colin, all businesslike. "Time to go. Weigh anchor! Crew to the foresail and crow's nest!" Reluctantly they jumped back on board. He revved the motor, concentrating excessively on his technology, while Andrei and Potempko cast off the lines. Colin steered the boat away from the dock without looking back. The three children clung to the stays and watched Aaron until he was only a sliver against the massing black forest of mountains.

Potempko took Andrei's bag and led them to a van parked on the gravel by the head of the dock. Andrei got in the back with Aaron. Instinctively they hunched down on the floor, making themselves invisible. Five minutes later the van, which was missing a muffler, roared into the driveway of a small, shabby house on the flank of a hill at the edge of the village.

"The neighbors may be awake", said Potempko. "Quickly, quickly."

He led them around the side of the house and went in by the back door. The kitchen was terribly messy and smelled of tobacco and beeswax candles. By now the sun had risen and the room was full of golden light, saturated in a curious peace. Potempko banged a kettle onto the range, clamped his teeth on the pipe stem, muttered, fussed about in his coat pocket for matches, extracted a breviary, a rosary, and a bag of candy.

"Little boy, you want a sweet?"

Aaron shook his head.

Wheezing, Potempko took off his coat, revealing a large belly in a black clerical shirt and a dirty white Roman collar. The shirt was punctuated with burn holes from tobacco sparks. He plunked himself down on a kitchen chair. His visitors did the same. They sat in silence, listening to the steaming kettle, watching Potempko shake his head from time to time. A radio played classical music low in the background. A candle flickered in a red vigil glass beneath an icon above the sink. Newspapers covered the table—several days' worth of *The Vancouver Star*. Andrei saw his face on one of them, the faces of the three Delaney children, and the words ABDUCTED: SEARCH CONTINUES.

Potempko swept the papers off the table onto the floor.

"Garbage!" he grumbled.

"It is very good of you, Father, to take us in", said Andrei.

The other priest shrugged. "It's nothing." He pointed at the headlines. "Lies! I can smell lies. You don't think I know propaganda when I read it?"

"You are taking a great risk."

Potempko shrugged again.

"So? Life is a risk!"

He got up and made tea. As he was banging around looking for mugs and sugar, he said over his shoulder, "You know, Andrei, it's getting to be like the old days. Something stinks, I tell you."

Andrei murmured agreement.

"You remember what they were like", Potempko continued. "You were in Sachsenhausen. I remember what they were like too. I was in Budapest in '56. They never change. They never give up."

"We will win some day."

"Maybe. Maybe", Potempko sighed.

"The Lord has already conquered. These are only the final convulsions."

"It's the same thing all over again. They've just got better manners these days."

"We must strengthen the things that remain."

"Yes, yes. You know, when they arrested Mindszenty, they tortured him. Imagine, torturing a cardinal. They broke him."

"They broke him, but he recovered. And now they have fallen."

"Yes, the Soviets are gone, the Nazis are gone, but they've been replaced by a different monster. Left, Right—it's all the same."

"The time will be short."

Potempko peered at him theatrically: "Let us hope so."

"It will be short", Andrei repeated with calm emphasis. He glanced at Aaron. "We must carry these little ones through to a better day."

"You know," mused Potempko, lost in his memories, "after they took Mindszenty in '49, I knew they were capable of anything. Anything. Then in '56 when all those boys and girls went into the streets to hurl Molotov cocktails at Russian tanks, I didn't know what I should do. Should I be like those 'peace priests' who cooperated with the régime, keep quiet, keep hoping the Church would weather the storm, be good, don't make the Russians mad? Or should I go out and die with our children? What to do! In the end I took a crucifix and went into the streets to stand with the youth. I saw many shot. I heard their dying words. They called out to Jesus and for liberty. But don't think too highly of me, Andrei. I am a coward."

Andrei smiled. "You are not a coward, Potempko."

Potempko laughed.

"I *am* a coward. I knew they were torturing priests. I'd seen them shoot innocents. I was so afraid of torture. I knew I couldn't hold out against pain. I'm not good at suffering. I knew that if I denied the faith many little souls would be scandalized. But there was nothing in me that was strong." He slapped his belly. "Look at me! God's pork barrel."

"God's dear jester", said Andrei.

"Oh, sure, sure, God's dear jester! You should say Pantalone! Punchinello! Scaramouche! When I was wandering around the streets in my cassock, with a cross in my hands, hearing the confessions of all those dying young people, blessing, encouraging, I just wanted to scream and run away. Many were getting across the border into Austria. Oh, how I wanted to get to the bridge at Andau! No such luck. Three Russian soldiers cornered me during a battle in an alley. They dragged me to a general. A general, no less. I was so frightened I just knew they would torture me and I would crack; my weakness would hurt the little souls, and I would lose my own soul as well."

"No, no", Andrei demurred. "God is merciful."

"Well, you are made of better stuff than me. But I knew myself. I know what I am. So these soldiers dragged me up to the general. He was busy putting bullets into the brains of the teenagers they had caught on the streets. They threw me down on the pavement in front of him. He spit in my face. 'Priest,' he said, 'what a pleasure it is to kill you.' Just like that. Suddenly, I was filled with joy. How easy it will be, I thought. There will be no torture. Only a quick death! Oh, how happy I was when he put the barrel of his gun to my forehead. I was grinning from ear to ear. He pulled back the trigger. I heard it click. I smiled and I laughed. Oh, this is easy martyrdom, I thought. I could not stop smiling. I was thanking God with all my heart. This general, he pointed his gun to the cobblestones and fired it. Bang! Pew! The stone exploded into little chips. I jumped out of my skin. Oh, I was sad, for I did not die. I was so disappointed. Then he put the gun to my head again, cocked the trigger, and now I smiled very big. Oh, thank God, after all I am going to die. He looked at me and put his gun down once more.

"He swore very bad. He jumped up and down. He kicked me. I was smiling. I was smiling, I was so happy.

"'You stupid crazy man', the general said.

"The other soldiers asked him why he didn't shoot me. He told them it is bad luck to shoot insane people. Communists have no religion, but they are very superstitious. He told the soldiers to take me to prison. On the way partisans made battle in the street, and I was set free by our boys. Forty-two years later, here I am. I make tea, eat sweets, say Mass, pray, make a safe place for crazy people like you."

Andrei smiled. "Well, Potempko, I am very grateful for that general."

Potempko shrugged. "Yes, yes, but I am still a coward."

"We will let God be the judge of that."

Potempko sat brooding.

Eventually Andrei said, "The Blessed Sacrament is here."

"Yes. How did you know?"

"May we pray?"

Potempko led them into the sitting room and beyond it into a small bedroom. In the corner, behind a curtain, was a brass box bolted to the wall. A large seven-day vigil light burned in a bracket beside it. The two priests knelt. Aaron imitated them. Andrei felt a wave of consolation from the Presence and turned inward, gathering strength from the stillness that filled him. After a few minutes Aaron began to fidget, and Potempko took him back to the kitchen while Andrei continued to pray. Twenty minutes later he was so absorbed in an interior recollection that he did not hear the *rap-rap-rap* that assaulted the back door.

Potempko, seated at the table with Aaron, who was drinking a mug of hot chocolate and liking it, put down his coffee cup and stared at the door. A large brown face was looking in through the window.

"Oh, my Lord!" Potempko uttered. "Charlie Manyberries!"

The face at the window was taking in the contents of the

room, implacable eyes analyzing every incriminating detail. It was too late to scoot Aaron to the bedroom and impossible to pretend that no one was home. Potempko knew it was all over. In an instant of finely shaved time, he saw himself in prison, tortured, Andrei dead, and the boy undergoing a long apprenticeship in ideology. There was nothing left to do but beg.

* * *

Charlie Manyberries was a man of immense dignity. When Potempko let him in, he stood by the door saying nothing, rolling and unrolling his heavy white wool tuque, his large pouting lips saying nothing, gazing at the scene somberly, as only Charlie could. Potempko hoped he would not recognize the boy but knew this was optimistic. Charlie and his wife, Rose, were news addicts. He was a handsome man in his early sixties, too tall for a coastal Salish, because in the year 1778 an ancestor had spent a night with a sailor in a longhouse covered with painted faces, while the frigate *Discovery* rolled at anchor on the tidal waters of the bay.

Charlie stared at Aaron, and the gravity increased throughout the room.

"Uh-huh", he said.

"Coffee?"

"Sure", said Charlie blinking.

"Would you like to meet my young guest?"

He gave one, great, pontifical nod and shoved a copper-colored hand at the boy. Aaron let his small white hand be absorbed in the larger one, then withdrew it discreetly.

"Uh-huh", Charlie said again.

Aaron went back to his mug of hot chocolate.

Potempko sat down heavily, and Charlie did the same on an empty chair. It creaked under him. He spread his legs wide so his three hundred pounds could settle more easily and unbuttoned his gray and white cowichan sweater.

209

"How can I help you, Charlie?"

"I got bad news. They arrested Rose's mum last night."

"Again?"

He nodded. Up and down, twice.

"The same as usual?"

Another nod.

"Poor Cecilia! What are you going to do?"

Charlie sighed and scratched his head.

"I dunno. Maybe take the ferry down to Vancouver. They're gonna put Seely in the insane asylum. I gotta get down there quick and explain she ain't crazy. She ain't drunk. She just doing what the Lord tells her to do."

"You want me to make a call?"

"Uh-yup. That's what I came to ask. Can you tell the cops she's okay? In the meantime me 'n' Rose is gonna catch the ferry later today. We're gonna bring her home—if they let us."

"I'll phone right now. Do you have the number?"

Charlie extracted a crumpled piece of paper from his back pocket and handed it to Potempko.

"There's a hearing this afternoon, Father. If we don't get there on time, they're gonna commit her."

"But there's no way you can get there on time!"

"I tried to tell them that, but they wasn't listening. Maybe they'll listen to you."

"They'll listen."

"If they don't, it's gonna be tough getting her out this time. We'd have to stay in Van a week, maybe more, working through all that paperwork."

"Maybe it's time she came home."

"I think so. Rose thinks so too. But try convincing that old lady. She says she's working for the Lord, and nobody's gonna stop her."

Potempko dialed the number, talked into the phone for some minutes, went red in the face, and hung up. He wrote down some information, lit his pipe, and sucked on it furiously. Then he dialed another number.

He talked into the phone again, while Charlie watched the boy with a severe expression, moving his girth only to reach for the cup of coffee. From time to time he sighed.

Potempko's right knee began a little dance under the table. He looked supremely irritated. "Answering machines!" he snarled. "The devil's invention! They guard the entrance to every circle of hell."

After three more dials he got through.

"You don't sound like electric voice to me!" he grumbled. "Tell me, young lady, are you a real human being? Yes! Wonderful! I strike paydirt!"

When Potempko hung up, he said, "It looks good. The social worker says they can waive the hearing if I vouch for her. But you and Rose have to pick her up at the detention center and bring her back to Bella Coola. They say if they catch her in the city again, she'll have to go to Essondale for a recovery program."

"Recovery program!" Charlie retorted, offended. "Seely ain't never touched a drop in her life. That sickness is a mean one. Makes her look drunk, and everybody thinks she's a crazy street lady. Nobody knows she's a saint."

"Well, anyway, that's what the social worker told me. She sounded mad. Said we'd better make sure someone's looking after her up here and not let her go down to Vancouver again. I told her there's no lack of people to look after Cecilia at Bella Coola. I told her she wasn't drunk, either, but the woman didn't believe me."

Charlie looked depressed. "Seely's been doing this for thirty years. You'd think she'd get tired of it. You'd think the Lord'd let her off the hook."

"It's a cross", said Potempko.

"Yuh, it's a cross", Charlie agreed.

They sat together without speaking for a few more minutes.

Potempko had learned through long experience not to rush conversations with Charlie Manyberries. He poured him another cup. Charlie drank it, staring at his rubber boots. Then he looked over at Aaron and said, "That's the missing boy."

"Yes, he is", said Potempko. He occupied himself with stuffing the bowl of his pipe with tobacco and lighting it with a butane lighter.

"Funny thing," Charlie went on, "him bein' here and the whole province lookin' for him."

"Yes", Potempko nodded, puffing thoughtfully. "Funny thing."

"How come he's here, Father?"

"It's a long story, Charlie."

"I got time."

Charlie always had time. Potempko heaved a great sigh. "Not in front of him."

"Trouble?" said Charlie.

Potempko nodded philosophically.

Andrei, unfortunately, chose that moment to return to the kitchen. He froze in the doorway. Charlie looked at him, said nothing, and looked down at his boots.

"It's okay. Come in", said Potempko.

"Big trouble", said Charlie.

No one knew what to say. *Yes*, they all thought to themselves, *very big trouble*.

"Funny thing", said Charlie, musing. "Last night Rose had one of her dreams. When she woke up this morning, she tells me she had a God-dream. I asked her is it about Seely in jail? She says, no, strange thing, it wasn't about Seely at all. It was about something else, something bigger. Some trouble. She said Our Lady came to her over the water carrying a sailboat in her arms. Then she tied the boat to the top of Nusatsum, and an old man and a boy came out of it onto the peak of the mountain. The old man and the boy ran away into the east, and Our Lady covered them with her mantle."

"A strange dream", Potempko mused. "What does it mean, do you think?"

"I dunno. Then Rose tells me I should come see you, ask you to help us get Seely out of jail."

"I see."

Charlie nodded sagely. "Uh-yuh. God gave Rose some of Seely's gift. Maybe a different gift."

Potempko introduced Charlie to Andrei. Charlie, still interpreting the dream, acknowledged Andrei's presence with a single handshake and a nod. He stared at the floor as Potempko got up to prepare a pot of tea.

"Funny thing", Charlie said eventually. "Funny thing, I sold all that salmon to the tourist from the States last week."

"What do you mean?" said Potempko.

"Funny thing I do such a thing. It's illegal", he said significantly. "Maybe I go to jail anybody finds out about it."

"We won't tell", Potempko assured him.

"Agh, good."

Charlie unrolled his tuque and put it on his head. He buttoned his sweater. He sighed. He stood himself upright with considerable effort. He took a wallet out of his back pocket, opened it slowly, and with much deliberation removed some money. He threw four fifty dollar bills onto the table and said, "Rose and me been meaning to give this to you. We sure like it you staying here in Bella Coola. Maybe this'll help buy some hosts and wine, some coffee and tobacco."

"Really, Charlie, that's very kind. But please, take it back. My needs are simple."

"You got company, Father. Maybe they're gonna stay for a long time. They got to eat."

Then he took out more money and handed it to Andrei.

"Maybe you'll go east", he said. "You got to eat too. You pray for Rose and me, and my wife's mother, Seely."

"I will pray", said Andrei, accepting the gift.

"Better I go get ready for the ferry", said Charlie. "Rose, she wants to stop by the reserve before we leave. She got a birthday present for Robbie. He's eight today. Same age as this boy, I'll bet."

He was halfway out the door when he stopped and turned around like a grizzly waking up in spring.

"You know, I think I'm getting old. Already I forget I meet these people here in your place."

"Thank you", said Potempko.

"And Father, you think you could phone those guys in Vancouver again? Tell them to be careful with Seely's stuff? That Red Flyer wagon was mine when I was a boy. And that statue of Our Lady belonged to Rose's grandma. Okay?"

"Okay, Charlie. I will."

When Charlie's pickup disappeared down the street, Potempko shook his head, amazed. He lit another pipe.

"Don't worry", he said to Andrei. "That is one of God's men."

"I can see that. Who is he?"

"Charlie is a deacon at the parish. He and Rose run the prayer group and the rosary crusade. They come to see me sometimes and assist at Mass."

"What was he saying about salmon?"

Potempko smiled.

"That was Charlie's way of telling us he's an outlaw too. Indians are allowed to catch salmon year round, but it's illegal to sell it to whites."

"Ah, civil disobedience?"

"Nothing so idealistic, I think. Just some extra cash. Many of the local men do it, and who can blame them? Work is seasonal; income is erratic. Their lives are not easy."

"Can he be relied upon not to mention our presence here?"

"I'm sure of it. That dream says a lot. Also, his visit may be fortuitous."

Andrei was not so sure it had been fortuitous. "Why do you say that?"

"We shall see", Potempko said through a cloud of smoke. "So? Tell me, what are your plans?"

"The boy's great-grandfather and his brother and sister are living in the hills of the Cariboo country. I must take him to them."

"It would be difficult. The police are searching everywhere."

"I know. We were almost captured near Fort George. At the convent . . ."

The two priests lapsed into a pain-filled silence, staring at the floor.

"They suspect I am in the coastal region with the boy. They will be concentrating their efforts in the south and possibly in the east, especially the North Thompson Valley."

"It's four hundred and fifty kilometers to the Cariboo. I guess you want to go to Williams Lake first. How much farther after that?"

"Potempko, forgive me, but I think it would be better if you don't know any details."

"Okay. You're right. I could spill the beans."

"I do not want to endanger you unnecessarily."

"Well, if it comes to that, you've already put me in danger. Why not do it up big?"

"No. If we are apprehended, you can at least plead ignorance. Also, there are three other people we must protect."

"I will take you to Williams Lake", Potempko said, as if it were nothing at all.

After hesitating, Andrei said, "I would be most grateful."

Potempko shrugged. "I'll drop you on the far side of town, maybe on the road to Horsefly? You want to go into the east Cariboo, don't you?"

Andrei nodded, wondering how Potempko had guessed. "Thank you", he said. "That would be perfect."

"Now, don't thank me. Thank God for sending Charlie Manyberries. If you'd asked me an hour ago to take you to the Cariboo, I would have said it was impossible. I don't have any money in the house, my bank account's empty, and the pension check doesn't arrive till next week. I don't believe in charge cards either, never owned one."

"So, you're saying that divine providence has been active here today?"

"Undoubtedly."

"I hope you're right."

"Where's your trust, Father? Of course I'm right. You have to get to the Cariboo somehow, and God knows it too. But I doubt there's a person in this province who hasn't memorized your face—and the boy's. So you can forget hitchhiking or the bus. Yes, yes, it's your only chance. No arguments now. Anyway, I go out once a month. This is a good opportunity for me to do some shopping. I'm low on my favorite tobacco, and the Bella Coola supermarket just doesn't understand my tastes."

He looked at his watch.

"It's nine-thirty. The trip isn't far as the crow flies, but the highway's up and down. It's slow. We should leave soon."

Andrei forced Théophane Nguyen's ten dollars on Potempko, who accepted it with reluctance. "Just in case", he said. He began to pack a lunch. Aaron watched with disgust as Potempko sliced raw bacon off a slab and spread it over black bread, adding a copious amount of paprika. Potempko noticed the boy's expression.

"You don't like this?" he said. "This is a Hungarian delicacy. How can anyone not like this?"

"I think Aaron would prefer peanut butter, if you have it. Or cheese?" said Andrei.

"Okay! Father Potempko is a patient chef. Peanut butter for the little boy. We got lots of apples too. How about some cheese on rye? A dill pickle for you? Maybe a cucumber sandwich? A chocolate bar? Yes? Pickled eggs? No? Oh, all right."

He packed everything into a portable cooler, added a liter bottle of red wine, filled a thermos with coffee, and donned his parka.

"You stay here, Andrei, wait for me. I'll go gas up the van and fill some jerry cans too. That way we don't need to stop anywhere before Williams Lake."

He took one last look around the apartment, blew out the icon candle, patted pockets to find missing car keys, matches, a plastic bottle of holy water, a rosary. He was almost out the door when he wheeled in alarm, slapped his head, and went rummaging through the apartment looking for his tobacco and spectacles.

He was back within twenty minutes, poked his head in the kitchen door, and waved frantically to Andrei and the boy.

"Hurry, hurry, nobody see us!" Five minutes later the van was chugging along the valley toward the mountain pass that led to the east.

* * *

About twenty-five kilometers out of Bella Coola, Route 20 curved around the base of a high mountain.

"Little boy", said Potempko, "You see that? That's Nusatsum. She is very old. The Nuxalk people say she saved their lives in the great flood. When God sent the waters of the heavens to cover the earth, the people tied their canoes to the peak. When the waters went down again, they made their homes on the Bella Coola River, between the sea and the mountain. Ever it is a reminder to them: The sea is the mother of life, for she gives them salmon and whale. And the mountain reminds them not to forget heaven."

"How blessed these people are", said Andrei.

"Yes. But they carry many wounds. Family life is broken. The angel-beast prowls here too. Alcohol, and now drugs."

"Do they not see the danger?"

Potempko sighed. "Of course they see the danger. But the young ones say the acid trips are ecstasy; they tell me they don't mind paying the price, fighting off the devils. Poor children, they have no sense! They have no armor! I pick up the pieces when the heaven becomes hell."

"It is good you are here, Potempko. The people need you."

"And I need them. There are saints among them. The old ones have not forgotten. The young are blind."

"We are creatures of heaven and earth", said Andrei.

Potempko, absorbed in a temporary melancholy, did not reply to that.

They travelled in silence as the road ascended through cathedrals of old-growth firs—thick, heavy, tall—the giants of the rain forest. At the village of Stuie the road began to climb steeply into the Coast Mountains. Aaron sat in the rear seat, looking up at the snow-covered heights, observing the rows of olive-colored firs and bluer spruce spearing the pale blue sky. He saw creeks cascading down the cliffs beside the highway, where they curled under the road through metal culverts. He saw two bald eagles and a black bear. He watched the mountains rise up on both sides like teeth set in a gigantic mouth opening itself to swallow them. The van barely survived several hairpin turns and crossed ravines on bridges that seemed too light, flimsy creations that someone had cast over the abyss with disdain for the force of gravity. In the narrow valleys it grew darker, though it was still morning. He saw a mule deer and several blue jays. The two priests in the front talked quietly about things he didn't understand, and after a time he ceased to hear them.

Potempko was not a good driver. He frequently careened back and forth over the line, and when he noticed the expression of mild discomfort on Andrei's face, he laughed.

"I've driven this road hundreds of times", he explained. "I know the bad spots by heart. I used to take the Bella soccer team to matches all over the province. Don't worry, we're in God's hands!"

Andrei forced himself to relax.

"The little one is very silent", Potempko said in Latin.

"He has endured much", Andrei replied in the same language.

"His mother and father dead! This is a great suffering for one so young."

"Yes. I am worried about him. His home was not a good one. His life has never been normal."

"Normal?" said Potempko sadly. "What is normal in these times!"

"Pray for him, Father. I have not yet told him about the death of his parents. It would be too much for him to bear at the moment. His world is in chaos. I will tell him when we reach his family. He can hear it when he is surrounded by love, by sanctuary."

They travelled without further comment for some minutes.

Reverting to English, Andrei said, "Will you be able to return to Bella Coola in time for tomorrow's Mass?"

"No one will miss me. I'll stay at a motel in Williams Lake."

"What of your parishioners? Surely they will be concerned."

"Didn't you know? I'm no longer the pastor."

"I didn't know."

"A month ago they retired me. It was long past due, the archbishop said. Time for a rest. Three years over the age limit. He asked me if I wanted to come to the city and live in the retirement home for old pastors. 'No thank you, Your Grace', I told him. 'Do you think I want to spend the rest of my life watching hockey on TV and gossiping with the other old fellers? Why don't you let me stay at Bella?' I asked him. 'I'm happy here. The people like me.'

"He said, 'Well, not everyone is fond of your ideas, Potempko. The people will miss you, but it's time for new blood.'"

"And so they have new blood?"

Potempko raised his eyebrows. "Oh, yes. He came six months ago to be my assistant pastor. I should have seen the handwriting on the wall. Bella is too small for an assistant. They were easing me out gradually. A newly ordained boy who never wears his collar. More than that, his theology is . . . funny."

"Funny?"

"You know—*funny*."

"I see."

"This new pastor, he's not a bad boy, you understand. Just young. But not young like the kids in Budapest were young. More like he didn't grow up. He doesn't know the cross. He says that the Mass is primarily an art form. When I tell him it's a Sacrifice, he says nothing and gives me a compassionate look. He doesn't like the Pope. Says the Pope was conditioned by his experiences under tyranny. Thinks the Pope's ideas are too pessimistic, and now is the time for positive thinking. 'Don't call me Father; call me Shane', he tells me. He insists on calling me by my first name, which even my sainted mother, God rest her soul, could never pronounce. He has a master's degree in theology from a . . . funny college. His homilies are spaghetti."

"Spaghetti?"

"Without meat sauce."

"You mean without substance?"

"Exactly. All sugar and starch, no ooomph."

"Heresy?"

"Oh, no, the archbishop would never tolerate heresy. But a little disobedience he can stand."

"Such as?"

"No one is allowed to kneel during the Consecration. He fiddles with the prayers of the Mass. He invents. He gives homilies all the way through. He says he wants to make the Mass real for the people. If only he knew—it's more real to them than it is to him. I just don't understand him! Doesn't he trust the power of Jesus there on the altar? A couple of weeks ago he told everyone that from now on the children have to have First Communions *before* their First Confessions. Some of the old people like Charlie and Rose are upset. They're afraid to talk to Father Shane about it, because he makes them feel foolish and ignorant. If they try, he gets very tense, and from then on they're invisible. They don't exist in his eyes. They asked me to mention it to the archbishop. I phoned him, even though I felt bad about doing that. The archbishop said he'd speak with Father, but I don't know if he ever did, because nothing has changed. I guess he can't keep his eyes on everything. 'I'm not a policeman, Father', he said to me. 'And neither are you. We have a shortage of priests. Just pray for him.' I felt like saying, 'Your Grace, if *you* won't rein him in, who can? It's your job.' But I didn't say it."

"The archbishop is a very good man", Andrei mused. "I wonder why he doesn't act."

"Me too, I wonder why he doesn't act. Maybe it's diplomacy."

Andrei knew that the archbishop was a true apostle. A much-respected member of the hierarchy, a doctor of theology, he had managed to remain a humble, unambitious man. He radiated a quiet dignity, an aura of Christlike authority that drew many admirers and reduced many a theological opponent to silence. He was a father figure par excellence. He had character in abundance. He was blessed with an equally warm heart, but he governed the flock like the sagacious old shepherd he was. He never tolerated heresy in his priests, refused visiting dissident theologians permission to speak on Church property, and regularly warned his flock in the archdiocesan paper about the spiritual dangers of certain conferences that took place in the city. His pastoral letters were expressed in predictably subtle language, but the content was strong and, some said, courageous. He regularly brought in Catholic evangelists to speak at the cathedral, inaugurated prayer rallies, eucharistic conferences, and days of fasting. He had played a part in cleaning up the sex scandals at the seminary, and the number of solid vocations had grown steadily ever since. A few modernists had made it through to ordination, but that was because they hadn't shown their true colors until the oils were dry on their palms. Men like Father Shane. Andrei supposed that the archbishop was trying to deal with them in a fatherly way, patient and long-suffering as he was.

"Did you speak to the new pastor about his disobedience?"

"I tried. He got tense, then cold, and now I'm invisible too."

"What can possibly be in his mind?"

"I don't know. When he preaches, it's all twists and turns that leave you thinking what he said was very clever. But there's something wrong in it, and you can't put your finger on it. You can't remember it five minutes after he says it."

"That is a pity, Potempko. How is the rest of the parish taking to their new pastor?"

"Most of them really like him. He knows psychology. He's a charmer."

"Can it last?"

"That's a good question. It depends on whether he's able to learn from experience. But he's not listening, which is a bad sign. Confessions are down. Those holy old Indian ladies aren't happy about him. They believe in sin. They believe in grace. The white families from the city like him a lot. I guess some of them are on the pill, and he makes them feel good about themselves. He thinks guilt feelings are a bigger sin than offending God."

"Does he pray?"

"Sometimes. But I never saw him use his breviary. That's another bad sign."

"Ah well, we must give him the benefit of the doubt. Perhaps he prays it privately."

"Perhaps." But it was plain that Potempko didn't think so.

"They gave me a big retirement party. They made wonderful speeches. They said I was a grand old missionary in the traditional style. They called me a *character*. They gave me a boat with a big Evinrude motor and a fishing rod. I hate fishing."

"Couldn't you ask for another posting? You are a healthy man."

"I tried. But the archbishop said no. When I pushed him for a reason, he got irritable. But he said I could stay for a while till they figure out what to do with me."

"How are you filling your time?"

"I pray. I study. I say Mass for some of the old ladies from the reserve. That made the new pastor mad. He told me to stop undermining his ministry."

"Did you?"

"I have no intention of undermining his ministry. But a believer can attend any Mass in the world, wherever he wants."

"How many people come to your Mass?"

"As many as can fit into the house. It's getting embarrassing. But how can I turn them away?"

"Indeed, you should not, especially if this new pastor has no faith in the Real Presence."

"It's hard to tell if he does or doesn't. When you try to get a straight answer out of him, he gets vague and theological. I can't understand the new theology. I told him so, and that made him smirk. He thinks I'm an ignorant old man, pre–Vatican II. Me—a man who wrote a theology textbook in 1961! Behind my back he calls me names."

"Really? How childish. What names?"

Potempko peered over at Andrei and said in a hurt voice: "He calls me the Battleship Potemkin. Can you imagine?! A Russian name!"

Andrei resisted a smile.

"So, what can one do?! I keep myself busy. Most of the natives here are Anglicans, but some of them have been coming to me for instruction. It's the Real Presence that's drawing them. I'm certain of it. A few Catholic families have moved down from Anahim. I hear confessions when anyone asks."

"It sounds a full life."

"Yes, much better than TV. And in spare moments I try to write my books. My unpublishable books. Tell me, do you know of a publisher who hopes to get rich on a cosmology written in Hungarian by an old duffer who studied in an underground seminary in the 1940s?"

"Not many. But I would wager that God appreciates your books."

Potempko laughed and slapped Andrei on the shoulder.

"Ha-ha-ha! It's sure good to see you again, Andrei!"

"Speaking of confession, Potempko, would you hear mine?"

"Eh? Sure", said the priest, looking surprised.

Steering the wheel with his knees (a practice Andrei thought might take them closer to paradise than he had intended), Potempko rifled through his many pockets and found a rolled-up stole. He draped it over his shoulders and clamped his hand on the wheel just in time to avoid a transport truck roaring down the highway toward them. Potempko swerved violently onto the right side of the line.

"Sorry", he said, smiling.

Potempko made the sign of the cross over Andrei and heard his confession. Andrei, returning to Latin, spoke about his anger at those who had killed Aaron's family and the nuns. He probed deep within himself for the root of imperfect trust in divine providence and confessed that as well. For penance Potempko instructed him to pray for the new pastor and for "God's dear little pork barrel".

"Okay, Andrei. Now you hear mine, please."

Potempko accused himself of overeating and criticism. The rest was a mixture of faults and imperfections of disposition. He received absolution and agreed to do penance by praying a rosary for the archbishop, for the new pastor, and for the persecutors of the Church in this land.

After Anahim Lake the road levelled out onto the Chilcotin Plateau, an undulating terrain of rolling hills interspersed with lakes, pierced occasionally by low volcanic mountains. The land was drier, and trees dried up with it, the rain forest giving way to swaths of thin lodgepole pine. Aaron saw a moose in a meadow. When it tossed its rack and lunged heavily away from the highway, he sat up straight and smiled to himself. For several minutes he bounced on the seat and watched the passing landscape with renewed interest.

They stopped to eat on the side of the highway just west of Kleena Kleene. Potempko ate a penitential lunch and drank a sip of wine from a plastic cup. He forced the rest of the food on Andrei and Aaron, who were only too happy to oblige. After Potempko filled the gas tank from jerry cans, they drove on. Beyond Chilanko Forks the pavement began again. The next hour was spent in silence. Andrei read the breviary aloud, then dozed for a time. He awoke as they were approaching Hanceville, where a washout detoured them onto the old highway. About eight miles south of Riske Creek they crossed the steep bluffs of the Chilcotin River.

"A sheep", Aaron cried—the first words he had spoken. He pointed to a wild bighorn ram perched on the ledge of a cliff. The two priests nodded appreciatively.

Farther on, as they approached a sign that read WILLIAMS LAKE 12 KILOMETRES, Aaron asked for a bathroom break. They pulled over to the shoulder. While the boy ran into the bush, Potempko lit a pipe and puffed on it intensely, obviously thinking hard.

"You know", he said, "when I didn't die that time in Hungary, everything after was a gift. God gave me forty more years. Forty years in the wilderness. The world is a desolation, isn't it?"

"Yes, it is desolate."

"The hearts of so many have grown cold. They look without

seeing. They listen without hearing. But I have been so happy. So happy. I try to tell them, look, Jesus is paradise. If you let him into your heart, you don't need anything else."

"If they have not experienced him, it is difficult for them to understand."

"How can we reach them? How?" Potempko sighed. "The words are too little to tell it. Sometimes when I say Mass it's so beautiful I can hardly stand up. Time evaporates. I want to lie down on the floor and just rest there in his light. He's so warm. Sometimes I think God is too beautiful!"

"I know how you feel. It's like that for me sometimes. When I escaped from Sachsenhausen I thought it was a dream. I had ceased to hope for life. When my life was given back to me, I could scarcely believe it. For me, too, everything that came after was a gift—everything—even the suffering."

"We must cling to this, Andrei. Maybe someday the young priests will understand."

"That is my hope."

Aaron jumped into the back of the van, and they drove on. The late afternoon traffic was increasing. One after another, three cars going west to Alexis Creek flashed their lights on and off.

"What does that mean?" said Andrei.

"I'm not sure", said Potempko, looking worried. "They could be warning us. Cops ahead, maybe." He slowed, rolled to a stop on the shoulder, and shut off the ignition.

"Do you think they're searching vehicles, looking for us?"

"It's possible. But I don't think so. Sometimes they have a radar trap here. They try to catch the drinkers and the teenagers coming down to the hotel bar at Williams Lake."

"If they stop us, they will recognize the boy and me instantly."

"Yes. This is not good."

They sat thinking.

"Andrei, we're only a few miles from town. I think you and the boy should get out here and go into the bush. Try to stay out of sight. Down below the embankment is an old cattle road. Nobody uses it any more. It crosses Highway 97 just below town. I'll go past the police check point alone and meet you there at the crossroads. It will take me ten minutes, but for you it will take an hour or more on foot. I'll wait until nightfall, if need be. If you meet difficulties and are delayed, find me at the Stampede Motel, a half mile south of the crossroads. You'll know my room by the van parked in front of it. If you don't come, I'll wait another day or two. After that I'll presume you have . . ." He did not finish his thought.

Andrei opened the passenger door and got out.

"We're going to walk now, Aaron", he said. The boy slung his knapsack over his shoulder and got out.

Potempko fumbled in his pocket and found the bottle of holy water. He sprinkled them liberally and made the sign of the cross over them.

"God go with you, my friend. God go with you, little boy."

Andrei blessed Potempko in return. "We'll see you in a while", he said. "An hour or so. Pray."

"I will pray. May the holy angels guide you. May they make you invisible."

"And may the Lord of all consolations be your constant joy, Potempko. Thank you for everything."

Potempko frowned, started the engine, and drove off.

Andrei took Aaron's hand and led him into the brown grass beneath a copse of leafless poplars. A stone's throw into the woods they came to an incline and went downhill through thicker stands of coniferous trees. Five minutes later they emerged onto the floor of a coulee that seemed more an abandoned trail than a road. It was overgrown with saplings, the earth unmarked by tire tracks or footprints. It cut through the low, tawny hills and plunged down toward the east. They walked in that direction for half an hour. From time to time they passed over dirt roads that crossed the coulee going north and south. Nothing stirred except rabbits and game birds that fled with shrill cries. The sun was low behind them, and, despite the cold, it warmed their backs.

Rounding a bend, Andrei stopped suddenly and pulled Aaron to his side.

"Be silent", he whispered.

Twenty yards ahead, a road cut into the coulee, and a police cruiser was parked there. Two constables sat on the hood of the car, drinking from a bottle. They were talking in low voices, joking, chuckling, looking the other way.

"Do not make a sudden move", Andrei whispered. "Walk backward, slowly. Do not stop."

Step by step they retraced their path. The sun was behind them, and Andrei hoped that the eyes of the constables would naturally avoid that direction.

"So the Staff Sergeant gets up on the witness stand and lies through his teeth", said one of the constables, laughing, tilting the bottle back and pouring.

"What else should he have done? What about the reputation of the Force, eh? Should we all wash our faces in dirt just because Jones beats up a drunken Indian. He thought he'd got the right guy. So what if it turns out he wasn't. They're all the same anyway."

"Right on, Craig", said the other. "Anyway, it's over and the fat lady's singing. The judge ruled our way. Better to forget it."

"Yeah, let bygones be bygones."

"It's five o'clock. Let's get our asses up on number twenty and bag some more speeders."

The bend was only ten feet away when Aaron's running shoe came down hard on a dead branch and snapped it loudly. Andrei and Aaron froze.

The constables both looked up the coulee into the setting

sun. They looked away, then looked back, shielding their eyes with their hands. One got off the hood and took a step toward them.

"A deer", said the other.

"Maybe."

"C'mon, let's go. The wife's got supper planned for six and a flick in town after. The babysitter comes at seven. I gotta go."

"Sounded heavy for a deer."

"Okay, a pissed-off grizzly then. Go have a chat with it, Doug, but I'm outa here." The constable slid off the hood and got into the driver's side of the vehicle.

The other one walked slowly up the coulee, shielding his eyes.

"Give me a minute. I wanna check this out."

When Andrei heard that, he made a split-second decision and turned off the trail, intending to go into the cover of the trees. The moment he did so, the second constable shouted, "Hold it right there."

Andrei kept walking. "Do not be afraid", he said to Aaron. "Just keep walking."

The constable signalled with his hand to his partner, who got out of the cruiser, ran along the trail, and stopped beside him.

"Hey, you, I said stop right there!"

Both men had their hands on the butts of their pistols. They started walking slowly toward Andrei and the boy.

Andrei waved at them. "Good evening", he said in a friendly voice.

The constables looked at each other. One scratched his head.

"Well, well. Obi-wan Kenobi and Luke Skywalker going for a stroll. In the middle of nowhere."

The constables came up close and looked them over. Their hands left the butts of the guns.

"Can you tell me the way to Williams Lake?" said Andrei. "We were hiking, and I'm afraid we're lost."

"Oh, yeah. Well, town's thataway. You're going in the right direction."

"Can I see some identification?" said the other.

"Doug, forget it", said the first constable. "The wife's waiting, remember? Babysitter? Flick-city? I'm history."

"Not so fast, Craigie. Can I see some ID, sir?"

Andrei patted his pockets. "I don't seem to have any with me. I'm sorry", he said pleasantly and smiled.

"This is private property. It's range land. The owner might not be too happy about people crossing it."

"Of course. I can understand how he would feel. I am sorry. Could you direct us back to the road, please?"

The constable didn't answer. He looked at Aaron.

"This your grandfather, boy?"

Aaron looked at the ground.

"He has trouble communicating", said Andrei. "His home life was not easy. There have been problems."

"Oh, I see. A foster kid?"

"No."

"You related to him?"

"I'm a friend of his family. His father is my friend."

Aaron looked up.

"Is that right, boy?" said the constable. "This man a friend of your dad's?"

Aaron nodded.

"And where's your dad?"

Aaron pointed east.

"We're going to see him", he said in a small voice. "He's standing on a mountain looking at me."

The constables exchanged glances.

"Okay", said one.

"False alarm", said the other. "You can be on your way now."

Andrei thanked them, took Aaron's hand, and walked toward the car. When they passed it, he began to breathe more easily. He heard the motor start and the rattle of gravel spewing as it reversed up the road. He didn't look back. He exhaled loudly. They continued down the coulee pretending nothing had happened, as the sound of heavy traffic gradually increased in front of them.

"The highway is not far", said Andrei. "I think we are safe now. But, Aaron, if there are more difficulties, we should be prepared. Did you hear what Father Potempko said about the crossroads and the motel?"

Aaron nodded.

"If we have any more trouble, or if we are separated, I want you to hide until dark and go to him at the Stampede Motel. Do you think you can do that?"

"Yes."

"Good boy."

Five minutes later they came to another dirt road. Andrei saw the flash of white in the trees, but the closeness of the highway, the imminence of rescue, had distracted him and dulled his vigilance.

The police cruiser was parked up the grade, and beside it stood the two constables, their guns drawn.

"Don't move!" commanded one.

"Hands in the air!" yelled the other.

Andrei did as he was told. Aaron, watching him, did the same.

The two constables came down the road, pointing their guns, hunkered slightly as they came, just in case the old priest and the child drew weapons and commenced firing. Their faces were hard but flushed with excitement.

"It's them, all right. The old guy and one of the missing kids."

"No doubt about it. I knew they looked familiar."

They frisked Andrei and Aaron.

"They're clean."

"Check the bags."

One of the constables opened Andrei's knapsack.

"Books, clothes, a box with a gold cup and dish in it. A stone."

"Far out! What kind of hike were you guys on?"

He felt around in Aaron's knapsack and laughed.

"Stuffed animals."

"All right, then," said the other, "you two just come on up to the car."

When they were locked into the back, Andrei felt his heart go cold with dread. He prayed silently. Aaron sat close, his face shielded by that dark *inside* look. He stared at the floor. The constables got into the front, one talked into a radio phone, and the other tapped on a dashboard computer. Andrei watched the monitor screen and saw his own face and that of Aaron appear there suddenly, followed by the faces of two other children, their names in fluorescent orange letters beneath their images.

"The kid's name is Arrow Delaney. Arrow? What kind of a name is that?"

The radio squawked, the computer beeped, the images dropped off the screen and were replaced by a paragraph of text.

"Detachment says they have to call in OIS. The gray and greens are in on it too. He says we're to stay where we are until further instructions."

"That's weird. Any reason?"

"Hold on. The rest is coming through now."

The screen filled entirely with text. The constables read it silently, looked at each other, then looked over their shoulders at the prisoners.

"So, where are your brother and sister, Arrow?" said Craig.

"I don't know."

"He don't know", Craig said to his partner.

"Do *you* know?" Doug snapped at Andrei.

Andrei shook his head. "No. I do not."

"He do not", said Doug to Craig.

The radio squawked again, ordering the constables to punch their geo-coordinates into the computer. They did so.

"They're sending a bird here real fast. Five minutes E.T.A. We're supposed to sit tight and keep our eyes open. They're going to take the old guy and the boy in, and we're going on a manhunt in the toolies. Detachment's sending out a cruiser to help beat the bushes for the other two kids."

"Damn! There goes my movie night."

"That's a real shame, Craigie. But think of it—we just won the lottery."

"Promotion city", said Craig.

"Yeah, right up the ladder to Vancouver."

"Kamloops at least. Staff Sergeant stripes for both of us. I guarantee it."

Craig looked into the back seat and said, "It's all over, buddy. Why don't you tell us where they are?"

"I don't know where they are. I told you that."

"Sure, sure. Listen, what kind of creep are you, anyway, kidnapping a kid? Kid, you want to come up front with us?"

"No, thank you."

"Did this old guy touch you?"

Aaron looked at him, puzzled.

"You know—like, did he make you take your pants down?"

Andrei leaned forward, angry. "Do not put such evil thoughts into this boy's mind."

"Shut up!" Craig barked. "Did he do that to you, kid?"

Aaron shook his head and stared as if he thought the constable was insane.

"Bad sad", he said.

"Huh?"

Doug gave Craig a significant look and muttered, "Wacko. Purebred wackoes."

"Yeah, they brainwash the kids in those groups. It's sad."

"Right", said Doug, disgusted. "*Bad* sad."

Just then a long, black helicopter soared over the treetops, practically soundless, circled, and landed lengthways in the coulee. It sat there, humming like a drone wasp.

"Beetles", Aaron whimpered.

Three men in gray and green uniforms jumped out and ran up to the cruiser. Doug and Craig got out too, exaggerating their country-cop poses and broadening their accents a notch as they gave the report.

Five minutes later they put Andrei through the side door of the helicopter. When they lifted Aaron inside, his eyes grew terrified. "Black beetles", he wailed.

Andrei said something to him, and he calmed down. They handcuffed Andrei to a clamp attached to his seat and pulled his seat belt tight. Aaron was not handcuffed, but he might as well have been; he was strapped in between two big gray and greens. One of them leaned over, stuck out his hand for a shake, and said, "Hi, Arrow. I'm Jack." He didn't offer to shake Andrei's hand. Aaron shook Jack's hand limply and dropped it.

"Ever flown before, Arrow?"

"No."

"You'll like it."

"Where are you taking us?" Andrei asked him.

Jack gave Andrei a neutral look and replied evenly, "Vancouver."

The treetops were sinking fast below them. Through the port window Aaron could see a town in the distance and beyond it the Cariboo range rising on the horizon in the east. The pilot looked back at Jack and said, "We'll need to refuel somewhere. Want to do it here or at Kamloops?"

"Kamloops. Call K division and have them meet us at the airport with hamburgers, fries, and milkshakes for five. Make it double burgers. The kid looks hungry."

Even as he was speaking into the radio microphone, the pilot tilted the helicopter toward the south. It zinged once, then shot like a black bullet along the undulating escarpment, following the serpentine track of the Fraser River. Ten minutes later it left the river, tilted at a terrifying angle, and lifted up over towering heights that were not quite mountains but too big to be called hills. On the other side it veered south-southeast in the dusk, heading for Kamloops.

It was dark when they landed at the airport's government compound. A car was waiting for them on the far side of the fuel pumps. The pilot went out the cockpit door, and Jack went out through the side door, shutting it firmly behind him. The third gray and green reached over and rattled the lever; it wouldn't move.

"Locked", he said with emphasis, looking at Aaron. Then he craned his neck and peered through the port window to see what was happening outside. An agent was walking across the tarmac with three big bags in his arms. He gave them to Jack. Jack and the pilot checked their watches, opened the bags, and took out hamburgers. They munched on them and walked with the agent back to the car.

The gray and green sitting beside Aaron looked miffed. He checked his watch.

"Six-thirty-five, and I haven't had a bite since breakfast", he muttered. He looked down at Aaron. "You're starving, too, aren't you?"

Aaron nodded.

"Okay, sit tight. I'll go have a word with my friends there and be back with a snack before you know it."

He smiled at Aaron and gave Andrei a cold look. He punched a code number into the door lock, and it sprang open. He got out and banged it behind him without looking. The door did not perfectly catch.

"Aaron," said Andrei nodding toward the door, "now."

Aaron looked at Andrei and understood.

"I bless you, child. May God go with you!"

"You come too", Aaron cried.

"I can't. They have tied me", he explained, rattling the cuffs against its clamp. "There is no way I can free myself."

"I'm staying."

"No. You are going. Fly, my little arrow-in-the-bow-of-God. He will guide you to a safe place. Go, Aaron."

Suppressing whimpers, Aaron edged toward the door and gently pushed it open. He flipped over onto his belly and lowered himself to the tarmac. The car, the gas pumps, and the gray and greens were all on the other side of the helicopter. He tiptoed away from it toward the darkness beyond the radius of the arc lights that illuminated the landing pad. He walked without haste, making no sound. Behind a row of fuel drums stacked at the perimeter of light, he found a chain link fence. He crawled under it and went on hands and knees through the dead grass into the range land that bordered the airport. When shouts and floodlights erupted around the helicopter, he was already a hundred yards beyond the fence, sliding down a slope onto a railroad bed. He ran along the tracks, stumbling from time to time. He looked back and saw the helicopter rise up over the airport and begin to zigzag, playing a high power searchlight over the fields. When the beam came closer and closer, he threw himself into the jaws of a metal culvert and huddled there without moving. The light passed on.

He shivered in the dark and wondered if wolves or bears lived in the culvert, even though it was on the edge of a city. He cried. He pulled Curious George out of the knapsack and hugged him hard. He stayed curled in a ball for so long that the stars changed their position in the circle of night at the mouth of the tunnel. Finally, when he felt so stiff and cold that he could no longer bear it, he crawled out of the hole and sat beside the railroad tracks with his head between his knees.

Shortly after, a freight train squealed, whined, and groaned out of the north and rolled slowly past. He stood up. He saw that some of the boxcar doors were open. He walked quickly beside the track, trying to keep pace with one of the cars, but it was too fast for him. He broke into a sprint and was able to keep abreast of it. He grabbed the bottom rung of a wooden ladder nailed to the wall beside the door. Holding onto it, he kept running, then pulled himself up. His feet left the ground. Hand over hand he climbed the rungs. The wind ripped at his jacket and froze his ears. For one terrifying instant his grip slipped and he fell, but he caught a rung with his other hand and climbed again. He swung a leg to the right, and it touched the floor of the boxcar. Then he flung his right arm out, his hand grappled the door frame, and he half-jumped, half-pulled himself inside.

It was a grain car. It smelled of dust and wheat. Empty, dark, cold. He pushed the heavy door with all his might, and it slid closed. The wind ceased rushing through the car. Feeling his way blindly, he stumbled into a heap of empty feed sacks and fell on top of them. He lay there for some minutes, catching his breath, trying not to cry again, missing Andrei. Eventually he pawed the heap of burlap together and pulled it over himself. He used Freddy-the-Teddy as a pillow, Leo at his back for warmth, and Curious George pressed to his chest for comfort.

He stared into the darkness, listening to the squealing and growling. He tried to remember everything. It was hard to believe so much could happen in a single day. This morning he had awakened on a sailboat in the Pacific Ocean, then crossed the mountains in a car, walked through the hill country, flew in a helicopter, and now he was in a train, going someplace. Where was it going? Toward his father? Toward his mother? He didn't know. He didn't care, as long as it was far from the people who tie up other people and take them away.

He loved trains. He remembered how he had watched them when he lived with The People; they passed within a mile of the village, rumbling like heavy old men with bad lungs, the coal trains and sulphur trains and wheat trains blowing their horns as they crossed the iron bridge over Salmon Creek, making the red fish flash in the sun, the frogs leap, and the pebbles shake with laughter.

* * *

Aaron knew it was morning because splinters of light were breaking through the cracks of the boxcar walls. The air wasn't as cold as it had been last night, though he could see his breath when he exhaled. He couldn't see much through the door crack, so he pushed it open another foot. It looked like the train was rolling slowly through flat country.

He was not sure of the train's direction, but he wondered if the warmer weather meant they were close to the coast. Sometimes the train curled around a bend, and when it did he looked in the direction of its tail. Above and behind the last car the sun was trying to burn a hole through the blanket of fog. Aaron remembered that the sun always rose in the east. Now he knew he was travelling west, alongside a wide, smooth, jade-colored river over which a heavy mist hovered. The river looked familiar, but it was hard to tell what river it was because he couldn't see the mountains behind their screen of fog. Gradually it began to lift. He saw the black northern range first and the higher southern range next. Then he saw a mountain in the south range that he recognized, Mount Cheam, which The People said was a sacred burial site of the natives. Yes, there was the beaver-shaped logging cut halfway up. They were deep into the lower Fraser Valley. He recognized everything, the creeks, the teeth of the foothills, and ahead, approaching quickly, the bridge at Salmon Creek.

He slung the knapsack over his back, climbed outside onto the ladder, and lowered himself hand under hand, until the toes of his running shoes were inches from the trackbed. He dangled over space for an instant, afraid to let go, gathering courage, swaying in the blast of wind. When the iron walls of the bridge had clanked past, he dropped.

His feet hit the ties running, but he tripped immediately, tumbled to the side, and rolled into the bushes. When the train was just a rumble in the distance, when he was sure that no bones were broken, he picked himself up, dazed, sore all over. He checked to see if the teddies were all right. They were. They smiled back at him. He pulled twigs and burrs off his sweater, pushed the hair from his forehead, and looked around.

This was the creek that flowed near the village. He knew that upstream he would find the dead red fishes and the green stones, the pool of blue water where he used to swim, and beyond it, the village of The People. Maybe Maya had returned. Maybe The People were there. He picked his way carefully down through the tumbled boulders of the bridge abutment until he reached the shore of the creek. He turned north and followed its course for half a mile, stopping twice to lie down and drink like an animal from the water—so cold that it hurt his teeth. He splashed some of it on his face and felt better. When he came to the pool he began to feel happy, and his legs broke into a run. He crashed through the bush, heedless of the devil's club and salmonberry thorns that pulled at his clothing and scratched his hands. He laughed when he saw the light on the trail ahead, knowing that the dreamfields were on the other side of the wall of cedars. He burst through and came to a halt on the edge of a wide square of black. The fields had been burned. They smelled of ashes and leaf fires and mornings in the yurt after a feast. He did not mind that the fields were burned, because he had always hated dream smoke and what it did to Maya. He ran across the first field, and the second, leaving a trail of black dust rising in the light wind. When he passed a burned pickup truck on the lane between the second and third field, he began to feel uneasy. Ahead, beyond the hedges, where there should have been ribbons of smoke rising from cook fires, the sky was empty.

He slowed his pace now, his heart beating faster. He pushed his way through the blackberry hedges. His feet pulled him to a halt. He saw crocus pushing up through the carpet of last year's leaves. Salmonberry and bearberry were shooting their buds among the spiked canes. Everywhere the smell of growing things and burned things competed for his attention. He frowned. Fighting an overwhelming reluctance, he pushed through the last barrier of bushes and walked out into the clearing where the village should have been.

The cabins were gone. The tents and yurts had disappeared. The grass was black. Here and there he saw the blasted corpses of machines—an exploded Volkswagen van lying on its side. A cream separator twisting beside the stone foundation of the milk house. Lying in the fallen trunk of the watchtower, a metal loudspeaker dented and scorched, the trumpet of a fallen angel bleating its last protest to the sky. A cracked iron pot upside down in the dirt. Ravens picking among white feathers in the heap of splintered lumber that had been the hen house—they lifted into the air when they saw him and arched toward the forest, beating their black satin wings, screeching their complaints.

He knew that Maya's yurt was situated at the north edge of the village. The beetles had come from the south. Maybe she had seen them coming and run away. Aaron looked across the patternless web of dwellings toward the place where the yurt should be. It was hard to tell if it was still there, because it stood apart from most of the other shelters, a short walk into the forest. He wound slowly among the black tent rings and charcoal heaps of cabins. He passed a dead dog with a bullet hole in its ribs. It was Ringo, the guitar maker's collie. Where were all the people? Did the men in the black beetles take them away? Did they take Maya away? He saw another dead dog, Timmie-leery, a Rottweiler owned by the crop-master. Its eyes were gone, and its tongue had been pulled into raw strings. A raven hopped backward from the carrion, scolding Aaron, then heaved itself into the air, *caw-caw-cawing*. Farther on he saw a doll with an arm missing, hanging from a wire clothesline. Then a book face down in a patch of moss. Maybe it was Maya's book. He knelt, turned it over, and spelled out the letters: *Doors of Perception: Heaven and Hell*. He knew what a door was, and Irene had used the word heaven. He flipped open the cover and saw the name of the shaman written on the flyleaf. He dropped it like poison, jumped to his feet, and ran hard for the north edge of the village.

Maya's yurt had not escaped. It too was a circle of charcoal. Hardly breathing, he stepped inside the ring and moved about in it, turning over pieces of debris with the toe of his shoe, raising the stench of burned wool. Stumbling over broken crockery, he fell into a pile of ashes. He got up, gasping, not crying. He had felt nothing so far. He had observed it all with a terrible numbness, disbelieving, hoping it was a bad dream.

Then he saw Rampa. The panda lay on his back in the exact center of the floor, his limbs and ears burned, cotton stuffing spurting from his seams, his glass eyes staring, his mouth open wide in a silent scream.

Aaron sat down in the ashes and whimpered. Rampa was dead. The dogs were dead. Maya was gone. Andrei was gone. The beetles had come and gone. They had burned the home of The People. They had killed Andrei's sisters, and nothing had stopped them. Maybe Jesus couldn't stop them. Maybe Jesus was pretend. Maybe God's bow was broken. Maybe he was an arrow that had fallen from the bow of God.

Then the wind blew into the circle of stones and raised a cloud of ashes that rose high around him and formed itself into a shape of a giant or a *windigo*.

He screamed and ran away into the forest.

7

The Queen of Junque

He crashed through the forest for most of the morning. He did not know where he was going. He understood only that Maya, if she had run away, would have gone north, deep into the mountains. Hardly anyone lived back there, and maybe she was hiding. He called her name several times, but only the hills replied.

By late afternoon he was completely lost, terrified, and very hungry. The sun was already starting to fall from the sky when he burst out of a wall of trees and fell over a cliff. He tumbled head over heels down a gravel embankment and rolled to a stop in the middle of a paved road. He cried briefly, picked himself up, and brushed the dirt off his clothes. The arms of his denim jacket were torn, one elbow was showing a red stain through the sweater, and it hurt. His nose was bleeding too. His heart thumped so hard his chest ached, and he was breathing in short, noisy gasps.

He needed to get back under the trees quickly before anyone saw him. He looked up and down the road, which cut between high embankments on both sides, a hundred yards in either direction. There were no houses and no cars. He tried climbing back up but fell down to the road again, followed by a slide of gravel that left his hair full of grit and his heart in a panic. He clutched his knapsack tightly and ran as fast as he could along the pavement toward a bend in the road.

He was crying again, and he had wet his pants without knowing it. The cold wind informed him, and shame was added to terror. The banks began to level off close to the bend, and then he was able to scramble toward the forest, pulling himself upward by grabbing at small bushes and the exposed roots of trees.

He lay down beneath a patch of dry ferns and waited for the hammering of his heart to subside. It took a while. He closed his eyes. When the sun inched through the perfumed fronds and touched his neck, he sat up. He hugged his knees and buried his face in his knapsack.

"My name is not Aaron", he said. "My name is Arrow."

He opened the flap and looked at Curious George. The monkey smiled back at him.

"Don't worry", said George. "It's an adventure."

But Arrow did not believe him.

Then he pulled out the chain around his neck and looked at the picture of the lady. She didn't say anything, but he felt a little better. It was late afternoon by now, and he wondered where he would sleep for the night. Hunger bit hard in his stomach, but there didn't appear to be any houses as far as the eye could see. There might be a grocery store or restaurant nearby, but he had no money.

Then he heard a sound that he knew well—the naahing of goats. Maybe they were wild goats, and he could catch them and milk them. He didn't think that was likely, because goats were fast and clever. But if they belonged to people, they might be tethered in the bush, browsing. Then he could catch them easily and milk them. His stomach tightened into a knot.

He got up, rubbing his aches, and walked through the trees in the direction of the goats. The going was easy, because the floor was carpeted with pine needles and there was little underbrush. He came to a clearing where the forest opened wide, overlooking a valley. Below him, beside the road, there was a store of some kind, capped by a big sign and a black satellite dish. There were gas pumps out front. Behind it there was a barn and a yard full of broken-down cars, piles of barrels, boxes, and other things that he could not identify. Across the road from the store the hill plunged down to the valley floor. A river snaked through it, and a white mountain range rose above it on the far side.

He crept slowly down the slope toward the goat noises. They were probably in the barn. Circling the property, bending low, he prowled along the outside of a sagging mesh fence, hoping the people were not at home. Hoping there was no dog to bark an alarm.

The sign on the roof read:

Queen of the Road Collectibles
We buy junque! We sell antiques!
Alice M. Douglas, Proprietress

He slunk away from the road and ran doubled over to the back of the property. Beside the barn he found a heap of rotting lumber. If he climbed over the fence, he could mount the lumber and hoist himself up to a small window beneath the eaves of the barn. He could get inside and find the goats without being seen from the house.

He climbed onto the mesh fence. As he lifted his leg over, it pulled away from the posts with a loud squeal, flipping him onto the lumber pile, which began to slide, rattling and banging on a corrugated metal sheet that was leaning against it. The sheet went down with a crash, smashing empty gallon jars against a rock.

Arrow narrowly escaped being cut. He lay sprawling in the dirt precisely between vertical daggers of glass and a wobbling, threatening stiletto of iron. He sat up, rubbing his sore head. Then to his horror he heard the back door of the store open on protesting hinges, slam shut, and a high-pitched, angry voice shout:

"What kind of trouble you brewing now, you idiot Poody-tat!"

Arrow crouched down on his belly and wriggled through the weeds into a maze of junk on the other side of the barn.

"Meow! Poody-tat! Poody, poody, poody-tat!"

The screech was closer. It was a witch's voice!

"C'mere, you mangy feline."

He ducked behind a rusting car, crawled on hands and knees toward a citadel of packing crates, squeezed between two upright boxes, turned left down a narrow alley littered with trash, and found himself in a dark cul-de-sac. He curled up inside a box and tried to quiet his breathing.

"Poody, poody, poody-tat!"

Through a crack in the box he saw an old woman stalking him. Her yellow face was very wrinkled, and she was scowling. Her flaming red hair went past in a trail of smoke. A dragon lady.

Arrow gasped in fright, and the old woman stopped, turned, and looked at the citadel suspiciously.

She spat a cigarette butt out of her mouth, ground it into the dirt at her feet, and squatted down on her thighs. She held a bowl in her hand and offered it to the crack.

"Don't make me chase you all over creation, you goldarned tomcat. Where you been for three days? Had me worried outa my mind. Shoulda neutered you long ago."

Arrow made himself as small as possible and did not move.

"C'mon, it's suppertime, Puss-in-Boots!" she snarled. "Get out here, you! Kitty-kibble, kitty-kibble!"

He forced himself not to breathe, which was a mistake, for when he eventually inhaled sharply, the witch face grinned and put her face to the crack.

Oh, it was horrible! A wrinkled red turkey eye peered at him. Then it drew back suddenly and said, "Well, I'll be jiggered."

She stood up, kicked over a crate or two, exposing Arrow's hiding place. He rolled into a fetal position and covered his face with his hands.

"I'll be jiggered", she said again. "You ain't no cat."

She bent over and poked his ribs with a long forefinger.

"Hey, don't look so worried."

She laughed. Arrow whimpered.

"C'mon, get out of there, kid."

He opened his fingers and looked at her with one eye. Then squeezed it shut and curled himself tighter.

She laughed again.

"I know, I know, I ain't a sight for sore eyes. But I won't hurt you. Trust me. Trust Queenie."

She grabbed his arm in her clawlike hand and yanked him out of the box. He twisted around, hurled himself to his feet, and tried to bolt down the alley.

"Hold on a moment, thar, you li'l . . ."

She tripped him. He lay in the dirt and sobbed loudly and hysterically. She watched this for a minute or two, then extracted a package of cigarettes from the breast pocket of her lumberjack shirt, lit one, and blew a long, blue stream of smoke into the air above her head.

"You lost, kid?" she said in a raspy voice.

Arrow sobbed harder.

"Run away from home?"

He shook his head.

"Good, good. First sensible answer I had out of you all day. Now, now, nobody's gonna hurt you, so just stop that caterwaulin' and look at me."

Arrow dried his tears on his sleeve and fell silent. He stared at the ground. He could not bear to look at her just yet.

"Yeah, I ain't your gramma. And I ain't no sweetie pie. But I'm all you got at the moment, and I mean you no harm."

Arrow flashed a quick look at her. She no longer looked like a witch. She had hard old eyes, but they looked sympathetic.

"When was the last time you had something to eat?"

"I don't know", he murmured.

"You hungry?"

He looked at the dish of cat kibble. She looked at it too, and a sadness came into her turkey eyes.

"What's your name?" she asked him in a quiet voice.

He looked down at the ground again.

"Okay, you don't have to tell me your name. But you're hungry, aren't you? I can always spot a hungry guy. You want some buttered toast? You like strawberry jam? Homemade?"

He nodded.

"Milk? Cookies?"

He nodded again.

"Maybe a hamburger with the fixin's?"

A horrified look crossed his face.

"I don't eat meat. We're vegetarians", he mumbled.

She made a face that said she was very impressed.

"Ooh," she said, "that's special. Real special. And who's *we*?"

Arrow looked away.

"Okay. Plead the fifth amendment if you want. But why don't you come inside and have supper with me and Nick?"

She stood up and walked away toward the back entrance of the store. Arrow watched her. He wondered if he should run for his life. She didn't look like she could chase him very far. But he was hungry. He decided that he would eat what she had to offer, then slip away into the forest when she wasn't watching. He followed her.

They went through a dark woodshed, past bundles of newspapers, piles of plastic garbage bags, and cases of empty pop bottles. The shed door opened into a kitchen. It smelled of cat urine and cigarette smoke. Arrow saw neglected geranium plants, unwashed dishes on the counter, an antique wood-burning stove, paperback books (several were cracked open, face down on a greasy kitchen table), and an empty whiskey bottle. Many flies buzzed against the dirty glass of the window. A big color television set on the counter by the sink was blaring noisy voices and laughter.

247

The old woman busied herself rummaging in the refrigerator.

"It gets kinda lonely out here", she muttered through another cloud of smoke, the butt dangling from her lower lip. "Nice to have company."

Arrow regarded her warily as she shuffled back and forth across the kitchen. She was not like anyone he had ever met before. The People talked with soft voices, even when they did bad sad. They were mellow. This lady was not mellow, and she dressed like a mean redneck. But she said she wanted to feed him.

She popped four pieces of bread into the double toaster.

The intolerable pressure of Arrow's anxiety, combined with hunger, opened a crack in his wall of silence.

"When does your man come home?" he asked nervously.

She pursed her lips and looked at him as if he were joking.

"My man? I don't got a man."

"You said Nick."

"Nick? He's not a man. He's out in his buggy in the back lot, snoozin'. He likes to nap until supper. You can meet him later."

"Is he your little boy?"

She snorted.

"Nah. He's a house guest, sort of. He don't talk. Poody-tat don't talk, neither."

"Is Nick a baby?"

"Nick's twenty-two and a half years old."

"Oh", said Arrow.

"Shuttup, Oprah!" said the old woman, who punched a button, turning off the television set.

"You like talk shows?" she asked him.

"I don't know", he said.

"What? Don't you like TV?"

"We don't have a teevee."

"Don't have a TV? Now that's special. Real special."

She cracked two eggs into a frying pan and set it on the stove.

She threw a stick of wood into the firebox and blew on the embers.

"Eggs won't offend your principles, will they?"

"We eat eggs", he said. "And fish."

"Well, I got a crate of sardines left over from Dubbaya-dubbaya Two. How about some of them?"

"Yes, please."

"Say, you've got nice manners."

"Thank you."

"Who taught you such nice manners?"

He hesitated. "Maya", he mumbled.

Seeing a chink in his wall of anonymity, she began to work on it with a chisel.

"Who's Maya?"

"My mother."

"Oh, and where's your mum?"

He looked at the floor and closed his lips.

"You dunno?"

He shrugged.

"And where's your old man?"

"The black beetles took him", he blurted.

"Huh?" she said, looking at him strangely. "Some black beetles took your dad? What's that supposed to mean?" She stood staring at him, genuinely worried, a spatula dangling from her hand.

"I don't have a dad", he explained timidly.

"Oh", she said. "One of those."

"They took Andrei."

"Is that some guy you know?"

He nodded.

"The black beetles burned the village", he added. "And they burned the crazy ladies' castle."

She squinted at him and lit another cigarette.

"You run away from a hospital, kid?"

He shook his head.

"So where you from?"

He closed up tightly again, but after the third piece of toast (slathered with jam), he ventured: "I'm from The People."

"The People?"

She thought about that.

"Oh, I get it. You're from one of them communes in the bush down by the river, right?"

He didn't answer, which she thought was rather odd.

"Yeah, yeah", she smiled. "Now I get it. You got lost in the woods, right? Hansel and Gretel."

He cocked his head at her like a quizzical pup.

"So, don't you worry. After supper, I'll call the cops, and they can drive you home."

The terror that flooded his face gave her a moment's pause.

After the sixth piece of toast she tried again.

"Well, you don't have to go home if you don't want to."

Relief in his eyes.

"But where you gonna go?"

"I don't know."

"You don't know? Look, just how old are you anyway?"

"Eight."

"Eight? You're a pretty big kid for eight. You look ten or twelve, and a sturdy lad at that. You got a tall dad?"

"I don't have a dad."

"Oh, yeah, you told me that, didn't you."

She tipped the frying pan. Two hot fat eggs slid onto his plate and sat there sizzling. He tore into them, wolfed them down, and cleaned up the last yellow streak with more toast. He drank a glass of milk. She refilled it. He drank that down too.

She stood over him, cranking open a tin of sardines, which she dumped onto the plate.

He picked them up with his fingers and ate them in three swift bites.

At that moment a large orange and white cat came in from the woodshed, pushing the screen door open with its head.

"Poody-tat, meet Stranger", said the old woman.

Poody-tat ignored her. It crossed the room unevenly. In passing, it glanced up at Arrow with a sardonic expression. It stopped in midstride, one paw extended in space, and stared at him. It was cross-eyed. It had a pretty coat, but its feet were deformed, bent sideways, with too many toes.

"Yep. There's my mouser. A fine figger of a tom. A victim of inbreeding. But he plays *Dueling Banjos* real good."

She chuckled mightily over her joke while Arrow ate another piece of toast without comment.

"It gets pretty cold around here after sunset. You can stay the night if you want. Sleep in Nick's room. I'll make up the spare cot. Then you can be on your way in the morning." She looked at him sideways. "And I won't call the cops."

He said nothing, but once again she noted the relief in his eyes.

"Nick!" she shouted, slapping her head. "I forgot Nick! His poor little addled brains'll be cookin' out there in the sun."

She hurried out the door, leaving it wide open. Arrow got up and followed her through the woodshed into the backyard, chewing on a piece of bread that he picked up on the way.

The sun was setting behind a row of swaying pines. Jays scolded, and the old lady nattered to something that lay inside a rusty shopping cart. She pushed it toward the shed, slowly, with many grunts and curses, because its wheels kept digging into the soft pine needles.

"C'mere, kid", she shouted. "Give me a hand with this!" He ran over, pulled the cart out of a rut, and helped her to drag it to the back door. They paused, catching their breath. The old lady reached down into the shopping cart, whipped a blanket off its contents, and said, "Nick, meet the Stranger."

Arrow glanced down into the cart, yelped, then jumped away.

"I know. He takes a little getting used to. But he's really nice. C'mere, don't be shy. Shake a paw."

Arrow looked down upon two of the most beautiful eyes he had ever seen. They looked back at him and smiled. The face and the expression were very sweet.

"Cute, isn't he?" she said drolly. "If you ignore the screwy bits."

If Nick was twenty-two and a half years old, he didn't look it. His body was the size of a big baby. His head, covered in mouse-gray fuzz, was two times too large.

"He's no knockout, but he's a brave li'l tyke—lived a long time in that body."

"What's wrong with his head?" Arrow asked, fascinated and shocked.

"He's retarded. He's hydrocephalic."

"What's that?"

"Water on the brain. He shoulda been dead a long time ago, but life's full of surprises, ain't it?"

"Where did you get him?"

"My favorite discount shop—the dump."

"Why was Nick at the dump? Did he get lost there?"

"Yeah, he got lost. Or should I say overlooked. A little accident. Those government fellers can be so careless."

Arrow looked at her, then at Nick, then at her again.

"Dumpster boy." She tickled Nick under the chin, and he gurgled. "There's my little dumpster boy."

She pulled Nick out of the cart, hefted him over her shoulder, and staggered into the kitchen. She gently laid him down on the table and patted him on the head in a rough approximation of maternal affection.

"Here, kid, you talk to him while I go warm up his pablum."

She set to work making Nick's meal, and Arrow, leaning over the table, sought to establish some communication.

"Hi", he said. Nick's eyes blinked. "My name's . . . Arrow." He whispered his name so the old woman wouldn't hear.

Nick's eyes gazed back at him, his mouth opened, but no words came out.

"Nicky-nick", Arrow said, making a funny face. Nick smiled.

"Dumpster boy, dumpster boy", Arrow said in a singsong. "Can you play with a toy?"

Nick's shrivelled arms convulsed with delight, his little fists opened and closed, his mouth erupted in a babyish gurgle.

"Hey, he likes you", said the woman.

She flipped Nick upright, pulled him onto her lap, and began to spoon-feed him. It was a messy job. Arrow didn't watch much of it.

After that she changed Nick's diaper, and Arrow didn't watch much of that either, though she made him hold the safety pins while she cleaned up.

After supper she laid Nick down in a crib in a back room, croaked a lullaby to him, kissed him on his enormous forehead, and shut out the light.

Back in the kitchen she pushed dirty pots and pans around in the sink, humming to herself, watching him out of the corner of her eye.

"Don'tcha wanna know my name?" she asked over her shoulder.

He pretended he didn't hear.

"Call me Alice or Queenie", she said. "Take your pick."

She told Arrow to sit down in front of the television set and handed him a large bottle of cola. Never having tasted cola before, he was amazed by its flavor. He sipped it steadily, disgusted and mesmerized by the taste. The old woman sat down beside him and flicked the buttons of a remote control. The set turned on instantly, and a series of hot liquid images flowed across the screen. She tapped steadily, and the channels changed in a hallucinogenic stream. Within the space of a minute Arrow saw more of the modern world than he had beheld during his entire life. He saw racing cars crash into each other and go spinning end over end in balls of flame. He saw a cowboy shooting another cowboy and space men doing the same thing, men and women in business suits slapping each other on the face, screaming insults, then tearing off each other's clothes.

"Oops—I guess you don't wanna see the Playboy channel, do you?"

Then monsters shooting each other with light beams and bleeding green blood. Followed by weather reports and more people wrestling without clothes on (*bad sad,* Arrow thought), and pictures of little brown people being blown up by bombs, and then people saying funny things to each other and many people laughing, though you couldn't see them (the words made no sense to Arrow, and he did not laugh). Then a game in which people ran around a field kicking a ball, another game in which people hit a ball with a stick, and another game in which they bounced a ball up and down. Then more weather, and more people talking, and, finally, some picture-animals moving and speaking as if they were alive, like people.

"Disney Channel! You like cartoons?"

He wasn't sure what a cartoon was, but after a few minutes of watching he realized that he liked it. He had never seen such a thing before, and it made him feel amazed and happy. The animals did many of the things that real people did, and just like the adults they said many funny things that were not funny. But when they made faces and jumped about, Arrow permitted himself a small smile. They were sometimes happy and sometimes sad. Not bad sad. Just sad.

He watched for an hour while the old woman read one of her thick, cracked pocketbooks.

"Nine o'clock", she said eventually, flicking off the television set. Arrow blinked the millions of hot colors out of his eyes and listened to the noises still buzzing in his ears. Gradually they faded.

"Well, the moment of truth, laddie. You're free to go, you

know. I won't stop you, and I won't call the cops. You want to go?"

"I have to go. I have to find Maya."

"Oh, yeah, your mum, right?"

Arrow nodded. "My father is standing on a mountain looking at me."

Alice screwed up her face. The kid had a father but didn't have a dad? Weirder and weirder!

"Okay", she shrugged. "But it's pretty dark out there."

She lit a cigarette and blew a steady series of puffs toward the ceiling while he thought about it. He picked up his knapsack and edged sideways toward the door.

"Thank you for supper", he said. "Please say good-bye to Nick."

"Okay", she waved. "So long. Have a nice life." She went back to reading her book.

She flipped a page.

"Course, if you need a place to stay, just for tonight," she muttered, not looking at him, "I don't mind."

He stood by the door, not moving.

She sighed and forced her body out of the armchair.

"C'mere, kid." She shuffled to a door at the end of a dimly lit hallway.

"C'mere, kid", she said again, beckoning with a wiggle of fingers. Arrow hesitated, then followed her slowly through the door that led into the store. She turned on an overhead light, illuminating a vast graveyard of old furniture and curiosities. She went through to another room, and Arrow walked behind, distracted by the exotic collection of wares that lined the aisles, bursting from every display case and shelf: cheap plastic souvenirs, fluorescent car decals, porcelain chipmunks, imitation totem poles made in Japan, the hats that rednecks wear (like Bill's), a Coke machine, a jukebox, an antique cash register (filigree silver) with a tab reading NO SALE jutting from the top, racks of cigarette cartons, thousands of cans of tinned food, chocolate bars, bubble gum, outdated lottery tickets, fishing lures, stuffed birds, axes, aluminum pails, kerosene lanterns, pictures of Queen Elizabeth's coronation, ornate tin boxes full of cigar bands, beaded moccasins, and teetering piles of back issues of *MacLean's* magazine, *Saturday Night, National Geographic, Time, Trucker's Monthly,* and *Mad.* Two stuffed beavers, nose-to-nose like bookends, holding up a row of video cassettes. Most exciting of all, a stuffed mountain lion prowling on a high shelf. It stared at him with glowing yellow eyes as he hurried through to the next room.

A sign over the door read: WAR SURPLUS, and beneath it in orange letters: *Everything must go! Half price!* The room was filled mostly with green clothing and old boots. But here and there were ranks of empty mortar shells standing at attention; on the far wall a locked glass case containing military medals; suspended from the ceiling an eight-foot-long white and black missile.

The old lady rummaged through a stack of pants, pulled an olive-colored pair from the bottom, and held them up to Arrow's legs.

"We're in luck. It looks like they got midget marines. These'll be a bit big on you, but you can roll the cuffs up. Better than those rags you're wearing."

She draped the pants over his shoulder.

She kept tossing clothing left and right, peering at the labels. "It says *Small*. I guess they'll be triple X on you, but that don't matter. You ain't into style, are you?"

He didn't answer. Next, a leather belt, T-shirts and underwear, and a light blue shirt with an anchor on the breast pocket. To top it off she popped a redneck cap on his head. He took it off.

"Hey, don't be fussy! This is a collector's item. Look at the badge—the Toronto Raptors. You like dinosaurs, don'tya?"

"No."

"You don't?" She stared at him, perplexed. *This is one weird kid*, she thought.

They went back into the main part of the store to an alcove beneath a sign that read: DEEP-DISH DISCOUNT CLOTHING—FACTORY REJECTS. It was mostly baby things, but she did manage to find pajamas, socks, and a pair of running shoes that fit. Loaded down, they went back to the kitchen.

"Okay, you go into Nick's room and put on those PJ's. Don't worry, I won't peek—Do I look like a preevert?—Now take your li'l butt in there and get ready for bed. I got the cot all made up for you. Here", she said, handing him his knapsack.

Nick didn't wake up when he went in. He was lying on his back with his arms beside his head as if he had surrendered. His eyes didn't completely close, but he was asleep, his breathing a low, steady whistle. Arrow sat down on the cot and clutched his knapsack tightly onto his knees. Alice went out, closing the door behind. Arrow opened the flap of his knapsack and withdrew Curious George, Freddy-the-Teddy, and Leo. He pushed them under the blankets. When he had changed into the clean, soft, cotton pajamas, he felt suddenly grateful for Alice. He wriggled far down under the covers and hugged the stuffed animals.

She knocked a few minutes later.

"Are you decent?" She poked her head in the door. "Do you wanna sleep with the light on?"

"No, thank you."

"I just thought maybe you might like it on tonight."

"No."

"You being so far from your mum and all."

"It's all right. I don't need it."

"Well, okay. G'night then . . . Arrow."

He looked at her sharply.

"How do you know my name?"

"I heard you tell Nick."

He looked worried.

257

"Relax. Nobody but you and me and Nick knows you're here. And nobody else is gonna find out. Poody-tat ain't tellin', neither."

He smiled.

"Hey, you got a nice smile, Arrow. Now, get to sleep and don't give an old lady no more grief."

She grinned at him with a hideous grin. He tried not to, but he liked it.

He fell instantly asleep.

* * *

She got a glass tumbler from the kitchen cupboard, put some ice in it, and covered it with whiskey. Then she dragged the big old armchair over to the stove, opened the oven door, and propped her feet on it. She sat for a while sipping the drink, trying to read her potboiler. But she couldn't concentrate. She watched the cat lick the sardine juice off the kid's plate, then stroked its arching back as it made itself comfortable on her lap.

It was unusual for her to sit for long without doing anything, but she felt weird tonight. Very weird. This arrow who had shot straight out of the woods into her life was a pretty big puzzle. He was obviously in some kind of trouble. Trouble with the law? Maybe. Trouble with his family? It didn't sound like much of a family. Trouble in his head? He wasn't your average happy-go-lucky eight-year-old, that was plain enough. She decided to let the whole puzzle set a spell while she digested it. Tomorrow she'd ask around, make a few calls, and see if a boy had gone missing. There were a lot of screwed up people living way back in the mountains; you heard about them from time to time. Druggies, culties, abusers. Now and then you heard about arrests. The world was pretty messed up these days, and she didn't like it complicating her life. She sipped her drink, grunted, and flicked the remote control.

Ten o'clock. Time for the CBC news.

It was the usual garbage. So and so did this, so and so said that. This terrorist bomb went off in London, Jerusalem, New York. This or that religious nut got assassinated. Another priest arrested for sexual assault. A stockbroker arrested for fraud. Missing kid. Update on right-wing terrorist group that wiped out a bunch of nuns. Immigration quotas for Hong Kong refugees. China testing missiles offshore of Taiwan again. Drug bust. New president of European Parliament.

Missing kid?

Oops, that one slipped by too fast. Now the commercials were yammering. She flicked to the other network. Luckily they had the news items in different order.

Suspected member of a right-wing group wanted for questioning. Andrei something or other, a guy with connections to some kind of Catholic lunatic fringe. Archbishop disclaims any connection to terrorist groups. Abduction case. Kids missing.

Kid missing? No, *kids.*

And there he was. The little arrow's face, younger by a year or two, a blurry photograph. Two other kids. Zöe and Tyler Delaney. Missing for several weeks. Their dad was a member of this cult too. Killed in a shoot-out with police. Mother dead in last week's drug bust. It was really ugly stuff! What had the poor kid been through?

Alice shivered.

He doesn't know, she thought. *He doesn't know his folks are dead, and he's still looking for them.*

She tilted the glass and drained it. She pushed the cat off her lap.

"Sick!" she said to Poody-tat. "Why do people do these things to kids?"

She got up wearily and went over to the telephone. She lifted the receiver and tapped a number. It was busy.

Well, this was a cut-and-dried case. No need to feel the usual guilt.

She pressed the redial button, and this time it rang. When the duty officer answered, she hung up without saying anything and couldn't quite explain to herself why she did it. She had her agreement with the crocodiles. She didn't mind feeding a creep to them now and then. The guilty feelings were all nonsense, of course, because she never turned anybody over to them who wasn't a real bad case. It was the crocodiles' job to catch the alligators, and the alligators' job to avoid the crocodiles. Even odds, fair chance. Sometimes she turned them in, and sometimes she didn't. She didn't like cops, generally speaking, and she especially didn't like the new boys in gray and green. Didn't like them thinking they had it all under control. She treasured her little secrets. It made life interesting.

The kid wasn't alligator or crocodile. He was a victim. What he needed was to get into a foster home and have a normal life. He wouldn't see it that way at first. He'd think she'd lied to him. She'd told him she wouldn't call the cops, and there they'd be in the morning, with their badges and their nifty cars and *I'm in charge here* written all over their faces, making the world safe for democracy. She sure didn't like those guys. She didn't like the guys they sometimes arrested, either—especially the dope pushers and neo-Nazis. But sometimes, after a few drinks, on certain kinds of long nights when she felt extra weird, she would wonder if everything was quite the way the well-fed crocodiles said it was. She would have her doubts. She would feel like Agatha Christie or Erle Stanley Gardner spinning a case full of misleading clues. Perry Mason was her favorite. She'd read dozens of his books, most of them more than once—*The Case of the Dangerous Dowager* five times, *The Case of the Gold-Digger's Purse* even more times than that. Junk food. Twinkies. But they kept the brain alive and offered a lot more thrills per minute than crossword puzzles. She just knew she was the Alzheimer's type and wanted to delay the disease as long as possible.

Alice began to imagine various plot lines involving a runaway boy. He'd escaped from a mental institution. Or he'd witnessed something the Mob didn't want seen. Maybe he knew where a body was buried, like that kid in *The Client*. Better still, he was the crown prince of a European kingdom, and his wicked step-uncle the Grand Vizier wanted him dead. She smirked. She really liked her imagination.

She thought about the kid some more, and about the news, and wondered if the whole bloody mess was an illusion created in everyone's mind, because the big people with the money and the power and the guns wanted it that way. A bit farfetched, but it could happen. She didn't like the way the gray and greens looked at her sometimes—the look that made her lip curl up sideways over her dentures. Oh, yeah, they were always *real* polite. They called her Ma'am. They thanked her for helping keep the peace. They tried to tell her what a great citizen she was. And yet you could read the unspoken messages they sent to each other with their slitty little bureaucrat cop eyes, their fake-friendly tone: they despised her. Nutty old broad, watchdogging the frontier for them, like a Doberman. She guessed there must be hundreds like her, keeping an eye on things from the grass-roots level. "Call us if you see anything unusual, Ma'am. Pushers, smugglers, survivalist types."

Ma'am! You could see they thought she was pretty stupid. She was no Ma'am. She was a sixty-eight-year-old former hair-dresser who liked cliff-hangers, Harlequin Romances, cats, goats, and booze, not necessarily in that order. An old reject with fireweed hair, bobbley-bangley earrings, and painted lips. She didn't care what they thought, but she did care about keeping creeps'n'crazies off the streets.

She liked the kid. He was in bad shape, but he wasn't a creep, and he probably wasn't all that crazy. He had teddy bears, and you could see he missed his ma. That said something about him, didn't it? And about her? On the other hand, the druggies were connected to the culties, and the kid's mind was probably royally screwed up no matter how many teddies he owned. When they broke up that commune he must have taken off with the old guy, and when they caught him, the kid just ran. Poor little gaffer, didn't even know he'd been rescued. That was the way with these groups. They brainwash you, and when you're set free, you think the devil's got you by the tail. Well, he was young. They'd give him therapy, and he'd be fine. He'd thank her one day.

She lifted the receiver, paused, and set it back down.

"Whoa. Hold on arf-a-mo, Alice girl. You better just take it slow. Real slow."

She poured herself another drink.

She flicked the channel changer to the news network. More bombs. More blabbing heads. Anchor ladies looking charming and trying to talk like men. Burning bus in Jerusalem. Some new politician giving a speech in Rome. And then a hotshot helicopter pilot in a gray and green uniform giving an interview about an arrest he and his buddies just made. Nice looking young hunk, the kind of guy she could really go for. Clean-cut. But he had cop written all over him. The look. The look in the eyes she didn't like. He was standing in front of a big gray and green whirlybird. She turned up the volume.

He was talking about the neo-Nazis and the other cults. About this missing guy named Andrei and the kid he'd abducted. They thought the kid might have escaped the kidnapper and got lost in the forest. All points bulletin. Province-wide search. Worried about the eight-year-old dying of exposure.

The background info went on for a minute, and while the lady reporter babbled her conclusion into a mike, two long, sleek, pure black helicopters rose up behind her and peeled off into the sky. Quick cut to the stock-market report.

Alice couldn't get them out of her mind. Spooky things, like flying scorpions. Bugs. Beetles. She shut off the big eye and sat in the dark listening to the crackling in the wood stove. Poody-tat began to sharpen his claws on the arm of the chair.

He was tearing it to shreds, what was left of it, but she didn't mind.

What had the kid said? Black beetles took away his dad and his pal Andrei. Black beetles burned his village. Black beetles burned the crazy ladies' castle. And just who the heck were the crazy ladies?

If what the kid said was true, how come the cops said this Andrei was still missing? How come they said the old guy had kidnapped the kid, when the kid seemed to trust the old guy and didn't trust the cops, and the kid said the cops had kidnapped him and the old guy? Confusing or what! Talk about a dog's breakfast!

She got up, found a flashlight, and went quietly into the bedroom. She sat down on the end of Arrow's bed and stared at him. He was asleep, sweating, whimpering, his eyelids twitching. She looked over at Nick. A ribbon of drool was spilling down his chin. She dried it with the cuff of her sleeve. Then she thought about the night she found him.

She liked to go to the dump after dark because she didn't want the locals knowing that Queenie did a good deal of scavenging. She had obtained some of her best items there. A nice chest of drawers. An RCA Victor gramophone that worked. Lots of used clothing. People threw away the most incredible things. She went every Wednesday evening, on garbage day, after the gate was locked. A high power army flashlight and a few bangs on a tin pot were usually enough to scare off the bears.

There wasn't much worth scrounging from the regular pit that night, and she was just about to climb back over the gate to go home, when she saw a fresh trail punched through the bush at the back of the site. There was a NO ENTRANCE sign posted on a tree beside the head of the trail. *Trespassers Will Be Prosecuted*, it said. Signed by some government ministry. She thought that was kind of strange. Her Agatha Christie instincts took over at that point, and she walked down the trail. The way the forest floor was chewed up, it looked as if a heavy vehicle had been through, something bigger than the pickups the local garbage company used. Maybe a back-end loader. Maybe an army truck. She wondered if maybe the local armed forces base had chucked some empty shells or outdated war gear.

After a hundred yards the trail came to an abrupt end at a ravine. She almost fell into it. She shone the flashlight into the depths and was intrigued to see a heap of sand that looked as if it didn't belong there. Tons of it. What the heck for? Why would they dump sand here? There were a million land-fill sites closer to the base, closer to town, closer to anywhere. Maybe they were burying something that they didn't want people picking through.

She decided to take a closer look. She didn't know why she did it, because she was pretty unsteady on her feet, and her night vision wasn't good either. But she had a curiosity streak that was insatiable. She scrambled down the embankment and came to a stop on the crest of the sand heap. The narrow walls of the ravine rose up ten feet above her on either side; below her there was a dry creek bed that looked as if it came from nowhere and was going nowhere. Bits and pieces of boxes poked up here and there out of the sand. The boxes were made of that heavy waxed cardboard grocery stores use for storing meat.

Not a very neat job. She kicked the corner of one with her foot. She began to feel weird. Very weird. She thought maybe she should go back up and get the heck out of there. Maybe this was radioactive stuff or poison gas cans or something and she'd be dead within the week. But she didn't go up. Crazy, of course—but she'd always been crazy.

What was in those boxes that would get you prosecuted if you saw it? She kicked the sand away from one and pulled it out. It was heavy. There was definitely something in there. She cut the tape with her car keys and pried open the lid.

She shrieked when she saw it. Then she threw up. It was full of small human body parts. Very small arms and legs. There were heads and faces too—that was the worst part. They smelled bad. She closed the lid, pushed it back into the hole, and kicked sand over it.

She stood up, unable to stay, unable to go. She felt like cursing, which was an old habit of hers. But she couldn't. She was just numb. Her upper lip curled back, and she wanted to hate someone or something. But she didn't know who or what to hate.

That's when she heard the noise. The whistle noise, regular in and out, in and out, just like Nick was doing now in his dumb little dreams.

Alice reached over and stroked the damp hair off his forehead. She wiped away more drool.

She was just standing there in the ravine, stunned, when a small cough was added to the whistling. She played her flashlight over the entire ravine, inch by inch until she saw a box behind a big rock, covered by a twisted dwarf pine. As she moved toward the box she realized that the sound was coming from there.

There was some sand on it, but not much. When the dumpers unloaded the boxes, this one must have tumbled down behind the tree. When they dumped the sand, the rock and the tree kept the box from being buried. It was invisible from above.

There was a hole in the end of the box and the noise was coming from it. She cut the tape and ripped the top off. This time she didn't scream. But it was just as shocking as the little body parts. There was a living face in this one. The eyes looked at her, blinking in the flashlight. Then they looked shyly away. Looked back. Then smiled at her.

"O God", she said. "O God."

He was naked as a blue jay, and there was a lot of blood on him. She stripped off her jacket and wrapped him in it. She hefted him in her arms. He weighed a ton, and she was no spring chicken. She couldn't remember now just how she got him back up the ravine, through the dump site, over the fence, and into her car. She laid him down on the seat beside her. All the way home she kept staring straight ahead through the windscreen, saying, "O God. O God." It wasn't a prayer or anything. She wasn't much good at praying. But it wasn't cursing, either.

He just kept looking at her and smiling. He didn't make a fuss. When she got him home, she cleaned him up and found some discount kid clothes to put on him. He had needle marks on his arms and a bad case of diarrhea. She found some diapers in the store, some safety pins and baby powder.

"Hey, I'm a mum at last", she said sarcastically as she was changing him. Then she cried. The crying lasted about five minutes, then she choked it down and never cried again. She prided herself on toughness. She had survived on toughness. She ate nails for breakfast, for crying out loud, and no gruesome little kid was going to win *her* heart.

She peeled a piece of yellow tape off the bottom of his foot, a gummed label with typed letters on it. She understood hardly any of it. The kid had no name, just a number. It said he was a "hydrocephalic" and was routed to something called "E Lab, experiment 36". The bottom line read, "Termination permit 48715". It gave his date of birth, which must have been a mistake, because he couldn't be anywhere near the age it said he was. He was a toddler, for heaven's sake, who didn't even toddle.

She'd had a boyfriend in high school who died in North Africa during the war. His name was Nick. The li'l factory reject from the dump needed a name. So she called him Nick.

Eighteen months ago.

She sighed and shone the light on Arrow's face. He whimpered again but didn't wake up.

"Who's writing a permit on you, kid?" she whispered.

266

The stuffed animals crushed under the boy's arms stared back at her. Button eyes. Goofy little smiles. They almost got to her. Then she saw that there was a silver chain around his neck, an oval medallion hung on it. It was a picture of a lady with her arms open wide and what looked like rivers flowing out of her hands. There was also a tiny crucifix on the chain.

She raised her eyebrows at that.

* * *

Next morning she was up before her usual hour, feeling well rested. She smoked her first cigarette of the day, watched the sun rise, and put a kettle on the stove to boil. After that she went out to the barn, fed the chickens, and collected the eggs. The three nanny goats seemed delightfully surprised to see her this early. She milked them, stripped the udders down extra hard and gave them double mash, hoping they would reward her with more milk tomorrow.

"Fork over, you guys", she snarled at them. "I got two mouths to feed now. I'm a double-mum!" They laughed at her. She patted their butting heads and went in to fix breakfast for the boys.

"*The boys!*" she snorted. "What next!"

The arrow was still asleep, but Nick was wide awake, smiling at spots of sunlight dancing on the bedroom ceiling. She changed him, fed him, then strapped him into his special chair by the kitchen window so he could watch the jays and squirrels attacking the bird feeder. She sliced up a loaf of bread, put some eggs in a pot, and set it on the stove to boil. She popped a tea bag into a mug of hot water and let it steep.

About nine-thirty the gas pump dinged, and she went out to fill a pickup.

It was Harry Bird looking grumpy, sipping from a plastic Dunkin Donut coffee cup.

"Morning, Queenie."

"Morning, Harry. You look chipper today."

"Aaaarrgh!" he said.

"Rough night?"

"Yup."

"Calves born?"

"Nope. They ain't due for another week. I was helping the constable on that search and rescue. Drove all the back roads last night with infra red scanners."

"The missing kid?"

"Yup."

"Find him?"

"Nope."

"Too bad. Go home, get some rest."

"No such luck. The wife wants me to drive down to the Squamish fair this afternoon. She's got pies in the contest."

"Tell Ellen good luck from me."

"Thanks. I'll tell her."

She clanked the nozzle back in the pump.

"Forty-two dollars, ninety-five cents."

He gave her the money and his air miles card.

She filled out the slip and handed it to him.

"Where you gonna fly with this, Harry?"

"Dunno. Might take the wife to Acapulco some day. Why? You wanna elope with me?"

"I might consider it. You're a good lookin' fella."

He chuckled. Harry was seventy-one years old, weighed half again as much as he should, had a heart condition, asthma, and was the kind of lad who wouldn't survive more than forty-eight hours without his wife.

"That's sexual harassment, Queenie. I'm layin' charges against you."

She gave him a loud bark of a laugh. He grinned at her, got in the truck, and gunned the motor.

"Have a good one", he said.

"You have a good one too, Harry."

She went inside just in time to see Arrow scooting out the back door, fully dressed, with his knapsack on his back.

"Hey, hey, hey", she said, catching him by the shirt tails. "Where you off to?"

"I have to go now."

"Oh. Sure. Didn't you want to say good-bye?"

"I said good-bye to Nick."

"But not to me?"

He looked at the floor.

"Did you think I'd stop you?"

He didn't answer.

"I wouldn't stop you", she said, folding her arms. "Go ahead, get out of here. I won't tell no one you came callin'."

"Thanks."

"Sure you don't want breakfast before you go?"

He looked indecisive. He shot a fast look at the stove. The eggs were boiling themselves into rocks. She popped the bread into the toaster.

"Only take a minute."

"All right", he said, but he didn't look too happy about it.

He sat down at the table but kept his knapsack on.

She put four eggs in a bowl and set it in front of him, with a fifth in an egg cup. Salt and pepper, butter, spoon. A plate of toast guarded by jars of strawberry jam, grape jelly, and lime marmalade.

He lit into it quickly and didn't raise his eyes.

"You know, they're looking for a lost boy out there."

"I know", he said. "I heard you talking."

"To who?"

"To the man in the truck."

"You heard that?"

He nodded. "The bedroom window was open."

"Oh, I see. That lost boy wouldn't be you by any chance?"

He didn't hear her.

Four pieces of toast later he said, "It's probably a different boy."

"Oh, yeah," she said reasonably, "there're a lot of lost boys running around the woods these days."

She went over to the radio and flicked it on for the eight o'clock news. The announcer repeated some of last night's items, with a few added details about the boy-hunt. Arrow kept eating, staring at his plate, but she could tell he was listening to every word. When the sports came on, she shut it off.

She sat down across from him, lit a cigarette, took a sip of tea, and gave him her most penetrating look.

"I watched the news on TV last night."

"Oh", he said.

"Yep. I heard a lot of things about a guy named Andrei and a missing boy, and dead nuns, and a village where a drug gang was doing some shooting."

"Oh", he shrugged, trying to look uninterested.

"I saw the boy's photo", she said quietly.

He looked up at her.

Then his wall just shattered, and he was suddenly a very small kid with no one looking after him. His lower lip trembled, and he stared at the floor with haunted eyes.

It took a good part of the morning. The story came out in broken bits. It was obvious he had some of it garbled in his head. She had to probe for missing pieces and do some fast sleuthing in her own mind, but by lunchtime she was starting to get the picture.

A native woman drove up to the pumps shortly before noon, six kids in the back without seat belts (Alice clicked her tongue at that). She bought five dollars worth of gas and asked Alice if she wanted to buy some beadwork. Alice had to say no. Business hadn't been good lately, she explained. Sorry. The woman understood and drove off.

Over tomato soup and baloney sandwiches (Arrow carefully

removed the baloney before eating the ketchuped bread), he told her about a shaman (what the heck was a shaman? she wondered) and a stone table with dragons, an old man with a golden box (Andrei, she guessed), and the crazy ladies. She figured out that the crazy ladies were probably the dead nuns and probably weren't all that crazy.

They were interrupted half an hour later when some teenagers drove up in a rusty gas guzzler. They wanted ten dollars worth of regular. She stuck the nozzle into the gas hole (no cap) and squeezed the trigger, watching from the corner of her eye as the motley crew piled out of the car, clomped up the porch steps, and went into the store. That made her nervous. Most of them (male and female, she suspected) had funny haircuts and rings in their ears, noses, and lips. She stared at the pink velvet dice dangling from the rearview mirror and hoped Arrow would have sense enough to keep out of sight. She hoped her customers weren't shoplifting. She memorized the license plate number.

She went inside and found them clustered around the jukebox, slapping the coin return, trying to make it sing.

"This thing don't work", complained one.

"It works", Alice growled. She kicked it in the right spot, and it played an Elvis tune. They dropped in some brass loonies, punched a Led Zeppelin, and then a Mick Jagger. Alice hated that stuff, but she endured it for the sake of the loonies. The chief of the teens boogied over to the counter and paid for the gas. A girl who looked like his clone ordered a dozen chocolate bars, a carton of Craven A filter, and a case of Pepsi. She paid for it with a hundred dollar bill that Alice investigated carefully before deciding it was genuine.

The rolling stones left a few minutes later. When their tail smoke had disappeared around the bend, Alice thought about them for a few minutes, squinting her eyes and dragging hard on a relit butt. Then she tapped the cop number into the phone by the cash register.

"Hi. This is Alice Douglas at Queen of the Road Collectibles. Look, some kids just drove outa here heading for town. They were flashing big bills, and some of 'em looked like they were pretty high on something."

Blather, blather—typical cop talk.

"Uh-huh. Well, it might be nothin', but I thought I should let you guys know. Maybe they're clean, maybe they're not. Check it out."

She told him the plate number.

"Sure, officer, don't mention it. If they're sellin' drugs, they get what they deserve. I had a niece killed herself after a bad trip a few years back. Pull 'em in. Throw the book at 'em!"

Blah-blah.

"Yeah, you too, guy. Have a good one."

Alice always felt queasy about squealing, even if they were creeps. But she told herself she was probably saving somebody's life.

She unlocked the jukebox, extracted the loonies, and pocketed them. Back in the kitchen she jangled the coins in her pocket and said, "Wow, this is one productive day. Three paying customers, and the sun hasn't even set. Now, where were we?"

Arrow told her that his father and great-grandfather and brother and sister lived somewhere "up north". He and Maya lived with The People. The crazy ladies lived somewhere else. Andrei lived somewhere else beyond that.

"How in the heck are all these folks linked up?" she asked him, growing more puzzled by the minute.

"I don't know", he answered solemnly. "Maybe they aren't."

She screwed up her face at that, because it sounded from the news as if they *were* in deep cahoots.

"Did the shaman know Andrei?" she asked.

"No."

"Did your mum know Andrei?"

"No. But he knew her."

"Huh? Okay, let's skip that part. Now tell me again about the crazy ladies. Did you know them?"

"No. I never met them, because they were dead."

"I see", she said, looking confused.

"Did they know Andrei?"

"Yes."

"And what about your dad? You said Andrei knew your dad?"

"Yes, that's right. But I never met him."

"You never met him? You never met your dad? But your closest friend knew him real good? Whew! Through the looking glass or what?"

Alice lit her thirtieth cigarette of the day.

"Did your dad know the nuns?"

"No, I don't think so. He was far away with my brother and sister."

"Zöe and Tyler", she suggested.

"Yes", he nodded. "But I don't know them."

"You don't know them", she repeated slowly. "Curiouser and curiouser."

The part about relationships was muddled, but she thought she had a handle on what had happened. All these people, knowingly or unknowingly connected to the boy, had been scooped up in some kind of big police action against counter-culture types. The hippies were no pals of the religious fanatics, to be sure, but they shared one thing in common—they all seemed uptight about the government.

The black beetles ran like a thread through everything. If what the kid had told her was true, they had raided the drug commune and destroyed it, wiping out the boy's mother. And despite what the news said, they had been at the convent of the murdered nuns. No one aside from this boy and the old man knew they'd been there. Mighty curious that the news said a secret religious sect had killed the nuns. Especially curious when she knew for a fact, knew with her own eyes, that it was government flyboys who manned the black helicopters. Black as night, no insignia, swift and quiet as a rustle in the grass.

"Welcome to Wonderland, kid!" she said gloomily.

He gave her his puzzled puppy look.

"Wonderland", she explained. "You know, like in the fairy tale."

He shook his head.

"No matter. Now look, Arrow, I know you don't know me too well yet, but you're just gonna have to trust me. Those guys in the black beetles are not nice men. You already know that. And they want to meet you, and I don't think that's a very good idea, do you?"

"No."

"So, what I think we should do is just tuck you away here in my place for a while, till this thing blows over. They're gonna forget about you some day. Then you can leave here and start your own life. What do you think?"

"I don't know."

"You step outside this door, and you're gonna get caught", she said intensely. "The cops are after you, and I don't want them to get you. Understand?"

"Why don't you want them to get me?"

"Because I don't like them either. They tried to kill Nick."

"They did?" For the first time she detected a hint of anger in his little poker face, and it encouraged her.

"Yep, they did. So I've been hiding Nick here for eighteen months, and nobody's suspected a thing. If you want to, you can have the same deal. All you have to do is be real quiet when anybody drops by for gas or groceries."

"I don't know."

"Yeah, well, I think you better consider it, because you don't have too many choices. You can't go home, and you can't live in the woods like a wild animal. Where would you go? Do you know anyone else 'round here who could look after you?"

"No."

"What about this great-grandpa of yours?"

"I don't know where he is. Andrei knows."

"Hmmmm. And where's Andrei? That's the million dollar question, isn't it? Maybe they'll let him out of the clink some day. We could track him down, and then you can stay with him. But for now, this is the only safe place for a guy like you."

He nodded, but he wasn't sure. He told her he had to find Maya.

She wasn't prepared to deal with that one. Somebody else could tell him the bad news.

"Where you gonna start to look for her?"

"I don't know. Maybe Andrei can help me find her. He'll take me to my great-grandpa and my brother and sister, and then we'll find my father too."

"Right", she said, her lips screwing up strangely. "Right. But that could take some time. Besides, an old lady like me can't run a place like this all by her lonesome. Good help is hard to find. Can you milk goats?"

"Yes."

"Wash dishes?"

"Yes."

"Split kindling?"

"Yes."

"Good. You're a life-saver. Nick'll like it too. He needs a friend. We don't get much company here."

Arrow's face brightened. "I can teach him to talk."

"Well, he don't talk, and I don't think you're gonna get him to. But he'd like it if you play with him and chat with him. Can you do that?"

"Yes."

She thrust out her yellow paw and shook his hand.

"You're hired!"

8

Nicolo Piccolo

The big secret was getting on her nerves. Pretending to the kid that his folks weren't dead wasn't easy. For two weeks she carried it around inside of her like a cancerous growth, while Arrow just got friendlier and friendlier. It made her sad, and she never was much good at hiding certain emotions. She was good at faking, but not this kind of faking. He was opening up a little more each day—short chitchats about his mum and Andrei, and a sailboat ride he'd had. Almost like real conversation. He and the cat became pals, as much as Poody-tat would allow. The goats liked him too, after a fashion. Nick really liked him. Her *two boys* (she snorted every time she thought it) spent a lot of time nose to nose, making sounds at each other that only a mother could love. In the second week Nick did something that knocked her for a loop. Arrow was making funny faces at him and whistling bird noises. Nick laughed. He had never laughed before. It was really something special. Alice went over to his chair by the bird feeder and watched.

"He likes it", said Arrow with a shy smile. He made another face, and Nick laughed again. It was a sweet little noise, like a flute.

"Nicolo", Arrow sang. "Nicolo Piccolo."

Alice went all muckle-mouthed, screwed up her eyes, and went for a long walk in the scrap heaps behind the barn.

Arrow was a hard worker. He never complained. Hard eater too, except for that vegetarian nonsense. She tried to smuggle meat into his omelettes and soups, but he always knew, pushed it away, sitting back, refusing to touch a bite. Tough little customer, tougher even than old Queenie, which was saying a lot.

She burned all the front pages of the newspapers that had stories about him and his family and kept an eagle eye on the television. She caught him a couple of times just sitting there staring at the screen during the six o'clock news, which she flicked off instantly in mid-babble. Once she came back from sorting *junque* out in the shop to find the set turned on, Arrow hypnotized in front of it, and a commentator launching into the story.

"Don't watch that crap", she barked at him, changing channels fast. Luckily he hadn't heard anything about his ma and pa getting killed. Each night after he was asleep, she would turn on the late news for an update. They always gave the background—the cult, the drugs, the conspiracy against the government, the child abuse, brainwashing, and so forth. She was pretty sure they were lying. It made her mad. Real mad.

She began to like him a lot. She patted him on the top of his head from time to time, washed his pee-sheets every morning in the automatic, and tried to force bags of candy on him whenever she ran out of ideas. He always refused.

"Sugar's bad for you", he informed her.

"Oh", she said. "That's good to know." *Weird*, she thought. *Real weird*.

Round about week number three she decided to make her monthly trip into Fort George. Every so often the supply trucks dropped off cigarettes and potato chips, gas, bread, and pop, but there was no delivery truck for mystery stories or whiskey. She had to pay bills at the bank too, make the deposit, get her hair colored and permed—she could have done a better job herself, but the lady on Main Street was good at gossip and kept a supply of henna on hand, just for Alice. It was nice to talk shop, get the inside track on how badly the world was doing, and to feel somebody's warm fingers in your scalp. She tried not to depend on it too much, but it had become a habit.

Alice had owned a car once. In fact she still had it out in the back lot, an '83 Ford Pinto with all tires flat and a bent bumper. It had come with the place when her brother Donnie died and left her Queen of the Road Collectibles. When she retired from the hair shop in Vancouver and moved up here, she had had no idea it would be this quiet. Just the birds and coons for company, and a customer every now and then. There wasn't much income, but she had her pension, and she adapted quickly. It was pretty isolated, so she taught herself to drive on the back roads. She killed a deer with the bumper and nearly killed herself a couple of other times. She passed her exam after five tries. But last year she gave up driving for good. She had nightmares about having an accident and leaving her secret baby to die of starvation.

When Alice quit driving, everyone who lived on the road between there and town breathed a sigh of relief. Ever since then they offered rides, and sometimes she accepted. Other times, she begged a lift out of the blue, and usually someone came right over and swept her off to the big city lights. They liked her, she could tell. She knew they considered her the local character. She always paid for the ride with crusty comments, jokes, wildlife lore, and crude humor of the less obnoxious kind.

Her closest neighbors were the Potter family, who owned a two-bit farm eight miles north on the upper Steelhead, near the power dam on Stave Lake. Mrs. Potter was a nice lady, the nicest of them all. She and her husband had seven kids, homeschooled, dirt poor, Bible quotes on the dashboard. They always asked her over for Christmas dinner, and she always found some excuse to beg off. Of all her benefactors, Beth Potter was the only one who didn't respond to crude humor. She was a friendly lady and appreciated jokes, but not Alice's kind of jokes. Ellen Bird, on the other hand, could always go Alice one better. Ellen the pie-maker was into *dirty* jokes, stuff that even Alice found a bit too much. Beth Potter was at the opposite end of the spectrum. The Potters were fundies.

She called Beth on the phone and asked if she was planning a trip to town within the next few days. Beth told her she was driving in later in the morning and invited Alice along. Alice told Arrow that she had to go for supplies and would be back in a few hours. Keep out of sight. Don't answer the door. Give Nick his mash and bottle at noon. Warm it up first, but not too hot. Make himself some peanut butter sandwiches. As a final thought, she firmly instructed him to leave the TV alone.

The Potter station wagon drove up just after ten o'clock and dinged the gas bell. Beth honked a polite toot, and Alice went out, locking up behind. Beth had three of the younger ones in the back, and the baby in the car seat beside her. She was a plain-looking woman in her late thirties. Dark brown hair streaked with early gray, cut in a bob, thin wedding band, long wool coat with worn sleeves, a tired face.

"Morning, Alice."

"Morning to you too, Bethie." She swept her eyes over the clan. "How's everybody t'day?" The kids looked back at her but said nothing. They were a little shy of Alice, mostly because of the fire engine hair, heavy make-up, and gravel voice.

"Mary-Kate's got a bad rash", said Beth. "Ted and I are wondering if it's allergies."

"Sorry to hear it, Mary-Kate", Alice said to the baby. She fussed, twisted away from Alice, and hid her face in her mother's coat sleeve.

"I've got an appointment with the doctor at eleven. It could take a while. Hope you don't mind waiting."

"Nah. Perfect timing. Gives me a chance to get my *coiffure* and do some other chores."

"Should I drop you at the hairdresser first?"

"Yeah, sure. How about I meet you at Food City sometime after twelve?"

"Sounds good."

Alice refrained from lighting up a cigarette, which cost her a grand effort of the will. The Potters did not approve of smoking. She read the Bible quote on the dashboard: *I can do all things through Him who strengthens me.*

Nice thought, Alice said to herself. *Wish it were true.*

"How have you been lately, Alice?"

"Oh, the usual. Nothing much ever happens to Queenie."

"Don't you ever find time long on your hands, all alone there by yourself?"

"Never."

"Never?"

"Well, I shouldn't lie to a good girl like you. Sometimes it's a bore. But I got the goats and Poody-tat. I read a lot."

"Any chance you'll be bored around Easter time?"

Alice mulled it over. "Maybe."

"You can't keep putting us off forever."

"Now, now," said Alice defensively, "I ain't putting you off. It's just, you know, at my age, it's hard changing my ways. I like your little tykes well enough, but it does things to an old gal to have them puke in my lap."

Beth laughed.

"Well, as long as you know the door's always open", she said.

"Yeah, I know that."

"And I'm not letting up. Eventually you'll give in."

"Yeah, I probably will", said Alice looking disgusted. "You don't ever quit."

"That's right", said Beth, firming her mouth with an expression Alice recognized as the gentle resolve of a woman stronger than herself.

"Don't get me wrong. I appreciate the things you do for me. Driving me into town all the time."

"It's not much."

"You're real good folks."

Beth didn't respond to that.

A squabble broke out in the back a few minutes later, and

280

Beth tried to deal with the guilty parties by calmly negotiating over her shoulder, keeping one eye on the road at the same time. She wasn't having much success. When Alice had had enough of that, she whipped her face toward the back and gave the kids her enraged turkey look, instantly reducing them to silence. Everyone looked out the nearest window they could find.

Beth chuckled to herself.

"Well done, Alice."

"Don't mention it."

"Ever thought of taking in boarders?"

Alice's heart skipped a beat. Then she grinned and said, "What? Me? I'd damage their cute little minds. I'm no good with kids."

"You sure about that?"

"Yeah, I'm sure."

"You never had a family, did you?"

"Nah."

"Never been married?"

"Came pretty close once. He got killed in the war."

"Oh, I'm sorry."

No more was said for a while. The car began to zigzag down the winding road that led to the valley floor. Alice was dying for a smoke. On the outskirts of town she said, staring straight ahead, "Bethie, why you wasting your time on an old sinner like me?"

Beth thought about it for a minute and answered, "It's not a waste."

"Oh? The painted lady gets religion?"

"We wouldn't be upset if you did. But it's not that."

"What, then?"

"I'm not sure. Ted and I discuss you sometimes."

"Hold onto your girdle, Queenie," whooped Alice, "and stop your ears!"

"We think you're real, Alice."

"Real? Waddaya mean?"

"Real, that's all. There are a lot of unreal things going on all around us. Lots."

"Like what?"

"Like the flack we get from the government about keeping our kids at home."

"They bothering you again?"

"Yes. We just endured the third inspection since January. They say Jonathan's not reading up to snuff, and his math's deplorable. They said society has an interest in the education of future citizens. Parents have to be responsible. They hinted that if we don't put the kids back in school, they might have Human Resources do an investigation."

Alice's lip curled. "Bastards!"

Beth flashed her a severe look.

"Pardon my French!" said Alice, looking chastened.

"They're just ignorant, proud, filled with all those theories about human behavior."

"Ignorant and very well paid, thank you very much. Look, Bethie, if they ever try to take away your kids, you just hustle down the road and hole up with me. I got . . ."

She clamped down hard on what she had been about to reveal.

"I got lots of room", she finished.

"We can't run forever", Beth sighed. "Someone's got to take a stand against them. They're not bad people, you see. They just don't have any sense. No foundation inside themselves. They do whatever comes into their heads that seems right. They don't understand they're destroying the things civilization's built on."

"Yeah, well that's a bit over *my* head. But I agree with you. I don't like what's happening either."

"What is happening?" said Beth with a somber look. "What do *you* think is happening?"

"What's happening? I ain't sure. Maybe it's just shadows in the bush."

"Yes, just like shadows. And no one thinks it's real until it comes out of the bush and bites him."

Taking a reasonable tone, Alice said, "You don't want to get all hot and bothered if there's nothing in the bushes. You don't want to start seeing bogeymen that ain't there."

Beth nodded. "Yes, that's a danger. Paranoia."

"Yeah, whatever you wanna call it. You been bit yet, Bethie?"

"No. But they're growling at us."

"Look, if they start snappin' at your ankles, you just toddle down the road to Queenie's. We'll look after you."

"Thanks", Beth smiled. "Who's *we*?"

"Me and Poody-tat."

"All right. We'll keep it in mind. But for now the best we can do is just try to be real, even if Jonathan never gets the better of algebra."

Alice got out on Main Street. The hairdresser did a passable job on her head and offered some juicy bits about a local civic scandal. She thought the new president of the European Parliament had done a good job stopping the war in Mongolia. Alice thought so too. The hairdresser *tsk-tsked* about the abducted kids, and Alice agreed it was awful. Later she did the banking, splurged on a new plaid shirt and black stretch pants, and bought three bottles of Newfie Screech at the liquor store. After that she got a bagful of whodunits at the secondhand book mart. Then she searched along Main until she found the health food shop.

She asked the grumpy old Swiss guy at the counter what a person should buy if you wanted to get off meat. He suggested soya bits, because you could spice it up and make burger patties out of it and no one would know the difference. He filled sacks with various stone-ground grains and told her that combined it made a complete protein. After much deliberation, she bought an automatic bread maker, a wizard contraption no bigger than a microwave. It cost a pretty penny, but she admitted to herself that she had a few pennies to spare.

He gave her a sample cube of tofu, which Alice thought tasted exactly like nothing at all, looked like white rubber, and had the texture of something repulsive you would squish under your heel if you caught it in your tomato patch. She bought several tubs of it and asked him to put everything in the plastic bags she had brought from home—he disapproved but obeyed, after lecturing her about hydrocarbons and recycling. He suggested a reusable canvas carryall with rope handles that he had on sale for $18.95. No thanks, she told him, she preferred plastic and had more to worry about than the ozone layer.

He gave her an argument.

She told him with a straight face that her favorite pastime was driving up and down the back roads setting styrofoam cups on fire, tossing them out the car window, trying to pollute the atmosphere and start forest fires at the same time. He didn't think that was very funny.

Sizing him up exactly, and feeling in the mood for a bit of sport, she said, "Oh, Lordy, a styrofoam in flames is a loverly thing!"

He stared at her in disbelief.

"But there's nothin' sweeter than them big green garbage bags. Burnin' garbage bags." She said it so loud that other customers began to notice.

The Swiss guy's disgust would never be permitted to erupt into unforgettable words, for there was nothing sweeter to his own nose than the smell of money. A person had to have priorities.

"When I lived in Vancouver," Alice continued, "I thought that carbon monoxide was how the world was supposed to smell. It was perfume to me. Nothing finer than a hot sunny morning on Davie Street, with the yellow haze rolling down to English Bay—I like to see the air I breathe, y'understand. Such a sight!

The gates of paradise, I say, with some Chinee freighter bobbing in the harbor, or maybe one from Japan or Libya, black and red on the silvery water, and those pampas grass and little palm trees in the yards of the rich folks—"

The old Swiss opened and closed his mouth. But Alice was one of those unstoppable women.

"I saw a submarine chugging out to sea once. I was crossing over the walkway on Lion's Gate Bridge, the year the hippies painted the eyes of the stone lions—must have used glow-in-the-dark orange spray paint—real bad for the ozone layer. Spooky or what! So, as I was saying, the submarine passes right under my feet, pumping a trail of thick, black diesel smoke out of its chimney."

Alice sighed. "That was the good life. Never a day went by without something interesting happening. That's over now. I make do with what I got."

But the old Swiss, his eyes blinking rapidly, was busy excising her from his consciousness. She asked him to hold onto the heavy things, said she would come by to pick them up within the hour. And interpreted his ferocious silence as assent.

Feeling proud of herself, knowing how nice she looked all dolled up, she walked to the Food City on Second Avenue and waited for Beth. The station wagon pulled up shortly after, and Beth got out. She looked upset.

"Alice, I have to buy groceries. Do you mind watching the kids until I get back?"

Alice didn't mind. She sat in the front passenger seat beside the sleeping baby, gave the monkeys in the back a turkey look, rolled down the window, and smoked three cigarettes in a row. Beth came out with a pack boy staggering under a load of paper bags. When they were stowed in the back, Alice asked Beth to drive back to the health food store for the tofu, cooker, and grain sacks.

Beth was agreeable, but something seemed to be bothering

her. She didn't utter a word all the way to Main. On the road home Alice said, "Out with it!"

"Out with what?"

"Whatever's eating you."

"It's nothing. Sorry."

"It don't look like nothing."

"Really, it's not important."

But the farther they got from town, the wetter Beth's eyes got, and the grimmer her mouth.

"C'mon, tell me. It's the baby, right? She's pretty sick, right?"

"No", said Beth quietly. "She's okay. I got some medicine at the pharmacy. It should clear up in a week or two."

"So what's the problem?" Without thinking, Alice lit a cigarette and exhaled out the window crack. Beth didn't notice.

"I am so angry", she said in an ominously quiet voice.

"Oh, hey, look, I'm sorry", said Alice, rolling down the window and firing the butt into the ditch. "I should know better. I won't do it again."

Beth looked over at her distractedly and said, "I didn't mean that. It's not you. It's that doctor."

"What she do?"

"It's not what she did; it's what she said."

"What she say?"

Beth took a deep breath. "Mary-Kate has a urinary infection. The doctor went through a checklist of possible causes. Proper handwashing, diapers, diet, how clean is our well water, etcetera. Then she looked at me with the most intimate, probing look and asked if there was a possibility of sexual abuse. I was so flabbergasted I just stared at her. I couldn't think what to reply to such a question."

"Sex abuse!" Alice snorted. "What right does she have to ask that?"

"I don't know about her right to ask it. It just bothers me that she would ask it. She's been our family physician for years.

286

She delivered most of the children. She knows us. She knows us!"

"Ah, you know what doctors are like. They have to ask all that stuff."

"Do they? She asked if Ted and I were having marital difficulties, of all things. And did I ever leave Ted alone with the girls."

"Is this doc-lady married?"

"Divorced. No kids."

"There you go. Probably doesn't like men. Just an educated dummy. Don't get hot and bothered about it. It'll go away."

"Will it? I just sat there looking at her, dumbfounded, wondering if I really knew the woman. I'd considered her a friend of our family. I thought she, of all people, would know what a great marriage we have. Ted and I love each other. Ted would rather die than hurt our kids, *any* kids for that matter. He's the finest man in the world!"

Beth began to cry soundlessly. She pulled the car over to the shoulder of the road and put her face in her hands. Alice felt very uncomfortable. She patted Beth's back. She said something crude about the doctor—aloud. Beth didn't reprimand her.

Looking up, Beth went on in a broken voice. "Then she asked me why I wasn't giving her an answer. I told her I was too shocked to think of one. She suggested maybe I wasn't facing something about Ted. She asked if we were homeschooling because something was wrong at home, and maybe we didn't want people to have access to the kids. If a family is 'dysfunctional', she said, the best thing they can do is get professional help.

"Then I did something very foolish. I gave in to the temptation to lose my temper. I told her in no uncertain terms that she was a very unhappy woman. I said she must have something wrong with her own moral life to suspect such vile things of normal families. She asked me why I was overreacting to a simple question. I said I wasn't so sure it *was* overreaction, that it just might be *under*-reaction, because what she was saying was sick, and I felt betrayed, not by my husband, but by her. That was a mistake. Before you could blink an eye, my trusty family physician became the most icy bureaucrat I've ever met.

"'And who will protect the children?' the doctor asked. I snapped back: 'Their parents will protect them. And those poor parents who can't or won't will answer to God.' When I said *God,* she rolled her eyes. When she did that, I lost all prudence. I told her that she had better be careful about playing God. 'Yes, there are some abused children in this world,' I said, 'and they should be helped. But people should be presumed innocent until proven guilty. If we presume guilt until innocence is proven,' I said, 'then the State will create a situation that will damage every family, every child. That is abuse on a colossal scale!'"

"What she say to that?"

"Nothing. She just kept watching me with that cold, officious look. Then she wrote out a prescription. There was no further conversation."

"Can she make trouble for you?"

"I don't think so. It's a bladder infection, for heaven's sake. Children get them all the time."

"Well, let's hope she leaves you alone. Sounds to me like she's got a bee in her bonnet."

"She does indeed; I found that out! She thinks she's saving humanity. She's rescuing children! The worst of it is, she and I are in the same quilting club. Also, she's on the food bank committee, and I volunteer there once a month. We cross paths all the time."

"Ooh, messy. Maybe she'll quit the club."

"She's not a quitter."

"Maybe you should quit."

"Maybe I should. I've just about had it, Alice. Is everybody going slowly crazy?"

"Not everybody."

"Can I trust anyone any more?"

"You could try me", said Alice lighting up another cigarette.

Beth dried her eyes, and looked at Alice. "You shouldn't smoke so much", she said in a motherly tone.

"I know."

"I do trust you, Alice. There's something true about you."

"Gee, thanks. I'm glad there's something true about me. Nice of you to overlook the other stuff."

Beth reached over and squeezed Alice's arm.

"You know what I mean. It's just that, well, sometimes I wonder if anything is what it appears to be anymore."

"Hell, lady, nothing in life is what it appears to be! How long you lived and don't know that?"

"I've lived long enough to know that lots of things are dependable. The Lord is. And some of his followers are too. You develop a sense about people. It's not always perfect." She laughed humorlessly. "Our doctor, for instance. I thought she was wise. Imagine! Wise!"

"Yeah, well, smart ain't wise, is it?"

"That's true", Beth said thoughtfully. "Quite true. That's what I mean about you. You know the difference."

It was a rare thing for Alice to be complimented, especially in the field of human character. She had never developed the knack for dealing with it graciously. She did the only thing she knew how to do in such situations. She shut up, lit another cigarette, and made an extremely sarcastic face. Beth understood it, started the car, and pulled back onto the road.

When they drove into the yard of Queen of the Road, Beth got out and helped her unload bags onto the porch. Alice thanked her for the ride.

Beth said, "Anytime. Just give me a call."

"Don't you forget, now", Alice scolded. "I'm always here if you want me to scare off them little government buggers."

"I won't forget", Beth said in the same tone. "And don't you forget about Easter! I'm after you, Alice."

"Painted lady gets religion, eh?"

"Painted lady gets a tummy full of baked ham, sweet potatoes, and spring greens. Pie, chocolate eggs, Ted's spruce beer."

"Spruce beer! I thought you guys didn't drink."

"We don't, really", Beth hastened to explain. "It's very low alcohol content. Really."

"Spruce beer! Yum! Now you're talking. I'll consider it."

"Good."

"No sermons?"

"Only a little."

"I guess I can hack it."

"I know you can. You're one tough customer, Alice."

"No match for you, Bethie", she said, and meant it.

She unlocked the front door, and dragged the bags through the store to the kitchen. Arrow and Nick were still by the window, gurgling at each other. Arrow hardly noticed her. The cat was sitting on the window ledge beside them, watching jays. Late afternoon sun was spilling pools of gold over them. She stood by the door watching the boys. She didn't know what caused it, but a huge contraction went off in the center of her chest. It felt good. Then her eyes got wet. That didn't feel too bad either. *The boys.* Sentimental or what!

Arrow had found a miniature chessboard somewhere in the store and shoplifted it. Of course she didn't mind. He had set up the pieces on Nick's tray. Nick's hand made a jerky swat and scattered the pieces. He blew his new flute of a laugh. Arrow laughed too and set up the pieces again. Swat, rattle, flute. Swat, rattle, flute.

"Nicolo Piccolo!" Arrow sang.

Swat, rattle, flute.

"Look, Alice, look what Nick can do!"

"Hey", she said, squinting her eyes at them. "Good stuff! You just keep him busy while I make us something special."

Swat, rattle, flute.

You could watch only so much of that. She unloaded the bags, put the delightfully vulcanized rubber tofu into the fridge, along with the intoxicating soya granules. Booze went into the top cupboard over the broom closet, tins of cat food wherever they would fit. She cranked one open and put it on the floor behind the stove, a move that Poody-tat noticed instantly. Then she searched through her cupboards for the fat cookbook that had a section on counterculture cooking. Sure enough, listed in the index under *tofu* were a dozen entries.

"Toad food!" she muttered. "Yummy, I can hardly wait."

* * *

In week four, the spring rains let up for a few days, and Alice propped Nick in his shopping cart for an outdoor jaunt. Side by side, she and Arrow pushed the cart, rocking and lurching, over the sandy soil and the pine needles, back and forth through the tangled lanes nearest the woodshed. It took enormous effort, but Nick loved it. He gurgled, squinted his eyes at the sun, practiced his voice flute, and grunted—his new sound for displeasure—whenever his head banged against the sides of the cart. Alice tried putting a man's hockey helmet on his head, but it wouldn't fit. Arrow suggested pillows. But Alice said Nick drooled too much, and his nose ran green sometimes, and she didn't want to have to add pillow slips to the daily sheets. They compromised with a five-inch-thick foam mattress, cut to size with a hollow whittled out in the middle for Nick's skull. It worked perfectly. From then on it was all flute and no grunt.

On rainy days, Arrow went out back in a slicker and rubber boots. Alice wasn't sure what he was doing in her treasure trove, but she was glad it kept him busy and out of her hair. He would come in for lunch, play with Nick for half an hour before Nick's nap, then gallop outside again, banging the screen door behind him. She never saw him again till suppertime.

"What you doing out there?" she asked a couple of times. "You ain't gettin' into trouble, are you?"

"No, Alice."

"You watch for broken glass, eh? Rusty nails too. I don't wanna have to do no explaining about you at the emergency ward."

"Okay, Alice. I'll be careful."

She liked the afternoons a lot. With Nick snoring in the bedroom, clangs and bangs wafting faintly from the junk yard, she could sink into her favorite easy chair, put her feet in the oven, call Poody for lap duty, and crack open a new mystery novel. She had just discovered Josephine Tey and loved her. Dorothy Sayers was okay too, but kind of brainy and upper class. Alice had always been able to detect the merest whiff of snobbery in writers, and real people too. She wasn't sure yet about Sayers, but she wondered if Sayers had deliberately injected the whiff for added spice. The wondering was as much a part of the mystery as the plot.

She was accustomed to drink a tumbler of whiskey neat in the afternoons, but since the arrow hit the bull's eye four weeks before, she had gradually weaned herself of it. Now she didn't drink until after eight in the evening, when *the boys* were snug in their jammies, sawing logs. She was beginning to enjoy her life. It wasn't exactly the roulette wheel at Las Vegas, but it sure kept Alzheimer's at bay.

Beth stopped by at the end of March. She told Alice that Ted was having trouble scraping together enough money to pay the income tax. Would Alice trade some frozen pork for a tank of discount gas? Alice said, "Sure, why not?"

As Alice was filling the tank, Beth got out and leaned against the side of the car, bouncing Mary-Kate in her arms.

"How's the infection?" Alice asked.

"All cleared up. But Adam and Jonathan have it now."

"Oh-oh. What's the doc-lady say about that?"

"She doesn't have anything to say about it. We found a new doctor. He's pro-life. He's got three of his own and thinks the medical system is in terminal meltdown."

"Sounds like our kind of guy. What's causing all the infections?"

"The well. We had the water tested. It looks like some runoff from the barn has been leaking into the water table."

"I hope the doc-lady apologized."

"Apologize? No. That would be losing face, wouldn't it? I had to restrain Ted from roaring into town to give her a piece of his mind. Can you see it? She'd say he was an abuser for sure if he did that."

"Sounds t'me like she could use a knuckle sandwich."

"Oh, don't say that, Alice! We have to forgive."

"Yeah?" Alice growled. "Well, maybe you do, but I don't."

"That's not true. We all do. If we don't, then they can really get inside us. The damage goes deep. This way it's just flesh wounds."

"So, you're gonna pretend everything's fine and dandy now between you and her?"

"Not exactly. Forgiveness doesn't mean pretending. You can forgive someone without trusting them. We just pray for her and hope the best for her."

"I'm hoping for a two-by-four across her ass."

That was too much for Beth, who fixed Alice with a severe look.

"I've resigned from the food bank. And I'll be quilting at home from now on. I've asked the ladies around Steelhead to come by our place; we'll try to start our own club."

"So, tell me. Did you ever get back to the doc-lady about that infection?"

"The other day I walked into her office and told her calmly that we wouldn't be needing her services any more. I put a sample bottle of the well water and a copy of the test results on her desk and walked out."

Alice chuckled. "Good fer you, girl! That must have put her shirt in a knot."

"I didn't wait to find out. Anyway, we had to drill a new well, which is why there isn't too much cash floating around our house these days."

Alice put on her tough lady mask. "Look, if you guys want some credit, that's okay by me. Pay me when you sell the calves in the fall."

"Oh, Alice", said Beth, overwhelmed. "That is too kind!"

"Nah, it ain't. Anything you need, just let me know. Gas, coffee, kids' clothes?"

"We do need some socks and underwear pretty badly, now that you mention it. The boys need new jeans and runners. I never saw children wear out clothes the way ours do."

"Well, c'mon into the emporium and take your pick. There's three million moths in there feasting on the stuff, and I'd rather see some human beans put it to better use."

Beth drove off with the back of her wagon packed to the hilt, not before making one more try at an invitation to Easter dinner. Alice refused, pleading bad nerves, bad digestion, a bad back, and just too much to do around the place to go trotting off to social events.

On Easter Sunday Arrow begged her to come outside and see the surprise he had made for her and Nick. It was a brilliant sunny morning with blue skies and a lot of songbirds making a racket. She dressed Nick in woolens, wrapped his favorite blanket around him, and sat him upright in the shopping cart. Arrow ran out the shed door ahead of her and yelled at her to stop right there.

He came galloping back with two old planks and laid them down over the sand like a railroad track.

"Come on, Alice, try it. Push Nick's buggy onto the boards."

He rushed off and returned a minute later with more planks. Foot by foot she progressed along this road, delighting in the smooth rolling of the wheels. Ten feet into the yard it joined up with a main highway of planks that curved nicely behind the Pinto and out of sight.

"This is great, kid! You get a gold medal for this one."

Beyond the Pinto, the track rounded another bend and entered a canyon where Alice rarely went. She stopped and gasped. For fifty feet the new road plowed straight through mountains of wreckage. Obviously Arrow had been tossing things left and right for weeks, cutting this trail. At the end of the canyon it veered to the left and made a wide circuit around the perimeter of the property, circled back through a few more canyons, crossed a ditch on a rickety bridge and finally deposited them all, safely, with much improved constitutions, back at the woodshed.

"Do you like it?" Arrow asked eagerly.

"Like it?" crowed Alice. "I'm crazy about it!" She whacked him on the back and mussed up his hair with her spidery fingers. He didn't mind.

"Is that what you've been doing out here all this time? Building this road?"

Arrow nodded proudly.

"Well, you're the cat's pajamas, boy. I'm just so knocked for a loop I'm gonna give you blueberries on tofu for supper. How about that?"

Arrow thought that was pretty nice.

They went around the circuit a few more times, hundreds of yards worth. Arrow went skipping ahead on the boardwalk, Nick played his flute, and Alice hummed to herself steadily, pushing the buggy full-tilt, smoke pouring out of her mouth like a steam engine. It suddenly struck her what an odd snapshot they would make and hoped no one would ever be in a position to take it. She chuckled. A video tape of the whole event would be worth a thousand pictures. *Oh well*, she thought. *Better than the funny farm*.

Eventually Alice tired. She groaned and sat down on an oil drum, rubbing her back. Arrow and Nick were flushed and happy, obviously wanting it to go on forever, but she'd had enough for one day.

"What's the matter, Alice?" Arrow said, watching her with a worried expression.

"Nothing serious. Just my bum knee and my old back. Lumbago."

A slow smile crept over Arrow's face.

"Lumbago lady", he said, peering up at her mischievously from under his eyebrows.

She grinned. "Hey, that's cute. I like that."

Then it dawned on her that Arrow had just made his first, his *very* first, attempt at joshing her. It was a joke. She recognized instinctively that it meant he felt at home with her, trusted her.

She produced a belly laugh; Arrow responded with a genuine chuckle; and Nick dazzled them both with a giggle. It was a great day. A really great day. From then on, it was Arrow's job to take Nick for a daily pushme-pullyou on the boardwalk.

In mid-April she planted tomato shoots in the raised bed of soil behind the woodshed. She tilted old windows over them for a makeshift greenhouse, and the seedlings shot up fast. Every night she threw a blanket over the panes to protect the plants from frost. She built another raised bed beside the tomatoes. Arrow hauled buckets of goat manure from the barn and mixed it with the loam. At the end of the month she planted marigolds. Tomato leaves and marigolds were her favorite scents.

She kept a daily watch on the late-night newsline. Somewhere between weeks three and four the missing kids dropped completely from public attention and didn't come back, but she slept with one eye open just in case. She didn't want Arrow getting any nasty surprises. She felt guilty about him not knowing. Somebody would have to tell him, sometime, but it sure as shootin' wouldn't be her. Alice hated emotion.

An R.C.M.P. corporal walked into the store one day when she was filling out her overdue income tax form by the cash register—it wasn't a problem, because she didn't owe the feds a penny.

"Good morning, Miss Douglas."

"Mornin', handsome."

He pushed his cap back and returned the grin.

"You mind putting this up by the door?"

"Course not. Give it here", she said, taking the sheet of paper dangling from his big meat-hooks.

It was one of those "Missing Persons: Have You Seen This Child?" posters. They always broke her heart. She couldn't bear looking at those little faces, wondering where they all had got to and what was being done to them.

She grimaced and sighed.

"Pretty sad", said the corporal, throwing a loonie onto the counter, twisting the top off a cherry soda.

"Yup, pretty sad", said Alice. "They ever find some of these kids?"

"Some. Not many. Usually if it's a domestic abduction. Divorces or separations. The dad takes off with the kids, or the mum takes off with them, against court orders. But those cases are the minority."

"The others?"

"Nobody knows", he said, looking depressed. She liked him. He was a good guy.

"I ain't religious," she said, "but I sure hope there's a hell for kidnappers."

"Me too", he said. He finished his pop, said so long, and left. Alice went around the counter and tacked the poster beside the others just like it on the bulletin board by the front door. The new poster had three little Delaneys in the top row.

* * *

Eventually she had to tell him. She tried to choose her timing, but in the end no time was right for this kind of news. It was a foggy Friday afternoon, with not much traffic moving on the road. Arrow had been playing that dumb chess game he and Nick invented—swat, rattle, flute—since lunch. It tore her up to see how happy they were together.

He was trying to teach Nick to talk too.

"Say Arrow."

"Wah! Wha! Woa!"

"Say Arrow", he coaxed. "Come on, Nicolo, try it again."

"Woa! Waoh!"

Over and over. She watched it for half an hour, chain smoking. She fixed herself an early drink and knocked it back. Then Nick dropped off to sleep about three o'clock, and Arrow begged a snack. She fed him a plate of cookies and a glass of milk. He sat there dangling his legs, wearing down the linoleum with his socks, smiling to himself. He asked her if she knew how to play chess—real chess. She said no. Bridge and canasta were her games. Then he asked her if he could look at some of the comics she kept in the used-book section of the store. She said okay, and he scampered off, returning to the kitchen with an armload of tattered DC Comics—Superman, Green Lantern, Archie, and Cyborg Wars of the Eighth Dimension. He didn't understand Archie, but he seemed to clue in to the cyborgs without a hitch.

She filled the plate again, and he ate the cookies distractedly, absorbed in the pictures. When he had finished the comics, she called him back from the eighth dimension and tried to give him the bad news. She wanted to do it as delicately as possible, but from the beginning she made a mess of it. She stammered. Started and stopped a few times. He gave her the puzzled puppy look. She dropped cigarette ashes all over the table, spilled her drink, wiped it up, and tried to calm her trembling hands. Then she told him.

He sat there staring at her, expressionless. She could tell he had heard her right because his feet stopped swinging. His mouth opened a little, and his eyes looked *way* back inside of himself. He put his fists between his knees. After a minute he looked up, stacked the comics neatly, inserted the chess pieces into the foam backing of the board and closed it. Then he got up and walked to the bedroom, went in, and shut the door without a sound.

Alice's heart did a double thump, which she knew wasn't healthy. She wished he had screamed. Thrown a tantrum. Had a big cry. Smashed a few tea cups if he had to. Anything would have been better than this.

She let him alone for a few minutes, while her nerves calmed down. She poured herself another drink but couldn't touch it. She lit a cigarette and butted it out after a few drags. She got angry at herself for not knowing how to talk to kids. She was no good at it. Never had been. She felt angry at soldier Nick for dying and at God for letting things get into such a mess and at the government for making everything worse. She was angry at Beth and Ted for having so many kids and being poor and sponging on her credit, at their idiot doctor for being a cyborg, at Donnie for leaving her this godforsaken place in his will, at Little Nick for being so damn heavy, and at Arrow for shutting her out.

When her anger had burned itself off, she felt an upwelling of the deepest sadness she had ever known. Her upper lip snarled spasmodically. A tear dropped like acid off her nose. She wiped it away and went into the bedroom.

Arrow was curled into a ball, with his hands tight between his legs, heels tucked up under his hind end, chin screwed into his chest. Face white, expressionless. No sound. No tears. Teddies on the floor.

She sat down on the end of the bed, reached out a hand and shook his shoulder. He didn't respond. Stiff. Coiled like a cutworm. She tried to pull him upright, but he was dead weight. She shunted herself toward him a little to get a better grip. She wanted to hug him, but she wasn't much good at that sort of thing either. She'd give it a try. What if he just lay there and never got up? Went catatonic? Starved to death? She took his shoulders in both hands and yanked. The dead weight yielded a little and fell back. It was no use. He was heavier than Nick, much heavier, with a heaviness that was unnatural in an eight-year-old.

She sat with him for about an hour. He didn't flick a muscle or an eyelid all that time. The window faded from light blue to dark blue, and then turned black with a faint star in the upper corner.

"Come on, kid, wake up", she said ferociously. "You can't lie there forever."

Not a flicker.

"Arrow! Answer me!"

He was gone somewhere, maybe into another dimension.

"Look, I'm sorry about your folks. It's terrible. It's the most awful thing could happen to you. But we gotta keep going in life, don't we. We can't ever give up."

No answer.

"Please, kid," she cried, "don't do this."

She shook him violently. No response. Nothing. She could tell he was alive only by the shallow breathing coming from his open mouth.

She sat for another half hour, wondering what to do, wondering if she should curl into a ball too. Maybe it felt good. She might like it. Wouldn't that be great! Then they'd all starve.

She put her face in her hands, bent over her knees, and cried. It had been a long time since she had done that, not since the day she found Nick at the dump. But this time she couldn't stop it. She hated the sound of her old lady's wail, going on and on, uncontrollable. Hated the stench of nicotine on her fingers and her whiskey breath. Hated the smear of lipstick on the palms of her hand. Hated herself.

It was hard to tell how much time passed. The sound snapped her out of it.

"Waoh! Woah! Wo!"

She flipped on the night light.

Nick was awake, not smelling too good. Somehow he had managed to tilt his head in the direction of Arrow's cot. He was peering through the bars, looking at Arrow's back.

"Awhoa! Woa! Wa!"

Alice was trying to choke it back, to dry her face.

"Awo! Awo!"

Arrow's mouth closed and swallowed. His eyes clenched and unclenched. His body uncurled a degree.

"Wo, wo, wo!" said Nick. "Wo, wo, wo!"

Arrow's hands came out from between his legs, the skin red and wrinkled from the seams of his jeans. He rolled over and faced Nick's crib.

When Nick saw him, he played his flute.

Arrow opened his eyes. At first they were still looking way back inside, but gradually they focused. Then Nick and Arrow's eyes met.

"Awo. Awo."

"Nicolo", Arrow whispered. "Piccolo."

Alice reached down and pulled him onto her lap. He wasn't so heavy any more. She wrapped her arms around him. He didn't resist. He kept staring at Nick. Nick kept looking back. She rocked him. He sank into her chest and buried his face. Then he let out a long, scary, really awful moan.

Nick stopped fluting.

"Awo? Awo?"

When the moan was finished, Arrow sobbed loudly. When that was over, he sat up, rubbed his eyes, and slid off Alice's lap without so much as a thank you. He knelt by Nick's crib, pressing his face to the bars.

"Awo?"

"It's okay, Nicolo", he whispered. "Everything's going to be okay."

9

Two Crowns

Father Andrei was surprised by the blandness of it all. He sat for a week in a windowless metal box ventilated by a fan in the twelve-foot-high ceiling, illumined by recessed lighting that was switched off by remote control every night and turned on again in the morning. The temperature was perfect. There were no disturbing sounds. Meals were inserted through a slot in the wall three times a day. The food was nutritious, well balanced, served on soft plastic trays, with equally soft cutlery. The room contained a comfortable sleeping pallet, a bathroom alcove, and a drinking water spigot. He felt himself to be incarcerated in the innards of a vast, benign, indefinable institution.

There was no interrogation, no torture, no psychological intimidation other than the uncertainty of his position. So far there had been nothing whatsoever. He had not been permitted to telephone a lawyer, nor was he officially accused of anything—in fact, none of the normal procedures of the legal system seemed to be operative. The guards who admitted him on the first day would not answer his questions. His request for his Mass vestments, vessels of the altar, and breviary was refused, impersonally but politely.

He was simply there, waiting. He supposed that the isolation and mounting tension were intended to soften his resistance, that his unseen captors hoped to increase his natural apprehension until it reached the level of pathological dread. This waiting for a crisis or a test of faith, for physical and psychic agony before a brutal martyrdom, haunted him a little. But he was sustained by the practice of mental prayer and by the gift that the Holy Spirit had granted him some years before. He was able to rest inwardly, in perfect stillness for hours at a time, moving back and forth across history to his brothers and sisters who were in prison or nailed to beds of sickness. His memory was richly stocked and his heart able to convert the growing sensory deprivation into a kind of Lenten sacrifice in his soul. He offered each day for the salvation of a hardened sinner or for imprisoned believers who were scattered across the planet, broken in body and mind. He thought especially about the children who were being tortured in front of the eyes of their parents by police and military of various nations—such men knew that there is no more horrible assault upon a mother and father than the sight of their child suffering intolerable pain because of his parents' religious or political convictions. This was the most diabolical torment of all, Andrei knew, and he resolved to offer his worst sufferings, if they should come, for these children.

He missed saying Mass. His longing for the Eucharist grew daily. For the more than sixty years of his priesthood, he had seldom been without it—only in Sachsenhausen and a few days in 1957 when he had been hospitalized for pneumonia. Now he made spiritual communions, uniting his heart to the perpetual Sacrifice throughout the world. This gradually filled an interior reservoir of confidence, a sure faith that the Savior was with him, despite the totality of the negation of freedom. He realized, also, that if the government merely wished to eliminate him, it would have done so shortly after his arrest. He knew, of course, that they would not be so foolish as to think they could reprogram him and release him as a reconditioned citizen, perfectly adapted to the absolute State. Clearly, the unseen powers that now controlled his exterior life wished to turn him to some use. They wanted information—the location of Aaron and that of Thaddaeus and the other two Delaney children; possibly the identities of remnant Christians living quietly in the belly of

Leviathan. If so, why had there been no interrogation? Aside from the fingerprinting and the small blood sample they had taken from him—a DNA print, he supposed—they had required nothing. From the moment the agents on the helicopter had deposited him in the compound of this prison, he had not had a single significant conversation with anyone. And for almost six days after that, he had not encountered a living soul, other than the mute presence that pushed the meals through the slot in the wall. No one had asked him to speak, to write, to fill out a form, to recant, or to debate. Total silence. He was merely a piece of State property waiting to be processed.

After breakfast on the morning of the seventh day, a guard opened the door and beckoned him out of the cell.

"Come with me, please", he said.

He took Andrei firmly but gently by the arm and led him down a brightly lit tiled corridor to an elevator, where another guard joined them. They went into the elevator, and the second guard punched a code into a wall panel, the doors closed, and the elevator descended. They emerged into a corridor identical to the one above and went along it past rows of what appeared to be office doors, all closed. At the end of the hall, they entered a small, carpeted room that contained two chairs facing each other across a conference table. There were no windows or decorations of any kind. One of the guards told him to be seated, and both went out. A moment later a woman entered.

She walked in and closed the door behind her with a no-nonsense air and sat down across from him. She did not greet him or look at him as she placed a yellow legal note pad on the table in front of her, arranged a set of pens beside it, and removed a file folder from her briefcase. She put on reading glasses and proceeded to scan its contents in an unhurried manner.

Andrei observed her carefully, wondering if she were a lawyer. She was about fifty years of age, dressed tastefully in a gray suit and white blouse. No jewelry, no wedding band, unpainted fingernails, well manicured. Her eyes were grave, concerned, detached. A professional.

"Good morning", she said absently, perusing the file.

"Good morning", Andrei returned.

She closed the file and laid it down in front of her. Looking him directly in the eyes, she said, "This is your first interface with the government under the new statutes. I have been appointed as the preliminary interviewer. I would appreciate your cooperation."

He said nothing.

"I think it in your best interests to offer us as much as you can. This will save you and us a great deal of inconvenience."

"May I ask, are you a lawyer?"

"I am a lawyer, but I am not here in that capacity. I am an officer of a federal security agency."

Andrei reached across the table and offered his hand. "I am Father Andrei."

She looked at it, then shook it once, reluctantly, looking away.

"And you are?" he prompted.

"My name is not an issue", she replied without emotion. "I am here in an official capacity to conduct a preliminary hearing. I cannot emphasize strongly enough that your present situation is uncertain. Your assistance will greatly affect the government's assessment of your case."

"I see."

"I hope you do see." Her mouth tightened, and she took the cap off a fountain pen.

"I wish to speak with my archbishop", he said cordially.

"Perhaps later."

"I want to obtain legal counsel."

Her mouth tightened still further, her brows furrowed, the eyes grew cold.

"That will not be necessary", she said.

"Why not?"

"Obviously, you do not understand your situation."

"Why may I not speak with a lawyer? I do not know why I have been arrested or what I am charged with."

"There will be due legal process."

"Tell me, please, what am I charged with?"

"That is not for me to say. You will be informed when it is necessary."

"This procedure is illegal."

She put her pen flat on the pad and exhaled through her nose.

"I am a busy woman. I do not have time to waste. Either you wish to cooperate, or you do not. Decide now."

"Perhaps if you ask me some questions, I will be able to decide."

"Fine. The missing children. Where are they?"

"I do not know."

"The child Arrow Delaney left the aircraft in Kamloops. Did you tell him where to go?"

"No."

"Did he tell you where he intended to go?"

"Of course not. He is eight years old, and he fled from your agents without any idea of where he was or where he would go."

"He must have gone somewhere."

"I have no idea where."

"I think you do know."

"I do not. I fully expect that at some point in this legal procedure you will subject me to truth drugs. I suggest that you apply them now, then we will not waste any more time in fruitless debate."

"I hope that will not become necessary. Those procedures are distasteful and avoidable. It's up to you."

"I am telling you as a priest, as a man of truth, that I do not know where any of the children are."

"Do men of truth abduct children?"

"I abducted no children."

"But you did. We have a witness."

"The shaman? Is that your witness?"

"Shaman?"

"The lone adult survivor of the commune. I am sure your records will indicate whom I mean."

She glanced down at her file.

"Ah, yes, R. Schwartz."

"A drug manufacturer and dealer? Is this your man of truth?"

"He observed you abducting the boy on the day of the incident at Salmon Creek."

"He observed me rescuing the boy from mortal danger."

"What was the nature of that danger?"

"There were shootings, killings."

"By whom?"

"By whoever invaded the commune."

"Do you know who did it?"

"No."

"Do you know the identity of any organization or group that attacked the settlement at Salmon Creek?"

He did not wish to answer. Clearly the government wanted to know if he knew about their involvement.

"No."

"I repeat, do you know the identity of any organization or organizations that were involved in the massacre?"

"I have no positive evidence."

"What are your suspicions?"

"It would be needless conjecture to say. I have no evidence."

"Yes, you said that already. You have no evidence, but you have a reasonable certainty."

He did not answer.

"Please respond."

Leaning forward, he said, "Who do *you* think is responsible for the murders?"

Her mouth became a hard line.

"All right. Let's leave that for now", she said in a clipped tone. "Tell me about the massacre at the convent."

"What do you wish me to tell you?"

"Everything. First, tell me why you were there."

"I was there after the massacre. I found only the bodies of the victims."

"We know you were there. We have a recording of your 911 call."

"Of course."

"But we really don't know when you arrived there."

"I arrived after the departure of the killers."

"Do you have any suspicions about who they were?"

He nodded.

"But you have no proof."

"That is correct. I have no proof."

"Why didn't you wait for the police to arrive?"

"Because I believed the killers might return."

"Don't you realize that fleeing the scene of a crime is a very serious matter?"

"Yes."

"You were present at the Salmon Creek massacre the day before, and then you were present at the convent massacre the following day. That is an extraordinary coincidence, wouldn't you say? Don't you find that just a little incredible?"

"No. I believe it was divine providence."

"Do you expect me to believe that?"

"I expect you to believe only the disinformation you have been given."

She grimaced and made notations on her pad.

"The crimes appear to be completely unconnected. Why were you present at both?"

"I was present only at the periphery of the Salmon Creek massacre and was not present at the convent massacre."

"But you said you were."

"No, I said I arrived at the convent *after* the massacre."

"Then why did you flee the convent? You had the Delaney boy with you, didn't you?"

"Yes. I was afraid the killers would return. I was certain we were both in danger."

"If you were merely rescuing him from the massacre at the commune, why did you hide from the police at the convent? Surely, it would seem reasonable that you would hand him over to them for safekeeping."

Andrei now understood the trap that was being prepared for him. If they so wished they could extract information from him—and thus he knew that the obtaining of information was not their primary objective. This preliminary interrogation must be for the purpose of recording his statements, for use in the media, to confirm the government scenario. He could so easily say things unthinkingly that could be extracted and rebroadcast out of context, a sleight-of-hand, cut-and-paste journalism that would settle the affair in the mind of the public and kill many birds with one stone: the fostering of anti-Catholicism and severe gun control, the elimination of dissident journalism and inconvenient witnesses.

"This interview is being recorded, isn't it?" he said. "This is for propaganda purposes."

Her lips betrayed the answer, though she did not reply.

"The crimes took place on the same day", he said. "Both massacres were carried out by agents of the federal government for political reasons."

She put the cap back on her pen, sighed, and got up, shaking her head. She gathered her papers and left the office without a word.

Two men in business suits entered as she left.

One sat down in the chair the lawyer had just vacated, the second sat on the edge of the table and swung a leg casually. Both peered at him with intense, disgusted expressions.

Andrei spoke first: "I think there is no more to be said, gentlemen."

"You're right", replied the one seated on the table.

The two agents looked at each other.

"Okay. Take him to level two."

Andrei did not resist. He stood and walked between them down the corridor and entered the elevator. A code was tapped into the console, the doors closed, and the elevator descended. When the doors opened, Andrei walked out into a shining white corridor. The two agents gripped him by the arms and nodded to a medical technician and a doctor who stood waiting for them. The technician rolled up the sleeve of Andrei's prison shirt, and the doctor injected him with a syringe. They laid Andrei down on a gurney. He raised his right arm and made the sign of the cross over the four men. He blessed them all in Latin and concluded in English by saying, "I forgive you."

"Another shaman!" said one of the men in the business suits.

"They're all the same", said the other.

* * *

It was like falling down a well. The air around him grew darker and the palpitations of terror increased as he plummeted into the unknown depths. But it was unlike a well, for as he inhaled the thick water, it became warmer and warmer, and he did not drown. Even in the submergence of delirium he understood that his mind was only a portion of his being, and not the greater part. His soul was awake. The pounding of his heart was like a snared animal. He felt pity for his heart, and his soul enfolded it as a child's hands would enwrap a trembling hare, until the stillness of enclosure would reassure the creature that it was not so much trapped as held in a merciful security. The security was grace, he knew. What the technicians were trying to do to his mind was occurring far above on the surface of his being and could not touch him. With dwindling scraps of consciousness he prayed that the holy angels would seal off the portion of his mind that contained the dangerous knowledge—the rough map of the Cariboos leading to Thaddaeus Tobac and the two young Delaneys. He did not know where Aaron was, but he knew that if certain words should escape from that sealed room, the lives of the innocent people who had given him help would be endangered—Bill and Irene, Julie and Colin, their children, Potempko, Charlie Manyberries. He asked God to take his life before that happened, begged him for permanent release before chemicals or pain would pry the lock.

He heard his lips muttering things far above. He spoke about the cross on the cathedral of Dresden and the fact that his mother was a Jewess and that he did not know how or where she and his father had died. He told the technicians about the mountaintop of ordination and the dark cellar of torture at Sachsenhausen and about the shining eyes of Maximilian Kolbe and how they had killed him by lethal injection at Auschwitz. Then he thought that he too must be in the saint's death cell, and he called out to him and told him how sorry he was that it had taken him so long to join him. He apologized that he had not been arrested when they rounded up the friars at Niepokalanow, that he was safe in the northern missions of Canada by the time the Nazis invaded Poland. Of course he had gone into exile under obedience to his superiors, even though the Mother of God had told him at Sachsenhausen that he must suffer martyrdom.

Maximilian pointed to the scar on Andrei's face, and the scars in his soul, and gazed at him with unfathomable solemnity, the purest expression of union. Two crowns floated across his vision, and he saw obedience and martyrdom commingle into one crown that flashed with unearthly colors, similar to Maximilian's crowns but different, radiant but less bright, the colors subdued and rich, and his own. The colors of the soul were waves of light streaming from the infinitely creative palette of God. There was no end to the spectrum; each soul was unique, never before seen, never to be repeated. Each life and each way of the cross, and each death, would be imprinted with the singular character of the one who offered it back to the prime Giver as an embrace returned, requited in a final consummation. It was called many things, but its most common name was love.

He saw Potempko's love for the people whom the world considered small and who were in fact among the great strokes of genius created by the Most High. He saw a phalanx of angels hovering over that people, the sons of heaven walking among the sons of earth, and was amazed to see that each angel in that vast host was unique. He remembered that mankind was only one species, but every angel was a unique species.

Then the voice of an interrogator reached down into the well and asked him names and places, but when Andrei opened his mouth to answer, nothing incriminating would come out of it.

"It is against the law", he said to the interrogator.

"We are the law", the voice said, a voice like a pale rider upon its pale horse, and the rider was Death.

"I do not know your law", said Andrei. "I know the law of Life."

"Ignorance of the law is no excuse," said the rider, "nor is it exemption. For I am the destroyer of peoples and worlds."

"You are but a chimera that will fade with the dawn."

"It is night. Night, absolute and irrevocable. I will swing my scythe across the four faces of the globe, and I will harvest all blood."

"For two times and another time and a half time", said Andrei. "But you cannot destroy it all, for the Lord has ordained that a remnant shall survive."

"Ignorance of the law is no excuse", the rider repeated. "For death is my law, and I reign supreme. Nothing escapes."

"And I say to you also, ignorance of the law is no excuse, for there is a higher Law that will soon defeat you. He has permitted you a final swing of the scythe before you pass away forever and are remembered no more."

"It is you who will be remembered no more", laughed the pale rider.

"There is one coming who will remember me—He Who Is Faithful and True. He rides a white horse, and in his train is an army riding upon white horses, and by them you shall be defeated."

Then Andrei saw a priest climbing a mountain in Italy who like himself bore the blood of the Old and the New Covenants in his veins, who like himself was penetrating the darkness of the Great Tribulation, naked, powerless, except for the sword of faith. Like Andrei, this old priest was grieving with the grief of fathers whose children are pulled down to destruction and crying out for light, crying for the grace to strengthen what remained, the grace not to abandon the good, begging for the words that would defy the universal triumph of negation. Then an angel walked out of the desert and took the old man by the hand and said, "Elijah."

The angel looked at Andrei and said, "Pray for him."

Andrei knew then that whatever he had yet to suffer must be offered for this Elijah, to assist in the accomplishment of his mission, hidden in the mysterious designs of God.

Then the voices changed, and the seasons, and the days. He saw a ship tossing on a heaving sea, like a toy, its hull dark blue and its sail saffron yellow, but this was inexplicable because the *Osprey* was white. He saw Colin's love through and through, as if he were a transparency, and understood the obscure nature of his unbelief and his nobility and saw his ship moving through many storms toward a safe and final harbor. He saw Julie's fidelity and her artist's soul, Charlie's kingship, and the flowering garden of dreams that grew out of Rose's heart. And though he had never met Cecilia, the old woman who pulled a wagon of grace through the streets of a cold city, he turned the eyes of his soul across the spiritual chart of the west in search of her. And when he found her, he fell back in shock at the radiance of her, for she was a very great saint, though she was only a fool in the eyes of the world. He suddenly knew her perfectly, and she knew him too, for she was in a tiny room in a cabin at Bella Coola, prostrate on the floor before a crucifix, weeping and fasting for him. With the eyes of her heart she sought him, and when she saw where he was, she doubled her supplications. She alone, of all the good people in the world, knew his exact situation and knew what she must do. She extended her old, aching arms in a cross and prayed several rosaries in that position, until Rose and Charlie found her and made her go to bed, where she continued to pray for him throughout the night.

Strength came into his soul, and though the chemicals and the interrogators battered at the sealed room, probing the lock with their questions, the hosts of angels flooded in and stood before the door and deflected them, and he could not speak.

When the technicians swerved away to other topics, he babbled about a king from a far country and dreams of fair pastures where all the beautiful, beautiful children ran up over meadows into horizons of blue. He told them about colors and prisms, about the mosaic of human souls who compose the unspeakably beautiful and tender and hidden face of Christ.

They gave him another injection at that point, and he felt his heart begin to falter. Then it stopped, and he was glad, for he knew that he was dying, and his soul told him that the room with secret knowledge was still sealed and that now they would never enter.

Then they put something on his chest, and a bolt of blue fire shot through his heart, and it started to beat again. After that he sank down into the bottom of the well, and an angel came and consoled him and told him that he would rest for a time.

* * *

Andrei opened his eyes two days later and saw that he was in a hospital room, his body linked by wires to monitors. Through a glass window in the wall beside his bed, he saw a nurse seated at a desk, making notes on a graph and checking the monitors. When she glanced up and saw that he was awake, she stood and rushed from the room.

A doctor came in, checked his pulse, and shone a light in his eyes.

"The government looks after its citizens", Andrei whispered.

"Don't talk", the doctor said. "You've had a pretty close call."

"I died."

"Only for a minute. You're very much alive."

"Ah, that is a pity."

"Try to rest now. You're not out of danger yet."

"Of that I am certain."

He spent a week in the intensive care unit of the prison hospital, then the monitors were disconnected, and they wheeled him down the hall to a room that resembled that of an ordinary hospital. Nurses checked on him throughout each day, took his vital signs regularly, and went away without comment. They uniformly failed to respond to any of his questions or attempts at small talk.

The lawyer returned in the third week, pulled a chair beside his bed, and sat down.

"You are better", she said, removing the yellow pad from her briefcase.

"Much better, thank you."

"Do you feel comfortable?"

"Quite comfortable, thank you."

"Are you able to talk without distress to your heart?"

"It depends on what you mean by the heart", he said.

"You have survived a serious cardiac trauma. But the medical

316

staff informs me that your condition has been stabilized. You can answer a few simple questions."

"I wish to speak to a lawyer and my archbishop immediately."

"Why are you refusing to cooperate?"

"Why have I not been granted my legal rights?"

"The law has changed. This procedure is perfectly legal. It would be better for you to tell us what we need to know. Then your case can proceed, and I expect you will be released into the custody of your archbishop."

"You and I know that is a lie."

She cocked her head at him and looked straight into his eyes. The coldness in her gaze almost made Andrei flinch, but he did not. He met her look with equanimity and prayed for her silently, until an irritable expression crossed her face and she looked down swiftly at her notes.

"The cult", she said. "Tell us about the cult."

Andrei smiled. "Ah, yes, the cult. Well, it has one billion members, and its head lives in Rome."

"That's not what I mean."

"Which cult do you mean?"

"The one in which you and Nathaniel Delaney were involved."

"We were not involved in any cult. I am a Roman Catholic priest, and Nathaniel Delaney was the editor of a quite reputable newspaper—that is, until your government made it a crime to speak the truth."

"The truth? Do you call incitement to hate crimes truth?"

"He never incited anyone to hate crimes."

"The evidence is overwhelming. During the final months of publication, his paper frequently referred to abortion and euthanasia as murder. That is incitement to violence."

"Is abortion not violence?"

"It is a medical procedure."

"So is sophisticated torture."

She ignored the comment.

"So is machine-gunning adolescents. So is the execution of a man without a trial."

"Nathaniel Delaney was shot during an exchange of gunfire. He fired upon officers of the law, who were forced to defend themselves."

"I doubt this very much."

She raised her eyebrows. "What are you insinuating?"

"Was he executed by the government for political reasons?"

"That is nonsense. Things like that don't happen in this country."

"It has happened many times during this century, in many civilized nations."

"Let's move on to another subject. You maintain you have no connection to the cult that liquidated the community of nuns at Fort George, am I correct?"

"That is correct. The sisters were my friends."

"I see. What precisely was your relationship with the sisters?"

"I heard their confessions. Sometimes they came to me for spiritual direction."

"Were you ever alone with individual nuns?"

"On occasion, when one or another wished to discuss questions of a spiritual or theological nature."

"Perhaps of a moral nature?"

"Rarely."

"And when you were alone with them, did you ever initiate . . . intimacies?"

Andrei looked at her, disbelieving. He shook his head sadly.

"Oh, my poor woman, what a barren heart you must have."

"What is that supposed to mean?" she snapped. It took her a few seconds to recover her professional mask.

"You should not project your misery upon innocent people", he replied gently. "They were like daughters to me, and I a father to them."

"Of course you would say that", she replied in a cool tone.

They remained in silence for a moment while each collected his thoughts.

"Do you know", Andrei began, "that though the world is immense, the full measure of the kingdom of life is even wider and deeper and higher—in fact, it is measureless. It goes on forever. But the gate that leads to it is narrow."

She laughed shortly. "We can dispense with the sermons."

"You live in a tragically stunted universe", he said to her. "You have grasped power over mankind for a brief time and would crush everything into your flat world, but it will not last. It cannot last."

She shot him a look of cold malice.

"There is love waiting for you", he said. "Fairest love. Indestructible."

She snorted discreetly.

"You have never known joy, have you?" he said, reaching out, intending to pat her hand in a gesture of sympathy.

"Don't you touch me", she said.

He closed his eyes and prayed for her. He saw a small girl soaring on a swing, falling off and bruising her right knee. A sweet little girl, very sensitive, very bright. She lay in the dirt and cried, but her mother did not come, for her mother was at her job, and her father had left them long ago. Then the child became a young woman, leaning against the wall of a gymnasium, listening to music, hoping a boy would cross the no-man's-land of the dance floor to ask her to be his partner in a fast jive. But none of them crossed for her. None asked for her. That night she decided she could not be loved, but she would be respected. She determined to become someone powerful and dangerous. She would prosecute the infidelities of men. She would be above them and beyond them and free at last of her enslaving need for them.

"You were very lonely", he said, as she wrote on her pad. "It began when your father left, when you fell from the swing and hurt yourself."

She looked up.

"You're insane", she said.

"I'm sorry. I don't mean to hurt you. I merely ask you to understand the true shape of things. You must try to see the form."

She raised her voice a decibel and said to the walls. "This is pointless, Gerry. There's no usable material here. Beam me up!"

The door of the room buzzed, the electronic lock unlatched and sprang open an inch. She stood, snorted again, and shook her head.

"Oh, boy, you are one classic case."

She went out and closed the door behind her. She walked down the corridor to the staff lounge, poured herself a cup of coffee from a machine, and sat for ten minutes, sipping, struggling to keep her exterior appearance in perfect control. She wrestled with alternating waves of rage and fear. From time to time, for no apparent reason, she rubbed her right knee.

* * *

A week later he said to a young doctor, "This is quite restful. I've been wanting a vacation for years."

The doctor gave him an ironic look but said nothing as he wrapped a blood pressure band around Andrei's left arm.

"How am I?" Andrei asked cheerily.

"Very good for a man your age, considering what you've been through."

"You don't like what you're doing, do you?"

The doctor fixed him with a look. "As a matter of fact, I do like what I'm doing."

"What exactly are you doing?"

"I am caring for the physical well-being of wards of the State."

"Ah, then, I am a ward of the State."

"It would appear so."

"Do they intend just to keep me here in these barren rooms until I die of natural causes?"

"You'll have to ask some of the legal people. I'm a physician."

"Do you terminate the lives of people whom the State no longer considers useful?"

"Don't be absurd."

"Do you know my name?"

"No. Your chart has a number."

"My name is Father Andrei."

"How do you do", the doctor laughed. "How nice to meet you."

"A pleasure, despite these unusual circumstances."

"Yes, a pleasure, I'm sure."

"And what is your name?"

"You don't need to know my name."

"Do you have a number?"

"Everybody has a number. Hold still now, please, I have to take a blood sample."

Andrei closed his eyes and prayed for the doctor. He saw a boy playing a piano, staring out windows, wandering alone through a graveyard, a mother working, an empty apartment, a dream of a sailboat.

"You should have gone to sea", he said.

"What?" the doctor smiled unevenly. "Roll over on your back, please. I have to read your arterial pulse now."

Andrei rolled over.

"Don't you remember when you walked through the grave-yard thinking that death was the end of everything? You were crying because your father had left and because you had wanted to build a sailboat with him and go to sea. He was going to teach you to sail, but he never did."

The doctor sat down on the foot of the bed and furrowed his brows.

"What color was it?" he said quietly.

"You wanted to paint the hull dark blue."

"And her sails?"

"Bright yellow."

The doctor's face screwed up, and he said fiercely, "How could you bloody well know something like that!"

"I'm not sure."

"Are you people psychic?"

"No, that is precisely what we are not. The willful attempt to gain unlawful knowledge through supernatural means is gravely sinful."

"What are you talking about?"

"Consulting psychic mediums, Ouija boards, tarot cards, fortune telling—these are forbidden by God."

"Then where does my boat fit in this? You think it's lawful, just poking into people's memories?"

"Isn't that what your technicians are doing to me?"

"Yes, but . . . you're the patient . . . I'm the . . ."

"You're the doctor."

"Yes, *I'm* the doctor!"

"Sometimes God sends a picture into my mind, as a kind of word or message."

"Message? What kind of message?"

"I think he is saying to you that, though you have felt abandoned all your life, there is a Father who loves you."

The doctor stood up.

"And the universe is larger than you think", Andrei added.

"I heard you spooked one of the legal staff last week. Well, you can't do that to me. I'm a scientist."

He left without another word.

In the fifth week Andrei began to feel much improved, almost normal. Though he found time long on his hands, he harnessed the experience to various prayer intentions, not the least of which was the mission of the priest Elijah climbing a mountain in Italy. He was returned to his cell, to his private thoughts, and to absolute solitude, for his contact with human beings was again reduced to nothing, save for the meals that came through the slot in the wall.

It was obvious that the attempt at chemical interrogation had failed, for they now knew that the drug dose necessary to extract the information they desired would kill him. They had probably also ruled out the grotesque cruelties of the torture chamber, for that too would have stopped his heart. How many methods of interrogation did they use? How many levels did the building contain? And what happened on the lowest levels? Was the "dungeon" on level three? Perhaps there was no bottom to this pit, and victims could look forward to nothing other than an unending descent into increasing agony. The mere thought of it would be sufficient to crack most people. He thanked God for his weak heart.

No doubt they were searching for a drug that would achieve their purposes without damaging his heart. Or perhaps they were searching for other methods, more refined, subtle, civilized. They might wait until the solitude disintegrated his mind, then walk in among the ruins and pick up the items they desired. They would be prepared to wait a year or two or more, he knew, for time was on their side. But they had failed to consider the fact that his solitude was not total—for there was prayer, and grace, and angels.

* * *

At seven o'clock on a Friday evening in May, a silver-haired man leaned back in his chair and stared out the plate-glass window of a twelfth-story penthouse in a government office building in the capital. The river below was in flood, and the hills on the far side were soft green with budding leaves. The sun in the western corner window was low, a harsh bronze that filled the room with blinding light.

The commuter traffic had declined to an occasional vehicle. The sky was washed with a blood-red hue. It would be dark by the time he reached the cottage in the Gatineau hills where he spent his weekends. There were a few telephone calls to make, and then he would be free. Most of the staff had gone home, but his executive assistant was still in the outer office, going over a report for the Prime Minister.

He buzzed her on the intercom.

"Suzette, I'll be leaving in a few minutes. Will the security summit report be ready on time?"

"Not to worry, sir. The secretary has finished typing the final draft. Do you want to deliver it yourself to the P.M.'s office?"

"No. You can send it by security courier as soon as you're finished. Call his office and see if he's still there."

A minute later she poked her head in the door.

"He's gone home for supper, sir. He's coming back to the Centre Block for a Privy Council meeting at eight-thirty. Will he need it tonight?"

"No, they're discussing the OPEC crisis tonight. These are strictly security matters. But he needs it on his desk by Monday morning."

"I'll see that his exec receives it by then. Probably to-night."

"Thank you. Have a good weekend."

"You too, sir. Get some R and R, will you?" she smiled at him. Suzette was infinitely loyal and exercised only the degree of maternal familiarity she knew he could tolerate.

"I promise."

"Right. I'll see you Monday."

"Oh, Suzette", he called her back. "I won't be in till Wednesday. Would you please call the Minister when he gets back on Monday. Tell him I've taken the OIS jet to Vancouver to check on the progress of the investigation."

"Oh, that abduction case."

"Yes. Tell him I'll check in when I'm back. We can discuss the security summit presentation then."

"Fine, I'll tell him first thing on Monday. Did you have a chance to read the first draft of your summit address?"

"Yes. It was excellent. Suzette, look through my talk at last year's Interaction Council. Some of it can be reworded for this address to the U.N. summit, especially the section on globalization, the need to confront overpopulation and balance it with the need for a healthy environment and the revitalization of the world's economy. Can you insert those items into the section on security issues?"

"That should be no problem. I'll have it ready for your signature when you get back from Vancouver."

"Fine, that should be all, thank you."

"Oh, also about the summit: Do you have any suggestions for the media release?"

"They don't need to know much. Describe it as an international forum at the U.N., the CEOs of world security agencies meeting to discuss coordination of efforts in global peace. You can extract some quotes from the preamble of my talk."

"All right."

"That's all for now, Suzette. Good night."

"Good night, sir."

He leaned back, put his feet on the sill of the window, and watched the hills turn deep blue. When he heard the electronic code tone of the outer office signal her departure, he removed his shoes, went to a cabinet in the hospitality annex of his office, and poured himself a light drink of Cinzano on ice. He loosened his tie, removed his jacket, and sat down on the charcoal-gray leather sofa.

When he had finished his drink, he touched the *Activate* button on the communications console beside the sofa. Then he pressed a second, marked *Operations Directorate*, then a seven-digit number that connected him to the head of the agency's West Coast division.

A recorded voice answered: "Your identi-code, please?"

He passed his hand over the scanner.

"Thank you", said a real voice, female.

"This is the Director", he said.

"The Chief of Ops is on another line, sir. Can you hold? I'll tell him it's you."

"That's fine."

A moment later a deep male voice came on line. "Maurice, how are you?" He pronounced it Morris, which the Director did not like.

"Good evening, Wade. I'm just leaving the office for the weekend. I'll be flying out to see you a bit earlier than expected, midmorning on Monday, your time."

"Okay, I'll have a car meet you. You want to talk? We could go to the Hyatt for lunch."

"This is much more important than the usual. I'm becoming rather concerned about the Delaney case and would like to see it concluded as soon as possible. Frankly, I cannot understand why there has been no progress."

"It's got me baffled too. We've put every spare agent in the west on it, and there's no trail leading anywhere. The grandfather and the two kids simply vanished in the North Thompson without so much as a footprint in the snow. Of course, the heavy snowfall didn't help much. The youngest one did a disappearing act at the airport in Kamloops, as you know. Not a trace. Where can an eight-year-old kid go?"

"It's a big province."

"I'll say, and a lot of vertical terrain it is."

"Has the priest divulged anything useful?"

"Not a single lead. A lot of religious gibberish. And he's given a few staffers a scare with his mental tricks."

"You almost lost him, Wade. I suggest that you move with

extreme caution. He knows something important. He probably knows where all of the fugitives are. If his heart gives out again, we lose our best chance of finding them."

"All right, boss", Wade said, masking the disappointment in his voice. "We're going as carefully as we can. The medical people say he's hanging by a thread, health-wise. Right now, we have him in isolation. It's the slow method, but it's effective. He'll start to unravel in a month or so."

"You don't know these people as I do. He's an old man who's been to hell and back, a concentration camp survivor, unafraid of death. I expect he'll unravel a few more of your staffers before he shows any signs of personality disintegration."

"You may be right. So, what's next?"

"I want to talk with him."

"You can give it a try, but I doubt you'll get much out of him."

The Director smiled to himself.

"Wade, that is precisely what I intend *not* to do. I'm not going to probe for a single piece of information."

"Huh?"

"I'm going to show him the kingdoms of the world."

That reduced Wade to silence.

"We'll visit the cities of the plain and discuss certain questions of a . . . philosophical nature."

Wade cleared his throat. "Oh."

"I'll have the pilot send your office our time of arrival once we're in the air. You should get it online around 7 A.M. PST, Ministry transport channel, top confidentiality."

"We'll meet you at the hangar. See you then, Morris", the voice trailed off.

The Director hung up and went down to the garage. He waited patiently while the officer on duty went to get his car, and when the dark green BMW came up to the ramp and parked, he took over the wheel and drove on alone through the exit, into the cool spring dusk. Five minutes later he crossed over into Québec on the Champlain Bridge and turned north-east onto the Gatineau parkway. There was little traffic, and the drive was restful. Beyond the village of Chelsea, he turned onto a side road and drove higher into the hills. Beech and maple trees thickened steadily, the number of cottages and farmhouses dwindled, and the stars came out in full force. Forty minutes from the city he pulled into a gravel-topped lane. He paused, letting the engine idle while he pressed the electronic key in his dashboard. It beeped, flashed green, and the black wrought-iron gate swung open. He drove through, and the gate clanged shut behind him. He rolled down the window, and night air scented with damp humus and leaf mold wafted in. The white flags of trillium flowers carpeting the woods reflected his headlights on either side. He kept the speed at ten kilometers per hour, enjoy-ing the soft crunch of fine gravel under the tires, the sensations of anticipation, relief, and the gradual approach of privacy.

The cottage was an old stone country house, two stories high, nested between towering pines on the shore of a lake that had been gouged by glaciers from the rock of the Precambrian shield. There were no other dwellings around the lake, for it was a government preserve. His main residence was a double condo-minium in the city, in the enclave of Rockcliffe Park. It was on the fourth floor of a large warren designed for high-level civil servants; it overlooked a park, was soundproof and luxurious, and very, very secure. But it offered not a single element of that mystique that even the Director recognized as true home.

There were no servants at the cottage. There never were. In fact only a few people knew of its existence, and they had not been invited to visit on a social level. The Minister and Suzette Lemieux were the only people who possessed the cottage's un-listed telephone number. As far as he could tell, not even the R.C.M.P. special services or the loyalty checkers at OIS had ever penetrated its interior—he had personally installed devices that would record such incidents and in the ensuing years had detected not a single intervention. Only once had there been a break-in, and that by a rather confused black squirrel that had come down the chimney. The other incident involved a party of drunken teenagers who had stumbled upon the lake, but their attempt to break into the house was unsuccessful and had been easily handled by the local police.

He checked the instruments now and, as usual, found that nothing had registered. Their sensitivity was such that if a spider crossed the living room carpet, the video cameras would automatically switch on and record its criminal activity. A bird hitting the picture window overlooking the bay would prompt a similar recording on the deck, accompanied by the flashing of lights and a siren that would turn off only after it had radiated the house and grounds with sonic bombardment. Other instruments recorded door and window entries. When he entered his code into the front door console, it opened to him with electronic politesse. He went in, accessed the security panel by the coat rack, and turned off the interior surveillance equipment.

Despite these measures, the cottage was a marvel of homeyness. The smell of old birch smoke lingered in the wood-panelled entry hall, the handwoven rag rugs on the bare oak floors welcomed, the log-cabin quilt on the wall reassured. A grandfather clock ticked down the passageway. He lit two kerosene lamps that stood on the antique buffet, one with a rose-colored base, the other of pale amethyst. Their translucent white chimneys glowed, illuminating their hand-painted flowers from within. He put on his slippers and carried the amethyst lamp into the kitchen, padding softly across the red brick floor, checked the refrigerator and found cold cuts and rye bread. He made a salad, spiced with sweet basil and garlic. He lit a fire in the ancient wood stove and stood by it warming his hands. These and other movements of rustic charm acted upon him as a balm.

He lit a candle on the dining room table, set out the Delft blue plate and silver cutlery, a crystal tumbler for spring water, a wine glass, and a cruet of French burgundy. He sat and consumed the meal slowly, savoring it, savoring above all the silence—no city bustle, no muted scurry of office staff, no hum of fluorescent lights, no timetable, no crises, no background tension of phones and computer communications poised to distract him at any and every moment.

The nation could take care of itself for one night, he decided.

After supper he listened to a CD recording of Samuel Barber's *Adagio for Strings*, and when it was finished he went outside onto the front deck. He sat on the railing that hung over the water, listened to loons throbbing their romantic insights from one to another, and watched a large silver moon rise. It was a moment of pure happiness. It was perfection.

Later, he went in, undressed, and sat for ten minutes in his whirlpool bath. His doctor had warned him that his blood pressure was a little high and that he should give himself no more than that.

You're in excellent condition, Maurice, he had said. *You're almost an octogenarian, and you have the health of a man in his early sixties. Remarkable, really. But you shouldn't push your luck.*

Maurice did not believe in pushing his luck. A lifetime devoted to avoiding excess had left him with a young mind and a body that performed as if it were just cresting the mellow strengths of late middle age. Yes, really quite remarkable.

He dressed in silk pajamas and robe and went into the den. There he lit the kindling in the fireplace, put a birch log on top of it, and settled himself in a wing-backed armchair upholstered in rose tapestry. The reading lamp beside him cast a warm glow throughout the room. He glanced around, enjoying each item of decoration—the maple bookshelves, the brass chime clock on the mantle, the original eighteenth-century oil of racing horses, the A. Y. Jackson landscape of a Laurentian farm in winter, the amber and garnet Persian carpet.

He put on his spectacles and opened a hardcover book—*The Enemy Within*. It was a Larry Bond mystery novel, a techno-thriller that Suzette Lemieux had given him at Christmas. He had not yet read the author, but the reviews were raving about him. He liked P. D. James and John Grisham well enough, but LeCarré was his favorite, because of the sophistication of his portrayal of convoluted British espionage and the sense of classical intelligence, in both senses of the word. He was not so fond of the inscrutable Len Deighton, author of *The Ipcress File*, which he felt was unnecessarily obscure. Tom Clancy was good, though his CIA character Jack Ryan was a little too much the all-American boy scout. Agatha Christie's tales he considered well done but womanish. G. K. Chesterton's Father Brown mysteries he loathed for philosophical reasons.

He read for an hour and enjoyed the book, but his attention began to wander after the chimes struck ten o'clock. The face of Nathaniel Delaney surfaced in his consciousness, and try as he might, he could not banish it to the archive of completed cases. He supposed that this was so because the man's children were still fugitives and because in that sense the case was not complete.

For the thousandth time he berated himself for the little experiment he had tried four months earlier—the telephone call he had made to Delaney, informing him that he and his children were about to be arrested. Why had he done it? A whim? No, he was not the sort of man who acted upon whims. Perhaps he had desired a fisherman's pleasure, observing a trout run with a hook in its mouth, believing itself free until the moment he chose to flick a switch on his casting reel and pull it in. Had he done it from sheer cruelty? No, he was not a cruel man. Had it been an irrational impulse? No, he was not an impulsive man. Most likely it had been motivated by curiosity, closer to scientific than to morbid, a desire to observe what a little man would do in a moment of panic, how the fugitive would scuttle along his escape route while Maurice observed it from a great height.

There had been, of course, an emotional factor. When the Prime Minister and the select committee on national security made the decision to arrest the few remaining dissident journalists, Maurice had had no objections. He knew that there would be little or no outcry from the public because the arrests would be covert. If by chance there were leaks and the media became involved, the arrests would be justified under the hate-literature laws, and any embarrassment to the government would be easily dispersed by the confusion created by disinformation. Even so, when he saw the name of Nathaniel Delaney among the names on the list, he had experienced a moment of emotional conflict.

Too many months had passed for him to untie the knot of his obscure motivation. That was now beside the point. The important fact was that, for whatever reason (a moment of ambiguity or weakness or some cause hidden in his subconscious), he had contacted a man sought by the Department of Justice and warned him to flee.

During that first and final conversation, Delaney had accused him of being a split personality.

"I thought you worked for them. Why are you telling me this?"

"Because the problem interests me."

"Which problem, precisely?"

"The dialogue between individual freedom and social order."

"Oh, I see. Tell me, then, if you are so interested in freedom, why you think it's perfectly all right to suppress civil rights in this country."

"I don't have time to argue that with you. More to the point, *you* don't have time. It's enough for you to know that unless you act now and go immediately to a safe place, you and your children will cease to be citizens."

"Come on, Maurice, this is too schizoid! What game are you playing? Are you some kind of virtuous mole who burrowed under a tyrant's skin or a bad guy who's having second thoughts?"

"I am neither."

"Then what are you? What the hell are you!?"

"What am I? I am a man who is trying to save your life and the lives of your children."

"But what for? You and your friends are trying to destroy everything that makes it worthwhile living."

"I didn't start out this way", he said in a low voice.

"I don't buy it. I think you're lying."

"No, I am not lying. This is real."

"You're trying to spook me, make me run!"

"If only it were that simple. Listen to me, listen, you fool. I'm telling you with absolute certainty that unless you take your children immediately and go, there is nothing that will prevent you from disappearing indefinitely into civilian internment camps or other subterranean government mazes. Do you understand me?"

Delaney said nothing.

"Understand this also", Maurice went on in a voice as cold and hard as iron. "Make absolutely sure that you do not, under any circumstances, mention my name or this conversation to anyone."

"Why not?"

At which point Maurice had hung up the phone.

Delaney had run, as Maurice knew he would. But unfortunately he had involved others in his dramatic little escape, and there was now no way of telling if he had infected them with the information—with the virus of Maurice's name.

That telephone call had been a mistake, he now realized. He had not carefully weighed the factors in the situation, but that was because he had been new to this work, had been the

333

director for only a few months before the plan was unveiled to him.

Had it been a test of the parameters of his own power? He wasn't sure now and couldn't remember. Perhaps it had been no more than an intricate chess maneuver, a private game that he had used to assure himself that he was not entirely owned by those above him in the hierarchy of the nation. For the time being he was subject to them, but he was rising, he knew, and he would continue to rise and rise. Soon, he would be above everyone in this miserable corner of the world, and he would walk beside the truly great, the ones who even now were moving into position across the planet. One day, in the not too distant future, they would sit together on decks hanging over the Riviera and discuss the hidden shape of the universe. When he was among the élite at last, he would learn his own true name and would know what he was for. He would come into the more perfect knowledge of his destiny, a destiny that had been ordained from before the foundations of time.

His star was rising. But Delaney as an individual was a closed document. A memory, a notation in a secret file. He regretted the necessity of terminating him.

* * *

The prisoner was stripped, and his body inspected. He was issued a gray cotton jumpsuit. A plastic identification bracelet was clamped around his left wrist. His name was not printed on it—only a bar code.

"My name is Nathaniel Delaney", he said to himself. Then he repeated it loudly to the police escorts. They ignored him.

His belongings were placed in a box that was then locked and sealed. Within minutes he was going through the night under armed guard, flying in one of the new helicopters. It was difficult to resist the thrill of it. Zöe would have called it *a real adventure*. He took pleasure in the lights of villages and lonely farms below him, though he became frightened as the helicopter approached the airport of a city. Upon landing he noticed a jet aircraft parked on the edge of the runway. Like the helicopter, it was gray and emblazoned with the green insignia of the OIS.

He was taken by car to the regional headquarters of the agency, and there he was placed in a cell in an isolation wing. He was fed a good meal, and the official who admitted him suggested that he try to sleep, because he would be formally interrogated in the morning. But he could not sleep and requested that the guard leave the lights on. He felt somewhat reassured by the respectful manner in which he had been handled since his arrest. His cell was well lit and comfortable. It contained a plain desk, chair, bed with a foam mattress, sheets, pillow, a wool blanket. A toilet alcove. The entrance to the cell was simply a door. When he rapped on its surface, he found that it was made of vinyl-covered metal and that it was locked. The walls were painted white, the ceiling was twelve feet high, and the entire room was lit by recessed lighting covered with steel mesh. There were no windows.

He sat at the desk and prepared numerous speeches of defense in his mind. He was pleased with his words and thought that they could not help but improve his situation. The authorities would see immediately that he was an upright fellow and no psychopath. His difficulty, if one could call it that, was political and not criminal. In time, he knew, they would release him, because there really was no evidence, and there were no witnesses. Furthermore, he was innocent.

He guessed that it was between one and two o'clock in the morning when a man entered. It was Maurice L'Oraison.

"I hope they're treating you well", he said pleasantly.

"Yes, just fine. When are you going to release me?"

He indicated that Nathaniel should sit on the bed and took for himself the chair behind the desk.

"You know very well that you can't be released until the legal process is completed. Even I can't waive that."

"What exactly are you?

"I am the director of internal security for the nation."

"Which means?"

"It means that I'm second to the Minister himself, and he, of course, is under the office of the Prime Minister."

"So, you're number three in the country. Congratulations, Maurice. By the way, can you show me to the nearest phone booth? I'd like to call a lawyer."

"I'm afraid that's not possible."

"I see. Just exactly what is this legal process we're going to try to complete tomorrow morning?"

"It will begin tomorrow. Eventually, there will be a trial by a panel of judges. You will be free to make any statements you wish, and they will be kept in the data bank."

"Not that anyone will ever see those records, right?"

"Some day, in another century perhaps, when historians are trying to assess what happened here."

"That's not very consoling."

"You can take some comfort in the fact that you're being treated fairly. There is law in this country and—"

"A boy is dead, Maurice. What exactly was he guilty of?"

"He fired upon a State agent with a dangerous weapon. Under the new statutes—"

"To hell with your new statutes. A boy is dead. A damn fine boy, too."

"That is regrettable. One can't always control decisions made under extreme pressure. The enforcement agents are, like you and me, quite human. But they are dedicated to preserving the new order, for the good of the people. One foolish boy with a gun cannot be permitted to run amok in a sane society."

"Maurice, let's pursue this question a bit, if you will. That boy was quite sane, if a little hasty. He panicked after your very human agent fired high-caliber machine-gun rounds at children."

"The agent was simply trying to bring you to a halt in order to take you into custody. No harm was intended. But if it's any satisfaction to you, the man involved has been reprimanded, and he will be facing an inquiry."

"Thanks, that's a great comfort!"

The Director did not reply to the sarcasm. He pushed his glasses up on his brow and rubbed his eyes wearily. He stared at the surface of the desk as if lost in thought. There was no trace of emotion on his face. Nathaniel observed him carefully, trying to assess the nature of the man. He must be more than seventy years old now, but he appeared to be several years younger. His skin was clear. His skull was bald except for two white fringes on either side. He was scented with an expensive cologne and was dressed in a suit of very fine quality. He carried his frame with dignity. The impression he created was one of immense calm and authority. The eyes were thoughtful, even kindly, though their color was a cool gray. His voice was cultured, measured, low-key. He resembled nothing more than an aging barrister or perhaps a retired professor of philology.

"Since your arrest, have you spoken to anyone about our conversation of four days ago?"

"No."

"Before that, did you mention my involvement with your attempted escape? To anyone?"

"No. No one."

The Director was an astute judge of men and saw that Nathaniel was not lying.

"What's going to happen to me? I want to make some statements."

"Anything you wish to declare will be filed in the data bank under a computer code-lock."

"Tom Swift and his ultrasonic cyclotronic data bank!"

"I warn you, any mention of my involvement should not be part of your trial, and I suggest you do not refer to it during the preliminary hearings."

"Why not?"

"Believe me when I say that it wouldn't help your situation in the least. It would ensure that you disappear forever into the labyrinth of the corrections system."

Something in the other's wording recalled Nathaniel to their first telephone conversation. He suddenly remembered the warning Maurice L'Oraison had given him. He was now grateful that he had not mentioned his name to anyone and hoped that the young R.C.M.P. corporal had not yet found the journal of his escape—the *Plague Journal*. If he had read it and was imprudent enough to let someone in authority know about it, it might cause him some problems, because it endangered Maurice. Though it seemed unlikely that the thoughtful, intelligent man seated before him was capable of anything draconian.

"You should sleep now", said the Director. "It will be a long day for you tomorrow."

"The condemned man had a good night's rest before torture!"

"Nothing of the sort. We are not monsters. You will be meeting with a series of State investigators and psychologists. You will have a government appointed lawyer. You will be meeting with him also, after breakfast. I suggest that you shut down that rather fertile imagination of yours!"

Nathaniel, despite himself, laughed shortly. "I see", he said. "Just some routine bureaucracy, and I'm a free man. Wonderful! It's always great to see the civil service chewing up paper like the busy little Canadian beavers they are."

Maurice ignored it. "There is a pattern to the psychology of detention", he intoned. "Fear, rage, defense mechanisms. It's really quite useless. By morning you will be very unhappy, and then we must try to converse with a frightened, exhausted

338

man. We have found that a mild sedative helps to relax the muscles and makes sleep possible. You will be thanking me for it tomorrow."

The Director smiled for the first time, a grandfather cajoling a truculent child.

Nathaniel assumed a cold, frightened, and defensive expression.

"No, thank you."

"Come, come, it's not poison."

He removed a plastic pill case from the inside pocket of his jacket and shook two small red tablets onto the palm of his hand. From a recessed wall faucet he poured water into a paper cup.

"Here", he said. "These are mine. I take them myself when I'm travelling in different time zones, when I get overworked and beyond sleep. They're quite safe."

Nathaniel took the pills, placed them on his tongue uneasily, and drank the water.

"This isn't what I expected", he said after a few minutes. "I thought it would be like the Lubyanka or Auschwitz."

"As I said, we are not monsters."

Nathaniel's tension was quickly draining away. The Director watched him.

"We can talk a short while longer, then I must go. Lie back on the bed if you wish."

Nathaniel did so. He was very tired. His lips were chapped and his face burning from the days of exposure. The desire to close his eyes became irresistible. His body did not wish to respond immediately to his commands, but that no longer mattered.

It's strong, he thought. But that did not matter either. He longed for the profound sleep of the exhausted. He was falling into warm, golden light. A beautiful white hart galloped into the snowfield of his imagination, stopped, tossed its antlers, and looked at him.

Then he felt the sting. He opened his eyes. The Director was seated beside the bed and injecting his arm with a hypodermic needle.

Nathaniel observed it carefully. It took much gathering of energy in order to form the words. Quiet, peaceful words:

"You're killing me."

The other shook his head.

"No."

"Yes. You needn't lie, Maurice. You're taking my life."

When the syringe was empty, the Director removed the needle and placed it on the table.

The two men looked into each other's eyes. The Director's face was expressionless. Nathaniel's was full of an emotion that was uncommon to him. It was the pity one feels when observing the anguish of a trapped animal. It was Maurice, he saw, who was that animal, not himself. Oh, yes, he was dying, he knew. But Maurice was the truly powerless creature.

He had often imagined moments like this. It had usually taken more horrific forms. The Director was right; he did have a fertile imagination. He had frequently wondered if his decision to take controversial stands in the public arena during a dangerous era might bring him to such a moment. He had never considered the possibility that the act would be committed by an old friend of his family, and in such a matter-of-fact manner.

"Do you remember once when I was in my twenties, you asked me to work for you at the provincial legislature?"

"You turned it down", said the Director tonelessly. "You wouldn't be where you are now if you had accepted."

"Wrong, Maurice. I'd be here. Except I'd be holding a needle and pumping it into some victim."

There was no reply. The other merely watched him.

A wave of cold iron swept upward from his stomach to his brain.

He reached out his arm and touched the other's sleeve. The Director stared at it but could not withdraw.

"I forgive you, Maurice."

"Don't say that!"

"I forgive you. I do forgive you."

Eventually the Director shook off the limp, cold hand. His face registered distaste.

He left the cell shortly after. He gave instructions to the officer of the guard to dispose of the body by cremation. In an upstairs office, he seated himself at a desk. He stared out a barred window for perhaps fifteen minutes without moving. He took a phone from his briefcase and tapped in code numbers that channelled the call through security.

It rang for a long time before a voice answered.

"Hello."

"This is the Director."

"Yes, I know, sir. Security told me you'd ring on this line. Sorry. I was asleep. I'm at home."

"I'm sorry to disturb you there. I wanted you to know that the situation has been resolved. The subject was apprehended a few hours ago. I have conducted an examination. His case has been terminated according to the provisions under section 97."

"I see, sir. I'll send a press release around to the media in the morning. Death while resisting arrest?"

"Yes. Fine. That will do."

"The other fugitives?"

"Nothing yet. A full-scale search and rescue is under way. There is some indication that the children have been abducted by a person or persons unknown."

"I hope they find them. These things can be messy."

"Yes. But I don't think it will take long."

"Do you wish me to convey any message to the Minister?"

"Yes. Would you call him at seven and advise him I'm departing within an hour. Please tell him to begin the meeting with the Prime Minister as scheduled at nine. If the traffic is light from the airport, I should be only a few minutes late."

"I'll tell him. Good night, then, sir."

"Good night."

The Director called downstairs for a car to take him to the airport.

The flight home was uneventful. He was the only passenger on board. He drank Turkish coffee. He read through several pressing reports. He slept until dawn and awoke refreshed. The sun was rising as the pilot banked the jet over the capital. The lines of commuter traffic below him were not heavy, and the hills in the distance were bathed in light. It would be a beautiful day.

* * *

Maurice L'Oraison removed his reading glasses, closed his eyes, and laid his head back. Delaney's last words floated in the air before him, an almost auditory hallucination:

"I forgive you."

Nathaniel Delaney, a verifiable enemy within, had forgiven him. So? What did forgiveness mean? It was no more than a final sentiment flung by a drowning man, a last testament from an old mythology. A little phrase. A *word*. When Maurice gave him the injection that had terminated that original error and assured the preservation of his role in the new world order, he knew that his own word was far more important, because it fostered a lasting benefit for mankind. Delaney's delusion was worth no more than the cries of the loons, perhaps less, for the natural world was balanced in perfect cycles of harmony, while Delaney's cult was a breeder of chaos.

It was regrettable; he had even tried to help Delaney escape, had not wanted it to end the way it did. He should have known that man's simplistic black-and-white morality would drive him to make all the wrong choices. He had brought it upon himself. Sociopathic forces were the antithesis of the order that was absolutely essential to the preservation of civilization. Delaney had suffered no physical pain; the psychological pain had been brief. It was merciful, really. He was unstable, dangerous, not only to himself and his children, but to the nation.

To take a life—an evil act? No, it had been an act committed in the interests of a higher good. For many years he had struggled with the vestigial conditioning of his childhood, the moralism and guilt, the conscience deformed by Catholic ideology, the endless nostrums produced by his ignorant, pious father and the crude jests of his not so ignorant stepmother, that fabulous griffin, Madame Turid L'Oraison, formerly Gunderberg, town hosteler and part-time concubine.

Maurice L'Oraison laughed.

What an obscure beginning! How ironic that a man such as he, a man from the lowest class in the nation, surrounded by fanatics, failures, and gnomes, reared in a liturgical feast of fools, should reach the heights of maximum influence. It had taken years to shed the indoctrination of his childhood. The 1990 trip to Russia had been a major turning point. There, in a deluxe Intourist hotel, surrounded by two hundred mystic Americans and a few prosaic Canadians, including the Member of Parliament who had invited him, he had opened his mind to the vision of the Spirit Masters. Neither the sensuous strumming of balalaikas nor the snickering of the vodka-soaked waiters could diminish the profoundly moving inrush of knowledge. After a lifetime of rejecting the existence of anything outside the physical world, to discover that the transcendent did indeed exist was a shattering revelation. It had opened for him a world of divine perfection, populated by spirits who loved mankind and who desired above all to bring the reign of peace to this wounded planet. No more war, no more division and duality, no more doctrinal tyranny, no more guilt.

The San Francisco conference in 1995 had removed the last reservations. Titled *Toward a New Civilization: Launching a Global Initiative*, it had brought together the most powerful figures in the world, former heads of state, press czars, financiers, mystics, futurists, ecology-gurus, and think tankers from a wide spectrum of movements. Barbara, an American woman he had met during the Russian trip, was one of the summit speakers. She informed the gathering of four hundred members of the global élite that humanity was now ready for "conscious evolution" and a "fuller awareness of the larger planetary being".

Another friend, a former assistant secretary of the U.N., gave him one of Barbara's books, which he read with growing excitement on the return flight to Ottawa. He was stirred by her bold, courageous cry for definitive action, for a cleansing of the planet of all those forces that blocked the path to global harmony:

> Out of the full spectrum of human personality, one-fourth is electing to transcend, and one-fourth is destructive. In the past these destructive seeds were permitted to die a "natural death". Now as we approach the quantum shift from the creature-human to the co-creative human, from *Homo sapiens* to *Homo sapiens universalis*—the human who is an inheritor of godlike powers—the destructive one-fourth must be eliminated from the social body.

The following spring he attended the Colorado retreat at the invitation of another friend, the director of an international power corporation. There in a small hanging valley suspended in the Rocky Mountains, in a glass and stone conference hall filled with rarefied light, Maurice saw the full import of the Plan, its magnificence, its utter necessity.

Barbara had been there too. In a private moment, over avocado salad and papaya juice, he asked her what exactly she had meant by "elimination".

Her face radiating compassion and intensity, she replied: "The elimination of suffering."

He pressed for more details. She did not immediately reply, examining his eyes with a thoughtful expression, her surreal calm assuming visionary proportions.

"Each of us has a part to play, Maurice," she said gently, "and some of those parts demand extraordinary courage. You are not responsible for the purification. We are. We are in charge of God's selection process for this planet Earth. He selects, we destroy. We are the riders of the pale horse, Death."

For years he had believed that the human condition was in urgent need of reconfiguration and that this would demand a concerted effort to break the cycle of poverty and abuse. He had assumed that a process of education and the application of tactical pressures would bring it about. But at the Colorado summit he had begun to understand the need for direct intervention, a quantum leap, a cleansing. A higher form of man was coming into being, but the emergence of this new proto-human could no longer be delayed without risking the loss of everything. Old Western man must go the way of the Neanderthal, who had enjoyed his place in the sun, his moment in time, before being swept away by the superior Cro-Magnon, who in turn was replaced by early civilized man. Followed by industrial man, then technological man, who in turn must surge forward to the next stage of evolution with the assistance of everything learned from the past.

Maurice realized that there now opened before mankind a window in time and that the power that had been slowly maturing through millennia must either be seized or be lost for untold generations to come. If the gifted ones did not move swiftly, then all that had been won would collapse back into chaos, and the cycle of development and destruction, rise and fall, complexification and regression, would repeat itself endlessly through the ages. Like primitive life-forms swimming in the hot primal seas, surfacing from time to time, eyeing the unknown land, moving toward it, extending brave tendrils into its more solid dimension, humanity was now probing the shores of the unspeakably immense spiritual cosmos.

Maurice inhaled sharply and felt the tremors in the atmosphere that signalled the coming of the masters. The air vibrated, as if shot with electricity. He turned off the reading lamp and waited for his personal guide to come, easing his mind, breathing ritually, quickening to the thrill of his approach.

Then a being stood before him like a blade of black fire, visible in his consciousness as a laser of presence from beyond the known spectrum of light. The pleasure he derived from this presence had grown with the years, for it was a sign that the heights of human government were but the foothills of vast ranges of spiritual authority and that, as he merged with this authority, it would lead him higher until he was gathered in among them, and became one of them, and ruled with them.

It spoke to him in a language that was beyond all human tongues. It informed him of the danger presented by the little priest in the prison in British Columbia; it warned of a shaking in the high echelons and of a disturbance in the low. It reminded him of his vows and of the singularity of his role, of the rewards that were coming to him, of the power that was his by right of the magnitude of his character. Yet it reminded him of one higher than he, who would be a companion to him in the great company of reformers. This man was already upon the earth, and the elder showed him his face. Maurice recognized it, for though the Christ of this age was not yet revealed in his fullness, he was ascending rapidly in global affairs and was known by all men of influence.

There were many enemies, the elder showed him, and many forces that warred against the triumph of this man's mission. Death was release for these misguided ones, and to bring death to them in a humane manner was a deep mercy, for those who were removed from the earthly realm would receive instruction on another plane and would not resent his mercy. The elder showed him the face of Nathaniel Delaney, who was now dwelling in the sphere of noble warriors who had misunderstood their times. Delaney was thankful to Maurice, the elder revealed to him, for he understood everything now, regretted his rebellion, and wished to speed the work that on earth he had resisted.

For this illumination Maurice was grateful.

"And what of my role?" he whispered. "Why am I chosen?"

The elder replied with an image. There appeared to Maurice, in his inner eye, the form of a small village in the mountains. Snow was falling upon it in a winter that was too long. The valley was dark, the people dismal and coarse, the broken and the poor of humanity. He had been born as one of them, and if it had not been for the death of his mother, he would have remained content to stay in the lost valley and dwell in mediocrity. He saw himself as he might have been, a retired small-town lawyer, bent, bitter, shuffling to the post office in a snow storm, hoping for his pension check, a dweller of bungalows, an unclean bachelor, still writing the unpublishable poetry that had been the passion of his youth, measuring out his nightly dram of cheap whiskey, and obsessed with the last scraps of health; then dying of prostate cancer, laid out in a plywood coffin surrounded by ugly mourners who would soon forget him.

And now, to his surprise, Maurice heard the thoughts of the elder. For the first time in his life they came to him as more than images from beyond, took shape within him as actual words, spoken.

"You see", said the elder, "that her death was a release from the terrible squalor of your family. Your mother is happy now, and her passing provided the doubt that dislodged you from the stronghold of the Judeo-Christian god. From then on you turned away from the old and began to search for what is true. You left the valley and the small people and began to know the great. We led you step by step until your greatness was unfolded as from a chrysalis. Now you will go even higher. Now you will fly."

10

Life, Politics, Crime, and
Other Matters of Significance

When Alice M. Douglas went out on the town, she liked to go in style. She spent a long time on her hair, painted her fingernails red, and dug up the black polyester pant suit she had bought for Donnie's funeral. The big rhinestone heart that she inherited from her mother looked just perfect pinned beneath her throat. The bobbley-bangleys on her earlobes were a bit daring, but hey, they made a statement—hand-carved green and orange parakeets perched on wire hoops—a saucy touch, Caribbean, doing the tango at the Copacabana Club. Not that she'd ever been to any place like that, but a girl can dream.

She smeared some Mary Kay skin cream over her face, though it didn't make much difference: it couldn't eliminate jowls or the triple bags under her eyes or the little nodule growing on her chin. She should have the damn thing removed some day. It made her look like a witch.

She stared into the mirror, and after a minute's appraisal she grimaced. Her shoulders slumped.

"Oh, Queenie, you're a wreck", she scolded. Then she cackled: "Ha, ha, ha, Dorothy, I'm gonna steal your red shoes and kill your little dog, Toto!"

Alice smeared her cheeks with rouge. Bright pink lipstick. Then more rouge. With enough paint she could easily scuttle their cute little dream of getting her into religion.

"If you're gonna look cheap, you might as well go all the way", she said to the face in the mirror. "Painted lady!"

She put Nick and Arrow to bed, warning Arrow not to answer the door or the phone under any circumstances, short of the Palace burning down. If the Palace did burn down, Alice said, he was to call her at Bethie and Ted's place, the number was by the phone.

Arrow didn't tell her he had never learned to use a telephone.

"I'm outa here, you guys. Back in a few hours. Sure you won't be lonesome?"

"We'll be okay, Alice."

"I know you will, kid. You're a smart one. If Nick needs a bottle or a change, you think you can manage it?"

"Sure."

"I knew y'could."

She went out into the store and picked a vinyl shoulder bag from a shelf in the ladies' section. It was old but clean. She was peeling the price tag off when Beth pulled into the driveway and beeped. Alice went out, locking up.

Beth never looked better. Her robin's-egg blue dress did nice things with her eyes, and her salt-and-pepper hair was pinned back with zebra barrettes. She had some paint on too.

"Hey, girl, you're a knockout."

"Thanks, Alice. You look great yourself."

"You shouldn'ta got gussified just for me."

"You look kind of gussied up too."

"Well, even hags get tired of looking like hags. I figure, seeing as how you finally got me to your place, I shouldn't frighten the kids."

Beth laughed and made no comment.

"So what we gonna do? Drink Ted's beer and talk about the weather?"

"A bit more than that."

349

"Oh?"

Beth broke the speed limit all the way to Steelhead, where the car made a right turn and went into the shadows of a heavy forest of firs. Beth flicked on the headlights.

"It's turning into a fine summer", Alice prompted. "But there'll be frost tonight."

"Speaking of the weather, you mean?"

"Yeah."

Three miles farther on they pulled into the long lane of the Potters' farm and bounced over the ruts until they came into the clearing in front of the house. Alice noticed several cars and a herd of pickups parked by the barn.

"Hey, what's this? You said it was just a party for me and you guys."

Beth winced. "Oh, Alice, you're going to have to forgive me. I didn't plan this."

"Plan what?"

"It's sort of a last minute thing."

"What sort of thing? You got a bunch of fundies in there? You gonna try to pray over me?"

"Of course not!" Beth looked agonized. "It's just that the man who's running for the new coalition party came into town unexpectedly. Ted's on the riding association, you know, and the candidate asked him if he could get a bunch of people together tonight to meet him."

"So? You could have called me. I could have come another time."

"Alice, you know darn well it's taken us years to get you here. Do you think I want to risk waiting another few years?"

"You could have given me a choice in the matter."

"Yes, I suppose we should have. But really, I think you'll like these people. Don't you get tired of never seeing people?"

"I see people all day long."

"You know what I mean. Seeing them socially."

"I ain't social, and you know it."

Beth got out of the car. Alice stayed put in the passenger seat. She lit a cigarette.

"C'mon, Bethie, drive me home."

"Oh, Alice, please. I think you'll enjoy yourself."

"What! With all them fundies in there? By the end of the evening, I just know it, you're gonna strap me down and exercise me."

"You mean exorcise."

"Yeah, exercise! Hell, you'll need a big cage for all the devils that'll come rippin' and snortin' out of me. I know what you're up to. I seen *The Exercist*."

"*The Exorcist*", Beth corrected.

"Yeah, right. Now take me home."

Beth got back into the car, turned the ignition key, and sat there staring ahead, letting the motor idle.

"What are you waiting for?"

"This is ridiculous", Beth muttered.

"My sentiments exactly."

Then Beth did something that Alice had never seen. Bethie, sweet little Bethie, got mad. Turning to her guest, she said in her firmest, most severe, motherly and sisterly voice, "Alice M. Douglas, you are a selfish woman!"

Alice laughed.

"You got that right. Now take me home."

"I am not taking you home. You are marching into my house, right this minute, and you are going to be nice to those people, and you are going to enjoy yourself. Do you understand?"

Alice, genuinely amused, gave a belly laugh. "Wow, that's quite an act."

"It's not an act."

"Oh, really", said Alice sardonically, intrigued and delighted. "You push your husband around like that?"

351

"All the time."

"You get away with it?"

"Most of the time. He doesn't have anyplace else to go."

"Well, that's great. You're a lucky woman havin' a fine guy like that wrapped around your baby finger. But listen, girl, I got lots of places to go."

Beth looked at Alice coolly and said, "Actually, you don't."

Alice didn't like the sound of that. She lit another cigarette and blew some smoke toward Beth. She dragged on it a few times and fired it out the passenger window.

"Take me home."

"I really like you, Alice M. Douglas."

"Funny way of showing it. I said take me home."

"You're a great person."

"First you bully me, then you butter me up."

"Nothing of the sort. I like you very much. I think you're something very special, and I wish you'd trust me."

"I don't trust nobody, girl."

"I know, and that's why somebody needs to kidnap you."

"Wow, what an honor."

"I'm kidnapping you, see."

"I'm scared skinny. What a great terrorist you woulda made."

"You haven't seen anything yet."

"Ooh, scarier and scarier."

"You don't like yourself, Alice. Really, you don't love yourself very much."

Alice snorted.

"I love you."

"Yeah, *all* the boob-tube preachers say that."

"Maybe they do. Maybe some of them are phonies. But I'm not."

Alice demurred. "I guess you're not. But that doesn't mean you have any right to drag me off to a fancy dress ball with a bunch of people who'll take one look at me and figure me out pronto."

"The people in there aren't like that."

"Really? That'll be a first!"

"Will it?" Beth said irritably. "Well, maybe you're the judger. Maybe you're the most self-righteous bigot between here and Fort George."

Beth regretted it the moment it was out of her mouth. She rubbed her eyes and bowed her head.

Alice screwed up her face. Then she opened the car door and got out.

"All right", she growled. "Let's get it over with."

Ted came out the front door just as Alice and Beth were going up the steps.

"Hi, Alice. Beth, what took you so long?"

Beth patted his arm and gave him an enigmatic smile. "We were talking."

"Girl talk", Alice grumbled.

"Everybody here?" Beth asked.

"Yup", said Ted. "Thank heavens you're back. It's kind of stiff in there. Go in and loosen things up, would you?"

"Okay. I'll do what I can. Kids in bed?"

"I said Noah and Janie could stay up till nine. They're trying to make themselves invisible."

Beth went ahead into the living room, while Ted found a hanger for Alice's sweater.

"What you mean stiff?" she asked him. "Aren't you all in cahoots?"

"Wish we were. There's people from different churches, and a few lone rangers, plus the candidate and his wife. They're all making horrible small talk to each other. Wish me luck."

"Better still, break open a case of that spruce beer, willya?"

"Later, Alice, later."

The large living room was crowded with about twenty-five

people, ordinary-looking farmers and shopkeepers for the most part. They occupied the easy chairs and folding chairs; a few individuals sat on cushions on the floor. The candidate, a man in his sixties with a pretty, silver-haired wife beside him, was parked uneasily on the stone ledge of the cold fireplace, making conversation with a minister of religion who sat on a straight chair to his left. The minister—pastor of the Lutheran church on Seventh Avenue in Fort George—wore a brown clerical shirt, Roman collar, and a blue blazer. The candidate looked nervous, the minister a paragon of public cheeriness. Alice was introduced all around, and no one seemed unduly alarmed by her presence. She recognized a few, because she filled their gas tanks from time to time.

The bulk of them, she supposed, were fundies. The Pentecostal minister and his wife were there, and the minister from Salvation Tabernacle (the Potters' pastor), plus a Catholic priest. He was introduced as Father Ron from Saint George's. He shook her hand and then returned to a private discussion he was having with a teenager—an oriental kid. The boy was translating for another oriental, a woman who gave Alice a dazzling smile and glanced shyly away—a Chinese lady in blue pajamas. She began to relax after that, relieved that she wasn't the only exotic person in the room. Beth made her sit down on the remaining vacant seat, the middle of the couch, where she tried unsuccessfully not to touch elbows with a very old woman who was the mother of Canon Briggs-Smythe (the Anglican minister) and a young man she recognized as the R.C.M.P. constable who handed out missing kid posters.

"Hi, handsome", she said, poking him in the ribs.

"Evening, Miss Douglas", he replied. He was dressed in civvies, but you couldn't wipe the cop off him. Different from the gray and greens, she noted. A nice cop, a good guy.

There was a teenage girl stretched out on the rug with her foot in a cast—Janie. Another of the Potter kids, Noah, squatted cross-legged by Father Ron, listening intently to the Chinese boy explain why his basketball team was going to win the cup from the high school across the river.

Ted stood up in the middle and cleared his throat. "Ahem, everybody."

The scattered conversations ground to a halt.

"It's really great you could be here on such short notice. Any more of you, and we'd have to move out to the barn."

"That's just what we'll do next meeting", said the Lutheran minister. People chuckled appreciatively, and the atmosphere thawed.

"Before I introduce our candidate, I'd just like to say that it really is moving for me and Beth to have you all come to a gathering like this. When you think that just a few short years ago it would have been hard . . . well, how shall I put it . . . *impossible* to get people of different denominations talking with each other, I'd say we're pretty blessed."

"It's that beer of yours we've all been hearing about", said the Anglican minister in a thick English accent. Almost everybody laughed outright at that, though a few looked uncomfortable.

"I'm sorry to say this is a dry party, folks", Beth interjected. "But anyone who's interested can come back for a sip another time."

That thawed things out some more.

"The times we're living in are getting pretty bad", Ted went on. "Those of us who have families know it, because we're the first to feel it when the government decides it's going for control. Most of the people in this country still think we need to build a society on family values. But the media and the kind of people who get into power aren't much interested in what we think. That's why we need a party to be our voice in Parliament. Without further ado, I'd like to introduce a man who has laid his future on the line for that purpose. He's a retired high-school teacher, the author of some of the better articles you read in our local rag, and a member of the Abbotsford Evangelical Free Church. He's a family man with six kids—is that right, Ed, six?"

"That's right, Ted, six. Plus eight grandchildren", the candidate smiled.

"I give you the next M.P. for Fort George-Dewdney, Mr. Ed Burgess!"

Applause all round.

The candidate stood, straightened his tie, and removed his glasses.

"I'm not warming a bench in the Commons yet", he began, earning some points for humor. "We have a tough uphill battle ahead of us, if we hope to get there. But I think we can do it. I know we can do it."

Speaking slowly and concisely, without a prepared speech, he described the gradual erosion of family rights that had occurred during the previous two decades, the rise of a new class of social "rehabilitators", and, most worrisome of all, the appearance of precedent-setting legislation that seemed headed toward the creation of a completely amoral society.

He spoke at length, without interruption. People generally felt that he was a smart man, principled, and determined. But he stumbled over his words at times, and his eyes seemed too kind, lacking confidence. The gentleness of his voice also gave them pause, and each of the listeners wondered if he would be capable of force on the hustings, and even (if the impossible should come to pass) in Parliament. But they admired his courage.

At the end of the talk, Ted and Beth applauded loudly, and the rest of the group followed suit.

"Thanks, Ed", said Beth. "We're going to have a coffee break right now, and then we'll come back for a question period and discussion. Goodies are in the dining room. Serve yourselves, everyone."

The men congregated around Ed Burgess and began to congratulate, comment, negotiate, make suggestions, and get acquainted. The women, understanding a different language, went off to the dining room. Alice saw her opportunity and bolted for the front door.

The stars were out in full force, as were the mosquitoes, but she didn't mind. She lit a cigarette and dragged desperately at it.

The door opened behind her, and someone else came out onto the dark porch.

Whoever it was lit his own cigarette and sucked on it eagerly. Puff, puff, puff—she recognized the pace.

"Hi, buddy. You dying for a smoke too?" she jabbed him in the ribs with the conspiratorial humor of the addicted.

"Am I ever", said a male voice.

"Here we are behind the high school at lunchtime."

"Isn't it too true. Is that you, Miss Douglas?"

"Ain't no other. Who're you?"

"Father Ron. Hi."

"Hi."

"I don't like to smoke in front of the young people", the priest said.

"That never stopped me."

"Well, I try to set a good example. It's a filthy habit."

"Ain't it though."

"It's my only vice. Don't betray my secret?"

"Don't worry, I won't squeal. We all got our little secrets."

"Thanks. What do you think of the speaker?"

"I s'pose he's okay."

"I thought he was great. He has convictions."

"Yeah? Good for him."

The door opened suddenly behind them, and light from the hallway spilled out. Father Ron threw his cigarette into the garden.

"Faddah Ron, Faddah Ron, you out here?"

357

"Uh, yes."

Father Ron unwrapped some chewing gum hastily and stuffed it into his mouth.

"Mum asked me where you go. She want us to talk with the lady in black."

"The lady in black is right here", said Alice, lighting another cigarette.

The boy looked back and forth between the priest and Alice. Father Ron chewed furiously on a mouthful of gum.

"Tell her I'll be there in a minute, Théophane."

"Okay", the boy said, looking whimsical. After a thoughtful pause, he said, "Faddah, you smoke?"

"Uh, yes, Théophane, I do sometimes."

Alice laughed shortly. The boy bobbed his head and smiled.

"Okay, see you in a minute, Faddah."

The priest sighed. "Well, if he had any illusions about my character, they're gone now."

"Huh? You mean cadging a smoke? That's nothing! Them Chinese people are used to opium smokers, aren't they?"

"They're not Chinese, they're Vietnamese. Excellent people. They would disapprove of opium. I'm not sure what they think of tobacco."

"I could tell the kid thought it was kind of funny, catching you like that."

"I don't think it's funny."

"No? You some kind of saint?"

"I'd like to be, Miss Douglas, I'd like to be. But my friends are real saints. They've had some trouble adapting to this country. They've seen a lot of evil in their lives, and I think they shouldn't be disappointed by simply everyone."

"Oh, come on! You're human."

"Absolutely."

"If they've seen real evil, pal, smokin' ain't gonna fizz on them a bit."

"I guess you're right", he said ruefully. "It's all that anti-smoking propaganda that makes a person feel guilty."

Alice laughed. "The eleventh commandment: Thou shalt not smoke!"

He chuckled.

"You should mellow out, buddy. *Don't worry, be happy*, like the song says."

"Thanks for the advice. I'd better go in now. You want to meet them?"

"Not really, but what the hell—"

The social arrangements inside the house had altered somewhat. The men were now in the kitchen; the women were having a famous time getting to know each other around the coffee urn in the dining room. Alice made a side trip through there and scooped up three date squares, a nanaimo bar, and a cranberry tart. Balancing a cup of coffee in one hand and the plate of goodies in the other, she made her way back to the living room. It was deserted except for the misfits.

The old Anglican lady, Father Ron, and the two Vietnamese were sitting together without talking.

Great, Alice thought. *Just my luck. This should be exciting.*

The old Anglican lady was staring at the rug, resigning herself to the stupor of the abandoned. Father Ron stared at the walls, examining the framed Bible quotes and a print of a sentimental nineteenth-century Jesus with purple lips and feminine features. The Vietnamese lady watched Alice approach, her small olive face poised and expectant, like that of a friendly vole. She was as small as a twelve-year-old girl, perched on the edge of an easy chair, her bare toes dangling a few inches off the rug. The boy sat beside her sporting an optimistic look, ready to interpret.

Alice sat down on the couch at right angles to them and began to tear into the goodies.

"My mum is glad you come here", the boy said.

"Oh, thanks. Me too. Nice to meet you people."

"Nice to meet you too, Missus."

"I'm a Miss, not a Missus."

"I am so sorry. Not very smart men don't want to marry you?" he said politely.

Alice choked, and exhaled crumbs.

"Hey, you got real nice manners", she said archly.

"Thank you", the boy replied, smiling.

When the mother and son withdrew into an animated conversation in their own tongue, Father Ron turned to Alice and said in a lowered voice, "Miss Douglas, I think there's a language barrier here. He meant to say that you're well worth marrying, and—"

"Hell, I know what he said. The laddie was just being nice. I can read these people fine."

"Manners are very important to them", Father Ron explained.

"I noticed."

"It's respect. We have a lot to learn from them."

"Oh, yeah?" she snorted. "Well I've met lots of nice-mannered people who'd slit your throat for a nickel. Phony through and through."

"These people aren't phony", Father Ron replied with a hint of severity. "Not at all."

"Okay, okay, don't get your shirt in a knot."

Alice reached over and shook hands with Théophane's mother.

"I'm Alice. Shake a paw."

"My mum's name is Thérèse", said the boy.

"Glad t'meet you, Treece."

Alice took a gulp of coffee. The woman looked at her son and fired a rocket of sentences at him.

"My mum say, she glad you not go back home tonight. She glad you listen to Mrs. Potter."

"Oh, did Bethie tell you about our little fight?"

"Fight? No, mum see it."

"I doubt it. What's she trying to say, anyway?"

"She just saying she glad to meet you."

More Vietnamese was exchanged.

"She say you a brave lady, and God is watching over you."

"Tell him thanks for me. I need watching in a big way."

"My mum is not understanding something. She say, when you come in here, she see a cloud over your head with lightning coming out of it. Then she see a bow and arrow."

Alice shook her head and wiped crumbs off her lap.

"Tell your ma I don't know where she gets her ideas, but I ain't got a bow and arrow."

The boy translated into Vietnamese.

Thérèse nodded, then looked back directly into Alice's eyes. Alice dropped her eyes, studied her plate, and went to work on the nanaimo bar. She felt uncomfortable.

"My mum say she sorry, maybe she didn't understand the picture from God. She see an arrow and a baby in a box."

Alice's heart did a flip-flop. *An arrow and a baby in a box?*

Alice, who spent a great deal of her life between the covers of cheap mysteries, knew a clue when she saw one. And if this was a real clue, then it was part of one whopping great Mystery— the kind that she'd rather not read.

Coincidence, she told herself. *Just a coincidence. Means nothin'.*

"Please don't think my mum's crazy. She's not crazy."

"Oh, I can tell that", said Alice sagely, not looking at him. "She's a real good person, your mum."

"Thank you", Théophane nodded modestly.

"But I ain't got no baby in a box."

Théophane tilted his head thoughtfully. "Ah, maybe we not understand it too good. You forget it."

"Okay, it's forgotten."

Father Ron, who had been following this exchange with a growing sense of puzzlement, stood and asked Thérèse if she would like some coffee.

"Tea, please, for her", Théophane replied, smiling broadly. The priest went out, and in the vacuum created by his absence, everyone reverted to silence. Eventually Thérèse sat up straight and said something else in Vietnamese. Then she watched Alice while her son translated.

"My mum say you not be afraid. God cover you and two babies."

Thérèse nodded up and down repeatedly. Alice stared back at her. But nothing more could be said because the jolly voters were crowding into the living room. Alice hardly heard a thing during the next hour. When it was over and most of the people had gone, except, of course, the misfits, she went to get her sweater from the hall closet. Finding her way like a sleepwalker, she hoped she wouldn't have any more nice little chats with the Vietnamese. She needn't have worried, however, because they passed her, bowing and smiling, without delivering extra messages from the outer limits. She waited on the porch for Beth to take her home and watched the teenage boy drive off with his mother.

Weird, she said, lighting a cigarette, *Real weird*.

Beth stepped outside with Father Ron.

"There's so much to clean up here, Alice, I really shouldn't leave it all to Ted. Reverend Ron could drop you off on his way back. Do you mind?"

"Do I mind? Hell, no, he's the only other smoker in the place."

Father Ron said, "Good night, Mrs. Potter. Thanks so much for asking me. I'll do what I can with my congregation. They'll need a little waking up, I expect."

"As do we all, Reverend. God bless you."

"God bless you too."

"God bless, Alice. See you soon", said Beth.

"Yeah, thanks for the great time. It was a hoot."

"Hope it wasn't too painful."

"Not too much. Next time crack open the booze, and you might just get me back."

"It's a deal."

"I'll second that", said Father Ron.

Bumping down the Potters' driveway in the priest's beat-up Volvo, Alice turned to him and said, "Your only remaining vice, huh? Sounds to me like you get into the suds too."

"Rarely. But it's permissible in my religion. All things in moderation—"

"I could get used to your religion."

"Don't try coming in for the fringe benefits."

"What's wrong with that?"

"Your second state would be seven times worse than your former."

"Huh? That's over my head. So, tell me, what do you folks think you can do with all this running around organizing yourselves into a party?"

"I don't know if we'll achieve anything, but we have to try."

Alice shrugged.

"Don't you think we should at least try?" he prodded.

"Go ahead and try. Me, I leave Life, Politics, Crime, and other matters of importance to you smart fellers."

"That's what my parishioners think too", he said. "That's why things are in such a mess."

She offered him a cigarette, and he took it. "You smoke too much", she said in a motherly tone, mimicking Beth.

"I know", he said gravely. "It's a filthy habit."

She took a few puffs to work up her gumption and asked him the million-dollar question: "You a preevert?"

"What?" he said.

"You know. Preeverts. All them priests going to jail."

He groaned. "The answer to that question, Madam, is no, I am not."

"Oh. Good."

363

"And 99 percent of my fellow priests aren't either", he said in a low tone, with anger quivering just below the surface.

She could tell he was mad at her.

"Do you just swallow everything you hear?" he said in a deceptively quiet voice.

"Hell, no!"

"Do you know what it's like being a priest these days?"

"Sure I do."

"I don't think you could begin to guess what it's like."

"So, tell me."

"You don't even want to know", he said bitterly.

"I'm all ears."

"Try imagining this, lady: you give your life away, at considerable sacrifice, and all you get for it is some stranger asking you if you're a *pree-vert!*"

"Look, I'm sorry. I don't mean nothing by it."

"Of course you meant something by it", he replied nicely. "Of course you did."

"I said I'm sorry."

"It's a sad state of affairs when a man's whole life is automatically suspect because he isn't married. I don't know a single priest who'd get into an elevator alone with a child these days. You hardly dare pat their heads for fear of a legal suit. All my brother priests feel the same."

"Don't blame me for that."

"I don't blame you, but maybe you could try to be a bit more sensitive."

"I ain't sensitive."

"You're blunt, I'll say that for you. Sometimes I wonder if there are any honest people left."

"Aside from you'n'me, of course", Alice chortled.

"Sometimes bluntness is a good indication of an honest person. Other times it's just a symptom of a person who couldn't care less about anything but themselves."

"Hey, you're kinda blunt yourself."

"I've been a nice priest for twelve years. Since my ordination I've hardly made a single convert—just the people who would've signed up anyway. I'm a caretaker. I've been in agony watching my parishioners gulp down the big hype about abusive priests. My people give one hour a week to God and about forty hours to that idol in the corner of their living rooms. How come there's no big foofarah when a teacher or a social worker abuses a child? Where are the statistics on those guys, eh?"

"Calm down, buddy, calm down."

"Don't tell me to calm down, Miss Douglas. I've been calm all my life—lukewarm, you might call it. I'm sick of it. Maybe it's time to start calling a spade a spade."

"Who's stopping you?"

He thought about that. "Nobody, I guess."

"Right! Sock it to 'em, padre. Give 'em a rip-snorter. Hellfire and brimstone. Scare 'em into heaven."

"Don't mock things you don't understand", he said tensely.

"Blunter and blunter."

"Look, Alice—may I call you Alice?—if we had about twenty years to play around with, I could come to tea at your place and make a habit of it. I could try to cultivate your buried religious sense, and you might even take a shine to me, your pet priest, if and when you ever became convinced I'm a normal man. I could wheedle you into knitting doilies for our parish bazaar and gradually tell you about my faith, and then maybe, just maybe, you'd start to ask a few of the right questions; and maybe, just maybe, when you're about ninety-five years old, you'd be on your deathbed and ask the doctor to call good old Ronnie, and we'd have a lovely chat about eternity and life and other really significant matters; and maybe then, just maybe, you'd let me pray with you, and in the most extreme scenario imaginable you'd ask to become a Catholic and go to paradise."

"Hey, that's an offer I can't refuse."

"The point is, we don't have time."

"Oh? How come?"

"You may not have noticed, but we're in a battle zone. It's guerrilla warfare at the moment, but it's heating up fast. My people are no way prepared for it, and I'd guess that most of the other ministers at the Potters' tonight would say the same about their congregations."

"Prepared for what?"

"Well, I'm not sure, but I think we just might be in the end times. Hardly anybody can see what's happening."

"End times? Look, padre, I went through the Great Depression in a slum in Toronto. I can tell you a few things about end times."

"No, you can't. You don't get it, Alice. As I said, if I had twenty years to work on you, maybe you'd come around. But we don't have time. *You* don't have time."

She laughed and offered him another cigarette. "Have a reefer."

"Thanks." His hands were trembling. She lit both cigarettes and handed him one.

"Go on. This is fun."

"Christ is real, Alice. He's coming back, maybe before you can knit a doily. Until then we're in a war. There's a devil too, and he wants your hide nailed to his barn door."

"Great stuff. I like your style."

"Think about it."

"Okay, I'll think about it."

The remainder of the trip was completed in a cloud of smoke and silence. Father Ron pulled into the driveway of the Palace and parked. They finished their cigarettes, then Alice got out.

"Thanks a million. You're an okay guy."

"You're okay too, Alice. God bless."

"Sure. See you around."

She slammed the door in a friendly way, and a piece of rust fell off the Volvo. She liked the sound of a car door slamming in the dark on frosty nights—it reminded her of a dance hall in 1939, the night when soldier Nick taught her the jitterbug. The night they held hands till two in the morning, and he took her home to her mother's front door, where she had her first and last kiss, a soldier's kiss, smelling of Burmashave, promises, and tragedy.

When the priest's taillights had gone down the road, she sat on the porch steps and lit another cigarette. Poody-tat peeked around the corner, meowing, and stationed himself beside her. Together they contemplated the stars for a while. She told him about the crazy Chinese lady, the baby in a box and the arrow, and the nutty Catholic priest. Poody wasn't impressed.

Alice didn't like Catholics, generally, but this one was okay. Then she thought some more about Nick the soldier. They had talked about getting married when the war was over. "I'll be back, Allie", he'd said. "I'm coming back for you." From way down inside a dusty drawer of memories, she pulled out a disturbing little item. She remembered that he had asked her to think about becoming a Catholic. *Oh, yeah, that's right*, she said to herself. *Nick was a Catholic!* Her mother hadn't liked that, and Alice hadn't been too enthusiastic about it, either. But she sure had liked Nick. A lot. Blasted to smithereens by a tank shell in North Africa. They never even found the bones. Sometimes tragedy was bigger than promises.

Alice butted out the end of her cigarette and stood up. She looked down at the cat and said, "Sometimes, Poody, sometimes life just hands you a dog-crap sandwich."

She unlocked the front door and went in, feeling her way through the *junque*, muttering, "This is one crazy day. One crazy day."

* * *

She didn't sleep well that night, despite a double whiskey. In the morning she called Arrow, who came into her bedroom rubbing sleep out of his eyes.

"Kid, can you get Nick up and make him breakfast?"

"Okay, Alice."

"I'm pooped. Need another forty winks. Will you change him too?"

Arrow didn't look too pleased by that, but he nodded.

Alice slept for another two hours, and when she got up she couldn't find the boys anywhere in the house or the shop. She dressed quickly, turned the *Closed* sign around to *Open*, answered a ding from the gas pump, filled a tourist's jeep, and when it had gone, went searching. She found the boys in the wilds of darkest junkheapia, Arrow grunting, trying to push the buggy along the boards, Nick blowing his flute and singing, "Awo, Awo!"

"It's broken", Arrow said, pointing to the right front wheel, which was bent at an angle. She knelt down to try to bend it straight, but it fell off.

"Criminy!" she barked.

It took a lot of effort, and a tearing feeling in her lower back, but she managed to pull Nick out of the buggy and carry him to the kitchen. She strapped him into his chair by the window, put some Lego in front of him, and sat down at the table, fuming to herself.

"Are you mad at me?" Arrow asked plaintively.

"Nah."

"I think you're mad."

"Well, hell, what am I gonna do now? Nick needs his constitutional, or he's gonna get sick."

"What's a constitutional, Alice?"

"Fresh air'n'exercise."

"I could carry him around the boardwalk."

"Nah, he weighs a ton."

"I'm strong."

Scowling, she muttered to herself, "What a wonderful life. When I think I coulda been a banana farmer in Labrador!"

"I carried him this morning. I put him into the buggy."

"Yeah, I guess you did. Think you can get him out of it?"

"I don't know."

"Wanna try?"

Arrow nodded.

Alice groaned, got Nick out of his chair, and hefted him against her chest, his big head half resting on her shoulder. Outside she nearly tripped on a board, but made it to the buggy without further mishap. She put him into it and stood aside.

"Okay, take him out, kid, he's all yours."

Arrow bent over, braced his legs, and pulled Nick out. He staggered back and forth with him in his arms, straining, sweating, but doing all right.

"Not bad. Wanna try getting him back to the house?"

Arrow weaved forward along the boardwalk, Alice bringing up the rear, rubbing her lumbago. When Nick was propped up in his seat again, Alice gave Arrow a bowl of yogurt and fresh strawberries. She watched him eat, sizing him up.

"You musta growed two inches since you came to live with Nick and me."

She felt his biceps.

"You're a tough little beggar too."

Arrow wiped a smear of white off his lips and squirmed with pleasure.

"I got an idea", said Alice. "How about I get one of them army backpacks and fix it up for you and Nick. That way you won't drop him."

She went out to the shop and returned a moment later with a big affair made of aluminum, green canvas, and white webbing. She made Arrow stand up and slipped the straps over his shoulders. They needed tightening, but it looked just fine.

369

"Feel okay?"

"Yes."

"Let's put Nick inside."

She tried to slither Nick into the sack, but he wouldn't go. His hind end jammed at the top, and she had to extract him.

"Awo? Awo?" Nick said nervously.

"It's all right, Nicolo Piccolo. It's all right. We're making something for you."

"Something special", Alice added.

Alice spent the rest of the day tearing out seams on the canvas sack, adding heavy cotton walls to both sides, cursing the treadle sewing machine, breaking needles, stabbing her fingers trying to get it just right, and, despite the fussing and fuming, rather enjoying herself.

Just before supper, while the tofu was simmering, she put the finishing touches on a hooded flap, which she sewed to the top of the sack. It had a string tie and elastic supports, triple thick, for Nick's head.

She put the thing onto Arrow's back, wrestled Nick into it, and this time he fit. It was snug enough to support his entire body without throwing any weight onto his spindly legs. Alice cinched the waist strap around the two boys and tied the hood around Nick's head. Nick smiled at her and laid his cheek against Arrow's back.

"Awo, wah? Wah?"

"He wants to go for a walk", Arrow said.

"Okay, let's go for a walk. Test flight. Don't kill yourself."

They went out into the evening sunshine, swatting mosquitoes and sniffing the yellow-orange perfume of the marigolds. Arrow made straight for the boardwalk, bending under the weight. She could see he was struggling but excited. He jiggled the load up and down, and it settled more comfortably. Nick giggled.

"Wok, wok!" he cried.

"Nicolo go walk-walk!" Arrow replied.

Arrow, in T-shirt, short pants, and sockless runners, pumped his sturdy little legs, brown and muscly from his summer in the trash heaps, and forged on ahead. A regular trooper, Alice thought. Cigarette in left hand, right hand on the back of her sore hip, she worked hard at keeping up, but it was a lost cause. The space between them gradually increased, and the boys suddenly rounded a bend into the valley of scrap metal and disappeared.

She called to them to wait for her, but obviously they weren't paying any attention. Every so often she shouted things like, "Slow down, goldarnit!" or "Hey, wait up for me!" to no avail. From time to time she heard giggles and "Choo-choo, Nicolo! Choo-choo!" and figured they must be all right. She suffered nightmare images of Arrow wearing himself out and tripping, pitching himself and Nick into a pile of broken bottles or tin— blood all over the place. But nothing like that happened. Eventually she figured out that Arrow was leading her on a merry goose chase and planted herself at the main intersection, where the boardwalk to the barn intersected with the line heading into the graveyard of dead cars. Sure enough, he emerged from there five minutes later, chugging along, sweaty as the little-engine-that-could, grinning from ear to ear.

"Choo-choo", Alice said.

Arrow put on the brakes and stood in front of her with bright eyes, huffing and puffing, face flushed. Nick started to bounce wildly in the back.

"Wok, Awo, wok!"

His face was flushed too. He looked great.

"Okay, you guys, that's enough for one day. It's Nick's beddy-bye. You can walk him again tomorrow."

"Can I walk him every day?"

"Every day of the week and twice on Sundays, if y'like."

"Hurray!" Arrow shouted.

"Way, way!" Nick mimicked.

After all that exercise and fresh air, it wasn't difficult to get either of them to bed. She made Arrow take a hot bath first and then tucked them both in. She thought for a split second that she might try saying something cute and Norman Rockwellish, such as, "Now I lay me down to sleep . . ." But she couldn't remember how it ended. She didn't want to do anything phony, like pretending to pray, though she figured it was a nice enough tradition. In the end she just turned out the light and murmured, "God bless, you guys."

Arrow didn't reply. But Nick surprised her by saying, "Guh buh!"

* * *

Not content with hiking around the trash heaps, Arrow begged her for permission to go exploring in the woods with Nick.

"Nix!" said Alice adamantly. "No way! You'd fall down a gully and kill yourselves."

"We'd be careful."

"I know you *think* you'd *try* to be careful. It's the surprises that get you. Bears, wolves, cops."

"There're no cops in the woods."

"The woods are crawlin' with 'em."

"No, they aren't, Alice. Please! Pleeeease!"

"Forget it."

"I'm tired of going in circles", Arrow protested.

"Drop the subject, kid."

"Why?"

She suppressed a smile. She liked the way he was fighting back. It was better than curling into a ball and squeezing his eyes shut.

"Why? Because I said so, that's why. Because I don't want you to make trouble for me."

"I won't be trouble."

"You're already trouble. Big trouble."

That hurt his feelings, she could tell.

"Look, I'm sorry. That was kinda nasty. I didn't mean it. I like your kind of trouble. I'm glad you're here. Really."

He wouldn't look at her.

"Hey, I got an idea. Why don't you and Nick go out to the end of the property, you know, right by the back fence, and make a playground."

He thought about that, and then his face lit up.

"That's a good idea", he said.

"Yeah, and if I like what you make out there, maybe I'll take you and Nick for a stroll in the toolies."

"We could make a path through the woods. A hiking trail. I'll get the axe!"

She grabbed his shirt as he tried to bolt from the room.

"Not so fast, not so fast. First things first."

"How do I do that?"

"You take Nick out to the spot where you want to make this playground and sit him up in a box with pillows. Then think about what you want to do, and then you and Nick can decide which comes first. Wanna dig a swimming pool?"

"That sounds big."

"Nah, I got an old inflatable in the shop. Never been used. There's a swing set in the hardware section too, never been out of its box. Course Nick couldn't use it, but it'd add to the atmosphere. But don't expect any help from me."

"I won't, Alice", he grinned.

"Okay, get hopping."

She dragged steadily on her cigarette, sipped her coffee, and watched him through squinty eyes. He struggled to load Nick into the backpack, which was leaning against the kitchen wall. And when that was done, he got down on his knees and turned around, hoisting the straps over his shoulders. With a few grunts and groans, he was on his feet and staggering toward the door to the woodshed.

"See y'later, boys."

"See you later, Alice."

"Watch out for bears."

"We will", he waved, banging the door as he went out.

"Whee wiw!" Nick burbled.

Poody trotted across the kitchen floor, meowed, stuck his nose into the crack, pushed the door open, and raced after them.

She chuckled. *Pretty clever, Queenie. That'll keep them busy for a few hours.* She sighed luxuriously, settled into the armchair by the stove, and cracked the spine of a new mystery.

Arrow found a cardboard box in the shed, grabbed the foam and pillows from the useless buggy, and made his way through the maze of the boardwalk to the back of the lot. Jiggling Nick from time to time to keep him happy, he walked the northern perimeter fence, which was a few hundred yards long. There was hardly a spot that wasn't cluttered with dangerous things (piles of scrap metal with jagged edges, spears of old iron fence post bristling in every direction) or ugly things (ten discarded wringer washing machines, missing their motors) or inconvenient things (a warren of woodchuck holes and a hill of red ants). He walked back and forth for about half an hour, trying to decide.

He considered a site about three-quarters of the way to the west corner, well hidden from the house, ten scissor steps from the boardwalk. But he wasn't sure about it until he explored every inch of the vast complex of refuse. Eventually he returned to the place he liked. It was a patch of bare ground about fifteen feet across, covered with brown pine needles baking in the sun. Three titanic pines hovered nearby, like guardians. He realized that it was perfect: some of the clearing had already been done for him; it was warm, just the right combination of sun and shade; and it was surrounded by junk that could be tossed back

374

without too much strength, merely a big investment of time. He could expand the circle to about twice its width and also clean up the path to the boardwalk, which was littered with pop cans and dead car batteries.

He threw the cardboard box down in the center of the clearing and put Nick into it, making sure that he was in the shade of the pines, so his brains wouldn't boil. Nick rolled his head and blew his flute. Poody strolled in, curled up beside Nick's box, and went to sleep.

He worked the rest of the morning at widening the circle. He pushed and pulled, carried and hurled a variety of junk. At first it didn't seem that he was making much progress. There was so much of it. Some of it was heavy; all of it was dirty. Nick fell asleep. Poody woke up and went off hunting. But when Alice screeched from the back porch, calling them in for lunch, he was pleased to see that the outer rim had been pushed back two or three feet all around. Even so, there was only just enough space for the swing set and swimming pool. He needed more room for a sandbox and a slide.

After lunch Alice put Nick to bed for his nap and told Arrow he could go get the pool and the swings from the store. The swing set was still boxed up, sealed with heavy staples and strapping tape. Alice found a razor knife and cut the cardboard off.

"You're going to have to assemble the dang thing yourself. Think you can do it?"

"I don't know."

He flung himself into the task at once, dragging the set out to his playground piece by piece. During a cookie and milk break about three o'clock, he said, "I need your help."

"Sorry. You promised you'd do it by your lonesome."

"Just a little, help, Alice. Please?"

She grumbled and admitted defeat.

She held an end piece while he set the cross bar in the socket, then helped him do the same for the other side. When it was upright, he threw himself into the air and grabbed the bar, swinging like a monkey. The set wobbled and almost collapsed.

Alice withdrew a pair of pliers, a screwdriver, and a wrench from her back pocket, handed them to the kid, and lit a cigarette for herself. She watched him try to tighten the bolts for a while, then threw down the butt and ground it out.

"Here, gimme those. You hold the wrench, and I'll turn the damn screwdriver."

After that it was fairly easy. She helped him to get the chains up and the seats hooked on just right. The contraption was still wobbly, so she went back to find the assembly instructions, thinking maybe they hadn't done something right. Sure enough, they hadn't. There were bracers to drive into the ground, straight through the base of the four legs, two spikes each. After that it was fairly solid.

There was a faint *bing* from the direction of the gas pumps, and Alice scurried off to answer it, leaving Arrow to do whatever he was going to do next. He spent the remainder of the afternoon digging a hole. Beneath four inches of pine humus, he banged into a layer of gravel and heavy rocks, which took the better part of two hours to excavate. He returned to the house shortly before supper, found the plastic swimming pool, and dragged it out back, refusing to take Alice's offer of apple juice and a piece of chocolate cake. He was sweating and scratched, slightly crazed with manic determination, but happy in his peculiar way. Alice let him go.

Later she took a plate of pork and beans (pork removed) and a thermos of milk out to the playground. She found him sitting on a pile of gravel, arms wrapped around his knees, smiling as if he'd swallowed the Cheshire cat, his eyes so bright she wondered at it.

"Surveying your vast land holdings?" she said.

"Do you like it, Alice?"

"It's great, kid. Really great", she said sincerely.

The pool was sunk into the ground, its rim flush with the surface.

"We can carry buckets of water and fill it", Arrow said. "Then Nick can float. He won't feel heavy."

"Correction: *You* can carry buckets of water."

"It's like the ocean. He'll be happy in it."

"It's a pretty small ocean, if you ask me. But he'll be happy in it", she admitted.

Arrow pointed to the circumference of the clearing. "I'll put up boards for a fence. You can plant flowers."

"Say, you're a pretty enterprising fellow", she said, and meant it.

"This is my mountain", he went on, patting the pile of gravel. "I'm going to throw the rocks away and bring my cars out here."

"Sure, why not. Take some of the sand pails and shovels from the store. There're some plastic trucks you can have too. I got a Tonka bulldozer there somewhere. It's all yours."

"Thanks, Alice."

"Don't mention it."

"There's only one thing wrong. Nick can't swing."

"Maybe we can do something about that. Why don't you get that butter crate from the antique room. It's got handles on both ends. We can tie ropes onto it and hitch it to the swing. Nick'll fit in that."

He jumped up, leaped over his untouched supper plate, and shot away before she finished her sentence. He was back in a few minutes with the box and a length of rope. They worked on it together and had it swinging in no time. Arrow went back to the house and returned, puffing, with Nick in his arms.

Nick loved his box-swing. He blew his flute, burbled and giggled, and ran through every one of his known sounds and new half-words as he swung back and forth.

"Not too high, kid. You don't want him doing a somersault.

Then he'd have a real exciting ride in an ambulance, and you'n'me'd have a nice little ride in a police car."

That cast a pall on things, but not for long. Arrow let Nick's box glide by itself until it slowed to a gentle roll, then he went off to find buckets. Alice brought lawn chairs, which she set around the pool. A few more items were added: a potted pink geranium, a beach umbrella, and a bridge table for her drinks and ashtray. She threw a yellow plastic duck and a fluorescent red tugboat into the pool, which was filling with painful slowness, bucket by bucket. She sat in the lawn chair, watching Arrow's determined efforts to complete his garden of earthly delights. Poody ambled in and deposited a dead mouse at her feet and sat down on his haunches, waiting for praise. Nick talked to flies. Swallows darted everywhere, and a warm breeze blew in from nowhere. She thought it was really nice and felt genuine admiration for what Arrow had accomplished.

When he threw himself down on his mountain, she said, "You're one sharp kid. I'm glad I got a guy like you around the place."

He rewarded her with a sweet smile, then ran off again to find his cars and trucks. By the time he got back, the sun was setting, and Nick was beginning to fuss. She took them all inside, gave Nick a sponge bath, made Arrow take a shower, and fed them both a snack in their jammies. Arrow fell asleep sitting up, and Alice had quite a job getting his little carcass into bed. She patted his wet hair, took a quick look at the medal of the lady around his neck, tucked him in, and turned out the light.

She had to clear her throat a few times to make the words come out right.

"God bless, you guys."

Arrow sighed in his dreams. Nick said, "Guh bluh, Awis."

She collapsed into the easy chair, lit a cigarette, and called Poody for lap duty. She turned on the television set by remote control but after a few minutes felt bored by what she saw on it.

She shut it off. As she stroked Poody's striped orange back, undulating and purring under her hand, she realized that she felt pretty good. Weird and happy—an odd combination. It had been a great day, she thought, a really great day. She didn't know why, but the image of the lady with water coming out of her hands lingered in her mind. Then it struck her that Arrow hadn't wet the bed in over a week, and she hadn't had a shot of whiskey in three days. The thought of the whiskey propelled her toward the booze cupboard, but halfway there she thought that maybe she didn't need it after all. Maybe tomorrow.

It was only nine-thirty, but Alice felt like going to bed early. She got into her nightie, brushed her dentures, and stared into the mirror. Her cheeks were rouged naturally by all that sun, and her eyes looked clearer. There were two and a half bags under them instead of the usual three. Her mouth twitched into a smile—*Almost a real smile*, she thought. She tried it again and liked it, though at first it seemed phony.

She lay awake for a while, staring at the dark, wondering what was happening to her. Eventually she said, "Guh bluh, Awis", and was asleep before she knew it.

11

Among the Exiles by the River Fraser

After the meeting at the Potters, Father Ron drove home to his rectory in a state of agitation. He was not so much upset by what Alice Douglas had said to him, because that was predictable, considering her unbelief, her loneliness, and, he supposed, her habit of imbibing media swill. He was more disgusted by himself, because he saw in a kind of stark clearing of vision what most people thought of him: possibly a pedophile but probably not; a nice priest, a harmless fool; in summation, an ineffectual minister of God.

Not that he hadn't preached the truth, not that he hadn't been faithful to Christ and the teachings of the Church and fulfilled the duties of his calling. He had been diligent in all of that. He was neither an active sinner nor a saint. That was the part that upset him the most, because he knew that God wanted a Church full of saints, and somewhere along the line he had gradually lost the original fervor, let the toxic vapors of the world seep into his soul. He loved the Lord, no doubt about it, and he believed that his priesthood was the foundation of his being. But little by little he had allowed himself to drift into a state of lukewarmness. He had begun to cultivate a weed patch in the garden of his character. He had taken up smoking, arguing that it wasn't a sin and that it helped to relieve the not inconsiderable stresses of parish administration. He had taken to watching three or four sitcoms on television every week, not the grossly immoral ones, just those that were semi-intelligent, funny, and diverting. He liked the police dramas too, but worried over the sex scenes (he closed his eyes during those or went to get a beer from the fridge). On especially busy days he bypassed the saying of his breviary, and he felt uncomfortable wearing his collar in public. Clerical dress was so . . . alienating. Neither did he make as many visits to the Blessed Sacrament as he used to. He was busy. He was always too busy. He wasn't a bad priest, he knew. He was probably fairly good in comparison with some of the other pastors in the diocese. But he wasn't happy. Alice M. Douglas, without knowing it, had revealed that to him.

Sometimes he recalled a girl he had been in love with before he entered the seminary. She was a devout Catholic; it had all been perfectly chaste; there were no big regrets when they broke up; he knew he was called to the celibate life. But sometimes, when he was exhausted or discouraged or both, he would think about her and wonder what it would have been like to take the other path of love. He imagined her face—a lot. He tried not to think of her too much but had fallen into the habit of pretending she was sitting on the veranda of the rectory with him, sharing a cup of coffee, having a spiritual conversation. He had been watching the screen of his imagination more and more lately, and she was always in the drama. Nothing romantic. Just friends enjoying each other's company. The thought of it was consoling.

Father Ron parked in the driveway and let himself into the rectory through the office door. He was tired from a long day that had contained three meetings, two Masses, a visit to sick parishioners at the hospital, three confessions (one of which taxed his knowledge of moral theology), a catechism class for the kids preparing for First Confession and Communion, and about a dozen telephone calls—even as he passed through the office into his apartment the answering machine was blinking its red warning light at him. He checked his watch. Ten o'clock. *NYPD Blue* was just starting on cablevision. He had a little wrestling match with himself, then went back to the office.

What if someone were dying at the hospital and needed a priest? He pressed the playback button and listened to the messages, all of which were routine matters to which he could respond in the morning.

By that time the police drama was well under way. He flicked the remote control and watched a crew of sophisticated actors work through their relationships, their egos, their passions, their ideas about justice and corruption, not to mention a good deal of hair-raising gore displayed with utter realism. After ten minutes he knew exactly how the plot would be resolved and turned it off.

Restless, desperate for distraction, he pushed a video rental cassette into the VCR and tapped the play button. It was an action drama set in Australia after a nuclear war. A hero named Mad Max, who called himself the Road Warrior, went about the devastated landscape fighting off swarms of hideous bad guys, defending an inordinate amount of scantily clad post-apocalyptic maidens. It was well done, but Father Ron couldn't concentrate. He turned it off after twenty minutes.

He sat in the darkened living room for a while, staring at the picture window. Then he put his forehead in his hands and tried to quell the riot of imagery culled from the day's events, including Alice's sardonic face and Thérèse's pure eyes, his imaginary girlfriend beckoning for a spiritual conversation, and a stab of guilt that he hadn't prayed his breviary for three days in a row.

He replayed the crazy John the Baptist stunt he had pulled on Alice. He had never done anything like that before. Why had he done it? He had probably driven the poor woman away for good. He decided he would phone her in the morning and apologize. *Alice*, he would say, *please forgive me. I'm not really like that. I was so exhausted. Frustrated, strung out, worried about what's happening in the country. Most of all I'm haunted by the feeling that time is running out for all of us. Would you come have a cup of tea with me? Would you knit a doily?*

He wanted to go to sleep. He wanted to wake up feeling energetic and enthusiastic, as he had during the first years of his ministry. He went to the bedroom, popped his collar, and threw it on the dresser. He stood looking at his face in the mirror and saw somebody staring back at him whom he didn't recognize: a thirty-seven-year-old man with troubled eyes, twenty pounds overweight, sagging at the shoulders, a few gray hairs, and a brain full of riotous imagery.

He wasn't exactly sure why he did it—nostalgia perhaps—but he suddenly reversed his steps, walked swiftly through the apartment, and went into the nave of the church. The exit signs, a bank of seven-day vigil candles, and the tabernacle lamp gave enough light for him to find his way to the sanctuary without banging his knees on the pews. He genuflected, made the sign of the cross, and went up behind the altar and knelt in front of the tabernacle.

He tried to force words of prayer through his mind, but they trailed off, lifeless. He just stayed there without moving until the riot subsided, and he was empty.

Then he sighed.

Then he cried.

He hadn't done anything like that for a long, long time. He was glad no one else was in the church. When it was over, he lay down on the rug in front of the tabernacle, face down. He remembered the day of his ordination. The joy, the exultation, the current of peace flowing through him. All gone now, frittered away in a million bureaucratic details, parish suppers, and bingo games.

He hated bingo.

He loved his people.

But he couldn't reach them. They came to Mass every week, hardly any of them missing their Sunday duty, most of them decent, law-abiding folk. There was only a handful of serious sinners, the kind who really needed his help. He liked them especially, because they weren't proud people and knew they needed a Savior.

He knew that he was proud, with the pride of the oh-so-humbly superior. The pride of the good guys. Small and decent and law-abiding, and quite resigned to be an unhappy caretaker priest. Knew that he was mediocre. Knew that he was a composer of drab sermons, knew that he would try to wake his people up at tomorrow's Mass, and would fail. Probably the other ministers in town would fail with their flocks too. No one listened. No one was interested. For years he had used the pre-packaged, processed, homogenized homilies provided by the national liturgical conference—liturgy as consumerism, he called it in low moments. Lately he had returned to writing his own. Neither approach worked.

"O God, I'm sorry", he whispered. "They needed a prophet, and they got a clerk."

He cried again and felt a little better for it.

Then he fell asleep in front of the tabernacle.

The dream was unlike any he had ever experienced. He was standing on a plain that stretched before him toward a sinister horizon, where storms were engorging into cauldrons of turbulent thundercloud. Lightning shot out of the cloud in all directions. The sky was an ocean of rolling black waves. He was dressed in priestly vestments, tattered and covered with filth. His hands were empty. *He* was empty. He was exhausted and terrified. The desolation that spread before him was absolute. Before him lay a million dead bodies, decomposing. Millions upon millions of bones, the offal of what had once been a great company of children.

Then a voice pealed from the thunder, "Son of man, can these bones come to life?"

"You alone know that, Lord God", he cried.

Then the voice said, "Prophesy."

"What shall I prophesy?" he said into the rising wind.

"Say unto what is dead, awake! Say unto them, see yet a little while, and I shall bring spirit into you that you may come to life, and know that I am the Lord!"

He prophesied as he had been told. And flesh returned to cover their bones, but there was as yet no life within them.

"Say unto the spirit, son of man, say: Thus says the Lord God: From the four winds come, O spirit, and breathe into these slain that they may come to life."

He prophesied as he had been told, and the spirit came into them; and they stood upright, a vast host of the living where once death had reigned.

"Son of man," cried the voice, "these are the bones of the whole house of God. They have been saying all hope is lost, our life is dried up, and we are cut off. Therefore you must say to them, O my people, I will open your graves and have you rise from them and bring you back to your own true home. Thus will you know that I am the Lord who saves you. I will do it. I have promised, and I will do it."

The whole company of the children of God raised their hands and praised God in that place and began to move as one people toward the distant land, there where the mountains rose upon the horizon, even as the storm cloud and the sky fire rolled toward them, to confront them, seeking to negate the word that the Lord had spoken.

Then he looked upon his own garments, and they had become as bright as shining bronze. He raised his arms, and in his hands was a monstrance, bursting with light from the Presence of the living God. And the Lord went before his people, raised in the hands of his priest, like a pillar of fire, into the growing dark.

On the edge of the desert, the priest hesitated, and he doubted the company of the children of God, but looking behind him he saw that they were indeed there, following. He looked ahead to the storm that was close upon them, and he feared. But the light from the Presence strengthened him, spirit came into him, and he lifted his head and sang.

The singing rose from a deep place within. It was a flood of peace, a river of harmony that was light and force and truth. It poured from him as a fluid word, which reflected the greater word that had been spoken when the Lord God brought his children to life. And though the song issued from his lips as a small rivulet, it swelled in the singing, and it grew until it was of immense breadth and depth and power. It filled the sky and made a path through the storm.

Then he saw a figure of light in the air above him, riding upon a chariot of the Lord, and the splendor of it was beyond all telling. The chariot and its rider travelled with him for a time, until it went up, went up unto the Lord. The rider was not the Lord but a servant of the Lord who was to instruct him for a time, twice a time, and a half time.

The music that flowed from his lips became solid words, and he cried, "Ezekiel, my father!" Then the chariot was taken up and was seen no more.

"Ezekiel, my father, is going!" he sang, and though the river was a torrent of grief, the grief was sweet with love and longing.

Then a voice cried, "Look again!"

He looked again, and a woman came forth from the gates of gold where Ezekiel had gone, and she came down and stood above the people in the sky. Upon her head was a crown of twelve stars, and in her hand was a mantle of blue, half as large as the sky, which she spread over the people that they might be protected and take strength and instruction.

Father Ron woke up, hearing the song still ringing in his ears, seeing the golden curtains of the prophet close within the clouds, seeing the mantle of spreading blue, seeing the host of the children of God moving toward the mountains under the mordant gaze of the sky.

"My God", he whispered. "My God."

He remained prone before the tabernacle for a time beyond measure, in awe, in wonder, in joy and exultation, until the river flowing from his lips declined and subsided into a rivulet and then grew still within him.

Then he worshipped the Presence.

The sun rose, poured through the east windows of the church, and bathed it with light. Mrs. Edwards, the lady who looked after the flowers, unlocked the side entrance, came in, and began to putter in the vestry. When she saw him lying in front of the tabernacle, she looked startled and patted her chest as if fending off heart failure.

"Are you all right, Father?" she asked, alarmed.

"I'm fine, Mrs. Edwards, just fine!"

Feeling a little foolish, he got up and went back to his apartment. His legs were unsteady, but his heart was elevated and tranquil, which he thought a curious combination. He laughed. All the fatigue was gone. The anxiety and discouragement had fled. He looked at his watch and saw that he had only an hour to prepare his homily.

* * *

There was hardly a soul in the congregation who didn't like Father Ron. Saint George's was one of those parishes that did not backbite pastors. At one time or another they had all observed him handle difficult people with tact and kindness and just the right amount of firmness. He never threw his weight around, but he wasn't a wallflower either. His youth group was small but puttering along, two of the altar boys had gone on to the seminary, and people had been trickling back to the sacraments, although some in the congregation were a bit uneasy about the characters Father had been pulling in lately, the welfare types, the families of criminals in the local prisons, the habitués of the bars on Main Street. Even so, the worst of the gossips could only come up with the judgment that Father Ron was too generous and let himself be used. They knew he was a self-effacing sort of priest, the kind who thought he was doing a poor job when he was actually doing a great job. He never preached errors, and his liturgy was straight. If they didn't always like him quoting the Pope every second homily, at least they knew he loved them. He never went on golfing vacations like other priests. You could always count on him to get out of bed in the middle of the night and go down to the hospital to administer the Last Rites, or to bring Communion to the homes of the sick. If you were unemployed, depressed, or generally messed up, he'd give you his salary, listen to your woes, lend you his car, or hear your confession at any hour of the night or day. Most of all, he was gentle.

That is why there was some surprise when he stood up to the lectern to deliver his homily and cried out in a loud voice, "Dry bones! Hear the word of the Lord!"

He stood there, letting the words echo around the room. The entire congregation shifted in their seats. A rustle like a soft breeze went through the crowd. Every face looked at the lectern with interest.

"Thus says the Lord God: See! I will bring spirit into you, that you may come to life! I will do it. I have promised, and I will do it, says the Lord!"

Father Ron swallowed hard and wondered what he would say next. He stood for several seconds looking at his congregation. They looked back, waiting. He felt a ripple of fear run up and down his spine.

A baby cried. A teenager giggled. An old lady coughed. Someone began whispering to his neighbor.

He opened his mouth. Nothing came out of it. He hesitated. He doubted the company of the children of God and closed his eyes.

Holy Prophet Ezekiel, Saint John the Baptist, Saint George, pray for me!

He cast a glance at the statue of Saint George sticking a big sword into the dragon. He opened his mouth again. Nothing came out. There was nothing in his mind. Nothing! He resisted a feeling of panic.

Holy Mother of God, intercede for me!

He felt a trickle of the river-song stir in some unknown reservoir within him.

Come, Holy Spirit! For the sake of thy people, Lord!

The river surged toward his lips, as the whispering spread like wind in a dry wheat field.

Dear Lord God, Holy Spirit, come into this dry-bone pastor, or I'm in big trouble!

"Awake, my people!" he roared.

A shocked hush fell upon the congregation.

"Awake! For you are asleep!"

This elicited perplexed frowns from many.

"There is a God!" he cried. "There is a Savior! There is a Holy Spirit, and they love you with an everlasting love. Our God is a consuming fire! Our God is coming soon to cleanse the earth, to end the things of death and to bring to life what is called to eternal life!"

Then the river swelled, and the current deepened and widened, and the force of it was great. His knees were shaking. He clasped the lectern with trembling hands to keep himself from falling.

"Too long have we sat idle while the world steals the little ones from us. Tired and defeated have we become, unable to speak the truth in the face of the lies that daily wash over us and would sweep us away in a flood. How easily we have made our truce with sin. And I am the worst of sinners, for I knew better but would not speak. For twelve years I have stood before you, afraid to preach the fullness of truth to you for fear of turning some of you away.

"But in my thirty-eighth year, on the first Sunday of the

fourth month, while I was among the exiles by the River Fraser, the heavens opened, and I saw divine visions. There in the land of our captors I wept and sang, and I lay down upon the ground while my Lord spoke to my heart, and the hand of the Lord came upon me.

"And he showed me that my people are like an army of dry bones; though some of you are alive, you are barely alive. And I am the worst of you.

"Then he showed me that a storm of darkness is soon to come upon us and that we are unprepared, save a few who have not listened to the spirit of this age. He showed me that most of you have closed the gates of grace. Many of you have mutilated your flesh to cut off the wellsprings of life, for fear that you will not have the good things of life, for fear that the burden of bearing new souls into existence would be too much for you, for fear of the cross. And so you have been deceived, for it was not the appearance of evil that the devil offered you but the appearance of life, though it was not life but death you tasted, just as he tempted our first father and mother, and they fell.

"He showed me that your hearts, though they yet retain a spark of love, are growing cold. You have little time for the stranger and the sojourner who come up out of the desert, forgetting that you too were once in bondage in Egypt. You have little care for the lame and the halt, for they are a burden to you, though they are precious in the eyes of the Lord and shall enter the Kingdom of Heaven before us.

"And he showed me that you have voted for politicians who promised a better life, who promised security, though they asked you to blind yourselves to the murder of the young within their mothers' wombs; and when you helped to put these people in the seat of power, they turned on you and made you pay for murder through your taxes, and you shrugged and said it was regrettable, but what can we do, and we must render unto Caesar what is Caesar's.

390

"O my people, the life of the innocent is not Caesar's. The life of the innocent belongs to God, and no law can violate it without calling down destruction upon the nation.

"And he commanded me to look at the nations, and at our nation, and behold I saw the shopping centers and the malls filled with the sated, weary consumer and the seats of government and law filled with the proud and the blind. I saw storm winds and black fire pouring from the pens of the mighty and corruption sold to children in the city of the merchants and the idol welcomed into every home.

"And you said unto yourselves, it is harmless, we must pick and choose. But your strength to choose grew weaker, and in time the idol began to rule you, O my people. And I too am one of you in this matter. I do not speak with the voice of the accuser but with the voice of your shepherd who loves you, who is a weak man like you, who has fallen and stands up again, though I am small.

"Many are the great shepherds and many the prophets whom the Lord has sent to us in these times, but we would not listen, I would not listen. Now we reap the dreadful harvest. Now the desolation is upon us, growing daily; soon is the abomination of the desolation to rise among us if we do not repent."

He bowed his head, made the sign of the cross over the congregation, and returned to the altar. An audible exhalation of breath came from the crowd, and a stir of bodies shifting after long concentration. If Father Ron had taken the trouble to observe their reactions—he didn't—he would have seen a scattering of individuals gazing at him with great affection, the lame and the halt, the mad and the afflicted. A slightly larger number were scratching their heads and communicating with each other across the pews with raised eyebrows. The majority sat there as if stunned, not sure of the meaning of what they had just heard. Out of the corner of his eye he did see Thérèse Nguyen nodding enthusiastically (catching the spirit of the event, he supposed). Théophane, his altar boy, was grinning from ear to ear.

After the final blessing, he came forward to the lectern again and said, "There are just a few announcements."

The congregation seemed relieved that he had reverted to his normal speaking voice.

"Beginning this coming week, we're going to have exposition of the Blessed Sacrament all day on Fridays. If enough people show up for it, we'll add a day a week, and maybe we'll have perpetual exposition here some day. I hope you'll come. I've heard that amazing things happen in those parishes that honor the Lord in this way.

"Secondly, the Cub Scouts will be meeting on Wednesday in the parish hall, 7:30 P.M. It's been changed from Tuesday. I didn't have time to put it in the bulletin—sorry.

"Also, would you pray for the soul of Gladys Thompson, who passed away at Fort George Seniors' Home yesterday, and for Paul Goodwin, who's back in hospital.

"Finally, I want to thank you for your patience with me this morning. I know it's a bit of a shocker, but it's what I believe the Lord wants of me. Those of you who have time after Mass, maybe you could join me in the parking lot. There's something else I have to do, and you might be interested in it. It'll take me five minutes to unvest, and I'll meet you there."

He gave them the final blessing, the dismissal, and as usual croaked his way through the recessional hymn. As he unvested in the sacristy, he could hear quite a lot of discussion going on as the people slowly moved toward the exits. He removed the chasuble and, dressed in alb and stole, returned to the sanctuary. He knelt for a few minutes in front of the tabernacle and prayed his thanksgiving. Then, he went directly to his apartment, picked up his television set by the handle, gathered a few more things in his free hand, and walked out to the parking lot.

He expected it to be empty. He was surprised to see that it

was full of cars. None of the usual jockeying to get out of the lot, no roaring of tires on gravel. Two hundred people stood around the main entrance waiting for him.

"Hi, everybody."

"Morning, Father", came a smattering of replies.

He walked to the center of the lot and put the television down on the ground. The people gathered around him in a circle.

He was fighting an urge to bolt back into the church when old Miss Dunwoody tottered out of the crowd and patted his arm.

"That was simply wonderful", she said. "It reminded me so much of my childhood."

"Thank you, Miss Dunwoody."

"Faddah real hot today. Hot stuff!" said Théophane Nguyen.

"Thank you, Théophane."

A few more came forward, mostly women, and Old Bud the caretaker, offering their approval in embarrassed but sincere terms. Most just stood back and watched.

"Well, my friends," he began, "every diocese has to have at least one crazy pastor, and I guess I'm yours."

There were chuckles and murmurs of reassurance. They knew he wasn't crazy, but something had happened to make him bounce off the wall, and they were curious to find out what it was.

Well, here goes, Ronnie, he said to himself. *If you're going to become a religious fanatic, you might as well go all the way.*

"Théophane, what is this at my feet?"

"That's a TV, Faddah."

"And what's this in my hand?"

"That's a hammah, Faddah", he said slowly.

"Right. Now watch this."

He bent over and smashed the head of the hammer into the screen. The glass shattered deliciously. Then he gave the box a few hefty bashes. It cracked in three places.

Total silence reigned over the people. There were a lot of furrowed brows.

"Well, I say!" exclaimed Miss Dunwoody. Mrs. Edwards' hand fluttered over her heart. Someone laughed nervously.

Father Ron nodded with satisfaction and stood up.

"Now, can anyone tell me what this is?" he said, holding up a metal can.

"That's lighter fluid for your barbecue", Old Bud answered.

"Correct."

He dowsed the shattered box with the fluid.

"And this?"

"A match?" someone suggested.

"Uh-huh, it's a match. Stand back, everybody."

When they had withdrawn a safe distance, he lit the match and tossed it onto the box. It went up in a whoof, and the black smoke of burning plastic churned skyward.

No one said much as the television set disintegrated into a heap of charred glass and gnarled electronic intestines. When only a thin noxious coil of smoke remained, he withdrew a small bottle from his hip pocket and held it high.

"Holy water", he said. "Very good for blessing and very good for exorcising." He sprinkled the ruins of the television and smiled.

"Well, that's that", he concluded. "Bud, I don't want you to clean this up. I'll do it myself, but we're going to leave it right here for a few weeks, until Pentecost."

"Okay, Father, you're the boss. But this sure beats all!"

"I know."

Phil Evans came out of the crowd, rubbing his chin, smiling. Phil was a lawyer and a major force on the parish council.

"Heh-heh, I kind of get it, Father Ron. Are you trying to tell us this thing isn't doing our families any good?"

"Exactly."

"But it's just an appliance."

"It's become an idol, Phil."

"Isn't that a little extreme? I mean . . ."

"I'm not saying you should all go home and burn your television sets. No, not at all. I'm just saying that for me, your pastor, this thing has become an idol, a drug, and a deadly distraction. I can't handle it, and I'm getting rid of it."

"If it's just between you and your tube, how come the theatrics?"

"I'll let you think about that."

"You mean, you believe we all should do likewise, but you don't want to push? You're setting an example?"

"Some of you can handle it, and some of you can't. Each of you can decide for yourself."

"It's not evil", said the head of the CWL reflectively.

"Of course not", Father Ron replied. "It's a black box with wires and tubes inside. But many of the messages that come into your homes through that box are definitely evil."

"What about Mother Angelica?" someone said.

"I love Mother Angelica", he replied. "I bought the satellite dish just so I could watch EWTN. And I think she's a saint—a flinty kind of saint. I think the Lord's doing something fantastic through her. And some of you can benefit by the public education channel too."

"What about Vision 2000?"

"The religious channel?" Father Ron replied. "I've watched it some. There are good things on it, all right, but have you noticed the amount of New Age and Newchurch programming they've been feeding us lately?"

"Yeah, I noticed that", someone agreed. "It gives me the willies. But then I thought maybe I'm getting too critical in my old age."

"I'd say you're right on track. I'd call it good old-fashioned discernment of spirits. Now look, I'm not against the polio vaccine or microsurgery, or telephones or jet planes. All I'm saying is, whenever I'm alone in the rectory, funny thing, I just don't get around to watching Mother Angelica. I turn on crime dramas and can't get enough of them. It helps me relax, watching all those people get shot to death. Do you think that's healthy?"

Some looked dubious, some shook their heads, quite a few sensed that the drama in the parking lot was over and headed for their cars.

"If you're able to keep one of these things in your homes and not let it take over, more power to you", he said. "As for me, I'm a weak guy, and it's time for me to get a life."

The remaining people laughed, wished him a happy Sunday, and left. The halt and the lame, the mad and the afflicted were the last to go. Théophane thumped him on the back admiringly; Thérèse bowed low.

"Anyway," Father Ron concluded, "enough said and done for one day. The idol stays here until Pentecost."

When he was alone in the lot, staring at the burnt offering, he wondered if he was genuinely unbalanced. In the end he decided that it didn't matter if he was. Feeling extraordinarily lighthearted, he went to the rectory, made himself coffee and a heap of pancakes, and after that went through his library in search of a good book.

* * *

The archbishop phoned about one-thirty, just as Father Ron was getting into chapter 2 of Willa Cather's *Death Comes for the Archbishop*.

"Good afternoon, Your Grace."

"Good afternoon, Father."

"I thought you'd be calling. You must have had a few complaints by now."

"Yes, I have. Some of your parishioners are worried. Someone thought you'd been drinking."

"I hardly ever drink. A sip of beer now and then. I wasn't drinking this morning."

"When was the last time you had a vacation?"

"Eleven months ago."

"Feeling burned out?"

"Fit as a fiddle."

"Then what's going on?"

"It's a long story."

"I have time."

Taking it from the beginning—the meeting at the Potters', the speech by Ed Burgess, the John-the-Baptist-stunt with Alice M. Douglas—and concluding with a vivid description of the NYPD show, he gradually set the stage for the shocking little incident in front of the tabernacle. He hadn't quite got to that part when the archbishop interrupted him.

"So, you're telling me that you're upset by the corruption in government and in culture?"

"Yes, that's part of it. But there's more."

"I'm inclined to agree with you that the State is making some threatening moves, and television is doing a lot of damage to our people. But couldn't you have gradually eased them into understanding it?"

"I've tried, Your Grace, God knows I've tried. I've given them years and years of subtly nuanced messages. Nothing works."

"Are you so sure?"

"I don't think the flock is in any great shape. Do you?"

"I think there are some very fine people in our congregations."

"I know it. But I took a long, candid look around the church this morning, and I asked myself, 'Where are all the young people?' I'd say 90 percent of them are sleeping off their Saturday night parties or are out on the sports fields. Then I asked myself, 'Where are all the children?' There must have been 150 families at Mass this morning. Do you know how many kids under twelve were there today?"

"How many?"

"Eighteen, counting babies."

"Is that so bad?"

"Wouldn't you think, with all those married couples out there, we'd have maybe an average of three to five kids per family? Saint George's should be bursting at the seams. It should be noisy and bouncing and full of life. It's becoming old and tired, and in a generation from now, unless the Lord does a fabulous intervention, we're not going to have enough people to pay the hydro bill. Worse than that, there're gonna be a whole lot of lost souls wandering around the malls on Sunday morning."

"I agree, Father, but is burning your television in the parking lot really the best way to evangelize them?"

"Probably not. But it was all I had at the moment."

"From what I hear, you gave a rather unusual homily."

"Uh, yes, I guess there was that too."

"If you're angry at the corruption in the media, you could have taken the set to the dump, written to the networks, done something constructive."

"I've done all the constructive things. Nothing changes. It struck me that this is more than a personal thing. I've got a congregation of really nice people here, really *great* people. But they're all hooked on the big electric drug, except for Mr. Creighton, who's gone blind. And most of them are deep into sin, only they've decided it's not sin, and a bunch of noisy theologians agree with them. They think it's perfectly reasonable to pump themselves full of chemicals to make themselves infertile, or tie their tubes, or cut off their testicles."

That was a bit too crude for the archbishop. The last remark was greeted by an ominous silence. Father Ron suddenly realized that he had lost his cool and regretted the indiscretion.

"Sorry, Your Grace, I get carried away sometimes."

"I noticed."

"But you know what I mean."

"I do, and it's a cause of no end of grief for me, I hope you realize that. You read my pastoral letter on the subject, I assume."

"Yes. It was great, right to the point. But when I read it from the pulpit, I watched about 60 percent of the congregation go glassy eyed, probably 80 percent of the parents. They just switched channels. That's what I mean, Your Grace. They've been programmed to change the station whenever the message doesn't suit them."

"I think you're being a little harsh."

"Maybe. But I love these people. It makes me ache to see what's happened to them during the past three decades. And I'm partly to blame. Sunday after Sunday, I kept telling myself, gee, they're under such stress these days, they can hardly afford their mortgages, and I don't want to turn them off. I told myself that, bit by bit, we'd inject some education, some pastoral programs, gradually turn them on to the vision."

"Surely, you've had some success."

"One success for every ten failures."

"So you think it's time to turn on the pressure?"

"Putting it that way, I guess I'd have to say yes, I do."

"And the ritual immolation of a television set was to catch their attention?"

"You could say it was to catch my own attention too."

"How do you mean?"

"I burned my bridges. It disposed of my addiction, or at least it was the beginning of the process. I'm suffering withdrawal pains today, but I sure feel good otherwise. More than that, I burned my bridges to the old Father Ron. You know—nice, safe Ronnie, who never disturbs anyone, puts everyone at ease, the kindly uncle who wants nothing more than to see the young folks have a good time. That Father Ron is gone."

"I see. A prophetic act?"

"Well, sort of, I guess. Of course, I fumbled the ball a little. I got Elijah and Ezekiel mixed up somewhat, but I don't think anyone noticed. The message was the same."

"Father, have you considered the fact that we are living in the era of the New Testament?"

"Uh, yes, I have. Next Sunday I'm going to preach on similar themes from Saint John and Matthew 24. The New Testament building on the old. Pretty much the same message, only clearer."

The archbishop sighed. "I hope it will be as clear to your congregation as it is to you."

A pregnant silence ensued.

"I'm sorry if I've brought any embarrassment to the archdiocese", Father Ron said, hoping to break the mood.

"Well, Christians shouldn't be strangers to embarrassment", the archbishop replied thoughtfully.

"Signs of contradiction?" Father Ron prompted.

"Yes, that. And fools for Christ, I suppose."

"It's certainly scriptural, isn't it?"

"Quite. You said there was more you wanted to tell me."

"Oh, yes, I was coming to that. This is going to be hard to describe, but I think I might have had a vision."

"A vision?"

Father Ron described his dream in front of the tabernacle, leaving nothing out. The archbishop sighed again.

"I see", he said.

"I know how it must sound. Really, I didn't want this to happen."

"I'll take your word for it, Father. But you know, of course, that you're talking about the realm of personal inspiration, or private revelation, if you like. That's rather dangerous ground."

"I know, but—"

"It's a very delicate thing. The subjective breaking into the objective. It can get very confused."

"I understand, Your Grace, and I see the dangers. You don't want one of your priests going off the deep end and leading the flock into la-la land. I understand, I really do."

"I'm glad you do. But do you understand that the evil one can also simulate visions and ecstasies, infiltrate the Church by giving powerful spiritual experiences containing marvellous truths and an ounce of poison? It's the poison he really wants to spread, you see, and what better way to inject it into the life of the faithful than to wrap it in a pleasing religious package."

"I know. And I want to ask you, if you sense the merest whiff of anything wrong in the message, to shut me up. Say the word, and I'll be silent."

"That's a good sign in itself. Let me ask you, are you willing to leave this new approach aside for a while, just to give it some time to settle?"

"I am, if you tell me to."

"Are you willing to accept my decision about burning things on church property?"

"Absolutely. I'll go out to the parking lot right now and clean it up, if you want."

"Hmmm."

This was followed by another considered pause.

"I give you my word, Your Grace, that I will abide in perfect obedience to you, even if a bunch of angels troop in here and tell me to do otherwise."

"I have your word?"

"Absolutely."

"That's good. Can I ask you this: Would you say you are a man who has a healthy mistrust of his own senses?"

"Yes, I think that's true of me. I trust you more than myself. You're Christ's shepherd in this diocese, and if I can't follow your authority, then I'm not much of a disciple, am I?"

"You believe in the hierarchical Church?"

"Of course. My allegiance is to my bishop when he is in union with the Vicar of Christ."

"Good. That is the true obedience." The archbishop paused and sighed. "I wish I had a hundred priests like you."

It was an admission of startling candidness. Father Ron's heart took a leap, and he began to hope that maybe he wasn't crazy after all.

"But you must understand", the archbishop went on, "that even the best of disciples can be misled. That's why we need a period of testing."

"What sort of test?"

"The greatest test of all. Obedience."

"I'm ready and willing if you are."

"Good. First of all, I'm going to ask you to spend two hours in front of the Blessed Sacrament every day. Will you do that?"

"I will."

"Do you pray your office faithfully?"

"Uh, well, to tell the truth it's been slipping lately. But I made a resolution just this morning—"

"From now on, you will not omit it for any reason."

"Yes, Your Grace."

"And I want you to pray very much before your homilies. Invoke the Holy Spirit regularly."

"Agreed."

"I also ask you to pray a rosary each day. I would be grateful if you would offer it for me and the archdiocese. Can you fit that in?"

"Yes. Anything else?"

"A few guidelines: I don't know for certain if what has happened to you is from our Lord, but I want you to proceed carefully. Try not to be impulsive. Think things through before you act. Every time you feel the urge to speak or do something dramatic, ask yourself first if you are being prompted by emotionalism or by a genuine movement of the Spirit. Call it a reality check. Make it a habit."

"I will."

"It's an acquired taste", the archbishop said dryly.

"Uh, anything else, Your Grace?"

"Yes. Now I come to perhaps the most difficult test of all."

Father Ron steeled himself.

"Do you like golf?" said the archbishop in an authoritarian tone.

"Actually, I despise it, Your Grace."

"All the better. Personally, I love golf. I see it as a form of meditation. You probably find that hard to understand, don't you?"

"Well, yes."

"Good. Now I'm giving you a strict obedience. I want to meet you at the Langara Golf and Country Club next Saturday morning, and you're going to go eighteen holes with me."

"Are you serious?"

"I couldn't be more serious. Are you willing to obey?"

"Uh, yes, of course."

"I'll rent you a set of clubs. Ten o'clock all right for you?"

"Just fine, Your Grace."

"Good. I'll see you then."

He hung up.

Father Ron was still staring at the telephone when it rang again.

"Father?" It was the archbishop.

"Yes, Your Grace."

"I forgot to say, I don't want you destroying any more appliances in public without checking with me first. But you can leave the burned set where it is for the time being."

"Really?"

"Yes, really. It might have an impact."

"That's wonderful."

"Well, we'll see how wonderful it proves. And by the way, don't suppress the Spirit. But pray before you speak, reflect carefully, then trust."

"Trust."

"That's right. Trust. I'll be praying for you."

"Thank you, Your Grace."

The archbishop hung up.

Father Ron smiled.

Well, he thought, *that was a surprise and a half.*

He had been pretty sure the archbishop was going to relieve him of his duties. He could have offered a sabbatical, a trip to a rest home for troubled priests, a series of counselling sessions, or free psychiatry. Nothing of the sort, as it turned out. He should have known the reaction would be fair, reasoned, and open to the surprises of the Spirit. The golf part would be hard to stomach, but obviously the archbishop wanted to keep a closer tab on him, get to know him better.

Father Ron admired the archbishop. Though he radiated a quiet authority, which most people respected, he never ruled like a Teutonic autocrat, always tried to negotiate, correct, and encourage. The young modernists laughed at him behind his back, and they worked hard to get their friends from across the country—feminist nuns and dissident educators—appointed to key positions in the archdiocese. A few of those had slipped through, but not many. The number of orthodox priests was steadily increasing, a breed of zealous young pastors who amazed both modernists like Father Shane (who wrote articles for *Catholic New World*) and moderates like Father Ron (who used *Catholic New World* only to start fires in the trash barrel behind the rectory). Father Ron had applauded the efforts of the new breed and wished he were like them but felt too old for zeal. He wasn't sure why the archbishop didn't rein in the other guys, guys like Shane, but maybe the archbishop was trying to do it quietly. Maybe he was being as patient with the rebels as he was with crazy pastors like Ron.

Throughout the following week he followed the archbishop's directives and felt the better for it. Attendance at his daily Mass increased. On Friday a group of seniors stayed after Mass and told him they were organizing the timetable so that the exposed Blessed Sacrament would not be left alone at any time during the day. After supper a few working men dropped in and prayed for an hour; the Nguyens were there, and even Phil put in a half hour on his way home from the office. At seven-thirty a grand total of twenty-five people gathered for Benediction.

On Saturday morning, the line to the confessional was longer than usual, mostly old women (virtuous class), harried housewives (heroic), and a retired fellow or two (struggling). He locked up at nine, hopped into his car, and raced for the golf club, hoping to meet the archbishop on time.

He was fifteen minutes late, but the archbishop didn't seem to mind.

They played nine holes of golf, which Father Ron found not unpleasant, mostly because the archbishop kept up a stream of friendly, inconsequential chat. The sun was warm and the breeze cool. It was a nice day, but he began to wonder what it was all about. He supposed the archbishop was meditating on some level deep below the small talk. Or perhaps he was merely sizing him up. Or it might have been just the old prelate's way of male bonding. A little father and son stuff.

The archbishop bought him lunch and gave him a few unsolicited pointers about the game. He talked a bit about a paper he had to give to a parliamentary committee in a last ditch effort by the bishops to stop the fetal experimentation bill. He looked sick and worried when he talked about that. Father Ron didn't have much to say in reply, but he promised to ask his parishioners to double their prayers on the day of the submission. They played nine more holes, and Father Ron felt mild pleasure at improving his swing, an accomplishment he in no way valued but enjoyed because of the rather touching way the archbishop patted him on the back. Grandfatherly. Patriarchal.

He could see that the archbishop really didn't know what to make of him but was going to give him a chance, to test the spirits, as he called it. On the way out to the parking lot, he turned and said, "Have you had any more visions?"

Father Ron shook his head. "No."

"Any plans for prophetic acts?"

"No promptings so far."

The archbishop put his chin on his chest and stared at the gravel, lost for a moment in his private thoughts. He looked up at Father Ron.

"So, how do you like golf?"

"Not much, Your Grace."

"Didn't enjoy yourself?"

"I enjoyed being with you."

"Thanks. Want to try next week?"

"Do I have a choice in the matter?"

"No", the archbishop smiled. Then frowned. His face was ruddy, but his shoulders looked burdened.

"Are you feeling all right, Your Grace?"

"I'm all right", he said gruffly. He paused. "I'm just tired. I haven't been myself since the sisters died. Such a horrible tragedy."

"Have the police found anything?"

"Just the traces leading to the cult in the U.S. But the trail has grown cold by now. There are other problems. So many."

"Can I help?"

"You can pray for me. My doctor says I've got high blood pressure. Told me to stop being a workaholic. What else can I be in these times?"

"A golf pro?"

"Wouldn't it be nice. No, who would do all the paperwork if I ran away? We're drowning in paper, Father, choking on masses and masses of documents from every direction. Problems coming out our ears."

"I think I added one more problem to your list, didn't I?"

"Yes, you did. But it's the kind of problem that has a bit of life to it. I like that. I like your courage, Father. But I do ask you to implore God for only his will to be done, not your own, not anyone else's. Promise me?"

"I do."

"I'm especially worried about the missing priest the police are looking for."

"Oh, yes, the sisters' chaplain."

"They say he may have been abducted by the cult. If so, he could be suffering, if he isn't dead. I think about him all the time. You can pray for him too."

"I have been."

"The police say there's another possibility. They think he may be involved somehow with a northern branch of the right-wingers. He may have abducted three children."

"I saw that on the news a couple of months ago. It seemed kind of a wild theory to me. Any sign of the children?"

"They've totally disappeared too."

"It's pretty ugly."

"Indeed. But lately I've been having some doubts. Sometimes I wonder if these scenarios are quite as cut and dried as we think."

"How do you mean, Your Grace?"

"Look what the media has done to us during the past few years. Look at the way Ottawa's been riding roughshod over civil rights. So far it seems to be low profile, but it's getting worse. There's a certain intelligence to the way it's all unfolding. Someone's got an agenda, I'd say, and a schedule. Also, certain facts in the case don't add up. For one, I happen to know the missing priest fairly well. Father Andrei, an old Polish man, survivor of the war, really quite a saint. The sisters thought a lot of him."

"I met him once at a baptism party. People named Wanna-makers in my parish."

"Close friends of his?"

"I think so. Or at least their daughter was. She was in the convent for a while."

"Would you go talk with them? They may have a lead. Even a scrap might tell us something."

"The Wannamakers left for California last month, and their daughter just went on a sailing trip around the world."

"I see. Well, it was just a thought. I'd better get back to the chancery now, Father. See you next Saturday."

"I'll be here."

"Good lad."

The archbishop got in behind the wheel of his sensible sedan, turned the ignition, and drove away with a wave. Accelerating to ninety kilometers per hour on the freeway, he mused on the character of Father Ron and realized that he liked him. The lad displayed just the right mixture of respect and self-possession. Not an obsequious bone in his body, nor a disobedient one. Pious, loyal, average intelligence. He obviously loved God and just as obviously didn't think too highly of himself. The kind of priest who would shuffle along to a respectable old age, dragging with him a haunting sense that he was weak, unsaintly, a failure.

The archbishop wished that another young priest in his diocese, Father Shane, were more like Father Ron. Shane was anything but average. He was bright and ambitious, a clever writer, artistic—maybe a little too artistic. The archbishop had hoped that a year with the native people and rubbing shoulders with Potempko would have a salutary effect upon him, but it didn't seem to be working out. Potempko was complaining about him; the devout natives in the mission were upset. He had called Father Shane on the phone a few times to rein him in on the major abuses, admonished him in as firm a manner as possible under the circumstances. But he was well aware of the priest shortage and wanted to give Shane all the time he needed to come to his senses, without aiming the big gun of his authority. Shane was young, proud, badly formed by the unorthodox seminary where he had begged the archbishop to send him. The archbishop regretted that decision now, felt a certain guilt about his own weakness in letting the man manipulate him. He had wanted talent in the archdiocese, new life, imagination. He'd got that, and a whole lot of trouble along with it.

Shane, political lad that he was, had quickly rallied a majority of his parishioners around him. Twenty or thirty letters had arrived at the chancery, praising the new pastor to the rafters and criticizing old Potempko for his "pre–Vatican II ways". The archbishop read the ploy with perfect accuracy but wasn't sure what to do about it. If he pulled Shane out, there could be a revolt. If he put Potempko back in, it could only appear to the "progressive" parishioners that he, the archbishop, did not understand their concerns. He knew that the orthodox would persevere through anything, pray for their pastor (no matter who he was), and arrive in heaven on schedule. He worried more about that larger group of vaguely compromised Catholics who were teetering on the edge of apostasy, who needed to grow in their understanding of the hierarchical Church, who could not yet understand the difference between his authority as bishop and the exercise of raw power. They were as much a part of his flock as the virtuous, were they not? You had to meet people where they were. There was no simple solution. He had agonized over the situation for weeks before realizing that any decision he made would do some damage. In the end he let Shane stay and let Potempko stay as well, hoping that the prayers of the saints at Bella Coola would have a good effect.

Hitting one hundred kilometers in the fast lane, the archbishop sighed wearily. He never should have been made a bishop, he said to himself. He should have remained a simple priest, an ordinary professor in a small, ordinary theology college. It wasn't such a bad thing to be ordinary. He wouldn't mind having a dozen *repentant* Father Shanes and a half dozen Father Andreis, and of course one Potempko was enough for any diocese. But he wished he had a hundred *ordinary* Father Rons. The kind of man the archbishop would have been if divine providence had not been so improvident as to pull him out of obscurity and put him into the episcopacy.

The difference between himself and Father Ron or Father Andrei was that he had not been blessed, or burdened, with mystical experiences. No visions or prophecies, no interior locutions or heaven-sent dreams. He was glad of that. Such phenomena were definitely treacherous. For a moment he wondered what it would be like to experience a brief parting of the veil that separated the divine from the mundane. There had been periods in his life when prayer had given him an inexplicable peace and, on rare occasions, a touch of interior joy that approached ecstasy. The brush of an angel's wing. Just enough to let him know that all the abstractions were connected to living realities. He lived by faith, not by phenomena.

There had been one exception.

Twelve years ago, on the day Father Ron knelt before him and received the oils of anointing, a voice had spoken to the archbishop. It came from outside him, but he heard it within. As he laid his hands over the young ordinand's head, he had heard the voice say, *Here is one who will feed my flock amidst many tribulations. Set him before me that I may increase him.*

That was all. Nothing more, nothing less. He had attributed the voice to imagination. He had spent much of the night before in prayer, imploring the Lord to send fit laborers into the harvest; he had boldly requested great graces for the young men who would become his priests on the morrow. There was nothing extraordinary about any of them, it seemed, and it was this lack of outstanding quality that had worried him most. The times demanded apostles, saints. These young men were devout Catholics—all of them—dedicated, idealistic, determined to be good administrators of good parishes in a good diocese. But the archbishop had reached that point in his life when the original fervor of his own episcopal ordination was fading a little, when the demands of bureaucracy were beginning to shunt aside the exigencies of apostolic passion, his longing to be high priest, teacher, and prophet to his people. He didn't like what was happening to himself, and he worried about the lack of zeal in the young generation. He hadn't slept well. Thus, on the morning of Father Ron's ordination, he had been greatly fatigued and not a little sobered by the limitations of the candidates. He had shaken off the voice and completed the ordination.

Now, twelve years later, if Father Ron's pedestrian nature proved anything, it was that the extraordinary was always latent in the ordinary. In the seminary the lad had never been exceptionally pious; he was an average student, average liturgist, average chum to his fellows, and an average candidate for an average pastoral life that would culminate in a quiet old age, filled with modest pleasures and small regrets.

Yet the Lord knew his chosen ones far better than did the judgment of men. Perhaps Ron had been chosen precisely because of his ordinariness. His smallness would be a protection against pride, and thus anything good the Lord did through him would be attributed to none other than its true source. He could be called up higher only because he thoroughly understood his low estate. The archbishop, who felt that he himself was unsuited to the episcopacy, understood the dynamic all too well. He suddenly felt reassured by it and looked forward to the coming Saturday.

* * *

On the Sunday morning after his first golf game, Father Ron rolled his body out of bed an hour earlier than usual. He felt groggy but knew that if he was to continue to build upon the foundation he had laid the previous Sunday, he would have to do some serious praying. He spent an hour in front of the Blessed Sacrament, going over the day's readings for the third time, asking the Lord to inspire him with the words of his homily. He didn't hear anything from heaven; there were no dreams or visions, but there was a new peace. He supposed it was a grace of some kind, mixed with the rush of expectation experienced by those who throw their lives away in a free fall without parachute. But it was mixed with fear, the continuous sting of self-doubts that attacked like an army of ants, each one rather small, annoying but persistent, distracting, threatening his sense of direction by sheer numbers. To combat them, he prayed every prayer of invocation and spiritual protection he knew, used holy water liberally, and felt a little better after that, but by no means certain of what he would say to his parishioners.

He remained kneeling in front of the tabernacle until he heard some of the parishioners arriving early to pray before Mass. He checked his watch. Nine-thirty. His sense of emptiness was utter, his efforts to refute panic growing feeble.

He considered reverting to the old Ronnie and quickly assembled a dull but insightful maintenance homily. After practicing it in his mind for a few minutes, he knew it was no good; rather, it was good but not what the Lord wanted.

"Help, God! Help!"

Then a voice spoke within him.

Take and eat, it said.

"Take and eat?" Father Ron replied.

He saw a hand stretched out toward him, though it was an invisible hand.

Son of man, eat what is before you, then go and speak to my House, which has eaten the food that does not nourish.

In the hand was a scroll.

"How can I eat it, Lord?"

Take and eat, the voice repeated. *Eat of the Word that I will speak to my people.*

A Bible lay on the floor of the sanctuary. He glanced down at it, picked it up, and wondered what to do next. Putting the Bible on his knees, he closed his eyes, and prayed to the Holy Spirit. He heard the words, *Revelation 6*, felt a breeze that came from nowhere riffling the pages of the book, and opened his eyes. The breeze was gone; the book was open at Revelation 6.

He was astonished at the coincidence. He hadn't made it happen, no, not in any way. He read through the chapter, then went to the sacristy and vested.

During the opening prayers of the Mass he noted that at least a dozen families were absent. Some of the people who usually sat in the front pews had moved to the rear. The lame and the halt, the mad and the afflicted had moved closer to the altar, with a few new faces among them.

After the Gospel reading, which reinforced uncannily the message of Revelation 6, he gripped the lectern. As on the previous Sunday, he felt panic and abandonment, then a surge of grace, and finally an anointing.

"My people!" he cried. "O my people, listen to the voice of One who loves you!"

Once again a shiver of attention blew through the congregation. Once again he stood before them, waiting, empty. He opened his mouth. Nothing more would come out of it.

Speak, said the voice.

"Speak what?" he prayed in his mind.

Speak the words that will warn and protect.

He looked at the hundreds of upturned faces, waiting for him to speak. He felt the quickening of the river-song, and as it rose toward his lips, he saw the fragments of meaning swim together and form the *word*, take up their position in the center of the stream, and when the stream surged out of his mouth, his confidence grew, and he spoke without effort or fear.

"We are the children of the last days", he cried. "But we do not know it."

Pause. Uneasy rustling, whispers.

"My brothers and sisters, while I was in prayer before the altar of the living God, I saw the souls of those who have been slaughtered because of the witness they bore to the Word of God. They cried out to the Lord in a loud voice, 'How long will it be, holy and true Master, before you sit in judgment and avenge our blood on the inhabitants of the earth?'

"Each of them was given a white robe, and they were told to be patient a little while longer until the number was filled of their fellow servants and brothers who were going to be killed as they had been.

"Then I watched while the Lamb broke open the sixth seal, and there was a great earthquake; the sun turned as black as sackcloth, and the whole moon became like blood. The stars in the sky fell to the earth like unripe figs shaken loose from the tree in a strong wind.

"Then the sky was divided like a torn scroll curling up, and every island and mountain was moved from its place. The kings of the earth, the nobles, the military officers, the rich, the powerful, and every slave and free person hid themselves in caves and among mountain crags. They cried out to the mountains and the rocks, 'Fall on us, and hide us from the face of the One who sits on the throne and from the wrath of the Lamb, because the great day of their wrath has come, and who can withstand it?'

"O my people, do you think the wrath of God is unjust? Do you think that his justice is not coming? Listen, then, my people, for the Lord would tell you that for many years he has sent you his prophets, but you would not listen to them; the seeds of their word were trampled underfoot or swept away by commentators and false prophets. For how long must the Lord pour out extraordinary graces upon you if they cannot take root in you, for

414

you desire both the comfort of God and the pleasures of Mammon? Your Lord is now giving you a final grace. In this time of patience, when the oceans of innocent blood spilled across the world cry out for justice, and the silent holocaust all around you cries out for justice, though it is hidden from your eyes in this land, he gives you a time of mercy. Do not waste this time, O my people, for it is short. Turn now to your Father in heaven, plead for the Blood of the Lamb to be upon the doorposts of your hearts and upon your families. Detach yourself from all sin. Run home to your Father who loves you.

"You ask, where is mercy in the wrath of God? I tell you, *now* is his mercy, and even though his wrath seems a terror to you, or an abstraction, I tell you it is coming. Even his wrath is mercy. The hand of the purifier is upon us, and if we do not let him form us into a true people, a true witness, then another will form us, and that other is the spirit of this age, which is not love and is not truth.

"Choose, my people. Choose the one who will form you. You will choose the will of the Father, or you will choose the will of the evil one who knows only hatred. Not to choose is to choose. Not to listen is to listen to the one who is all deceit. Not to obey is to obey the one who would lead you into destruction.

"The Father is mercy and truth. Do you think it unjust that he would permit fire to cleanse this sick planet? Think of it, my brothers and sisters. Think of the oceans of agony that men have filled with blood and degradation. The victims of Stalin, Hitler, the victims of the doctors of our lands, the many wars and rumors of wars. Think of China, where at this moment your brothers and sisters are being herded into prisons and executed, which is even now preparing in secret an abominable war. Think of the former Soviet Union, where chaos reigns. Africa and Asia, where other demons fill men's hearts and drive them to mass murder. Do you think that evil on that scale can never come here, protected as we are by seas and wealth and power? Wealth can vanish in an instant, power disintegrates easily, and even the seas are no longer wide. Think of Europe, great daughter of the faith, where little remains, where paganism rules. Latin America, where slavery exists under other names. North America, where men kill countless souls and spread their corruption to the farthest reaches of the earth. Do you think my words are extreme? How mild they will appear to you when the reign of evil in our land erupts from beneath the crust that covers it. In that day will you say to me, why did you not warn us? Why were we not prepared? The sins of mankind are now greater than the times before the Great Flood, but worse is yet to come. Why should we expect that judgment will not fall upon us, just because we are a nice people, a very nice people? Evil must cease. God will not permit it to devour everything. This is mercy. The time is short! Repent!"

Father Ron's final word rang throughout the room.

He tried not to notice the small group of people heading for the exit, tried to ignore the distinct odor of discontent in the church. He returned to the altar and proceeded with the Mass.

Later, when the church was empty, he stood up from his prayer of thanksgiving and went out into the parking lot, hoping to chat with any parishioners who might still want to belong to Saint George's. There weren't many cars left in the lot; about forty people stood talking together in quiet voices by the entrance. They greeted him in a subdued manner, but their attitude seemed positive. Someone pointed to the place where the television had been burned, and Father Ron was delighted to see five sets stacked on the ashes.

"Some of us have been thinking, Father", Old Bud said. "We think you're right. There's my new Sony ready for the torch."

"My set too", said Miss Dunwoody.

"Ours too", said Théophane Nguyen.

"Wow", said Father Ron. "God bless you! You mean you don't mind being crazy like your pastor?"

"As long as we're in this thing together", said Mrs. Edwards.

Théophane ran to get the barbecue fluid, someone else supplied matches, and Bud lit the fire on his own initiative. As the smoke and flames rose higher, one of the men brought a cardboard box from the trunk of his car and threw it onto the heap.

"What's that, Tom?"

"Don't ask, Father. Let's just say it's magazines. The kind I buy . . . only for the articles."

"Oh, that kind of magazine."

"Yeah, that kind of magazine. Pray for me."

"I will, Tom."

"And, uh, Father, d'you think you could hear my confession after the wiener roast?"

"Sure thing."

Théophane pulled a few cassette tapes from the pocket of his jacket and threw them onto the flames.

"Bad music, Faddah. Wall of noise. Break my head."

"Break your head?"

"Heavy metal."

"Oh?"

"No more Mister Cool", he grinned.

Father Ron withdrew a package of cigarettes from his pocket with agonizing slowness. He gazed at it wistfully, then added it to the pile.

"Good for you, Father", someone said. "Right on!" said another.

"Uh, yeah, right on", Father Ron muttered. "Pray for me, will you, people? I'll be going through the tortures of the damned for the next week or so."

"Maybe the tortures of purgatory", Miss Dunwoody corrected, patting his arm.

"I hope you're right", he said.

He spent the next four days resisting the urge to leap into his car and race to the supermarket for a package of cigarettes. He had a few bleak moments scrounging for old butts in an ashtray, smoked them, and then felt so disgusted that he went out for a brisk three-hour walk that left him refreshed. On the fifth day the craving was cut to about a third of what it had been on Monday, and he began to enjoy feeling physically better. The smells in the garden were sharper, his lungs seemed clearer, and food tasted great. He slept deeply each night and awoke with an enormous appetite. He gained too much weight at first but balanced it with increased exercise. He began to anticipate his daily outing and gradually increased the pace, loping along the sidewalk like an ungainly bear. There were moments of depression, irritability, rage, and whining self-pity, but bit by bit these were replaced by a sense of accomplishment.

It was raining heavily on Saturday morning. The archbishop phoned to cancel their golf date. He mentioned to Father Ron that he had received more phone calls and a few irate letters. Father Ron described the homily in detail and asked the archbishop if he thought it was out of order.

"Not really", said the archbishop, musing. "And I must admit you tied it into the readings of the day rather well. But perhaps you should go more gently for a while. Have you lost any parishioners?"

"I may have. Maybe ten or twelve families. I tried phoning the ones I think have flown the coop. Most of them wouldn't discuss it. A few told me what they thought in no uncertain terms. Said I was scaring the children, depressing the people, acting like I thought I was better than everybody."

"What did you reply to that?"

"I said I certainly don't think I'm better than anyone else. I told them I think I'm kind of a weak, self-indulgent guy and figured it's time I took what the Lord says in the Gospels seriously. I told them it finally hit me after all these years that things are getting pretty intense in the battle between good and evil. I told them I need a Savior every day of the week and finally woke up to the fact."

"Nothing out of line there. Did you harangue them?"

"I guess you could say the homily was a strong exhortation. But harangue, no."

"One of your parishioners said you called her up and blasted her. Said you tried to frighten her."

Father Ron sighed heavily. "Not true, Your Grace. Not true. I don't know who it is you're referring to, and I don't need to know. But there was one lady who tore me up one side and down the other. I tried to make peace, told her I respected her need to step back and think about what I've been saying. But I was quite gentle. She blew up. She accused me of trying to terrorize her. Said she'd discussed me with her women's group, and they were certain I had really serious mental problems. I was a paranoid schizophrenic, wanted to drag the Church back into patriarchy. That sort of thing."

"You're sure you were perfectly respectful?"

"Absolutely. *She* was the haranguer."

"All right. I'll take your word for it. But don't you see where all this is leading?"

"I do now. I should have seen it coming. But look what happened to the Lord when he spoke the truth."

"Father, do you think that's who you are?"

"No. Just a scruffy little disciple."

"Any repetitions of the fire in your parking lot?"

Father Ron hesitated.

"Please, be honest, Father."

"Uh, yes, Your Grace. There was another fire after last Sunday's Mass. But I didn't start it."

"Who did?"

"The parishioners themselves."

"I see."

419

An uncomfortable silence stretched between the two men, until at last the archbishop broke it, saying, "I'm not happy about this. It's going to get out of hand."

"To tell you my honest opinion, Your Grace, I think it's going to peter out. I made my point, and they'll think about it, but it's basically up to them to do what they think best for themselves."

"I hope you're right. We'll leave it be for the time being. Don't try to chase after people who leave. They'll only interpret it as harassment. They feel defensive. Give them time to reconsider. Things will settle down."

"All right."

"And let's pray the weather clears up so we can meet at Langara next Saturday. Still willing?"

"Yes. I'll be there."

On Sunday he delivered another exhortation but took extra care to relate it to the Gospel readings of the day and to the new *Catechism of the Catholic Church*. The church was three-quarters full, and the collection amounted to two-thirds of the normal donations. More familiar faces were missing, but several new ones were present.

On Monday he went through the parish library and was rather surprised to find how much questionable material was in it: catechisms with vapid content and thinly disguised dissent from the Magisterium, an overdose of psycho-theology and self-help books that seemed to promote psychology as salvation, and a primer on New Age Catholicism that needed to be handled with asbestos gloves. He burned that one and packed the rest into a garbage bag destined for the dump. The periodicals rack also needed pruning. He spent the next two days on the telephone and the Internet tracking down sources for orthodox publications and was further surprised to find that in the past few years there had been an explosion of outstanding material. He ordered a selection of it, charging it to his personal credit card. He cancelled subscriptions to those magazines and papers that served watered-down Catholicism, ordered a half dozen of the bright new orthodox journals that were springing up everywhere, and charged those too. He wrote it off as his contribution to the parish. He hadn't ever given much in terms of money and thought it was about time he did so. The total amounted to a few hundred dollars more than his monthly salary, but he had some money saved and dipped into it a little.

It was a busy week in other ways, because confessions climbed steadily, though the number of penitents wasn't in any way overwhelming. Daily Mass attendance was increasing as well. An anonymous donation for a thousand dollars arrived in the mail, a bank draft, postmarked Fort George, B.C., accompanied by an unsigned note that said simply, *For parish needs.*

On Friday he typed out the Sunday bulletin and ran it off on the photocopier. It was twice as long as usual, because there were a lot of announcements:

> My dear parishioners, there are many practical things we can do to help bring more life into our parish. The following are just some of the changes I intend to begin during the next few weeks.
>
> * First of all, let's each of us ask ourselves if the *spiritus mundi*, the spirit of the world, has seeped into our thinking. A stringent self-examination is needed by every baptized believer, beginning with your pastor. Each of us must repent and "go and sin no more."
>
> * You won't see me being "creative" with the words of the Mass any more. I have realized lately that if a man cannot be obedient in "small" things, he will not be so in great things. From now on I'm going to be completely faithful to objective norms of worship in the liturgy.
>
> * We will be returning to the regular practice of Benediction and "holy hours" during which the Blessed Sacrament is exposed for public veneration. In many places this practice is bearing an abundant harvest of conversions and vocations to the priestly and consecrated life. That we are astonished by this is perhaps one of the signs of how far we have drifted from what was once considered normal Catholicism.

* I intend to restore the hour for confessions before all Masses. As usual, please do not hesitate to ask for confession at any other time.

* Beginning this coming Tuesday, Saint George's will be offering ongoing classes for adult education in the faith, using the *Catechism of the Catholic Church* as a primary teaching tool.

* Classes will soon be available in the parish for the education of parents in effective methods of "family life formation" and the formation of a truly Catholic vision of sexuality. Workshops will be conducted on a regular basis. I ask you parents to avail yourselves of such assistance. There is urgent need for restoration of full obedience to the Vatican's directives on sex education. Guidelines have been widely misinterpreted and in many places directly violated. Parents, educators, and pastors must work together to restore the authentic Catholic vision, rescue it from the mass-processing of children in this most sensitive area of their formation.

* The parish is now offering the services of at least one couple capable of instructing parents in Natural Family Planning, and within the month we hope to expand that to three teaching couples.

* The parish library is filling up fast with Catholic classics (old and new) and audio-visual material that is evangelical, educational, spiritual, and social in content, selections from the vast wealth of solid material that is available. Go browsing. Take some home. Let's get good Catholic culture flowing into our families again.

* I will be leading a Bible study in the rectory for anyone interested, on Monday nights at seven. Members of the parish are organizing a Rosary Cenacle and a Youth Cenacle. Come on out! Don't be shy!

* CWL and Knights of Columbus will continue to meet at their regular times.

And so forth.

He played golf on Saturday and after a few holes decided he could tolerate the game if it meant having time with the archbishop. The archbishop was rather quiet at first. There was no inquisition. His small talk was pleasant, and there were no reports of further complaints. He seemed distracted, however, and told Father Ron that he was still working through the death of the sisters.

"I'll never get over it. In the beginning I was just shocked, numb. It's so horrible you can't feel much at first, then it starts to sink in."

He was sleeping poorly. His blood pressure was higher.

At the ninth hole he stated, "Father Andrei is still missing."

The presentation to the parliamentary committee hadn't gone well. The bishops were treated with exquisite politeness by the members of the committee, but their papers had obviously been "thrown onto the compost heap" (as the archbishop put it) that committees use for material that contradicts their prearranged decisions.

"It's a charade. They go through the motions of listening to our submissions, but it always, I repeat *always*, goes their way. We lose every time."

One of the committee members, a virulently anti-Catholic ex-Catholic, had run up to the bishops and pumped their hands, congratulating them on their subtly nuanced presentations, telling them how their approach would contribute to the climate of "pluralism and tolerance" in the country. The archbishop had reminded her that *his* paper expressly stated that murdering a child in order to use his brains for experiments was a heinous crime and that any lawmaker who approved of it would stand before the terrible judgment of God some day. The committee member made a sour face, turned her back to him, and engaged a less difficult bishop in friendly conversation. The archbishop wondered if he had made a mistake.

"I think you did the right thing", said Father Ron. "Bravo, Your Grace. Bravo!"

To which the archbishop did not reply.

On Pentecost Sunday Father Ron delivered his fourth exhortation, which was about the need to invite the Holy

Spirit into family life as teacher, consoler, purifier, and advocate.

"My people, in the Gospel of Matthew we read about a meeting between Jesus and the Pharisees. Desiring to test him, they asked, 'Teacher, which commandment in the law is the greatest?' Jesus said to them in reply, 'You shall love the Lord, your God, with all your heart, with all your soul, and with all your mind. This is the greatest and first commandment. The second is like it: You shall love your neighbor as yourself. The whole law and the prophets depend on these two commandments.'

"Parents might take the seasons of Lent and Advent each year as periods of gentle but firm self-assessment. Ask yourselves, 'Do I put the love of God as the first and greatest commandment in my life? In the life of my family?' I have begun to ask myself this question every day, and sometimes the answer makes me uncomfortable. But God never promised us a tame religion, a safe religion. He isn't a tame God. And it's time we stopped trying to make our church into an extension of our comfortable living rooms. It's time for us to fall on our knees and *worship!*"

He proceeded through an examination of conscience, asking the families in the congregation to focus on fidelity to the Church's teaching on conjugal love, to persevere in prayer, Scripture reading, and sacraments, and to consider the many ways they could renew the culture of the family. He concluded with a ringing exhortation:

"O my people, hear me! Have we forgotten that one day we will be called to render an accounting to the Lord?"

He thanked God heartily during his recollection after Mass for the return of about half of the disappearing faces. As on the preceding Sunday, there were also a few new faces. He went out to the parking lot afterward and was startled to see eighty people gathered around the black heap of the "Baal-pit", as he had taken to calling it. This time there were eight television sets, a drift of paperback books, a clutch of CDs and cassettes, and a bottle of pills waiting for the torch.

People greeted him with shy smiles. A few jokers tried to normalize the mood, and Father Ron joshed back with equal skill. When it came time to do something, a young mother came out of the crowd and said, "What are we waiting for?"

"I'm just a guilty bystander from now on", said Father Ron.

"Fine", said the woman. "Mind if I throw these on?"

She showed Father Ron an armload of books. They were children's catechisms, the ones he had always felt uneasy about. Big omissions, doctrinal truths turned into vapid, useless pap. Spiritual flatland. No heresy, just the smell of something not right, an unstated message that the faith was boring and thin and no better than any other religion. He had not dared to think of these books as candidates for the fire, but now that this bold mother had stepped forth, he saw that she was right.

"Do you mind?" she repeated.

"I don't mind", said Father Ron.

"I'm cleaning up our own house", she said. "I'm not saying anybody else should do this, just that I've been dying to do it for a long time. This is junk food, and I'm not feeding it to my kids any more."

She threw them onto the pile with steely determination. Bud supplied the lighter fluid, and a young father stepped forward.

"Here, allow me", he said calmly, flicking a butane lighter.

Surrounded by his three sons and two daughters, he lit the edge of a theo-babble journal (as he called it) and threw it onto the pile. This was followed by the now familiar loud whoof and a roar of flames. Followed by a cheer from the crowd.

"Way to go, Dad!"

Then everyone laughed nervously. The nervousness dissipated quickly, but the laughter and banter continued, until Father Ron saw it would soon become necessary to invite them into the rectory for coffee. There were too many of them for that, so the ladies got busy in the kitchen of the parish hall, and they all repaired to the rectory garden for donuts and coffee on the lawn. There was a party feeling in the air, lots of handshaking and hugs, much animated conversation, and suggestions for getting together sometime. It lasted an hour, and then everyone went home to enjoy their day of rest.

On the following Sunday, a few more dropouts had returned, though not all. There weren't as many new faces, the donations were up to almost normal, and the reaction to his exhortation was not nearly so uneasy as it had been until now. People were obviously getting used to it. He worried about that. Maybe they shouldn't get used to it. But he decided in the end that his job was to speak the word, and the Lord would look after the rest.

There was another conflagration after Mass, attended by about half the parish. The things thrown on the Baal-pit were various and sundry, but the television set was still the number one item. There was a lot of humor and some good-natured jostling for the privilege of igniting the heap. Ed Burgess was there, campaigning full tilt. And a reporter-photographer from the local paper was snapping photos and interviewing parishioners.

A badly written article, obviously the product of a naïve journalism student bent on rising in the trade, hit the streets on Wednesday. There were a few crank telephone calls after that, references to Nazi book burning, a few pleas for spiritual direction from non-Catholics, to which Father Ron readily agreed, and a call from the religion editor of the *Vancouver Star*, asking for an interview.

"I'll have to check that one out", Father Ron replied. "I'll get back to you."

On Saturday morning the archbishop was not his usual self. When Father Ron met him in the parking lot at Langara, he saw that the man was upset. The archbishop held up a copy of the Fort George paper.

"What is this, pray tell?"

"Let me explain, Your Grace."

"Yes, please do."

"The reporter came on her own. I didn't even see her in the crowd until it was too late. If she'd asked, I wouldn't have given my permission for those photos."

"I knew it would get out of hand. It's turning into a joke. They're making us look like fools."

"Is that such a bad thing? They did the same to our Lord—"

"Don't give me that. The *Star* phoned me yesterday to ask for my comments; they say you've agreed to an interview."

"I did no such thing. They're lying. I intended to ask you for permission this morning."

"Was that really your intention?"

"It was. Do you believe them or me?"

The archbishop fumed silently, rubbing his face.

"I believe you, of course."

"Thanks, Your Grace."

"Don't you see where your prophetic thing is getting us? Not content with crushing the morals out of the people, they want to make the one moral voice left in the country look like pyromaniacs and fanatics."

"If they do, it's on their conscience."

"Yes, yes, but think of the consequences."

"I am. If the Lord wants something done and we don't do it, think of the consequences."

"All right, you have a point. But why do you and the other priests like you have to make it look so bizarre. Can't you do it with dignity?"

"Uh, what other priests?"

"You and the others", the archbishop said shortly.

"I'm sorry," Father Ron said, shaking his head, "I don't know what you mean."

"Surely, you've been in contact with the other pastors who are starting these fires."

"No. I thought I was the only one."

The archbishop looked genuinely perplexed.

"You mean you haven't been in communication with those priests in Ontario and Québec? The prairies too have—"

"No, Your Grace. What's going on?"

"I thought you could tell me."

"I don't know a thing about it."

"Well, well", said the archbishop, eyebrows raised high. He whistled softly. He smiled, then frowned. "Isn't that interesting."

"What, Your Grace? I'm completely in the dark."

"The archbishop of Toronto phoned me two days ago to chat, and he tells me he has three priests doing exactly what you're doing. Slightly different approach, but same message, same Scriptures, idols, fire, etcetera. When I told him about you, he was sure there was some kind of new priests' movement starting up, some extreme evangelical wing. He said it's happening in a few other dioceses in the east. There have been similar incidents south of the border. The bishops are getting worried."

"Why are they worried?"

"For the same reason I'm worried. Because it could so easily just go off the rails and become another private revelation nightmare. The devil could step in wherever there's a weak spot and use it to confuse our people totally."

"Your Grace, with all due respect, may I suggest that our people are already very confused."

"You underline my point. Do they need more confusion?"

"Isn't the tree judged by the fruit? What's the content of the messages? Is the word in them strengthening our people's faith? Are these other priests obedient?"

"Yes, and again yes. That's the odd thing. They're all faithful priests, down-to-earth types who've suddenly got bit by this bug, or vision, or whatever. Now I'm not going to rule it out as supernatural in origin, and neither are the other bishops, but it's definitely unstable ground. We're worried. Of course we're worried! Why shouldn't we be?"

"I guess that's your job", Father Ron agreed.

"I'm your shepherd. I've got to think of everything."

"You've got a heavy load on your shoulders."

The archbishop looked up at Father Ron and fell silent.

They walked slowly back toward the clubhouse, neither of them able to produce any more conversation. When they reached the archbishop's car, he turned to Father Ron and said, "I just don't know what to think. Give the *Star* its interview, if you must, but make it a condition that they send you the text for final approval before it goes to print. Demand the right to veto it. Don't let them warp it. If this is really a movement of God, it would be a real victory for our enemy if he could use it against us."

"I'll do what I can. But even if the enemy tries to warp it, he can't stop what's happening in our parishes. It is getting out of my hands, Your Grace, just as you said, but I think that's good, because there's some kind of wonderful grace flowing. I haven't seen my parishioners so energized in a long time. Actually, never."

"I hope you're right."

The archbishop blessed him and drove away, shaking his head.

12

The Cities of the Plain

Prepare yourself.

Father Andrei awoke in the dark and sat upright in bed.

Prepare yourself, the voice repeated.

"For what should I prepare myself?"

The tempter approaches. He will try to sift you like wheat.

"How shall I prepare myself, O Lord?"

Pray and fast.

"For how long?"

Throughout forty days you shall be put to the test.

"I am much weakened, my Lord. How shall I resist him?"

Trust in me. Be vigilant, but do not fear. Have the words of Scripture upon your lips.

Father Andrei remained awake, praying, pondering, listening to the silence that ensued. He felt a certain fear but resisted it by reciting the psalms and many other prayers, especially the Our Father, lingering over the words, "Lead us not into temptation, but deliver us from evil."

He calmed the irregular thumping of his heartbeat, made repeated acts of faith, hope, and love, thanked God for brief touches of peace, which he recognized as bursts of fortification. Each of these was followed by a hush during which the darkness of the room seemed to intensify, and the necessity of absolute faith become ever more obvious to him.

Whatever was coming would gain power over him to the degree that he did not trust completely in God's providence. He understood the various weaknesses of his character and the less-developed areas of the intellectual dimension of his faith and knew that both would be probed. He was neither a theologian like Potempko nor a mystic like the old Indian woman Cecilia, who had appeared to him in his drugged delirium, nor a saint like Maximilian Kolbe. He knew that he was a small man, poor and often empty. His one personal treasure was to have always chosen the way of perfect obedience. Weakness was his strength. The weakness of his physical heart had defeated the assault upon his mind, as if the breach in the outer wall had proved to be the most effective defense of the citadel. He prayed that the same paradox would apply to spiritual warfare, that the vulnerability of his nature would turn him again and again to divine assistance, that he would not rely upon his own little satchel of strengths, that he would not be so foolish as to regard himself as impervious to temptation. He did not understand why it had to be this way, but he had observed the pattern often enough in his life to place some confidence in it. Ultimately, this was a confidence in God, for the paradox was dependent on the reliability of grace. During his very long life, Father Andrei had found it to be entirely reliable.

He wondered if the temptation would take the form of some new brutality but dismissed that as unlikely, because his captors knew the torment of his flesh would quickly end his existence on this earth, which would be a blessed relief for him. Psychological torment? Perhaps. But they would realize that this also had its repercussions in the heart and would speed him on his way, out of their hands. Consummate masters of the psychology of victims, they would no doubt seek a more subtle form of disintegration.

Intellectual seduction? Yes, he thought. This would probably be their approach, combined with an invisible spiritual assault upon his judgment, his loyalties, his perceptions—all of which they would try to accomplish without arousing in him any sense of undue alarm.

431

The lights came on, and fifteen minutes later a breakfast tray slid through the aperture in the wall. He pushed it back.

The unseen waiter on the other side pushed it toward him again. Once again he rejected it. He did the same with the other meals that were served that day. He repeated the unspoken dialogue on the following day as well, and on the morning of the third day, when the breakfast tray arrived, he said into the slot: "Please take it away. I cannot eat."

He was very hungry, and the rejection of the food was beginning to cost him a certain effort.

He supposed that an invisible camera was monitoring his behavior, watching for signs of physical sickness. When they came to take away the tray, a voice spoke through the microspeaker above the slot: "Are you feeling ill?"

"No", he replied.

"Would you like to see a doctor?"

"Thank you, that will not be necessary."

"Is this a hunger strike?"

"No. I simply do not wish to eat."

There was no reply to this. Five minutes later a second voice, which Father Andrei recognized as that of the young doctor who should have gone to sea, said, "You must eat."

"I do not feel able to eat at present."

"Why not?"

"I really can't say. However, if you could give me a little wine and some unleavened bread, I will be able to consume that."

This was followed by another silence. After what seemed an interminable delay, during which Father Andrei prayed fervently, a tray containing a plate of three biscuits and a small plastic cup of dry red wine was pushed through the slot.

He could barely contain his jubilation.

Sitting on the end of his bed, he celebrated the most interiorized Mass of his life. He guessed that the monitors would be observing every movement of his hands, every sound that escaped his lips. He tried to prolong the elements of the ritual so as to present the appearance of an old man lingering over a meager meal. The prayers and liturgical actions were canonical but whispered, muted, disguised as casual gestures of a purely practical nature. After the consecration of the bread and wine, he felt the presence of Christ before him on the plastic dish and closed his eyes, worshipping, his entire being concentrated into a beam of adoration. After Communion, he felt the Presence inside himself as a radiant fire of such exceeding sweetness that all sense of time and every sensation of anxiety disappeared. At first he spoke with the Presence, discussing his situation, his concerns about the areas of vulnerability that the enemy might probe, about the welfare of the other fugitives, and concluded by asking God to forgive his captors. Eventually all articulate words subsided into a current of communication flowing like a river of love between Lord and servant, between Creator and creature, between Friend and friend, Lover and lover. The union was so utterly complete that the old priest sat immobile in perfect recollection for a time that existed beyond time.

At the end of it, or more accurately, floating in that level of being that he recognized as a thing the human mind called *completion*, he returned slowly to linear time and recited the final prayers. He raised his right hand and blessed the humans on the other side of the walls.

"The Mass is ended", he whispered. "Go in the peace of Christ to love and serve the Lord."

He is coming now, said the voice.

The electronic lock buzzed lightly, and the door sprang ajar. An elderly man entered the cell and stood in the center of the room gazing at Father Andrei. He was tall, silver haired, dressed in a tailored blue suit. His buttoned-down white shirt was appointed with a multicolored tie. His shoes were expensive oxfords, dark brown. A hint of cologne and barber's talc lingered in the air. There were no rings on his fingers, but a gold watch flashed at his wrist.

His face was dignified without a trace of pomposity, the eyes were kind, almost melancholic, the mouth sensitive but firm, set in an expression of concern and universal understanding, yet well accustomed to issuing commands. He exuded the kind of authority that need never resort to force. There was a crystalline quality to the glance, a serene intelligence that took in every detail of the bent, scarred old prisoner seated on the bed before him and analyzed it with discomforting accuracy.

He drew the single chair toward the bed and sat down upon it, facing Father Andrei. The two men regarded each other without speaking.

This is the tempter? Father Andrei said to himself. *An important man.*

This is the priest? the visitor said to himself. *A small man.*

The visitor withdrew a black plastic object from the breast pocket of his jacket, pressed a button, and pointed it at the four corners of the ceiling. He pressed another button and pointed it at the four walls.

"There", he said. "We can speak privately now."

He reached out and offered his hand. Father Andrei shook it.

"You are Father Andrei."

"Yes. And you are . . . ?"

"I am the federal Director of Internal Security."

"I see."

"Father, I know exactly what you must be feeling. What I have to tell you will be difficult for you to accept. I'm going to ask you to suspend your disbelief for a moment."

"I think you would like me to suspend my belief for a moment."

The visitor smiled appreciatively. "Actually, no."

"Then what is the reason for this visit?"

"I want to help you."

"Ah", Andrei said.

434

"Let me first tell you that I understand precisely how we appear in your eyes. You have been apprehended under highly unusual circumstances by an agency of my Ministry. You have been held under the new statutes without recourse to legal counsel. You have not been allowed contact with anyone outside of this institute. You have been subjected to medical interrogation procedures. You are probably frightened—"

"I am not frightened."

"Excuse me, I expressed that badly. I expect that you are concerned about your status and what is going to happen to you. Am I correct?"

"Not really. In an ultimate sense I am unconcerned. I expect to die here."

"I am here to see that you don't. If you will grant me the benefit of the doubt, I want to reassure you that I am doing everything in my power to see that you are released as soon as possible, without any prejudice to your freedom of action."

"I am glad to hear it."

"Of course you do not believe me. That is to be expected under the circumstances. But I assure you that my authority is not inconsiderable, and I fully intend to have you released, probably within the month." He glanced at the ceiling. "Unfortunately, I am under certain constraints imposed by the tiresome machinations of bureaucracy and the objectives of the new statutes. So you see, it will take a little time. If you are patient and trust me, I will see that you are released as soon as possible."

"As soon as I divulge the information that you are seeking."

The Director held up his hand.

"That is where you are wrong. You are still misreading me."

"I do not know where the children are."

"I will accept that. I know you are a man of your word."

"Then you will have no further use for me, will you? It would be a mere formality, would it not, to have me released this morning?"

435

"Not as simple as it might seem. Let me explain."

Andrei rested his back against the wall. The Director crossed his legs and removed his glasses. He glanced around at the walls and lowered his voice.

"As difficult as it must be for you to grasp, I am not in complete sympathy with the methodology of the justice system as it is presently functioning. Of course, under the emergency measures we are strictly within the legal parameters of our mandate. However, I personally have grave reservations about the far-reaching consequences of this approach. I am disturbed that a man such as you has been inconvenienced by it."

Andrei listened carefully but said nothing.

"I wish to apologize for this inconvenience. I will try to do what I can to dispel the confusion that has developed."

"Confusion?"

"The mistakes that inevitably occur when several levels of administration attempt to cope with an emergency situation in too short a time frame. It will take some unravelling. You see, if I simply walk out of that door with you and take you through the labyrinth of security that surrounds this institute and liberate you, that would really accomplish very little."

"I would be pleased to consider it very great indeed."

"I know. But we have a situation here that is much larger than the fate of a single individual, and it is more ominous than it appears. There are other prisoners, there have been some abuses of civil rights, and most importantly there are other levels of action pending in the nation. I think it in the interest of a higher good that for the moment we not compromise my position by a premature exposure of my sympathies."

"What are your sympathies?"

"In a word—freedom."

"Forgive me, but it strikes me that actions speak louder than words."

"Yes, they do. And you will soon be able to test my sincerity by the nature of my acts."

"You are going to set me free?"

"Yes."

"When?"

"With your cooperation, within the month."

"I see—with my cooperation."

"Do not jump to conclusions. I do not for an instant mean cooperation by betrayal of your conscience."

"How then?"

"Let me first explain further the situation in this country. You are not guilty of any crime. You are an innocent bystander who has been swept up in a movement of the State that has many dimensions to it. I control only one such movement, and of that only a fraction. And yet my power is not inconsiderable. However, if I were to release you summarily, my own credibility would be weakened, and I would be unable to work for the preservation of civil rights."

"That is your primary objective?" Andrei said doubtfully.

"Yes, it is. Of course, you cannot believe me at this moment; I understand perfectly why you cannot believe me. You will have realized that the department that engages in medical interrogation has come to an impasse because of your physical health. Thus, only a simpleton would fail to interpret my visit as a ploy to wheedle information from you in a subtler way. But the truth is, I do not want the information. I am, in fact, asking you not to reveal what you know, *if* you know anything."

"I repeat, sir. I do not know the location of the children."

"Fine. Then there is no problem. It won't cost you a thing to trust me."

"That remains to be seen."

The Director sighed. "You will see. You will see in due time."

"Tell me," Andrei said thoughtfully, "why are you so powerful

437

in a régime that is already displaying many of the traits of totalitarianism?"

"People bandy that word around far too easily. It conjures up visions of torture chambers and extermination camps. The fact is, we are passing through a period of instability in the social order. Some of the new measures are simply a case of overreaction. I am trying to combat the extremes. I am working to moderate the militant elements in the Party—the political philosophers, the conditioners."

"The conditioners?"

"The ones who would bring about reform by force. You must realize that such an approach is completely abhorrent to me. I believe in social evolution through reeducation."

"What if the people do not desire to be reeducated?"

The Director pursed his lips. "Most do desire it. Few deny that the condition of the social contract is in a state of degeneration. There is a consensus in the population about the need for corrective measures in order to stabilize society and advance it toward the common good. The problem at the top levels is philosophical. There is much debate among us regarding the degree of State intervention necessary to redirect the evolution. I am a minimalist. I believe in low-intensity intervention, strategic, nonviolent, a reliance on gradual processes. By contrast, the Prime Minister and my Minister, both of whom are deeply involved with several globalist organizations, believe that a maximal intervention sustained over a short period is the most effective approach."

"You disagree with them?"

"We are able to discuss it. However, other levels of authority are involved here, higher than national, higher even than continental. Thus, my position is complex. If I hope to achieve any mitigation of the intensity of what is coming, I must move with great caution. It cannot be seen that I make summary decisions that are at variance with the overarching goals of the process, even though they may be within my rights as Director. I may save an individual here or there, such as you, but only if it can appear that in doing so I am achieving much more for the process than—"

"Than simple torture, extraction of information, and execution?"

"Yes. That is precisely what I am trying to avoid. I have no more than nominal control over those activities. If I were to try to stop them, I would be immediately suspect and dismissed from my position; I would be replaced by someone as intent on radical surgery as my superiors. I would have gained a little and lost much."

"I think I understand. You wish me to cooperate with you in such a manner that you will prove to your superiors the reasonableness and the fruitfulness of your approach?"

"Correct. But I want to reassure you once again that by cooperation I do not in any way imply that you should compromise your conscience."

"That is most laudable. Still, I do not see how I can help you in practical terms."

"That part is not complicated. I would like to create the impression that you *have* compromised. This will take time, because the psyche profile staff know you would not readily do so. I want it to appear that I have gradually influenced you to come over to our side, that you have agreed to participate in a long-range program of analysis of the status of dissident movements in the country. I want them to think that you have been tempted and have fallen, that I have convinced you that you are saving people by an act of compromise."

"What do you mean?"

"It's an old tactic, is it not? I could never succeed by offering you alleviation of pain, or your life, or even some blatant evil. They will think that I have offered you a higher good and that you have fallen for it."

"That would make sense. I mean, that *is* your tactic, isn't it?"

The Director paused and peered searchingly into Andrei's eyes.

"That is one of our tactics, I will grant you. But it is definitely not what I am doing at the moment."

"Ah, so you merely wish your colleagues to think that you have used this device and that I have been deceived?"

"Yes, exactly."

"So, how will that be accomplished without . . . without compromise of my conscience, as you call it?"

"I wish to take you on a series of excursions. You are going to be a consultant to our department. Our rationale will be this: We need someone who is familiar with the inner workings of the institutional church, who understands its psychology, someone who can predict its responses in various crisis situations. The government will soon move to a new level of social reconstruction. The church must cooperate. Pressures will increase. All tax exemption for charitable institutions of a religious nature will end. There will be more arrests of clergy. There will be penalties for refusal to conform to State-defined concepts of social responsibility. This will throw the churches into an uproar of debate that will distract them, as it usually does, while we proceed with our more important goals."

"Such as?"

"Last year we launched an experimental program in computer-based economy. A satellite city of Toronto was chosen as the pilot project. Within its confines no cash was accepted as currency. As an incentive, the government arranged for large, forgivable loans to small businesses, in some cases doubling their projected net profits for the fiscal year. Residents and visitors wishing to make purchases within the city limits were required to use bank cards in order to make purchases. Cash was useless. Every government employee was required to accept the imprint of an identification code on the palm of his hand, using the new technology—an experiment within an experiment, if you will. It worked surprisingly well. The statistics proved that the new model reduces crime, poverty, duplication of labor, and time. The experiment is now in its pilot stage in six major cities, despite some protest in religious circles, notably from the fundamentalists, who are superstitious and see in this development a characteristic of the Antichrist."

"They may have a point", said Father Andrei.

"The new world order is not the Antichrist", the Director smiled patiently.

"How do I fit into this?"

"It is predictable that as the new economic structure becomes universal, there will be increasing protests from religious extremists. Certain portions of the population will attempt to create counter-economies, a kind of black market based on barter of goods and services. There will also be philosophical objections, counter-propaganda in the media, though only the vestiges of the conservative press will be able to mount any kind of serious protest, and that for only a short while."

"I am already thinking of a few objections."

"That is your right. However, in the interests of what I hope to achieve, I would be grateful if you would hear me out."

"Please proceed."

"If and when they finally stop their endless bickering, the churches in this country, with the exception of the liberal denominations, will probably make a few attempts at organized resistance—mass rallies, economic boycotts, food banks, possibly a tax revolt. These protests will be ignored. We can count on a few religious leaders to make some pathetic public gestures, uttered in suitably prophetic language. They will go to prison. Then, if there are any remaining dissidents, they will go underground."

"May I ask, are your sympathies with such people?"

The Director paused. "No. Such people are merely ignorant."

"Then what are we discussing here?"

"A larger problem. After the short burst of corrective measures, stability will return. I wish to ensure the reemergence of democracy."

"Why do you wish to preserve it?"

"Because people like me—and you—people of high ideals, would not survive in a totalitarian state. The lessons of this century are sufficient to prove that the revolution inevitably moves on to liquidation of the first wave of revolutionaries."

"If so, why assist the revolution in any way whatsoever?"

"Ah, that is where your religious sentiments always prove inadequate in the face of real crises. In your simplicity you believe that there are only two choices, good and evil. Am I correct?"

"Fundamentally, yes—though the forms that the choices can take are many and various."

"I see things from a higher perspective, one might even say a cosmic perspective."

"There is no perspective so cosmic, indeed, so supra-cosmic, as Catholicism."

"Of course you would believe that. But the world is teeming with mythologies that embody in symbolic fashion the universal truths. Catholicism has preserved in fossilized form certain intuitions of these truths, but it has placed limitations on them. It is exceedingly narrow. My approach leaves the widest avenue possible for the preservation of the truths that will lead mankind to peace."

Father Andrei shook his head. "I cannot agree."

"Be that as it may, Father, the problem before us is this: as we move to the next level of intervention, the church has already been characterized in the mind of the people as a repressive belief system that encourages overpopulation, eco-destruction, civil disobedience, and poverty. What remains of your church will soon be driven underground. My ruse, if you wish to call it that, will be to convince the authorities that in exchange for your life, you have agreed to be a consultant in the search for underground communities. Having been a fugitive, you will know the mentality of the fugitive; having been a captive, you will know the inevitability of submission. *Total* submission."

"I am *totally* confused. What are you trying to do?"

The Director smiled. "I am trying to preserve diversity."

"While appearing not to?"

"Exactly."

"To what purpose?"

"World revolution destroys much that is good, especially when it approaches the level of totality. I am not against this revolution, you must understand; I merely wish to nudge it in the direction of moderation. We should not eliminate the church entirely."

"Why not?"

"Because Christians are an interesting subspecies."

"You mean, like a small, vanishing tribe in the rain forest? You wish to preserve us as animals in a zoo?"

"Not animals. A sociological phenomenon that has spent its last resources but should be preserved for historical interest."

"What an amazing concept!" Andrei exclaimed.

The two men stared at each other. Andrei closed his eyes.

Interiorly, he saw a log cabin in a clearing in a snow-covered forest, a dead woman lying on a bed—a mother. A man weeping. A boy walking through a winter forest, clutching a white canvas jacket about his chest. A blue dog whining about his ankles. A woman followed the boy along a footpath through the trees. The woman was Anne Delaney.

Father Andrei looked up sharply, surprised. He examined the face of the Director. The man's features bore a strong resemblance to those of Camille L'Oraison.

"I know you", he said wonderingly. "You are Maurice."

The Director frowned and tensed his shoulders. He did not answer.

"Yes, you are Camille's son."

The Director scowled.

He crossed his arms and said, "I've heard about this ability of yours. I understand you've already unnerved two of the staff."

"It *is* you."

"Yes, I am Maurice L'Oraison."

"This is astonishing. What providence that our paths should meet!"

"I prefer to call it coincidence, or, as Dr. Jung calls it, *synchronicity*."

"Are there really any accidents in the universe, Maurice?"

"Your ingrained belief in the sovereign power of cause and effect, of some higher *plan*, creates so many useless difficulties. When will you people learn that whatever is not controlled *by man* falls back into chaos?"

"The universe is much larger than you think."

"My universe is larger than yours."

"No, Maurice. It depends on how one understands its structure. Seeing the form."

"I agree—it is a problem of perception. You and I merely follow two different interpretations. Yet we share many ideas in common."

"Such as?"

"As I said before—diversity."

"Yes, I too believe in diversity. A creative universe is impossible without it."

"So, you see, we are on the same side."

"Unfortunately, we are not", Andrei replied sadly. "A truly creative universe is a moral universe. You seek to undermine its moral structure, and in the resulting collapse of creativity you strive to maintain an illusion of diversity. But it is a controlled diversity, the exotic animal in the zoo, the pygmy in the artificial reserve in the Congo. Do you really think Christians can be summed up by calling them a dying cult playing

444

apocalyptic games, running about the landscape in search of sanctuary?"

"The sanctuary you dream of does not exist. My vision is to create a world that is total sanctuary."

"A global game preserve? Oh, Maurice, you will need many bars and many fences to enclose it."

"There will be no need for bars and fences."

"Still, when everything has become captive, you will have the pleasure of observing its small life, as you would derive pleasure from the antics in the monkey house."

"No. I wish to preserve freedom."

"Freedom only on your terms. Like the monkey, we will have no responsibilities. In this global zoo of yours, we will lack nothing, except our dignity."

"Where is the dignity in famine, misery, sickness, insecurity?"

"You would eliminate poverty by eliminating the poor. You are already doing it in Africa and Asia."

"There will be bread for everyone."

"At what cost?"

"They will not even notice the cost."

"For myself, I prefer hunger."

"We are straying from the point."

"Oh, no, we are focusing on the central point: What is man?"

"If I had days to discuss this with you, I would do so. But I have a full schedule, and I have already overextended my visit. I will return next week to discuss this further."

He stood up and offered his hand. Andrei shook it and held onto it with both of his own.

"Maurice, you are a human soul. Leave this deceiving cloud. Come into the light."

"Ah, it is you who dwell in darkness. I say unto *you*, come out into the light."

He pulled his hand away, went to the door, and turned to the priest. "Please eat something. You mustn't starve."

"I am not starving."

"If you live, you can save many people from what is coming."

"So that they may fill their stomachs as they lose their souls?"

"No. That they may go through these difficult times to the era of reconstruction. Perhaps, if enough of you survive," he smiled, "you will rebuild your church and convert the world. Please consider my offer."

"I will consider it. May I ask a favor of you?"

"Yes?"

"I would like to have the vessels of the altar from my belongings, the missal, wine, and hosts."

"I'm sorry, that is not possible."

"Why not?"

"Because it would undermine the illusion that you and I will create. However, I will see to it that you have a cup of wine and some biscuits every day." He laughed. "That way you can continue to say your clandestine liturgy without alerting the staff."

"You saw it?"

"Of course. Everything is observed and recorded. Do not worry. I am the only one capable of deciphering your inscrutable gestures and mumbled prayers. You are safe."

Andrei stared at him.

Maurice pointed his black box at the ceiling and walls and pressed buttons. Then he aimed it at the door, which sprang ajar. When he had gone out, Andrei sat down on the bed and covered his face with his hands.

"My Lord," he whispered, "it is more complicated than I thought it would be."

He sat in silence for some time. Lunch came, and he rejected it. Supper came, and he rejected it as well. By now he was feeling hunger gnaw harshly at his belly. He drank several cups of water.

That night, after lights out, he lay on his bed and replayed the conversation. In the quiet dark it was easier to sort out the architecture of the argument. He knew that it was a very danger-ous thing to dialogue with temptation. The great spiritual writers cautioned against it with utmost severity. To debate with the devil was to cede him ground. To admit that he had any ground to stand on, which he did not, was to give him the first move.

But Maurice L'Oraison was not the devil. He was a human being, and, moreover, one connected to Andrei's own past and, through an obscure stroke of divine providence, to people he had loved. Anne Delaney, for example, had always felt a certain responsibility for Maurice. He was her student; she had been at the cabin on the day the boy's mother died. Andrei had never met the young Maurice, who had been at university studying law when Andrei was pastor in the North Thompson during the War. But Anne had mentioned him often. She had worried over the way the young man had become silent and bitter after the death of his mother; she regretted that his first attempts at po-etry—childlike but gifted—were displaced by an almost super-human drive to rise above the squalor of his surroundings. His ascent through the echelons of power could only partly be ex-plained by ambition. Such success could not be attributed en-tirely to the fact that he was handsome and intelligent—the sort of man people are always drawn to and rarely understand—or to his skill in reading human personality, or to his ingenuity at finding his place in causes and forces that carried him ever higher. The hidden dynamic was almost certainly spiritual. The pressing question was, had God so arranged this amazing coinci-dence for the purpose of providing an unexpected rescue at the end of the age? Or had he arranged it for the sake of Maurice's immortal soul? Perhaps both.

And what of the question of dialogue? During the tempta-tions in the desert, Christ refuted Satan's arguments with the authority of Scripture, but it was in no way a discussion. It was the utterance of a primary Word against an anti-word. In other passages Christ was silent before Herod, yet he engaged Pilate in

447

a thought-provoking exchange. He patiently explained things to his apostles. He called sinners to follow him before they had properly discussed the job description. He debated the scribes and the lawyers of the Pharisees. Clearly, the Gospels offered plenty of examples of Christ's willingness to dialogue with man. Maurice was a man, nothing more, nothing less. So too were the people who ruled above him in the network of international authority.

Andrei knew that his real struggle would be with the demon, but in the center of their struggle was a human soul. He would cooperate with Maurice's game only to the degree that truth permitted. He entertained no illusions that he could rescue Christian lives from the coming scourge. He suspected that Maurice was lying to him and that this was no more than bait thrown out to entice him. On the other hand, there was a slender chance that Maurice was sincere, in a distorted fashion, that he believed in his idealistic agenda. In either case Andrei resolved to speak no lies and to create no false impressions. It was up to Maurice to think whatever he wished. He would walk with him in the desert beyond the Jordan, and they would debate. If God willed it, and if Maurice's soul permitted, he would draw him slowly but inexorably out of darkness.

* * *

A week later the door of the cell opened, and Maurice L'Oraison walked in. He drew up a chair, sat down, handed Father Andrei a sheet of paper, and watched as the priest read it. On it was written:

> The staff of the Institute would suspect something amiss if I were to deactivate the surveillance technology twice in a row. They presume that the first breakdown of the technical support system was purely coincidence. We are being observed. From now on we must proceed with that in mind. Do you agree?

Andrei nodded.

Maurice tapped the paper. "This is an outline of the proposed objectives. Do you wish to cooperate?"

"Yes."

"Good. You will save many lives for your church."

"Thank you, Director, for offering me this opportunity."

Maurice took the paper from him, folded it, and put it into his pocket.

"I believe it will serve both our interests quite well", he said.

"It may be so. What do you want me to do?"

Maurice looked at the door and said, "You can bring it in now."

The door sprang open, and a guard entered, bearing an armload of men's clothing. He laid it on the end of the bed and went out. Maurice told Andrei to remove his prison uniform and to dress in the slacks, short-sleeved polo shirt, and light cotton jacket. When Andrei had completed this task, Maurice placed a peaked cap on the priest's head.

"There, your disguise is perfect. That is the sort of attire that elderly gentlemen wear at recreation."

"And when haunting the shopping malls."

Maurice permitted himself a short smile.

"Or on their way to execution", Andrei added.

Maurice shot him a warning frown. "Nothing of the sort is going to happen to you."

"Ah, good. Now, what do we do next?"

"We are going for a pleasant ride."

Maurice led him out into the corridor and down the hall to an elevator. The door was open, held by a guard whose face was expressionless.

"Good morning", said Andrei.

The guard ignored him and punched a code into the elevator console.

"Do we ascend?" Andrei asked. "Or do we descend into another circle?"

"I doubt if our personnel have ever read Dante", Maurice said. "And I am not Virgil."

"Yet the resemblance is uncanny."

Maurice twisted his mouth in an approximation of humor and said to the guard, "Admissions floor."

"Yes, sir."

The elevator ascended, and the door slid open at a corridor similar to the floor of Andrei's cell, identical in all aspects except for the sound of chamber music and the tapping of computer keyboards in an office adjacent to the front desk. The walls were white, unrelieved by decoration of any sort. The fluorescent lights hummed just above the level of sound, and the air conditioning breathed softly. There were no windows, no screams of pain from unseen prisoners, no clang of bars or lash of whip, just the atmosphere of an ordinary office building. The only other staff in evidence was a businesslike woman, seated at what Andrei supposed was the admissions desk, staring into the screen of a computer monitor. She wore a photo identity badge on a cord around her neck. She looked up and smiled at Maurice. She did not acknowledge Andrei's presence.

"Good morning, sir. The print-out will be here in a second."

"Fine. Can you call the garage and have them bring my car to ramp two?"

"It's done. It's waiting for you."

"Thank you."

The printer beside the monitor rolled out a sheet of paper. The woman gave it to Maurice, who signed it and handed it back.

"Status confirmation: extern subject seventeen", the woman said. "Approved. Estimated return, 1400 hours PST?"

"That is correct. Send out a search party if we aren't back by then."

The woman laughed. "Right. I'll get a posse together. Oh, just one moment", she said, glancing at her screen. "High priority message through apex ministry net, just coming in. It's for you."

She swung the monitor around on its axis so that he could read it.

"Got it", he said. "Please send the following message to the Minister's office: Am returning OIS flight this evening, arrive security terminal 2300 hours EST. Meet you at A.M. conference on hill.—M."

"I'll transmit that now, sir."

"Very good."

Andrei followed Maurice down the corridor to a set of double doors. Maurice put his right hand onto a scanner by the code lock, and the doors swung slowly outward. At the next set of doors he slid a card through a scanner; at the third, he typed in a code. They proceeded through two more security barriers, arriving finally at a large dock beside a ramp in a windowless cement room that looked like a warehouse. A charcoal-gray sedan idled on the ramp in front of a large garage door. Maurice held the front passenger door open, and Andrei got in. Then Maurice got in the driver's side and took the wheel. The garage door rumbled up.

Andrei nearly lost consciousness when the blast of green light, fresh air, and bird song blew in through the door. It had been weeks since he had seen or heard anything from outside the confines of his synthetic prison. He closed his eyes.

Maurice pressed a button, and the passenger window closed.

"A bit of a shock?"

"Yes."

"You'll get used to it."

He drove the car up the ramp and out through the doors. They travelled along a winding access road enclosed on both sides by twelve-foot-high mesh fencing, on which signs appeared at regular intervals.

"Electrified", said Maurice pointing at the signs. "It keeps children and raccoons away."

"A preliminary model of your wildlife sanctuary?"

"That's only the inner perimeter. No one ever gets in this far."

"Or out?"

"Or out."

They passed through the gates of two more rings of fencing, the guards saluting Maurice without demanding a clearance check. As they passed the outermost gate, Andrei glanced back and read a sign on the lawn:

National Research Institute
Authorised Personnel Only
No Admittance

The gate shut behind the car, and Maurice turned left onto a paved highway. The traffic was light, coming from nowhere, going nowhere. Andrei wondered where he was. Some place in British Columbia, he supposed, probably near the coast. The overcast was swollen with unfallen rain. Thick coniferous forest rose on both sides of the road. Distant mountain ridges climbed above the serrated crest of the trees.

"We can speak openly", Maurice said.

Andrei cast about in his mind, searching for something to say. His mind was empty, overwhelmed by the inrush of sensory impressions.

"Before we begin, there are a few things you should know", Maurice said. "First of all, I am certain that, given your personality and beliefs, you will feel compelled to try several means of escape during our sojourns. You can make the attempt if you wish, but it will always prove futile. Please understand that it will only serve to delay what we hope to accomplish, you and I. It would be counterproductive."

"Counterproductive?"

"Time is running out for your people. Timing is of utmost importance. How many do you wish to save?"

"I do not know if I can save any", Andrei replied thoughtfully.

"Neither do I. Everything depends on how well you understand this situation."

Andrei turned to Maurice. "What is this bizarre charade really about? Why are you doing this?"

"For the reason I explained during my first visit."

"I find that difficult to believe."

No more was said for some minutes.

Eventually Maurice said, "You must trust me."

"That is impossible."

Maurice reached over, picked a microphone off a radio console, and said into it, "The subject is reacting as foreseen. Escort, can you please advance into visibility?"

An automobile roared up close to their rear bumper and honked. Maurice honked twice in reply. The tail car fell back a hundred yards.

"Those are agents assigned to this exercise. Standard procedure. Our clients usually try to escape during the first few excursions."

Andrei made note of this useful piece of information: there were others like him. Other prisoners.

"Air escort," Maurice said into the microphone, "please show yourselves."

A black, unmarked helicopter veered toward the road, just above the tree line on the right, flying parallel to the car. Another approached from the left. They advanced ahead of the car and crossed over the road, a hundred feet above the pavement.

"Thank you. Return to regular flight plan", Maurice said. The helicopters banked and disappeared instantly.

"That is for show. A display of power, for your sake. They will accompany us a little farther, then return to the Institute. Ground escort will be with us all the way."

"I see that you do not dare to take chances with one old man."

"A rather unusual old man."

"I have no strength. I cannot run far."

Maurice smiled to himself. "I have heard that said before, by people sitting in that very seat."

"How many of your experiments have failed?"

"None. They all run. Hide. Evade—some are more cunning than others. They all return to the Institute eventually. Remove your jacket."

"What?"

"Remove your jacket."

Andrei did so.

"Look under the flap in the rear of the collar. You see that tab? It's a microelectronic homing device. Every article of clothing you wear carries one. Although our escorts cannot hear a word of our conversation, they know where you are at every moment."

Andrei quickly ran through several escape possibilities in his mind.

"Oh, yes, you can find a public washroom and strip yourself naked. So many have done that. Climb out windows, crawl down ventilator shafts, leap into subway cars, flee to a phone booth, stop a shopper and stammer out your predicament . . . It's the stuff adventure films are made of, isn't it? But it's not reality. I think we can bypass all that. Such a waste of time."

Andrei said nothing.

"If the impulse to irrational behavior persists in our consultants, they must submit to a surgical insertion of the device. I find that degrading, and so do they. It is really quite unnecessary."

"How reasonable of you."

"Try the door."

Andrei unlocked the door and squeezed the handle, but it refused to open.

"We wouldn't want you to hurl yourself out of the car. Such a waste."

"It would end my difficulties."

"Yes. And for the ones you could have saved, it would create many difficulties."

"You keep referring to these hypothetical ones whom I may save. I do not believe they exist."

"They exist. I assure you, they exist."

"You think I don't understand your plan? You hope to play out this complicated scenario until you are sure you have convinced me of something or other, and then you will release me. Thinking myself free, I will run straight to the nearest group of underground Christians, and you will track me with your little electric toys. Then you will scoop up many, many lives in your infernal net. Well, it will not work. Take me back to the Institute. Kill me, if you must, but I refuse to play your games."

Maurice reached over and patted Andrei's shoulder with a look of amusement.

"Well done, Father", he said quietly.

He saw that the old priest's face was calm but controlled, his eyes fixed straight ahead, staring at the smoked glass of the windshield, his lips moving in prayer. Maurice let him stay like that for a while.

"Take me back. I refuse to cooperate."

"You are exhausted and hungry. Soon your people, thousands of them, are going to be exhausted and hungry. We can feed them."

"Man does not live by bread alone, but by every word that proceeds from the mouth of God."

Maurice tilted his head thoughtfully. "Father Andrei, I am not the devil. I am not the Antichrist."

Silence.

"I am here to help you."

"That is absurd", Andrei said.

"The agents who follow this vehicle presume that I am conducting you through a classical exercise in psychological reconditioning. This is standard operating procedure. The profile of your reactions is utterly predictable to them. They have studied many cases such as yours. There is only one factor in this equation that they do not know. They think they know, but they do not."

"And what is that?"

"*I* am the unknown factor."

The highway bent around a stand of fir trees and branched into the onramp of an eight-lane superhighway. The car accelerated and mingled with the flow of traffic. Maurice moved it skillfully into the fast lane.

Andrei studied the overcast but could not discern the position of the sun. East or west? Into civilization or away from it? Gradually the forest receded, the number of farms and villages increased, and the mountain ranges spread apart. Ahead lay the coast.

"Where are you taking me?" he said quietly.

"To the Cities of the Plain."

* * *

The spires of the metropolis jutted toward the heavens, ranks of office towers, lances in a cavalry poised to hurl itself into battle. Thousands of transport trucks, buses, commuter vehicles, roared in every direction. Screeching tires, honking, exhaust fumes, swarms of pedestrians.

"Look into their faces", said Maurice. "See their tension. See their isolation one from another."

"The spirit of this world has done it to them."

"Yet they do not know."

"That is correct", Andrei said sadly. "They do not know."

Maurice drove through the downtown core at a leisurely pace, until he came to a main intersection. He parked at the curb and turned off the ignition. The escort vehicle drew up and parked behind. A traffic policeman sauntered over to the car and rapped on the window.

"You can't park here", he said.

Maurice said nothing. He opened the window and showed the policeman a card. The man read it carefully and nodded.

"We won't be long", said Maurice.

"That's all right, sir. Take as long as you need."

He backed away with a strained expression on his face.

"See the masses who are in bondage to their labors and their incomes", said Maurice. "See their millions upon millions of ambitions. Above all, see their despair, which is hidden even from their own eyes. See the little churches squeezed between the basilicas of commerce, your gospel dwarfed by our gospel. Those churches that do not promise an earthly paradise are emptying; those that do are half filled. See the servants of your god. They have grown soft, their faces full of fear, their courage eroded."

"You have done this to them."

"Yes, we have done this to them. But they do not know it. See also the crowds of women scurrying to and from their places of work, their faces full of anger and their wombs barren."

"You have done this to them", Andrei said.

"Yes, we have done it to them, but they do not know. They think they have chosen it and are free, which is our master stroke."

"They know. In their hearts they know."

"See the old, who wander aimlessly, haunted by their decline, puttering in the shops, contemplating death, afraid of their children, afraid of the final needle, for they are unloved and unwanted. See the young, who glory in their flesh, clinging to their senses and despising the old, who are a reminder of mortality. They too are afraid, desiring power and pleasure as an antidote to death. We have done this to them, though they do not know it. See also the children, those few who remain. Let them come unto us, for we shall care for them."

"And I say unto you, Maurice, do not despise these little ones or violate them; it would be better for you if a millstone were hung about your neck and you were cast into the sea."

Maurice smiled. He turned the ignition key and eased into traffic.

Trying to read Maurice's obscure designs, Andrei turned to him and asked:

"Why are you doing this?"

Maurice did not reply.

"First you tell me that you want to help my people, and now you are telling me openly that you are determined to destroy them."

Maurice frowned. "Play the game, Father. Play the game."

Five blocks farther along, the car entered a section of the city core that was run down, dirty, crowded with poorly dressed people, each bearing the marks of a damaged life. Again he parked.

"See the beggars, the drug addicts, and the alcoholics", he said. "See the insane who plague the streets and the native Indians who have no home. See the prostitutes and the thieves."

"If they seek the truth, they shall enter paradise before you."

"None of them seeks the truth. None shall enter your paradise, for it does not exist."

"It exists."

"Soon, all of these shall be removed from this plane of existence, for they are the offscouring of the world."

"They are damaged but beloved in the eyes of God."

"They are the failed experiment."

"They are each created in the image and likeness of God."

"Behold the image of God", Maurice said, pointing to an old street woman shuffling past, pushing a shopping cart filled with bottles and rags.

"No matter what you think of her, she is created in the image of God."

"What of him?" said Maurice, pointing.

A thin young man bounced past the car; he was naked except for a pair of transparent plastic shorts, his eyes crazed, his lips painted purple, his walk a parody of femininity, his breasts pierced by rings. Around his neck a dog collar, connected to a chain, which was held by a muscular bald man who strolled behind him in studded black leather clothing.

"The master is walking his pet", Maurice said.

"He too is the image", Andrei replied.

"And that one?" Maurice inquired, pointing to a native boy, sullen, eyes blazing, stopping men and women, muttering the price of his body.

"You can buy a child for a few coins", said Maurice. "Or for a syringe full of paradise."

"Yet, he too is a son of God."

"Where *is* your God? I do not see him."

"He is coming."

"Look—there are more children of God."

Girls danced past in saffron robes, chanting, shaking bells, clanging finger cymbals, offering incense and wilted flowers for sale.

"Their god is coming too," said Maurice, "always coming, never arriving."

"They were intended from the beginning to be children of the true God, though they are deceived by a false god."

"Are not all men deceived by their hopes for paradise?"

"Not all, Maurice. Yet each of us is blinded, our will is weakened, our judgment distorted."

"You make my point for me."

During his commentary up to that point, Maurice's expression had exhibited neither malice nor contempt. If from time to time a note of irony crept into his voice, it was always counterbalanced by a tone of compassion.

"The image is damaged but not destroyed", Andrei said quietly.

"We shall perfect the image."

"You are not God."

"And those who cannot be perfected on this plane shall be taken up to another, where they shall be completed."

"By force?"

"The captive must sometimes be freed against his own will, for he knows nothing outside his own bondage."

"And you, Maurice. Have you ever considered that you are in bondage?"

"I am a free man."

"You are more in bondage than any of these broken people."

Maurice smiled. "Father Andrei, you delight me. I am endlessly amused by the predictability of your responses. Now, let us move along to our next observation post."

He circled the block and headed back to the city's center of commerce. He parked in front of a towering office complex.

"Do you see this building?"

"Yes. What is it?"

"That is the stock exchange. Here we find an army of cunning, ambitious men who would make themselves rich."

"Ah, they too are free men?"

"Here we find man in an advanced form, though still focused on the self, upon petty individualistic desires. He no longer believes in your paradise and seeks to make his own."

"Just as you do."

"You are wrong. The world we are shaping is not the pathetic utopia of the suburbs. It has nothing to do with their trips to Disneyland or Paris, their yacht clubs and barbecues, or their sexual exploits."

"Ah, then your paradise is for the enlightened only. A spiritual utopia?"

"Yes, it is", Maurice replied simply. "It is coming. Behold, it is coming soon."

The absolute conviction in his voice, and the biblical style, disturbed Andrei deeply.

"Do you see these well-dressed men and women going in and coming out of that building like ants?" Maurice went on. "Their passion is money. See their hunger? See the anxiety in their eyes? How many of them would hesitate to lie in order to make a dollar, building their fortunes on illusion, on gambles, and on the losses of others? Are they too created in the image of God?"

"They too", Andrei replied. "Yes, even they. And among them are some who try to do good."

"These are the flat men who think they rule from on high, as high as their towers. We use them."

Probing the driver's eyes with a lucid glance, Andrei said, "Why these contradictions? Are you two men in one body?"

"Play the game, Father", Maurice answered. He pointed to the stock exchange. "Behold the bright young millionaires besotted with lust. They are our creations."

"You are not God."

"Not as you conceive God to be."

"Babylon the great is fallen!" Andrei said.

"It is not fallen."

"And all the merchants of the earth grieved!"

"The merchants are rejoicing."

"Their day is drawing to a close."

"*Your* day is drawing to a close."

"Fallen, fallen is Babylon the great! She has become a haunt for demons. She is a cage for every unclean spirit, she who spread her corruption throughout the world. For all the nations have drunk the wine of her licentious passion. The kings of the earth have had intercourse with her, and the merchants of the earth grew rich from her drive for luxury."

"We will use her, and she will take pleasure from us", said Maurice. "Then we will discard her."

"And the merchants of the earth will mourn for you, O Babylon, when they see the smoke of your pyre, because there will be no more markets for their wares, because your merchants were the great ones of the earth, and all nations were led astray by your magic, because in you was found the blood of the prophets and the saints, and all who had been slain on the earth. Alas, alas, great city, in one hour your judgment has come!"

"*We* are judgment."

"Rejoice over her destruction, you holy ones, apostles and prophets. For God has judged our case against her!"

The two men relapsed into silence.

Maurice drove on. Rounding a corner, he pointed to a huge stone building.

"Magnificent, isn't it? Solid stone walls, baroque architecture, bronze statues of *Iustitia* and *Veritas*. Justice and Truth defending the people. In this place the judges of the land do our bidding, but they know it not."

"Their pride deceives them. Their minds are darkened."

"False witness finds a forum. Truth becomes the poetry of madmen."

"And lo, the unjust judges shall be judged with an everlasting judgment. And all they who defame the truth, they also shall go down to perdition."

"Tell me, Father Andrei, who will judge the judges?"

"The Lord God shall judge them."

"No. *We* shall use them, and *we* shall judge them."

"Then you too shall be judged."

Maurice smiled to himself and drove on. Now the car left the central region and went out to the dwelling places where the people of that city lived. He parked at the curb in front of a small house on an ordinary residential street.

"A quarter of a million dollars to purchase a shelter for a family of four", said Maurice.

"How can this be?" Andrei protested. "It is not a mansion!"

"Buy and sell, buy and sell, profit heaped upon profit, riches upon riches—so do the men and women of these times aspire to be like kings of old."

"They become rich, not by the labor of their hands, nor by the sweat of their brows, but by speculation", Andrei murmured.

"These are the homes of the slave class that thinks itself wealthy. These are the ones who force the prices upward. Even an apartment in a slum demands a prince's ransom. Only the family that is not a family can buy a home. Two incomes. Two labors. A token child, two at the most. Let the little children come unto us, and we will teach them the ways of prosperity."

"You did this to them."

"They did it to themselves."

"They chose because they thought they had no choice."

"We offered them bread. They accepted."

"They are not happy. Their marriages fail in droves. They covet each other's wives and houses and goods."

"They are content", Maurice countered.

"Bread and circuses, purchased by blood."

"What blood? I see no blood."

"A river of secret murder flows beneath this prosperity."

"Where is murder? There is no murder. See how calm are the suburbs, sleeping in heavenly peace."

"You say, peace, peace, where there is no peace."

"Security."

"There is no security. You have destroyed the nation!"

"The nation is quite well, thank you."

"It is sick unto death!"

"It is peaceful and productive."

"Where are the children? Where are they? They are no more, and we have even forgotten how to weep for them, because you hid them from our eyes as you swept them into the sewer. You see this vast estate, Maurice, these hundreds of thousands of homes spread before our eyes?"

463

Maurice nodded. "I see it."

"You have forced them to eliminate children in order to purchase a box in which to put their nonexistent children."

"A stroke of genius, wouldn't you say?"

Streams of water flowed from Andrei's eyes.

"I know your works, O my people. I know that you are neither cold nor hot. Because you are lukewarm, I will spit you out of my mouth. For you say, 'I am rich and affluent and have no need of anything', and yet you do not realize that you are wretched, pitiable, poor, blind, and naked!"

"All is calm. All is bright", Maurice said.

"Usury! Greed!" Andrei cried.

Maurice started the car and drove away. He saw that the old priest was upset. They travelled in silence, reached the superhighway, turned onto the access ramp, and travelled at a leisurely pace toward the east. Forty-five minutes later, when the car drove through the gates of the National Research Institute, Maurice was pleased to hear the instability in Andrei's voice when he said, as if to himself, "Man does not live by bread alone, but by every word that comes from the mouth of God."

* * *

Maurice, eyes closed, reclined in his chair before the glowing fireplace in his cottage. He felt the trembling in the atmosphere and welcomed the master.

You have revealed too much, said the black flame.

"I thought he would see the extent of our influence and capitulate."

You sought to win him, but you have instead steeled his will against us.

"He is powerful", Maurice replied. "He deploys his counterarguments with skill."

He has no skill. He is merely simple.

"I felt . . . I felt a force in him."

The adversary struggles in his final moments.

"But their Christ is not real! Need we struggle against a false idea?"

This false idea yet retains its influence. A small god has small powers.

"How shall we break its hold over men's minds?"

Break their god's best servant.

"Can you tell me the route to his soul?"

Force will not accomplish it. Pain will not, nor intimidation.

"What then?"

Shake his confidence in his god.

"I am already trying this, as you know."

Shake him well, show him that we have already won.

"And if this fails?"

Confusion.

* * *

A week later Maurice returned and took him for another ride. Entering the city, he said, "You like to quote Scripture, Father."

"In the beginning was the Word."

"The light shines in the darkness, and the darkness has not overcome it", Maurice completed the passage for him.

"That is so."

"What you call darkness is another dimension of light. You limit the light by your ignorance. And for this reason your 'light' is in fact a kind of darkness. Our light cannot be overcome, for it is the fullest meaning of the word."

"Your word is the false word. It is darkness. It is already defeated."

"Is it? Come, I will show you."

"Where are you taking me?"

"To the temple of culture."

The car went down a ramp into an underground parking lot. The tail car followed. Escorted by Maurice and two agents,

465

Andrei was taken up in an elevator to the main floor of a public art gallery.

"Behold the word", Maurice said. "Acres upon acres of words."

He led Andrei through a door into a corridor that linked the numerous galleries of the vast exhibition space.

"Where do we begin?" Maurice wondered. "There is so much to see."

Passing through a series of displays of abstract painting and sculpture, without pausing to reflect on any of the images, Maurice said, "Let us not waste time here, for this is the word in its purest form, distilled into spiritual essence. Few are enlightened sufficiently to read it."

"A bare canvas is a bare canvas", Andrei replied. "Its word is Emptiness. It is desolate and barren!"

"Do you long for Fertility?" Maurice countered. "Come, let us return to the womb."

In a vaulted room a giantess lay naked on the floor, a papier-mâché nude, thirty feet long from head to toe, flat on her back, limbs spread from wall to wall. The belly arched like a beached whale; below the navel a portal invited the lovers of art to penetrate.

"See the springs of life", Maurice said. "Enter and search for the source of the Nile."

Maurice entered the body of the giantess.

Andrei wheeled and strode toward the exit. The two escorts caught up with him, took him by the arms, and conducted him firmly back to the sculpture.

"Go inside", one commanded.

"No."

"Now!" said the other, looking over his shoulder. He signalled to a gallery guard, who positioned himself at the entrance of the room. The guard turned his back and explained to a crowd of schoolchildren and their teacher who were about to enter that the exhibit was closed for renovations.

Andrei cried to them feebly, "Help! I am a prisoner."

The teacher and children looked anxiously at him. The escorts smiled, and one said, "Our grandfather isn't feeling well." Turning to Andrei, the other said, "You'll have to go back to the hospital, Gramps."

"They are lying", Andrei called. The gallery guard murmured explanations to the crowd and moved them out of sight.

"Inside", said the first escort.

Andrei clamped his eyes shut. The escorts looked disgusted and shook their heads.

"You tough old sunuvabitch!"

Maurice came out and said, "What's the matter?"

"He won't go in, sir."

"Bring him in."

They dragged him inside.

"Open your eyes", Maurice commanded.

Andrei whispered prayers.

"It's just a sculpture!" one of the escorts said.

"It's art!" the other laughed sarcastically.

"*Mulieris dignitatem!*" Andrei cried.

"Open your eyes. You will stay in here until you open your eyes."

"I will die in here, if I must. But I will not look upon the degradation of the image of woman."

"Open your eyes and look, or we will find a real woman and degrade her in front of your eyes." This threw Andrei into confusion. Could he allow himself to be responsible for the violation of a woman, merely because of a fine point, because he could not bear to look upon an anti-word?

"Open your eyes."

He opened his eyes. They led him farther into the interior. In the place where the womb should have been was a large glass sphere, a terrarium in which live snakes writhed, devouring frogs.

467

"I know what you are doing", Andrei said angrily. "You put vile images into the minds of children."

"We are demythologizing the archetypes. Soon, every school-child in this city will have walked through these portals."

"You are already defeated, Satan. The woman shall crush your head."

"What grammar!" Maurice smiled. "You continually mix your tenses."

"They are precise", Andrei replied. "You are already defeated, and you shall be crushed."

"We are not crushed."

"Revelation is unfolding. Your time is short!"

"Let us move along to our next revelation", Maurice said.

As they walked along the corridor to another gallery, Andrei mentally formulated a cry for help. If he met any more people, he intended to shout, "My name is Father Andrei. I am alive. Tell the Roman Catholic archbishop!" The escorts would clamp his mouth shut, of course, but that would create a scene, and the message would be released. Somehow it would reach the archbishop.

But they met no more people, for the gallery guards went ahead, clearing the rooms.

The next gallery was bare except for a long, black sports car in the center of the room.

"This is your apocalypse", Maurice said. "See how low your word is fallen."

"It is an automobile", Andrei said.

"It is a word."

"What is this word?"

"Its title is *Trans-Am Apocalypse No. 2.*"

"It makes no sense."

"This is the quintessential muscle car. The dream of boys, the toy of adolescent men. With this do they aspire to strength. In this do they ride forth to conquer the nations. Come closer. Read."

Words were scratched into the surface of the black paint. Familiar words. Passages from the revelation of Saint John the Evangelist.

"You see? We have taken your apocalypse and turned it into a myth. The fundamentalist harangue of the television evangelist, the death-loving lyrics of the heavy-metal subculture of youth, the ravings of madmen, and the dry wastes of the theologians all draw upon this book."

"And yet this word is the proclamation of your defeat."

"We are not defeated. Read the pamphlet that accompanies it."

Andrei looked away and closed his eyes. Maurice handed the pamphlet to one of the escorts, who read aloud:

The artist recognizes the widespread popular obsession with power. For the underprivileged urban male, this car represents affluence, dominance, and escape. The artist has chosen to cover the vehicle with a hieratic text, scratching the letters into the body with a nail, digging deep into the metallic flesh like a modern scribe with his stylus. He creates a statement that blends ancient archetypes with a modern symbol of transcendence. Reaching deep into the shadows of the male psyche, he has effectively blended the macho-man, the mediaeval knight upon his black charger, and the dreaded horseman of the apocalypse, merging them into an icon of the follies of the male ego.

The destructive duality of the male, his violence, his uncontrolled passion for domination, are here exposed by the artist in one masterful stroke of juxtaposition and integration. The fearful imagery of the apocalypse has its source in the male's incompleteness. His cosmic terror, his alienation, his failure to integrate the feminine and the masculine, his inability to heal the destructive split in his personality, must necessarily lead him to dogmatism of one kind or another. The dogmatic nihilism of the young urban criminal is but the reverse image of the dogmatic religious extremist; both are mutated forms of the same dynamic.

Please do not touch the work. Oil from skin will damage the painted surface. On loan from the National Gallery of—

469

"Now, to our next revelation", Maurice said.

In a room off the main entrance, three images:

"Behold your word", Maurice said.

A photograph of the Pope sealed within a glass case. The case was filled with yellow liquid that foamed and bubbled.

"Read the title", Maurice said.

"I will not read it", Andrei replied.

"*Pisspope, No. 7*", the escort said, smirking.

"You understand?" said Maurice.

"I see only the crude malice of the sandbox. I see the infantile and the silly. Do you think you can defame a great man with this?"

"Yes, we can. It is sufficient to demythologize your guru."

Andrei shook his head.

"This does not shock me. It only moves me to pity for you, and for the artist."

"Ah, then let us move to the next image."

A crucifix, debased and ridiculed. The title was as vile as the blasphemy.

"Are you shocked by this?" Maurice asked tonelessly.

"Yes. Shocked most of all by the blindness of man."

"How much pity do you feel now for the artist?"

"Even more."

"I was hoping for outrage."

"You elicit only my prayers for him."

"Ah, then you must observe the next work of art."

A mockery of the Eucharist in images of utter degradation. Andrei turned away. The escort read the title to him. Andrei tried not to hear it.

"You understand?" Maurice inquired.

"I understand that the artist's soul is captive. I see also that those who control the organs of public culture are weak, deluded, filled with hatred for what they do not understand."

"We have humiliated your word."

"And by doing so, you tell everyone how important it is."

"I don't think so."

"Why do men hate it? Men do not hate a mere nothing."

"They hate a nothing that has masqueraded as something."

"Why not just ignore it?"

Maurice hesitated. "Because your religious totems have power over men's minds", he replied grudgingly.

"Power? This image of divine humility? This weakness?"

"The captive mind must be set free."

"I agree, Maurice. But who is the captive?"

They led Andrei back to the car, passing not a single soul to whom he might have bleated his cry for help. During the ride to the Institute he kept silent, staring out the passenger window, straining to find in the passing scenes a hint of normality. The hot, black, fast highway, the manicured residences and farms, the perfect rows of fruit orchards, and the exalted heights of the distant mountains all seemed to contradict the writhing imagery that had been implanted within his mind. He felt both nauseated and hungry. Very hungry. The controlled hysteria of the freeway made him dizzy. The drivers of expensive cars zipped in and out of the lanes without regard for their mortality. The hard, handsome faces of the young males, the equally hard faces of beautiful young women. Scowls, rude gestures. Transport trucks barrelling down on smaller vehicles, intimidating, honking, passing too close. Police cars cruising by at unthinkable speeds.

A mobile home passed on the left, the faces of children at the window, each of them plugged into a Walkman. The logo of the vehicle—*Security*—blatantly proclaimed its highest ideal. A child riding within it, catching Andrei's eye, stuck her tongue out at him. He looked away.

Her face was added to the day's images that had coiled and twisted and slithered through cracks in his defenses—they bit, injecting their poison into his bloodstream. He desired to weep, to vomit, to shout a final word of protest. He felt a wave of terror wash over him, spilling into portals, invading the womb of the soul.

Darkness. Light. Darkness. Light. Endlessly circling each other in the cockpit of existence.

Maurice, watching him out of the corner of his eye, said, "I was particularly interested in the way the gallery authorities justified the last exhibit, weren't you?"

"I can imagine."

"They call him a modern Goya."

"Another of your strokes of genius? Goya protested against the violation of the world. Your artist celebrates it."

"Of course. It is propaganda."

"You know this, and yet you approve of it?"

"I find the crudity distasteful. But you see, it is the only way to shatter the power that your myth holds over the captive mind."

"It is not a myth."

"If not, why so easy to humiliate it?"

"God is humble. He is love. He is patient. He grants us time to hear him. He waits for us to say yes to grace."

"There is no such thing as grace. There is only knowledge. Those who know, transcend. Those who cling to your ignorant word will go down into total humiliation."

"Not total."

"Soon, unless you reconsider, it will be total. Help us, and we will leave you a remnant."

"I will not help you. God himself will provide the remnant."

"Your God is a thought that has dissipated on the wind."

"My God is the one true God. He is a blazing fire. He who was, who is, and who is to come. The light of him is like unto the sun."

"The sun is a medium-size star, a ball of atomic fuel. Your God is a metaphor. A minor star. Your star has consumed its

472

fuel and is close to extinction. The star of the abyss is ascending."

"The star of the abyss will drag you back with him into the abyss. Unless you repent—"

"Unless *you* repent, Father Andrei, your light will be extinguished completely, your word utterly banished from this planet."

"In the beginning was the Word, and the Word was with God, and the Word was God. All things came to be through him, and without him nothing came into being. What came to be through him was life, and this life was the light of men. The light shines in the darkness, and the darkness has not overcome it." Father Andrei spoke with simplicity and conviction. There was no fear or intensity in his voice, no passion or drama. It was a statement of fact: "The Word became flesh and dwelt among us, and we saw his glory, the glory of the Father's only son, full of grace and truth."

"Glory?" said Maurice. "Where is your glory now?"

"The Son of Man is glorified on the Cross. He reveals it in the Resurrection."

"I see no glory. I see no resurrection. Where is this savior?"

"He is coming."

"Always coming, never arriving."

"Our God saves."

"Look all about you. Do you see any evidence of resurrection?"

"I see it everywhere."

"Point out an example to me."

"Am I not, in my own flesh, a small example?"

"You are the last devotee of a dishonored myth."

"Yet I live."

"You live because of *my* mercy."

"No, I live by the mercy of God."

"If so, why does your God not rescue you?"

"He rescues my soul even as we speak."

"We shall see", Maurice said, taking the exit from the expressway, turning onto the secondary highway that led to the Institute. He picked up the radio microphone and said, "Escort, return to center. The subject is secure. Over."

"Returning now, sir. Over."

The escort car passed them, accelerated ahead, and disappeared over a rise in the road.

Maurice and Andrei travelled in silence for several minutes.

"You can escape", Maurice said.

"I beg your pardon."

"I am going to release you."

Andrei stared, struggling to believe him.

"What do you mean?"

Maurice slowed the car to forty miles an hour.

"If you wish, you can leave the vehicle. I will not try to stop you."

"Do you mean it?"

"I mean it absolutely. Try the door. It is unlocked."

Andrei tried the handle of the door. It opened a crack, and the wind whistled in. He glanced at Maurice.

"I don't know why you're doing this, but I thank you."

"Don't thank me. Thank your God."

"He will bless you for it. I also bless you for it."

Maurice drove on without decelerating.

"Where do you wish to drop me?" said Andrei.

"Anywhere you like."

"This will do fine. Stop here, by these woods."

"Oh, no, I cannot stop."

"I don't understand."

"If you are a son of God, and if he is a God who saves, you can throw yourself out of the car as it moves, and he will keep you from harm."

"I begin to understand."

"Is it not written, 'He will give his angels charge of you, to guard you', and 'On their hands they will bear you up, lest you strike your foot against a stone'?"

"You must not tempt God", said Andrei.

"Throw yourself out. Let us test this glory you say you believe in."

Andrei closed the door firmly and said to him, "It is written, 'You shall not put the Lord your God to the test.'"

Maurice did not reply. Five minutes later he drove through the gates of the Institute and returned Andrei to his cell.

* * *

"How are we today?" Maurice asked when he returned the following week.

Andrei, lying on the bed, turned his face to the wall.

"I hear they saw through your liturgical ruse. That is unfortunate. You must miss saying your prayers and eating your biscuits."

Still no answer. The old priest rubbed a bandage on his arm.

"Surely you must feel better now. The intravenous feeding wasn't so bad, was it?"

"You cannot win", Andrei said.

"Do you feel up to another excursion?"

"No. We have nothing further to discuss. Please go away."

"Unfortunately I can't do that. Besides, I think you will find today's trip interesting."

Maurice and a guard took him up to the roof of the Institute, onto a pad where a black helicopter was waiting. The wind was sweet, sighing through the forest beyond the perimeter fence. Birds called. Andrei stopped and raised his head, drinking in their music hungrily. His legs trembled, and he stumbled. The two men took his arms and put him into the hellcop. When he was strapped into a seat, Andrei said, "Where are you taking me?"

475

"To the temple of understanding", Maurice replied.

The machine hummed and rose straight up, banked, and shot into the west.

The windows of the aircraft were shuttered, so Andrei could not see where they were going. He guessed that the flight lasted more than an hour and thus determined that the destination was not Vancouver. There were at least four Cities of the Plain within the radius of the flight, though he argued with himself that the hellcop might be making complicated maneuvers to disorient him. If so, to what purpose?

When his body registered the sensation that one feels in a descending elevator, and the craft ceased to hum, he knew it had landed. Maurice took him out onto a pad on the roof of a high office tower in the core of a city that Andrei did not recognize. It was a large metropolis, shining brilliantly in the dusk, the muted roar of evening traffic surging up from the streets below. Accompanied by Maurice and the other agent, he was taken down in a code-lock elevator and conducted onto a street. He opened his mouth and cried for help, but none of the passersby paid any attention, and Maurice pulled him along the sidewalk by the arm.

Three blocks down they came to the wide-open front doors of a neo-gothic cathedral. Organ music, singing, and the light of hundreds of candles burst out into the hot night. He was taken into the foyer, where he saw that the church was packed with people. Figures moving about the distant altar were lighting tall candles.

Maurice guided him into a room adjacent to the foyer, its front wall a sheet of glass facing the nave of the church. A sign on the door read, *Mothers and small children only, please.* The room was empty, save for two pews. Maurice shut the door and locked it.

"The crying room", he said, rapping the glass with his knuckles. "Soundproof."

"Is this a Catholic church or Anglican?" Andrei asked, scanning the front of the nave, searching for a tabernacle. He could not find one.

"Oh, it's very much a Catholic church. Tonight you will see a bishop and a prophet."

At that moment the organ swelled triumphantly, its trumpets carried to the room by the speaker system. The escort pressed down on Andrei's shoulder until the old priest took a seat.

"Observe carefully", Maurice said.

A mitered bishop, carrying his shepherd's staff in one hand and wearing liturgical vestments, entered the church through a side door and moved in stately procession up the side aisle toward the rear of the church. Beside him walked a priest in alb and rainbow-colored stole.

"The shepherd and his prophet", Maurice said.

As they passed the glass window, Andrei tried to stand and thump on the window, hoping to attract the bishop's attention, but the hands of Maurice and the escort were firm on his shoulders, restraining him.

Ahead of the bishop a troupe of adolescent girls in white tights danced in unison, twirling and leaping, waving streamers of brightly colored ribbons.

The bishop and priest turned and entered the central aisle, then moved toward the sanctuary. Behind them came two rows of children dressed in red robes, the boys swinging the chains of incensers, the girls holding bronze bowls of smoking incense high above their heads.

The organ music surged full volume, pumping into the church an atmosphere of exultation, passion, and triumph. The crowd stood, cheering, then burst into song.

"We are sons of the morning, we are daughters of light", they sang. "We will build the city of God, we will scatter the shadows of night!"

The song ended as the bishop and his prophet ascended the steps of the sanctuary.

A hush fell on the crowd, and the people sat down.

The bishop went to the lectern, leaving the priest standing beside the altar.

"My friends," he said into the microphone, "today in this cathedral God is doing a wonderful thing. He has brought to us a teacher and spiritual leader who has suffered much for the kingdom. Few have been maligned as he. Few have labored as diligently as he has to bring about a healing of the sectarian hatreds that have wracked us for so long. Heavy on his heart are the feuds that divide human beings from each other—Christian and Muslim, Jew and Gentile, black and white, oriental and caucasian, rich and poor. This valiant defender of the rights of the oppressed is the author of many books, some of which are used in our seminaries. He is a doctor of theology and the founder of a prophetic new college that seeks to heal the dualism that has tragically wounded our church for two millennia. Yet he is also artist, singer, poet, visionary, and mystic—all of these and more.

"In the name of the church I ask pardon for the sins that have been committed against this man by my own denomination. I ask pardon for the vestiges of the Inquisitional church that still linger in the shadows of our congregations in distant Rome. I ask pardon for our dogmatism and judgments. I ask pardon for the silencing and the fear, for our inability to hear the cries of victims, the voices of the poor. Before you tonight is their spokesperson, their champion. He has been commanded to keep silence, but he obeys a higher law. He will no longer remain silent. Indeed he *cannot* be silent, for the spirit of God is upon him.

"Tonight, at this opening liturgy of the Association of Pastoral Educators, he will celebrate with us the birthing of a new age for the churches and for humankind, which even as we speak is spreading like holy fire throughout the world. Listen to this man! Hear him!"

478

The bishop inclined his head to the priest and took his seat on the episcopal throne. The little dancers and the altar servers sat down on the floor about the sanctuary. A stir of expectation swept through the congregation as the priest walked to the lectern.

He smiled at the crowd and spread his arms wide.

"My sisters and brothers", he said in a strong, quiet voice. "In the words of the historical Christ I say, 'How I have longed to eat this feast with you. How I have longed to gather you together under my wings.'"

The voice was deep and melodious. The face, young and handsome, despite a shock of silver hair. The eyes, deep set and sensitive. His body tilted at the angle that denotes dignity, humility, and resolve.

"This gathering is an ecumenical one. You, the members of our association, for the most part, are chaplains and counsellors in the institutions of our land. Your ministry is to the schools, hospitals, prisons, and asylums for the victims of our materialistic society. Some of you are ministers in the sister churches. Some of you are priests and religious. Some of you take no label upon yourselves, though you are no less teachers and prophets among us.

"Tonight I ask you all to come into the light. Come in from the cold, from the exile to which my church has condemned you. I say unto you, we are one people, we are one humanity, and no longer can we walk in the ways of division. For this reason I have asked representatives of the various religions to concelebrate our liturgy as a sign of the harmonic convergence that is approaching. Will you please come forward now—Dr. Muhktari of the Hindu Reunification Church, Pastor Miriam Okazawa-Jones of the Christian Spiritualist Church, Most Reverend Anthony Trevor of the Anglican archdiocese, Talya Starfield of the Gaia Centre for Spiritual Renewal, and Reverend Meg Symes, Moderator of the United Church of the Americas."

The concelebrants went up into the sanctuary and seated themselves on chairs behind the altar. The priest bowed to them, and they returned the gesture.

"You see before you on the high altar a magnificent rainbow. The bishop tells me that the children of his diocese made it as a gift to commemorate this great moment. The rainbow contains all the colors of the visible spectrum. Such are we—for *we* are the many-colored light of God, incarnating the divine illumination among the people of our times. We are to be a sign, pointing the way to a third covenant that is soon to be revealed.

"The first covenant was intended for the formation of a chosen people who would be ready to receive the second covenant, which was the coming of the historical Christ. The people of that era proved themselves unprepared, and so the Christ of that age was not understood. Even so, over two millennia, mankind has again been shaped and molded in anticipation of the long-awaited dawn of the third advent—the revelation of the cosmic Christ. We are the blessed generation. We are the chosen. But like our forebears, we too can miss the day of his visitation. We too might turn away like the rich young man. We too might misread the signs of the times and fail to recognize him for who he is."

The priest bowed his head and let the tension build. Looking up suddenly, he cried with controlled passion, "I am not he!" More dramatic silence. "I am a voice crying in the wilderness, preparing the way of the Lord!"

He bowed to the bishop. "Neither is this great and good shepherd the one. Your bishop is a prophet, and long have I sat at his feet, learning the ways of discipleship. Yet even he is but a prefiguration of the one soon to be revealed."

The priest went on at some length describing just what constituted a great prophet. It took little effort for all present to conclude that the speaker himself fit the description quite nicely. He urged them to return to their flocks with the news that the dawn was no longer far off. Urged them to open the interior *chakras*, the portals of their souls, to the shaping spirits who would guide them to the Christ of the new age. The priest was masterful in his use of language, simultaneously poetic and precise in addressing contemporary issues (war, ecology, various forms of oppression). His face and his manner were spiritual, passionate but not theatrical. His words radiated power.

"No longer can we define church as hierarchy, that rigid, linear archetype in the minds of men whose hearts have never known passion. No longer can the will of the people be suppressed by those who wall up the garden of paradise. For the garden is all about us, my sisters and brothers. The traditional church has been oblivious to *theosis*, the divinization of the Cosmos. The church's obsession with fall and redemption, sin and repentance, has destroyed justice! It has torn the web of cosmic union! It has built walls. This must cease!"

The last word was shouted.

"It must cease!" he shouted again. "Tear down these walls!"

Father Andrei stood. His heart beat hard. The anguish he felt struggled to burst from him, but no words would take shape on his lips, for the rising fear choked them back.

"Tear down these walls! Let us join hands! Let us dance the ineluctable modalities of fertile life, which is the eternal Circle Dance!"

Maurice, mildly amused, observed Andrei's reaction. The old priest had been born in another era and had spent most of his life in remote missions or ministering to nuns and had never seen anything like this in a Catholic church.

Andrei staggered to the plate-glass window and slammed his hands on it.

"Stop", he cried.

"We are potent and passionate, my sisters and brothers", cried the prophet. "We are pregnant with the new age. Let us reclaim our garden! Let us restore Eden! For paradise is within us and all around us, and nowhere else can it be found. All walls are illusion!"

"Thief and liar!" Andrei shouted to the prophet. "Go in by the straight path. The narrow gate."

Maurice and the escort watched, saying nothing. Maurice smiled to himself and let the old man rant. No one could hear him. All eyes were on the prophet in the sanctuary.

Father Andrei slammed his hands again and again on the glass.

"Open your hearts to the light!" cried the prophet. "The light that reveals to us the presence of the Cosmic Christ. It comes from the Light-bearer, who offers you wholeness, who offers you freedom."

"False apostle! False prophet! False light!" Andrei sobbed. "Black light of Lucifer!"

"The old church is moribund", said the prophet.

"She is the Bride!" cried Andrei.

"The old church is a perverter of hearts and suppressor of liberty!"

"She is bleeding from many wounds!"

"There is only one tyrannical régime left on this planet—the Vatican!"

The crowd roared its approval, leapt to its feet, and cheered wildly.

"She is despised and rejected", Andrei groaned.

"The aristocracy of the sterile men must come to its appointed end", shouted the prophet.

"We looked upon her as a thing of no account, without beauty, with no looks to attract our eyes", Andrei cried.

"Let us build the City of God!" shouted the prophet, and the crowd burst into the lyrics of the song.

"The City of God will not be built by man", Andrei whispered. "It will come down from heaven as a gift, after the devastation of the earth by sin and error."

482

When the song was over, the prophet said, "Sister Debbie will now give us the first reading from Scripture."

A nun in a diaphanous lavender gown strode to the platform and took the microphone offered to her by the smiling prophet.

"We are children of joy", she said sweetly. "We are free to play on the marriage bed of our Mother-Father-Creator." Then, clearing her throat, she intoned solemnly, "A reading from the Book of Teilhard de Chardin."

This was followed by "a reading from the Psalms of Praise to the Earth Mother from the *Book of Knowings,* by Talya Starfield" (with a bow to the author).

When it was finished, she said, "Brother Ryan from Inner City Alliance of Gay Ministers will now present the second reading."

She sat down cross-legged beside the children.

A young man in a black body suit clinging to every part of his anatomy bounded up the steps and executed a somersault in front of the altar. The crowd laughed appreciatively.

"Thanks, Debbie", he said in an exquisitely gentle voice. "Our second reading is from the Book of the Prophet Carl Gustav Jung."

This was followed by an old woman in a long white dress, who flowed with ceremonial grace up the steps of the sanctuary and took the microphone.

"A reading from the Gospel of the Egyptians," she proclaimed, "containing the Revelation of the Great Seth."

Andrei cried out loudly, "No! You do not understand what you are doing!"

"They know", said Maurice. "They know very well what they are doing."

The thumping on the glass drew the attention of a few people sitting in the back pew, and though their curiosity was aroused for a few seconds, they did not wish to miss a word from the pulpit and turned to face the front.

"We have seen and heard", Maurice said. "It is time to go."

They went out the main entrance. Andrei, his eyes cast down, heart in agony, moved slowly down the steps assisted by the two men. At the bottom they encountered a cluster of people kneeling on the sidewalk—twelve.

"Behold the apostles", Maurice said.

Three children, four old women, a mother and father, a middle-aged man in a wheelchair (his mouth covered by a wide strip of duct tape), an old nun dressed in traditional habit, and a young priest. They were praying the rosary aloud. The man in the wheelchair caught their eye and lifted a sign for them to read:

> Abomination of the Desolation
> Do not listen to false prophets!
> Pray the Rosary!

"Here is your remnant", Maurice said.

"They are the Lord's little ones", Andrei replied in a shaken voice.

He stumbled over to the priest before Maurice or the escort could stop him, grabbed the man's arms, and stammered, "Please, help me. I am a priest. I am a prisoner!"

The young priest stood up. "What's that?" he said. "What did you say?"

Maurice and the escort grabbed Andrei and pulled him away, covering his cries with their own loud interjections.

"Grandpa", said the escort. "Don't bother these people. C'mon, it's time to go home."

"He has Alzheimer's disease", Maurice explained with a compassionate smile. "He doesn't know where he is. He thinks he's a priest."

"Maybe he is a priest", the young cleric said, his eyes flashing from face to face.

Maurice laughed. "He isn't. Come on, Andy, time to head home. Mum's waiting."

"Go to the archbishop of Vancouver!" Andrei shouted. "Tell him I am alive. My name is—"

But the last word was swallowed by the noise of a bus roaring by.

The young priest took a step forward. Maurice drew Andrei away and began to pull him briskly along the street. The escort stepped in behind them.

"What is your name?" the young priest called to their retreating backs. He could not hear Andrei's muffled reply.

Maurice and the escort hustled him along the sidewalk without any more embarrassing incidents, went into the office tower, and took him in the elevator to the top. Faces grim and controlled, they conducted him to the corner of the roof and held him there with his toes over the edge.

"That was very unwise", Maurice said coolly.

"I am prepared", Andrei said. "I offer my life for those foolish people in the cathedral. Lord Jesus, receive my soul!"

Maurice laughed. "Do you think we're going to throw you off? A scene from a fright film? A brutal end to a trite crime drama? Oh, no, it is not so simple as that."

"What do you mean to do?"

"I mean to make you think."

"I have thought. I have seen. It is perfectly clear."

"You understand nothing", Maurice replied. "Look."

He extended his arm and made an arc over the cityscape that lay before them. The many splendored lights of the city were dazzling.

"Behold the City of God."

"That is the City of Man."

"Behold the kingdoms of the earth and the glory thereof. Do you not desire them?"

"I do not want them."

"Your church wants them. I will free your church from the forces that oppress it. Your religion will enjoy a revival and spread throughout the world. There will be no more atheists. There will be no more persecution. The people will worship in spirit and truth."

"And what is the price?"

"You will go down and merge with the crowd in the cathedral and become one of them. You will worship."

"What do you want me to worship?"

"You will worship the Christ."

"I worship the one true Christ and no other. He who was, who is, and who is to come."

"The Christ who is to come is already among us."

"Jesus is the Christ! He alone!"

"He was a foreshadowing of the Christ of these times. Fall down and worship the Christ of the new age!"

Andrei stared at him with horror and pity. "I will not."

"If not, then you, and you alone, are responsible for destroying what little remains of your dying church."

"That is a lie. You are the destroyer."

"I offer you life."

"You are the death-bringer."

"The world has become an arid wasteland, a cold desert of unbelief, immersed in hatred, division, and darkness."

"*You* have done this."

"No, priest, you and your church have done this, for you have failed to bring the light into the darkness of men's hearts."

"We brought them the light, but they have preferred darkness. Yet the light is still among us. Until now our faith has freed mankind from the terror of demons. But if the redeeming light of the one true Christ should go out, the world would fall again into terror and hopelessness."

"Terror and despair grow daily", Maurice replied. "Give them hope. Give them faith."

"Faith, you say? What kind of faith? There is a thing far worse than the desert of atheism, and that is false religion—to worship an idol in the desert."

"Consider well. Is it not better for you to open your temples to the new worship? If you are right and we are wrong, if your Christ is greater than our Christ, then you have nothing to fear. Your Christ will win."

"Falsehood! Deceiver! In this way has the enemy seduced mankind from the beginning. Your Christ grasps for thrones; ours accepts a cross upon his back and dies for us."

"That is the way of the Old Age. Now is the time when religion comes into its full inheritance. I will give you authority and glory and power to bring men back to the light."

"Our full inheritance belongs to Jesus alone. He will give it to us when we come into his kingdom, in paradise."

"Paradise is all around us. The kingdom is unfolding even as we stand here."

"Jesus on the Cross is the gate of paradise."

"That is finished. It happened two thousand years ago. You are locked in a pathetic obsession."

"And I say unto you, Maurice, that you are the prisoner, for you call life that which is death, you call freedom that which is bondage, you call savior the one who is the destroyer."

"He is the elder brother of the Nazarene, given authority over the kingdoms of this world. Now are the two brothers reconciled; now does the elder ascend to his rightful place, the throne of godhead."

"Be silent!" Andrei cried, his voice shaking.

"Worship the elder not the younger, the greater not the lesser, the cosmos not the reflected light of the moon."

"This is blasphemy. I will hear no more."

"You will hear this: Now is your choice. You can save or destroy."

"The salvation you offer is total destruction."

"Choose."

"Begone, Satan! for it is written, 'You shall worship the Lord your God and him only shall you serve.' "

Neither of Father Andrei's captors replied to this. Fully expecting to be hurled from the roof, he closed his eyes and prayed. He was greatly surprised when they pulled him away from the edge and took him to the helicopter that stood warming its engine on the landing pad. They put him inside, strapped him to the seat, and accompanied him back to the Institute without a word.

13

Hiatus in Arcadia Deo

When Father Ron left the rectory on Saturday morning, the sky was overcast. As he pulled into the parking lot of the golf club, a light misty rain had begun to fall. He hoped that when the archbishop arrived he would cancel the game. No such luck. His Grace was wearing a waterproof jacket and a look that said, neither-sleet-nor-hail-nor-rain-shall-impede-our-course.

"Good morning, Father", he said jauntily.

"Good morning, Your Grace. Dirty weather today."

"Not at all. The forecast says blue skies later in the morning. Why don't we tough it out?"

"I didn't bring a jacket."

"That's all right. I brought one for you."

Father Ron grimaced and put on the jacket.

The course was almost deserted except for a few diehards. As they walked to the fairways, the archbishop went through the usual question-and-answer checklist for fanaticism. Father Ron had little to report. The fanaticism was performed by his parishioners now. A few more television sets had been burned that week, but it looked like the wave had crested. He told the archbishop that he was puzzled by the fact that most of those who burned their sets were the very people best able to live with one. Those who needed to unplug were clinging tightly to their *TV Guide*s.

"What else is being burned?" the archbishop inquired.

"A lot of books and magazines. And a growing number of pills." He added that he hadn't looked closely at the packages but guessed they contained contraceptives and anti-depressants in about equal proportions.

The archbishop shook his head. "Why are so many of our people depressed, Father? Are they really so unbalanced! Did you know that mental illness almost disappears during wars? The asylums become empty."

"Are you sure about that? What about all those soldiers who get shell shock or battle fatigue?"

"Yes, I suppose we have to consider them. But that's reasonable insanity, isn't it?"

"Reasonable insanity?"

"I mean," said the archbishop, choosing his words carefully, "war is fundamentally insane, and it's to be expected that people on the front lines will crack under pressure. What has perplexed me for the past several decades is why so many people who are living more or less normal lives are victims of neurosis and psychosis."

"Maybe we're in a war zone?"

"Yes, I think so. A silent war that is producing far more victims than have the violent wars of this century. You see, I think there is something in the psyche, one might even say in the soul, that can cope with a visible enemy but not with a constant sense of dread and chaos, the source of which is invisible."

"So, people either break down or . . ."

"Or what, Father? That's the question. Or what?"

"Well, I suppose the alternative is to try to find meaning for their lives. Get some stability, order, peace."

"Absolutely correct. That's what most people strive for. But it's not working very well, is it?"

"No, Your Grace, not very well."

"So, when that fails we see a third option beginning to materialize."

"Which is?"

"Control."

"My parishioners control the intolerable pressures by upping their entertainments and cutting back on burdens . . ."

"And responsibilities."

"Yes, and responsibilities. Raising children is the first thing to be jettisoned."

"Correct. At the grass-roots level, our most precious gifts, our children, have come to be considered burdens. That should tell us something about the nature of this war. But I'm trying to get at something else. I'm beginning to see that the dynamic of control must eventually reach all the way to the top of the power structure. As the dread approaches a high level of intensity, the control will necessarily become absolute."

Father Ron looked sideways at the archbishop. This was extreme talk coming from a master of moderation. He maintained a judicious silence while the archbishop mused.

"The foundation of democracy is conscience—personal responsibility. The society that abandons moral absolutes must eventually degenerate into a police state. Well, this nation *has* abandoned morality. Is it realistic to think we can avoid the consequences?"

Father Ron shook his head.

"These people, whoever they are," the archbishop continued, "will more and more suppress civil rights in the name of security. But they're going to make mistakes from time to time. They're human too. There are going to be some leaks."

"Do you see signs of that happening?"

"Until now I wasn't sure. I try not to jump to conclusions. Imagine, if you will, the specter of a paranoid archbishop. The worst thing that can happen to a flock is to stampede and run hysterically in every direction. It's my job to prevent that."

"I don't envy your position, Your Grace."

The archbishop smiled wryly. "I don't envy my position either."

"May I suggest a thought?"

The archbishop's glance said, *You're going to suggest it whether I say yes or no.*

"Your Grace. Isn't there a worse scenario? What if the wolves are closing in on the flock but are disguised as lambs? What if a few of the wolves are already among the flock?"

"All right. You have a point. But let's for the sake of argument just switch metaphors here a minute. Let's say I'm driving a runaway stagecoach; the horses are out of control. What should I do? If I suddenly throw on the brakes, the coach will crash, destroy itself, and kill everyone inside."

"But what if the coach is stampeding toward a precipice? Surely to slam on the brakes is the only thing you can do."

"Are we stampeding toward a precipice, Father? That's the crucial question."

"I think we are."

"I know you think that."

The silence yawned uncomfortably. Eventually the archbishop said, "How am I to know? I don't hear voices. I depend on reason. I depend on faith."

"Isn't the Body of Christ composed of many different gifts, Your Grace?"

"Yes. Why do you ask?"

"I mean, isn't your gift to teach and defend, using all the resources of faith and reason? But the body has many organs. It couldn't survive without your reason and faith. But neither would it do very well without spirituality and all the rest."

"Ah, you mean we need prophets."

"Yes. Prophets working hand in hand with sober minds like yours, who have the gifts to measure the vision against revealed truth."

"I agree. Tell me, how am I to discern whether or not your vision is genuine prophecy?"

"Does it fit with Tradition and Scripture?"

"So far, it does—at least yours does. But you know as well as

492

I that there have been aberrations. There are a lot of bizarre messages coming from every direction."

"I know. Maybe they're a smoke screen, to confuse and distract the flock from genuine prophecy. Wouldn't you expect the devil to pull a stunt like that?"

"Yes", the archbishop replied slowly. "My problem is, Father, are you Noah or Chicken Little?"

Father Ron sighed. "I don't know. Maybe I'm Noah Little."

The archbishop chuckled. Then he laughed. He slapped Father Ron on the shoulder and said, "Let's go get some lunch."

He bought a copy of the Saturday *Star* at the restaurant desk. They found a seat by the window overlooking the fairway and ordered hamburgers. The archbishop read the religion section while Father Ron perused the international news. From time to time the archbishop beetled his brows and sipped from his coffee cup.

"Well, we've made the headlines", he said at last, passing the religion section to Father Ron.

"Oh-oh. What did they do to us this time?"

"It's not so bad. Read."

The headline—*Fire in the Grass Roots or Opiate of the Masses?*—didn't bode well, but the contents were better than expected. It wasn't a hatchet job. A few swings of the blade here and there, but on the whole a balanced approach. Several quotes from articulate pastors and members of various congregations. The snideness was left to a few liberal commentators.

The author approached it from the angle of sociological phenomena. The burning of television sets, books, and other material had erupted spontaneously, it seemed, and none of the churches involved could claim any motivation other than the desire to return to a focus on the basics of the Gospel. Although the author took pains to classify the "movement" as fundamentalist, he qualified it by saying that its most puzzling characteristic was that it seemed to cut across all sectarian boundaries; and it had happened without any organization or coordination, indeed, with nary a word passing from congregation to congregation. Moreover, the phenomenon had erupted from no identifiable source, like a subterranean root fire springing up in all sectors of the Christian community. Evangelicals, Catholics, and Pentecostals were involved throughout the country and abroad, and incidents had occurred even in that most reasonable of reasonable circles, the liberal mainline Protestant denominations. The Catholics and the Evangelicals were the largest statistical group, the liberal Protestants the smallest, and everyone else was somewhere in between. Religious sociologists were utterly perplexed, because the statistics demolished some behavioral and psychological templates that had heretofore been accepted as authoritative by the social sciences.

"Did they let you proofread it first?" the archbishop said.

"Yes", Father Ron admitted. "What they faxed me was fine. I okayed it. But it looks like they put in a lot of stuff I didn't see. Swift move."

"Even so, it doesn't make us out to be hysterical. We should be grateful for that."

"I don't like the sly little reference to Nazi book burning. But I like the quote they used from your office: 'A spokesman from the Roman Catholic archdiocese of Vancouver told reporters that the archbishop wishes to maintain the scriptural precedent of not stifling the Spirit, while at the same time keeping an eye on the potential for excess.'"

"That's not exactly what I said, but it's close. Reporters aren't trained in theological nuance, it seems. What really bothers me is the other episcopal voices."

"You mean this quote from the Anglican archbishop? Hmmm. Not very nice."

"And the Catholic bishop next door."

"Even worse. But look, Your Grace, at the end they quote a cardinal. He seems positive enough. Same approach as yours."

"The statistics are interesting. Most interesting."

"Uh-huh. Looks like we're not the only crazies on the block."

"Read them to me again."

"Fifty-seven R.C. parishes in the country have had 'incidents'. Wow!"

"A little more than one percent of our parishes", said the archbishop.

"Not exactly overwhelming. But listen to this—an auxiliary bishop in Toronto is also involved. Pastoral letter exhorting all the faithful to remove New Age material from their homes and destroy it. He set up a hot line for people to phone in to check out titles and authors. Hey, that's great!"

"Read on", the archbishop prompted.

"It says here that four priests in Vancouver are involved." Father Ron looked up sharply. "Who are the other guys?"

"Don't you know?"

Father Ron spread his hands and shook his head.

"Old Father Kim at Our Lady of Grace, the Korean parish. He was in prison under the Communists, you know. Also, Father Anthony, the Vietnamese curate at Saint Michael's—he's been in prison too. Our saintly Father Don out at Saint Gabriel's in the east end. And you."

Father Ron mused on that. "Any others in the archdiocese?"

"Well, there is Father Potempko up in Bella Coola. But I'm not too surprised by that. He's rather eccentric. The pastor there, Father Shane, is having a fit. He wants me to pull Potempko out."

"Are you going to?"

"I'm not sure."

"So what does all this mean?"

"Do you see the pattern? Three of these men have been in prison under Marxist dictatorships. The question I'm asking myself is this: Are they overreacting to something in their pasts? Are they . . ."

"Paranoid?"

"I hate to say it, and I'm getting just a little sick of that word, but yes. Maybe they've been looking for something like this to vent their irrational fears."

"Where do I fit in?"

The archbishop skewered him with a penetrating look. "I don't know."

Father Ron waited.

"You're not the only factor here. There's young Richie Benson."

"The deacon?"

"Yes, the deacon. He's become a bit of a problem."

"Why do you say that?"

"He's the brightest seminarian we've ever had in this archdiocese. He's scheduled to be ordained to Holy Orders next summer, if the seminary graduates him. After what he's done, I'm not sure they will."

"What did he do?"

"Last month, shortly after you began your parking lot experiment, Benson went through the college library with a few of his fellow seminarians and weeded out the heretical material."

"And . . .?"

"And they had a little bonfire."

"Oh, I see."

"Do you? This is a very serious matter. What he did is quite different from a pastor burning his own possessions."

"Obviously he did it without permission."

"Obviously", the archbishop said dryly.

"Oh, dear."

"Yes, oh, dear. The administration is up in arms. Richie handed the president of the college a letter of explanation and an envelope containing enough money to cover the cost of the books he had destroyed. That money didn't come easily to him.

He works every summer as a stevedore on the docks to pay for his education. But that's not the point. It's the objective nature of the act that's in question, and also what it tells me about his personality. They suspended him. They're probably going to refuse him his degree, but they're hesitating. It's somewhat embarrassing for them, you see, because Richie won the medal for philosophy a few years ago and just won the national award for merit in theological studies. The president wants *me* to do their dirty work for them. He demanded—demanded, mind you—that I drop him and send letters to every diocese in the country and the U.S., informing the bishops of Richie's unsuitableness as a candidate for the priesthood. If I do that, there isn't a diocese in North America that will accept him."

"They may have a point. Is he suitable?"

"I talked to Richie over the phone. He was sincerely apologetic. Didn't know what came over him, he said. Promised me it would never happen again. I told him that I was thoroughly disappointed in him and that his ordination was now in grave doubt. Told him that no matter how orthodox he considered himself to be, his act was just as foolish as liberation theology."

"How did he take it?"

"He agreed. Admitted that what he'd done was precipitous. Said he'd acted on impulse, was overtired and just sick to death of having to fake liberalism in order to pass his courses. Said that this kind of fakery was a scandal and that no faithful Catholic called to the priesthood should be forced to play a double life. I told him he should have been more diplomatic, told him I've been trying to make the administration of the college come to its senses about curriculum. He replied in no uncertain terms that he doubted if I could make them come to their senses. He said to me, 'They're not moderate liberals, Your Grace. They're dedicated Modernists.' "

"Are you going to ordain him?"

The archbishop gave Father Ron a harsh look. The look said

that Father Ron should be careful not to presume upon their growing familiarity.

"Sorry, Your Grace."

"I don't know what I'm going to do with him. He'll have to apologize to the faculty, of course. If they accept his apology, maybe, just maybe, he'll be allowed to get his degree, and then I can pack him off to Rome for his doctoral studies without too much flak from the academic community here in Canada."

Father Ron cleared his throat. He tried to say something but thought the better of it. It was a tricky situation. The archbishop had been one of the founding professors of the college and was a close friend of the dean of theology, one of the few members of the faculty who was still orthodox, strictly speaking, and who it was rumored would soon be offered the presidency of the college. After that he could begin to turn things around. If he or the archbishop blew it now, it could take another generation to get things back on track. And who knew how many dissident priests and nuns would be pumped into the system before that happened?

The archbishop looked exasperated.

"It would be so much easier if Richie were just another garden variety troublemaker", he said.

"He isn't?"

"There's my dilemma. He's young. He's impetuous. But he's pure gold. Finest mind I've seen in years. Really a holy kid. Loves to laugh and has lots of friends. Plays hockey and reads von Balthasar with equal zest. Sends his spare cash to the Sisters of Charity and works with street people on the weekends. I won't bore you with a list of his other fine qualities."

"I see your dilemma."

"Do you? I wonder if anyone realizes the complicated webs we bishops have to maneuver through these days."

"Your Grace," Father Ron said, taking his life in his hands, "is the Gospel complicated? Maybe when faced with a spider web we should just cut through it. Not get stuck in it, if you know what I mean."

"I know exactly what you mean", the archbishop replied coldly. He glanced at his watch. "Look. I'm a bit tired. Let's call it a day. I should get back to the chancery and do some work."

Father Ron, feeling chastened but grateful for liberation from the remaining holes, said good-bye and drove home wondering if he had made a mistake by attempting that kind of frankness. To lecture a bishop of all things! What was happening to him? Was this prophecy business going to his head? Had pride seeped into his heart? He could not excuse himself by pleading the misplaced zeal of youth. And he certainly wasn't brilliant or holy. Nor did he have enough energy for zest. He wasn't interested in hockey, and he rarely spent his leisure time reading theology.

Yup, he'd blown it, he said to himself. What would the archbishop do next?

* * *

In the late afternoon the archbishop spent an hour putting the finishing touches on the next day's homily. The chancery offices were deserted, and he was able to work quietly without interruption. After that he climbed the stairs to his apartment. Situated on the fifth floor of an old brownstone apartment block, his suite of rooms was decorated in simple style, reflecting his unsophisticated tastes. He lit a candle beneath an icon of the Mother of God, bowed to it, said a brief prayer, and went into the kitchen. The housekeeper had left a meal for him in the refrigerator with a note taped to the cellophane wrap, instructing him to heat it up for five minutes in the microwave. He obeyed and set the steaming veal cutlet, rice, and broccoli on the dining room table. He said grace, poured himself a glass of cranberry cocktail, and ate without paying much attention to the contents of his plate. He ignored the rhubarb pie, remembering his cholesterol level.

After a single cup of decaffeinated coffee, he washed the dish and utensils off in the kitchen sink and went into his living room. He sat in the easy chair for some time, watching the sky fade into purple dusk and the lights of the downtown core winking on. It was a hot, muggy night, and the air conditioner was broken. He opened the window wide and listened to the sirens of ambulances and police, the raucous cries of a group of teenagers cavorting on the street below, and the rumble of trolley buses. He fell asleep and dreamed.

A garden. A beautiful garden of fruit trees, arrayed in a mysterious pattern within a high stone wall. The trees were heavy with buds, blossoms, and fruits of many kinds, the species of which he had never before seen. Gold and silver orbs predominated, but all the colors of the spectrum were also present. In addition, there were colors that the human eye had not seen, each of them an epiphany of light in which there was no darkness, for they were colors of the spirit—something he understood while he was in the dream but that later, upon waking, made no sense to him.

At the center of the garden there was a tower of ivory, with twelve open doors from which streams of water flowed, and upon the height of the tower was a jeweled crown of great magnificence, surrounded by a corona of twelve stars.

The garden was filled with playing children, their laughing-singing voices intertwining with brightly feathered birds that swooped and arched through the branches. The children ate of the fruit and drank from the streams of water. Then they entered the front door of the tower and prostrated themselves before a dazzling light coming from a throne on a high altar. Upon the throne was a Lamb. Five ruby jewels pierced its body, and rivers of blood flowed from them. As the five streams poured down from the altar, they divided and formed twelve rivers of clear water that went out into the garden and watered it.

Then an angel came from the sanctuary, and in his right hand he carried a sword. Beside him stood another angel of a different kind, though he too was in the service of the Lamb, and in his hand was a stylus.

Go forth from this place, said the voice of the Lamb. *Go forth to purify the earth, but do not do so until you have sealed the foreheads of all those who seek me with their whole minds and hearts and souls. Begin first with those who are closest to the sanctuary. Begin with those who night and day grieve over the state of the household of the people of God.*

Many angels proceeded from the throne of the altar and went out through the doors of the temple, accompanying the flowing rivers as far as the gates of the garden wall. Beyond the gates was a field surrounded by a ring of outermost wall. Its twelve gates stood open, and before each portal many angels wrestled with demons, and some of these, seeking to enter, were felled by the angels' swords, while others entered into the outer court, though none was able to enter the inner. Flowers of all kinds grew in the outer court, and many of these were crushed by the writhing of the serpents that had gained entrance. The light of that region was dimmed, and the rivers that flowed from the throne were unseen by the multitudes that ran this way and that, their hands stretched out before them as if blind, searching for entrances that were exits and exits that were entrances, not knowing where to find sanctuary, refuge, or eternal joy, or food to eat, or water to quench their thirst. The angels of the inner gates stood waiting, observing the battle in the outer court, biding their time. While they watched, they wept over the darkness of the world, grieved as the rivers poured out into the night where vast numbers of people stumbled over each other, wailing and gnashing their teeth and hurling contempt upon the garden and the rivers and upon the children who sang within.

And the angels cried to all the corners of the earth:

Come, my children! Come into the light! Sanctuary! Refuge! Peace and eternal joy! Come out of the dark, my children, come out of it, my people, lest it pull you down into the abyss from which there is no return!

But the malice of the people in darkness waxed full, and about their eyes and hearts there coiled many serpents whose names were jealousy and hatred and all the deadly sins. Then a great trumpet blew, and the angel scribe and the angel with a sword went forth, the former first, followed by the latter, and the scribe marked the sign of the cross upon the foreheads of many who were struggling in the field of the outer court. Among them were shepherds, and some of them the angel marked, and some of them he did not. The archbishop was with the shepherds, carrying his miter and crosier, but strangest of all he was only ten years old. When he saw the two great angels, he knelt down and covered his face in shame, for he believed that he was one of those not chosen, that he was unworthy, that he had failed to protect the flock. Yet the angel approached him and inscribed upon his forehead the sign of the cross.

Here is one who has defended his flock amidst many trials, cried the angel with a voice like a trumpet. *All of his labors are seen and recorded, his sacrifices, his suffering, and his courage. Yet I have this to say of you: Too readily did you falter and not trust. Too much did you rely upon yourself, your strength, and your own mind. Too much did you expect from the City of Man. Too little did you trust the heart of the Father. Too easily have the deceivers played upon your kindness and bent you to their ends. Even so, they have bent you but a small measure. Stand up now, be firm, and strengthen the flock that remains.*

The archbishop awoke. His heart was beating hard, his emotions turbulent with an impossible mixture of joy and anguish. He sat upright and put his hand to his forehead. It was hot, and he wondered if he were coming down with the flu. He told himself that the imagery was an imaginative mixture of various books of the Bible and was probably somewhat garbled. The stars were obviously derived from a scriptural source, and the garden was, of course, a mixture of Genesis, Revelation, and various other references to the New Jerusalem. He pondered the theology and symbolism and didn't quite know what to make of it. A fevered imagining? A temptation perhaps? A nightmare? But a strange sort of nightmare, if nightmare it was, for it both alarmed and consoled.

He got up and went into the private chapel beside his bedroom. He genuflected before the Presence in the tabernacle and knelt praying for guidance about the dream and about the many questions plaguing him. How to strengthen the flock? How to deal with the serpents and wolves? The situation in the archdiocese was becoming too complicated. The spider web, Father Ron had called it. But what could he do? Swing a sword without regard for where it came down, upon guilty and innocent alike? He couldn't see invisible crosses on foreheads! God didn't speak to him! There were no voices, no visible angels guiding him, no manuals, no blueprints, no maps!

Still the dream would not fade. It remained in the center of his consciousness like a mute messenger delivering a telegram, with a foot in the doorway, unwilling to depart. Was the dream a product of the fever, or the fever a symptom of the disturbance he felt over the dream? It had been many years since he had experienced a dream of that intensity. He had a vague sense that he dreamed every night, but such night visitations always faded a few seconds after he awoke and could not be remembered. This was different. There was a lucid radiance to it that had startled and alerted him even in the stupor of sleep, that presented itself as something more than the ruminations of the subconscious. He had read enough psychology to know that the mind contained untapped reservoirs, image banks into which the soul could dip from time to time for symbolic insight. At other times, the soul prompted the eruption of symbols into the conscious mind, as a kind of language, relaying through the message center of the brain whatever was picked up by some hidden faculties of the spirit. He would never be so bold as to presume that they were direct messages from heaven. That sort of thing happened to saints and mystics, he argued, not to administrators.

He remained immobile for several minutes, unable to form words of prayer, unable to shake off the images of the dream. Then, for no reason, a memory rose up within him. He was ten years old, walking through the poplar woods at the edge of his father's fields. It was early summer on the prairies, the sun was hot, and the grasshoppers were clicking madly. He was skipping through the underbrush, singing a Hail Mary. He was very happy that summer, because he had just made his First Communion and also because he had been given a battered bicycle by a cousin who moved to the city when the bank foreclosed on the farm of his uncle. He did not understand why the grown-ups were so unhappy.

He skipped and sang all the way to the pool in the creek where brown trout spawned and stopped there, watching them play. Then a boy of the same age as he walked out of the willows on the far side and stood facing him, smiling at him. He had flaxen hair and a fine face, with eyes that looked as old as a grown-up's, but not sad. He held an orange in his hand. He smiled again and threw it across. The archbishop caught it. Sitting in his armchair in a distant city sixty years later, he could still feel the round fruit in his hand and wondered at the sensation.

"It's for you", the boy said. "You can eat it."

He had sat down on the grass and peeled it. It was a very large orange. Its color was gold, but when the sun struck its surface, it was red.

"What's your name?" he asked the stranger.

"My name is Joachim", the boy replied.

"That's a funny name."

"It means, *God prepares*."

Joachim watched him as he stuck his thumb under the thick skin and curled it back. He had never seen an orange like it, for in the midst of the Great Depression such marvels were few and far between. The previous Christmas he had found at the bottom of the sock tacked to the foot of his bed a rosary made from knotted white string, a pencil, and a small, sour, wizened orange.

He finished peeling the marvellous orange and looked up, intending to offer half of it to the stranger, but the boy had disappeared. Who was he? For most of his life the archbishop had assumed that the strange boy had been a visitor at a neighboring farm, though when he inquired at all the farms for miles around, no one had seen or heard of a child named Joachim.

Not understanding why he did so, the archbishop bent his weary joints and laid his body down on the floor, facing the tabernacle.

Like the day of my ordination, he thought.

Oh, such a day! Such joy. Peace flowing straight through his heart. And that smile on his mother's face at the reception. He was her eleventh child. She had nearly died giving birth to him. He was her darling. The farm folk gathering around his parents had drowned them in praise, but she had remained solid in her heavy, humble, Old Country way. He could still smell the scent of pies and rose perfume clinging to her gaudy floral dress, purchased with egg money from the Sears catalogue.

"This must be the proudest day of your life, Minnie", someone had said.

She smiled gently. "I'm as proud as the day he was born", she had replied. His mother—a farm wife, the kind of simple woman who would be roundly despised today. Uneducated. Unambiguous. A workhorse. Matriarch of a clan of serfs. The wisest woman on earth, she couldn't read or write. He thanked

God for her and for his stolid father and, curiously, for the mysterious boy who had given him the orange.

The archbishop lay still, letting himself float in a state of inner quietude. Memories and dreams blended and faded, leaving only the feeling of the host in his fingers during the first Mass. A burst of awe, the brief flash of a transient light, both tactile and transcendent. Tears barely held back so as not to embarrass the family. Wanting to weep with wondrous love. Wanting to remain kneeling before the miracle forever. But the liturgy must proceed, no theatrics allowed, no mysticism, please. The great golden fruit of purest faith floating within him, sweet on the tongue, sweet in the belly, sweetest of all in the heart.

Silence fell in the archbishop's chapel. Time ceased. He rested in a perfect stillness of soul, without thoughts or desires.

Zeal for thy house consumes me, said a voice. And it was the voice of the mysterious boy.

The telephone rang, tearing the weave of tranquillity. The archbishop ignored it. But it rang and rang. He began to count the rings. After the fifteenth, he worried that it might be urgent and got up with much creaking and aching of his joints.

"Hello."

"Is this the archbishop's office?"

"Yes. This is the archbishop speaking."

The caller gave his name and told the archbishop he was an assistant parish priest in a neighboring diocese. He named the diocese. The archbishop frowned.

"How can I help you, Father?"

"Your Grace, I'm not sure you can. Something rather odd has happened, and I think it concerns you. Do you have a few minutes?"

"Of course."

The priest described an incident that had occurred in front of the cathedral of his diocese on the previous night. He had been praying with a group of his parishioners, protesting the presence of a heretical theologian who was speaking there with the approval of the bishop. During the liturgy three men had come out of the cathedral. One of them, a very old man who seemed distressed, had come up to him and said he was a priest and a prisoner, and that the archbishop of Vancouver should be informed.

"Did he tell you his name?" the archbishop asked.

"He tried to, but I couldn't hear. The other two men whisked him away pretty fast. They didn't look any too pleased, either."

"What did he look like, the old man?"

"Just an old man. Short, limped slightly, had a scar on his cheek."

"Did he speak with an accent?"

"Now that you mention it, I guess he did. German or Slavic, maybe Russian."

"I see. Can you tell me about the other two?"

"Well, they seemed to have him pretty tightly in hand. There was a distinguished older man with him, lots of dignity, expensive clothes. He seemed to be in charge. The other one was in his thirties, ordinary suit, smart-looking but not too smart, if you know what I mean. They both made out that the old fellow was suffering from Alzheimer's and was totally confused. They pulled him away against his will, saying they were taking him home to his wife."

"Was there anything about them to indicate who they were?"

"No", the priest replied, puzzled.

"Nothing at all? If you had to make an educated guess, what kind of men would you say they were?"

"I haven't given it much thought. At first I wondered if they were criminal types, but that doesn't hold water. They looked too clean, too confident—establishment. They weren't Mafia. They didn't look like kidnappers. These were definitely high-level guys, I'd say."

"High level?"

"Well, I'm just guessing, but I'd say the classy guy was civil

507

service or maybe a banker or college professor. The younger one looked like plainclothes police or private eye. Do you know who the old man was? Was he really a priest?"

"I'm not sure. But thank you, Father, thank you for phoning me."

"If I can help in any way, Your Grace, just let me know."

"I will. In the meantime, I suggest that you don't mention this to anyone else."

"All right", the priest said slowly. "What's it all about?"

"I don't think I can discuss it. But I'm going to do what I can. Pray for me, will you, Father?"

"Of course I will. Of course."

The archbishop hung up and sat thinking. Then he picked up the ecclesial directory and found the telephone number of the young priest's bishop. He did not relish the thought of having a conversation with this bishop, for he regarded him as a major instrument of division within the Church in North America. It was sometimes difficult to control a feeling of disgust, and dismay, whenever the bishop spoke at meetings of the national conference. A clever theologian, but proud and ambitious. Frustrated in his desire for a cardinal's hat, he seethed with barely concealed resentment against Rome.

The archbishop had to navigate through three intermediaries before he reached the bishop. When he answered at last, the bishop was polite.

"Good evening, Your Grace", said the bishop, absolutely without a hint of warmth.

"Good evening", the archbishop replied evenly.

"What can I do for you?"

"First of all, I must apologize for interrupting you so late in the evening. Like me, you're probably putting the finishing touches on your homily for tomorrow's Mass." The archbishop chuckled artificially. The bishop did not reciprocate. He waited for the archbishop to continue.

"Actually, I'm just calling to confirm something that has been reported to me."

"And that is . . .?"

"Well, I received a rather unusual telephone call this evening, from a man who says he's a priest of your diocese. I wanted to ask you about him—"

"What did he say his name was?"

The archbishop told him. The silence on the other end radiated an answer that needed no words.

"Do you know him?" the archbishop prompted.

"Yes, I know him", the bishop replied irritably. "Whatever he told you, you can be sure it was distorted. The Pastoral Educators' liturgy was completely within the acceptable limits of—"

"Excuse me, he didn't speak about that. He was calling about an entirely different matter. He seems to have met one of my priests who happened to be in your cathedral last night. The man has been missing for some time, and I thought—"

"Well, I don't know anything about that. But you can be sure, whatever he told you was unreliable. I have had no end of trouble with him. My consultors and I have been discussing whether or not we should suspend his faculties. He's done some very irrational things lately."

"Such as?"

"He's an incendiary!"

"Incendiary?"

"Burning church property, inciting parishioners to do the same. Criticizing diocesan policy from the pulpit, creating panic among the people with apocalyptic theories."

"That sounds rather extreme."

"Oh, yes, he's an extremist all right. An ultra-traditionalist. I suspect he's secretly in league with the conservative schismatics."

"Are you sure?"

"No, but it would be in character."

"You mean, his sympathies lie to the right of center?"

"Exactly. He's doing his best to undermine the spirit of Vatican II. He causes division wherever he goes. I'm sure you know the type."

"Yes, I am quite familiar with the type," the archbishop replied carefully, "but in my diocese this type usually operates on the other end of the ecclesial spectrum."

He counted the seconds while the bishop thought of a reply. When it was not forthcoming, the archbishop said, "Well, thank you. I'm sorry to have bothered you."

"Not at all. Good night."

"Good night."

The archbishop hung up and sighed. Well, it had been worth the chill. Father Andrei was alive. But where was he? And with whom?

He was digesting this when the phone rang again.

"Hello, Your Grace. This is Potempko."

"Hello, Father. How are things in Bella Coola?"

Potempko gave one of his profound Hungarian groans. "They're okay."

"Just okay?"

"You know. The usual."

"Father Shane?"

"Yes."

"Do you have a complaint to make?"

"No, no. No more complaints. I already said my complaints to you."

"Any improvement in the situation?"

"Some yes, some no. Little things yes, big things no."

"I'll speak with him again."

"Thanks." Followed by a Potempko silence.

"Just phoned to chat?"

"No."

"Something you want to discuss?"

"I didn't phone to complain, and I didn't phone to chat."

A double long silence. The archbishop began to feel impatient.

"Father," he said eventually, "people usually don't phone an archbishop at ten o'clock at night to listen to him breathing."

"Ha-ha", Potempko laughed. "That's a good one, Your Grace. Ha-ha."

But the laughter was thin.

"What's the problem, Father?"

"Trouble."

"Trouble?"

"Big trouble."

"What kind of trouble?"

Potempko paused. Then he said quietly, "Father Andrei."

The archbishop's heart thumped, and he sat up straight.

"Do you know where he is?"

"No. But I saw him."

"You saw him! Where?"

Potempko related the story of Father Andrei's arrival with a boy on a sailboat, the drive into the mountains, and the road-block.

"That was the last time I saw them. Father Andrei and this little boy went into the bush outside of Williams Lake. I drove on and stayed at a motel on the highway waiting for them, but they never came."

"Were you aware that the police are looking for them?"

Silence.

"Didn't you report it to the police?"

"No."

"Why not?"

"I don't trust the police."

"You don't trust the police? When did this happen?"

Potempko told him.

"What!" the archbishop erupted. "Three months ago! And you've said nothing about it all this time?!"

511

"I'm sorry, Your Grace."

"You're sorry! Don't you know I've been worried sick over Father Andrei?" The archbishop raised his voice. "Didn't you think? What is wrong with your mind?"

"I'm sorry", Potempko repeated meekly.

"I'm asking you a question. Why didn't you tell me?"

"I'd rather not say, Your Grace."

"You'd rather not say?"

The archbishop's face contorted, and he sat back. Potempko maintained a ponderous silence. They listened to each other breathing.

"All right, then, tell me where Father Andrei went with the boy."

Potempko told him they were going to find the boy's great-grandfather in the hills of the Cariboo country. They were running away because Father Andrei was convinced the police or the government or some army group had killed the sisters, and he and the boy knew about it, and they knew that they knew.

"Wait, wait, wait a minute", the archbishop interrupted. "Tell me slowly. Who killed whom?"

"Father Andrei said he saw black helicopters kill the people at the commune where the boy lived. Then the killers flew across the valley and shot the sisters on the same morning. He said they were working for the government."

"That is absurd. It was criminals and hate groups."

"He didn't think so. He saw them."

Potempko explained what little he knew. How Father Andrei had called the police at the convent, and five minutes later the black helicopters had returned, looking for him.

"No ordinary police ever came. He hid in the bush and watched. He waited and waited, and they never came. You see, Your Grace, the black helicopters were the police."

"He told you this?"

"Yes. I swear on it. Upon my sainted mother's grave, and upon my—"

"All right, I believe you. Or at least I believe that's what he told you."

More breathing.

"Now, Father, I'm giving you a strict obedience. You must tell me why you did not advise me of this as soon as it happened."

"I . . ."

"Speak plainly. I want to know."

"I . . ."

"Was it because you didn't trust me?"

No reply.

"I want an answer, Father Potempko."

The reply was muffled.

"Speak clearly."

"No."

"No what?"

"No, I didn't trust you."

The archbishop shook his head in disbelief.

"You didn't trust me? Why not?"

"Nothing personal, Your Grace. I didn't trust anyone, not after what Father Andrei told me. Everything was so confused, everybody was believing the news."

"And you assumed I would be like everyone else."

"I regret to say—"

"You regret to say. Tell me, then, why are you coming to me now, three months too late, to let me in on your secret?" The archbishop was having difficulty restraining his anger.

"I had a dream."

"You had a dream? Tell me about your dream."

"Last night, I saw you in a dream. You were in a garden with angels and snakes. The snakes were trying to bite the kids—you know, eat 'em up. You were lying down on the ground. You couldn't see what was going on. You had too much on your mind. Then an angel gave you this big orange or grapefruit or something, and he touched your forehead, and you stood up. Then you were strong after that. You hit the snakes with your crosier. It was a good dream."

Now it was the archbishop's turn to be speechless.

"Well, I told you", Potempko said in a sad voice.

"Yes, you told me", the archbishop answered quietly.

"I guess I'll say good night."

"Good night", the archbishop mumbled. Potempko hung up.

The archbishop closed the window, shutting out the sirens and the screeches of the teenagers. He went into the chapel and knelt down.

Agitated, feeling deeply hurt by Potempko's lack of confidence and not a little upset that he had contributed to that lack, the archbishop tried to calm his nerves. The events of the evening swirled through his mind: serpents, voices out of nowhere, children singing, oranges, angels, crosiers, his homily, his blood pressure, prayers, arguments, the face of Fathers Andrei, Shane, Ron, the priest in the neighboring diocese, the bishop, snakes, angels . . .

More private revelation, he muttered to himself. *Just what I needed!*

He prayed as much as he was able, resisting the undertow of hurt, bitterness, and discouragement. Eventually the tumult subsided into a profound sadness. Later, he tried to sleep but could not. He went downstairs to his office in pajamas and bathrobe, and sat at his desk rewriting his homily. After that he prayed in the chapel until dawn.

* * *

The parishioners at the ten o'clock Mass were surprised to see the archbishop process to the altar in full vestments, mitered and crosiered, accompanied by the two assistant pastors of the cathedral parish and the chancellor. The archbishop looked uncommonly tired, but there was in his face the grim determination of a tough old shepherd.

That morning he delivered one of the more outstanding homilies of his life, holding the entire congregation in rapt attention as he proclaimed in a strong, steady voice, and in the clearest language possible, the end of the era of compromise. Years later, people who were there that day remembered the tone more than the exact details of what he said. Key phrases stayed with them, however, and were curiously present whenever they needed to recall the Church's directives on various issues. They remembered especially how his voice had thundered when he exhorted them to be signs of contradiction. *Signs of contradiction?* they wondered. *What was that? How do we do that?*

He told them what it was and how to do it. *Truth*, he said. *Love*, he said. Beckoning the Monsignor who held the archbishop's crosier, he took the shepherd's staff from him, held it firmly, and thumped it three times on the hardwood floor of the sanctuary. *Tough love!* he said on the last thump. Then, finally, the roar of his voice: *Leave the darkness, my people! Come into the ark of the New Covenant!*

No one was more shocked than he when the entire congregation jumped to their feet and applauded him heartily as he stepped down from the pulpit. Nothing like it had ever happened in his cathedral. He wasn't fond of outbursts or lack of decorum. But he had to admit he had finally done something to move them. That was all well and good, he thought. The real question was, had he done anything to change them?

On Monday morning he met with the senior partners of the archdiocese's law firm and had them draft a formal letter of inquiry to the federal government, stating that the archbishop had reason to believe that a priest of his diocese, therein named, was being held without due process of law by an agency of the State. He demanded the priest's immediate release or the laying of a formal charge. In the latter case, the archdiocese demanded the right to defend the priest against any and all charges the State might bring against him.

The lawyers were of conflicting opinions regarding the letter. If indeed the government did have him in custody, and if some of the more questionable measures of the new statutes were applied, the letter just might bring the full force of the law down upon the archbishop and the archdiocese. Did the archbishop really want to risk that?

"Yes," he insisted, "I very much want to risk that."

"If your informant is correct," rejoined a partner, "and the government is moving toward some kind of martial law, and if unconscionable elements are in control of corrections facilities, it could endanger the life of Father Andrei. Do you want to risk that?"

"If that is the case," replied the archbishop, "and I'm beginning to suspect it is, then we are all at risk. If we back down now, we hand everything over to them without a fight. Our only hope is to awaken the country as quickly as possible. That means risk. I believe it's a risk Father Andrei would want me to take."

Duplicates of the document were sent to the Prime Minister, to the leaders of the opposition parties in Parliament, to the Commissioners of the R.C.M.P., and to the Minister of Justice. Copies were forwarded to every bishop in the country, to the papal nuncio, and to the newsrooms in every major city.

When he returned to the chancery, he asked his secretary to make an appointment with the nun in charge of religious education for the morning of the following day. He dictated several letters, then called the nun in charge of Catholic hospitals and arranged another appointment. He wrote out a check for ten thousand dollars (from his personal account, the last of his family's inheritance) and sent it to the provincial pro-life defense committee. He asked the janitor to replace the defective air conditioner, prayed his breviary, said the five o'clock Mass in the cathedral, and went to his apartment for supper. At seven he phoned Father Shane and told him that he was being transferred immediately to Our Lady of Grace in the city, where he would spend the summer as Father Kim's assistant, ministering to the Korean immigrants.

"But they won't understand a word I say", Shane protested.

"That's right", the archbishop replied. "You can bring them Christ in the sacraments. And while you're there, I want you to learn a few things from Kim. He has a lot to teach you."

Furthermore, the archbishop went on, in September he was to proceed to a small monastic college in the eastern United States, where he would take a year's sabbatical, studying spirituality. Shane was not pleased. He knew that the rector of this college was a friend of the archbishop's, a man of great learning and sanctity, who knew how to minister to dissident priests. He had enjoyed amazing success with them. He was famous—no, *notorious*. Father Shane used every bit of guile at his disposal to get out of it, but as he exhausted all of his ploys, one after another, the archbishop hardened his resolve. When Shane finally blew his cover and began to threaten and rant, the archbishop told him in no uncertain terms that this was the moment of choice. Either Shane obeyed, or his faculties would be suspended. Shane, to the archbishop's relief, obeyed.

After that the archbishop phoned Potempko and asked him if he would be willing to return to the parish as pastor. Potempko was surprised but happy to comply.

It was nine o'clock by that time. The archbishop got out the ecclesial directory and looked up the phone number of the young priest who had seen Father Andrei at the cathedral of the neighboring diocese. He punched in the number and was answered by a recorded message that announced Mass and confession times, holy hours, prayer meetings, and sundry other edifying items. He left a message, asking the priest to call back.

The archbishop prayed a rosary, pleading for guidance from the Holy Spirit, hoping that his new approach was not the biggest mistake of his life. The phone rang just as he was singing the Salve Regina.

It was the young priest returning his call.

"Father, I want to thank you again for yesterday", the archbishop began.

"Glad to do it, Your Grace. It's what anyone would do."

"I'm not so sure about that. I enjoyed your recorded message. Sounds as if you have a lively parish there."

"We do our best."

"I suspect you don't get much support."

The priest hesitated. "Support?"

"Your situation is not the easiest in the world, is it?"

"It's not so bad. We've all got our crosses." His voice was suddenly guarded.

"Father, you don't know me, and considering your situation, you're probably wondering if you should trust me. But I'd be grateful if you would trust me enough to answer a few questions."

"All right." The priest was now distinctly uncomfortable.

"May I ask, are you a supporter of the schismatics?"

"Uh, which ones, Your Grace?"

The archbishop named them.

"No, I'm not. I guess you could say I'm neither left nor right. I'm just with the Holy Father, that's all."

"The true center?"

"Uh-huh. The true center. Why do you ask?"

The archbishop paused.

"It's okay, Your Grace. I understand. It makes sense you'd want to check out a guy who calls you up from nowhere."

"You are a humble young man."

"Thanks. That's not entirely accurate, but the Lord's working on me."

"He's working on all of us, it seems, and moving quickly."

"I think so too. The time is short, if you ask me."

"I would like to ask you what you think on that subject. Do you preach apocalyptic theories from the pulpit?"

"My bishop really gave you the rundown on me, didn't he?"

"I'm sorry, I have to ask."

"That's okay. The answer is, no, I don't preach it. I don't rave in the pulpit like Savonarola. But whenever we have readings from Revelation at Mass, I try to get my parishioners to think. I ask them questions, get them to look around at the world. Personally, I believe these are the times the prophets were talking about, but I don't overfocus on it. I just try to put the tools of discernment into my people's hands. That's all."

"Do you have fires in your parking lot?"

After a long pause the priest replied, "No."

"No?"

"We have them in the garden of the rectory."

"I see."

The priest sighed. "There goes my credibility!"

"Don't jump to conclusions, lad", said the archbishop, smiling to himself.

"Yup, I'm an arsonist. Certifiable."

"Has your bishop instructed you to stop the burning?"

"Yes."

"And . . .?"

"I stopped."

"Why did you stop?"

"What's my life all about if I can't obey? There was nothing sinful or erroneous about his order, so of course I did what he told me to do."

"No more fires since then?"

"Well . . . actually, my parishioners are doing it on their own."

"Television sets?"

"Yes. How did you know?"

"A lucky guess. What else?"

"Pornography, contraceptives, drugs, bad videos, some CDs—that sort of thing."

"Books?"

"Uh-huh, a few books, magazines."

"Catechisms?"

"Just the slimy kind."

"Slimy kind?"

"Mind benders."

"I see, mind benders."

"With all due respect, Your Grace, why are you asking me all this? I saw one of your priests. I told you what happened. That should about wrap it up."

"Listen, my son, I realize this is somewhat outside the normal lines of communication, but I want to tell you that I'm proud of you."

"Proud . . . ?" The priest stumbled over the word and swallowed audibly.

The archbishop hoped that he hadn't made a mistake. This was another bishop's priest. This was a stranger. He had called him son, a rather trite exercise in cliché paternalism. But it had felt good.

"I think you have a lot of courage. I have five arsonists just like you, and they're among my best men."

The priest was at a loss for words. Eventually he cleared his throat and said, "That means a lot to me. I'm a bit of an embarrassment around here."

"I'm sure you must be."

"Have any suggestions for a pyromaniac like me?"

The archbishop mentioned a few of the cautions he had given to Father Ron. The priest listened without interrupting and thanked him for the advice.

"I have to go now, Father. As you are well aware, this conversation is somewhat unusual. May I ask you to keep it confidential?"

"You can count on it."

"Also, I'd like you to call me if you need any help. The times are confused, aren't they?"

"Very."

"If you should find yourself . . . well, how shall I say it . . . if you find yourself unable to practice your ministry, for whatever reason, come and see me. We can talk about it."

"Okay." The word was barely audible. "Thanks."

Next morning, Sister Connie, director of religious education, arrived for their appointment. She gave him her usual hug, inquired about his health, and reported a few routine developments in her office. When that was out of the way, she gave him her best smile and asked if there was something on his mind. The archbishop replied that there was a great deal on his mind. He outlined for her a change of policy in the archdiocese that was effective immediately. The archdiocesan catechism program was to be scrapped, the defective catechisms (he named them) removed from every classroom in parochial schools.

The sister gave him a look of gentle consternation and replied that this series had been produced by a national catechetical team with the highest credentials. Did he really want to take such summary action? Yes, he did, he replied. He authorized her to order a catechetical series from an orthodox publishing house in the U.S., an interim measure until they could develop a program suitable to the needs of the diocese.

"They're very American," she replied thoughtfully, "and rather conservative."

"Actually, Sister, I had them send me a set of the children's texts, plus the parents' and teachers' manuals. I went through them carefully. They've got more substance and are much clearer about the faith than the ones we're currently using. Not a hint of flag waving, plus beautiful illustrations and wise pedagogy. It's a wonder to me how we could have overlooked them."

She pointed out in a tactful tone that the publishers did not enjoy a good reputation in Canada, that they were somewhat reactionary to the spirit of the Council. The archbishop replied that he had been a *peritus* at the Council and had found the publisher to be fully in tune with the authentic spirit of the Council. He further added that the publisher was a victim of the anti-Roman prejudice in the country. The series was excellent, he concluded, and she was to order it immediately.

A note of tension creeping into her voice, she advised him that the cost of replacing their current textbooks would be prohibitive. He asked her what was the price of a soul? She replied that he might be overstating the case. Furthermore, she believed that parents would not be receptive to the program and that Catholic education would suffer in the archdiocese. He replied with a smile that he believed Catholic parents would welcome the new approach as soon as the fruits of it became evident.

Upping the tension a fraction, she advised him that there would be resistance among the better quality of educator. In answer, he regarded her calmly for a full minute, saying nothing, until she blinked and looked sideways.

He informed her that the wholesale mass-processing of children in "family life formation" was to be withdrawn from all schools until he could study the subject of sex education with greater attention. She looked seriously alarmed at that, tightened her mouth, and offered a few objections.

"The Vatican's guidelines are quite clear on the subject", he rejoined. "Are we going to obey, or are we not?"

Using a reasoning tone, and addressing him by his first name, she reminded him that the directives of Vatican congregations were not *ex cathedra* and that people of various nations and cultural backgrounds needed to adapt the directives in order to implement them more effectively. She concluded by appealing to *inculturation*.

"Ah, inculturation", the archbishop smiled.

"Yes. Hasn't the Holy Father strongly affirmed the need for inculturation?"

"We are not discussing African liturgy here, Sister", he replied. "Nor catechizing native peoples. Surely you realize we are immersed in a social revolution."

She nodded. "All the more need to reach the young people where they're at."

"How do we do that?"

She looked down, thinking.

"I mean, Sister, should we inculturate them into a culture of death?"

"No, of course not."

"Let me give you an example. It has come to my attention that for the past few years, our schools in the archdiocese have been teaching an AIDS prevention course. Now I was very surprised last week when I read the manual for the first time. If you recall, you and your committee examined the material and advised me that it was thoroughly in line with Catholic moral teaching."

"Which it is."

"Which it is not", the archbishop replied solemnly.

"Are you calling into question my competence?" she asked in a quiet voice.

"Is any of us infallible?" The archbishop paused for the briefest moment. "As I was saying, I was quite impressed by two-thirds of the content, traditional material on chastity, the meaning of conjugal love, and so on. But the final chapter was disturbing."

"Yes, I wondered if it would be. But we're dealing with a crisis situation in the high schools and even the upper levels of the elementary schools. Many of these children are sexually active. Can we abandon our responsibility to them? Can we face God knowing that a child has died because we kept him or her in ignorance?"

"The course strongly encourages young people to live moral lives and warns them of the dangers involved in breaking the Commandments. Then, in the final chapter, the authors inform the children that, despite everything said, if their morality fails, they should use a condom."

"I realize that's problematic. But it will save lives."

"Will it?"

"Statistics prove—"

"Actually, Sister, statistics prove the opposite. The young think of themselves as immortal. They do not grasp the reality of death. By offering them a device that implies 'safe sex', we give them a false sense of security. Recent medical studies have shown that the condom actually increases the incidence of sexually transmitted disease, teenage pregnancy, and infection by HIV and AIDS."

"I would like to see those studies."

"I have copies for you." He handed her a thick manila envelope. "So you see, for several years now, we have been giving our children mixed signals here. Moreover, we have been contributing to the death of children. Are you ready to stand before God and explain that?"

"Statistics can be manipulated to prove anything", she snapped.

"An insight that works both ways, doesn't it?"

She did not respond.

"Regardless, we are withdrawing that program as well. We are going to revise the material, and we are going to shift the educational focus in these areas from school to parents. I am putting together a committee that will produce a program that can be implemented in every parish."

"I'm sorry, but that won't work."

"Why not, Sister?"

"Because a majority of our Catholic parents are no longer active in parish life."

"That is a deep grief to me", the archbishop replied slowly. "I wonder if they would be more active if the parish were a place where bold, clear teaching was customary, where they could go to find support and advice."

"If you scrap these school programs, you will effectively marginalize a large portion of the next generation. How else can we reach these people?"

"By direct evangelization. I intend not only to implement certain reactive measures but to develop several *proactive* measures."

As the tension increased between the archbishop and the director of religious education, their discussion ranged far and wide over several levels of Church administration and the state of society. The nun's discomfort increased steadily. From time to time, whenever the archbishop seemed immovable on this or that point, tears filled her eyes.

Two hours into the conversation, he asked if she would like a cup of coffee. He went to the kitchenette beside his office and returned with two brimming cups. He offered her some delicacies from a tin of biscuits. She declined. When they were once more seated, sipping from their cups, she reminded him of the reputation he enjoyed in the country, that he was considered one of the most reasonable and "well-balanced" bishops, that the staff of the college (which he had helped to found) often mentioned how grateful they were that he was not a conservative bishop, that he was a moderate. She told him how much his support had meant over the years, that she had obtained her master's in theology and her doctorate in educational psychology only because of his encouragement.

"Do you return to the college often, Sister?" he asked harmlessly.

"From time to time. As you know, I gave the Dewey lecture there last autumn. And, of course, I see some of the professors at conferences."

"Theological conferences?"

"Yes."

He asked her how she felt about recent developments at the college. She replied that she wasn't entirely in agreement with some of the professors, who she felt were drifting away from moderation into liberalism.

"Perhaps into modernism?" he inquired.

"I wouldn't go so far as to say that", she mused. "I think it's more a case of pushing back the frontiers of theological in-quiry."

"A broader vision?" he prompted.

She shrugged, finished her coffee, crossed her legs, and folded her arms.

"I wonder if it is as deep as it is broad", he remarked casually. "Perhaps we have put too much emphasis on psychology."

She looked dubious but said nothing.

"I wonder if we have really developed a profoundly Christian psychology", he went on. "There have been some mistakes."

She murmured agreement but added that mistakes were in-evitable.

"Mistakes can be measured in terms of souls", he said. "There have been grave mistakes."

It went on for another two hours, and by the end of it, his probing had revealed to him that she was a completely sincere, intelligent, slightly confused victim of academic inculturation. They had been friends for years; she had been like a daughter to him. He knew that she had a few wounds from her childhood and a few others from the difficulties her order went through during the period of adaptation after the Council. He knew that his mentorship had helped to heal some of those wounds. He had prided himself on sensitivity to women but now saw that the damage was extensive and that his compassion had been manipulated.

He did not want the meeting to end the way it did. When she burst into tears and flooded him with accusations, he felt a moment's terror, a desire to hide, to recant, to give her many reassurances. But for some reason he refrained from these habitual reactions to weeping, accusing nuns. He told her that he loved her as a father but that he was also a shepherd of souls, that it was time to rethink a great many things. Would she be willing to take a new journey of discovery with him? he asked. Would she work with him to implement programs that were consistent with the mind of Christ?

He was stricken with pain when she snapped at him, "The mind of Christ is not necessarily the mind of the institutional church. The institutional church has made mistakes, *grave* mistakes. And *that* can be measured in terms of human souls!"

The final sentence was delivered with a cold intensity that took him completely off guard. They sat together in silence. She dried her eyes while he tried to collect himself. They made another attempt at discussion, but in the end her face contorted with rage, and she stormed from his office.

The next morning he found her letter of resignation on his desk, a move that he had not anticipated or wanted. He wrote a note of acceptance but reminded her that if she could see her way clear to rethink what they had discussed, his door was always open.

The web was thick, and as he cut through layer after layer, he began to see that practically every level of ecclesial life had been affected. It had occurred largely because he had not understood the nature of the "inculturation", the dynamics of ideological invasion. Most of all he realized that he was at fault. He had allowed his kindness, his compassion for unhappy religious, his self-doubt, and, yes, his fear of being rejected to be manipulated by many people who understood his temperament only too well. As he cut through the webs, he hoped that the instrument in his hand was a scalpel, not a sword. He felt that he was trying to perform surgery in the dark but prayed with growing fervor for the light of the Holy Spirit.

In the afternoon he met with the elderly nun who was the director of Catholic hospitals in the archdiocese. A wise, tough old superior of a nursing order of sisters, she answered every one of his questions directly, especially those that concerned the practice of medical ethics. She reassured him that there would be no abortions, euthanasia, sterilizations, or contraception referrals in her hospitals, and if some of the doctors tried anything "funny", they would do so over her dead body.

The archbishop and the director thought about her choice of terms and laughed.

"Let's hope that isn't prophetic, Mother", he said.

She brought up the subject of the new socialist government of the province, described the bill before the legislature that proposed that all hospitals should be required to establish departments for the servicing of "women's needs".

"Read abortion, sterilization, and contraception", she said.

"If they try that, they're in for a fight to the death", he replied.

"Let's hope that isn't prophetic, Your Grace."

She described a situation that had arisen just over a month before: a doctor—a *Catholic* doctor, she emphasized—had tried to push back the limitations on removal of life-support systems. In collusion with the daughter of a prominent local family, he had ordered the suspension of food and water from the woman's mother. The mother had Alzheimer's disease but was alert and peaceful, a beautiful presence in the extended care unit. The situation had been brought to the director's attention only because a nurse had complained that she thought something wasn't right.

"I rarely go down to the wards," the nun said, "but I thought

I'd better check it out. Sure enough, they'd decided, the doctor and the daughter, to terminate the mother. I suspended him on the spot and gave the girl a piece of my mind. She's a lawyer, married, no kids, earns a six-digit figure every year. She'd set the date for her mother's cremation and was planning to fly off to Costa Rica on a holiday the day after the funeral. Oh, was she mad as a hatter. Dragged in her personal theologian to try to change my mind. I gave that one a tongue lashing she'll not soon forget."

The archbishop nodded. "What did the doctor do?"

"He gave me a fight, threatened a legal suit against the order and the archdiocese. Said that it was morally permissible to remove support systems if death was imminent. I reminded him that the Church's medical ethics guidelines say that water and food are not 'support systems'. They're fundamental rights. They can be removed only if death is imminent within hours *and* if hydration and feeding would create more suffering than it was worth. He replied that this wasn't so, that the imminence argument left room for personal judgment on the part of the doctor. I told him that death would be imminent for *anyone* if you deprive him of water and food."

"What did he reply?"

"Well, he really didn't have much to say, did he? They're still consulting with their lawyers. Been at it for weeks, trying to scare us into backing down, I guess."

"They're sadly mistaken if they think they can intimidate us. They obviously don't have a clue about your nerve, Mother."

She laughed.

"Nerve can take you only so far, Your Grace. We've got a catch-22 situation here. We need your firm hand on this mess."

The archbishop wrote down the names of the doctor and the family and decided he would read the riot act to the theologian, who was, he was chagrined to hear, a graduate of the college he had helped to found.

529

"How is the woman with Alzheimer's?"

"Recovering very well. I ordered the doctor to reinsert the tube. Four weeks have gone by. Her mind's as usual, but otherwise she's as healthy as a horse. After I stepped in, she started smiling again, her muscles relaxed. The nursing staff say she had been distressed ever since the daughter made the decision to terminate her. The daughter and the doctor must have discussed the whole thing right in front of the old woman; they probably thought she couldn't understand a thing. She understood. She understood all right. What a horrible suffering. But she's fine now."

The archbishop assured the director that she had his full support and that he would be organizing a team of Catholic doctors to give lectures on medical ethics to the staff of every medical facility in the archdiocese. He would also issue a pastoral letter on medical ethics that would be read from every pulpit in the archdiocese. It would contain clear directives and would advise any person who violated them that he could expect *immediate* excommunication. Dissenting staff would be suspended pending an inquiry; acts of direct violation would result in dismissal.

When the director had gone, the archbishop telephoned an old friend, the owner of a large corporation in the east.

"I've got a crisis on my hands, Cal", he explained. "I'm trying to clean up my house, and some of my people don't like it. There are going to be legal suits. The government's probably going to put on the pressure too. They might go as far as cancelling our tax exemptions."

"How much do you need, Your Grace?"

"You and Rosemary can add an extra rosary a day. How's that for starters?"

"You got it. Now, down to plain talk. I have my checkbook in front of me. How much?"

"Conservative estimate, a million and a half."

Silence.

"I'm sorry. I realize that's a lot of money."

"Shhh, shhh, Your Grace."

"Listen, if it's not possible, I understand."

"Quiet, please, I'm writing. Oops", Cal murmured. "Darn, my hand slipped. Looks like I wrote down the wrong figure. Oh, well, it's just petty cash. Is two million okay?"

The archbishop gulped.

"Yeah, you're right. Why be niggardly? How about three million? Ouch. Hey, stop twisting my arm! Three and a half million."

"Cal, that's too much."

"Okay, okay, you sure do put pressure on a guy. Four million, then. Let me know if you need more."

"Thanks." The word was so hopelessly inadequate that the archbishop didn't try to embellish it.

"Don't mention it", Cal laughed. "Looks like you scooped up my tithe for this year."

"You're bowling me over! This is too easy."

Cal's voice suddenly lost its bantering tone. "Your Grace, if you don't mind me saying, this has been long overdue."

The archbishop could say no more.

"Now tell me, have you given any more thought to that little golf tour you promised you'd come on?"

"Sorry. I've got my hands full here", the archbishop stammered. "But we must get together. Maybe next year."

"Sure, sure, you always say that. Well, I'll send you a postcard from the Carolinas."

"I'll keep my eye on the mailbox. Give Rosemary my love."

"I'll do that. And, uh, look, don't burn yourself out driving the money lenders from the temple, eh?"

"I'll try not to."

"We need you."

They bantered for a few more minutes, and then Cal hung up.

The archbishop ate a simple supper in his apartment, then retired to his armchair. He turned on the air conditioner and let the cool breeze waft over him and lay back wondering what he would have done if Cal hadn't offered the safety net. He dozed for a while, but there were no dreams. When he woke up, he turned off the conditioner, opened the window, and sat for a long time listening to the noises of the street.

The telephone rang at ten o'clock. It was a cardinal archbishop in the east. He fielded the cardinal's oblique small talk for ten minutes, then asked him point blank what he was calling about.

"Your director of religious education contacted me this afternoon, looking for a job. What happened between you two?"

The archbishop explained. The cardinal hemmed and hawed and then told the archbishop that he had offered her a middle-management job in his office of education.

"How could I refuse? She's an old friend", the cardinal explained.

"She seems to have quite a few old friends", the archbishop replied.

"Sorry. Hope it doesn't rub you the wrong way."

"Not at all. Not at all."

"I'll keep an eye on her."

"Yes, you should. She's a good woman, but a bit confused."

"Speaking of confusion, what's going on in your corner of the world? The good sister seemed pretty upset. Said you've been behaving strangely, shooting from the hip, loose cannon on the deck."

"She said that?"

"I'm afraid so. Of course, she's upset."

The archbishop said nothing.

"You and I are old friends too", said the cardinal. "Can I make a suggestion?"

"Go ahead."

"I want you to know that your name is being touted around as an ideal candidate for the next president of the national conference."

"Oh?"

"A lot of the bishops think you're the one who can hold it together."

"That's generous of them. I'm willing, if they are."

"Of course, if it gets around that you're making some . . . how should I put it . . . some problematic moves, there are going to be a lot of nervous people around here."

"That would be a shame."

"Yes, I think so too. I'd like to see you get elected. We could do a lot of good, get things back on track."

"I suppose that's true. What are you suggesting?"

"Go slowly. Don't make any sudden moves."

"I see."

"I hope you do see. There's a lot riding on this one."

"Your Eminence," the archbishop said calmly, "I fully intend to proceed as I have begun. There are a lot of souls in this archdiocese. A lot of souls riding on this one."

Silence. "All right. Not to worry. I'll put in a good word for you."

"Thanks."

The conversation wound down directly, and the archbishop hung up, knowing that he would never be elected to the presidency of the conference. He felt a moment of pain, of regret, of doubt. But he got up, went to the refrigerator, and found an orange. He ate it in the dark. Then he stood by the window, listening to the sirens and the screams.

14

Small Boys Can Gum Up the Works

Just when things were beginning to look as if they might turn out all right, Arrow got sick. About three in the morning, Alice awoke, checked the red glow of the digital clock on the dresser, and sat up. Groans were coming from the other bedroom.

Bad dream, she told herself. *The kid's having a bad dream.* She lay back and listened for a few more minutes, hoping he would quiet down, but he didn't. The groans became little cries, then accelerated to a high, persistent whining that dug into her nervous system like the wail of a vacuum cleaner about to blow its motor. She gave it another five minutes, sure that it would go away, but it didn't.

Then Arrow yelled, "Maya!"

Alice muttered a bad word, threw off the bedcovers, and planted her bare feet on the floor. She rubbed her face, deliberating about whether or not she should pop her dentures in, and decided against it. Her gums were sore. She lit a cigarette, sucked on it hard, and exhaled. She coughed. She got up and went down the hall to the boys' room, fully expecting to spend half an hour settling him down, blowing away his nightmare with puffs of smoke and a few shoulder pats.

She flicked on the overhead light as she went in.

He was lying stiff in bed, hands floating over his belly, his eyes wide with fear.

"Mummy, it hurts!"

"Okay, okay, Arrow", she said, sitting down on the end of the bed. "It's me. It's Alice. What's the problem?"

"It hurts, it hurts", he wailed. His face was flushed, not sweating. She put a hand to his forehead and found it hot. She was no great shakes as a nurse, but she knew that kids got night sweats, chills, and fevers from time to time. They also got belly aches. They also had bad dreams, and they usually survived anything more serious.

"Put the lid on it, kid. You'll wake up Nick."

But Nick was already awake, trying to roll his head sideways, staring at Arrow through the bars of his crib.

"Awo? Awo?"

"It's okay, Nick", Alice said in a tone that approximated reassurance. "Arrow's okay. He's just got an upset stomach."

But she wasn't so sure. This didn't look like your average green apple two-step. For supper last night he'd had a cheese omelette and fish sticks washed down by fresh goat's milk. Same as she and Nick had eaten. Two Oreo cookies for bedtime snack. She'd had one too. But all day yesterday he had been dragging himself around like a puppy with worms and had complained of a stitch in his side when she tucked him in.

He wouldn't stop the noise. Whimpering, then cries like splinters of broken glass. Then more whimpering. The bed smelled like the kind of rug an old dog would lie down to die on. It wasn't Arrow's usual odor, the oops-I-had-an-accident smell. This was a new brand of perfume, and it made her uneasy. Very uneasy.

Attar de Rover décomposé, she quipped mentally, trying to steady herself with a bark of twisted humor. But the joke didn't come off, and she felt her heart chug into a higher gear.

"Where's it hurt? C'mon, tell me. Where's it hurt?"

"Here!" he gasped, waving his hand over his midsection, above the belly button, not touching it. She put her hand lightly on the waistband of his jammies, and he howled, twisting away.

"Awo? Awo?" Now Nick was whimpering. Poody ambled in and jumped onto the end of the bed. He began to lick his paws as if nothing whatsoever of interest was happening. Alice batted the cat off the bed.

"How about an ice pack? Yeah, let's try that."

She trotted to the kitchen and got one of those blue jellied freeze packs out of the refrigerator's ice cube compartment, but when she put it on the boy's sore part, he shrieked even louder. Then she tried a hot towel, but that got the same results.

"Water!" he said, his dry tongue rasping across his lips.

Alice went to the bathroom, rinsed out her tooth mug, and filled it from the tap. She tilted his head, and he gulped the water down. "More", he whined. Then he threw up all over himself and a part of her nightgown.

"Crapola!" she snarled. "Double crapola!"

It took five minutes to clean up the mess. He didn't want to cooperate, because every time she tried to move him, his mouth became an air raid siren. All he wanted to do was lie there without moving.

"You feel better?" she asked him. "You tossed your cookies, and that should help."

"It's worse", he whispered. "It's down there now."

He pointed to his lower right abdomen. Alice wondered what the hell was going on inside there, how such a granddaddy of a pain could shift so suddenly and drop about six inches and move to the right. Bowels were tricky things. Thirty feet of sausage links. It *had* to be cramps.

He began to scream, jerking his hands over the pain, afraid to touch it. Alice stared at him, at a loss for what to do. She went back to the kitchen, hoping that some solution might present itself. She stood in the middle of the room, panicking, turning this way and that. She reached for the door of the booze cupboard and stopped herself. She sat down, lit another cigarette, and left it abandoned in the ashtray. She got up, sat down, and got up again.

"This is the pits!"

Arrow was crying even louder now, and she went back to him, trying to calm him, and herself, with futile words. But they didn't penetrate the wall of noise.

It might be nothing at all, she told herself. It might be only a case of stomach flu. He would probably drift back to sleep and wake up in the morning with an embarrassed smile, if he remembered it at all. Kids got this sort of thing all the time. No sweat. Nothing to lose sleep over.

It was the sort of thing that made her glad she was an old maid. Teething, colds, diaper rash—Uh-uh, that wasn't her idea of a good bridge party. Once in 1952 she'd sat up with her sister Kurly in a cheap apartment in Saint John's, Newfoundland, while Kurly tended her daughter, Baby Sue, through a night of croup. Nasty stuff, but Sue had pulled through just fine, had grown up to be a smart, sexy seventeen-year-old who threw herself off a bridge on a bad acid trip in 1969.

He wouldn't stop screaming, and the trouble brewing in his lower belly sure didn't look like the croup.

He needed to see a doctor.

But her doctor, Murdo the King of the Geriatrics, had retired two months before, and Alice didn't know anyone else. Maybe the Potters' lady doc? Nope, that was a hard apple for sure. She'd want to know who the kid belonged to, and then the fur would fly. Bethie had said something about having a new doctor, somebody she trusted, but how could she wheedle the information out of Bethie in the middle of the night without arousing suspicion.

No way. No way could she call Bethie.

Alice weighed the factors carefully. That belly looked like appendix trouble. Maybe, maybe not. But could she risk it? If it was his appendix, and it blew, Arrow could die. She'd read an article on it in *Reader's Digest*. Easy to fix, but if you didn't fix it, it was bad news. Baaaad news.

She couldn't drive him into the emergency ward, because the

Pinto was parked in her own personal intensive care unit, and even if she did get it started and the tires pumped up, she might kill both herself and Arrow anyway, considering her driving skills.

She lit another cigarette.

Maybe she should call an ambulance. But what would she tell them? "Uh, sorry, fellas, the kid doesn't have a health card. No, I don't know who he is, couldn't tell you. Just a kid who wandered in here and happened to be sleeping in my spare bedroom. Don't ask *me* how he got in. Where'd those jammies come from? Oh, I guess he musta brought his own supply. Name? Uh, golly, I don't know."

Yeah, right. About as believable as a three-dollar bill.

The medics could save his life, *if* his life really was in danger. She wasn't sure if it was, or if this was all a big to-do about nothing. That would be a laugh, wouldn't it? The boy was as hot as a stolen pistol. Should she blow his cover over nothing more dangerous than a case of cramps? If she did, somebody sure as shootin' would identify him. A boy with no name and no family would set off a whole bunch of firecrackers real fast, a pack of care-givers scrambling for their make-work projects. Maybe they'd take Nick too. Maybe they'd say she was a kidnapper and throw her in jail. And . . . well . . . the truth of that matter was, she *had* nabbed Nick, and she *had* kept Arrow hidden away here, which was the same as kidnapping, wasn't it? Did they still give you the electric chair for kidnapping? Nah, in Canada it was hanging.

Alice stroked her neck distractedly.

But what if this was his appendix? If it was, and he just lay there and exploded, she'd have killed him. As sure as if she'd poisoned him.

Alice didn't think it would be right to do that, and she didn't think she could live with herself if she did. But what could she do? Arrow kept screaming, and now Nick was crying hard too.

She'd never heard him do that before. She wanted to jump up and just walk out, go buy a condo in Florida—not that she could afford it—and spend the rest of her life getting a tan, drinking orange juice, reading mysteries, and sleeping through the night.

Except, if she did that, she'd never sleep again.

Alice said another bad word.

Then she creaked down onto her knees and put her forehead on the edge of the bed. She folded her hands—little-girl-praying hands.

"Look", she whispered. "Look, God, you know I ain't spent much time on you the past sixty, well seventy, years. But this situation don't look too good. This here is a fine kid. Maybe he's even a great kid. But even if he wasn't, he is a *kid*, and he doesn't have a mum and dad and an insurance card. Seems to me you picked a mighty funny place to drop him—here in my lap, I mean. Right now I need some help for Arrow, and pretty da . . . uh, darn fast. Please. I'm askin' ya."

Feeling foolish, she creaked her bones off the floor and sat on the bed.

Then a thought flashed into her mind. *Call Beth Potter.*

Taking her life in her hands, she dialed Beth's number. It rang three times.

"Hello", said a woman's voice, sleepy but awake.

"That you, Bethie?"

"Yes, this is Beth. Who . . . is that you, Alice?"

"Yeah, it's me", Alice replied unsteadily.

"Are you all right?"

"Yeah, yeah, I'm fine. Hate to bother you in the middle of the night, but look, I got a little problem."

"A problem? What kind of problem?"

"It's kind of hard to say. I . . ."

"Do you want me to come over?"

"Willya?"

"Of course I will. Are you having heart trouble?"

"Nah, nothing like that. But I ain't feelin' too good, I can tell you that."

"Oh, dear! Now, Alice, just you lie down, and I'll be right over."

"It ain't me, Bethie. It's . . ."

"Alice, you don't sound like yourself. It's not prowlers, is it?"

"Prowlers? I guess you could say that. Two li'l prowlers."

"Oh, Lord! I'll call the police. I'll wake up Ted. We'll be right there—" Beth made hanging up noises.

Alice stopped her by yelling, "Don't hang up! And dang it, Bethie, don't call the cops!"

"Why not?" Beth said slowly.

"Well, these prowlers . . . they're friendlies, you see—"

"I'm afraid I don't see, Alice. Are you in some kind of trouble?"

"Yes and no."

"Yes and no? Is it bears? Ted can bring his gun."

"Nix on the gun. Nix on Ted. There's no danger, nothing the cops need to know about. But I do need some help here. I hate to ask you—"

"Don't worry. I'll be there in fifteen minutes." Beth hung up.

Twelve minutes later Beth's station wagon screeched to a halt beside the gas pumps. Beth flew out the car door and ran up the front steps. Alice, in nightie and dentures, puffing frantically on a cigarette butt, opened the door of the Palace and let her in. Beth's hair was undone, a frayed winter coat thrown over her jeans and pajama top, bare feet in rubber slip-on boots.

"What is it? Tell me!" she urged, holding Alice's hands in her own, her face a study in anxiety.

Alice shook her head. "I guess there's no sense hiding it any longer. Damn, but small boys can sure gum up the works!"

"I beg your pardon?" Beth said, wrinkling her brow.

"C'mon. Follow me."

The two women went through the door behind the cash register counter and entered Alice's living quarters.

"What on earth . . . ?" Beth said when she heard the combined cries of Nick and Arrow.

"They're in there. *The boys.*"

"The boys?" Beth walked into the bedroom slowly. She stopped in her tracks, and a shocked look spread over her face. Her eyes went directly to the small form screaming on the single cot.

"That's Arrow. I don't know what's ailing him, but it looks bad."

Beth sat down on the edge of Arrow's bed and reached out a hand to his forehead. She touched it. She looked down at his exposed belly in slow motion, then up at Alice wonderingly.

"Who? What . . . ?"

Then Nick cut in with a big caterwaul, and Beth looked across the aisle to the crib. She gave a yelp and a jump and looked even more perplexed.

"What's going on here, Alice?" she asked, looking at the old woman as if she were a specter.

"It's a long story."

"I think you'd better tell me."

"I been looking after these two kids. They don't have any folks."

"Are these your prowlers?"

"That's right. Now this little gaffer here is in a bad way. The trouble is, he doesn't have any medical, and he doesn't need to get fouled up with the law, for reasons that are too screwy to tell you right now."

"Who is he?" Beth looked sideways at the crib. "And who is that . . . child?"

"Like I said—later, Bethie, later. We don't have time to chinwag. This pup could have something serious. Maybe he does.

Maybe he doesn't. But I figured I'd better call an expert like you. Waddaya say, Supermom. He look bad to you?"

"Whatever it is, it's serious all right. It looks like it could be appendicitis. Alice, you'd better call the ER at Fort George hospital. Get them to send an ambulance out here quickly."

"I don't think that'd be too smart."

"Alice!" Beth snapped. "Call the ambulance!"

"Can't do it."

"You can't do it? Why not?"

"Trust me on this one, Beth."

Beth stood up. She stared at Alice as if she didn't know her.

"This boy may be in serious condition. He's got to get to a hospital."

"I know that. I just don't want anybody knowing he was here."

"Why not?!"

Alice inhaled deeply. "He's the missing kid. The one the TV's been blabbing about for the past six months."

Beth looked down into the boy's face. Then her eyebrows raised very high, and her mouth made a small, silent o.

"You mean . . . ?"

"Yup. I been lookin' after him."

"But Alice, that's insane. It's . . . it's bizarre! What's going on here?"

Alice pulled Beth by the coat sleeve and took her back to the kitchen, sat her down in the armchair, and gave her a thumbnail sketch of the situation. Every so often Beth shook her head. She looked more and more worried by the minute.

"Are you sure about all this?" she said eventually. "Maybe you've misinterpreted it."

Alice told her Nick's story. When she came to the dump part, Beth's face went cold with deadly maternal fury.

"I see", she said quietly, looking at her own reflection in the black window.

"Try to believe me, Bethie. It's taken me months to figure it out. It's a jigsaw puzzle, but when you get enough of the pieces, it starts to make a pretty dirty picture. They're lying to us. The feds and the cops and the anchormen been spinning us a line. A big line."

"But how do you know that?"

"Because everything the kid's been telling me adds up. And everything the professionals tell us is full of holes."

"How can you be sure?"

"I ain't a hundred percent sure, but it stinks to high heaven. They tried to kill Nick—I know that for a fact—and the kid says they tried to kill his mum and those Catholic nuns across the valley and a guy named Andrei and his pa. The government did it all."

Beth stared at the open palms of her hands for a minute, trying to sort it out.

"All right. If what you say is true, then this is much too big for us to handle. What can we possibly do?"

"Well, the painted lady got religion and prayed. How's that for starters? Maybe you're an answer to prayer, Bethie."

"Me?"

"Yeah, you."

"This is so strange", Beth mumbled. "Very, very strange. Something woke me up about three this morning. That almost never happens. I figured the Lord wanted me to pray for somebody, some anonymous person in need of prayers at that moment. You might not believe me, Alice, but you were the first person who came to mind. I'd been awake about half an hour, praying for you when the phone rang. Coincidence or what?"

Alice pursed her lips. It was a lot to take in at once.

The sound of two crying children in the back room recalled them to the problem at hand. Beth stood up suddenly and said in a firm voice, "I know what we'll do."

"What?"

Beth opened a big fat wallet, rifled through a stack of plastic cards, and extracted one.

"Yes, here it is. Noah's health card. The ministry of health has been transferring over to photo IDs, but they haven't got to the P families yet, thank God."

"Huh? What you talking about?"

"I'm adopting this boy—what did you say his name is?"

"Arrow."

"No, it's not Arrow. I'm adopting him, you see, and I'm re-naming him. His name is Noah."

"Holy smackers, Bethie, you're the cat's pajamas!"

"Aren't I just. Now quickly, Alice, we've been wasting time."

Beth strode back into the bedroom. Alice followed. Beth un-furled a blanket and spread it beside Arrow's body. He watched her with large, white eyes, whimpering. Moving slowly, she lifted the boy's legs onto the bottom half and then tugged the top half under his upper body. She instructed Alice to take the bottom while she grabbed the top, and they snapped it tight under Arrow.

"We'll use this as a stretcher", she said. "We're going to put him in the back of the station wagon. Try not to bend him."

Beth draped another blanket over the boy, and then, giving the signal with her eyes, she and Alice lifted him in the blanket, forming a kind of soft, straight basket, and staggered out the bedroom door.

Alice gasped and swore as they maneuvered through the apartment and the store, but her tough old turkey arms were able to bear the weight as far as the front door. They put him gently on the floor, and Beth ran out to open the tailgate and flip down the back seat.

Arrow's screaming had stopped, replaced by steady moaning.

When they had him horizontal in the back of the wagon, Beth slammed the tailgate shut and ran around to the driver's door.

"Call emergency", she ordered. "Tell them I'm bringing in a child with an appendix that's going to rupture any minute. There'll be an intern on duty, but I don't know if he can do this kind of surgery. Call Dr. Stevenson. He's in the directory. He's our new family doctor, and he's a surgeon. Tell him to get himself down to the OR fast!"

Beth jumped in, gunned the engine, and roared out of the lot in a spray of gravel.

Alice went back inside and dialed the hospital ER number on the store phone beside the cash register. She told the nurse on duty that Beth Potter was racing for town with an appendix. The nurse asked her to say that again. Alice's tongue tore a strip off her hide. The nurse's tone stiffened but became cooperative.

"Gimme the number of Dr. Stevenson!" Alice snapped. "He's their doctor."

"Dr. Stevenson is on call tonight", said the nurse. "I'll have him here in about twenty minutes."

"Thanks. You're a great gal", Alice replied in a conciliatory tone. "And, hey, look lady, I apologize for my language. I was upset. I didn't mean what I said about your mother."

The nurse, exercising heroic restraint, did not reply. She hung up.

Alice went in, fixed a bottle of warm milk for Nick, fed it to him, dried his tears, and pitty-patted his forehead until he drifted back to sleep.

When he was down at last, she flicked off the bedroom light, went back to the kitchen, threw a birch log on the coals in the firebox, called Poody for lap duty, rejected a craving for a double whiskey, and sat in the armchair. She stared at the black window until it turned to charcoal, then purple, then mauve, then blue.

* * *

Beth arrived at the hospital parking lot at about a quarter past four. She spun the wheel and circled around to the emergency wing, braking under the canopy in front of the entrance. She jumped out and opened the tailgate just as a nurse and a young intern hustled through the sliding glass doors, pushing a gurney between them.

"Are you Mrs. Potter?" the intern asked.

"Yes. Did my friend call?"

"A few minutes ago", said the nurse. "Dr. Stevenson should be here shortly."

The intern and the nurse pulled the blanket out carefully, loaded Arrow onto the gurney, and wheeled him inside. Beth trotted along behind them, keeping a firm hand on Arrow's shoulder.

The ER reception area was empty.

The intern looked at Arrow's face, felt his forehead, and asked him to stick out his tongue.

"Dehydrated", he said calmly. "Nurse, would you hook him up to an IV hydration solution. I want blood and urine tests too. See if you can get the lab people moving."

She scurried off.

"Your tummy pretty sore?" he asked.

Arrow nodded, gasping.

"Where does it hurt?"

Arrow pointed to his lower right abdomen.

"Any vomiting?"

Beth related to him everything Alice had told her.

The nurse returned with a rolling intravenous stand, flipped up an arm of the gurney, put Arrow's left arm onto it, fastened the boy's wrist with a Velcro strap, and inserted the needle. She took his temperature and pulse.

"Temperature elevated, pulse racing", she said evenly. Then she drew a vial of blood from Arrow's forearm.

The intern carefully tugged down the elastic of Arrow's pajama bottom. He applied a gentle but firm pressure on the lower abdomen and held it for a few seconds. He released the pressure suddenly. Beth expected Arrow to scream in acute pain—real agony—but he merely whimpered.

"Good", said the intern. Then he worked with Arrow to obtain a small urine sample. Beth looked elsewhere during that part. When it was finished, the intern handed the sample to the nurse and told her to take it and the blood for immediate lab tests.

She was back in two minutes. "They're on it. They'll have results ASAP."

"Right, thanks. Where *is* Doctor Stevenson?"

The nurse checked her watch. "Mrs. Potter," she said, "I'll have to admit your boy now. Can you come with me? There are forms to be filled . . . "

"No", said Beth. "I'm staying with him."

She rummaged in her coat pocket, withdrew her wallet, and handed Noah's health card to the nurse. The woman frowned but accepted it without an argument and went away to the ward desk.

Dr. Stevenson flew through the entrance at that moment, his thinning brown hair askew, his eyes red. He nodded at Beth.

"Prognosis, intern?" he asked.

"The child complained of soreness in the epigastrium earlier this morning, then vomited, and the pain shifted to the right lower quadrant of the abdominal wall. Followed by acute pain."

"Sounds like the real thing. No swelling, I see. Thank God for that."

"No, sir. I applied pressure on McBurney's Point, but there was no rebound tenderness. Still, he's in a lot of pain."

Dr. Stevenson put his hand to Arrow's forehead and looked into his eyes.

"You're going to be fine, son. Just fine", he said with a reassuring smile. Beth was glad he was the sort of doctor who had already been broken in by three of his own.

A lab technician came down the hallway in high gear and stopped at the foot of the gurney. The physicians looked at her.

"Small amount of blood in the urine, doctor, raised white cell count in the blood."

"Thank you. All right, intern, that's it. Let's get him into the O.R. I'll scrub and meet you there in five minutes."

"Right sir." He wheeled Arrow through a green double door. A sign on it said MEDICAL PERSONNEL ONLY: NO ADMITTANCE.

"Is he going to be all right?" Beth asked tremulously.

"I think we've caught it in time, Mrs. Potter. The appendix hasn't ruptured yet. But it could be close. If it does, he'll be fighting peritonitis, which is a serious matter. I'd better get in there now."

She thanked him profusely, and he strode through the green doors.

Beth sat down on a waiting-room chair and prayed.

* * *

She called Ted on the public pay phone at seven-thirty.

"Beth! Where are you? I've been worried sick wondering where you got to."

"I'm sorry, hon. But it was an emergency. I didn't want to wake you up, you were so tired last night—"

"Emergency? What emergency?"

She told him what had happened, leaving out certain details.

"You've got to be joking! Why didn't you wake me up? I never would have let you go driving off in the dark, into some crazy situation."

"I know you wouldn't, Ted, dear. But somehow I knew I had to do it, and do it fast. I—"

"But Bethie, who the heck is he, this kid?"

"A guest of Alice's", she explained. "He should be coming

out of the operation any time now." Her voice faltered. "Pray for him, Ted. This is a whole lot bigger than I can tell you over the phone."

"Huh? What's going on?" he asked, puzzled.

"I'll fill you in when I get home. Get the porridge on, will you?"

"It's already bubbling."

"I love you, Ted."

"Love you too, Bethie."

"See you when I get there."

"Yup." His *yup* was pretty glum.

"Don't worry, sweetie, I'll be home in a couple of hours."

"Oh, that's good to know." Glum and hurt.

The emergency ward was filling by then, the morning shift arriving, along with a few new patients. An old woman with cardiac arrest, a teenager with drug overdose, and a mill worker with a crushed hand. Beth watched in a daze but managed to pray silently for each of them.

At eight-thirty Dr. Stevenson came out through the green doors with a big smile and stood over her.

"He's fine. Just fine. You can see him in the recovery room for a few minutes. Then I suggest you go home and get some sleep."

"Thanks", she breathed. "Thank you so much, doctor. You'd better take some of your own advice."

"All in a night's work. Comes with the territory. I'll look in on Noah later in the day."

She nodded and stared at the floor. Dr. Stevenson had never met Noah—the real Noah. Noah was a healthy boy, thank the Lord.

"Can your husband be here when Noah wakes up? He'll be under for another couple of hours. Why don't you go home?"

"No, I want to be here."

Beth Potter never lied. Never. It was a difficult moment—a *conscience* moment. She hadn't yet thought about this part of the

549

problem. If he asked her . . . ? If he asked her the question she hoped he wouldn't ask, what would she say?

But the doctor assumed she was merely overcome with emotion; he squeezed her arm and left.

The day nurse led Beth to the recovery room. Arrow was still under the anaesthetic, breathing easily, his face quietly resting, good color, the agony lines smoothed out. Beth put her hand to his forehead. It was warm, normal. She said a silent prayer over him.

She suddenly changed her mind about staying. She needed to explain everything to Ted in case the hospital phoned to tell him that his son Noah was recovering just fine from surgery, and then Ted would say, "Huh? Noah's sitting right here at the table doing his math." Then where would they be? A nice mess that would be. A mess and a half.

She jangled her car keys like a normal mother and went out to find the wagon. On the way back to Steelhead, she stopped in at Queen of the Road Collectibles and told Alice the good news. Alice's tough-lady mask dropped for about thirty seconds, and a tear rolled out of her left eye. Then she put on the mask again and lit a cigarette. Sitting across from each other at the kitchen table, they sipped black coffee and made a pact that for the next three or four days, while Arrow was in hospital, he would be Noah Potter. Neither of them would mention Alice's involvement. Beth would go back into town later in the morning and try to get a few moments alone with the boy. She would explain what was going on. Tell him that he was adopted temporarily.

Alice assured her that the kid had his head screwed on straight, was sharp as a tack, and would play the game to the max. When he was released, Beth could pick him up and bring him home to the Palace.

"Unless . . ." Beth hesitated. "Unless you'd like Ted and me to take care of him for a while at our place."

Alice shook her head. "Naw. For better or worse, the little laddybuck's been dropped in my lap. I like him. I got a duty to him."

"Raising a child is a big responsibility, Alice. And it looks to me like you've got more than one . . . child."

"Yeah, I'm a double mum", Alice replied sardonically.

Nick woke up just then and began to burble, "Awo? Awo?"

Alice brought him into the kitchen, patting his little back with one hand, holding his enormous head with the other, squinting from the smoke that blinded her, a butt dangling off her lower lip.

Nick smiled shyly at Beth. Beth smiled back.

"Hi", she said.

"Ha", Nick replied.

Then Beth cried. She didn't even feel it coming. She bent over suddenly, put her face in both hands, and sobbed. Nick watched the blue jays at the window. Alice watched Poody batting an empty cat food tin across the linoleum.

When the flood was over, and Beth was drying her eyes on the sleeve of her coat, Alice said, "Feel better?"

Beth nodded. "What's happening, Alice? What's happening? This is all too strange."

"Yeah, I know. Ask me about it. We're in the Twilight Zone, Bethie. You'n'me."

"You and me", Beth echoed weakly.

* * *

Beth drove into Fort George about eleven that morning. It was a crisp autumn day, the sky clear, sun trying to burn off patches of September frost that hid in the shadows of the pines. Beside her on the front seat, situated between a badly stained baby carrier and a box of library books, sat a plastic bag full of scrounged Playmobil parts, some Bible stories, and cards the children had made. Bless their hearts, they felt sorry for the sick boy who had been staying at Alice's.

"His name's Noah", Beth had told them. "Just like our Noah." *Temporary*, she had added silently. *Temporary Noah*.

The kids had addressed their Get Well cards to "Noah", drew them with varying degrees of skill, ranging from crayon scribbles by Mary-Kate, a cowboy shootout by Li'l Dan, an excruciatingly feminine garden of wildflowers and butterflies by Janie. Noah made a very clever ark, complete with pop-up giraffe and elephant.

"He'll get it", Noah said, grinning. "He's a Noah too."

Arrow was reclining in bed, staring at a slash of sunlight that was sliding across the far wall. He turned and looked at her as she entered the room. He was the only patient in the children's ward.

"Hi", she began softly. "Remember me from last night?"

He nodded his head.

"Feel pretty sore?"

He shook his head. But Beth knew children well enough to see that he was hurting. There was a half-full glass of 7-Up and an empty pill cup on the bedside table. Pain killers, probably.

She sat on the end of the bed and opened the bag.

"I'm Mrs. Potter. You can call me Beth."

He said nothing, merely watched.

"I'm Alice's friend."

"I know", he answered—his first words.

"My kids made these cards for you. When you're feeling better, in about three or four days from now, I'm going to pick you up and take you back to Alice's. Okay?"

"Okay", he nodded.

She spread the cards on the blanket beside his leg. He moved an arm limply and fingered them. She reached over and opened Noah's trick card. The elephant and giraffe jumped to attention.

A flicker of a smile passed across Arrow's face. He picked up the card and looked at it carefully, opening, closing, opening, closing. Slowly, without betraying any more emotion, he looked through the others.

"When you get home, you can come and visit us. We have lots of kids at our place."

He ignored that.

She put the Playmobil parts on his lap. Tim's plastic igloo, a dog team, and an unconvincing Eskimo. A pirate ship. A Wild West Indian. A miniature rifle. A pistol the size of an ant.

Arrow picked up the pistol with his thumb and forefinger and pointed it at the door.

"Bang", he whispered, totally without expression.

That worried her.

"I brought you some books too. Want me to read them to you?"

He shook his head and put down the gun. He went back to observing the beam of sunlight.

A nurse walked into the room, bustley-cheery, and said, "Hi, there. You must be Noah's mother. He's doing real fine", she said. "Real fine."

Beth swallowed hard and answered, "He's a strong boy. Thanks for looking after him so well."

"Our pleasure. Maybe after lunch Noah's going to talk to us, aren't you Noah? He hasn't said much, Mrs. Potter, but that's normal. He's been through quite a trauma. He'll perk up in no time, just you watch."

Beth smiled back at her, hoping it didn't come across as completely phony. Then she reminded herself that the nurse would be expecting only a worried mother trying to produce a polite response. The illusion was all on her side, she realized. It wouldn't cross anyone's mind that the situation was other than what it appeared to be. The best protection would be to let things take their normal course. No lies. The less said the better.

After the nurse left, Beth watched Arrow dismantle the igloo and put it back together. A good sign, that.

"Arrow," she said quietly, pointing at the plastic band on his wrist, "did you read what's written there?"

He shook his head and read it. He looked up at her curiously.

"It says Noah Potter, doesn't it?"

He nodded, staring at her with solemn grown-up eyes.

"Alice told me that some bad men . . . some very *evil* men . . . are looking for you. I don't want you to worry, but I think you should understand that they know your name. Your real name."

No response. Blank stare.

"So for a few days, just while you're here in hospital, we're going to pretend that you're my son Noah. Is that okay with you?"

He looked at the band on his wrist, then down at the igloo. Again, he dismantled it slowly and reassembled it.

"Arrow, is that okay, honey?"

He nodded.

"So, can you tell me, what's your name for the next few days?"

"Noah", he whispered.

She patted his arm and held it. "Good boy."

He picked up the tiny rifle and held it in the fingers of his left hand.

"And maybe whenever there's anybody else around, if you want to say something to me, you shouldn't call me Mrs. Potter, okay? Do you think you could call me Mum?"

He thought about that, then nodded.

"Can you say it?"

"Mum", he whispered. Then brushed everything off his lap, turned away from her, and stared at the wall.

Beth sat back, absorbing it, trying to grasp what it meant. She watched the boy without making any further attempts at strained conversation. Obviously he wasn't interested in homey repartee, nor did he seem to want any maternal surrogates. Where *was* his real mother, she wondered. Where was his home? And just why wasn't his family looking for him? No doubt Alice knew the answers to those questions. Last night, when she had explained the situation to Beth, she hadn't really supplied many details. Just the rough outline: parents in trouble with the law, father a dissident of some kind. Federal agents trying to nab the boy for all the wrong reasons. Illegal arrests. Big brother stuff. Suspicious government moves. But murder, fires, guns, media lies? What did it all mean? What was the true picture? So far, it was just a crayon scribble. No trick cards with self-explanatory pop-up characters.

Alice would explain. Alice watched television news. Alice read newspapers. Alice liked to keep abreast of the world's slow slide into self-destruction. Alice would show her the puzzle, assembled, no missing pieces. But she'd better show her *soon*, and convince her, because something like this, deceiving a ministry of the government, could land a person in a very big mess. And life was hard enough without legal problems.

She stood up to go.

"Bye for now . . . Noah."

He turned his head and looked at her.

"Bye", he mouthed.

"I'll be in again soon."

"Is Alice coming?" he said slowly.

"Yes, this afternoon."

"Can she bring George?"

"George?" Now who was George? Another pop-up character in a trick tableau? Another unexpected guest?

"My monkey. My teddy."

"Oh, I see. Sure, I'll ask Alice to bring him too." She patted his foot. "See you soon."

She was going down the hall before he thought to whisper, "Bye . . . Mum."

* * *

Ted wasn't very happy about what was happening. He kept pacing from living room to kitchen to dining room to barn and back again, shaking his head, doing a slow boil, saying things like, "This is going to get nasty, Bethie. This is going to blow up in our faces."

He warned her that they were probably already on a few short lists in various government offices, branded as Christian counterculture types, lunatic fringe types, probably-brainwashing-their-kids types. Homeschooling was considered an almost subversive activity, wasn't it? Did they need any more problems? Did they need this?

"The real question is, Ted, dear, does the Lord want this?"

"But how can you tell what he does or doesn't want?" he asked, throwing up his arms.

"The same way we always tell. Pray. Read what the Word says. Listen to our hearts. I've done a bunch of all three since last night, and I think Jesus does want us involved in this. Don't ask me why. We don't have any pull in this world, no money, no power. But we've got him watching over this thing."

"Well, not much I can say to that, is there?"

"Not much", she shot back, smiling. She went over to him and cuddled into his ample arms. She laid her head on his chest, his red checkered bush jacket exuding the smells of hay and sawdust.

"Tell me, Ted, what do you make of the fact that something woke me up to pray at 3 A.M. last night? Eh? What about that part? How come the Lord prompts me to wake up and pray for Alice precisely at the moment she's having the biggest crisis of her life. Then she phones me, at considerable risk to herself, a few minutes later, asking for help. Coincidence or what?"

"All right. You got me there, woman. Sheesh, the weaker sex!"

They laughed together and hugged hard. Then they prayed, and Ted felt more peaceful.

Just after two-thirty Beth drove into the Palace lot, parked by the pumps, beeped her horn, and waited. Alice came out the front door and locked up.

"Hey, Bethie, how's the girl?"

"Tired. How about you?"

"Tired. But I think it's gonna work out. Looks like we're gettin' away with it."

"I hope so."

Alice got into the passenger side, carrying a paper shopping bag, a stuffed monkey, and a jam jar crammed with marigolds. Some of the water sloshed onto the seat.

"Sorry."

"No problem."

Beth turned the ignition key, then paused.

"Alice, what about the other . . . boy?"

"Yeah, what about him?"

"You're not going to leave him alone, are you?"

Alice shrugged. "He's napping. He'll be out cold till suppertime."

"I mean, really, a responsible parent shouldn't leave a child alone by himself in a house, don't you think?"

Alice raised her eyeballs in mock disgust. "Spare me", she said. "Me and Nick been doing just fine without the babysitter police."

Beth wasn't convinced. She fixed Alice with a severe look. The two women regarded each other with irritable expressions, but neither could find anything to say. Then Beth shook her head and put the car in gear.

"All right. There's not much we can do at the moment, but we're really going to have to pull together from now on. I'll bring Janie over to babysit any time you need to get out."

"Nick ain't a baby", Alice grumbled. "He's twenty-two and a half years old."

Beth gave her a perplexed look and decided not to pursue it. They had enough to think about without yet another bizarre detail.

They rode in silence for a few minutes, until Alice opened her window a crack, lit a cigarette, and said, "Sorry for being a bit cranky."

"That's okay. Sorry for being Mrs. Fussbudget. I guess we're both pretty worn out."

"Yeah, I guess we are."

Beth let it hang in the air for another minute, then asked Alice to describe in detail everything she knew about Arrow and his situation. She also wanted to know what Alice had deduced from her media watch during the past few months.

Alice told her everything, black beetles, nuns, druggies—the works.

"So, whaddaya think?" she asked when finished.

"I think it's a very dirty picture. Very dirty. And I think you and I are two of the few people who've had a look at some of the puzzle pieces."

"So what are we gonna do, Bethie?"

"I'm not sure. Probably the best thing is to just get through the immediate crisis, get Arrow back safe and sound to your place, and take it from there."

"One day at a time. Easy does it."

"Right. As for the long-range view of things, I'm not so sure. You might be able to go on for quite some time hiding the boys, but eventually there'll be another medical problem, not to mention your own health going downhill. The other one—Nick, is it?—I'm sure with that condition of his he'll be needing special treatment."

"Got any more spare health cards?"

"None that would fool the people down at Fort George General. We got away with renaming Arrow because most little boys look pretty much like one another. But Nick's a boy with a big difference. He'd stick out like a sore thumb."

"Then we're sunk", said Alice sullenly.

"Oh, I'm not saying that. Not for a moment. We mustn't discount God."

"Better get on the blower to him, then, 'cause we need rescuing in a big way."

"Why don't *you* talk to him? You've already done it once, and the Lord seems to take special interest in newly hatched prayer warriors. He wants them to know he's really there. So pray away, Alice, and we just might stumble upon some unsuspected solutions."

Alice didn't like the sound of that. She lit another cigarette, crossed her legs and folded her arms, and stared out the side window with a worried look.

"Don't get any wrong ideas here, Bethie. I ain't never gonna be a fundie."

Beth chuckled.

"Absolutely not", she said, trying to squelch a grin. "Painted lady."

* * *

Beth and Alice spent a lot of time together during the following three days. Mornings and afternoons they drove in to see Arrow at the hospital. He was recovering well, smiled each time they came into the ward room, smiled his biggest (which wasn't all that big) when George arrived on the first day, said "Thank you, Alice", for the marigolds and the comic books and the battery-operated rabbit with the tin drum (it was babyish, but he seemed to enjoy it). Alice made toughlady small talk with him (which he also enjoyed). The clichés flew about the room like shrapnel at a terrorists' picnic. It was such a return to normal dialogue (Arrow's and Alice's version of normal) that Arrow began to look almost as if he were just another kid recovering from minor surgery.

The nurses were friendly, the sun shone steadily through the big picture windows at the end of the room, and Dr. Stevenson came by on rounds every morning, winking at Arrow and hinting that he'd go home by Tuesday.

On Sunday afternoon, the Catholic priest, Father Ron, poked his head in the door and waved. He had a purple stole around his neck, doing his own kind of rounds, Alice supposed.

"Hi, Alice! Hi, Mrs. Potter! I heard you had a boy here. How's he doing?"

"Fine, Reverend", said Beth.

"What's your name, lad?" Father Ron asked.

Arrow, Alice, and Beth stared back at him until the priest began to feel as if he had committed an indiscretion.

"Uh . . ." said Beth. She never lied. Never. Especially not to ministers of God, however misguided they might be.

Arrow looked at the rabbit and flicked a switch on its bottom, filling the room with a pleasant, distracting *ratta-tat-tat*.

"Noah", said Alice. "His name's Noah. Right, Noah?"

Temporary Noah, thought Beth, trying to maintain the moral equilibrium in the room.

Despite the odd delay, which Father Ron attributed to Protestant mistrust of Catholics, he smiled brightly and said, "That's a great name. Wish I had a name like that. Big time."

"Yeah, big time", said Alice overenthusiastically, with a full display of dentures. Beth decided that Alice would have made a very poor con artist.

On Monday morning, Dr. Stevenson stopped by the ward, checked Arrow, and said, "Lookin' good! I think we can let you go home tomorrow."

Arrow responded with a jumpy smile that faded before it had barely begun.

"After you're feeling better, why don't you get your Mum to bring you over to our place. My son has a new air hockey game. He's about your age. Would you like that?"

Arrow looked at Beth.

Beth looked back at Arrow.

Arrow nodded solemnly.

Dr. Stevenson wondered about it but assumed that the boy was still a little low from the surgery.

"What do you think, Beth?" the doctor said (he had dropped the Mrs. Potter business on the second day).

"Fine by me if it's fine by Arr . . . by Noah."

"Great. Call me when he's up and running, and we'll get the boys together."

"How long will that be, doctor?" Beth asked. "I mean, should he stay in bed when I get him home?"

"He should get plenty of rest, and no heavy lifting, no fooling around on the monkey bars, but I think he should just try to live his usual routine. In six to eight weeks, it'll be as if it never happened."

He winked and was gone with a wave.

"Whew!" said Alice. "Close call." She lit up a cigarette distractedly. When Beth gave her a scolding look, Alice popped into the washroom, turned on the ventilator fan, and closed the door. Five minutes later she was out again, the nicotine level in her bloodstream back to where it should be.

On the drive home they did some more figuring.

"It could be uncomfortable trying to pretend that Arrow's my little boy. He's out of the attic now, and someone's going to put two and two together before long."

"Yeah, well, you could just give the doc the cold shoulder", Alice pointed out.

"I suppose I could. But he's such a nice man, and Arrow does need friends."

"Well, you got a whole barn full of kids, more than enough for Arrow."

"Yes", Beth said uncertainly. "We'll work on that angle all right, but eventually our gang is going to chatter about their pal down the road, and they could do it when the wrong kind of ears are listening."

"Snoops, you mean?"

"Or just friendly, curious people, who watch life and think about other people. Nothing malicious, just the way people are—you know."

Alice looked sarcastic. "Yeah, don't I know."

"So eventually, someone is going to ask someone else, maybe one of our neighbors, who's that boy the Potter kids were talking about. It's hard to stop leaks. They're children, and children speak without thinking."

"You could tell 'em not to let the cat outa the bag."

"I could. But it wouldn't stick. The little ones can't keep secrets, and the older ones would give it away by looking silent and mysterious whenever a hint of the secret pops out of some younger one's mouth. It's going to happen, I just know it. And we can't keep our kids in quarantine."

"I see what you mean. Maybe it would be better if we don't start hooking Arrow up to other kids."

"It hurts to say it, but that seems our only solution right now."

"There's no problem, Bethie. We just bring Arrow back to my place tomorrow, and life goes on as usual."

"Except it isn't usual any more, is it? Children need to grow, Alice. They need friends. They'll wither up and die if they're kept in a cage."

"My place ain't a cage", Alice grumbled. "I treat him right. He's got Nick as a friend, and plenty of places to run and jump out back."

She told Beth about the boardwalk and the garden of earthly delights Arrow had made in the wilds of the junk heap.

"Why that's wonderful", Beth said, brightening up considerably. "Then he does have some space to stretch and some challenges. More than that, it tells us that inside those protective barriers of his there's a very smart, enterprising young man."

"Yep, he's that, all right."

"I think he's going to do well, Alice. Very well indeed."

"If you say so."

"Why don't we try this: When he's up and running, as the saying goes, I'll bring Noah over—the real Noah—to meet him. I'm going to take a week or so preparing him. Janie too. She's the oldest, and really quite wise for such a young lady. Noah's like his Dad—extroverted but solid as a rock, and wise in his own way. I'm going to have to explain the situation to them, and they're going to have to make some leaps in understanding to accept the fact that we intend to deceive the government."

"Some leaps? I'll say!"

"But they love an adventure."

"Bethie, take it a bit more slowly. You know your kids better than I do, but is that really such a smart idea? How much adventure can they take?"

Beth considered this objection.

"It *is* a gamble", she mused.

Alice shook her head. "Nah, it's too risky. The lads and me'll get along okay by ourselves. If I can keep the arrow from shooting into the store at the wrong moment or making noises while I got customers, we should be hunky-dory for a long, long time."

"It's worked so far."

"Yeah, but that's pure luck. We've been careless. Real careless. It's time to start getting our act together."

"What if at some point someone gets suspicious? They could phone the child welfare office . . . or the police. Have you made any contingency plans?"

"Huh? Continget . . . what?"

"I mean, if someone does discover him, what will you do?"

"I hadn't thought of that." Alice lit a cigarette. "I guess we'll call you. You could come down and pick him up, adopt him temporary again. How's that?"

"That would work if we can get him away from the store in time, without anyone seeing. The problem would be if somebody phones the officials without you knowing. What would you do if a squad of police cars just roars into your parking lot?"

"I'd lock the doors! I'd tell them to go to hell!"

Beth gave Alice a pitying look.

"Okay, okay. I better get real, right?"

"Uh-huh", Beth nodded. "We should think of everything that might go wrong and make a plan for it."

"We'd go out the back door."

"What about Nick? How far can you carry him?"

Alice rubbed her bad hip. "I see what you mean."

"Any escape routes?"

"We got the maze out back. We could hide."

"They'd go through it with a nit comb."

"Yeah, I guess they would. Well, maybe me and Arrow can make a secret path through the maze. Then, anytime we need to, we could hightail it into the bush and go through the woods to your place."

"That's a long walk, Alice. A very long walk for an elderly woman, a little boy, and someone with Nick's problem. There are swamps and miles of impassable bush between your place and ours."

"Yeah, scratch that plan."

"But let's say you make that secret getaway path through your maze. Let's say you can get into the forest without being seen. Maybe you could just go through the big pines parallel to the road, a half mile or so. You could tie a red scarf to a tree, and I'll drive back and forth between your place and ours until I spot it. Then I'll park and honk. You can hustle down to the road and into the car lickety-split, and I'll bring you to the farm."

"Sounds perfect", Alice mused. "I don't have a red scarf, but I got a blue one."

"Good enough."

"One problem, though. How in tarnation are you gonna know that I run away? How you gonna know you need to drive over and look for a scarf on a tree?"

"I could keep tabs on you, maybe. Why don't I phone you before breakfast and after supper every night, and if you don't answer I'll hop in the car and drive down? Sound like it could work?"

"Yeah, it just might work."

"It might mean you'd have to spend a few hours in the bush waiting for me. It could be a long wait."

"It'd be a longer wait in a jail cell."

"Alice, here's another plan—if you have a bit of warning, let's say a few minutes or so, you could call me and say, *Blue scarf time.* Then run for the bush."

"Okay! I love it. Trixie Belden and the Case of the Blue Scarf it is!"

Beth chuckled. "Let's hope it doesn't come to that. Dear God, I hope not."

"Nah, the whole thing's pretty far out. Still . . ."

"Yes, still . . ."

"Better to be prepared. That's what the Boy Scouts say."

Alice stretched her left arm along the back of the seat and put her hand on Beth's shoulder.

"You're good folks, Bethie."

Beth smiled but kept her eyes on the road. "Thanks, Alice. You too."

"You're really putting yourself out for me and the boys."

"Happy to do it, happy to do it."

Alice did not remove her hand. "You're the best thing happened to me in a long time, girl", she said quietly.

It was said in a tone completely devoid of the many vaudevillian artifices of which Alice was capable. The old face was sad and grateful, and itself. Beth tried to form a word of response, but her throat wouldn't let her do it. Both women stared straight ahead, and they drove up to the Palace a minute later having said no more.

* * *

Tuesday morning, after breakfast, the hospital phoned Beth to tell her Noah was being discharged at eleven. Dr. Stevenson would do a final checkup, and then her son was free to go. Beth phoned Alice, and they drove down to Fort George.

Arrow's room was bursting with golden sunlight when they walked in. Dr. Stevenson was sitting on the end of the bed, chatting with Arrow, who was standing beside him pulling a striped T-shirt over his ribs. He was already wearing the clean faded jeans, gym socks, and green runners Alice had brought for him the day before. He looked chipper, though he winced as he tucked in the shirt.

"Morning, Beth", said the doctor. "Noah's got his engines revved up, all ready to go."

"Hi . . . Mum", Arrow whispered.

"Hi, sweetie", Beth replied unsteadily, smiling with barely concealed relief.

"Hi, Alice." Arrow flashed a look at her.

"Hi, kid."

Alice decided to take a back seat on this one, saying no more, leaning against the open door frame. Dr. Stevenson handed Beth a small white cardboard box. "Here're some odds and ends that'll come in handy. Gauze, tape, saline solution. You should change the dressing once a day. Bring him into the clinic on Friday, and I'll take those stitches out. Keep your eye open for infection. If the incision starts to look angry, give me a shout, and we'll nip it in the bud."

"Fine, thank you so much, doctor", Beth said, taking both of his hands in hers. She pumped them up and down. "So much."

566

He patted her shoulder. "Not at all. Line of duty. You've got a great trooper here. Just make sure he stays quiet for a week or two, then it's business as usual."

He turned to Arrow and made a mock stern face. "No climbing trees for a while, buddy. Promise?"

Arrow nodded. The doctor grinned, stuck out his hand for a shake.

"Take care, Noah."

No one saw her come in. No one realized what was going to happen until a few seconds after she said it.

"That's not Noah Potter." The voice was low and cold.

Beth, Alice, Arrow, and Dr. Stevenson turned in unison and stared at a middle-aged woman standing just inside the doorway.

"Who is he?" the woman said. Both her hands were in the front pockets of her white lab coat. Clipboard under her arm. Stethoscope around her neck.

"I said, who is he?"

No one answered. Dr. Stevenson laughed. "This is Noah Potter, doctor."

The woman's lips compressed and twisted at an odd angle. "No", she said very quietly. "No, I don't think so."

Beth looked stricken, her face blanched, eyes widened. Alice tried to create a diversion. She lit a cigarette. The woman doctor scowled at her and told her to put it out. Alice blew a puff in her face and kept smoking.

"Just who are *you*?" the woman demanded.

"A friend", said Alice nonchalantly. "I came in with Bethie to pick up Noah. Keep her company, like."

This was a mistake.

The woman looked at Arrow's face, then at Beth, then at Dr. Stevenson.

"This isn't your concern, doctor", said Stevenson evenly. "I'm in the process of discharging the boy."

"Yes, but what boy? I used to be their family physician, and I'm telling you that's not Noah Potter."

"It certainly is Noah Potter", Stevenson countered. "Now, if you don't mind, we'll just proceed about our business, and I suggest, Margaret, that you do likewise."

"Don't bully me, Bruce. There is something irregular here. And I doubt if the ministry would be pleased by it. There has been far too much fraudulent abuse of the medical system. I don't know who this child is, but someone has pulled the wool over your eyes."

"That is ridiculous", Stevenson said, frowning. He turned to Beth and raised his eyeballs in disgust. "Beth, will you please reassure the good doctor that this is your son."

Beth gulped and stared at him, red-faced.

Alice took in the whole scene and analyzed it accurately.

It's the hard-apple lady-doc in full battle gear, Alice said to herself, slipping out the doorway backward. Making as little noise as possible, she went down the hall in the direction of an EXIT sign.

* * *

After Alice found her way out of the building and into the parking lot, she clamped her purse in her right hand and walked as fast as she could up the hill to Fourth Avenue. She turned onto it, going east, and was hustling along, scared and angry, when an old rusting car pulled over to the curb beside her and sat there idling. The passenger window rolled down, and a teenager's face popped out.

The Vietnamese kid.

"Hi, Missus. You need a ride?"

Alice looked up and down the street nervously, then answered. "Uh, yeah. That'd be real nice."

She got in, and he roared back into the main lane. "Where I take you?"

"I gotta get back to Steelhead", she said, forcing her words to come out slow and easy.

"Oh, I am too sorry. I got a class in ten minutes. I'm gonna be late if I take you all the way there. How about I drop you at the turnoff?"

"Better than nothin'", Alice replied pleasantly. He turned left at the traffic lights, and the car labored noisily up the steep incline. The boy tried to make "Nice weather we having, eh?" comments, but she merely grunted the responses. Once, she shot a glance at him, and the startling contrast of the scene at the hospital and his implacably grinning, inscrutably happy face stabbed her with a feeling of unreality. Normal people just kept on doing normal things in their hideously normal lives, and her world was going to hell in a hand-basket.

He dropped her at the corner of the road that led to Steelhead, said, "Bye-bye, Missus!", did a screeching U-turn, and rumbled like a tank back down the hill, leaving a cloud of blue exhaust hanging in the silence.

"Bye-bye", Alice muttered. Pulling her jacket tight around her neck, she hoofed along the gravel shoulder in the direction of home.

Five minutes later, a battered once-red pickup lurched to a stop beside her, its box piled high with feed bags. It was Harry Bird.

"Alice, darlin', what you doin' out here all by your lonesome?"

"Gettin' my constitutional, Harry."

"Need a ride?"

Alice shrugged, "Sure. I've had enough aerobics to last a lifetime."

What the hell am I going to say to him? Alice wondered, climbing up into the passenger side of the cab. She needn't have worried. Harry supplied the entire conversation all the way back to the Palace, ranting about the price of dairy mash for fifteen utterly forgettable minutes.

"So long, old gal!" he yelled at her as he drove away from the gas pumps. "Have a good one!"

She bored a hole into his tail pipe with her eyes.

"Have a good one", she snarled.

She let herself in the front door of the store, locked it behind her, pulled the blind, made sure the *Closed-Open* sign was hanging the right way, and went in to see how Nick was doing.

He was lying in his crib, smiling at sunbeams.

"Ha, Awis."

"Ha, Nick", she answered. She got him up and dressed and into his seat by the bird feeder, fed him lunch, and when he was finally content to amuse himself, swatting and rattling and playing his flute, she went out to the cash register, banged the NO SALE key absentmindedly, and had a trembling fit.

Bethie was no squealer, but if they did break her down, it was the chain gang for Alice for sure, and maybe another meat box for Nick.

But there was nothing she could do about it. Run? Where to? Out into the woods with a blue scarf? Uh, sorry! Bethie won't be able to pick you up right now, Miss Douglas. Maybe next week, maybe never.

Even if Bethie could fake her way through the grid-lock, what about Arrow? They sure weren't going to let a no-name brand kid just go toddling off down the street hand in hand with his fake mum after cheating the health-care system, were they? Would anybody identify him? The best thing that might happen, the *very* best, would be Arrow getting confiscated and put into some Human Resources holding tank. But it wouldn't take long before somebody checked the no-name face against all the missing faces on the posters and figured it out. That little face was by now one of the three most famous faces in the province. Posters everywhere.

And how could she blame him if those smarmy social workers pried the information out of him? "I lived with Alice M.

Douglas and her cat and goats at Queen of the Road Collectibles at Steelhead outside of Fort George, B.C., for a long, long time. She was very nice to me. Yes, she knew my name. Uh-huh, she knew that you'd killed my mum and dad, and uh-huh, she has another little boy living with her."

Baaaad news!

But where could she go? Donnie was dead, and hey, he got her into this mess in the first place. Kurly in Saint John's? And just how would she get a big-headed baby across three thousand miles of open land. Bus, plane, train?

Alice went into the kitchen, checked Nick (he was chuckling at the blue jays now), and poured herself a whiskey. She drank it down in three sips and made another one. She nursed this one more carefully, and the effect seemed to ease the stab wound in the center of her chest, reduced the hand-trembling to a mere quiver.

Taxi?

Hardy-har-har! Can you imagine it? Tottering down the front steps with a suitcase and one heck of a strange infant in her arms. *Take me to the bus station, wouldya, cabbie. Baby's got a cold, had to wrap his head. What's the matter with you, haven't you ever seen a baby with a head twice the size of his body? Kootchy-koo!*

Alice was on her third drink and fourth cigarette when the phone rang. She decided not to answer it, but it just rang and rang and rang until it nearly drove her crazy. Then she wondered if it was Beth calling and picked up the receiver.

It was Ted.

"They took her, Alice." His voice was shaking.

She didn't reply.

"They took her and the boy."

Alice cleared her throat. "Who took her?"

"I don't know. The police . . . I think."

"Take it easy, Ted", she said, trying to calm him. "You mean you don't know for sure who took her?"

"Not really. Dr. Stevenson phoned here a few minutes ago and told me what happened. He was pretty upset, upset with me and Beth, that is. Told me he couldn't understand why we'd pull such a stunt. There was nothing I could say to that—nothing."

"Did he tell you what happened after the lady doctor blew the whistle?"

"Not much. I suppose she went off to phone the ministry and the police. Stevenson says he doesn't know who the people were who came to sort out the mess. I asked him where Beth was. He said he wasn't sure, but he thinks the R.C.M.P. wanted to have a talk with her, get a statement. He guesses they'll probably be driving her home later in the afternoon."

"They're not arresting her, are they?"

"I doubt it. I mean, technically it's illegal, but so is parking by fire hydrants. I don't think it's in the criminal code. Maybe they'll fine us or hand us a bill for the operation. Anyway, we'll try to explain it some way that makes sense to them. We could say he was just a troubled kid who wandered in out of nowhere. It was an emergency. His life was in danger. We'll tell them we thought that pretending he was Noah for a few days would bypass all the red tape. They might go for it. It's a lie, of course . . ."

Alice could tell that the falsehood was sticking in his throat like a chicken bone.

"Don't worry, they'll buy it, Ted. What about Arrow? Did Stevenson tell you anything?"

"He said the Child Welfare people or someone from Human Resources came out and took him away. He thinks there'll probably be a custody hearing if the boy can't tell them who he really is. We'll probably have to testify about our part in the affair."

Alice paused. "Uh, did you mention my name?"

"No", he answered woodenly. "No, I didn't mention your name."

She stared into the receiver.

"No, not at all", he repeated, coldly. Then he hung up.

Alice began to feel sick and guilty and ashamed. It surged up inside her like a jet of black muck from a cracked septic tank. She pushed it down angrily. There was Nick to protect, wasn't there? Wasn't there?

15

A Parliament of Disasters

After talking with Alice, Ted made a couple of calls, the first to his pastor, who listened without a word and told Ted he would pray and not to worry, Beth would probably be home before he knew it. He asked if Ted had a lawyer. Ted, who had never needed one before, didn't know any. The pastor said maybe he should find one, just in case there were complications. He suggested a young lad he knew, fresh out of law school, who had recently joined the congregation. He was married, had a baby daughter. Ted took the lawyer's number and called him.

The lawyer's voice sounded as if it came out of a fourteen-year-old's mouth, but the mind behind the voice was well-stocked and scalpel sharp. He made an appointment to meet with Ted the next morning. It didn't sound like much, the lawyer assured him, just a misunderstanding. But it would be better to check out all the legal ramifications. He gave Ted his unlisted phone number and asked him to call him at home when Beth returned.

Ted then called the local R.C.M.P. detachment, but the duty officer hadn't heard anything about Beth. He took Ted's number and agreed to call him immediately if she was brought in.

By now he was in the beginning stages of panic, trying to crush the frantic feeling for the sake of the kids, pacing, snapping instructions at Janie and Noah. They hopped to it and began to forage in cupboards, looking for supper fixings.

He could see they were worried but acting calm and brave.

"Don't worry, Dad. Mum'll be home soon", Janie said in a grown-up voice.

He nodded joylessly and said nothing.

At 4:35, the phone rang—it was the corporal from the Fort George detachment.

"Mr. Potter? This is Bill Murphy. You remember me? I was at the Coalition Party meeting at your place a few months ago. Your wife is here. There's a bit of confusion going on. She might have to wait until some of the legal people from Vancouver arrive. Do you want to come down and stay with her?"

"How long will it take? She'll be driving herself home, won't she?"

"Probably. But I thought you might want to be with her. She's looking kind of upset."

"I'll be right there."

He went out the front door in a rush, jumped into the cab of the pickup that he used for hauling firewood, and turned the key. It *grr-grrred*. He tried it again. Nothing. The battery was dead. He slammed the wheel with both fists and said something he instantly regretted.

It took another ten minutes to get the tractor warmed up, backed out of the shed, and the jump cables attached under the hood of the truck. The battery seemed deader than a doornail, but it sparked eventually, and the old 450 engine burped, sputtered, then roared.

Ted broke the speed limit all the way to town.

He remembered to ease back on the gas pedal half a block from the police detachment but pulled into the parking lot too fast, lurching to a stop by the cement steps with an inch to spare.

He banged the front door wide open, stomped into the reception foyer, and stood there, bull-eyed, chest wheezing.

"Where's my wife?" he demanded of the corporal who stood at the desk with his mouth hanging open. The corporal looked back at him with a sympathetic expression. He was a young man with a brush cut, a serious, guileless face—long, tall, and stupid, Ted thought.

"Hello, Mr. Potter. I'm Bill Murphy." He stuck out his hand, and Ted shook it distractedly, eyes flashing around the office.

"Where's Beth? Where's my wife?"

"You wanna come inside here and sit down, Mr. Potter?" the corporal said slowly. "Why don't you c'mon in here, and I'll get you a cup of coffee."

"No, thanks. Where's my wife?"

The corporal's shoulders sagged a fraction. "I tried to call you. Your daughter told me you'd already left. It looks like your wife had to go into Vancouver for some more questioning. They left about fifteen minutes ago."

"What!" Ted shouted. "Where are they taking her?"

"Relax, Mr. Potter. It's just routine stuff. I guess they want to find out a bit more about that missing boy who was with you. There's been a big manhunt for him for months, and—"

"Why couldn't they question her here?"

"I don't know, Mr. Potter. Maybe—"

"Stop calling me Mr. Potter!"

"Okay", the corporal said apologetically. "I'm sorry . . . sir. I know you're upset."

Ted stared at him. "Yes, I am very upset", he said, one word at a time.

"I know it's an inconvenience, but I don't think there's anything to worry about. It's just one of those things. Everybody hates bureaucracy—I know I sure do—and why don't you let me get you that cup o' coffee. Cream and sugar?"

"Forget the cream and sugar. Forget the coffee. Just give me the phone number of wherever they're taking her."

The corporal said, "Okay, it'll take a minute." He flipped through a Rolodex file on the desk, found a card, and jotted down the number on a slip of paper. He handed it to Ted.

"Thank you", Ted said shortly. "What is this place? Is it the city jail?"

"No, sir. It's just an office downtown. The guys who came in for your wife were from a special division that deals with federal matters. They're called S and I."

"Federal matters? Isn't this just a mix-up with the provincial ministry of health?"

"I guess it is, really", said Murphy, scratching his head. "But that boy's been the subject of a nationwide search, you see, and maybe they just want to check out any leads to where he's been all this time."

"You don't think Beth and me abducted him, do you?" Ted snapped.

The corporal shook his head, remembering the meeting at Potter's farm. He'd had a look around the place that night and had a pretty good idea of what the family was all about.

"Do you?"

"No", the corporal replied. "Definitely not. I think it's probably just an accident that you got involved in this. You don't have to tell me anything, because I know what the legal system is and how things can get snarled up. Your lawyer isn't here right now, and I don't think we should be discussing the details without him present. Maybe you should call him as soon as you get home."

"I've already called him. Now, what about my wife?!"

"Don't worry, they'll sort it out soon as your wife explains things. They probably just want to know anything that could throw light on the boy's whereabouts while he was missing. He was part of a drug commune, you know."

That sobered Ted up quickly. He shook his head. "I didn't know."

"It's a pretty sad tale, and I think he's seen some bad things, if you ask me. I'm sure they just want to ask your wife if she can tell them anything that might give them a lead. They'll probably bring her back to your place later tonight and ask you the same questions they ask her."

"I see." Ted nodded slowly. "So all this foofarah isn't really about us not telling the medical people he wasn't our son."

"I don't think so. Of course, it seems to me you and your wife made a mistake not telling the staff at the hospital, but that's not a federal matter. Personally, I think you were just being good samaritans."

Ted revised his opinion of the corporal. He pushed the farmer's cap far back on his head, took it off without thinking, and twirled it in his hands—Kelly green, *John Deere* in yellow letters—its message plain for all to see: I'm a regular workin' man, don'tya know, honest as the day is long.

He swiped away a cowlick. He began to twist the cap in his hands, as if wringing it dry.

"Lord, what a mess", he groaned. "I knew this was going to blow up in our faces. I just knew it."

The corporal said nothing. Ted Potter had broken the law, and that was not good, but he hadn't intended to hurt anyone, he'd just been trying to help. They were good people, the Potters. They'd made a mistake. People made mistakes all the time. It could happen to anyone.

"Look, tell you what. They should be getting into Vancouver in about forty-five minutes from now. I'll phone the S and I office and tell them you were asking for your wife. I'll get them to phone you. They'll put her on the line. Okay?"

"Okay", Ted said, feeling embarrassed by his grand entrance. "Thanks, officer. What did you say your name was?"

"Murphy. Bill Murphy. Call me Buzz, for obvious reasons."

It was Ted's turn to extend his hand. They shook hands and liked each other for some reason that was inexplicable to both.

"Sure I can't get you that coffee?"

"All right. Cream, no sugar."

"Coming right up. Cream, no sugar."

While the kids were eating supper, Ted made a few more phone calls: the first to Beth's parents in Alberta. They took the news calmly, but their voices betrayed confusion and suppressed fear. They promised to pray, and Ted assured them he would phone back as soon as he heard anything. Then he called his pastor again, and the man promised to get a prayer chain going. Then another to the boy-lawyer, who had been doing his homework and said that Ted and Beth would probably be facing some bureaucratic discomfort for a while, possibly a fine, and almost certainly the surgery bill, but not to worry. He took the S and I number and offered to give their office a call. He would, if necessary, drive to Vancouver and stay with Beth until her interview with the feds was completed. Not to worry, it probably wouldn't come to that.

Next, Ted dialed the number that Buzz Murphy had given him. The feds S and I. It sounded like a grocery store or a savings and loan company.

It was now early evening, and Ted expected to bang into an answering machine, but the phone rang once, and a female voice answered.

"Security and Intelligence."

Security and Intelligence? Ted wondered. He identified himself and asked for his wife.

The voice on the other end of the line said pleasantly that there was no record of such a person as Beth Potter at that office.

Ted insisted that she had left Fort George over two hours before, heading directly for the Vancouver S and I office. A one-hour trip at the most.

"There must be some mistake, sir. Who gave you this number?"

Ted told her.

"Well, local R.C.M.P either gave you the wrong number or they misunderstood."

"Misunderstood?" Ted echoed, feeling a rivulet of dread snaking down his spine.

"Why don't you check with the Fort George detachment, sir, and see if they gave you the proper information?"

"All right", he said calmly.

Murphy checked the Rolodex file again and told him that the original number was correct. "Looks like some snafu between various agencies, Mr. Potter. I'll try to do some tracking and get back to you."

Ted hung up the wall phone, sat down at the kitchen table, and waited.

Fifteen minutes later his lawyer phoned.

"Ted, I don't know what's going on, but S and I doesn't have any record of her clocking in at the Vancouver office."

"I know. I called them myself."

"It could be Buzz Murphy didn't hear right or jumped to conclusions."

"Then where is she?"

"I don't know. Let's go through what happened again, step by step. Don't leave out a single detail."

Ted told him everything he knew.

"And you say Beth told you that the boy is the missing child who was involved in that cult?"

"Uh, drug commune", Ted corrected.

"Drug commune? I thought it was a cult."

"Maybe it was both."

"Maybe. Now how did he come into your . . . possession?"

Ted told him, leaving out Alice's name.

"This woman he was staying with, I think you'd better tell me who she is."

"Nobody needs that info. She's—"

"But what do you know about her? I mean, she might be a member of this cult."

"Her? No way! The lady's not that type. Believe me."

580

"What's her name, Ted? She might have been duping you. Maybe she's a front, running a safe house for cult members."

"What's that mean . . . a safe house?"

"Espionage term, means a clandestine refuge, totally anonymous, where spies and terrorists and the like can lie low for a period of time or move across the country without leaving paper trails."

"Sure doesn't sound like this lady."

"You're certain about that?"

A ponderous silence ensued, during which Ted wracked his memory for anything about Alice that looked in the least sinister. In the end he concluded, *Crude, yes. Sinister, no.*

"Not a chance", he told the lawyer. "The kid just wandered out of the woods, and she took him in like a wounded bird. She's just an innocent bystander like us."

"Okay. Looks like this is going to be a busy night. I'll start checking every law enforcement agency in the lower mainland. I'll get back to you as soon as I hear anything. Sit tight and don't worry."

Ted put the little ones to bed, called Janie and Noah to the living room, and asked them to pray with him. He didn't explain much, just told them that there was a mix-up and no one knew where their mother was. Not to worry. It would sort itself out. After some valiant attempts at spontaneous prayer, they fell silent. Finally the two teens got up and returned to their homework. Hoping to convince himself of his own optimistic words, he remained alone on the couch and tried to read the Scriptures for a while, but his eyes had trouble focusing on the text.

At nine o'clock he told Janie and Noah to get ready for bed.

"No arguments, *tout de suite!*" he said.

"Toot-sweet", Janie replied.

They kissed their father good night, trying to mask their anxiety. Their wind-down routine seemed to stretch far too long, Janie brushing and brushing her teeth for an age, hanging around the kitchen phone in her nightie and bathrobe and pink, fluffy-doggy slippers. Noah came out of his bedroom at ten, scratching the backside of his hockey-star pajamas.

"Can't sleep", he mumbled.

In the end the three of them just sat at the kitchen table, waiting. Around midnight Ted told them to go to bed.

* * *

After a fitful sleep, Ted awoke to the sound of the kids rummaging in the kitchen, clanking cereal bowls and rattling spoons, whispering and giggling. He sat up on the couch, where he had fallen asleep around three o'clock in the morning. He checked his wristwatch. It was a quarter to six. Janie came into the living room, joggling Mary-Kate up and down in her arms.

"Mamma, Mamma?" Mary-Kate sang.

The feeling of cold dread returned full force.

"Should I change her, Daddy?"

"Yes, please, honey, and get her dressed too, willya? Tell Noah to feed the pigs. I'm going to milk Moonah."

It was raining hard and cold when Ted went out the back door. He hiked his coat up over his head and ran for the barn. Inside, it smelled of manure, hay-perfumed, but chilly. Puffs of white breath were coming from the cow's green mouth. She was chewing cud, giving him a reproachful look over her shoulder, a little irritated with him for being late.

He filled her manger with alfalfa, shook a bucket of mash under her nose to catch her attention, and she set to work on her breakfast. He tied her tail to the stanchions with a length of baling twine so she wouldn't thwack him in the eyes with it and spent twenty minutes pulling a gallon and a half of rich, warm milk out of her. He squirted a little at the mob of calico barn cats who had gathered, and they went away licking their chops.

The phone rang as he was filtering the milk into a stainless steel can on the kitchen counter.

"Buzz Murphy here, Mr. Potter. Hope I didn't wake you up. It's my day off, but I wanted to get back to you."

"Have you found her?"

"I'm sorry, I just haven't been able to find a trace. The other guys here at the office haven't heard anything, either. None of us can figure out what's going on. It's not the usual way we do things around here, I hope you know that."

"But *someone* took her away", Ted said into the phone, controlling his emotions. "Who was it?"

Buzz stammered. "I don't know. They *said* they were S and I, but those guys don't leave calling cards. We just assumed—"

"You just assumed?"

"It was all regular procedure until the moment they walked out with her. They were law enforcement officers, all right, no doubt about it, but I can't for the life of me tell you why they've just disappeared into the woodwork."

"You've lost my wife!" Ted shouted. "You've lost my wife!"

The children stopped eating and chattering and stared at their father. Mary-Kate whimpered.

"Listen to me, Murphy", Ted roared. "You just get busy and find her. Find her real fast, or there's going to be such a stink you'll wish you were . . ."

There was silence on the other end of the line for several seconds. When Murphy responded, it was in a gentle tone that left Ted wrestling with a mixture of shame and rage.

"I know how you must feel, Mr. Potter. I feel terrible. If it was happening to me, I'd be going out of my mind. Look, I'll go down to the detachment right now and see if anything's turned up. Then I'll go into Vancouver and start knocking on doors. She might be in any one of a number of agencies, Customs and Excise, OIS, Missing Persons Bureau, she might even be with the boy, trying to help him adjust to a temporary foster home that Human Resources arranged—that sort of thing."

"If it was that sort of thing," Ted barked, "she would have phoned me."

"Yeah, I guess you're right about that", Murphy replied slowly. "But look, Mr. Potter, I'm going to head into the city now, and I won't leave any stone unturned."

Ted felt like crying. He shook his head, held the receiver away from his face, wanted to smash it down on the hook, yell at long, tall, and stupid Buzz-for-obvious-reasons-Murphy.

"Okay," he muttered, then added a strangulated, "thank you."

He hung up.

Alice phoned a few minutes later, sounding stiff and scared. Ted told her what he knew, which was almost nothing. She asked him again to keep her name out of it. That made him angrier than ever, and he hung up on her without saying good-bye.

The lawyer called ten minutes after that.

"Anything yet?" Ted asked.

"Nothing so far. I tried everything I could think of last night and got nowhere fast. S and I won't return my calls any more. They insist they've never heard of her. I talked to a few people higher up at the agency, and they think Beth must have been picked up by somebody else. They suggested that whatever happened is strictly kosher, because R.C.M.P. in Fort George did their job right. It's just that there's a missing component somewhere along the way, and no one, simply no one, knows what it is."

"Or someone, simply someone, is lying."

"I haven't discounted that", the lawyer replied uneasily.

"What do you mean?"

"This is purely conjecture, Ted, but Beth may have been detained under the civil order statutes."

"The what?"

"Some new statutes have been passed by the federal cabinet that make it possible for people to be held for an indefinite period without being charged if there's a suspicion that national security is at risk."

"Huh!" Ted almost laughed in disbelief. "Beth? A risk to national security?"

"I know, it's ridiculous. But it seems they have the authority to do it. It's real, it's legal."

"That's incredible! I never heard about that!"

"Precisely", the lawyer replied, his voice turning sour. "Not many people have. There's been a rather odd media silence over this development. Our brave defenders of free speech are proving ever so selective these days."

"But where does that leave Beth and me? If they're holding her, how do we get her out? How do I contact her? What about our family?"

"As I said, it's a wild guess on my part. Right now there's no way of knowing if she has or has not fallen under the scope of their mandate."

"Scope of their mandate? What is that?"

"Their crusade, Ted, their crusade."

"What are we going to do?"

"First of all, I want you to stay at home and wait till I get back to you. Don't go anywhere, don't do anything rash. Don't go charging off like a wounded moose, Ted. That won't help in the least, do you hear?"

"All right. But if what you say is true, how come they haven't come out here to our place? How come they haven't asked *me* any questions? I mean, if Beth were a security risk or something, wouldn't they be checking me out too?"

"You would think so, if our scenario *is* correct. If it is, it's totally baffling why they haven't pulled you in as well. The entire Potter family of Steelhead, British Columbia, would be suspects, babies and all."

"I don't get it. What's happening?"

"I'm not sure. I'm going hunting for her, and if I find that those bastards have harmed a hair of her head, or made a single wrong move legally speaking, I'll make them pay dearly for it."

"Thanks", Ted whispered. "Thanks."

"Now don't worry. Just sit tight and wait."

"I have been waiting." Ted's voice broke. "I've been doing nothing but waiting."

"I'll talk to you later", the lawyer said, and hung up.

* * *

Ted sat tight for just under an hour. That was all he could take. He picked up the phone and dialed his Member of Parliament.

Ed Burgess was sitting alone in the Members' restaurant of the West Block on the hill in Ottawa, reading a handbook of parliamentary procedure, sipping from a cup of herbal tea. It was midmorning coffee break time in the east, but he still hadn't adjusted to the time zone, and he was prone to nervous stomach, hypertension, and ulcers. He spoon-fed himself a dish of plain yogurt, fighting regret that he had won the by-election three weeks before. Here he was, he thought to himself, an elderly gentleman, retired high-school teacher, sometime preacher, and full-time flycasting addict, wishing he were back at the cabin at Harrison with nothing bigger to worry about than whether or not he was getting the threads properly around a blue lightning. He looked up from the book and stared lovingly into a deep pool of glacier-fed lake water just waiting for the long arching zing of a cast.

Sixteen-vote margin. That wasn't a great majority. That was definitely not a secure seat, especially with the next election looming only eight months from now. His party had twenty-three seats in the House, another unimpressive count, in fact, no majority at all. But combined with the other two opposition parties, they made a formidable stumbling block in the path of the big government steamroller party. David and Goliath. Five smooth stones.

586

The little box clipped to his waist flashed red and beeped.

"Yes, Miss Theriault."

"*Oui*, Monsieur. It is a phone call from a constituent. He is very upset."

"Is he on the line?"

"*Non*. He is hang up. He leave his number."

"Did he say why he was calling?"

"He not want to tell me."

"I'll call him back. I'll be up to the office in a few minutes."

Ed Burgess sighed, closed the book, and said good-bye to the lake, to flycasting, to fresh salmon, and to a leisurely old age.

Back in his office on the third floor, he closed the door to the inner office so that Miss Theriault wouldn't overhear how incompetent he was at this sort of thing. Then he settled into the padded leather chair behind his desk and tried to make believe that he was a real M.P. It didn't suit him, he decided; hopefully he would be defeated come the election.

He dialed the number.

The constituent was a man he had met some months before at a campaign meeting near Fort George—Ted Potter. He remembered the Potters well, because it had been an unusual gathering, top-heavy with church pastors and the marginalized. The man was very upset indeed, and what he had to say was disturbing. Ed sat up straight and put his elbows on the desk, listening intently, asking questions for clarification from time to time.

"Are you sure? You've checked every agency?"

"Every one, Mr. Burgess. So has my lawyer. He's in Vancouver right now, going from office to office trying to get personal appointments with the various cops the government keeps on tap out here. There sure are a lot of them, more than I imagined. I don't think he's going to get any cooperation—he hasn't so far. We're getting stonewalled, I'm sure of it. There's something fishy going on."

"That's an understatement, Ted. Your wife has been apprehended by some unidentified federal agents, and no one knows where she is? That's more than fishy. That's downright dangerous."

Ed listened to Ted Potter's anxious silence, his heavy breathing and muted anguish.

"Is there anything you can do, Mr. Burgess? Anything at all?"

Ed exhaled loudly. "Yes", he nodded. "Yes, I expect a lowly M.P. can still do a lot in this country. I can't promise you anything. There are three hundred of us here on the hill, and the civil service is a rabbit warren, but I'm going to see what I can do."

"Couldn't you mention it in the House of Commons?"

"It's no easy matter getting a slot to make a speech, Ted. Question Period might be the best time to throw it into the public forum. I'll see if I can't arrange for it this afternoon. If the police have gone beyond their limitations, we just might scare them enough to cough up your wife."

"But what if . . . ?"

"Yes?"

Ted's voice trembled. "If they *are* doing something illegal, they might try to silence her—you know, get rid of her."

"I don't think things are as bad as that. They wouldn't dare. Not if we turn on the spotlight and get the media involved. If we can make a case that the government has kidnapped a citizen and won't explain itself, and won't give her back, then we just might accomplish something very important. It would scare a lot of people into mistrusting what the party in power is trying to do to the democratic process. They could very well lose the next election."

"This is my wife you're talking about. This is Bethie! Dammit, I won't have her being used as a political pawn or lever or wedge, or whatever you think she is."

"Ted," Ed said calmly, "if I could trade places with her, I would."

Ted knew that he meant it.

"I know that politicians don't count for much these days", Ed went on. "But some of us are men of principle. My first priority is to find Beth and to bring her back. My second objective is to find out why this has happened and make sure it never happens again. I know you're a praying man, so I'm going to ask you to pray like you never have before."

"Already have been . . . ", Ted murmured.

"As soon as you hang up I'll call my constituency office in Fort George and get them to phone every church in the lower mainland. We'll get them praying. Then we'll get them off their hind ends and into the arena. Next, I'm going over to the Centre Block and have a little chat with the Minister of Justice. He's a clever young Rhodes scholar with puppy-dog eyes and the heart of a barracuda, but he's also a realist."

Silence.

"It's the best I can do."

"Okay—" Long pause. "—Thanks."

"There are a couple of other things I'm going to pursue."

But Ted was unable to say anything more. He hung up. Ed sat there, staring out the window at the red and gold hills of the Gatineau across the river, clutching the hot receiver in his right fist, feeling somewhat unnerved but rather excited. *This is my first real challenge*, he said to himself. *It should be interesting.* He was bothered a little by an odd sound on the line, a faint double click, followed by the usual electronic burr.

He swivelled his seat to gaze fondly, with a feeling of farewell, at the blue lightning fly framed and mounted on the wall beside the window. But the odd clicking sound stuck in his mind like a hook. On a whim he called his wife, Marjorie.

"Hi, love, what's for supper?"

She chuckled. "Eddie, I told you this morning."

"Oh, that's right. Meatloaf and roast potatoes. Caesar salad."

"Uh-huh. You're not going to break your promise, are you? You'll be home at five? The House isn't sitting tonight, is it?"

"No. But I might be a little late. Probably around six. Mind?"

"I'll keep it warm."

"Thanks."

After she hung up, he listened carefully to the receiver. No odd clicks. Just a regular burr.

He made three more innocuous calls, none of them concluding with the clicks.

Then he dialed Ted Potter's number. A girl's voice answered.

"Daddy's in the barn", she told him.

"Okay, honey. Please tell your Dad that Mr. Burgess phoned, and I hope to have something to tell him soon. I'll phone back when I find out anything about your mum. Okay?"

"Okay. Bye." She hung up. Followed by the double click.

He pondered that for a minute, then called his constituency office in Fort George.

"Hi, Dotty", he began. "This is Ed. Oops, I've just been interrupted. Can I call you right back?"

"Sure boss." She hung up. No double click.

He dialed her again. "Sorry for the delay. Look, I think we've got some unpleasantness brewing here. A family in the riding is being harassed by electronic surveillance. Their phone's bugged."

"Oh, that's terrible!" Dot gasped. He could see her in his mind's eye, the moral outrage of stenographers, the whispered gossip over coffee break, her hand tightening the button at the collar of her sensible blouse.

"Dot, I'm going to ask a favor of you. First of all, you mustn't breathe a word about this to anyone, not even to the other ladies at the office, understand?"

"Sure thing, boss."

"I want you to drive out to Ted and Beth Potter's place at Steelhead; they have a farm this side of the dam, you can't miss it, name's on the mailbox. Tell Ted that his line has been tapped, and if he needs to make any sensitive phone calls, he should find a public phone booth somewhere."

"All right, I'll tell him. But what's going on? Is it Mafia?"

"No, it's not Mafia. Just give him the message, will you?"

"Okay. Mum's the word."

"Right, mum's the word. God bless, Dot."

"God bless, boss."

After that he walked through the underground tunnel to the Centre Block and tried to track down the Minister of Justice. He wasn't in the House or his office. His secretary advised Ed to make an appointment. There was an opening, she said, a week from tomorrow.

"It's much more urgent than that", Ed replied. "I need to see him today."

The secretary looked bemused and tilted her head apologetically. "Sorry, Mr. Burgess. It's not possible. A lot of people want to see the Minister every day of the week, and they all feel their concerns are pretty important."

Ed asked for a memo slip, wrote the name *Beth Potter* on it, and slid it across her desk.

"Perhaps you'd be so kind as to give this to him when he comes in. I think he'll want to call me when he sees it."

"All right", she replied.

Then he went to pay a visit to the leader of his party.

He knew that lunch hour was approaching and that Question Period was only three hours away. Using sparing language and speaking in a tone of calm urgency, he told the leader what had happened. Then the leader brought in the party whip and the justice critic. Ed repeated the story, the leader tilting back and forth in his chair, playing with a pencil, tapping his teeth with it from time to time, listening carefully to how Ed told it a second time.

When he was finished, Ed removed his glasses and said, "Well, what do you think?"

The leader said nothing, watching the others; the whip shook his head and crossed his legs; the justice critic took a deep breath and raised his eyebrows.

"Any thoughts on the matter, gentlemen?" Ed pressed.

"Ed, are you sure this isn't just a case of a constituent blowing off steam?" the whip responded. "It could be just an ordinary missing person case."

"I don't think so. Let me replay the chain of events carefully for you—"

"That's not necessary", the leader interrupted. "It's quite obvious from what you've told us that there has been some kind of inappropriate intervention by a federal agency or agencies. But it could be a simple communications error on their part, or it could be the wife was released after she was questioned and was distressed, went home to mother without telling her husband. You say you know these people. What's their marriage like?"

"I don't know them well, but from what I've seen they're the kind of grass-roots married folk who keep this country alive. I'd wager my seat in the House on it."

"Would you wager your seat on this being a violation of human rights?" the justice critic asked.

Ed nodded. "Definitely."

The other three men lapsed into silence, staring this way and that, thinking.

"If you're wrong," said the whip, "you'll have egg on your face."

"I can take it", Ed replied. "I used to teach high school. I've had egg on my face before—literally."

"I'm not so sure the Party needs that kind of make-up", the whip countered. "The press has already characterized us as right wingers, gun-totin' bigots, prone to alarmism."

Ed leaned forward. "I know, but if the fox *is* in the hen house, the sanest reaction might be to sound the alarm."

The whip leaned forward, resting his elbows on his knees. He looked at the leader.

"Sir, we know that they've been making some highly questionable noises in committee, and the emergency measures statutes are at best a latent danger, always there, ready to break out like the plague. The Potter case may be a preliminary sign that they intend to move toward the worst-case scenario."

The leader nodded but kept his counsel. The justice critic spoke for him: "We've discussed this many times. The potential is there all right, but I think it's going to have to be a lot more conclusive than this before we stand up in the Commons and make like Paul Revere."

"Or the boy who cried wolf", the whip inserted.

"Excuse me, aren't we losing sight of something here?" Ed said. "A woman has been apprehended without regard for her rights. Isn't that the issue?"

The leader stood up, walked to the window, and looked out for a full minute.

"Ed's right. That is the issue. That's why the electorate put us here, to ensure that this sort of thing doesn't creep into government." He turned and faced his two lieutenants. "We're not the official opposition party. But we are part of the third function of Parliament—checks and balances, watchmen for the rights of the people. This is not a character defect, gentlemen; it's not carping criticism; it's not about scoring political points. It's our duty."

The whip and the critic agreed but advised tactical caution.

The leader listened to their insights, then said, "Al, see if you can get the leaders of the other opposition parties together right after lunch, let's say about one-thirty. Sweeten the pot by telling them we're onto something that could bring the government down a little earlier than we had anticipated."

"Should I get the caucus together?" the whip asked.

"No. For now, let's keep it between the four of us. I want to see how the other leaders respond. If our parties make a concerted stand in the House, the boys in power are going to go scrambling for cover. If we can't get a coalition together in such short order, we can at least bring the subject of Mrs. Potter to Question Period and embarrass the hell out of the Minister of Justice and the P.M."

"Maybe we should wait till next week", the whip suggested. "By then the facts may be clearer, Mrs. Potter may have shown up at home, and we'll have saved ourselves some embarrassment. Sir, you have a speech scheduled for Monday on the Order Papers. That might be the opportune moment."

"In the meantime," the leader responded, "Mrs. Potter may be going through a great deal of *embarrassment* in some institution that the government has failed to bring to the attention of the public. Or she might be suffering something worse. No, the time is now."

"Could I bring a private member's bill before the House this afternoon?" Ed suggested tentatively. "Something to the effect that no citizen detained by federal agencies may be held without legal representation, that their names and whereabouts have to be made public within twenty-four hours . . . something like that."

"There are already plenty of statutes covering that ground", the whip said.

The justice critic looked at Ed sympathetically. "Ed, you're the new kid on the block here. I guess you didn't realize it, but only five or so private member's bills a year make it to the floor, and usually they're harmless things, like naming a bridge or a street or proposing a national day in honor of motherhood or beavers."

"I think Question Period is the place to start", said the leader firmly. "Today is Wednesday. If Ed is fast on his feet this afternoon, and the Speaker recognizes him, he can ask the Minister of Justice where she is. The Minister will probably deny any knowledge of her, but he'll have to get back to the House tomorrow to give an account of what the Ministry has done to try to locate her. Then on Monday I'll follow it up in my speech, hammer them until the media starts to take notice."

"The media!" the whip snorted. "Do you really think we can count on them? They're like pet ferrets on government leashes who think they're taking their masters for a walk. They hate us."

"Most of them do," the critic argued, "but not all. I have some contacts. I'll try to cash in a few poker chips and see if we can't get an article in some big daily. It's not too likely we'll get a front page. The newspaper czars are dedicated to the government's agenda and only play at being objective. I don't hold out much hope for the TV networks, either."

Ed shook his head in dismay. "The fifth estate or the fifth column!"

"You have to understand the game, Ed", the whip explained. "We politicians tend to think of ourselves as the ones with the power. We consider the media a necessary evil; they're our natural adversaries. The media people like to think of themselves as the ones with the real power, keeping guys like us in check. We're *their* necessary evil. But it's kind of like an ocean liner; the captain and the crew may squabble about details, but the ship just keeps sailing in a certain direction."

"Our party excepted", the leader interjected with a smile.

"Yeah, our party excepted", the whip grinned.

"Everyone plays the game, Ed", the justice critic said. "Politicians, the media, the money people—they all play because everyone gets his own kind of reward. It's a system that works."

The leader demurred: "It works if the captain and crew don't get so distracted by their petty ambitions that they stop keeping an eye open for icebergs."

"If that's happening, then we're just rearranging deck chairs on the Titanic", the critic replied.

"My constituent isn't exactly a deck chair", Ed said.

"I have a friend on the board of the education network", the whip contributed. "We might get Mrs. Potter some exposure there."

The critic laughed humorlessly. "Great, Dave, four hundred kids see her face on *Learn about Your Government*, then forget her the moment they head off for the mall."

"Cynical, Al, cynical."

"Gentlemen," the leader interjected, "I want to get moving on this. Try to organize a meeting of opposition leaders for one-thirty, and, God willing, we'll field an offensive that will make the party in power plenty nervous. Al, I want you at that meeting. You too, Ed. We may have to spell it out for them. Some of our counterparts only read lips."

Ed returned to his office, where Miss Theriault told him the Minister of Justice had called. She gave him the information with a big excited smile and raised eyebrows. He smiled back and went into his inner office. He sat and waited. He opened the lunch box Marjorie had packed for him that morning. The sight of a bottle of skim milk, diet biscuits, and a thermos of bland soup was not enthralling, and he left it untouched.

A few minutes later, the Minister phoned.

"Mr. Burgess," the man began warmly, "welcome to Parliament Hill. I haven't had a chance to meet you yet, but I've seen you in the House. Are you settling in all right?"

"Fine, sir, just fine."

"Good. We must get together for lunch some day."

"Fine", Ed said. "When would you like—?"

"My secretary tells me you've been in to see me. I try to make it a point to respond to new members as quickly as possible, no matter what their political persuasion." The Minister chuckled in a friendly manner, and Ed tried unsuccessfully to match the sound.

"The note you left contained a rather cryptic message. Could you explain it?"

"It's the name of one of my constituents, Mrs. Beth Potter of Steelhead, British Columbia. I have reason to believe that she has been detained by an agency under your Ministry and has been held without legal counsel. Her family has not been informed of her whereabouts, nor have any charges been made against her."

"And . . . ?"

"And I would like to know where she is."

A long silence.

"That's reasonable enough", the Minister said eventually. "I'll get some people right on it. If she's somewhere in the system, they'll find her. But really, I think it's farfetched. No honest citizen can be held without legal representation in this country."

"My constituent *is* an honest citizen, sir. If she's in *the system*, it's probably as a result of a bureaucratic error, and I expect she'll be released immediately. Can you assure me of that?"

The Minister's tone stiffened. "If she's there, and if she hasn't committed an indictable offense, she has nothing to worry about."

"Good", Ed said in a subdued tone. "I'm glad to hear it."

"I can assure you of that." The Minister's voice, rendered with perfect calm, could not hide a certain tension. "You're a new member, I realize. The House is presently clogged with bills, and Question Period has been a zoo lately. I think we can avoid an unnecessary waste of time and the taxpayers' money. This sort of matter is usually handled privately."

"Oh, I see. I didn't know. I'm still working my way through the members' handbook."

The Minister chuckled again.

"Great, Ed. Thanks for bringing this to my attention. I'm sure we can straighten it out in no time. Have a good day."

"Right, sir. Thanks for calling."

"I'll see you in the House."

"See you in the House."

597

Ed met the party whip in the private members' restaurant in the Centre Block at one o'clock, and they shared a quick weight-watcher's lunch. Ed related the conversation he had had with the Minister. The whip smiled grimly.

"Very interesting," he said, "*very* interesting."

"How so?"

"I can tell you for a fact that this particular Minister doesn't call up backwoods backbenchers and invite them to lunch. Never."

"Never? Maybe he was just being friendly."

The whip laughed and wiped his mouth with a napkin. "Yeah, real friendly. It's a good sign, Ed, a very good sign."

"You think we've made them nervous?"

"Oh, yes, I think so", the whip said enthusiastically. "The Minister especially doesn't call up backbenchers from opposition parties, unless it's for an earth-shattering reason. Come to think of it, I've never known him to do such a thing, and if it *was* some earth-shattering problem, even then he'd probably get one of his lackeys to handle it."

"I see", Ed said, troubled. "You called it a good sign. But it may be a bad sign for Mrs. Potter. It seems to confirm our hypothesis."

"It's pretty fair evidence, I'd say, circumstantial though it may be. It's going to be an interesting afternoon in the House."

"Yes", Ed sighed. "I think I'll do ten laps around the hill to burn off some adrenaline."

"Stage fright?"

"I'm afraid so."

"Don't worry. You'll do fine. It's a zoo."

"Yes, the Minister called it that too."

"Did he?" the whip grinned. "He was probably thinking we're going to feed him to the animals."

Ed managed to complete three brisk walk-laps around the hill. It was a sunny afternoon, but the day was cool, and he tied his old plaid scarf (the one his granddaughter had knitted for him three Christmases ago) around his neck and flipped up the collar of his tweed jacket. Red and gold maple leaves tumbled in loose wind-rows across the huge front lawn of Parliament. He stopped for a few moments behind the library building, leaned on the black iron railings at the edge of the cliff, and watched the river surging below. The water was sheet-metal gray, choppy. Small children, shepherded by mothers and nannies, walked the promenade in both directions, bouncing, running and shouting, going east and west. From sea unto sea. *A mari usque ad mare.*

Ed prayed, then went in.

They met in the hospitality room annexed to the office of the leader of the official opposition party. Drinks were poured. Ed declined. It was his first experience of power politics. He had heard a lot about smoky back-room wheeling and dealing and had prepared himself to give them all a piece of his mind if they tried any of it on him.

The meeting began with good-natured sparring and some in-jokes and took off from there. Psychology played a significant part in the process, and Ed was surprised to see how adept his leader was at that kind of psychology. Most of all, it was crude horse trading. His leader was by far the most ethical of the traders in the room, but he did his fair share of dickering. That dismayed Ed, who was an intelligent, forthright man but not gifted in reading people's motives. He mistrusted subtlety. The *art* of compromise, he supposed they called it.

At just the right moment, the leader called on Ed to tell Beth Potter's story. No one said much when he was finished. One by one the other leaders voiced the same kind of objections that the whip and the justice critic had raised, then added a few more.

"The whole thing hinges on whether or not this woman has really disappeared", the leader of the official opposition pointed out. "And whether or not the government is involved with full knowledge."

"With or without full knowledge," Ed's leader replied, "it's a black mark against them. It shouldn't happen. Ever."

"I agree", said the leader of a party that was smaller than Ed's own, a woman who enjoyed a reputation for feisty combat in the House. "We could score a minor victory if we demonstrate that they aren't keeping a close watch on civil rights. Even if they plead ignorance, even if they *are* ignorant, it's a symptom of breakdown on some level. It's going to cost them."

"We could win a bigger victory", said the leader of the official opposition, "if they do have full knowledge and have been covering up. But we have no proof of that."

"That is true", the woman replied. "But at the very least we can raise a doubt in the mind of the public. A flesh wound it might be, but they're going to bleed."

"*If* you can wake up the media", someone said.

"The media!" eight people said in unison, rolling their eyes in revulsion.

Ed kept silent and watched the consensus gradually develop.

It went on for a half hour more, then the bell rang for Question Period.

"We've just run out of time", said Ed's leader. "We haven't touched on tactics."

The leader of the official opposition smiled. "Or what kind of horses you're trading for this."

Everyone laughed.

"Let's pull the bastards down first," said the woman, "then we can all get back to the hustings for our usual free-for-all. Right?"

The articulation of that thought sobered everyone up, though of course it had never been far from their minds.

"Look", said Ed's leader. "We have our disagreements with each other. But we are agreed on one issue—that the present government is making dangerous moves in the field of civil liberties. None of us wants that. Remember the Weimar Republic. All those parties in Germany could have stopped Hitler's rise to power if they had just once got their act together. We have an opportunity here, gentlemen . . . and lady."

The bell kept ringing.

"Mr. Burgess," said the leader of the official opposition, "may I suggest that you try to raise the question of Mrs. Potter during Question Period? We haven't had much time to prepare, and I have a number of backbenchers who want to raise questions on the floor today. I'll try to meet with our party whip in the next fifteen minutes and have him spread the word that our members should hold off. But we may not have time. If the Speaker doesn't recognize you today, I'm sure every one of us will speak to our caucuses and you'll have a clean deck tomorrow afternoon. How's that for a deal?"

Ed and his leader nodded simultaneously.

"Thanks", said Ed's leader. "Now let me look at your teeth for a minute. Are you really as young as you say you are?"

Everyone laughed and hurried off toward the House.

* * *

Ed and the party whip entered the Commons side by side and walked down the aisle to their desks, third row from the front, far right. No pun intended, as one caucus wag had told Ed on his first day.

"Question Period is our moment in the sun, Ed", said the whip. "It's the task of opposition parties to use this time to keep the party in government on their toes. Critical function is the third role of Parliament, after legislation and financial matters. No one loves a critic, but it's the saddle we're wearing until the next election. Then the roles will be reversed. Hopefully."

"God willing", Ed corrected.

"Uh, yeah."

Ed played with a pen on the green blotting paper of his desk, eyed the red light of the television camera in the communications booth, and tried to calm his nerves. The proceedings of the House of Commons were broadcast live on cablevision, and Ed said a silent and somewhat fatalistic prayer that all twenty-eight million residents of the nation would be watching today. The House was half full when the Speaker entered and took his seat. The Prime Minister was not at his desk, nor was the Minister of Justice. After the procedural preliminaries were completed by House functionaries, the whip gave Ed the thumbs up sign and whispered, "Go get 'em, tiger."

Ed was the first to his feet, but five other members were a split second behind him. He stood at his desk waiting to be acknowledged. The Speaker did not recognize him, and one by one he called on the other members, who raised questions about the cost of public works projects, the naming of a coast guard ship, an aberration in the redesign of an electoral boundary in Nova Scotia, and so forth. By then the opposition party whips had managed to get the word around to their members present in the House, and Ed found himself standing alone.

"The member for Fort George-Dewdney", the Speaker said.

Ed cleared his throat. "Mr. Speaker, I would like to address this question to the Minister of Justice, but I see that he is not here today. Neither is the Prime Minister present. In their absence I address this to the acting Prime Minister. It has come to my attention that a person living in my constituency, Mrs. Beth Potter of Steelhead, British Columbia, has disappeared after being taken into custody by agents of the Department of Justice. She has not been charged with any crime, nor has proper legal procedure been maintained in her case. It would appear, Mr. Speaker, that this person has been lost by the federal government . . ."

From the corner of his eye, Ed saw the stenographers look up, interested. His words would appear in tomorrow's *Hansard*, the record of the Commons proceedings. All the members in the House looked up from their newspapers, correspondence, and notebooks and stared at him.

"Does the member have a question?" the Speaker prompted.

"Uh, yes, Mr. Speaker. I would like an assurance from the acting Prime Minister that he will investigate the matter and report to this House about the location and status of Mrs. Potter."

Ed sat down.

The acting Prime Minister stood and smiled indulgently. "Mr. Speaker, this is rightly a question for the Department of Justice, but I will be speaking with the Minister later in the day, and I can assure the member for Fort George-Dewdney that every effort will be made to check into this matter. The Minister will be here tomorrow for Question Period, and he will report his findings to the House, if indeed there is anything to report."

He sat down.

There was a hush for a few seconds. It was a rare moment. Most of those present had never before witnessed a Question Period during which not a single member stood to raise an issue. The television technicians were marvelling over their first experience of dead air time in the Commons.

"Are there no more questions?" the Speaker queried.

Ed's leader stood. The Speaker recognized him.

"Mr. Speaker, on a supplementary question: I would like to assure this House that the member for Fort George-Dewdney has not raised his question frivolously. There is considerable evidence that the woman has disappeared while in custody of agents of the government—"

"Would the honorable leader of the Coalition Party please express himself in the form of a question", the Speaker interjected.

"I am coming to that, Mr. Speaker. I address the acting Prime Minister in the absence of the Prime Minister and the Minister of Justice and would like an assurance from him that his government does not at present, or in the future, intend to weaken civil rights in this country—"

Several backbenchers on the government side began to rumble and raise their voices, one or two of them shouting across the floor, cutting off Ed's leader.

"Order! Order!" said the Speaker. Silence fell.

"Thank you, Mr. Speaker. Can the acting Prime Minister assure me that his party has no intention of weakening civil rights in this country, rights that many have died for in time of war and in the ongoing pursuit of justice?"

The rumbling and shouting was louder now. Ed's leader sat down. The acting Prime Minister shook his head and stood up.

"Mr. Speaker", he began in a patient tone. "In response to the question from the honorable leader of the Coalition Party, I can assure him that this government never has, and never will have, any intention of undermining the rights and freedoms built into our system of government. If he is hoping to score political points . . . [here the opposition benches began to rumble] . . . if he is hoping to score political points with rhetoric in the guise of a question, he will surely be disappointed. Open debates are scheduled on the Order Papers for next month, when the House will discuss the findings of the Committee on Law Reform. There have already been extensive debates in this House regarding the Prime Minister's Privy Council bills to restrict irresponsible use of firearms. Neither of these, I repeat, neither of these is an erosion of civil rights. On the contrary, they are intended to ensure the preservation of the civil rights of *all* citizens. But perhaps the honorable member merely wishes to promote the special interest rights of gun owners."

Yelling broke out from all directions.

"Order! Order!" the Speaker demanded. It took a few minutes to silence the members; two backbenchers who refused to comply with the Speaker's wishes were escorted peaceably from the Commons by the Sergeant at Arms.

Ed's leader rose to his feet. "On a point of order, Mr. Speaker. I do not believe the acting Prime Minister has adequately responded to my question. I would like a yes or no answer from him, not his own brand of rhetoric disguised as an answer."

More bedlam. The television technicians were grinning.

The acting Prime Minister stood, the indulgent smile gone. He gave the leader of the Coalition Party a long, cold look across the aisle.

"The answer to the honorable member's question is: No, we do not intend to undermine civil rights. The government's intention is to preserve those rights for the people of this great nation. Our intention is *freedom!*"

"Mr. Speaker", Ed's leader replied, standing. "That is an impressive assurance from the honorable acting Prime Minister. I thank him for it. And when Mrs. Beth Potter of Steelhead, British Columbia, has been reunited with her family, I will thank him again. I will have become completely reassured."

"Hear, hear!" cried dozens of voices on the opposition side, many of them thumping their desk tops enthusiastically.

The moment was over. Several members jumped to their feet, unable to contain their own issues any longer. The Speaker recognized the first, and Question Period went on as usual.

Ed exhaled loudly and went out in search of a cup of herbal tea. He met the leader of his party in the reception foyer.

"That was impressive, sir."

The leader grinned. "Child's play. You could dance rings around that whippersnapper. By the way, you did just fine, Ed, just fine."

"Thanks. Now what?"

"We wait. They've got some egg-foo-yung on their faces, and they'll move quickly to wipe it off. Tomorrow's Question

Period will be predictable, but it will be most pleasant watching them squirm."

"We may make them squirm, but is it going to help Beth Potter?"

"We're shaking the bushes pretty hard, and these guys know an election is looming. They're not going to want a scandal, not even the hint of a scandal. It just might scare them into quietly releasing her . . . *if* they have her."

"They have her. I know they do. I feel it in my bones."

"I hope your bones aren't playing tricks on you, Ed."

Ed returned to his office in the West Block, a determined bounce in his walk, nursing a feeling that he just might enjoy politics after all.

* * *

Late in the afternoon Ed phoned the Ottawa bureau of one of the nation's largest daily newspapers and asked for Peter Stanford. Pete was from a small town in the lower mainland; Ed had taught him history and civics way back in the 1960s.

When Pete came on the line, Ed reintroduced himself, half expecting his former student not to remember him.

"Ed, great to hear from you. I read about you winning the by-election. I've been meaning to call you."

Ed let it pass.

"So, how do you like the shenanigans on the Hill?"

"It takes some getting used to, but I think I'm feeling my way around all right. Made my first speech in the Commons today."

"Hey, pretty good."

"Well, it wasn't exactly a speech, just one minute during Question Period."

"Not a bad place to start. What were you asking?"

"That's actually what I'm calling about. I've got a tricky

situation shaping up in my constituency, something that may have repercussions for a lot of people. And I wanted to get your advice."

"Advice? Oh, you mean you want to get some exposure in the press, right?"

"Not exactly, though I wouldn't mind that. It's something bigger. It could be very big."

"Dangling a carrot in front of the newshound, are we? All right, I'll bite. What's it all about?"

"I'd rather not discuss it over the phone. Can we meet somewhere?"

"Sure, why not. How about the National Press Club? It's on Wellington, right across from the Hill."

"I'll find it. Is five o'clock okay for you?"

"Five o'clock it is. Meet you in the bar on the third floor."

At ten to five Ed bid Miss Theriault good night and walked out into the dusk, which was brightly illuminated by street lamps and a vault of cityglow in the sky. He walked across the street and located the Press Club building, a granite-faced monolith a few doors down from the American Embassy.

On the third floor he found the bar, which seemed almost deserted, spotted a middle-aged man sitting at a corner table, and went up to him.

"Peter Stanford?"

The man stood up and shook his hand, grinning. "Edward Burgess, I presume?"

"It's been a lot of years, Pete, a lot of years."

"Yeah, a lot of water under the bridge. But you look hale and hearty."

"Oh, I guess I've lost most of my hair and added a few pounds since I last saw you, but I do feel good for an old fellow."

Ed noted that Pete didn't look so hale and hearty. He seemed older than his years, ashen, with bags under his eyes and receding hair that was completely gray. His trench coat was rumpled, an expensive foreign tie dangled askew at his open-necked collar, and he needed a shave. He had once been the heartthrob of Abbotsford High, girls dropping in ecstasy whenever they passed him in the hallways, a fine athlete, serious about his studies, a quiet but popular student. He had taken Ed's oldest daughter to a few hockey games and once to a dance. She had told her father afterward that Peter Stanford was a very good guy, no messing around, no funny business, just friends. "He's a nice boy", she said. "But we don't have the same interests." And nothing more had come of it.

Something had happened to him in the ensuing years. A lot of water under the bridge, Ed supposed, some of it muddy, some of it turbulent.

"Siddown, Ed. I'll order you a drink."

"I'm not much of a drinker", Ed apologized.

The waiter came to take their orders.

"How about a Moosehead draft?" Pete offered. "Molsons? A Blue?"

Ed asked the waiter if the bar served herbal tea. Pete laughed. The waiter looked amused.

"We don't have herbal tea, sir. We do have decaf coffee and soft drinks."

"I'll have a ginger ale then, thank you."

Pete ordered a large draft of Guinness stout. When the drinks arrived, he fixed Ed with a bloodhound look.

"Okay, tell me, what's up?"

"I don't suppose you saw today's Question Period on cablevision, did you?"

Pete shook his head. "Nope. I hardly ever watch the kids fighting in the sandbox. I'm at the diplomatic desk here."

"It will be in *Hansard*. I'll ask my secretary to send you a copy of today's and tomorrow's proceedings. We only scratched the surface of the problem in the House. I expect that's all we're going to be able to do. But the issue is bigger, Pete. Potentially very big."

"All right. Fire away. I'm all ears."

"Before I begin, can you promise me you'll keep this conversation off the record?"

Pete nodded. "You have my word."

Ed told him the story of Beth Potter. Pete listened attentively, his eyes growing more and more serious as the details mounted. Halfway through he ordered another draft for himself and another ginger ale for Ed.

When the story was completed, Pete stared at the tabletop. He took a sip of his beer and thought some more. He looked up slowly at Ed.

"May I ask why you're telling me all this?"

Ed threw up his hands. "I'm not after anything. I'm not trying to use you, Pete. I think you know that."

"I know that. You're not the type."

"But you are a journalist, and I thought you could give me some advice on how I should go about getting the public interested in the case."

"Didn't you ask the bigwigs in your party about that?"

"They made some suggestions, but they sounded pretty lame to me. People across the street don't seem to have much respect for your profession, I'm sorry to say."

Pete laughed abruptly. "And for good reasons", he said with a bitter note.

"What do you mean?" Ed removed his glasses and inserted one stem into the corner of his mouth.

"You have no idea how happy I'd be to get out of my line of work."

"Can't you?"

"Not right now. I make good money, but most of it goes to taxes and child support payments."

"You have a family?"

"Had. Had two, in fact. Twice divorced. I made two women very unhappy and left two sets of kids without a resident dad. I was never home, you see. Always away chasing a scoop."

"I'm sorry it hasn't turned out well for you."

Pete shook himself and sat up straighter. "Yeah, well, it's water under the bridge. But look, back onto the subject: I wish I could help. If national issues were my turf, I'd certainly write a story about it. But as I said, they've got me strapped into the embassy circuit."

"Do you know any other writers who might be interested?"

"I could rustle up a couple", he said, musing. "The real problem is the publisher."

"The publisher?"

Pete took a long look into Ed's honest, somewhat simple face. "Oh what the hell, I might as well tell you. You're a grown-up."

"Tell me what, Pete?"

"I think you've lived long enough to know that the things you taught us in civics class are a bit more complicated than they appear. If you've spent any time watching what goes on across the street since you arrived in the capital, you know that there are a lot of games being played over there. And sometimes . . ."

"Sometimes truth gets lost in the process?"

"Exactly. Sometimes truth gets lost in the shuffle. Well, it's pretty much the same on this side of the street. We play by slightly different rules, we have different aims and motives, some of them idealistic and lots of them not quite so idealistic. Ego and reputation are hot commodities in our estate, as they are in yours. But essentially the character of the players isn't all that different. No one on our side likes to admit it, but objective reporting and commentary are not the bottom line."

"What is the bottom line?"

"Agendas."

"Agendas?"

"Yeah, long-range tactics. Reshaping the nature of the game itself."

"I guess I'm not following you, Pete."

"There's too much deep background to tell you about here. Most of it would be incomprehensible to you anyway. Let me just say . . . by the way, is this conversation totally confidential?"

Ed nodded. "You have my word."

"Let me just say that this country is run on several levels, more levels than we thought way back in Abbotsford High. The most visible level is, of course, the infrastructure of government. After that comes the world of finance, right? Not quite so visible, and often murky, but still out in the open, more or less." Pete paused. "Then you look deeper and things start to get blurred. You see shapes that move under the surface. You pick up things that look meaningless at first glance, but then you find out that they're connected in some indefinable way to other vague but powerful hidden currents. Years go by. You see more and more of it, but it never steps out into the open. You never get a handle on it. It just quietly slips and slides away into the shadows. More years go by. A few things happen that don't sit right with you. Nothing you can put your finger on, nothing conclusive, nothing illegal, nothing that could ever feed the fondest desires of conspiracy theorists. But it's there. It's just there, like a subsonic background noise. Or maybe it's a sixth sense you develop, like hearing things in the attic of your mind, or seeing them with the heart."

Ed listened without interruption. Pete signalled to the waiter and ordered another draft. Pete watched him go away and lowered his voice.

"Ever see things with the heart, Ed?"

Ed nodded slowly. "Yes, I think I do sometimes."

"Well that's how it's been going with me for the past couple o' years. I've started seeing that way. When my second marriage failed, I took a good hard look at my life. I saw the hundreds of articles I'd written over the years and knew that a few of them had done some good in the world. But most of it was just copy, sheer filler. Clever verbiage."

"I can't agree with you, Pete. You've been very good at making the people aware of what's going on in the world. You have a lot to be proud of."

Pete shrugged. "Oh yeah, lots. Until I blew it and lost my foreign correspondent status, lost my. . ." He stopped himself. "There's a helluva lot I didn't do. I ignored many stories over the years, prime stories that badly needed to be out there on the front page. But I knuckled under to the publisher, took his advice on this or that issue, advice he always couched in the subtlest, friendliest, most nonauthoritarian manner. It wasn't hard for me. After all, I was the one of chain's fair-haired boys. I was rising in the trade, and hell, they even hinted I might be foreign editor one day. I thought I was a first-class get-the-facts-nothing-but-the-facts, old-time fightin' newsman bound for stardom. But inside, I think I always knew I'd betrayed something somewhere along the line but for the longest time hadn't wanted to notice. A few years ago, maybe after the second marriage cracked up, I finally noticed. It ate at me then, and it's eating at me now. It's guilt, Ed. Good old-fashioned guilt. By the way, are you still a Puritan?"

"I guess you could say I am."

"Good, Ed", Pete said sadly. "Don't ever change. Drink your ginger ale." Then he swirled his mug, put it to his lips, and emptied it to the bottom.

Ed left his own glass standing in its wet ring on the table. He looked at Pete and saw the boy he had once been. Gathering every latent power of the fatherhood resting in his old heart, he said quietly, "What is it, Peter? I'd like to know."

Pete shook his head. "You don't want to know."

"You can trust me."

"I know I can trust you. It's not that. No, not that at all."

"What, then?"

"It would be better for you if you didn't know."

"I'll risk it."

Pete's face broke into a half smile. He gave the old man a look of grudging admiration. "Puritans never give up, do they?"

Ed smiled back at him. "Never."

Pete closed his eyes and remained silent for several seconds, then he inhaled suddenly and looked at Ed with eyes that were tired, troubled, and full of self-doubt.

"I'm not a conspiracy theorist", he said obliquely.

"I didn't think you were."

"And I'm not a paranoiac."

"That neither."

"Ed, have you ever toyed with the idea that the lunatic fringe just might have got a few things right?"

Ed pursed his lips judiciously. "It has crossed my mind."

"Now don't get me wrong. I'm not saying they *have* got it right. I'm not even saying they've got the major part of it right. But they might have stumbled onto something."

"Are you trying to say that even if what they've stumbled onto is small, it's really not all that small?"

"Exactly. If they're reading even a fraction of this stuff correctly, we've got some serious problems on our hands."

"So far I'm with you."

"Even with a big fraction, a person could interpret it fifteen different ways and still get it wrong. All I'm saying is that there are things going on beneath the surface that powerful people don't want us knowing about, but what those things really mean is pure conjecture."

"Okay, Pete, we've set the ground rules here, so let's have a look at what the players are doing out there on the ice."

16

Eskimos, Plane Crashes, and Poker Chips

Three years before, Peter Stanford had been at Toronto International Airport, waiting to pick up an aunt who was returning from a trip to Spain on a flight from the Canary Islands via Kennedy in New York. The flight had been interrupted by mechanical trouble, and the plane had landed safely in Pittsburgh. The passengers were rerouted on several other flights out of Pittsburgh, via Chicago to Toronto, but there was a two-hour delay before his aunt's flight arrived. Pete had taken the afternoon off, had time to kill, and spent the first hour in the bar, drinking Scotch and perusing *Barron's Weekly* and *Forbes*. He had just completed reading an article on models of the emerging global economy when he looked up and saw one of the world's most influential men walk past the lounge window.

Was that who I think I saw? he asked himself.

He had to look twice, and even then he wasn't sure if he had seen correctly. But scenting news, he paid his bill, scurried along the concourse, and went out the exit just in time to see the man getting into a limousine with two aides. It was he. The Man. Mr. Big. Former American cabinet member, political philosopher, and grand facilitator of international think tanks.

By the time Pete reached the curb, the limousine was pulling away into traffic. He thought it was interesting but shrugged it off, reminding himself that The Man regularly travelled about the world on whatever sort of business he did.

He went back to the bar and was flipping through the magazines again when a certain financier walked past the window, a multi-billionaire, philanthropist, and globalist.

Mr. Bigger, Pete thought to himself. *Coincidence number two for the day.*

Ten minutes later he noticed a top presidential aide from the White House. At that point he closed the magazine and started observing closely. By the time his aunt's flight landed, Pete had counted a head of state from a foreign nation, two former heads of state, a world class media czar, and the Secretary of State for Canada.

The scent of news had become a full-fledged climatic front, which had moved in, it seemed, without anyone appearing to notice.

His aunt, a retired grade-school teacher from Mississauga, Ontario, a witty and devil-may-care soul, came out of the Customs gate wearing a sombrero and a red bullfighter's cape, did a fancy twirl, shouted "*Olé!*" at him, and collapsed into giggles. He tried to laugh. He had a hard time concentrating on the tales of her many adventures as he drove her home. He dropped her at her apartment, begged off her insistent offers of supper, and raced back to the office.

Most of the staff had gone home, but the foreign editor was still on duty. He had no idea why so many movers and shakers were in town. He was fascinated but completely in the dark. Was Pete sure he had seen The Man? And all the heads of state? I mean really sure? Pete was sure. The foreign editor said it didn't make sense; there were no summits scheduled, no press releases about any conferences. It didn't add up. He suggested that Pete phone some of the big hotels in town and try to find out which one had a top-level convention under way. He spent two hours doing that and came up with nothing. He phoned every contact he could think of and again came up with nothing.

On a whim, he drove back to the airport, sat unobtrusively by the VIP gate at Customs for another few hours, and watched.

Half a dozen more big names walked through, including the scion of a European royal family, the director of an influential New Age foundation in San Francisco, and yet another media czar. When a certain English Lord, a world class banker and NATO luminary, appeared, Pete knew he was on to something very big. He hadn't yet attempted to approach any of the visiting dignitaries to ask why they were here in sleepy old Toronto. Smart lad that he was, he realized they were here on the quiet and probably wanted to keep it that way. He was still trying to figure it out when he spotted someone very important indeed (so important that Pete declined to mention his name to Ed).

Bigger and Bigger! he said to himself.

He followed the man out of the terminal, watched him get into a limousine, memorized the license number, and jogged to the parking lot to get his own car. The limousine was in no hurry, and five minutes later Pete caught up with it on the expressway. From then on he tailed it, staying a respectful four cars behind. It took the exit to a satellite city west of the metropolis and eventually arrived at a super-hotel down the street from the convention center of the country's largest commercial bank.

Pete parked in the non-VIP lot and scurried into the lobby, only to see the very important man entering an elevator, surrounded by bodyguards. He went up to a bellhop and asked if he knew why the man was there. The bellhop looked at him suspiciously and replied that he had no idea, sir. Pete then inquired at the desk. He was rewarded by more suspicious looks—this time from three clerks and the assistant manager. The latter pressed a button on the desk. Then the manager walked out of his office, staring at Pete. Pete flashed his press card, which didn't help at all. It made things worse. The manager informed him that the identity and personal affairs of all guests were confidential and that if Pete had no further business in the hotel he should depart.

Pete ambled out of the lobby with as much dignity as he

could muster and went around a corner of the hotel to the street entrance of its deluxe lounge. He seated himself in a dimly lit alcove, twenty feet from the entrance to a banquet hall that was cordoned off by braided purple ropes hanging from silver posts. Two uniformed butlers stood on either side of the doorway. Pete ordered a Scotch and nursed it slowly, hoping to pick up any information that might waft past. In the course of the next half hour, he saw a minion of millionaires and a baggle of billionaires disgorged from a private elevator, then conducted by bodyguards into the hall. Pete was glad he had read *Barron's* and *Forbes* earlier that day, otherwise he would not have recognized many of the faces. The guards eyed him carefully, as they did the other guests in the outer lounge, but Pete was an expert at appearing innocuous and disinterested.

He was just getting a little pad out of his jacket pocket in order to make some notes when the manager walked into the room, spotted him, and strode to his table. Politely but ominously, he said that he would appreciate it very much if Pete would depart, and do so immediately, otherwise he would be forced to call hotel security. Pete departed.

By then it was after eleven. Pete went home to his downtown apartment and typed up a story. There wasn't much to the article other than the facts he had spliced together around the main strand, namely, that a startling number of the most powerful figures in the world were converging on Toronto, and no one seemed to know why. But he managed to stretch it out to two thousand words, tying in some of the curious things he had learned from *Barron's* and *Forbes* (pure speculation, mind you, but enough to qualify the story as a news analysis piece). He printed out a final draft just as the dawn sky was graying in the east. He hadn't slept at all, but he was no stranger to espresso coffee. He drank half an urn full, took a hot, hot, hot soapy shower, whistled something from *La Traviata* while he was towelling off, shaved, dressed himself, straightened his tie, and said

Olé! to the sun that was breaking into the canyons of the city's skyscape.

He drove through rush hour feeling elated (it had been a long time since he had had a scoop) and dropped the article off at the foreign editor's desk. Then he went to his own cubicle on the editorial floor and turned his attention to other stories. The foreign editor called him in shortly before noon, asked after his health, asked if he had won anything on the lottery draw two days before, asked if Pete still planned to take in tomorrow's Blue Jays game, asked if he still wanted to go on that special assignment to Africa. Pete said yes to the latter and waited.

Then the foreign editor said casually, "Oh, by the way, that piece you dropped off isn't really newsworthy."

Pete raised his eyebrows, wondering if he had heard right. "Run that by me again?" he said.

The foreign editor shrugged, "So, a few names arrive in the city. But where's the story?"

"That *is* the story", Pete countered.

The foreign editor chuckled. "Not much of story, Pete. You get any sleep last night?"

"Not much", he admitted.

"You look awful, guy. Why don't you go home and get some rest. I think your mind's been playing tricks on you."

Pete shook his head. "No, it hasn't. Not at all. But it's starting to play tricks on me at this very moment. I think I just heard one of the best journalists in this country tell me that one of the biggest stories of the year is no more important than a traffic jam or a flock of geese landing on the grass strip at the airport."

The foreign editor stared at him without a word. He leaned way back in his swivel chair, crossed his arms behind his head, and put his feet up on the desk. Then he cleared his throat. "Pete, this is not a story. You can't make soup out of deer tracks."

"Hal, I agree that we don't exactly have soup here, but these aren't ordinary tracks. Try to imagine, if you will, finding the

618

spoor of forty or fifty bull elephants who've just passed through the lobby of the Royal York Hotel. We got elephants here, big game tracks, crap all over the carpet, and no one blinks an eye. Doesn't that intrigue you?"

"Not in the least."

"Not in the least? Last night you were fascinated, and this morning you're bored. Am I hearing right?"

"Uh-huh. You're hearing right."

"That's ridiculous!" Pete raised his voice.

The foreign editor spread his arms as if to say, how unreasonable can you get, what can I do with a guy like this?

Pete wasn't exactly sure of his status, but he knew he was valuable to the chain, and somebody higher up might regret the loss of a fair-haired boy over an issue as minor as deer tracks. He decided to risk everything on one roll of the dice.

"It needs to go in", he pressed. "And if it doesn't go in, I'm going to make it a resigning issue."

That made the foreign editor mad. His feet hit the floor. "Oh, come on! Get real!" he growled.

"I mean it, Hal." Pete stared back hard.

"Forget it! There's no story, and it's not going in."

Amazed that he had lost the gamble, Pete shook his head, uncomprehending. "This is nuts. I'm going to thrash this out with the editor."

"Have it your way", the foreign editor said to his back as he stomped out of the office.

The editor in chief was on the phone when Pete barged in after running an obstacle course with the man's secretary. The editor mumbled a few "Uh-huhs" and "Yeah, okays" into the phone and hung up. He gave Pete his Hail-to-the-Chief stare, then smiled artificially.

"Sorry. It's not going in."

"Why not?"

Another editorial shrug.

"I asked why not and I want an answer, or I'm outa here. History. It's no skin off my nose if I do go, because your competitor recently offered me a job at 20 percent higher salary than you're paying me. I turned him down because I figured our paper is more interested in real journalism than his. Prove to me that I made the right decision—Chief."

The editor laughed. For a full minute he pondered what Pete had said. Then he offered him a drink.

"No, thanks."

"C'mon, relax. It's after noon hour."

"I said no, thanks, and I want an answer."

Another shrug.

Pete wheeled and left the editor's office, tossing over his shoulder, "So long, Phil. I'll be in my cubicle loading pens and paper clips into a cardboard box, then I'm history, ancient history. Watch out what you step on, the carpet's a mess."

He was loading his belongings into a cardboard box when his desk phone rang. It was the publisher himself.

"Hi, Pete. Do I hear a caffufle going on downstairs?"

"That's right, sir. Our noble editor filled you in on the details, no doubt."

"Yup. You know what Phil's like. He's a fine editor, the best. But sometimes he's a heavy hitter—that's why I hired him—and once he's made his mind up there's no arguing with him, right?"

"Right, sir."

"Why don't you come upstairs, and we'll talk about it."

"I was just packing."

"Now, now, don't blow your cool, Pete. You're too valuable a man to get in a huff over this sort of thing. The other team could never treat you nice the way we do."

Pete let a few seconds pass.

"I mean it, we need you here. The chain needs you. *I* need you."

Pete fought with his emotions. He could feel himself cooling down. Despite himself, his resolve weakened.

"When?" he asked.

"Come up right now. I've got a few minutes."

Pete rode the private elevator to the penthouse office suite, *all* the way up—it was a long ride—shaking his head, muttering to himself, feeling honored, feeling wanted, feeling grateful, but still confused.

The publisher gave him that special smile and hale-fellow-well-met handshake that he reserved for presidents and prime ministers and film stars and ushered him into his inner office. On the wall above the long, dark green leather couch, where the publisher indicated Pete should sit, there were plenty of signed photographs of presidents and prime ministers and film stars, the aforesaid gentlemen and ladies shaking hands with or embracing the publisher, who was, of course, wearing that special smile he reserved for such occasions.

Margaret Thatcher and Mikhail Gorbachev. Desmond Tutu and Katharine Hepburn.

Special, Pete grimaced. *Real special.*

If the boss intended to woo him, he thought to himself, he had better present candy and flowers, and the biggest sweet of all had better be a page-one article on the secret conference. Or else. Or else what? Or else he was history, *ancient* history!

The publisher, oozing masculine charm, humor, and utter calm, brought him a glass of Irish coffee that had just the right amount of whiskey in it. Understated. Elegant, like the boss himself. Making small chat, he offered Pete an expensive Cuban cigar from a polished mahogany box. Pete declined. The publisher lit one for himself.

"Castro sent me these for my birthday", he commented lightly. "Which is a funny thing for him to do because the bearded wonder knows I'm an old-time capitalist. It's pure politics, Pete. Pure politics."

"Viva Fidel!" Pete mumbled humorlessly.

The publisher guffawed and choked on smoke. When he had cleared his lungs, he grinned. "And that, my dear Stanford, is why I need you."

"Beggin' yer pardon, sir?"

"What I mean is, there are a whole lot of people on the floors below who are scared spitless of me. Some of them are your regular no-nonsense press guys, like the editor and foreign editor and some of the desk people. But there're a lot of sycophants too, young ambitious types who want to advance their careers. You don't care about that, do you?"

"Sure I care about it, but not enough to play cards using my integrity as a poker chip."

"Well spoken", the publisher mused, looking at the ceiling, blowing two thin streams of smoke out his nostrils.

Pete said nothing, watching the publisher decide what approach to take with him. Pete leaned forward.

"Sir, the story goes in, or I go out. It's as simple as that."

"Actually, it's not as simple as that", he replied, not unkindly. "I know and you know that this is a story, Pete. But it's larger than I am. The problem is, I've made a promise to preserve the confidential nature of the conference, in the interest of the public good."

"To whom did you make the promise?"

"I can't answer that." The publisher smiled. "Among your many talents, you're a damn fine investigative reporter."

"So why the secrecy?"

"It's not secrecy. It's discretion. I have to preserve confidentiality. The people who arrived in the city yesterday are committed to preserving democracy, to ensuring the social order of the West. But they're not going to be able to function if they have to trip over TV cables every thirty seconds or deal with a media blitz whenever they go to the bathroom."

"Doesn't that come with the territory?"

The publisher shrugged. "Who says it does? Is there some law that says it does?"

"No, sir, but there's an unwritten law in democracies that ensures the accountability of people in power. It's a check and balance system. The media . . ."

"The media!" the publisher said, disgusted.

Perplexed, Pete tilted his head. "Sir, *we* are the media."

The publisher waved away the comment with his cigar hand. "I know, I know, Pete, of course we are. But there are times when we have to restrain ourselves in the interest of a higher good. If we want to preserve the democratic process and the capitalism that ensures freedom of the press, we have to see things from a broader perspective."

"What could be more important to the preservation of a free society than laying the truth out on the table?"

The publisher thought hard about that. Eventually he answered: "Because if we lay everything out on the table, it slows down the process."

"Is that such a bad thing? Maybe the slow method gives people time to consider all the factors. To avoid mistakes."

"Yes, and no. People so often misunderstand—"

"Isn't that the risk democracies take?" Pete interrupted. "Isn't our mandate here at the paper to ensure that people have an opportunity to judge for themselves? Even if they do misunderstand, isn't it better than the alternative?"

The publisher stubbed out his half-finished cigar. He leaned forward and said firmly, "In all truth, sometimes it isn't. These are transitional times. You don't know all the risks involved here."

"So, clue me in."

"It's a long story. It's complex."

"I've got all day."

Suddenly, the publisher did not seem as infatuated with Pete's lack of fear as he had when the conversation began. All traces of good-natured bonhomie vanished.

"Unfortunately, I don't have all day", he said coldly.

Pete slapped his knees and stood up. "Fine, sir. Thanks for the interview. I'll be on my way now. Thanks for the fun, thanks for the many interesting experiences over the years, thanks for the grossly inflated salary. I'll miss it."

A portion of the publisher's amusement returned to his face. "Sit down! Come on, sit down."

Pete sat down, giving the publisher one last chance to think about flowers and candy.

"I'm going to ask you to trust me on this one. The people at this meeting are good. They're the best and brightest in the world. They need confidentiality because time is running out for all of us. I can assure you that their goals and motives are the highest. It's nothing more than a think tank, and people can't think clearly if a pack of *paparazzi* are dogging their every step. It's simply distracting. That's the problem—distraction. So cut them a little slack, will you, and hell, while you're at it, why don't you cut out the damn adolescent act. I need you on staff because you're very good at what you do. But you're not indispensable, not even you, Pete. If you walk out of this office like an outraged Victorian maiden who can't bring herself to say the word *sex*, then you'll be making the biggest mistake of your life."

Intrigued, Pete shot back, "Will I?"

"You will. You'll be throwing away a career that has every promise of rising indefinitely. There's no ceiling for a guy like you. No upper limits. I don't know what's making you jump to such ridiculous conclusions or why you're mucking about in paranoia, but maybe it has a lot to do with your marital problems."

That stung. "My marital problems?" Pete answered slowly.

"Yeah, your marital problems. You're a bit strung out, guy. You've been distracted for the past few years getting it sorted out."

"My marital problems are all sorted out", Pete countered. "They're over, both of them."

"They're never over", the publisher replied in a melancholy voice. Pete knew that the boss had his own problems in that department.

The two men sat in silence, looking at the walls.

"I'm asking you to stay. And I'm asking you to let the story pass. And I'm offering you a twenty-percent increase on your salary."

Pete sat back on the couch.

"Think about it", the publisher added.

Pete did. Then he shook his head. "I'd be content to keep the salary I've got, *if* the story goes in."

The publisher shook his head. "Sorry."

"Okay, boss. See you sometime." He stood up and walked to the door. The publisher watched Pete open it before he spoke.

"Oh, hell, all right, all right", he growled. "I guess it's not such a big deal. Put your damn story in!"

Pete tried unsuccessfully to suppress a smile. "You mean that?"

"Yes, I mean that! You also get the raise, hotshot."

"Story on page one?"

"Don't push me that far. You get space inside. But I doubt our beloved readers will so much as sit up and take notice."

"That's great, sir. Thank you. Can you give me the green light on a follow-up?"

"*If* the public notices your first piece, then and only then, can you go ahead and waste your time and my money on follow-ups."

The publisher glared at him.

Pete walked back into the room and shook his hand. But the boss didn't look any too happy. Pete left him staring out his floor-to-ceiling window at the towers of the city.

On the way down in the elevator, it struck him that the publisher had said something about jumping to conclusions and paranoia, which was strange, because the article had not jumped to any conclusions, nor had it raised any issues that would feed anyone's paranoia, even that of the paranoiacs. But he dismissed the publisher's comment as the kind of meaningless chaff that blows through any conversation in which there are unknowables.

He was unpacking the box in his office when Phil stepped in.

"I'm back!" Pete smiled ruefully.

"I noticed. Where are the ghostbusters when you need them!"

"Sorry for the snit, Phil."

"Don't sweat over it. By the way, can you lend me a shovel?"

"Huh? A shovel?"

"Yeah, I got elephant crap all over my carpet."

Shortly before five, Phil buzzed him on the office intercom.

"You still want to go to Africa?"

"Sure", Pete replied. "What's up?"

"All hell is breaking loose in Rwanda again. More massacres, and it's spreading into neighboring countries."

Phil told him more details, and Pete agreed to go. "When?"

"Tomorrow morning. Nairobi via Amsterdam. Then you can catch a shuttle flight into Kigali."

Pete, who was now thoroughly exhausted from lack of sleep, felt a moment of suspicion.

"What about my article on the visiting dignitaries? It's still going into tomorrow's edition, isn't it?"

"Yeah, yeah, it's going in on page two of financial."

"Why not front page? This is news!"

"The boss said financial; financial is what you get. If there's reader interest in the piece, maybe you'll move closer to the front next time. Now look, can you get to the airport by seven? Your ticket'll be waiting at the KLM counter."

"I'll be there. What's the angle?"

"Angle?" Phil asked carefully.

"The Africa angle. Geopolitics, tribal dynamics, human rights, or what?"

"Don't ask me, you're the roving reporter. If the boss thinks you deserve special treatment, special treatment is what you get. He just called down to tell me you can handle it however you want. He thinks Africa is going to become a strategic point in global power plays: mineral resources, plagues, ecology, rights of women, the limitations on UN peace-keeping—that sort of thing. You've got carte blanche. Take all the time you need, he says."

"That's great."

"He thought you might consider taking a side trip to the Balkans too. You could tie in some of the same themes, UN forces, tribalism, and balkanization, pardon the pun."

Pete had been hankering for the trip for months, trying to convince Phil that on-site bureaus often missed things that a fresh eye could spot. He was excited.

"Now get your duff on home and have some shut-eye."

"I'm on my way. Uh, just one thing, Phil. Can you give me my shovel back?"

The editor laughed and hung up.

Pete arrived in Kenya two days later. In the bar of the Nairobi Hilton he met a group of international journalists, and they agreed to let him squeeze on board the small Citation jet they had chartered for the flight to Kigali. They drank and joked far into the night; much of the humor was barbed commentary about their respective publishers, but the gaiety burned itself out toward the end of the evening with the thought of all the people who were dying hideous deaths only a few hundred miles to the west. The next morning he was standing on the airport tarmac, roasted by heat and humidity even in his cotton tropicals, savoring the palm trees and the cries of exotic birds.

627

The other journalists were already on board, and the pilot was flicking switches in the cockpit. There was a high-pitched warm-up hum from the aircraft. The day promised to be a beautiful one, with light winds and sharp blue skies across which a few low cumulus clouds scudded, trying to engorge, hoarding their meager load of moisture.

A reporter from UPI stuck his head out the passenger door and signalled for Pete to get in. Pete had one foot on the bottom step when a young woman dressed in a jeans jacket, T-shirt, khakis, and hiking boots, carrying a tote bag and cameras, juggling sunglasses and a water bottle, ran up to the plane and in good but heavily accented English begged for a ride. UPI apologized but said the flight was already over-full. The woman was from the Reuters news agency, late-twentyish, and eager for what was probably the assignment of her life. She looked utterly deflated.

Wondering why he did it, Pete nobly stepped back and offered the woman his seat. She was effusively grateful. The Citation took off, and Pete strolled toward the terminal, wondering where he could find another charter into Rwanda on such short notice. There were some corrugated iron sheds offering older prop planes for hire on the outskirts of the airport, and he thought he might be able to rustle up a Cessna on company expense. He was wondering to himself if the little African cargo fleets took VISA or Mastercard when he heard a tremendous explosion and saw a fireball unfold like the petals of an orchid a thousand feet above and a mile beyond the end of the runway. Right where the Citation should have been.

It was the Citation.

Pete could never remember how he eventually made it into Kigali. There was a vague image of a Beechcraft, a black pilot, and mile after mile of rolling hills, tawny-colored savanna, giraffes lumbering along under impossible necks, herds of unidentifiable beasts stampeding, the mountains of the Great Rift escarpment, the silver sheen of Lake Victoria, then forest canopy hiding everything below, under which the heart of darkness was making itself visible.

He saw many horrifying things during the following weeks, vomited when he entered a church full of butchered women and children, tried to cope with the memory of the vaporized journalists who had died on the jet, met with field commanders from both sides, interviewed UN troops, faxed his articles to Toronto, and suffered from nightmares every night. The memory of the secret convention in Toronto faded to almost nothing beside the enormity of what he saw in Africa. Back in Nairobi he heard that Kenyan authorities were still investigating the Citation accident, as they called it. At the Hilton he got quietly drunk, read his mail in that condition, and noted only in passing that his article on the think tank (which seemed to have occurred three or four hundred years ago) had been drastically edited down to a quarter of the original text and had been inserted on page six of the financial section. He felt mildly irritated over the fact that Phil hadn't kept his word but reminded himself that Rwanda had scrambled his brains, his emotions were in anguish, and his body was thoroughly hung over. Besides, the paper had given his series from Africa high priority, page one and two for weeks in a row. There were a lot of things to worry about in the world, and a think tank wasn't one of the major ones.

Half-recovered, he flew to Rome, slept a lot, sat at outdoor cafés and watched Italian women, walked through the streets for hours on end, and went to the opera (he couldn't remember which one—*Rigoletto*, he thought). Later in the week he took a flight to the city of Mostar in the former Yugoslavia. There, he met with more UN commanders and picked up a lot of grumbling about how the UN needed more authority if it was to do an effective job of policing the madness. He went into the hinterland with Canadian troops and saw more churches full of butchered men and women and children. He faxed his stories back home. One evening, overcome with claustrophobia, he went strolling on the streets of Zagreb after curfew. Someone took a potshot at him with a real gun. With a real bullet. It happened two more times during his month in Bosnia and Croatia. His hands began to shake all the time. He drank every night, whiskey, neat, lots of it. The nightmares wouldn't go away. He wrote more articles, feeling a growing dismay over the condition of humanity. He faxed them back to the head office, and two months after his departure arrived home exhausted and thoroughly dispirited.

Then he had a minor nervous breakdown. Pete spent three days in the psycho ward of the Toronto General, but a doctor eventually informed him that he was basically a sane man, just shaken up. He prescribed Prozac. The publisher advised a paid sabbatical. Pete went kayaking on the Coppermine River in the Northwest Territories with an old college buddy. They had a fabulous time, grew beards, ate a lot of pink-fleshed Arctic char broiled on willow sticks beside cold, fast, green, absolutely clean water. They arrived at the mouth of the river just as the tundra was turning flaming orange with early northern autumn. Pete threw the last of the Prozac into the Arctic Ocean, hoping that no innocent char would find it.

At Coppermine he and his friend hitched a ride on a two-prop Otter full of American fishermen and paid for it with war correspondent stories. At Cambridge Bay they connected to the regular DC-9 flight south.

Back at the office on Monday, Pete felt fit as a fiddle. The publisher called him upstairs and asked him how he was. Pete said fine, just fine. Then the publisher offered him a new job.

"You're still recovering, Pete. How about you take over as diplomatic correspondent in Ottawa? Try it for six months, see how you feel, then I think we'll have something better for you. Much better", he added cryptically.

Pete thought that might be the best way to ease back into the saddle. He still felt a little shaky, he told the boss, but didn't need medication any more. He moved to the capital, where he had remained for the past year and a half.

* * *

Ed Burgess looked at his watch. "Good heavens! It's past eight. Marjorie was expecting me at six. I'll have to give her a call. Back in a minute."

As Ed stood up Pete grabbed the sleeve of his jacket.

"Just a sec! Before you make any phone calls, I'll ask you not to mention this conversation to anyone."

"Not even to Marjorie?"

"Not even your wife. In fact I'd appreciate it if you didn't ever mention to anyone that we met."

Ed looked around the room. It was full of journalists.

"I think a few people already know", he pointed out.

"Yeah, but no one knows who you are. When you get back from calling your wife, we'll go find someplace more private."

When she answered, Marjorie's tone was tense.

"You're two hours late for supper, and not a word from you."

"I'm sorry, love. You have no idea what this day has been like. It's beyond description. I'll explain when I get home."

"And when will that be?"

"I'm not sure. Please believe me, it's very important. Will you pray for me, and for the person I'm with?"

Her tone softened. "Of course, Eddie. Sorry for being a bit miffed. Did you eat?"

"I'll buy a sandwich."

"You can't run the country on a sandwich, dear. And I hope you haven't been dipping into the coffee."

"No backsliding so far. I've fallen hard for ginger ale though. I'll try to be home soon."

"All right. I love you."

"I love you too. Pray?"

"I will."

Pete had his trench coat on and was standing by the elevator when Ed hung up the pay phone.

"We'll go to Satchmo's", he said. "It's a place down on the market. Got a car?"

Ed nodded.

"Great", Pete said. "I lost my license a few months ago for impaired driving."

Fifteen minutes later they were seated at a quiet corner table of a restaurant on a back street of the trendy Byward Market, a few blocks east of Parliament Hill. The atmosphere was an eclectic blend of black cultures. The walls were covered with brightly colored East African cloth and West African ebony masks that Ed thought looked demonic. A recording of Paul Simon singing with a Bantu backup chorus was playing softly on the sound system. The waiters and waitresses were black, their facial features distinctly Sudanese. There was a photo of Louis Armstrong behind the cash register, Malcolm X and Nelson Mandela flanking him on either side.

Pete insisted on ordering some dishes from central Africa for both of them, a Scotch on ice for himself and yet another ginger ale for Ed. While they were waiting for the food to arrive, Ed asked if there had been any follow-up on his article about the think tank.

"Zilch. Zero", Pete replied. "It got lost in the wave of horror stories from around the world. Oh, a few right-wingers put up a fuss for a day or so. An anonymous reader sent me a copy of an obscure patriotic weekly from south of the border, down Washington way. It was right on target, blew the cover off their agenda, named all the people in attendance, and even managed to get some poor chump to pretend he was custodial or catering services into the center. He did a good job, brought out a lot of interesting information, but nobody was very interested."

"That's all?"

"Not quite. I was safely dispatched to Rwanda at the time, somewhat distracted by the heaps of dead children, so it took a long time after I returned to Canada to begin to figure out what had happened. When I was finished with my little nervous breakdown, and later when I got back from the north, the trail was cold. All the elephant tracks had been swept away. Business as usual."

"Surely other journalists were interested?"

"Yeah, well, it seemed for a while that they weren't. Whatever they had managed to pick up on the grapevine was squelched from the top down, or swept away, or just didn't make it into print, or got neutered like my article was. But that feisty little patriotic rag smelled something bad on the carpet and mailed a press release about the meeting to every major paper in the country. A friend of mine, the guy I went kayaking with in the Arctic, works for my paper's major rival. He has very sharp olfactory nerves, and he smelled something unpleasant on the wind. When his editor did to him what mine did to me, he was as befuddled as I was. But he's a tougher kind of guy than I am, and he didn't give up. He did one hell of a lot of research on the quiet, and two days after my little eviscerated article appeared, he used it to lever his own editor into reconsidering. He lied to him, told him that the Toronto bureau chief of the *New York Times* had got together a full-page report on the conference for the Sunday *Times*, and wouldn't the Canadian papers be caught with their pants down if they didn't breathe a word about a world-class story happening in their own front yard. His editor agreed that, if that were the case, it would mean a loss of credibility with the readership. Maybe this editor was just as perplexed by the hush-hush from his superiors as I was, maybe he was sick of the trade and wanted to retire early. Who knows why, but against company orders he let my friend's article go to press. Then for three days there was a flurry of articles in the major city dailies. Nothing came of it. The dignitaries went home, and everyone forgot it had ever happened.

"My friend's editor retired, my pal got a slap on the wrist and a holiday with half pay. That's when we decided to go kayaking. He told me the whole story on the Coppermine River, at a place called Bloody Falls, where the Eskimos slaughtered a band of Indians in the last century. A hauntingly beautiful spot, high bluffs, thundering cascades, the backs of huge red fish slicing through the pools below the falls, the stars so bright at night they make you blink. It was a great place to discuss man's inhumanity to man, pardon the cliché."

"So, until then you had no idea that the suppression of news was widespread?"

"Exactly. Up to that point I thought it was just a quirk or some private deal my publisher had cut with the visiting dignitaries. When my friend and I started comparing notes, we both began to get the feeling that something very big and very ugly had happened."

"But you had no proof."

"Precisely, we had no proof."

"Didn't the American press report it?"

"Hell, they were the worst of all. It was unbelievable. Usually they're Johnny on the spot when it comes to this level of public events. No way, not a word, not a whimper. The only people who reported it in the States were the little right-wing patriots, and nobody respects them very much, do they?" The question was obviously rhetorical.

"Last year I was in Paris and had a few drinks with Sylvie Mercredi; she's a foreign correspondent with the French national broadcasting system. She was hopping mad about the Toronto meeting and asked me point-blank why the Canadian press had dragged its heels on a story of that magnitude. I said I didn't know why. Then she said maybe we'd been bit by the same bug that hit the good ol' U.S.A. I asked her what she meant.

634

"She told me that an agreement had been hammered out by the American Newspaper Publishers' Association to keep the lid of 'privileged secrecy' on the meetings of *L'Alliance Mondiale*. It has more than one name, but that's what she called it. Later, I checked it out. I called Ames, the Toronto bureau chief of the *Times,* and asked him why his paper hadn't published a report on the meeting. He pretended not to know what the upsurge of interest was about, said that the *Times* didn't do a story about it because it had been decided it wasn't news. After that I called the *Washington Post*. Their foreign news section referred me to their financial section, and when I called their financial section, it referred me to their foreign news section. Round and round it went, and where it stopped nobody knows." Pete took a long drink from his tumbler of Scotch.

"Nobody knows", he repeated, looking down into its depths.

He stared at the table and finished his drink. Then ordered another.

"Sylvie's a great gal", he said. "She's an old friend. But that night I could see she didn't have much respect for me any more."

Pete sighed, embarrassed and depressed.

"The *Alliance Mondiale* is off limits to the media in America. It would have been off limits here too if my aunt hadn't been possessed by a whim to see a bull fight."

"You refer to them as the *Alliance Mondiale*. Who are they?"

"Ah, that's the real question, isn't it? Who are they? They call themselves 'the Alliance' and the 'Global Council', and a few other endearing terms, but they usually refer to their work as 'the relationship'. They were founded in Europe just after the War. Their annual meetings have moved around the Western world from place to place ever since, always secret, always erecting a wall of impenetrable silence."

"You said a janitor or caterer was able to penetrate it?"

"Well, I'm guessing about who the mole was. It could have

been anyone. The long and short of it is we now have a rough handle on what they're about."

"Which is . . . ?"

"You have to remember, Ed, that these are the most powerful people on the planet, the richest, the most influential in politics, finance, media, and culture. These are the folks who shape the world, and for the past forty years or so they've been slowly but relentlessly planning to reshape it radically. There are at least three hundred of them at any one time. It's all documented. It's real. Their agenda is to bring about a new economic order, and when that's in place, a new global political order will follow, and after that a new worldwide religious order. But the precise details are beyond me."

"Worldwide religious order?" Ed asked, wrinkling his brow. "That sounds rather beyond the scope of bankers and politicians."

"Doesn't it though. I doubt if that scheme will ever amount to much. It's the economic and political goals that worry me. The religion is probably just their attempt to make up a philosophy for the new world order. You know, window dressing."

Their meals arrived. Ed suddenly no longer had an appetite.

"Pete, it could be that the economics and politics are actually window dressing for the religious goals."

Pete, who was suffering no loss of appetite, was spooning up a bowl of yellow mash seasoned with red peppers.

"Yeah," he said after swallowing, "I guess you Puritans would worry about something like that. But really the bottom line for these people is money. Good old filthy lucre."

"Why have I read nothing about this organization, if it's so important?"

"An excellent question, my man. An excellent question. The answer to that is, they own the media, with a few exceptions. Did I mention that while my pal and I were munching on broiled fish, playing primitive in the wilds, he told me he had spent a lot of time standing on the public sidewalk at the entrance to the conference center? Did I mention that our Prime Minister gave a welcoming speech to the members of the Alliance? And did I throw in the inconsequential detail that my very own publisher was also present at the meetings?"

"What do you think it means, Pete?" Ed asked quietly.

"To tell you the truth, I don't know. But I know for sure this is not just a think tank. As I said before, I'm not a conspiracy theorist, and I'm not paranoid. But something of major historical proportions is taking shape under our eyes with hardly anyone noticing." He pointed his spoon at Ed for emphasis. "And that is not good."

Ed nodded. *Definitely not good*, he thought to himself.

"I'd like to tell you another interesting tidbit. But first some background: Did you know that the members of the Alliance are drawn from the major power points on the planet? The UN, the Council on Foreign Relations, the World Bank, the Trilateral Commission, the Club of Rome, the American Federal Reserve Board, the major banking institutions of Europe and America, several royal houses. The list goes on and on and just doesn't seem to stop."

"If they're that powerful, why did they permit the flurry of articles in the Toronto papers?"

"I don't think they wanted it. But after it started oozing through the cracks, they realized that a few token articles couldn't do them serious harm. They probably figured some minor exposure would be necessary to avoid any potential nervousness in the public."

"Also," Ed interjected, "if they *are* moving to a new stage of global power, they might want to introduce the public to the idea bit by bit, like an inoculation."

Pete pursed his lips. "I never thought of that, but yeah, it makes sense. That might have been their thinking, after the fact, so to speak. Plan A sprang leaks, so they moved to Plan B. These are no dummies, Ed."

"I had already gathered that. But you said you wanted to tell me about a tidbit."

"Uh-huh. Have you ever seen one of those three-dimensional chess games?"

Ed shook his head.

"It's like a cube, with gridwork. You don't just play the pieces forward and backward, you also plan your moves upward and downward. It makes the game so much more fascinating and challenging. It's not just adding a dimension; it increases the complexity in an entirely different way. It's not two plus two, which equals four; it's two *times* two *times* two, which equals eight. Do you see what I mean?"

"I don't think I do."

"Look, I've got one at my apartment. I'll show it to you some day. All I'm saying is that these interlocking organizations are each in themselves like a chessboard. Put them together, and you have a very complex game, and you need to have a fairly high IQ to play. The interesting thing about the global game is that there's no black team or white team. All the players are on the same side. Only the pawns remain ignorant. That's you and me and the average citizen, Ed. We're the pawns."

"Is that the tidbit?"

"I'm coming to it. Now a few years ago a U.S. congressman named Larry McDonald stumbled onto some dirty linen the globalists left lying about, and he didn't like the odor. He started doing some research and published some stuff on it. But it didn't attract one iota of interest in the press. That's a consistent pattern, by the way. No interest, no media exposure, no public response. McDonald was so frustrated he began to speak about it all over the States, and a grass-roots revolt started to spring up. All of that came to an end in August 1983, when the Korean Airlines Boeing 747 was shot down in mysterious circumstances by the Soviet air force. McDonald was on that plane. Media reports of the incident were flimsy and short-lived, and no mention was made of the fact that a prominent congressman had been on board, a man who had been leading a congressional effort to unmask an international conspiracy.

"This is only one of several similar stories. Want to hear more?"

"There's more?" Ed asked uneasily.

"Oh, lots, lots more. Let's go back a little. In the 1920s and 1930s a U.S. congressman named Louis McFadden, chairman of the House Banking and Currency Committee, was a strong critic of the Federal Reserve System. He called it the most gigantic trust company in history and believed that putting this kind of power into the hands of unelected people was dangerous, especially because the Reserve was an old boys' network of colossal proportions and impact. Three attempts were made on McFadden's life.

"In the fifties the Reece Committee conducted a thorough investigation of the biggest tax-exempt foundations—Rockefeller, Ford, Guggenheim, and Carnegie—but Congress just couldn't bring itself to believe what it found, that the wealth and power of these foundations were staggering and linked to the international money cartel.

"In the sixties and seventies Congressman Wright Patman, the chairman of the House Banking Committee, investigated the foundations and the Federal Reserve and sounded an alarm in Congress, loud and clear, called for a repeal of the Federal Reserve Act, called for audits of the Reserve. But none of this attracted media attention. Patman said that his committee's exposés of the Federal Reserve Board were shocking and scandalous, and he couldn't understand why they weren't reported in the press.

"Then, in the seventies and eighties Larry McDonald picked up the torch, and of course it came to very little, again with the help of a media blackout. I already told you how he ended up. After him came Senator John Heinz and Senator John Tower, both of whom had at one time been members of the Council on Foreign Relations, an organization that has one world government as its primary aim. Don't look so dubious, Ed, this is all documented. Read their own journal, *Foreign Affairs*; it's all there in black and white. Some of the U.S. presidents have belonged to the CFR, and a majority of their Cabinet members have come from there as well, not to mention the major people in government departments. It just goes on and on. Am I boring you?"

Ed shook his head.

"You're sure? I know this is info-overload, but I think it throws some light on the shadows in our own country."

"Go on, Pete", Ed prompted in a quiet voice.

"Anyway, to continue: Tower and Heinz were no longer with the CFR and had become quite critical of it in public. Tower wrote a book about it. Shortly after the book was published, he died in a plane crash, in April 1991. The day before, Senator Heinz also died in a freak plane crash outside of Philadelphia."

"Are you saying they were murdered? Surely not! Are you saying these people did it?"

"As I said, I'm not a conspiracy buff. And all these networks of power are composed of law-abiding citizens, aren't they? Many of them are law *makers*. All I'm saying is that the men who died were onto something potentially very damaging to the international power structure and that they died in mysterious circumstances. That's all. I'm not making any guesses about who did or did not do it. It's just a fact, and I keep it filed away, here." Pete tapped the side of his head. "For future reference."

Ed slid into a profoundly troubled silence from which he could not extract himself.

"Another tidbit", Pete went on. "Can you explain to me why a character as slimy as the current President of the United States of America just keeps floating above the many scandals that swirl around his ankles? A generation ago a man like that would never have made it to a campaign platform, let alone got himself elected to the presidency, not just once but twice. And tell me why there have been such an improbable number of plane crashes and suicides of people who could have given sworn evidence against him. He just keeps smiling and smiling, like a gray-haired Boy Scout, while the stink of rotting corpses gets worse by the day."

Ed stirred uncomfortably. "That's a very strong accusation, Pete. It does seem suspicious, but there's no real evidence."

"Of course not. Of course there's no real evidence. By the way, did you know that he's a member of the Alliance, has been since way back when he was a minor politico in an insignificant little state. Here's another tidbit—"

"Are you sure about this plane crash business?" Ed interrupted. "These could be just unfortunate coincidences."

"Maybe. Maybe not. But I've paid quite a lot of attention to unfortunate coincidental plane crashes since narrowly missing my own demise a couple of years ago. And the statistical odds are staggering. Much, much bigger than a simple chess game. Two times two times two, Ed."

"Equals eight?"

"Usually. Usually it does equal eight. But we're talking about many hundreds of key players, possibly thousands."

"Pete, let's say for the sake of argument that someone did try to kill you in Africa. Why didn't they try again?"

"I think they did. They tried three more times in the Balkans. But by then the wind had blown the elephant tracks away, and I was having a nervous breakdown and had taken up kayaking. Maybe someone figured it would be less trouble, and less of a scandal, to let me drink myself to death. I live a quiet life now, doing the rounds of the embassy parties, writing very insightful, very safe articles, avoiding noises that would make waves in the shadow world."

"I see", Ed said sadly. "You're telling me that you can't help me."

Pete's eyes were red, his words beginning to slur:

"Look, Ed, there's no such thing as an independent press any more. There's not one of us hacks who'd dare to write a no-holds-barred article about the sacred cows, and if we did, it would never appear in print."

"Are you sure? There seem to be quite a few blunt columnists in the country."

"Oh, sure, blunt as hell. Clever, funny, pointed—real iconoclasts. They can lampoon the bosses a certain amount, and it reassures the country that all's well with democracy. Court jesters twigging the king. The king likes a little of that, don't you see. Within limits, of course. But I guarantee you, if my honest opinions were to appear miraculously in an issue of my paper, I'd be out on the streets looking for a job within twenty-four hours."

"Is it really that bad?"

Pete laughed bitterly. "Ask the young journalism graduates, and they'll tell you I'm fulla crap. They'll say I'm just another burned-out old newshound sounding off. But get the veterans alone, Ed, and get them trusting you, and you'll hear a different story."

"Perhaps you and others like you could start a newspaper of your own", Ed suggested tentatively.

"Say, that's a great idea! Can you lend me ten million dollars? I'll pay you back. I promise."

Thoroughly chastened, Ed kept silent.

"My mission in life, as I interpret it, is to fawn at the feet of mammon. Ah, but I've learned to fawn with such dignity. I sell the country for my daily bread. I'm a jumping jack. They pull the strings, and I dance. Take a good look at me, Ed. Memorize the face. I'm an intellectual prostitute."

Ed leaned forward. "No, you're not", he said severely. "That's a lie."

Pete shrugged, raised his arms, and dropped them in a gesture of helplessness.

"I don't think I can help your lost lady. Not if what's happened to her is connected to shadows. You can't fight shadows, and even if I did try to box with them, what would that do for her? It might just push them to get rid of her. No one would ever see her again."

"There is another possibility. If we make a loud enough noise, it might just start a snowball rolling, might arouse the public, put the shadows on the defensive. That's what light does, Pete, it pushes back the shadows. If we throw enough light onto this case, it could arouse so much public outcry that the quiet revolution would feel threatened by the scandal. They might release her, in order to demonstrate that all is well with democracy."

"You could be signing this woman's death warrant."

"Not if we prove that the government took her and kept her and now cannot or will not explain her disappearance. We can do it."

"Hey, Ed, you're quite a genius at agitprop." Pete ordered another drink and mused over it for some minutes. Ed let him play with the idea. He looked at the ebony demons and thought to himself, two times two times two *always* equals eight.

Finally Pete looked up. "Oh, what the hell, I'll see what I can do."

"Wonderful, wonderful!" Ed reached out and clamped Pete's hand in his own. "God bless you for it."

"I'm not promising anything. And you can be sure if I can get something into the papers, it won't be under my by-line."

"That's fine. It's the exposure we need."

Ed drove Pete uptown and dropped him at the lobby of the Lord Elgin Hotel, a few blocks south of the War Memorial. Pete said he had agreed to meet a lady friend there. Ed felt disapproval but kept it to himself.

"I'll phone you tomorrow sometime", Pete promised.

"Don't call me at my Commons office. How about we have lunch together?" Pete suggested they meet at the McDonald's on the Mall. Ed knew it was across the street from the nation's most infamous abortuary and shuddered, but he realized that the noon hour pedestrian traffic would be heavy. Good cover.

When he let himself into his apartment shortly after eleven, he saw that Marjorie had already gone to bed. She had left a note on the kitchen table:

> Meatloaf and potato in the fridge.
> Put it in the microwave for 3 minutes.
> Can't keep my eyes open.
> Fill me in on the details in the morning.
> I prayed. I love you, Eddie.
> M.

He put on his slippers and dark blue cardigan while the food was warming up and tried to eat some of it but couldn't. Then he went into the living room, turned on a lamp by his reclining chair, and sat down. He closed his eyes and sighed, rubbing his face. *Old,* he thought. *I'm getting old.* He told himself that he had good reason to be tired. In all of his sixty years he had never before experienced a day so crammed with unusual events.

Then, remembering that he had skipped his morning prayer time in the rush to get to the office, he pulled his family Bible onto his lap, a large leather-bound volume bequeathed to him by his grandfather.

He prayed for protection for Beth Potter and for Peter Stanford, for himself and Marjorie and all the family. He prayed for Ted and his children. He asked for wisdom.

"Dear Jesus," he whispered, "you have put me into the path of the adversary, and I ask you to make me fit for this battle. Be my shield and strength. Confound the enemy with this your small servant. I'm so tired, Lord, and I'm not strong. Nor am I smart at this politics business. Please grant me the grace to know and do your divine will."

Then, with an increasing sense of peace, he found his bookmark at the passage in Isaiah, chapter 8, where he had last been reading. These were the words he read:

> Call not alliance what this people calls alliance, and fear not, nor stand in awe of what they fear. But with the Lord of hosts make your alliance—for him be your fear and your awe.

Slowly, he read them over again, savoring the new meaning they now seemed to hold. New meaning and confidence. Where was that passage he had seen just recently, the one about waiting in patience for the coming of the Lord? His fingers seemed drawn to it like a magnet—James, chapter 5:

> Come now, you rich, weep and wail over your impending miseries. Your wealth has rotted away, your clothes have become moth-eaten, your gold and silver have corroded, and that corrosion will be a testimony against you; it will devour your flesh like fire. You have stored up treasure for the last days. Behold, the wages you withheld from the workers who harvested your fields are crying aloud, and the cries of the harvesters have reached the ears of the Lord of hosts. You have lived on earth in luxury and pleasure; you have fattened your hearts for the day of slaughter. You have condemned, you have murdered the righteous one; he offers you no resistance.
>
> Be patient, therefore, brothers, until the coming of the Lord. . . . Make your hearts firm, because the coming of the Lord is at hand.

* * *

Over breakfast Ed gave Marjorie a brief outline of the situation, omitting Pete's name. He also refrained from mentioning the deaths of the American legislators but described the Potter case in detail. She looked worried and begged him not to succumb to the temptation to bolster his energy with stimulants.

"Remember that stomach of yours", she warned him. "I'll be praying", she said as he went out the door.

Forgetting the time zones, he phoned Dot in Fort George and apologized for dragging her out of bed at that hour of the morning. She told him that she had called all the churches in the area—there were an incredible number of them, she pointed out—and many of the pastors had agreed to attend a meeting that would be held tonight at the Potters' church. He asked her to put together a press release on Beth's disappearance and send it by fax to every newspaper in the province, no matter how small. A few preliminary phone calls to reporters might help, he suggested. When she hung up, he was startled to hear the faint double click on the line.

He then dialed the number of a rug-cleaning company in the capital, made an appointment to have the broadloom at the apartment cleaned, hung up, and listened. A double click. Realizing that his own line was now being tapped, he walked down the hall to the whip's office, explained the click problem to him, and asked if he could make a call or two. There were no double clicks on the whip's line. The whip offered to call Parliament Security and have Ed's line checked but figured it wouldn't do much good, because snoop technicians could tap in practically anywhere in the system, and it would be a nightmare trying to catch them, especially if they worked for the system.

Ed called Pete's office, reconfirmed with him their lunch appointment, and hung up. No double click. That was a blessing, he said to himself.

At noon he walked out of the West Block into a freak shower of snow flurries. He pulled his duffle parka tight, buttoned his collar, and walked the one block south to the Mall. Saying a prayer for the closing of the abortuary across the street, he went into McDonald's and found Pete huddled over a cup of coffee in a corner, his back to the door.

"Wanna Big Mac?" Pete asked. "Not as exotic as last night's feast, but it'll keep body and soul together."

"No, thanks", Ed replied, smiling wanly. "Have you had a chance to work on the case?"

"No. I've been working on my resumé all morning. If I'm lucky, I might be able to land a job on the *Daily Grunt and Bugle* in Upper Moose Pelvis, Saskatchewan."

Ed didn't smile.

"Any news about the disappearing lady?" Pete asked.

"Nothing so far. I've arranged for press releases in B.C., and my constituency office organized a meeting of the pastors of lower mainland churches tonight. If they respond, they may light a fire under the pews and make Ottawa very, very nervous."

"Those are mighty comfortable pews, Ed. I wouldn't count on too much."

"We'll see. In the meantime, my phone line's been tapped."

"You're kidding!"

"Wish I were."

Pete bit into his hamburger, eyebrows furious. "It's a good sign, Ed", he said with a full mouth. "Nah, a really *great* sign."

"You think so?"

"Uh-huh. It means we've made someone very, very nervous. It means we're right on track."

"Any progress with media exposure?"

Pete's face grew sphynxlike. "A little. The lady I met last night at the Lord Elgin is on the national desk of a TV network. She isn't promising much, but she's going to talk to a few people on the quiet and see if something can't be slipped in. We'll see how your moment in the sun during today's Question Period goes and take it from there."

"Anything else?"

"Possibilities. I still have some friends in the trade, and I hope to cash in a few poker chips. Call in some favors. You know, the usual despicable garbage."

Ed thought it best to leave Pete's business to Pete.

At five before two, Ed walked through the tunnel to the Centre Block and took his seat in the House. There was just barely a quorum that day—most of the opposition members were present, but the government party seats were practically deserted, except for the Deputy Minister of Justice, who kept glancing across the great divide toward Ed. The Deputy Minister's face was absolutely blank.

When the Speaker opened the floor, Ed stood up. Not a single member on his side of the House stood. The moment was his.

"The Member for Fort George-Dewdney."

"Thank you, Mr. Speaker. I would like to address this question to the Deputy Minister of Justice in the absence of the Minister. Can he tell this House and the people of Canada if his department has been able to locate Mrs. Beth Potter of Steelhead, British Columbia?"

The Deputy Minister rose. "Mr. Speaker, in response to the question from the Member for Fort George-Dewdney, and to his inquiry on the same subject during yesterday's Question Period: At the request of the Minister, I have conducted a thorough investigation into the matter, and we are happy to report that, contrary to the suggestion made yesterday in the House by the honorable member, Mrs. Potter is not presently detained in any facility under the authority of this department."

The Deputy Minister sat down.

Ed stood. "A supplementary question, Mr. Speaker: Can the Deputy Minister tell me whether or not Mrs. Potter was detained for any period of time, however brief?"

"Yes, Mr. Speaker", the Deputy Minister replied. "I can tell him. The woman was detained by the R.C.M.P. for an hour of questioning, then released. Her present location is unknown to us, and I believe that since she is now in her own custody, the matter is one that pertains to the private life of citizens and is therefore no longer an issue that need concern the House."

Ed wasn't sure what to reply to that. He wasn't sure if he had the right to reply. He was flustered and confused. Dare he irritate the Speaker? Were members allowed to do that? And yet no other member stood to sweep the Question Period in other directions. All eyes in the opposition parties were on him.

But what were they thinking, Ed wondered with a jolt of anxiety. Were they asking themselves if he, a raw, green back-bencher, an amateur politician, had parlayed an unwieldy coalition of parties for the purposes of drawing some attention to himself? Did they think that the Potter case was, after all, just a mere nothing, a tempest in a teapot? And if so, surely they would be angry at being used, at being deflected from their ordinary work, from their own constituents' problems, just to support a question that was based on unfounded suspicions. Most of all, they would be angered by the egg that had splattered them all. The Minister had answered clearly and cordially. The matter was settled.

Curiously the anxiety faded to nothing, and Ed felt a current of resolve harden within himself. Everything Pete Stanford had told him the night before flashed through his mind, and the sound of double clicking echoed in his ears. He stood.

"Mr. Speaker, I have documented evidence that the person in question is, in fact, still in the custody of the Department of Justice. I—"

"The member will restrict himself to questions", the Speaker interjected.

"Thank you, Mr. Speaker. I wish to ask the Deputy Minister of Justice to restate his answer. Is he absolutely positive that his department claims no knowledge of her present whereabouts?"

"Mr. Speaker, that is not a question. I have already answered his question. Her Majesty's government has gone to great lengths to investigate his question of yesterday, and the matter has been resolved conclusively. I would remind the Member for

Fort George-Dewdney that this is not the place for cheap publicity stunts—"

The House began to roar. Shouts from the opposition side hurled across the great divide.

"Order! Order!" the Speaker commanded.

"I had hoped to avoid embarrassment for the opposition parties", the Deputy Minister went on. "I had especially hoped to avoid public embarrassment for the family of the woman. But since the member is pressing me on this matter, I must unfortunately point out that the constituent he is defending at national expense is a suspect in a fraud case. She and her husband were involved in an attempt to defraud the health-care system of the Province of British Columbia. She was released in her own custody, pending an inquiry. Local law enforcement in British Columbia is preparing to lay charges. If she has disappeared, I can only assume she has decided to embark upon a flight from justice. This would, I believe, be consistent with the character of people who lie and steal—"

Ed leaped to his feet and shouted, "You are assassinating this woman's character! You are presuming her guilty without a fair hearing!"

"Order! Order! The member for Fort George-Dewdney will please be seated."

Shouts and a dying rumble from the opposition were met with more demands for order.

"Thank you, Mr. Speaker", the Deputy Minister went on. "If the member has, as he suggests, documentary evidence on this matter, this department would like to see it."

He sat down.

A rare silence ensued. Several members from the other opposition parties were frowning at Ed. Ed felt thoroughly deflated.

The leader of his party had sat through the preceding events, observing it all with calm, cool eyes. Ed felt certain that he would not be asked to run in the next election. They might even offer him a plane ticket home, right now, which Ed thought he would gratefully accept.

"Mr. Speaker," Ed's leader said in a strong, clear voice, "I address this question to the Deputy Minister of Justice in the absence of the Prime Minister and the Minister of Justice." He paused and gazed around the House, then turned back toward the Deputy Minister and fixed him with a penetrating stare.

"Where is Beth Potter? The government took her, and they haven't given her back—"

"Order! Order!"

"Where is she?"

The Deputy Minister threw his hands in the air and stomped from the House. The Speaker took over and instructed the members to move on to other questions.

Marjorie phoned Ed an hour later while he was puttering aimlessly at his office desk.

"Oh, Eddie, I saw it all on cable. You were terrific, darling! Just terrific. I managed to get a video cassette into the machine, but I missed some of it. I'll have copies made and send them to the children. They'll be so proud. I'm proud too."

"Thanks, honey", Ed mumbled. The extravagant praise did little to raise his spirits.

She blew him an electronic kiss, which was followed by two damnable clicks.

He sent Miss Theriault out later in the afternoon to collect newspapers, and upon her return he went through them carefully. It was too early for there to be anything about the Potter case, but he hoped to find signs of the government preparing the public for a potential scandal. There wasn't a hint of that, and he supposed they believed they had successfully put out an insignificant spot-fire.

However, on the evening news journal of a major network, there was a two-minute info-bite about the case, including a twenty-second clip of the Deputy Minister's urbane, sneering rebuttal and a shot of Ed looking glum and foolish in his seat at the House. The woman reporter approached it from the angle of, my, how our elected representatives do cavort. Then a quick shot to an interview with a health official in B.C., a grave, fatherly looking man who gave details of the pending charges and told the interviewer that it was time to crack down on abuse of the health-care system. Honest citizens could no longer be expected to pay for the dishonesty of others when the security of the system itself was lamentably weak.

Ed and Marjorie groaned, realizing what the network had done with the story. Marjorie's lips tightened dangerously, and she got up to switch off the television.

"Leave it, Marj", Ed said. "If they're going to shaft us, let's see the whole thing."

Then, to their surprise, the commentator directed her beautiful eyes straight into the cyclops eye of the camera and said:

"Reliable sources on Parliament Hill inform us that there is documented evidence that the government detained the missing woman and cannot or will not adequately explain where she is. The outcry in the House of Commons this afternoon will not be the last we hear of the case. 'The Government took her,' said a spokesperson for the opposition parties, 'and they haven't given her back.'"

The woman held the audience with a two-second pause and concluded with all the power of her gender, "*Where* is Beth Potter?"

Ed and Marjorie looked at each other and smiled.

Five minutes later the phone rang. The caller didn't identify himself, but Ed recognized the voice. It was Peter Stanford.

"Sometimes a pawn will fall off the chessboard", Pete said, and hung up.

* * *

The pastors' meeting was held in the basement of the Salvation Evangelical Tabernacle in Fort George at seven-thirty that evening, Pacific standard time. The fluorescent lights were too bright, buzzing loudly until they warmed up. The conversation among the twenty-one pastors was buzzing as well, and the promising coffee smells coming from the industrial strength urn in the hall kitchen put everyone in a perky mood. Most of the pastors had met each other before, and as they sat chatting, trying to compare notes on what they had managed to learn of Beth's disappearance, there developed a sense of common purpose. Few of them neglected to use the words "the Lord", and "pray". They were seated in a large circle of folding chairs around a low table on which a Bible lay open beside a burning candle.

Pastor Bob, the host and the head of the Potters' congregation, noted that there were four other evangelical ministers from around the valley, one Lutheran (brown shirt with Roman collar), three Catholic priests (black shirts with Roman collars), two Pentecostals, three Mennonites, a Free Evangelical, two Baptists, one Presbyterian, and one very uncomfortable lady from a new congregation called the Reformed United Church. No one was exactly sure whether the term *reformed* meant she was a liberal or a conservative. There was a single "high-church" Anglican in a cassock, who looked more Roman than the papists, and a "low-church" Anglican who had just arrived in town. The latter was a man in his mid-thirties who was married, had seven children, and was the owner of a pair of Birkenstock sandals, a light gray shirt with Roman collar, a charcoal gray tweed jacket with leather elbow patches, a divinity degree from Oxford, and a shy, winning smile. It was rumored that he was more conservative than the Archbishop of Canterbury and more pentecostal than the several other charismatics present. Most of the silent speculation in the room focused on him and the lady pastor from the Reformed United.

Ted Potter and his lawyer were also present. Ted looked as if he hadn't slept in three days. His eyes were red, and he swept a cowlick off his forehead every few minutes.

Pastor Bob called the meeting to order and asked the low Anglican to lead them all in a prayer. The young man stood up and prayed aloud from the heart in flowing, impassioned, articulate language. A chorus of *Amens* sounded throughout the hall.

Pastor Bob then called on Ted's lawyer to give an account of what had happened to the Potter family. The lawyer looked so young that several in the room wondered if he had graduated from high school. For a moment they were worried. But when he spoke, it was evident that inside the boyish appearance there was a brilliant mind and a man's character. He explained the sequence of events in detail to the hushed audience, then went on to inform them of recent developments in the law and civil rights test cases. Then he described the legwork he had done in Vancouver, the phone calls, the letters he had sent to various government agencies, painting a vivid portrait of the stonewalling he had encountered. His presentation took the better part of forty minutes, and no one interrupted.

There was a generalized shifting of body language and some coughing after he sat down.

"Any questions?" the lawyer asked, looking around the circle.

The first questions probed the very real problem of why the Potters had tried to fool the staff at the hospital. Ted bent over and put his face in his hands. The lawyer explained that Beth and Ted had made a mistake. It was a hasty decision, prompted by their concern for the safety of the child with the appendix problem. The boy was the victim of a series of suspicious moves on the part of the government. Once again the lawyer explained the new emergency powers of the federal government, emphasizing that it now appeared that more than one citizen had fallen through the cracks in the rising climate of fear. He cited an article in this week's edition of the newspaper of the Roman Catholic archdiocese of Vancouver, recounting the disappearance of a certain Father Andrei. The archbishop had demanded a response from the government, and the feds had countered with the same kind of denials they were now using in the Potter case. Furthermore, the archbishop's concerns had received no exposure in the secular media, which was remarkable, considering the facts of that case.

The lawyer then went on to say that the boy had witnessed some illegal acts by government agents, and under the circumstances the Potters had felt he might be in danger if he were identified and taken into custody. They thought there was a possibility that someone in the government was intent on silencing him, and thus they made the only decision they felt was open to them at the time.

There was more silence after that, during which it was obvious that every pastor was immersed in his own private thoughts, trying to match the lawyer's account with his own reading of current events. Things looked as if they would degenerate into an impasse. Pastor Bob stood up and invited everyone to take a break. Coffee was being served on the tables by the kitchen, he said. Help yourself, please, everyone. Shaking themselves as if they had been asleep, some of the men got up and ambled over to the coffee urn in groups of twos and threes, talking quietly.

The young Anglican minister, Father Ron, and Pastor Bob went over to Ted and his lawyer. Ted made an effort to acknowledge their words of encouragement, but it was a losing battle. Trying to control his emotions, he walked off in the direction of the men's washroom.

The lawyer and the three ministers made half-hearted attempts at discussion, but clearly there was a feeling that things weren't going well. The specter of a totalitarian state was just too outlandish for most of the people in the room.

Finally, Father Ron broke the spell. He turned to the lawyer and said, "I think your analysis of the situation is right on. One hundred percent right on. I've been praying a lot lately, asking the Lord for insight into what seems to be shaping up. I'm hearing some pretty strong words from heaven."

Pastor Bob smiled at him. "I heard about the fires at your Baal-pit, Ron. Pretty strong stuff. Think you can handle it?"

Father Ron returned the smile. "I think so, with the guidance of the Holy Spirit. By the way, Bob, did I see an eerie light in your backyard last Sunday evening?"

Pastor Bob colored and grinned. "Maybe you did, maybe you did. Don't tell anyone."

"My lips are sealed", Father Ron shot back conspiratorially.

The young Anglican glanced back and forth between them. "What are you two guys talking about?"

Father Ron and Pastor Bob laughed and invited him to stay after the meeting. They promised they would tell him the whole story when the others went home.

At that point a woman's voice broke in. "May I join you?"

It was the lady from the Reformed United.

Introductions were made all around.

"I know you're probably wondering about me", she said. "I want you to know I've felt for a long time that things are going wrong with people, seriously wrong. I see it on the streets. I read about it in the papers. And worst of all, I see it in my own congregation."

The other ministers nodded. "We see it in ours too", said Father Ron.

She turned to Ted's lawyer. "We're a mixed bag of theology here, but I don't think there's a person here tonight who hasn't been moved by Beth's story. Some of us may have doubts about certain details, about how things have been interpreted. But all of us, I believe, have a sense that what you've told us is basically the truth. We've got a problem here that's going to affect all of us, and I suspect it's much bigger than we imagine. Perhaps when coffee break is over, you could suggest some practical ways we can respond."

The lawyer thanked her and told her he would do just that.

The pastors were taking their seats again when the hall door opened and a small elderly woman hobbled slowly in, supported by a cane. She shuffled and tapped her way across the room, every eye upon her. She nodded at the young Anglican minister and sat down beside him.

"Hello, Mrs. Briggs-Smythe!" he greeted her.

"Hello there, everyone", she replied. "I took a taxi. Guess I got the time all mixed up. Am I too late for the fun?"

The Anglican minister smiled at her and said, no, she wasn't too late for the fun.

Father Ron recognized her as the mother of the older Anglican minister he had met at the Potter farm several months before. She was a small woman, blessed with twinkling eyes, many wrinkles, and a sweet smile. Her white hair was tied in a bun, topped by a frumpish hat with shiny black pins sticking out at odd angles. She wore overlarge, uncomfortable, brown pumps, wool stockings the color of Band-aids, a flowered print dress that might have been stylish in the 1940s, and a cameo at her lacy throat. She looked like a pin cushion, Father Ron thought. No, a human tea-cosy.

"Is Canon Briggs-Smythe coming?" the young Anglican asked her.

"I wanted to give him your message about the meeting", she replied shamefacedly. "But I forgot. I don't think it makes any difference, though, because he couldn't have come tonight anyway. Thursday's his Lodge meeting, you know."

The young Anglican's face went very still, expressionless. All conversation in the room suddenly ceased.

"I'm sure he'll be disappointed when he hears I forgot to tell him. But he'll be very pleased that I came in his stead."

She looked around the room. "You can tell me what it's all about, dears. Don't worry, I'll pass on anything you want me to tell him."

She smiled at them all in such a motherly way, with an expression so good and kind and so utterly naïve that several of the pastors looked in other directions, pulling a veil of charity over the appalling revelation.

"Uh, Mrs. Briggs-Smythe," the young Anglican said, "which lodge does your son belong to?"

"Oh, my dear, I can never remember what he calls it. But he did say something about being thirty-three degrees. That must be one of their games or projects. They have so many projects. They do a lot of fund-raising for children's hospitals, I think."

Mrs. Briggs-Smythe was very proud of her son, who was evidently the low Anglican's superior. The young Anglican began to feel very low indeed.

Ted returned from the washroom, drying his eyes, and sat down by himself, staring at the floor.

Pastor Bob cleared his throat.

"I think we'll get started again." He glanced down at Mrs. Briggs-Smythe, who was looking up at him in a most unsettling way, her entire demeanor exuding interest and approval.

He cleared his throat again.

The young lawyer rushed to his assistance. "Pastor Bob, considering the situation, might I offer some more information about the precise limits of federal, provincial, and municipal laws?"

"Yes, please do." Pastor Bob sat down. The lawyer stood up and for the next fifteen minutes delivered a mind-numbing dissertation on statutes and precedent cases. By the end of it, the old woman was asleep in her chair, her head resting on the young Anglican's shoulder. He smiled at the group and whispered, "Let's get on with business. Tactics."

During the next hour it was unanimously agreed that each of

the pastors would return to his congregation and strongly exhort his people to get involved. They would try to spark a letter-writing and phone campaign and a word-of-mouth grass-roots revival that would, God willing, keep on gathering momentum until it shook the nation. They would urge their congregations in the strongest possible terms to badger the media about the disappearance of Beth Potter until they had to cave in and give the story the exposure it deserved. If the media refused, the pastors promised to urge their people to cancel subscriptions and inaugurate boycotts. Combined, members of their congregations numbered in the tens of thousands. That would mean a sizable loss of revenue to the press. It might work. *If* they could get their congregations to respond.

When the meeting ended, people took their time leaving, drank more coffee, and seemed aroused by a quiet sense of purpose. The young Anglican asked Father Ron if he could take a rain check on the Baal-pit story, then gently woke up Mrs. Briggs-Smythe and drove her home.

* * *

On Friday morning Ed Burgess arrived at his office in the West Block shortly after eight, just in time to catch the tail end of a long scroll of paper purring out of the fax machine beside Miss Theriault's desk. It was a report from Ted's lawyer, detailing the exact chronology of the Potter case, written in impressive legalese.

When his secretary arrived, he asked her to make photocopies for every opposition member and instructed her to hand deliver them before Question Period.

"Oh, Monsieur, it is very hard, because Question Period is in the morning on Fridays. But I will do my best."

True to her word, she did her best. And when Ed walked into the House, several of the members on the opposition side gave him the thumbs-up sign, even a few who were traditionally his party's most vitriolic opponents. His party's platform was conservative, theirs libertarian, but it seemed they had found common ground in their opposition to the government's questionable civil rights amendments—which Ed's leader called "soft totalitarianism" and the libertarians called "crypto-fascism".

The Speaker opened the session, and once again, to the government's surprise, not a single member stood to be recognized.

The Speaker's eyes glanced up and down the rows of the opposition side.

"This is most unusual", he said. "Am I to conclude that there are no questions the honorable members of Her Majesty's opposition parties wish to address to the government? If there are no questions today, then Question Period will be closed until Monday."

Ed stood up. The Speaker hesitated a moment before recognizing him.

"The member for Fort George-Dewdney."

"Mr. Speaker, I address this question to the Prime Minister. Can he tell me if his Department of Justice has made any progress in its investigation into the whereabouts of Mrs. Beth Potter of Steelhead, British Columbia?"

The Prime Minister, after a swift glance at the television cameras, stood. "Mr. Speaker, I was not in the House yesterday, due to my meeting with the Vice President of the United States. However, the Minister of Justice has drawn to my attention the facts of the case and also described the discussion in the House during yesterday's Question Period. The answer to the member's question is, the Department of Justice has no knowledge of the aforesaid person's whereabouts. A thorough investigation was conducted, and it was found that after questioning by regional law enforcement officers, the woman was released. If she has disappeared, the government, of course, wishes to express sympathy to her family. However, it is clear that her disappearance is not a situation involving criminal activity. People regularly disappear in a country as large as ours, and they usually do so for personal reasons. I do not think this is a matter that comes under the purview of the federal government. I would remind the honorable member that this question has already been answered satisfactorily by the Deputy Minister of Justice."

The Prime Minister sat down.

Ed stood up. "Mr. Speaker, I would like to thank the Prime Minister for his forthright reply. However, since yesterday's sitting of the House, I have received documented evidence that Mrs. Potter was detained by federal agents, without recourse to her civil rights, and that she has not yet been released."

After a stunned silence, the government side began to rumble and throw comments across the floor.

The Prime Minister stood. "In the interests of justice, I would like to see this documentation, and if there is any indication in it that the honorable member's constituent has been denied her civil rights, I will initiate further investigation."

Ed stood. "Mr. Speaker, I wish to table the documentation before the House."

The Speaker nodded, and a clerk came up the aisle to Ed's desk. Ed handed him the notarized dossier.

From the corner of his eye, Ed saw his party leader writing a note, five desks away. The leader signalled to a young page, who brought the note to Ed.

On the note was written: "P.M. is a talented actor. Cool as a cucumber, but he's nervous. Press him hard."

Ed stood.

"The Member for Fort George-Dewdney."

"Mr. Speaker, a supplementary question to the Prime Minister: As the tabled documents will clearly demonstrate, there has been a grave suspension of civil rights on numerous occasions. This is a growing phenomenon. It is becoming a pattern—"

"Order! Does the member have a question?"

"Yes, Mr. Speaker. I ask the Prime Minister why, during the past two months, there have been more than a dozen incidents of this nature throughout the country."

The government backbenchers erupted into loud catcalls: "Shame! Shame! Innuendo! Slander! You have no proof!"

"Order! Order!" the Speaker raised his voice.

The Prime Minister stood. "The Minister of Justice will examine the member's documents and see if there is any truth to his allegation. There are twenty-eight million people in this country and many thousands of employees of the various agencies of the Justice Department. If there is evidence of misdemeanor or mistakes resulting in discomfort to citizens, the offending civil servants will be facing an inquiry. Is the member satisfied with that?"

Ed stood. "I will not be satisfied, nor will the people of this nation be satisfied, until the missing persons detained by the government (loud catcalls and desk thumping from every side)—"

"Order! Order!"

"—until *all* missing persons have had their liberty restored." Ed paused, stared intensely at the Prime Minister and shouted, "*Where* is Beth Potter?"

The ensuing uproar took five minutes to quell, and three members (one from the government side and two from opposition parties) were escorted from the House by the Sergeant at Arms.

When he was finally able to make his voice heard, the Speaker insisted that the question had been adequately answered and informed the members in the House that he would not allow any more discussion on the matter until the government had an opportunity to examine the documents.

Ed stood. The Speaker did not recognize him. No other members stood. Ed remained on his feet for several minutes, waiting, unrecognized, while a disgruntled tension built among the members. The Speaker appeared to be reading a document that a page had handed to him.

The feisty leader of the libertarian party stood. The Speaker recognized her.

"Mr. Speaker, I address this question to the Prime Minister: Where is Beth Potter?"

More uproar.

The Speaker instructed the Prime Minister that he need not answer the question and asked the woman to leave the House. She refused, and the Speaker instructed the Sergeant at Arms to escort her out.

Ed's leader stood. "Mr. Speaker, Where *is* Beth Potter?"

The leader of the official opposition stood: "Mr. Speaker, *Where* is Beth Potter?"

The leader of yet a third opposition party stood. "Mr. Speaker, Where is *Beth Potter?* "

But by then the Prime Minister had stormed from the House, and the Speaker closed the Commons for the day.

* * *

Ed and Marjorie watched the evening news on a major network and were delighted to see a thirty-second replay of the worst of the shouting and screaming that had occurred during Question Period. The commentator treated it as a joke but concluded with, "Some are calling it antics in the fun house, some call it the zoo, but the question raised today by all opposition parties remains: Where is Beth Potter?"

The other networks did not mention the antics or the missing person.

On Saturday, Ed left the apartment and braved a freezing rain, drove to the Chateau Laurier, and bought copies of every paper sold in the smoke shop. One Ottawa paper, a populist working man's daily that habitually enriched its editions with bikini-clad beauties and scandal stories, printed an amusing account of yesterday's doings in the House on page six, beneath a half-page story about the city's ongoing bus strike.

A small conservative Christian weekly came out with a special edition that soberly described the case, giving it four pages. Ed had sent them a copy of the dossier by courier on Friday morning.

An equally small libertarian journal, distinctive for its hard-hitting political commentary, biting sarcasm, and black humor, ran a full-page editorial on page three, under a trick composite photo of the Prime Minister's snarling face superimposed on a muscle-boy's body, wearing nothing more than a leopard-skin bikini and sunglasses. He was portrayed on a field of snow, valise in hand, nose to nose with a surprised-looking polar bear. The headline: "P.M. Promises to Investigate Rumors about Canadian Gulag". Beth Potter was mentioned twice; Ed's question in the House was quoted. Three other missing persons were named, including an editor from a small-town paper in the interior of B.C., an investigative reporter from northern Manitoba, and a Catholic priest, all of whom had been missing for months.

Ed suspected that the journal had been contacted by Peter Stanford.

One of the Vancouver dailies printed a short, newsy article on page twelve about a woman who was missing from the lower mainland area of the province, but it did not mention the uproar in the House of Commons. It said only that she was wanted by police for questioning in a fraud case. The photo of Beth that ran with the story was not helpful. She looked mean and worn, her stringy hair in need of a wash, eyes burdened. The sort of woman you would expect to write bad checks or stuff pipe bombs with gelignite. Weeks later Ted told Ed that the photo was definitely from Beth's driver's license; she had posed for it two years before, after staying up all night nursing Li'l Dan through the measles.

Only one of the Toronto dailies carried the story, an op-ed piece, quarter page, written by the man with whom Pete had gone kayaking. The column was primarily concerned with civil rights developments in federal legislation, but it described Friday's revolt in the zoo and referred briefly to Beth and the other missing people. The national news section had nothing, nor was there anything by the parliamentary correspondent. There was nothing about the case in any of the other dailies. Searching through Pete's paper, Ed found an item under Pete's by-line on reactions among Ottawa's diplomatic community to revisions of the North American Free Trade Agreement. The article was a model of objectivity, weighing the arguments from both sides and ending inconclusively.

On Saturday evening, a priority courier dropped off a package at the apartment. It was from Dot and contained three of the small-town papers that were published in the vicinity of Fort George. One of them trumpeted a banner headline on page one: "Steelhead Woman Missing: Local Pastors Accuse Federal Government of Complicity". There were more articles about the case on the inside pages, none of them offering conclusive proof, but all of them detailing the not inconsiderable circumstantial evidence. The other two papers treated the story in the same way, one going so far as to publish a half-page opinion piece by a priest in Fort George (Ed vaguely remembered meeting him at the Potters' and winced ever so slightly when he recalled a fire the priest had lit in the parish parking lot). But the article was noninflammatory and concluded with the question, Where is Beth Potter? There was a column on the religion page, written by the Potters' pastor, lambasting the character assassination of a member of his flock who was, he maintained, an honest citizen. His wording was not as erudite as the priest's, but the message was the same, and it also concluded with, "Where is Beth Potter?"

Ed thought it was a fairly significant victory. Combined, the three papers probably had about thirty or forty thousand sub-scribers. It was a start.

* * *

After the Sunday morning service at Salvation Evangelical Tab-ernacle, Pastor Bob invited Ted and his cluster of subdued chil-dren downstairs to the hall for the regular coffee and donut hour. Ted had wept quietly throughout the service, trying not to humiliate his kids. He was very depressed, but during the get-together afterward (attended by more than a hundred members of the congregation), he was buoyed somewhat by the many people who came up to him with words of encouragement, Scripture quotes, and small sealed envelopes that they pushed into his jacket pocket.

Several of the ladies told him they would be dropping off meals later in the day. He was hugged frequently, and everyone made a fuss over the children. The boy lawyer told him that there was no news about Beth as yet, but the public was getting interested. He also told him to forget about retainer fees. A few people showed him the front page with the banner headlines. Pastor Bob gave him a check for five hundred dollars on the quiet, drawn on the church account. Ted thanked everyone with mute nods and drove home in silence, feeling a trickle of hope beginning to run through his despair.

Later that afternoon, he and the kids sat around the television set, watching a children's animated Bible video, the little ones mesmerized by blind Samson's muscular prowess at the pagan temple, Ted and the older ones just watching it, staring for the sake of staring at something other than their own thoughts. The doorbell rang, and Ted answered it. It was the Catholic priest from Fort George—Reverend Ron.

They made uncomfortable passes at conversation for a while, the priest said a few encouraging things, told Ted that he had asked all of his parishioners at the weekend Masses to pray for

Beth and the family and had exhorted them to write to their M.P. and the newspapers. He said that many of the ladies in the parish wanted to know if Ted could use some meals on wheels. Did he have room in his freezer? Ted said to thank the ladies very much, but it looked like the ladies from Salvation Tabernacle had already gone overboard. He didn't know if he and the kids could eat one more chocolate brownie, and there was enough lasagna and shepherd's pie in the freezer to feed them for weeks.

Father Ron declined Ted's offer of coffee, put an envelope on the table, and left. The envelope contained eight hundred and thirty-six dollars and change (collected for the Potter family at all the Masses) and the priest's personal check for five hundred dollars. A bright yellow post-it note was stuck to the check. Ted read:

> From your brothers and sisters in Christ.
> Hope it helps with legal and medical expenses.
> God bless you.
> Fr. Ron and the congregation at Saint George's.

* * *

On Monday afternoon Ed's leader stood in the House to deliver his scheduled speech. It was listed on the Order Papers as an address on the topic of national unity. He read for twenty minutes from his prepared text, weaving in many of the issues that concerned the public, including the dissatisfaction felt by Western farmers, the recent protests by the fishing industry in the Maritime provinces (both of which his party supported), the chronic agitation for Québec sovereignty (which his party opposed), and the problems of implementation of the North American Free Trade Agreement (which his party also opposed). He built to a dramatic climax with an incisive analysis of the working papers of the Committee on Law Reform, whose proposals would be debated by the House next month.

He emphasized that the government's response to the many crises now facing the nation was simplistic. The party in power, he said, was positing an either/or situation. It was telling the people of Canada that they had only two choices: on the one hand, a continuing degeneration into crime and other forms of social "dysfunction" and, on the other hand, an increase in federal control of private life. This was a false choice, he said. In fact it was no choice at all. The government was not thinking creatively, and it clearly did not exhibit much faith in the integrity of the people. It was an insult to their intelligence to be offered only these two unacceptable solutions: social chaos or the growth of a police state.

There were only twelve members of the government party sitting in the House that afternoon, but they managed to create a short-lived ruckus. The Prime Minister and most of his cabinet were absent. The acting Prime Minister looked up from his newspaper, then looked down at it again and resumed reading.

The leader of Ed's party was not perturbed. The television cameras were broadcasting live, as they did every day. The press gallery was a quarter full.

He laid the papers on his desk and said, "Mr. Speaker, I will depart from the prepared text, as there is a need here to underline the foregoing points with solid evidence."

The backbenchers on the opposite side of the House produced loud boos and calls of, "What evidence!", "Shame! Shame!", "Leave the politicking to the hustings!", and "You're off the topic!"

"Order! Order!"

"Thank you, Mr. Speaker. I wish to expand the focus of this address only insofar as it pertains to the topic at hand—national unity."

"The honorable leader of the Coalition Party may proceed", the Speaker replied.

"Mr. Speaker, a nation retains its identity to the degree that it is a federation of persons who willingly agree to work together for common interests, who enjoy equal rights before the law of the land. This is a heritage that untold people have fought for and died for; it has been won and preserved at the cost of great human sacrifice. It cannot be neutered by the stroke of a pen. The people will not tolerate that. A free society will not survive it. We must no longer call the parliamentary system a 'democratic experiment', the term used so frequently and so loosely by this government. This nation's system of government is not a democratic experiment, it is a democratic *necessity*."

Much thumping of desk tops and many cries of approval from the opposition parties.

The leader went on to describe the most questionable aspects of the proposals being formulated by the Committee on Law Reform. He was interrupted by the Speaker, who reminded him that debates on that topic would be held the following month.

The leader begged the Speaker's patience, arguing that these were matters directly related to the topic at hand, and with the Speaker's forbearance he would demonstrate how this was so. The Speaker acquiesced.

For the next fifteen minutes the leader outlined in detail the several abuses of civil rights that had come to his attention during recent weeks. He named more than two dozen people who had simply disappeared during the past year and pointed out that these were citizens who had directly or indirectly found themselves in the path of agencies of the federal government, people who had committed no crimes. Where were they? Where, indeed, was Mrs. Beth Potter of—

The Speaker interrupted him and sternly instructed him to refrain from the topic of Mrs. Potter, a topic that had disrupted the House during the previous two days and that had already been answered by the government.

"Thank you, Mr. Speaker. I will continue without reference to the missing woman. I will continue without reference to the more than two dozen missing persons who have disappeared without explanation after encounters with federal—"

"Order!"

The leader collected his thoughts and began again. "This nation faces many vital issues in the coming years. Not the least of these is the question of Québec sovereignty. The government knows, as do all opposition parties, that the peaceful solution to this constitutional crisis will depend upon the faith that the people of Québec have in the people of Canada. If it is seen that the federal government is quite willing to resort to the Emergency Measures Act, to its War Powers, and to the recent Orders in Council, in order to suppress dissent against its social engineering programs, what will that communicate to the people of Québec about the government's respect for *their* civil rights? I must ask, in addition, why has this government signed several UN Conventions giving virtual override powers to a nonelected organization, granting them the right to supersede the laws of this nation? Why has this government done it, knowing full well that our people do not support such an executive action and do not understand its full implications? I maintain, Mr. Speaker, that this government is engaged in highly questionable activity that has not been approved by the House or Senate and that will destroy the confidence of the people. This is not a question of liberal policies versus conservative policies. This is not a question of opposition parties versus the party in power. This issue is absolutely fundamental. It calls into question the very nature of democratic government and the nature of society itself. Moreover, it calls into question this nation's identity in the international community. If we do not soon begin to address these issues, we may well find that we have become a large carcass, dispatched and quartered, to be consumed by less conscionable nations, desirous of our land and resources. We may wake up some morning and find that we are no nation at all."

He sat down. Loud thumping and many cries of "Hear! Hear!" from the opposition benches. A few scattered *boos* from the government benches. The acting Prime Minister folded his newspaper and walked unconcernedly from the House.

* * *

The major television networks highlighted the speech on the evening news. Some of the West Coast evening papers, three hours behind the east, carried excerpts. It wasn't front page, but it was something. A daily newspaper in Calgary ran it on page two under the headline: "Leader of the Coalition Party Accuses Government of Civil Rights Abuses". The Prime Minister was in New York and unavailable for comment. A hybrid mix of wild and judicious commentary from Québec was quoted.

The next day most of the English-language dailies in the country featured articles on the speech, a majority of them poo-pooing it as right-wing alarmism. All the big papers in Montreal and Québec City devoted serious consideration to it, and their consensus: The problem was real, and Francophone voters should consider it a significant factor in the upcoming federal election.

The French national broadcasting system devoted a half-hour special documentary in prime time to *Le Problème Québec*, and the host, a foreign correspondent for the system, used the missing persons issue liberally. Ordinarily a missing person story (unless it was about a famous missing person) would never achieve more than provincial exposure, let alone reach the foreign media. But more than one Québec paper had collated the curious pattern of disappearing persons, linked it to allegations that the federal government was moving to expand the already broad powers of the State, and related it to the issue of Québec separation. Would the government suppress the civil liberties of

French Canadians in an attempt to prevent the break-up of the nation?

And thus by a quirk of politics, of history, a photo of Beth Potter was seen by an estimated twenty million residents of France. The wires began to hum between Paris and Ottawa and Québec City. Where exactly were the missing Canadians? And what did their absence signify?

Then Reuters picked it up. They treated the story badly, dismissing the allegations as rumors that had been planted by separatist political agitators. But the news spread that not all was well in good old sheep-like British North America. Then the lower levels of the British press picked it up, the most scurrilous of the tabloids screaming that Canada would soon revert to its condition in the 1960s and 1970s, when separatists were bombing mailboxes and kidnapping British consuls. Canada would become the new Nicaragua, the new Chile, the new Iran, with secret police running amuck, plucking women and children and solid citizens off the street like the sons and daughters of the Mad Mothers of the Plaza de Cinco de Mayo. Said one tabloid: It has begun! Now they are even abducting the Mothers!

The hysteria did not help. The establishment press in Britain and Canada published dryly amusing, intelligent, condescending articles about the statements by the inflammatory press, turning *that* into the story, giving plenty of space to the worst of the distortion. A number of them discussed the phenomena of "urban myths" and "millennialist myths", and demonstrated how the pulp press was exploiting a latent mass hysteria for the purpose of financial gain. The establishment media czars accused the junk-press barons of tapping into subconscious neuroses, turning perfectly explainable disappearances into sinister events. It was really a tempest in a teapot, a vast catharsis, an airing of irrational fears. Public reaction to the controversy, they said, displayed all the classic characteristics of myth-making.

The hysteria had not helped, Ed thought to himself a week to the day after Beth's arrest (or abduction). It had simply sparked the establishment reaction that pushed the real story to the sidelines. Both were fuelling a psyche-war that was shunting aside the public's interest in the objective facts of the case. Nevertheless, he reminded himself that more than a hundred million people had now seen Beth Potter's face and were wondering where she was. Perhaps millions were praying for her. He didn't know if there was that much faith left on the earth. But he thought there might be.

On the eighth day after Beth's disappearance, the London *Globe* launched a five-part series of articles titled "Democracy in Transition". The *Globe* was one of the few independent newspapers in England; although it was not the largest of the dailies, it was growing rapidly and was widely read. During its three years of publication it had avoided both establishment condescension and tabloid hysteria. Part one, "The Future of Human Rights in the West", probed the vulnerable points of democratic government, not the least of which was its tendency to overconfidence. Blind faith in its purity of intention, the author argued, weakened its capacity for self-examination. A number of civil rights abuses by Western governments were cited, including cases in Philadelphia, Athens, Milan, Los Angeles, Manchester, Belfast, and British Columbia. The Potter case was examined in detail.

On the tenth day after Beth's disappearance, the largest Paris daily published a page-two story on civil rights in Canada, focusing mainly on the future of French-speaking citizens in that country. Under a quarter-page photo, a caption read:

Qui est Madame Beth Potter? Où est elle?

Ed would have liked the story to spread throughout the world press, but the world had a great many other things to worry about that week. He noted that on the whole journalists tended to focus on numbers, on shock value, on the size of catastrophes, and not on endangered principles. He was pleased, however, to discover a few exceptions.

One of the Dublin dailies published several photos of the missing people (including Beth) under a bold headline:

WHERE ARE THE MISSING CANADIANS?

And a New Delhi daily, *The Star of India*, published an editorial under a headline in the Hindi language:

IS CANADA SAFE?

A REPORT ON THE STATUS OF INDIAN EMIGRANTS

There was no *Daily Grunt & Bugle* in Upper Moose Pelvis, Saskatchewan. Indeed, there was no such place. But in the cities of Moose Jaw and Regina and Saskatoon, there were a series of stories about the missing Manitoba journalist, comparisons made to the known facts of the Potter case, hints about secret "civilian internment camps" in the northern regions of the prairies (no one was quite sure where), and heated editorials demanding accountability from the government. In the last election, Ed's party had won a majority of the federal ridings in that province. That was a help.

The big American networks and newspapers ignored the story. The right-wing patriot journals gave it front-page coverage, shook it like a terrier shakes a rat, and wouldn't let go. The left-wing establishment journals ignored it. A few of the smaller left-wing fringe journals thought they smelled a rat but weren't sure. One anarchist journal was very sure, but its readership numbered 127 subscribers.

Two Catholic "end-times" magazines (subscribers totalling 65,000) mentioned the case in the context of the global development of anti-Christian forces. Three national Catholic papers (readers totalling close to 400,000) published special reports on human rights issues around the world and referred to the Potter case. Approximately 1 percent of American Catholics read about it. The diocesan papers wouldn't touch it. The story was too foreign, too political, too dangerously alarmist. It was much the same with non-Catholic churches. Between 2 and 3 percent of all Protestants in America heard about it.

Staff at Mother Angelica's satellite network read about it in the Irish press. EWTN broadcast a two-hour documentary on the subjects of one-world government, New World Order, and Freemasonry, linking the themes to the new phenomenon of North American missing persons. Several cases were discussed, including Beth's. Three or four million American Catholics watched the program, which was aired repeatedly, five days in a row. EWTN had just been denied its fourth application for a license for cable broadcast into Canada, but a few people in the Great White North had dishes in their backyards. They recorded the program, made duplicate videos, and sent them around to many parishes. It all helped.

But none of it answered the question:

Where is Beth Potter?

17

A Breath of Windigo

On the afternoon of her arrest, Beth was taken to Vancouver in an unmarked police vehicle, riding between two silent men who sat on either side of her in the back seat. Neither they nor the driver would answer any of her questions. She prayed silently all the way in, most of the words a scramble of pleas from the psalms.

"Yea, though I walk through the valley of the shadow of death, I will fear no evil", she repeated to herself.

They arrived at a downtown office building in the city about the time the rush-hour traffic was swarming for its daily exodus.

I will fear no evil, she repeated over and over again, calming her nerves, trying not to cry.

They took her up in a private elevator to a seventh-floor office complex, passed through three security checkpoints, and arrived finally at a long, windowless corridor. There were no signs to indicate the name of the bureau, nor did there appear to be any of the normal bustle of clerical staff—indeed there was no staff. They took her into a small room (this did have windows, overlooking the harbor) and asked her to be seated on one side of a conference desk. Feeling weak in the knees, Beth sat down. The two men took seats across from her. No one said anything for a minute or two until an elderly man entered through a side door and took the seat at the end of the table. The three men regarded her with unreadable expressions.

She asked if she could make a telephone call to her husband.

676

The elderly man said no, perhaps later she might be able to. She asked if she could call a lawyer. Again he said no.

"Why have you brought me here?" she asked in a small, frightened voice.

They didn't answer, just reverted to their intimidating silence, staring at her until she opened her purse, withdrew a linen handkerchief, and began to twist it in her hands. She observed herself doing it, wondering why they wouldn't speak. She couldn't look at them for the longest time, dreading the three pairs of cold, inquiring eyes that seemed to want nothing but to bore into her. As fear began rising in her heart, she tried to counter it with the name of Jesus, which she repeated again and again, soundlessly, the intensity of her cry reaching a climax that would have become a scream if she had opened her mouth.

Were these the people who were looking for Arrow? The very ones who wanted to kill him? That was unreal. Had Alice really got things straight about the death of the nuns and the people at the drug commune? Perhaps these were quite reliable policemen who were simply trying to investigate the crimes and were wondering, naturally enough, if she had been involved in them.

Taking the positive approach, she looked up.

"I . . . I don't know what this is all about. I don't know why I've been brought here. I made a mistake telling the hospital that was my son, but I didn't mean any harm by it. Really, I didn't." Then she began to sob noiselessly, wringing the handkerchief, burying her face in her chest.

They watched her do it, and, when she had collected herself, the elderly man leaned forward.

"Mrs. Potter, I think you had better explain how the boy came to be in your custody."

She dried her eyes, sniffed, and felt some of the fear ebb away. The question seemed to indicate that these were concerned civil servants, professionals, who merely wanted to know what had happened.

"He was just a lost child. He came out of the woods one day and needed help. We don't know much about him, other than his name."

"What is his name?"

"Arrow. That's all I knew—just Arrow."

"You didn't know his last name?" one of the men asked her. She shook her head.

"When did you first see him?"

"The night he had the appendix attack."

"That is extraordinary timing", the elderly man said. "It was fortunate that he wandered out of the woods just as he was about to have an appendix attack."

Beth looked down at her hands. She knew she couldn't lie, but she also knew there was no moral duty to tell them *everything*.

She didn't answer.

The three men said nothing, just kept watching her.

Eventually the elderly man glanced at his wristwatch and said to one of the others. "It's after six. Why don't you ask services to bring a meal for Mrs. Potter."

"Oh, I couldn't eat a thing", Beth erupted. "But if I could have a cup of tea, I would appreciate it."

One of the policemen went out. When he returned with a mug of tea, she sipped at it nervously, trying to bolster her courage.

"Why did you lie to the hospital staff?" the elderly man asked.

"Well," she replied hesitantly, "the boy didn't seem to have a family, and he had no identification. Also, he was in extreme pain. I thought it would be the quickest way to get him looked after by a doctor. You know what red tape is like these days . . ."

678

"Then why didn't you—" one of the younger policemen asked sternly.

The elderly man silenced him with a glance. "I will conduct the interview", he said quietly. "This must be very confusing for you, Mrs. Potter. If you can answer our questions, I think we can see you home to your family in short order."

She nodded gratefully and gave him a flicker of a smile. "I'll try to answer anything you want to know. But I don't know much."

"Can you tell us", the elderly man said pleasantly, "why you did not inform the staff as soon as the boy was out of surgery?"

"I thought . . . I thought . . ."

"What did you think?"

Beth searched for an answer. "I thought he was a child in trouble."

"What do you mean? What sort of trouble?"

"Well, I wondered if he was in some kind of . . . danger."

"What kind of danger?"

"I wasn't sure." (Beth reminded herself that this was true. She *hadn't* been sure at the time. It had crossed her mind that the boy's story might have been a figment of Alice's imagination, produced by too many mystery novels, too much solitude, and the loneliness of an unfulfilled spinster.)

"Mrs. Potter, you must have suspected some kind of danger, if you decided to take such an unusual approach."

"He seemed so unhappy, and lost, and afraid. I suspected that someone might be looking for him . . . to harm him."

"Did you have any idea who that might be?"

"No. There are so many troubled children these days. There are so many abuses."

"This still doesn't explain why you chose not to contact Child Welfare or the police. That would have been the reasonable approach in such a situation, would it not?"

Beth's fear surged again, and her lips trembled. "Yes, I suppose it would have. I guess I wasn't thinking."

"Surely you would have thought of that."

Beth shook her head, and tears welled up.

"You needn't be afraid, Mrs. Potter. Why are you afraid?"

The tears spilled over, and she buried her face in her hands.

"I'm asking you a question. Why are you afraid?"

"Because I don't understand why this is happening. Because I don't understand why I can't call my husband."

The three men exhibited various forms of silent irritation. The elderly man pressed his lips together.

"Were you aware that this boy was the object of a nationwide missing-person investigation?"

She nodded. "I know now", she replied meekly. The three men looked at each other.

"How do you know now?"

"I read about it."

"Where did you read about it?"

"In an old newspaper. Gradually I put two and two together and realized this was the boy who had disappeared."

"Why didn't you contact the police at that point?"

She struggled to find an answer to that. "I was confused."

"You were confused?"

"Yes, I thought it was getting too complicated. I didn't know what had happened to him. I wondered . . ."

"Were you aware that he was the witness to a crime?"

"Yes."

"And is that why you wanted to protect him?"

She looked up and sniffled. "Yes, I suppose that's why. The situation was so unclear. I thought if his name became known, the criminals might track him down and . . . hurt him."

"Oh, I see. Didn't you feel the police would provide sufficient protection for the boy?"

"No."

The three men regarded her soberly. "How did you know he was a witness to a crime?" the elderly man asked.

"I . . . I don't know. Maybe I read it in the paper."

"Why did you think that a private citizen would be able to protect an endangered person better than police agencies?"

"I don't know. I've read about people being hurt, even in prison. Like in *The Godfather*."

The three men smiled grimly.

"You know—like the movie?" Beth raised her eyes hopefully. "The Mafia?"

"Let's return to the question of deceiving the hospital authorities. Were you aware that was an act of fraud?"

Beth's reply burst out in a rush: "I'm afraid I didn't give it much thought. It was an emergency. There was no time to lose. I'm very sorry it happened, and I'm sure my husband and I can take out a loan to pay for the operation. We will, I promise you. We're really sorry for making such a mess of things. I guess I just supposed that the health-care system covers everyone anyway, that it was just a technicality, bookwork. I assumed they would have gone ahead and okayed the operation regardless, and I thought that by giving my son's name it avoided delay. And then after the operation, when I realized he *was* in danger, I didn't know what to do. I just thought I needed more time to think, needed to protect him until the situation was cleared up."

Perched on the edge of her chair, her face anxious, shoulders hunched, cheap purse clutched in her nervous fingers, dressed in a frayed pale-blue winter coat, scuffed running shoes barely touching the floor, she seemed the quintessence of motherly protectiveness. She hoped they would believe her. What she had told them was true enough, and it was no sin to leave out certain details.

"Mrs. Potter," said the elderly man, "I'm afraid I don't find your explanation very believable."

"You don't?" she stammered. "Why not?"

Her question hung in the air like a feather floating slowly downward.

The elderly man looked at one of the other men and said. "See that she's admitted to the special unit."

Beth's face went white.

"What is the special unit?" she cried.

"You have no need to worry", the elderly man said. "It is a temporary detention center. We need to ask you some more questions, and until then—"

"Am I being arrested?" Beth wailed. "Why? What for? I want to call my husband!"

"We will inform your husband."

"I want to phone a lawyer. It's my right!"

No one answered her. The elderly man nodded at one of the agents. The latter took an electronic device from his breast pocket and pressed a button on it. A moment later two women entered and escorted Beth from the room.

It was the most humiliating experience of her life. The women (dressed in nondescript suits, no uniforms or badges) took her down in the elevator, through a series of checkpoints, and into a garage in which a van with tinted windows was parked by a ramp. One of the women took Beth's arm, firmly guided her into the back, and locked the doors. The other sat beside Beth. The passenger section was separated from the front by a wire mesh and a visual blackout screen. The single side-window was tinted, and Beth could see nothing of the passing streets as she was driven out of the city toward somewhere, to-ward nowhere. She cried and prayed and cried all the way, aching for her children, wondering if Ted were going into panic, willing herself to be strong for his sake, assuring herself over and over again that this was a misunderstanding and that as soon as she had told the police what they needed to know, they would let her go back to her family. But in her heart she was not convinced.

"I will fear no evil", she whispered aloud.

An hour after leaving the downtown office, the van stopped, and its doors were opened from the outside, revealing the interior of an underground concrete receiving area. None of the half-dozen women who admitted her to the institution (whatever it was, wherever it was) spoke to her. No one asked questions. No one would reply to hers.

There was another elevator ride upward into a completely sterile, windowless maze, several security gates, barred doors, cold metal walls enamelled white. No signs anywhere, absolutely nothing to hint at the identity of the place. In a small empty room, three women surrounded her and instructed her in a businesslike fashion to disrobe. Beth pulled the lapels of her coat tight together and refused. Stunned, she allowed one of the women to take away her purse.

Another woman, who looked as if she did not tolerate nonsense, said, "You will remove your clothing, or we will be forced to sedate you and remove it by force."

Beth had never been naked in front of any stranger's eyes outside of the delivery room where the babies were born— even then she had been only half naked. Before that, it was only Ted, and before that was the time her mother had changed her pajamas when Beth (age nine) was sick in bed with chicken pox. She thought about Jesus being stripped in front of the eyes of hundreds of cruel mockers, and this helped her to endure it. Then some kind of medical professional (a woman, thank God) came in and did some probing. Beth asked God to give her strength. He did.

She sat in a cell for two days, being fed and watered like a creature in a pet store. The main difference between herself and a budgie bird, she thought, was the absence of bars. She couldn't look out, and customers couldn't look in. The room was clean, and the bed comfortable. Her clothes had been taken away, and she wore only a gray and green cotton jumpsuit. She prayed continuously and repeated Bible passages aloud in the interim. She didn't feel the closeness of the Lord, but her terror gradually eased and an inexplicable calm seeped into her. As she pondered what was happening, it struck her that Alice's analysis of the situation was probably correct. The government was out of line here, greatly out of line, and it was a sign that everything Alice had told her (mystery-mentality or not) just might be on the mark. Beth remembered what Alice had told her about Nick—the meat box at the dump and all the murdered children—murdered by the State. She was beginning to think that the same fate was a very real possibility for her.

She told herself that there was a slim chance she just might make it through the system and be reunited with Ted and the children. She tried to recall passages in Scripture about people who had been miraculously released from impossible situations of imprisonment. She felt vaguely that there were many such stories in the Bible but couldn't put her finger on them—only Peter being released by an angel. But that was a pretty unique event, and she supposed that Roman prisons had been a lot simpler than modern ones.

She wept and trembled, calmed herself, prayed, got angry, got depressed, prayed more, quoted Scripture, resisted the undertow of panic, made mental acts of faith and hope, and gradually arrived at a state of calm acceptance. She worried a little about beatings, but there were none, not a single threat. In fact no one seemed to pay much attention to her whatsoever. Her meals were delivered with frigid impersonality. Her daily trip to the shower room was no more significant than a sheep dip. She worried also about rape, but reminded herself that probably no one would be enticed by a frumpish, overweight woman who had begun to lose her looks 'round about her fourth child, and she had had *seven*, for heaven's sake! The thought of her children made her cry hard. She didn't like the way two of the female guards ogled her undelectable body and smirked whenever she had a shower. But they didn't really bother her with anything other than their devouring eyes. She pitied them. She even managed to say a prayer for them. That wasn't easy, but it helped.

On the morning of the third day, she was taken from the cell and conducted to a room on another floor of the facility. It was a windowless room, barren except for a desk and three seats.

The elderly man entered with a well-dressed middle-aged woman carrying a yellow legal note pad and a tape recorder.

By then Beth had figured out that Alice's version of what had happened was accurate and that if she breathed a word about Alice and Nick, Alice and Nick would disappear. There was nothing she could do about Arrow now, but she could, God willing, contain the damage.

The elderly man and the woman with the yellow pad interrogated her for hours on end, asked her hundreds of questions that seemed to have no bearing on the case. For example, they wanted to know anything she could tell them about her pastor.

"He's a good man", she replied. "I'm a friend of his wife, Valerie. No, they didn't know anything about Arrow. No, they weren't involved in any discussions about defrauding the health-care system."

They also asked about a man named Edward Burgess.

"He's my M.P.", she replied. "He spoke to us at a political meeting at our place a few months ago."

Did Burgess belong to any subversive organizations?

"Of course not!" she replied curtly. "He's a high-school teacher, or used to be."

Was he active in any cults?

"He's active in his church. That's all I know about him. Are you people out of your minds?"

Did she have any contacts in the press or television media?

"Who, me? No. None."

Did she have any relationships with the murdered nuns at the Catholic convent near Fort George?

Beth looked shocked. "You mean that horrible business? I knew their convent was there, of course, but you realize our interpretation of the Bible is quite different from theirs. I felt really terrible when they died, but we didn't have much in common. I never met any of them."

Did she have any relationships with the residents of the Salmon Creek commune?

"The what commune?"

The drug commune, where the massacre by drug gangs had occurred.

"No, of course not. We have *nothing* in common with people like that."

Was she sure that she had not known the boy, Arrow Delaney, or his family?

"Absolutely not. The first time I laid eyes on him was the night he had his appendix operation."

Did she have any knowledge of his whereabouts between January, when he disappeared, and the night in October when he reappeared?

Beth hesitated. This knowledge was precisely the information she could not divulge. She shook her head.

"Are you sure?" asked the woman.

"All I can tell you is, he wandered out of the bush, and he was in very poor condition when I met him."

Beth prayed that they would jump to the conclusion that Arrow had wandered out of the bush at the farm, not someplace else.

The woman and the elderly man stared at Beth, trying to read her mind. Her momentary hesitation had alerted them to the possibility of more information.

"Do you have knowledge of any person or persons with whom the boy was residing during that period?" the elderly man asked.

Beth looked away.

"I think you had better tell us, Mrs. Potter. There are very dangerous criminal elements undermining this country, and this child has been involved with them. You must tell us anything that could provide a lead."

"I've told you all I can."

The elderly man's eyes probed her.

"That is correct. You have told us all you *can*," he said, "but not all that you know."

Beth burst into tears. "Why are you doing this? I don't know any criminals! I don't! I just don't! Why are you holding me here without my rights? This isn't democratic! What is happening in this country?"

The woman looked inquiringly at the elderly man. The man returned her gaze coolly.

"I think that is all for today, Mrs. Potter", he said. Then, as an afterthought, "Thank you."

A guard came in and returned Beth to her cell, where she wept uncontrollably for an hour. Only after much effort of the will and renewed attempts at prayer was she able to return to a state of sad tranquillity.

On the seventh day after her arrest, she was again taken to the interrogation room. Three men, including the elderly man, sat facing her across the desk. All of them looked very important and very serious. They asked her the questions she had already answered countless times and many more questions that were new, some of them totally perplexing, such as her connection to a Catholic priest in Fort George and the Catholic archbishop of Vancouver. That was easy: there was no connection. Other questions were not so easy: for example, the identity of a woman who had once accompanied her when she visited Arrow in hospital.

Beth replied that she couldn't say, that the woman was just an acquaintance she had met in the hall of the hospital. That wasn't a lie, Beth told herself, because Alice had made a side trip into the tuck-shop that day, to buy herself a pack of smokes, and they had met a few minutes later in the hall outside of the children's ward.

Once again Beth was able to walk the fine line between truth and prudence. The interrogators weren't satisfied, but they didn't press her about the identity of the old woman who had been smoking in the children's ward.

After an hour and a half of questioning, the elderly man looked at the other two interrogators and said to them, as if Beth were not present, "She's obviously using the mental reservations these people use to justify falsehood. There's more here, but we've obtained everything we can by this approach. I suggest we move to medical interrogation."

Beth thought that probably meant torture. Her heart fell through the floor. She stared numbly at the men, as if they were three dark angels bearing a message of loathsome tidings.

The elderly man gazed back with a look that was perfectly expressionless but colder than absolute zero.

"We can avoid that if you tell us what you know", he said to her.

Resembling a fierce mother robin defending the chicks in her nest, staring down three menacing cats, she leaned forward. She felt amazingly calm. She did not know how she did it or where the grace came from or why they were unable to stop her.

She looked deep into their eyes, one after another. "I will tell you what I know", she said quietly. "I will tell you what you need to know."

She paused, praying silently.

"Yes? What is it?" the elderly man said.

"Just this: There is a God. And he always has his eye on the sparrow. There's a hell too, and you gentlemen should realize that *that* is the prison where you are going if you don't think twice about the things you're doing. You can kill me, and you can kill Arrow, and maybe you can take away my children. You can even take away a million children from their parents. You can break a million hearts and destroy a million minds. But there won't be enough jail cells in all the world to hold the families that will rise up against you. And even if you do succeed in keeping the whole world in chains for a time, it won't last. In the end you're going to lose. The Lord is coming soon to judge between the just and the unjust, to judge between the sheep and the goats, for the cries of the sparrow are going up unto the court of the Lord. Lo, these cries are *already* heard in the court of the Lord, and his day is coming; behold, it is coming soon. And it shall be as a day of wrath for the ungodly, for all those who afflict the poor and the weak; and all those who distress the flock of God shall go down unto eternal darkness where there is wailing and gnashing of teeth and unending torment and fire."

The elderly man motioned with his hand. A guard came and took Beth away.

Later in the morning three guards and a young man in a white medical uniform escorted her to a new cell. She was strapped onto a hospital bed and given an injection. Beth felt the effects within minutes, and she prayed as she went down into the places of the mind or the soul where secrets are kept. But because she was aging and exhausted and suffered from a tendency to hypothermia (Beth always wore sweaters, even when taking the kids to swimming lessons at the rec center) and because she also had a borderline case of maternal diabetes (which had grown steadily worse after her fourth pregnancy), the injection did not achieve the desirable effect. Her vital signs did not respond in a predictable way. She felt as if she were floating on a warm cushion, suspended in a golden light, resting in a profound tranquillity, prepared to tell them anything they asked, all fears melted, all inhibitions faded away.

She mumbled and gushed for two hours, telling them every-thing and nothing. The *everything* was composed of knitting pat-terns and unpaid bills, her many little worries about her children's personalities, snatches of hymns, quotes from the Bible, and the innermost secrets of the blessings the Lord had given to her in prayer.

When they asked her about where Arrow had been for nine months, she thought that they must be referring to one of her children, because they had all spent nine months in her womb, and yes, he *was* her child, *Temporary Noah* in the womb of her heart. They asked where he had lived, and she kept saying over and over, "At the palace, with the queen!" She was raving, of course, they could tell by the way she garbled Bible stories and children's stories, crying alternately "The giraffes are too big for this ark!" and "Just ask Alice!"

They varied the doses during the following two days, but it was always the same—everything and nothing. Different drugs were applied, but one made her semi-comatose, and the other made her babble like a mad prophetess.

On the tenth day of her captivity, they returned her to her cell, where she slept and woke groggy, fearful that she had revealed everything. No one came to question her further, and she assumed that it was all over. Alice and Nick were taken. Maybe Ted and the children were in trouble too. She was almost sure of it, yet the strangest peace surrounded her and filled her. When she was back to what passed for normal in this facility, they stopped feeding her. She knew then that her life was over. She was permitted three small plastic cups of water each day for three days in a row, but not a crumb of food. She prepared for death and felt very peaceful, grieving not for herself but for her husband and for her children and what they would suffer without her.

On an evening fourteen days after her arrest, two female guards came into her cell and pinned her to the bed. A young doctor entered, looked at her without expression, and injected her with a syringe. She was certain it was the moment of her death. Her voice was weak, but she managed to say to him, "I'm sorry you feel you have to do this. You're somebody's son. You've got a mother somewhere, and I think if she could see this, she'd be very sad. I don't hold it against you. I'm going to my Savior now, and I'll ask him to forgive you."

Then the room spun, and Beth was sucked into a tornado.

Several hours later, at three o'clock in the morning, a police constable patrolling for drinking-driving teenagers in the back streets of Chilliwack, British Columbia, a town forty miles east of Fort George, found a semi-conscious woman lying in the weeds beside the baseball diamond at the sports center. He called an ambulance on the car radio, and the woman was taken to the emergency ward of the Chilliwack General Hospital. The constable took a good look at her face and realized she was the missing woman whom the papers had been screaming about for a week. He called the Fort George detachment, and they notified the woman's husband. Then he called the Missing Persons Bureau to tell them that she had been found.

The ER doctor checked her over and found that she was hallucinating, completely out of it. She was dehydrated and suffering from exposure and malnutrition. Her clothing looked as if she had spent a week or more sleeping in the bush. Her pale blue coat was very dirty, torn in many places, and covered with burrs. Her running shoes were soaking wet and torn. Her legs were scratched from brambles.

When Ted arrived an hour later, he was careening between feelings of elation and frantic worry. He stayed by Beth's bed until dawn and throughout the remainder of the morning. He called Dr. Stevenson and asked him to drive upriver to Chilliwack to see Beth, but the man refused. He was still angry. The Potters' pastor arrived at eleven, bringing with him his own doctor, who was a member of the congregation. The doctor tried to get a response from Beth, but she was still hallucinating. Suspecting drug abuse or a "mushroom toxin", he sent a blood sample off to a lab in Vancouver for a drug screen, prescribed an antipsychotic medication called Haldol, and advised the Chilliwack doctors to continue the hydration and intravenous feeding, to do everything they could to reverse the hypothermia.

The following day articles appeared in papers throughout the country announcing that Beth Potter had been found. It made the evening television news programs, which quoted local search and rescue authorities, who surmised that the woman, frightened by pending legal charges for fraud, had fled into the forest, where she had lived at a subsistence level for two weeks, reappearing in a delirious state, suffering from exposure.

Beth continued to hallucinate for another day after that, and neither Ted nor the doctor could make any sense of what she told them. On the third day she was transferred by ambulance to Fort George Hospital, and the children came in to see her later in the afternoon. Beth recognized them and smiled at them through cracked lips; her eyes brightened, and she held out her arms to them. They hugged her en masse and everyone in the room wept.

A hospital administrator took Ted aside in the hallway later on and informed him in a businesslike fashion that the Ministry of Health had decided not to press charges (this also was reported in the media) because his wife was obviously suffering from mental instability, and that had no doubt been a factor in the attempted fraud. Ted said nothing; the man went away. There was no sign of their ex-physician, the lady doctor, but their other ex-physician, Stevenson, nodded coolly at him, once, passing in the hall.

A reporter from the local paper tried to get an interview, but Ted fended her off with only a little steam escaping from his lips. The steam was not reported. Within a week the story faded from the minds of most people. Ed and Marjorie Burgess sent roses, the ladies at the church dropped by in dribs and drabs. The room began to fill with flowers for Beth and boxes of candy for the children. Meals on wheels kept arriving at the farm. At church the following Sunday Ted stood up in his pew after the service and delivered a choked thank you to everyone for the help they had given.

Their new doctor told Ted that Beth was recovering well, the hallucinations over, the disorientation and depression lifting, the effects of hypothermia and malnutrition minimal. The lab in Vancouver reported trace elements of an unknown drug in her blood, but a second and third screen showed that they were now washed out of her system. She was still weak but could go home in a few days if she felt she was ready.

Whenever Ted or the doctor asked Beth about where she had been during her absence, she strained her mind, trying to think. But there were disconcerting gaps in her memory. She could tell them only that she had talked to the police for a while, had ridden in a van without windows, then she had taken a lot of showers, something about a budgie bird and a hospital bed.

"Where?" Ted begged her. "What hospital?"

Each time he probed, she shook her head, feeling sad and confused. "I don't know", she replied vaguely. "I just can't remember."

"It sometimes happens", the doctor told Ted. "The trauma has erased some things, is my guess. But her memory will return bit by bit."

It would be almost a year before the fragments of memory revived and floated together into a coherent whole, but even then there were missing pieces.

Alice Douglas phoned the Potters' place one night, a few days before Beth was discharged. Ted didn't feel much like saying anything to her. The double clicks were gone from their line, but Ted wasn't sure he trusted anything any more. He refrained from blaming the whole affair on her. Yes, he reassured her, Beth was coming out of it fine. She couldn't tell them much about what had happened, but the doctor said her memory would gradually return. No, Beth hadn't said anything about the boy with the bad appendix. No, Ted was sure about that. And maybe, for a while, he suggested, the Potter family needed to be left alone; they needed a healing time. No offense, Alice.

Alice tried once more a week after Beth came home. She phoned one evening when Ted was out in the barn. Janie brought the extension into her parents' bedroom and plugged it into the jack by the bed. Beth was dozing, a Bible lying open on her chest. Janie shook her mother gently awake and whispered, "It's Alice, Mum. Do you want to talk with her?"

"Oh, Alice", Beth smiled. "Yes, I'd love to talk to her."

Alice and Beth chatted for a while, Alice uncharacteristically quiet and careful about everything she said. Beth strained to recall what had happened, but only elusive wisps of imagery surfaced—nothing that meant anything really. Alice asked about Arrow. Had Beth seen him?

Beth puckered her face, then she remembered who Alice was referring to. "You mean the boy. Temporary Noah. No, Alice, I never saw him after that day . . . that day in the hospital." Then Beth began to cry. Alice said so long and hung up the phone without a sound.

When Ted came in from the barn and heard that Alice had been bothering Beth, he went out to the kitchen, told the kids to make themselves scarce, and dialed the number of the Palace of Junque.

He told Alice in no uncertain terms that Beth was not yet a well woman and that Alice's part in it had brought a lot of pain to his family. He didn't blame her, he said. He knew she'd just been trying to help a lost kid. But until Beth was back to her old self, Alice calling would churn up too many painful memories. Alice didn't have to worry about him telling on her. He hated the cops and the social engineers more than she ever could, and he would be the last person in the world to throw her to the wolves. But for now, it would be better if they didn't see her for a while. Hoped she didn't take it the wrong way. Hoped she understood.

Alice understood.

* * *

In mid-October, shortly after Beth Potter's mysterious liberation, several seemingly unconnected events occurred:

Ed Burgess was audited by the income tax department, something that had never happened to him before. It cost him some nervous sweat, long-distance telephone calls, a cancelled speaking engagement, lost hours at the House (and a few votes because of it), and a good deal of effort calming down his wife. In the end it turned out that the government owed him $212.95. Which was some satisfaction. It covered the cost of the phone calls, with enough left over to take his wife to dinner at the Chateau Laurier.

That same week his brother-in-law was audited and found to be equally honest. Ed's daughter, a grade-school teacher in Vancouver, was also audited. Unfortunately, it was discovered that she owed the ministry of revenue just over three thousand dollars. Clearly, she had made an honest mistake on her tax return a few years back, and some clerk had failed to catch it. Ed's daughter was mortified and paid the outstanding taxes, narrowly escaping a colossal fine and a prison sentence. It made a splash in the lower mainland papers for a day or two, however, and cost Ed a few more votes in the next election. Ed lost count of the number of family members who were audited that year.

Then the federal election boundaries committee redesigned the shape of his riding, cutting off a third of his rural voters, shifting them to the next riding west, leaving Ed to the mercies of a largely hostile urban bloc.

Peter Stanford was transferred to the Asian Desk of his newspaper and relocated to Hong Kong, where he died of a pulmonary embolism the following year.

The hard-apple lady doctor was promoted to chief executive of the provincial hospital board. She invested in a time-share condominium in Fort Lauderdale, Florida. She dropped quilting and took up Mah-Jongg. Her club became popular with local ladies, and four of the members, including the doctor, went on to win the Western Canada cup.

Dr. Stevenson underwent an inquiry and was found innocent of complicity in the Noah Potter case. The following spring he moved to the United States with his family, and there he became quite wealthy.

Alice M. Douglas was smoking three packs of cigarettes a day, sleeping only a few hours each night, and quelling panic attacks with more than her usual consumption of whiskey. At one point she begged a ride to town from a neighbor—not the Potters; she gave the Potters a wide clearance—and brought back a case of Screech and a bag full of whodunits. The whiskey helped only a little, and she was unable to concentrate on the mysteries.

The Roman Catholic archdiocese of Vancouver lost its tax-exempt status under the anti-discrimination and hate-literature laws. The archbishop and his lawyers were appealing the decision. Other legal problems were cropping up. A former employee, a nun, was suing for compensation for unjust dismissal. A doctor was suing the Catholic hospital for defamation of character. Several members of the laity were in prison for blockading a fetal experimentation clinic in the city, and the archbishop was paying for their defense.

Also during that week of October, Richard Benson, a young seminarian who had been denied his master's degree in theology by a Catholic seminary, sat in his parents' home in North Vancouver, staring at the rain through the living-room window, brooding, praying, and toying with the idea of becoming either a member of the Russian Orthodox Church or a follower of an ultra-conservative schismatic group headquartered in France. In the end he did neither, because on All Souls Day the archbishop rang the front doorbell, smiled at him, stepped inside, and asked Richard for a cup of coffee. Three weeks later, the young man was in a jet bound for Rome, enrolled in the master's program under a private tutor in an orthodox Roman college.

Father Shane was in a New England monastery, hating it.

Father Ron took up smoking again and felt terrible about it. The fires at the Baal-pit declined in number and size but never entirely ceased. His homilies continued to keep people awake.

Father Potempko was in the hospital for a few days with serious burns, having fallen asleep in bed with his pipe lit. The bed had to be replaced. Potempko gave up smoking forever. The archbishop ordered a new set of clerical shirts for him. Potempko converted the home-care nurse, who became quite a force for good in that region.

*

Charlie Manyberries was fined for selling salmon to whites.

Cecilia Manyberries caught pneumonia but recovered.

*

Julie and Colin were sailing down the west coast of the Baja Peninsula under the stars. They had departed San Diego four days earlier and hoped to cross the Tropic of Cancer by midnight. It was almost ten o'clock Pacific standard time, and Julie felt an urge to bring the battery-powered shortwave radio up on deck, so that they could catch up on news from Canada. She sat down on the stern seat in the cockpit while Colin stood at the wheel, guiding the *Osprey* a degree or so to the east. Sometime before dawn they would pass the southernmost cape of the peninsula and would swing toward the coast of Mexico, aiming for the resort city of Mazatlán.

Julie spun the dial until she found English. There was plenty of English on the band and lots more Spanish. Some Portuguese and French. Even something that sounded Chinese. She crossed a blast of static in which the word *Fort George* was embedded and spun the dial back to find it.

"—state that the missing woman has been found— (static) — Mrs. Potter, a resident of Fort George, had suffered from mental instability, which was aggravated by exposure—" (more static) "—are not pressing charges—" (static and Spanish) "—from the capital of beautiful British Columbia, we wish you good night and easy listening—"

"Fort George, B.C.!" Julie said to Colin.

"What's that, honey?"

"I caught a shortwave broadcast from Canada. A Victoria station. Something about someone from Fort George. Did you ever know any Potters?"

"No, none that I can remember. What's it about?"

"A missing person. But she's been found."

"She okay?"

"Seems like it."

The breeze was warm, but she snuggled beside Colin at the wheel and zipped up her windbreaker. They stood in companionable silence for some time.

"Penny for your thoughts, Cap'n."

"Low-grade brain waves. Nothing much to report."

"Anything will do. Doesn't have to be fancy."

He stared straight ahead, eyes on the forward horizon.

"I dunno, I guess I've been musing about all this—the trip, I mean—and how we made such an early start."

"Father Andrei and Arrow, you mean?"

698

He nodded.

"Are you glad we did it?"

"Yeah, I'm glad. I miss that old man."

"Me too. Miss the brumby?"

He nodded again. "He was a nice kid. He should have come with us."

"Maybe we should have argued harder."

"He reminded me of myself a lot when I was his age."

"In what way?"

"Just a boy from nowhere, needing a dream."

"He'll be okay. He's in good hands."

"I hope you're right."

Colin's eyes swept up toward the stars.

"Life's a complicated thing, isn't it, Jules?"

"Sometimes."

"A person's a complicated thing too, wouldn't you say?"

"Uh-huh, sometimes."

"I've been doing a lot of thinking on this trip. I've been trying to make sense of what I am, or who I am, or . . ."

"Come to any conclusions?"

"This is all the sense I can make of it: I was a lost kid—with nobody to ask for directions, no maps, nobody with his hand on the wheel of my life. I was hungry for a dream, and I fell for a bad one."

"You mean back there in Sydney and San Francisco? The tribe?"

"Yeah, the tribe", he echoed sadly. "The love-bombers. I guess I fell for it so hard because I needed something badly."

"Any idea what that might be?"

He shrugged. Julie prayed silently, yearning for him to say the things she had wanted to hear for many years.

"When I finally saw I'd taken a bad hook, I spat it out. Tore it out, would be a better way of saying it. I hated what it had done to me. After that I went hard to starboard, as far as I could get. I told myself that all dreams are lies. I went to pure science, pure logic, you know what I mean?"

She squeezed his arm. "I know what you mean."

"But a real life's not like that. A real life's like deep water. It's like the ocean. It can't be all port or all starboard because, if it were, you'd just go round in circles till you foundered on a rock and sank. So, it's got to be port *and* starboard, doesn't it?"

"Yes, it does."

"It's got to be reason *and* dreams. It's got to be things you can know and things you can't know."

"That's true, Colin. And maybe the knowing and not knowing goes all the way up. Maybe there's no limit to it."

He thought about that.

"Maybe", he said at last.

"A captain is master of his little boat", she said. "But who made the sea, and who made the stars?"

He glanced at her, then away, and said no more.

Julie kissed the captain good night a few minutes later and went below to bed. She was tired from a day of sun and wind and from the tension of keeping the children from stumbling overboard and becoming shark snacks. She should have fallen asleep easily but instead lay wide awake in the honeymoon suite, staring at a circle of stars that dipped up and down on the wall.

She wished Father Andrei were there. He would know how to answer Colin's questions—unanswerable theological questions—his spiritual hunger disguised as philosophical musing. She hoped she would see the priest and the boy again some day. She hoped they were still missing. It had been months since they had dropped them at Bella Coola. There was no way of knowing where they were or if they were safe. She prayed for that, hoped for it. But a nagging feeling had continued to worry her for a long time now, growing steadily. She always pushed it back down into the bucket she defined as "the repository of neurotic fears". But tonight the feeling was like the needle of some inner seismometer, scratching its unwelcome message on a graph. She sighed, reached for a rosary hanging on a peg above the bed, and prayed.

*

That same night Bill and Reenie Wannamaker lost more than two hundred dollars at the game tables in Las Vegas. "*American* dollars", Bill grumbled. Reenie won back fifty-eight dollars from a one-armed bandit. "*American* dollars", she reminded Bill as they drifted off to sleep, arm in arm in the Winnebago.

*

Also in October, the two corporals of the Williams Lake R.C.M.P. detachment who had arrested Andrei and Arrow were promoted; one was transferred to Kamloops, and one to Surrey, a suburb of Vancouver. Neither of them advanced far in the Force after that. Two corporals of the Fort George R.C.M.P. detachment were transferred to northern Saskatchewan without notice and without promotion. Corporal Murphy remained in place, being too slow of wit to be of much concern to anyone.

*

On the eve of All Saints Day an old man living high in the Cariboo mountains enlisted his two great-grandchildren to gather moss, and they spent the day rechinking the logs of his cabin. Winter was coming. They had dried a large amount of fish on outdoor racks of willow poles over a birch fire. Each night they prayed a rosary together, and once a week, on Sundays, the old man walked through a forest path to a village eighteen miles west, where he attended Mass in a tiny mission church. There were only half a dozen parishioners, mostly old native people like himself. The visiting priest gave him extra Communion wafers, and he carried them home in a pyx under his shirt.

He felt bad that the two young ones could not accompany him to Mass but decided that charity demanded they remain hidden for a time. It would not be charity to throw them to the wolves to keep their Sunday obligation. If he did that, they would never receive Communion again.

*

In late October Ted and Beth Potter received surprise visits from, in turn, the Child Welfare branch of Human Resources, the regional inspector of education, and the provincial health department. Ted's little hog business was deemed insufficiently hygienic for renewal of his sales quota; the children were pronounced normal-with-reservations and the family subjected to a recommendation for periodic social assessment; the children's academic levels were also tested and found to be superior to peer-test profiles, with the exception of Jonathan, who seemed incapable of mastering mathematics. The inspector instructed the boy's parents to enroll him immediately in a school, which they did. They chose a small, private Christian school across the river. It cost a lot (Beth's parents contributed to the fees) and meant a good deal more driving. The school itself was subject to an inordinate amount of low-grade bureaucratic harassment, but the staff kept the worst of the social-engineering curriculum from infecting the students. Even so, Jonathan began to arrive home every night with a chip on his shoulder and a hankering for rock stars and questionable videos. He began to complain about being forced to go to church. His math skills did not improve.

On October 30, Ted listed the farm with a local real estate agent. He sold it the following March for half of its market value, after which the Potters moved to southern Alberta. There they lived for six months in an old farmhouse on Rosebud Creek with Beth's sister Pam and her husband, Willum, who was an easygoing, not overly convinced Mennonite. The two couples discovered that they were compatible. The Potters bought part interest in Willum's poultry business and moved into a trailer on the acreage behind the metal breeding sheds.

The mobile home was crowded, but the family was happy. Jonathan's math improved, and the chip blew away forever in a warm chinook wind. Whenever Beth chanced to look west toward the snow-crested Rockies on the horizon, her mouth tightened a little and she shivered and turned east.

18

The Altar of Sacrifice

Father Andrei was curled up on the bed of his cell, facing the wall. His eyes were closed, and he was praying. The words of Psalm 102 repeated themselves over and over in his mind. His thoughts were not as clear as they had once been, but more than sixty years of praying his daily office now stood him in good stead:

> Lord, hear my prayer;
> let my cry come unto you.
> Do not hide your face from me
> now that I am in distress.
> Turn your ear to me;
> when I call, answer me quickly.
> For my days vanish like smoke;
> my bones burn away as in a furnace.
> I am withered, dried up like grass,
> too wasted to eat my food.
> From my loud groaning
> I become just skin and bones.

He tried to remember the rest, but it slipped away, just beyond his reach. He sighed, searched, remembered:

> I am like a desert owl,
> like an owl among the ruins,
> I lie awake and moan,
> like a sparrow on the roof.
> All day long my enemies taunt me;
> in their rage they make my name a curse.
> I eat ashes like bread,
> mingle my drink with tears . . .

> But you, Lord, are enthroned forever;
> your renown is for all generations.
> You will again show mercy to Zion;
> now is the time for pity.
> The nations shall revere your name, Lord,
> all the kings of the earth, your glory,
> Heeding the plea of the lowly,
> not scorning their prayer . . .
>
> The Lord looked down from the holy heights,
> viewed the earth from heaven,
> To attend to the groaning of prisoners,
> to release those doomed to die . . ."

Andrei wondered for a moment, as he had countless times during the past few months, if a miraculous liberation would come. Then he recalled the vision he had received of the Mother of God in another prison so very long ago. A single vision, a burst of light, a consolation. A distant memory, like someone else's grace recounted in a dry martyrology. He had been offered the crowns of obedience and martyrdom. His lifetime, spent in a myriad small obediences, was gradually approaching the fruition of this final obedience. The seed, the root, the stalk and branch, the flower, and then the fruit. At first the fruit was bitter. In its early stages it was so harsh on the tongue it could not be swallowed. But then, beneath the invisible rays of the sun, it swelled and colored and sweetened, and one could taste its sweetness. He would swallow it, and it would feed his soul unto eternal life.

"Eternal Father," he whispered, "you have called us out of darkness into your own wonderful light. Nourish us unto eternal life . . ."

Andrei managed a small smile. An old owl he was, trying to chirp like a sparrow on a roof. So easily distracted he was. What was the end of the psalm? Oh, yes:

> Of old you laid the earth's foundations;
> the heavens are the work of your hands.

They perish, but you remain;
they all wear out like a garment;
Like clothing you change them
and they are changed,
but you are the same, your years have no end.
May the children of your servants live on;
may their descendants live in your presence.

He sighed. Yes, that was it. The end of the psalm—minus a few missing verses, he felt sure. But he had remembered the foundation. The structure of the universe. Seeing the form. The passing things of man, the transience of the earth; all the pride of human intelligence and power and wealth that would fail in the twinkling of an eye. But God remains.

May the children of your servants live on . . .

Yes, my Lord, may the children of your servant live on. Forever and forever, exulting in the light of indestructible love.

Would the owl among the ruins always lament for the absence of joy? Would the sparrow's small heart always burst with longing? No, all longing and lament would cease. But in the interim how many would be lost? How many? Small, small, oh, I am so small. I could not save it all, my Lord. It was too big. It was too big for me. I tried to bring a few back to you. Some were moved by the owl's plaintive lament, some were drawn by the sparrow's longing for things unseen and yet to come. But the falcon took so many in mid-flight; some died with a swift, killing blow, others in slow torment.

The agony. The tearing of a father's heart. I am a father unable to defend my offspring. They are all my children. All, *all* of them, but they do not know. They do not hear. They would not come when I sang for them.

And now they have numbered my bones, and my days are like a lengthening shadow, and I wither like the grass. They cast lots for my vestments. They silence my song. They contain my grief within these six panels of white metal. No doors, no windows. They will not let me lift you up on the altar, for they hate the light. They hate. They hate. O pierce this unspeakable darkness in their hearts. Do not let them destroy everything!

Sustain my spirit, O my Father. Sustain me, and if it is your will, do not release me from this prison. Ignore the groaning of my old mouth. Do not hear my complaints. If you need this sacrifice, if you need this last song, unheard, unknown, unlamented, then take it and use it to feed another.

"My little ones", he whispered to the white metal walls. "My children."

With power greater than he had felt on the *Osprey*, he saw the children of his heart come before his eyes: Julie and Colin and their small flock, embarked on their voyage, plunging on high seas; the Pope kneeling in the privacy of his bedroom, weeping over the Church; Arrow frightened, curled into a ball in a room without windows and without doors; Pawel Tarnowski wrestling with a mad dog that sought to tear the golden antlers from a red deer; the mysterious priest named Elijah; another unknown priest who was lifting high a monstrance from which the light of the Presence radiated to the children dwelling in darkness on a plain full of dry bones. Other priests, so many, many priests. Some known to him, some not, some living and some dead.

He saw Nathaniel Delaney, Thaddaeus Tobac, Tyler and Zöe, Cecilia Manyberries, Potempko . . . so many, many beloved. A young woman named Kateri riding a train into the west, carrying a flame in her heart. A man named Joseph walking out of the north, crossing the frozen tundra with a pack over his shoulder and a staff in his right hand, dressed in fur-covered rags, carrying in his heart an icon of true fatherhood. A one-eyed man named Enoch seeing with two eyes. A baby with a tiny body and the head of a giant and the heart of a soaring dove; a bitter old woman thinking new thoughts, hoping, because she now knew that she had been made for true love and that it was still possible.

They were real to him, the ones he knew and the ones whom he had not met but knew in the secret communion of the saints. It came to him that in the sacrifice of his own obscure blood, united to the eternal Sacrifice, they would be sealed and consecrated as his children forever. Their faces streamed before him like a line of pilgrims, winding through the city of man like a eucharistic procession on Corpus Christi day in the streets of Dresden, Dresden destined for burning. But the souls of these children were not destined for burning. In fact, no human being was *destined* for burning, if he would but listen to the small sparrow's voice piping in the dawn, just before the rising of the sun, when man sleeps in deep unheeding.

Some would awake. Some. How many? How many?

He saw their weaknesses and their beauty, the awesome glory of them, even as they moved through the time of distress, the *endlösung*, under lengthening shadows, in mourning, naked, powerless, feeling themselves to be nothing. He saw them leaving the great cities of the world, which is Babylon, saw them streaming out into the fields and the forests, departing the illusory securities of man, seeking, faltering, falling, then rising again and pressing forward against the fearsome night.

With many faces passing before the eyes of his heart, Father Andrei began to pray the rosary. He pondered the divine mysteries of the Incarnation, the redemption, and eternal life, until a guard shook him from his meditation and pulled him to his feet.

He was taken from the cell and led to a bare room on a floor in the lower levels of the Institute.

Maurice L'Oraison was waiting for him there. He gestured to the side wall, and a panel slid open in it, revealing a tinted window. Andrei looked through the window and saw a small boy dressed only in underwear curled in the fetal position on a bed in a white cell. It was Aaron.

"You see, we have him", Maurice said.

The guard forced Andrei into a chair and bound his wrists and ankles to it with handcuffs.

"You must release this child," Andrei said, "or the full wrath of God will fall upon you."

Maurice smiled. "I don't think so."

Speaking in Latin, Andrei raised his voice and prayed a blessing over Arrow. The boy did not stir. Maurice walked over to the panel and banged it hard, once, with his fist. The boy did not move.

"He cannot see or hear anything through this glass. Your superstitious incantations do not penetrate."

"There are no physical barriers to grace. There are no walls in the Kingdom of Heaven."

"There is no Kingdom of Heaven."

"It exists. I assure you it exists."

"You must abandon your mythology, Father Andrei, if you want to save your pathetic little remnant."

"If I were to abandon my faith, the remnant would be weakened. Yet you are mistaken, for though it is small, it is strong beyond all human strength."

Maurice shook his head. "You think so? I can demolish it in a breath."

"You may capture some. You may even succeed in frightening a majority into apostasy, but they will not cease believing what is true."

"With every word you sink deeper into your blindness", Maurice replied sadly.

"The truth endures. Earth may pass away, but the truth endures."

"There is no truth. There is only knowledge. There is only power."

"With every word, Maurice, you sink deeper into your blindness."

Maurice leaned against the glass panel and regarded Father Andrei wordlessly for a few moments.

"This is your last chance, old man."

"You too are old, Maurice. Soon you will be standing before the judgment seat of God."

Maurice smiled but did not reply.

"My time has come. I do not fear it", Andrei said.

"In a few minutes from now, or a few hours, or possibly days, I will decide to end your life. You will go on to another plane of existence where you will discover how wrong you have been about the shape of reality. The masters will instruct you. You will understand what a waste your resistance has been, how much suffering you have caused because you would cling to this cruel and ancient mystery religion of yours."

"The Kingdom of Heaven is not cruel. Though there are crosses for those who would seek it, the grace is always given to carry those crosses. Though they are at first bitter, they become sweet, and the fruit of them is eternal joy."

"Ah, theology."

"More than theology. Truth. The light of the mind of Christ. He who is the creator of reality, who loves it and redeems it."

"Look carefully at the world, priest, for it is more and more unredeemed each day."

"You have made an eclipse of the sun, Maurice. Yet a little while, and it shall be over. Never can it destroy the light of the sun. The sun bides its time, but when it comes, the shadows will flee. When he comes, there shall never again be eclipses. When he comes, it will be for us as if the shadows never existed. They will be remembered no more."

"When will he come? I tell you, he is always coming, never arriving. He never arrives because he does not exist."

"He exists", Andrei replied in a voice that was calm and peaceful.

"I am willing to release you."

"I do not think so."

"I will also release the boy."

"Of that I am uncertain. But I know you would exact a price."

"Oh, yes, I will exact a price."

"You needn't tell me, because I will not pay it."

"You will pay it."

"No. The only wealth that has ever been mine is my life. I gave it away long ago. I have nothing."

"You have knowledge."

"I do not know where Aaron's family is."

"Aaron?"

"Aaron Nathaniel, an arrow-in-the-bow-of-the-Lord."

"Ah, I see. You have renamed your little proselyte."

"In the sight of God he is Aaron. Strike him, and God will strike you."

Maurice shook his head again.

"You know, priest, it's really tragic that a man as strong-willed as you has fallen prey to irrationality. Think of the good you could have done for humankind without your dysfunctional religion."

"The fruit you offer is the same fruit offered in the garden of Eden. At first it would be sweet on the tongue, then the taste of it would be bitter indeed, and when swallowed it would not nourish but would lead unto eternal death."

"Ah, the snake in the grass!" Maurice laughed. "Listen to me: there is no God, and there is no snake. These are symbols of the psyche, archetypes, projections of the dynamics of the subconscious."

"You are mistaken."

Maurice, with surprising strength, pulled Andrei's chair around, facing away from the glass panel.

"If we are mistaken, why are we so strong? Why are you so weak?"

"Because God permits it", Andrei answered simply.

"Why would your omnipotent deity permit such a disaster? Tell me why?"

"In order to bring a greater good from it."

"Pathetic", Maurice murmured. "Utterly pathetic!"

"The mystery that confounds the mystery of iniquity."

"Listen, do you realize what we are going to do? We have shattered the claim that your deity holds over the captive mind of man. All your commandments are broken. The stone tablets lie trampled beneath the feet of the golden bull."

"You may shatter stones. You may shatter churches; you may shatter minds. Yet the Word of the Lord remains. It is indestructible. It is written in human hearts, even though you convince them that it is no longer there."

"And if we destroy all human hearts?"

"What kind of victory would that be for you?"

"Those who destroy are the true rulers of the universe. We will reshape mankind in the true image and likeness of the godhead."

"You would reshape it into the image of Satan."

"Satan!" Maurice snorted. "There is no such being. He is a symbol of the shadow. When the shadow is integrated at last, the world will know peace."

"If you were to succeed in that, the world would become hell."

Maurice waved away the thought. "Enough mythopoeia. Enough. You cannot frighten me with your old priest tales, as if I were a child."

"Once you were a child with a pure heart. You were Camille's son. When did you begin to forget?"

"I have forgotten nothing. I have learned and learned, and I will not cease to learn."

"If you persist in this path, Maurice, you will not cease to learn until you have become filled with Satan. That will not be the godhead. That will be unending torment."

Maurice chuckled ruefully. "Oh, you are good at this. But all your apologetics amount to nothing. We are breaking down the brittle mental constructs of pre-technological man, his political, social, and religious consciousness. The human misery this causes is not a pleasure for me. But it is necessary if we are to evolve into the new man."

"You are not God."

"All the commandments of your god have been broken and are forgotten. Where they are remembered they have become no more than dishonored myths. And still your god does not come to rescue you."

"The outcry against Sodom and Gomorrah and against Babylon is so great, their sin so grave, that God will destroy them unless you repent."

"Ah, John the Baptist is among us once again! Or are you Elijah? Jeremiah? Isaiah perhaps?"

"The days of the city of sin are numbered."

"There are not even ten just men in this city, and still God does not destroy it."

"Behold he is coming. His eye is on the sparrow."

Maurice looked startled by these last words. He crossed his arms, inhaled sharply, and stepped back. He seemed to be brooding over some private thought. But the moment passed.

He jabbed his forefinger at Andrei. "Only the élite, the enlightened, using their godlike powers, can reestablish cosmic harmony, eliminate dysfunction and poverty, restore peace."

"You say peace, peace, where there is no peace."

"Precisely. We will establish it."

"At the price of freedom. Worse, at the price of men's souls."

"What kind of god would demand that his devotees jump through so many hoops? Why would such a god make it so difficult for souls to experience divinity? Why does he make it so easy for souls to be destroyed?"

"He did not intend it to be thus. It is your masters who made it so. The one true God knows the full measure of our identity. He calls us out of darkness into eternal light, but it is your masters who trip us up at every turn. God longs to give us true peace and endless love and the freedom to share in the life of his divinity in a way that will reveal your 'godlike powers' for what they are—"

"And what, pray tell, is that?"

"Your so-called godlike powers are stolen fruit that will rot in your hands and poison you as you bite it and destroy you as you swallow it. These are the furtive cruel powers of the Gestapo. These are the dark powers of the fallen angels. Leave them, Maurice, I adjure you. Leave them. They hate you as much as they hate me."

"The masters do not hate me. They are not fallen."

"I do not bargain for my life, not even for Aaron's, not even for the life of the visible structure of my Church. But I plead for your eternal soul. You are standing on the edge of an abyss."

"An abyss? I stand on solid ground. The old ways are crumbling. There is one among us who is coming soon to his throne. He lives. He will reign over the whole world. After the collapse of the visible structures that presently sustain ordinary life, we shall provoke a formidable social cataclysm, which will show clearly to the nations the effects of absolute atheism."

"I do not understand."

Maurice bent over and put his face close to Andrei's. "Understand this: We are not atheists. I am not an atheist."

"You are not an atheist?"

Maurice shook his head. "We who love peace shall reap the harvest of the disintegration of the old order. We call it critical instability, management by crisis. The mass of men will find themselves unable to defend themselves against criminals and terrorists, hunger and disease. The vast majority will have become disillusioned with Christianity, for your god hasn't come, you see. As the world collapses into chaos, they will finally realize that he never will come. The leaders of your church, those who remain after the heresies and schisms and persecutions have decimated it, will be without credibility or direction. The multitude, restless for a solution to the chaos, longing for an ideal to cling to, will then be open to receiving the Light that has remained in obscurity until our age, known only by the elect."

"You speak of the anti-Church. A false light, an illusion of light!"

"What is true light? Rather, *who* is true light, if not the one who embraces all of the spectrum, dark to light? The forgotten son of God, the elder brother of the one you call Christ."

"Then you do believe in God!"

"Not as you perceive him to be. He too is an archetype of higher truths."

"There is only one Son of God. His name is Jesus!"

"You are making declarations of doctrine. The Hindus have doctrines, the Confucians have them, the Marxists and the Fascists have them, the most primitive witch doctors on the remotest isles have them also. I tell you that both Christianity *and* atheism will disappear."

"Your utopia will be religious?"

"Absolutely. Totally."

"Tell me, how do you propose to enforce universal belief?"

"There will be no need for force. Mankind will give itself heart and soul to the Lightbringer."

"You mean Lucifer?"

"Yes", Maurice nodded.

"Lucifer is Satan", Andrei protested.

"The myth of Satan was invented by the old religion to promote the Judeo-Christian messiah. The one you call Christ is in fact Adonai, the lesser brother."

"Speak no more!" Andrei shouted. "For the sake of your immortal soul, Maurice. This is blasphemy!"

Maurice shrugged. "It is *gnosis*. It is pure knowledge."

"It is a lie. It is the lie that would suck the entire world into hell if God were to permit it. For your sake, for your sake alone, we will speak no more."

Andrei closed his eyes and prayed for the deliverance of Maurice L'Oraison. Maurice leaned forward, grabbing the arms of Andrei's chair, putting his face too close. His eyes were blinking rapidly and his face was flushed.

"What remains of your church is going to be handed over to the elder brother, to its rightful Lord."

"God will not permit it."

"Your absent god has already permitted it. Your progressives gave it over to the Christ of this age long ago. There are so many of them. How easy it was to convince them. They are useful but of little worth, like cheap metal. Then there are the lukewarm of your faithful, those who still believe but are frightened and willing to capitulate; they will be as a semi-precious stone in the crown. But the prize—the ones you call orthodox, your little remnant—these are the jewel in the crown that will be placed on the head of the Christ of this age."

"These you will not take."

"We will take them, and you will assist us."

"Never."

"Yes, you will. I give you a choice. Do you see that boy there? He has not spoken since we captured him. He curls into a ball. He wets the bed. His mind is fragile. His trust is close to nothing. Unless you assist us, I will order my servants to demolish what remains of his personality."

Andrei felt the old dread return, but now it was a tidal wave. Struggling to resist the horror of what was being suggested, he prayed desperately for strength. Calming his heartbeat, he stammered, "Is that the kind of thing your new order proposes for mankind?"

"Of course not", Maurice replied in a reasonable tone.

"Then why—?"

"The new order will be for the benefit of mankind, but there will be casualties."

"Where is your love of humanity now?"

"It is unfortunate but necessary that some must suffer. The vast numbers of functionaries in the social project are ignorant of what will transpire here. If we retain a small group of less desirable employees for the purposes of weeding out the dysfunctional from the social organism, it is to ensure the stability of the ignorant multitudes. The weeders will themselves be weeded when their work is complete. The three depraved men I will soon call into that room know their work. They are good at what they do."

"If you order them to do it, know that you are choosing hell."

"No, *you* are choosing. You will make me do it."

"No, Maurice. That is a lie. You are choosing it."

"They will violate him in so total a way that his stunned mind will never recover. I will make you watch them as they perform their arts. You too would never recover from the sight of what they do to him. They will eject him from this Institute when they are finished with him, and he will wander through the world in perpetual agony, shattered in mind and body, without a personality, believing that he is worthy only of abandonment and degradation. He will *be* degradation itself. He will be insane. He will be not only insane but possessed."

Struggling for a counterargument, Andrei retorted: "Then you do believe in the existence of evil spirits!"

"Not as you understand them. He will be filled with a legion from the lower level of beings that are the unintegrated shadow. It is permitted for a time that these beings roam the earth until the final integration."

"You and your servants claim to be the defenders of children. How can you think of such a thing?"

"The human species has bred like rats for millennia, and your church has encouraged it. What does it matter if a few suffer for the good of the whole?"

"No good can come from evil means!"

"Ah, that is where you are wrong. Good always comes from what you call evil means. Evil is merely the reverse side of the moon. It is the same orb, the same sovereignty, the same light, for darkness and light are one."

"The darkness cannot overcome the light!"

"Unless you agree to participate in the establishment of the new church, I will give the command now."

Andrei, struggling against a ferocious assault upon his mind and emotions, cried out, "What is it you want of me?"

"Very little, really."

"What is it? Tell me!"

"First I want to know where the rest of this boy's family is."

"I tell you before God as my witness, I do not know."

Maurice regarded him thoughtfully for some moments. Then he said, "I believe you."

"Take my life", Andrei cried. "But do not touch the boy."

"It's not as simple as that."

"What do you want of me?"

"Do you know if secret communities of Christians are being formed in North America?"

"Perhaps somewhere they exist."

Maurice considered. "Surely they exist. Where else would the children be hiding?"

"Listen to me, Maurice. Listen. The number of underground communities may be few or many. I do not know. But I tell you solemnly, if you lay siege to the camp of the saints, there will be no hope for you. If you destroy it, there will be no hope for mankind, and it could mean the end of all human life on this planet."

"I doubt that."

"Fire will rain down from heaven upon you and all the works of evil."

Maurice smiled patiently.

"For lo, the Lord shall come in fire," Andrei cried, "his chariots like the whirlwind, to wreak his wrath like burning heat and his punishment with fiery flames. For the Lord shall judge all mankind by fire and by sword."

"A Scripture quote?"

Andrei nodded. "Yes. The entire Scripture is ablaze with such passages."

"I have read the Bible. Have you read the *Upanishads*? No? Perhaps you have read the *Tibetan Book of the Dead*? No, possibly the *Egyptian Book of the Dead*? Or the *Gnostic Gospels*?"

A long silence ensued as the two men looked at each other.

"Choose", Maurice said at last.

"What do you want me to do?" Andrei replied in a broken voice.

"As I said before, very little. When you have done it, you will walk out of this Institute and never return. You will be a free man."

"What is it?"

"I wish you to speak into a video camera. It will probably take you no more than ten minutes. Then one of the employees here will drive you to any place in the lower mainland that you prefer. Why, you could even be taking tea this afternoon with your archbishop."

"What am I expected to say into the camera?"

Maurice put on his reading glasses and extracted a folded sheet of paper from the inside pocket of his suit jacket.

"You are free to express it in your own words, and I urge you to speak in as natural a manner as possible. That may be difficult under the circumstances, but you will repeat it until it's just right."

Maurice opened the paper and read from it.

"You will look into the camera and say the following:

"I wish to thank the federal government and the Office of Internal Security for rescuing me from my abductors. The people who held me hostage are members of a religious cult and were responsible for the murder of the nuns at Fort George, British Columbia. They are a right-wing Catholic underground sect that believes in the imminent coming of the messiah; they are armed and expanding a secret militia, which is small but dedicated to the overthrow of law and order. They have connections to other violent terrorist groups in North America and abroad.

"I wish to apologize to the people of this country for the many mistakes the institutional Roman Catholic Church has made, for the way it has fostered in its social theories and its doctrines a dualistic understanding of the world—the very philosophy that has encouraged the growth of violent antisocial groups. At this time I would also like to thank the many good lay Catholics and bishops who have fought against backward tendencies in the Church. These forward-looking believers have done everything in their power to encourage a climate of tolerance and pluralism. This group is best exemplified by Bishop ——— (Maurice named the man) and Cardinal ——— (also named), who represent the true spirit of Catholicism. I also would like to encourage my Church to participate in the Organization of World Religions, recently established under the auspices of the United Nations. Such efforts will help to make the world safe for children and ensure that experiences such as mine are never again repeated."

Maurice looked up.

Andrei bowed his head. "Give me the paper", he said.

"You agree?"

"I will speak to the camera."

Maurice snapped his fingers. A guard entered, bearing Andrei's brown Franciscan robe and rope belt. He removed the cuffs from Andrei, and the priest stood up, rubbing his arms.

"Put on the robe and the belt", Maurice commanded. Andrei did so.

They took him to an adjacent room, pleasantly furnished and decorated, and seated him at a table. Above him on the wall hung a painting of the Last Supper. Facing him, a video camera on a tripod. The guard left and shut the door. Maurice placed a stone cross on the table in front of Andrei.

"You can hold this in your hands as you speak. Make a reference to the cross if you like. It adds to the atmosphere."

Maurice smiled encouragingly, sat down in an armchair behind the camera, and crossed his legs. He reached forward and touched a button on the camera, and a red light winked on.

"It's recording", said Maurice. "You may begin."

Andrei held the shaking papers in his right hand, the cross in his left. He looked down at them, then up, then down. He closed his eyes and prayed an act of contrition.

Then he looked calmly into the eye of the camera and said:

"Praised be to Jesus Christ, the King of Glory!"

Maurice jerked forward.

"He is coming soon to judge the whole earth. My children, do not believe the lies told to you by the government and the media."

Maurice jumped up, but in his haste he tripped over his feet and stumbled sideways, taking a second or two to right himself.

"I have been abducted by employees of the Office of Internal Security, and I will die at their hands. But you must live. Glory to God in the highest! Glory be to the Holy Trinity! His word endures forever!"

Enraged, Maurice kicked over the tripod. The camera fell off. He grabbed the tripod and raised it over the old man.

"You fool! You idiot!" he screamed.

Andrei gazed solemnly at the cross, holding it firmly in both of his hands. The Presence that had come to him in the Sacrifice of the Mass for sixty years now came to him in the offering of his own life.

Maurice smashed the tripod down on Andrei's head. Blood spurted. The priest crumpled.

"I forgive you", he whispered.

"You can't forgive me!" Maurice roared. Again and again he smashed the tripod on the head. Up, down, sideways. The priest slid off the chair and collapsed onto the floor. A pool of blood spread, soaking his robes, the cross, the papers.

Andrei gazed at Maurice calmly, seeing the face of the enraged man only for a second, until blood filled his eyes, and the children of his soul streamed by in procession and were replaced finally by the sisters rushing forward to greet him.

Consumed with fury, Maurice howled curses, kicking the body and the head until the body ceased to move and the eyes stared lifelessly up at the Last Supper.

Realizing what he had done, Maurice took a step back, dropped the tripod, huffed, and straightened his jacket. His face contorting with malice and loathing, he crossed the room, picked up the camera, tore it open, and extracted the cassette.

He stared at the body of the priest and hurled more curses at it. Gradually his breathing slowed, and the color drained from his face. He pulled a silk handkerchief from his pocket, sat down in the armchair, wiped the blood from his shoes, and threw the soiled cloth onto the floor.

Holding his brow in his left hand, he removed his glasses and inserted them into his breast pocket. The rage seeped away. Self-control returned.

He had lost his temper. He had destroyed a valuable resource. The masters would not be pleased.

"Who are you to forgive me?" he growled at the inert form of the priest.

A knock at the door.

"Yes, what is it?" he barked.

"Is everything all right, sir? We heard noises."

"Come in here."

Three men entered. They looked around the room and gazed at the details without any show of emotion. Indeed, they felt none.

"Clean up this mess. Dispose of the body."

"Yes, sir."

"Take it down to forensic section. I want this body cremated, the bones ground into powder, and the ashes scattered to the four winds. Now!"

"Right away, sir. Uh, after that, should we go ahead with the kid?"

Maurice rubbed his brow, frowning.

"No. Don't touch him. The situation has changed, as you can see. The boy is our only link to the others."

Three sets of eyes flashed messages to each other. They would never dare to express disappointment to the Director of Internal Security.

* * *

Maurice L'Oraison strode from the room, leaving the three men to dispose of the body according to his instructions. He took the elevator to the top floor and from there passed through into the north wing of the Institute complex. He placed his right hand on a series of scanners, walked through the security doors that slid open before him, one after another, and entered the private visitors' section. No one else was in residence that night, and he was grateful for that. He did not want to speak with anyone. He wanted to be alone.

He went to his room at the end of the hall, put his hand to the scanner, and the door sprang open. He went in, shut the door, and removed his shoes. He reminded himself to have them cleaned and polished in the morning. The room was lit by a pleasant glow from two ceramic lamps beside a sofa upholstered in embroidered silk. The rug was thick amethyst pile. A framed print from Picasso's blue period hung over the entertainment console. Another print, something semi-abstract but colorful from the German expressionist period, provided the perfect counterpoint, brightening the room considerably. On the rosewood coffee table there was a piece of valuable porcelain, a bonneted woman in a long, wind-blown gown, carrying a flower basket.

He went into the bathroom and turned on the Jacuzzi nozzle, then went to the bedroom while it filled and slowly undressed. He left the clothes in a heap. They would have to be disposed of.

He felt disgust and anger. He had lost his temper. The priest had tricked him. The priest had pushed a button within him that he had not known was there—had not suspected was there until tonight. He had personally terminated five other cases during his career, but those had been done without emotional excess. Injections only. For reasons of State security. The brutality of tonight's business was shocking, but he reasoned that he had been under tremendous pressure in recent weeks. The priest had provoked him, had drawn him into a painful and at times bewildering debate that had taxed his mental and spiritual reserves. There were other unconnected cases hanging in the balance, none as close to his personal history as this one, but they too were complicated and possibly disruptive. There were leaks in Parliament, mere rumblings, but potentially troublesome.

Although the immediate danger had been contained, Delaney and the priest both dead, the children were still at large. The fugitives had now been missing for nine months, and there was no way of knowing if Delaney had informed them about the involvement of the Director of OIS in their escape. If he had, there was no telling how many others they might have infected with the knowledge. That single moment of weakness had set off a chain of events that he had not foreseen. Why, why had he done it? He supposed that he had made the mistake —phoning Delaney to warn him—from a misplaced sense of loyalty, some inexplicable eruption from his subconscious memories. At the time he had not yet seen the spirit flame of the master, had not yet heard his voice, though of course they had conversed interiorly for many years. How much easier it would have been if the master had spoken more clearly, had warned him of all the dangers, had revealed his face visibly before the situation began to unravel.

He reminded himself that it was not good to doubt the wisdom of the masters. They knew best. They saw all, understood all. Soon he would rise, and soon he would enter the next level in the stratigraphy of power. When he was among the great, he would recall this unfortunate evening with a tinge of sadness, would recall that it had been done hastily, poorly, but that it had been necessary. Despite this reassuring thought, it struck him suddenly that if he, the most powerful man in the Ministry, had no qualms about culling the undesirable elements employed by his department, then others higher up, more powerful than he, might one day consider culling the Director himself, if they considered him unsuitable. The continuing absence of the fugitives was definitely a failure on his part. Failure in minor ventures was permissible, for no human being was yet perfectly integrated. But failures of judgment that threatened the entire masterwork were not so forgivable.

He went into the bathroom, turned off the Jacuzzi tap, and lowered himself into the whirl of steaming water.

Once again he repeated the question he had asked himself countless times: Why had he done it? Why had he made that phone call? Perhaps it was only a scrap of debt thrown to the memory of Delaney's grandmother, the old Englishwoman, the first editor of *The Swiftcreek Echo*, the teacher. Anne was her name.

What debt?

He recalled the day in 1921 when she had stepped off a train into the mud of Swiftcreek, he a scruffy bush-boy and she a proper lady clutching a maroon fountain pen and a leather-bound book of poetry as if those things could push back the wall of dark trees, could ever defeat the ignorance of children bred to clear a forest and harvest fur and die their insignificant deaths in obscurity.

What debt?

She had been there on the day his mother died. She had pitied his loneliness, his grief. She had looked deep into his soul and appreciated the untapped greatness she saw there, loaned him books, and encouraged him to write his doleful little poems in the twenty-five-cent scribbler she gave to him one Christmas. She had taught him heroic poems by Tennyson and Whitman. She had loved him with a special love, he felt sure, and for years he had worshipped her behind a mask of a mute, unspeakable longing. Then she had married an Irish trapper and descended into her own kind of obscurity, no longer a porcelain lady from an exotic alien civilization, just another bush wife buried under the crushing labors of life on the edge of nothingness.

Then his father, a man of no education, had married a harridan, hoping to replace the long, blue, cold body of a dead mother with a fat, hot, mouthy, female ship's cook of a woman who had never read a poem in her life—Turid Gunderburg! Even her name was big and gross and spilling all over like her bust. Turid had sold her rooming house in exchange for permanent companionship in a bed, for a captive audience around a kitchen table, and to trade her hideous goats for a real cow. And though she had used some of her money to send Maurice to college, he knew that she had done it to get rid of him.

What debt?

Perhaps it had been only a lingering nostalgia for what might have been. If Anne had not married, if she had continued to be the teacher at the one-room village school, if his mother had not died of disease and poverty, if his father had understood there were other places and other ways to live, if he had not met a certain man at university who initiated him into an esoteric club, if . . . if . . . if. There were too many ifs, too many choices made too long ago, most of them forgotten.

He glanced down at his toes and noticed with a start that small threads of red were uncurling from the nails. Some of the priest's blood must have penetrated his shoes and socks. He quickly got out of the tub, stepped into a shower stall, and washed himself thoroughly. He washed and rinsed three times.

Later, robed in a black silk dressing gown, he stood by the living room window, sipping from a small glass of brandy. The night was blustery, the thick blue spruce trees beyond the fence of the Institute's perimeter were lashing, though no sound penetrated the apartment. He pushed a CD into the music console and felt his tension ease as the strains of a Mozart concerto filled the room.

His eye was distracted by sparks shooting up from the chimney of the incinerator in the forensic wing. He scowled and closed the curtains.

* * *

On the evening of Father Andrei's death, a strong wind blew in from the west, tore down trees in the lower Fraser Valley, disrupted power transmission in some areas, and kept most people in their homes.

Police reported that not a single violent crime or automobile accident happened in the city and valley that day, nor were there any on the following day—which for the region was an unprecedented event.

*

Théophane Nguyen braved the gale-force winds and drove down the hill to Saint George's church. He found Father Ron kneeling in front of the tabernacle. He asked the priest if they could talk. Sipping coffee in the rectory, they discussed the music ministry's song sheet for next Sunday's Mass (Théophane played keyboard, and two of his younger sisters sang in the choir). They also discussed minor difficulties they were having with some of the young people in the Youth Cenacle. But Father Ron seemed very distracted. Théophane asked him if anything was wrong. The priest told him that an hour before he had been doing bookwork in the parish office when an interior prompting had urged him into the church. He didn't know what it was about, but he felt he had to pray for someone who was in trouble.

Théophane suggested that they pray together for whoever it was, and Father Ron agreed. They prayed a rosary and a final prayer to the Archangel Michael for protection of the unknown person.

Then Théophane said he had been thinking a lot about the priesthood lately. Maybe a guy like him wouldn't make such a bad priest. His academics weren't too good, but with some help he could get through the first year at the sem. What did Father Ron think? Father Ron told Théophane that it was a terrific idea. He'd see what he could do.

After Théophane left, Father Ron returned to the church and knelt in front of the tabernacle. He made a commitment to the Lord to give up smoking again, as a sacrifice for Théophane's possible vocation and for the unknown person who had needed prayers this night. But his feeling of uneasiness would not subside. Restless, increasingly agitated, he tried to reason with himself, arguing that on any given day of the week there was always someone in trouble and that the mood was probably caused by nothing extraordinary. He was just feeling a little overworked and tired out from wrestling with doubts about this prophecy business.

Unable to shake off the feeling, he got up and made a telephone call to the archbishop.

*

The archbishop of Vancouver had gone to bed early that night. A bad cough was coming on, and he was exhausted from giving testimony in court that morning. The judge had decided in favor of the archdiocese, because the archbishop had saved Sister Connie's letter of resignation, proving that she had not been dismissed. He had been able to give his testimony in calm, clear, charitable language. He thanked God he was blessed with a personality that impressed people, for this had often helped him whenever he was defending difficult truths. But he also felt saddened by the realization that many legal cases were decided on the basis of impressions. Facts had become secondary for law professionals and juries, and that was a dangerous thing. It had worked in his favor today, but it could just as easily work against him in the future.

He was drifting off to sleep when the bedside phone rang. It was Father Ron. The young priest congratulated him on the court decision, then lapsed into silence.

The archbishop waited.

Father Ron cleared his throat.

"Is there something else you want to discuss, Father?"

"Well . . . uh."

"I'm rather tired this evening, fighting a touch of the flu. I'm afraid I don't have much energy for digging. Better tell me what's on your mind."

"Your Grace, I'd like to ask you what you really think about the whole prophecy thing. I've been having doubts."

"Doubts? What do you mean, doubts?"

"I mean, even I don't know for sure if it's real or not", he said anxiously. "Look at me, here I am Mister Visionary, and I don't have a clue. You'd think the Lord would give me some kind of certainty if I'm supposed to go out on a limb like this."

"Not necessarily—"

"Maybe it's just something from my subconscious. Delusions of grandeur or whatever they call it."

"Do you really think that's the case?" the archbishop replied carefully.

"I just don't know! I just don't know!"

"You seemed fairly certain a few months ago."

"I know. It's just—"

"To tell you the truth, Father, it would be a relief to me if that's all it were, just a case of overactive imagination or emotional disturbance. But this is larger than both of us now. You should keep in mind the possibility that your experiences are quite genuine. If so, you can expect to be assailed by doubts from time to time. You can also expect that our Lord wishes you to go step by step, in faith."

That calmed Father Ron a little.

"Tell me, what are your voices saying to you?" the archbishop went on.

My voices? Father Ron winced.

"The general drift of it is much the same. A crisis and a test is approaching for us all. I'm supposed to wake up my flock, feed them, strengthen them. How can I do that when I'm not even doing it for myself?"

"An excellent question. Perhaps that's where you should begin. Just how well are you feeding yourself—spiritually, that is?"

Father Ron hemmed and hawed. "Well, since this renewal of the parish started, I've been busier than ever. And the temptation to ease off on prayer has been pretty steady."

"There is your solution, I think. Cling to the Lord in prayer, Father. He will show you the way."

Father Ron sighed. "I know you're right. I know it. Why do I get so distracted?"

"We both know the answer to that, don't we. Now, aside from the general themes of these . . . visions or locutions . . . do you discern that the Lord is asking anything specific of you?"

"Uh, yeah", he mumbled. "Maybe that's what sparked the latest doubt."

"Why don't you tell me about it?"

Another sigh and a pause. "It's extreme."

"I've heard a few extreme things before."

"Well, I had this dream the other day. It was like my first one, the one where I took a crowd of children who'd come back from the dead to some distant mountains. Remember?"

"I remember."

"The second dream is like the first, but the number of people is smaller, and it's all incredibly realistic. The first dream was, you know, sort of mystical and symbolic. But this was . . . like watching a movie."

"What happened in the . . . movie?"

"There was a persecution going on, a persecution of the Church. I was ministering as an underground priest, a farm laborer. I moved from place to place saying Mass, hearing confessions, baptizing, marrying, all in secret. Then, when things got really bad, I led some people to a place of refuge in the mountains, somewhere up north in the Rockies, I guess. A saint guided us."

"A saint. Which saint?"

"I don't know."

"What kind of place was it?"

"I'm not sure."

"You called it a refuge."

"It was far away, in the mountains and forest, very primitive. There were angels covering it, to keep anyone from seeing it."

Both men said nothing. Father Ron broke the uneasy silence with, "Maybe it's just wishful thinking."

"Perhaps it is", the archbishop said eventually. "It sounds rather like a fantasy to me. Refuge? My, how I would love to find a little of that! I have three hundred thousand baptized believers in the archdiocese. The unbelievers are also my children—millions of them. That's a lot of souls. Tell me, Father, where are *they* going to find refuge?"

"I . . . I don't know", Father Ron stammered.

"All right," the archbishop said, "if anything else comes to you, please let me know."

"I will. Believe me, I will. Pray for me?"

"I do every day. Pray for me also."

After he hung up, the archbishop rubbed his forehead.

Refuge? he thought. *Where would these millions find it? And how would they find it?* Feeling profoundly disturbed and quite ill, the archbishop went to his private chapel and knelt before the Blessed Sacrament, unable to formulate mental prayers. At considerable physical cost, he bent over until his forehead touched the floor. At first the swirl of impressions revolved mercilessly, and he felt himself to be little more than a human shell containing the random debris of anguish and confusion. Gradually it subsided under the gentle currents of the Presence of the Lord, until in the end he was empty and waiting.

He had wanted answers. He had wanted solutions. He had hoped for a plan, but none came. This absence of practical direction would have renewed his anxiety were it not for a palpable stillness that enfolded him and filled him with peace. The actions of grace were silent, he knew, and usually without sensible effect. This mysterious dialogue of the soul had intrigued him all his life, but he had learned to recognize it as a real communication, or rather as a communion with the Lord.

The Lord wanted trust, above all trust. And this trusting was the foundation of the personal holiness from which right action flowed. By seeking solutions before the foundation was firm, he had been wanting to bypass faith and to grasp at knowledge, as if knowledge alone could save. This was an old error, a subtle one, part of fallen human nature. It was like building a house on sand, and he now saw that in his anxiety to preserve the flock from trials, to build a shelter for them, any shelter, he might have fallen into the trap of operating solely from fear. What was the nature of this fear? That trials were so annihilating that they must be avoided at all costs? That God could not, or would not, save? That he was not with his people?

He understood that the divine economy affirmed man's need to build secure dwellings in the midst of the instability of a damaged creation; knew that God willed man to use every reasonable and moral method to avoid evil and do good. But at some point every soul was put to some ultimate test, each must turn and face its eternal foe in a definitive struggle between radical terror and radical faith. And in such combat ordinary human strategies would always prove to be ineffective; moreover, by relying on them, one could easily be misled into a state of false security—and thus be doubly defeated.

Of course he was called to teach, protect, warn, feed the flock with sacraments and Scripture—that would never change. But if Father Ron and the other "prophets" were correct, the present situation was truly extraordinary. It might be no longer merely a case of individual struggle with evil. It could very well be the moment in history when the Church and the anti-Church, the Gospel and the anti-Gospel, entered the final phase of confrontation.

What, then, was the Lord saying to him?

Should he rally the flock of Vancouver and like Moses lead a quarter of a million people or more out into the desert?

Should he issue yet another pastoral letter exhorting his flock not to be conformed to the spirit of this world? Would they be any more receptive to it than they had been the last time?

Should he issue a pastoral letter on spiritual warfare?

Should he begin to make contingency plans for an underground Church?

Arrange escape routes for his clergy?

Prepare for martyrdom?—*Martyrdom?* Would it really come to that?

The archbishop's questions took shape in his mind as forms rather than words, and he laid them one by one before the Lord.

With each question the awareness grew in him that the time was close but was not yet; that the Lord would answer him when it was necessary for him to know, and then only as much as he needed to know. He supplied only enough manna for one day at a time. This was the perennial way of faith, the path of absolute abandonment to the will of God. This, and this alone, was the sure foundation.

Still, it was hard to feel so helpless.

There had been few times in his life when he had experienced prayer as a sensible force within him. He could count them on the fingers of his hands, the major crises, the great turning points, the opening of decisive chapters. His prayers were usually mental exercises, containing all the conviction of a converted will but devoid of passion or spiritual anointings. Rarely had he felt all faculties of his being converging like streams into a mighty river. Now, however, his heart and mind surged into a single current, and his arms were raised.

"Jesus, Savior of the world, have mercy upon us!" he cried aloud.

Over and over again the holy name burst from his lips, tears streaming from his eyes as he implored divine assistance.

"Please, my Lord, do not let this flock suffer because of my many lacks. Give me the heart of a true shepherd! Grant me wisdom! Send me courage! Lead us and guide us, for the night is growing dark!"

Then the voice that he had once heard so many years ago spoke to him from the interior of his own soul:

My little son, you have the heart of a true shepherd, though you have grown weary under the increase of trials. Come to me always. Seek my heart in silence. You are always within the plans of my providence. See, but a little while and I will strengthen you for the work that remains. Take the staff in your hand and grip it firmly. Do not hesitate to speak the truth, though many will not understand. Do not fear, little one, for I am with you always.

Be patient, my child. You are mine. Much has been done already, and much is yet to come. Guard well the flock of my Church. Teach my children to seek me in the innermost tabernacle of their souls. The only indestructible refuge is in the heart, where I dwell. There they will find me.

Bathed in the warmest peace he had ever experienced, the archbishop felt his anxieties falling away, and in the moments that followed, he remained immersed in the presence of the One who had spoken. There were no more words; none was needed.

He went back to his office and dialed the number of Saint George's parish. The phone rang a long time before Father Ron answered.

"I've had some more thoughts on what we discussed, Father."

The priest noted that the archbishop's tone was markedly different from what it had been an hour before. It was gentler. Strong, of course—the archbishop always radiated strength— but now there was an uncharacteristic tenderness.

"We talked about refuge."

"Yes, Your Grace, we did."

"If the Holy Spirit has been preparing you for some work, if he has been speaking to you about finding sanctuary, then there is probably real danger approaching."

"You mean . . . you mean you think the dream was from the Lord?"

"Let me ask you this: In a situation of danger, which is the worse reaction—the psychology of hysteria or the psychology of denial?"

It took the priest a few moments to think of a reply.

"Neither of them is good. But if I had to choose, I'd say the psychology of denial is the more damaging."

"I agree."

Father Ron remained silent, at a loss for words.

"Do you recall the passages in the Gospel where Jesus tells the disciples about the coming persecution and the signs of the end?"

"You mean Matthew 24?"

"Matthew relates it also, but in Luke 21 Jesus says an important thing that is often overlooked. After telling the disciples about all the terrifying events that are to take place at the end of the ages, he says, 'But when you see these signs begin to happen, stand erect, lift up your heads because your redemption is at hand.'"

"You mean we should have hope?"

"Yes. This is our refuge. God is always with us. He loves us. The necessary graces will be given, whether or not we are called to flee to a safe place, or to undergo martyrdom, or merely to stand erect in our positions in the field. It's not for us to inquire curiously into the path the Lord ordains for us. Do you understand?"

"I think so. You're saying we have to trust all the way."

"That's right. If we try to arrange our own protection in advance, we will get many things wrong."

"Are you saying we shouldn't prepare?"

"I'm not saying that at all. We can and must take certain measures, whatever is prudent and reasonable. However, that is not the foundation."

"And the foundation is . . . ?"

"To so love the will of God, to so believe in his mercy, that whether or not we live or die, we accept as a great gift whatever form our trials may take. This is the refuge."

"You mean faith?"

"Father, the only indestructible sanctuary is in the heart."

"The heart", Father Ron repeated.

"We are his priests. We gave our lives to him. And do you know what that means? It means sacrifice. We live in the mystery of his eternal sacrifice. If we are the Lord's, isn't it up to him to decide when and how we are to be part of that sacrifice?"

"I guess it is."

"We are all connected in the Body of Christ. Your sacrifices, my sacrifices, may be bringing about a tremendous good in the world, affecting the lives of countless people whom we may never meet in this life. What looks like darkness and pain to us may be, in fact, a source of light for others."

"You're right", Father Ron replied in a tone that could not hide a certain shame.

"We are human. Fears will come, doubts will come. But whenever they come, we must run to him and hide ourselves in his heart." The archbishop paused. "Teach your people to give themselves totally to God. Teach them to find his heart."

"You mean you want me to focus on getting people back to devotion to the Sacred Heart?"

"Yes. But more than that, I want you to teach them to find him in their own hearts."

Father Ron paused before replying. "As you taught us so often, Your Grace, a pastor's ministry is always specific. What exactly am I supposed to do . . . uh, in practical terms?"

"Begin with your own heart."

The priest sighed. "My emotions are a bit like scrambled eggs these days—"

"Emotions are only the surface of the heart. I mean the heart of the soul."

"It's a beautiful concept . . ." Father Ron's voice trailed off.

"I think you're telling me, Father, that it's a pious platitude." The archbishop smiled to himself.

"Oh, no, I didn't mean to imply that. The idea is beautiful, all right. I appreciate it. But I can't just tell them to go to their hearts. They wouldn't know what I'm talking about."

"You might be surprised."

"But I've got to give them something concrete. Something real."

"This is the ultimate real."

Father Ron's perplexity increased, even as he noted the archbishop's surreal calm. *Surreal?* he thought. *Maybe more like ultimate real.*

The archbishop went on: "Don't you remember your theology, Father? The 'indwelling Trinity in the souls of the just'? In the deepest recesses of our souls there is a place where Christ waits for us, where no physical or geographical calamity can take him from us. The heart of the soul is an interior tabernacle. The time may come, as it has for many nations, when it will be difficult, if not impossible, for the faithful to have access to the Eucharist. Churches may be closed, tabernacles empty, priests few in number, in prison or in hiding. Where, then, will our people find Jesus?"

"You're saying we need to prepare now."

"That is correct. Not just devotion to the Eucharist, but profound *union* with him in the Eucharist."

"But our people aren't mystics!"

"I know. But Christ dwells in them. They will find him."

"But how? I couldn't even begin to teach them about mystical theology. I don't know much about it myself!"

"My son, this is where we so often get bogged down. We trip over a misconception and never recover."

"What misconception is that, Your Grace?"

"The error of thinking we have to make a success of it by ourselves. Thinking we have to make it work."

"Don't we?"

"No. The initial impulse comes from God. We are called by Love himself. Our task is to come to him. He will lead us to the tabernacle of the heart. We need only ask."

Father Ron said nothing.

"Trust him, Father. Go to him. He will do the rest."

The two men said good night and hung up.

The archbishop, though he was sustained by the extraordinary peace, felt feverish and suddenly weak in the legs. He took two extra-strength Tylenol and went to bed. He was drifting off to sleep when, for no reason he could discern, he was suddenly wide awake. He sensed that something very wrong was happening somewhere in the archdiocese, an act that was evil and absolute but beyond the reach of human cognition. He got out of bed, went into the private chapel, and knelt before the Presence. He begged God to prevent the evil, but asked that, if it could not be prevented, God would bring a greater good from it.

* * *

In a marina of the resort city of Mazatlán, on the west coast of Mexico, the *Osprey* rocked gently in the water, and Julie awoke. Music from a hotel discotheque was pulsing against the porthole window of the cabin where she and Colin were lying in bed. The music was not loud enough to have awakened her. Colin was snoring, and there was nothing unusual in that. The children had had a wonderful day cavorting like porpoises in a hotel pool, and they too were sound asleep.

Julie turned over on her back and stared at the darkness. For no reason she could discern, she remembered the top of Father Andrei's scarred head as she had seen it on the first morning of their voyage to Bella Coola. Her heart began to beat wildly, and she grabbed her rosary from under her pillow.

The next morning, she and Colin and the children took the bus from Mazatlán to Mexico City. When they arrived in the capital that night, Colin decided they should be extravagant for once and rent a room at the Hotel Grande on the plaza across from the cathedral. The desk clerk looked like an Aztec god and the hotel owner a Spanish conquistador. A mariachi band in three-foot-wide sombreros surrounded their table in the restaurant and *oy-oy-oyed* to the strumming of a variety of guitarlike instruments. Their suite was palatial, the television hypnotic (the children were amazed to hear Bugs Bunny speaking Spanish). Each of them remarked on the odd sensation caused by a floor that did not tilt back and forth. They enjoyed long baths and showers before turning in for the night.

Colin and Cub were awakened at 6 A.M. by the sound of drums and bugles. They jumped into their clothes and dashed down the regal staircase and out the hotel's main entrance. Father and son returned an hour later with an excited account of the morning flag raising in front of the presidential palace.

"The flag was as big as a football field, Mum, and you never saw so many soldiers in your life!"

"There were people sleeping on the sidewalk", Colin added in a reflective tone. "Covered by rags and cardboard."

"Dad gave an old lady a hundred pesos", Cub proudly informed his mother.

After breakfast they crammed into a Volkswagen taxi that seemed to be held together by chicken wire and optimism and were taken in it to the shrine of Our Lady of Guadalupe. It was All Saints Day, and the plaza was crowded for the feast. Julie and Colin were moved by the fervor of the Mexican people, their brass bands, their flowered pageant floats, their colorful clothing, the gusto of their singing, their poverty, their beautiful children—children, children everywhere—the shining faces of tens of thousands of pilgrims streaming into the shrine of Our Lady of Guadalupe. Achingly young teenage soldiers ringed the immense plaza holding machine pistols and shotguns, shooing beggars away from the *touristas*. Guarding everyone from what? Julie wondered.

When Colin looked up at the miraculous image of the Mother of God, he took a step backward, steadied himself, and frowned. Julie wept; the children were awestruck. And for the first time in their lives, Colin attended Mass with them and knelt at all the proper moments, though his mouth remained silent and his eyes troubled. At the Consecration his eyes widened and filled with tears. After Mass he went to the gift shop and purchased a bag of miraculous medals. For the remainder of the day he walked about the plaza giving them away to anyone who would accept one.

*

On the night of Father Andrei's death, Alice M. Douglas was in her kitchen, trying to read, feeding the firebox of her wood stove from time to time, stroking Poody-tat's back, feeling distressed. She had been fighting waves of stark fear and a steady plunge into depression ever since Arrow's disappearance. No matter how hard she tried, she couldn't concentrate on the mystery story and threw it down on the floor. The siren song of whiskey washed through her bloodstream, but for once she refused to give in. Her gums were sore; her eyes were sore. She turned off the overhead light. She sat in the dark, chain-smoking, getting up only to check on Nick. Nick was making unhappy sounds, but he was just dreaming. A baby nightmare probably. He whimpered and said, "Awo!", then lapsed into silence.

Alice returned to the kitchen, not knowing what to do with herself. She paced back and forth for ten minutes, Poody-tat following her steps, tippy-tapping his claws on the linoleum, meowing at her every so often, as if he weren't sure why they were doing this and wanted to know what it was for.

Alice threw herself down into the armchair and hid her face in her hands. The anguish built and built, until finally she sobbed, "Where is he? Where is he?"

Deep groanings of the heart shook her. Her sobs became a wail.

"Please!" she cried. "Please, don't let them hurt him!"

She looked at the booze cabinet for a split second, then turned her eyes away from it. She stared down into the cupped palms of her hands.

"Please", she said again. "I know I'm no good. I know I ain't worth nothin', and I don't have a right to ask. But I am askin' you."

She shuddered with the bottomless grief of it, with the hopelessness of it, with the silence that greeted her plea. Yet a strange peace trickled in and began to calm her.

"I'm askin' you, God", she concluded in a choked voice. "I'm askin' you."

Eventually Alice's gaze fell on three cardboard boxes stacked behind the stove. They contained old papers and useless books that she had found in a storage room some months before and had hauled out to use as fire starter. It was Donnie's stuff, letters and bills, back issues of *Mechanics Illustrated* and *Consumer Reports,* a few Louis L'Amour westerns.

Not knowing why she did it, she opened the top box and dug through it. Halfway down she found a battered, well-thumbed King James Bible.

Donnie? A Bible thumper? Not a chance! She remembered him when he was a kid, a little fat guy wiping snot from his nose. Always begging Mum for a new hockey stick. Always wearing that torn T-shirt with the Toronto Maple Leafs decal on it. She was always tying the squirt's shoelaces for him, always forking over a nickel so he could buy a Coke. He was always, always, bugging her. The brat.

Alice opened the Bible to the front page and saw her own twelve-year-old squiggle handwriting on it.

"Dear Don, Happy Berthday. Hope this Good Book keeps you outa trubble. Your darling sister, Allie (Moose)."

Drying her eyes, Alice smiled crookedly. It was the first time she had smiled since she had lost Arrow.

She sat down in the armchair and by the light of the open firebox began to read.

*

Also on the night of Father Andrei's death, a young woman

742

named Kateri was travelling on a passenger train that was rolling out of the rail terminal at Winnipeg, Manitoba, heading west. She felt an agony seize her heart, withdrew a rosary from her skirt pocket, and began to pray.

*

During that same hour a man named Joseph, who was camped in the boreal forest beside a river to the east of Great Slave Lake in the Northwest Territories, sat up and threw back the fur robe that covered his sleeping bag. The embers of his fire had died down within a glowing circle of stones. The hare he had cooked for supper rested in his contented belly. But his heart was uneasy.

The stars were very bright. He could see the Milky Way spread out like a sheet across the vault of the night. A wolf howled, foxes barked. The river chattered at the underside of its ice cover. A breeze blew through the jack pines, which began to sway, creaking and groaning.

The man threw more wood on the embers, the flames licked it and flowered. Then, gazing up into the unfathomable waters of the universe, he prayed.

*

In Bella Coola, British Columbia, Potempko stayed up all night reading a book on cosmology, a Latin edition published in Budapest in 1934. He thought it would help him sleep. It didn't. He was irritated. He never suffered from insomnia. Never. There was also an unpleasant bubbling sound in his lungs that he attributed to smoking cheap tobacco for so many years. He was coughing up black phlegm. He missed his pipe. The burns from his silly accident were healing well, but they still hurt. He blamed the sleeplessness on this and offered up the discomfort for Father Andrei.

*

In a cabin in the Cariboo mountains, Zöe Delaney woke up and cried, waking her brother and great-grandfather. She told

743

Thaddaeus that she had a stomachache, but the ache faded as the old man rocked her and whispered soothing words. She cried in his arms for an hour, a dull, wracked sobbing that resisted every attempt at reassurance. She did not know why she was crying.

Her great-grandfather asked if she had had a bad dream. Zöe said maybe she had but couldn't remember it. She fell back to sleep around two in the morning. Tyler drifted off shortly after. Thaddaeus sat down on a bench beside a cupboard made from a wood packing crate. The family altar, he called it. A framed holy card was perched on top, and beside it a glass jar containing the stub of a red Christmas candle decorated with a wax snowman carrying an armload of poinsettia. He lit the candle. He prayed. He did not sleep.

*

In Italy, several hours later, a priest named Elijah and a cardinal opened a pyx that the cardinal always carried on his person. Beneath the velvet-lined bottom of the interior they discovered a miniature radio transmitter and thus learned a great deal about the intrigues of their adversary.

*

Neither did Cecilia Manyberries sleep. She knelt on the cold plank floor of her bedroom in Charlie and Rose's house and prayed until dawn. She alone, of all those who had known Father Andrei, understood what had happened. She saw it all. Shortly before the sun burst over the coastal range, he appeared before her. His face was radiant, and he smiled at her with great love.

19

The Falcon and the Sparrow

In the morning a woman came into Arrow's room and sat down at the end of his bed. He knew she was there but did not uncurl his body or otherwise acknowledge her presence. She shook his arm and said his name. He did not want to look at her, but he knew he had wet the bed again and didn't smell very good.

"Come on there, son", she coaxed. "I'll bet you don't feel comfortable."

No, he didn't, but the lump of sick fear in his throat was stronger than discomfort.

"You're going to get ill if you don't eat", she went on in a sweet voice. "Why don't you open your eyes? I've brought you a clean set of clothes. You can go into the bathroom and clean up, and then I'd like you to get dressed. Okay?"

Arrow squeezed his eyes shut more tightly.

"You're going home", she said.

He heard her get up and leave the room, closing the door behind her.

Going home?

And what had she said about a bathroom? He didn't understand. There was no bathroom in the room, only a toilet in the corner. He opened his eyes and saw that a door stood open in the wall at the foot of his bed, in a spot where there had been no door when he fell asleep last night. He sat up and stared at it.

Going home? Maybe they were going to let him go. Maybe they had found his brother and sister and his great-grandfather,

745

and they would take him to meet them. He would see what they looked like. He would go and live with them.

Taking the clothing with him, he went into the bathroom and gingerly lowered himself into a tub that was full of warm water. He soaped himself, rinsed, and got out. Then he put on the plain blue shirt, clean underwear, brand new green corduroy pants, striped socks with the labels still on them, and a pair of running shoes with bubbles in the heels and tiny red lights that circled around the white rims. There was a switch on the heel that turned the lights off and on and off and on. Alice sold shoes like this in the Palace of Junque, batteries included. Arrow put them on.

He sat on his bed and waited.

A few minutes later the woman returned, patted him on the shoulder, and gave him a tray on which there was a plate of toast and strawberry jam, a glass of milk, a bowl of Nabisco shreddies sprinkled with brown sugar, and an orange. He bolted it down, every bit of it, even the orange peels.

When he was finished, she came back and told him he was going for a ride.

He opened his mouth and tried to speak, but only a small scraping sound came out of it. He had not said a word in more than two weeks, not even when a doctor had taken the stitches out of his tummy. Not even when they wheeled a television set into his room and asked him what kind of cartoons he liked best.

He tried his voice again. "Am I going to see my great-grandpa?" he rasped.

She replied that she didn't know anything about that, but maybe the nice man who was going to take him for a drive could tell him.

Downstairs, in a lobby full of potted plants, marble floors, and big glass windows, the woman introduced him to an old man.

"Are you my great-grandpa?" Arrow asked shyly.

The man looked uncomfortable for a moment.

"No, I'm not your great-grandfather", he replied in a kind voice. "But I want to take you to him. I'm hoping you can help me find him." He reached out a hand and ruffled the boy's hair. "Do you think we can do that, Arrow?"

Arrow nodded enthusiastically.

They went outside, and the man opened the front door of a car that was parked at the end of the walkway. Arrow looked up at the sky. He inhaled the fresh air. The lump of sick dread was gone, and in its place there was a throb of excitement. He got into the passenger side, and the old man got in behind the wheel.

The man talked to him in a nice voice. They drove through three sets of gates and down a lane onto a paved road. Arrow could hardly answer any of the man's questions because he was obsessed by the beautiful sky and the tall trees that were swaying on all sides.

The road came to a ramp leading onto a highway. Many cars and trucks were roaring in both directions. The man pulled over to the shoulder and stopped, letting the motor idle.

"I'm going to need your help from now on, Arrow", Maurice said. "Do you know where your great-grandfather lives?"

Arrow shook his head sadly. "No, I never met him."

The man frowned. "Do you know where your brother and sister live?"

Again he shook his head.

"Weren't you staying with them?"

"No."

"Someone looked after you. Do you remember who?"

"Father Andrei."

"Oh, yes, he looked after you for a while, didn't he? But that was a long time ago. Where did you live after . . . ?"

"After the black beetles took him?"

"Yes, after the black beetles took him. Where did you go?"

Arrow told him about a train ride, how he had jumped out of a freight car onto the banks of a creek and then how he had run through the bushes to where The People live. It was a long story, full of dead fishes and something called a windy-go and a doll with a missing arm, a cat, goats, and a baby on a swing.

"Oh, I see. You stayed with Mr. and Mrs. Potter."

"No, I never stayed there. I didn't know her. I only saw her in the hospital. With the igloo."

"Can you remember, Arrow, where you were living when you got sick? Who was looking after you?"

"A lady."

"What is her name?"

"Alice."

"Can you remember anything else? Her last name?"

"Queen of Junk."

Maurice looked at the boy and tightened his lips.

"Where does she live? Is it near Fort George?"

"I don't know. I don't know where Fort George is."

"It's the place where the hospital is, where the Potters live."

"Oh . . . I didn't know."

"Try to remember, Arrow. What did you mean about the Queen? That's not her name, is it?"

"She's the Queen of Junk. It's on her sign."

"I see. And where is the sign?"

"In the mountains above where the red fish play and the green pebbles laugh."

Maurice groaned silently. "And where is that?"

"Near where Maya lived."

"Maya? Oh, yes, your mother. Near Salmon Creek."

Arrow nodded. "Above there. Back. Far."

Maurice put the car into reverse and backed up until he was clear of the on-ramp, then drove under the expressway to an access highway. He turned east and fifteen minutes later took the cut-off to Fort George. When they crossed over the river on the Fraser bridge, Arrow spotted the marina. He craned his neck and raked the rows of boats with his eyes. But the *Osprey* was not there.

"Do you remember now? Which direction should we go?"

"I'm not sure."

"Where does the Queen of Junk live?"

"I can't remember." Arrow looked to the right, to the left, up the mountain, down the river.

Maurice pulled over to the curb, stopped, and let the motor idle.

"Try to remember", he said in a stern voice of command.

Arrow looked up at him, surprised by the tone. The old man's eyes were cold, cold, and Arrow felt a seed of fear swell in his throat. The eyes bored into him. Arrow pressed himself against the door.

He smelled dead things. He felt a breath of *windigo*, just like the time the wind had kicked up the ashes in Maya's burned yurt.

Maurice looked away from him, turned the car left into the town, and drove along Main Street until he found the R.C.M.P. detachment. He parked, told the boy to stay put, and got out, locking all the doors by remote control.

A solitary corporal stood at the reception desk, tapping a pencil, staring distractedly at a stack of files before him, swaying to pop music playing softly on a transistor radio.

Maurice bypassed formalities. He flashed his OIS badge. The corporal took one look at it and stood uneasily to attention.

"I'm trying to locate anyone who might call herself the Queen of Junk", Maurice said tonelessly.

"The Queen of Junk?" The corporal scratched his head. "Rings a bell. An alias? Some local pusher maybe?"

"No, not a pusher. This is a federal security matter. Does the name Alice ring a bell?"

"Alice . . . Alice . . . Let me see . . ."

Then the corporal's eyebrows raised and his mouth tilted into an odd diagonal smile.

"You don't mean Alice Douglas, do you? She's got a store up by Steelhead, about twelve miles from town, on the north road."

"That's probably the one, corporal. By any chance does the store contain used merchandise?"

"Well, yes, I guess it does."

"A junk shop, perchance?" Maurice intoned patiently.

"That's right. People up there call her Queenie. A funny old bird, but harmless. I don't think she'd be involved in a federal security problem . . ." He paused and looked wonderingly at Maurice. "Is she?"

Maurice frowned. "Thank you, corporal. That is all. This pertains to intelligence matters, and I will hold you personally accountable if any mention of my inquiry, or my presence here, goes beyond this room."

"It won't, sir. Absolutely not. You can count on it."

"Where are the other officers on duty?"

The corporal chuckled. "It's Halloween, sir. They're checking out a party at the high school. Later, I guess they'll be chasing teenagers and scraping rotten eggs off doors. I go home at five, but I can tell them you were in, if you need to talk to them."

"I won't need to talk with them. I won't need to return here, and you won't mention this investigation to the other officers. Do you understand?"

The corporal gulped. "Yes, sir, I understand."

"Very good."

Maurice turned on his heels and returned to the car. Arrow was sitting where he had left him, shoulders hunched, eyes closed, hands squeezed between his knees.

Maurice unfolded a road map and located Steelhead on it. He drove back down Main Street, turned left at the traffic lights, ascended the steep hill on which the town was built, and a few minutes later reached the north road that led into the mountains.

He drove on for three miles, going slowly because a thin rain had begun to fall; it was freezing on the windshield and slicking the road. The car swam across the line once or twice, and he geared down for better control. He glanced at the boy, but Arrow was curled into a semi-fetal position, as much as the seat belt would allow, his eyes squeezed shut, face white.

Abandoning all semblance of niceness, Maurice snapped questions at the boy in a threatening tone. He especially wanted to know if the woman called Alice knew where the great-grandfather was. Arrow did not respond.

The boy would tell him. Or the Queen of Junk would tell him. Either way, the problem would be eliminated shortly.

He rounded a curve and braked hard, just in time to slide to a long, skidding stop in front of a rusty old Chevrolet sedan that was blocking the road sideways.

Maurice cursed and banged on the horn. There was a human form inside the steamed windows of the other car. A small woman, by the looks of it. She was obviously shaken by the near accident, head bowed over the wheel, grinding the vehicle's ignition key. Its engine caught and spewed a cloud of black smoke out the exhaust. The car lurched forward a foot, then spun sideways on the ice, almost denting the front bumper of the OIS car. It stalled.

The woman got out of the driver's side and stood in front of Maurice's car, babbling incomprehensibly.

Maurice got out, taking care to lock the car doors behind him.

"What's the problem?" he snapped at the woman.

More babbling. She threw a diminutive hand into the air and clutched a silver crucifix at her throat with the other.

"Caw, bad caw! Too much ice!" she cried. "So sorry."

He looked at the woman in disgust. Perfect, he raged silently, just perfect. Who better to impede efficiency? Who better to block the path of progress? Of course, it would have to be one of the useless ones. Three strikes against her: she was female, oriental, and religious—moreover, she was *that* kind of religious.

"You get in and drive", he ordered. "I'll push."

He went around to the rear of the Chevy, putting on his leather gloves, detesting the thought of the mess that would cover his trench coat, the spatters of mud on his shoes. She tried to start the engine again, but its battery merely groaned.

"Come on, come on", he muttered. He stared at her car in revulsion, its leprous body, its bald tires, its filth. It would be an act of mercy to destroy it.

Four strikes: she was poor, pitifully poor, if indeed she deserved pity. She did not deserve it. She was the offscouring of the world. There were too many of them. Soon, this type would disappear.

The woman turned the key again, the motor caught and fired. Smoke blasted out of the exhaust pipe. She threw the shift into first gear too quickly, making the car lurch and revolve on its screaming tires. Maurice pushed hard on the trunk lid until at last the car began to inch forward, sliding in an arc. When it stalled again, it was now parallel to the yellow line. He could drive around it and go on to Steelhead.

As he walked toward the OIS car, the woman jumped out of the driver's seat of her car and came up to him.

"Bettah, Mistah. It bettah now. Tank you. Tank you."

"You're welcome. Now I must be on my way."

Then she stopped. A look came over her face that meant nothing to him. It expressed no emotion that he was familiar with, nothing he had ever read on a human face. He tried to get into his car, but the look held him. Something else held him also, and he felt that time itself had slowed, the needle-rain

752

falling now like soft feathers, while above him birds were suspended in midflight, a falcon and a sparrow performing a mysterious slow-motion choreography through a tunnel of warped matter, the trees swaying in a funeral march from which all music and all energy had been bled, sound sliding into a low sigh that blurred every meaning.

Her eyes looked deep into his soul, black almond eyes, shining agates, a drop of water crossing her cheek like a snail traversing a planet, mouth opening and closing, opening and closing.

What had she said to him?

"You no do it, Mistah. You no do it."

He forced a current of absolute zero into her eyes. She flinched but resisted it. There was something in her that was stronger. She grabbed the sleeve of his coat. He tried to pull away, but he had no strength.

"God see it. God see it", she said.

Then more of her foreign babble.

He shook his arm loose and swore at her. Time and sound shifted into high gear, a roaring in his ears, the needle-rain piercing his skin, the falcon and the sparrow spiraling upward on the wind.

She closed her eyes and raised both arms above him, her tiny palms exposed.

Five strikes: she was insane into the bargain.

"Get away from me!" he shouted, and opened the door of his car.

"Precious in my eyes are my beloved!" she cried in her child's voice, inexplicably fluent. "Precious in my eyes are my beloved!"

He got in and started the car. Arrow was frozen into a ball of unseeing. Maurice shifted into drive and moved his foot to the gas pedal. But the madwoman had run around to the front and was standing in his path. He powered down the window and barked at her, "Get out of my way!

"His eye is on the sparrow! His eye is on the sparrow!"

Startled, he glared at her.

"They forgave you!" she cried. "The man forgave you! The Faddah forgave you! Missus Pottah forgave you!"

Panicking, Maurice bellowed at her: "Move!"

He pressed the accelerator, and the car crept slowly forward, bumping into the woman as if she were a body floating in the South China Sea, shunting her aside. She hop-skipped out of the path, dropped her arms and opened her eyes.

"Forgive your muddah! Forgive your faddah!" she cried as he roared away.

His hands gripped the wheel fiercely, shaking, clammy; his breathing heavy, eyes snapping . . . in what? Rage? Fear?

What did he have to fear from a woman like that? Nothing!

But the fear increased, containing a dread suspicion that there was more at work in the situation than he had supposed. Trying to calm himself, he argued that the woman was nothing other than a mouthpiece for the other side, the angels of the half-light. They could play their mental tricks on him if they liked, but it would make no difference. They could manipulate, they could flash illusions across the screen of consciousness, say things to unsettle the ignorant and naïve, deflecting them from their proper course. But he was not so ignorant. He could not be fooled. He was strong, full of the *gnosis* that the masters had shared from their storehouse of knowledge. She was a nothing, a shell, a trumpet used by her own spirit masters, and they too would soon disappear with the coming of the fullness of the spectrum.

Forgive, the idiot had said. They all said that, *all* of them. Part of their programming, no doubt. Brainwashed, cowering before their tyrannical deity, seeking to please him with a final heroic gesture that meant nothing in the end.

The world was teeming with mindless fools. Generation unto generation of them. From early childhood he had understood

what they were, beginning with the children at the Swiftcreek school who had mocked him for his solitude, his poverty, his poetry, his superior intelligence. Tormented him
because he would not run like a rat through the maze of a
social hierarchy that was defined by muscle and ignorance,
could not play their small, mean, mating games and their
playground politics.

He had been the kind of boy who stood on mountaintops,
seeking relief from all human company, despising their follies
and their ugliness, wanting to ascend into the high places,
watching eagles gather in the upper spaces where he would one
day be transformed into the shape he desired, though its actual
form would be decades in coming.

Always, they had pulled at his limbs, his mind, his heart,
dragging him down from the heights, away from the sky, back
from the zone of freedom where there were no other faces to
shame his own face, none to demand that he become a shape he
did not want, or mock him for what he was. Hands grabbing
and pulling, mouths whining and accusing, wanting everything
from him, giving nothing.

They took my mother, he thought. *Death took my mother.*

But death, in the end, was not as powerful as he had first
supposed. No, in time he had mastered the knowledge of death
and the tools of death and become death's master. He was above
it. Taking wing, he was free.

He had been a small boy in a world of exile, there where
winters fell heavily upon the soul, grinding men's lives into
powder and scattering it to the four winds. The graveyard of
Swiftcreek was spilling over with children and women dead of
plague and childbirth and men cut off in their youth by the
many dangers of their crushing labors. Trees falling on fathers,
arms sliced off in mills, eyes gouged out, ears deafened by the
roar of primitive machinery, bleeding to death, freezing to
death, sickened unto death by virus and despair.

His own father weeping, weeping, *Mon Dieu! Mon Dieu!*, terrifying the cluster of white-faced children gathered around the long, cold, blue body of a dead mother.

He *had* to escape it, had to ride the dual serpent of rail that took him out of it. Out of it! Out of the darkness of the forest forever! Forever and forever out of that insufferable, interminable weakness!

Forgive his father? For what? Forgive him for being a weak, weeping man who was too small for the exile to which fate had condemned him?

Forgive his mother? Forgive her for the weakness of the flesh that destroyed her as surely as it had destroyed his father's character?

No, say rather that he should *not* forgive. Say rather that he should not forgive anything, all the way up the celestial hierarchy to a throne where a mythological deity had chosen to make man into a weak thing, a race of vermin.

"Maurice", said a child's voice.

He shook off the voice. A mirage, a phantom, a deceit of the enemy.

"Maurice."

Ignoring it, he saw a sign flash past his left window.

Get Everything You Want at Queen of the Road Collectibles
We buy junque. We sell antiques.
Alice M. Douglas, prop.
3 Km ahead

The pavement ended, and gravel began. Road repair signs, fluorescent orange cones, an abandoned tar-making machine, a sign:

Slow!
Province of British Columbia
Ministry of Highways
Building a Better Tomorrow

The gravel spattered noisily under the tires, and he decelerated.

"Maurice."

He looked at the boy. Arrow's eyes were open, watching him. His body was uncurled from the fetal position. His hands rested on his lap.

Maurice stared at him, barely noticing the right tires slide dangerously onto the shoulder. He jerked the wheel, and the car returned to the road.

"What did you say?" he asked the boy.

"I said Maurice, but I don't know why."

"How do you know my name?"

"I don't know your name. Is that your name?"

Hair rising on the back of his neck, Maurice pulled over to the shoulder and parked. Ahead on the right he could see a gas station, half a sign on its roof appearing through the heaving branches of giant pines:

> Queen of the Road Col
> We buy jun
> Alice M. Dou

"Why did you say that?" Maurice demanded in a low voice.

"I don't know. I saw a man standing on a mountaintop. It was my father. He was looking at me. He said Maurice. So I said Maurice."

"You saw it?"

"In my mind, like a picture."

"You say he was standing on a mountaintop?"

"Yes, watching eagles flying. There was another man too. Across a valley, far, back, up, in a place I never saw. There were two mountains. My father stood on one. The other man stood on the other. My father looked up and saw one thing. The other man looked up and saw a different thing."

Maurice's hands began to tremble. "Why are you telling me this?"

"I don't know. The picture feels good. It feels good when I tell it."

"Who are you?" Maurice bellowed.

Strangely, the boy did not cringe. "I'm Arrow", he answered calmly.

"Aren't you afraid of me?"

Arrow shook his head. "I was before. Now I'm not."

"Why not?"

"Because I saw my father, and he was looking at me."

"Don't you know that I can hurt you?"

Arrow looked out the window and kept his eyes fixed on the trees. "Yes", he answered.

Maurice stared ahead through the windshield. Confusion and rage circled each other in a desperate dance.

"My father says the words can be undone."

Maurice turned his head and stared at Arrow. "What?"

"The words you said, far away, a long time ago, in the dark place."

"Where?"

"I don't know where. A dark place. With shadows and fires and many people. You said words. You made a promise. The words were from the *windigo,* and you breathed them in, then you blew them out your mouth, but they stayed inside."

"What words?" Maurice insisted.

"I can't hear the words. I can't say them. They are bad."

"What else did you see?" Maurice demanded through gritted teeth.

"My father says a garden. Two trees."

"Shut up! Don't say any more!"

Arrow looked out the window again.

Maurice turned off the ignition. He closed his eyes. Then he too saw a vision of trees. Two trees. The antique doctrine, the

758

discarded myth—a junk theology. A man and a woman naked together in the garden, and a serpent coiling into the garden, whispering, whispering, whispering, now this way, now that, a spirit that was no more than shadows taking the form of a creature of cunning and speaking through it.

Do not believe, do not believe, it whispered, whispered, whispered, coiling about their minds. *Did God really say that? No, God did not really mean that!*

Then the serpent whispered into the ear of the woman, and she believed what it told her. The woman took of the tree of knowledge of good and evil and ate of it, then she bid her husband to eat, and he too ate of it. His was the greater error, for he was the firstborn, the father of the race, the husband and shelterer.

Then they were cast out, ashamed, doubting everything, most of all themselves, driven into a world of thorns and cold and hunger and death. A cherubim was stationed at the gates of the garden with a fiery sword that flashed and revolved unceasingly, to guard the way to the tree of life.

The banishment was bitter. The exile was hard, and the man and the woman hated it. They blamed each other, and they blamed the serpent, and for a time they blamed the One who had made them. The woman said to the man, "It is not fair that he should punish us so, for we did not know that his word was true." And the man replied, "Remember how he loved us, and in that love we knew that he was true. See also, my wife, that love does not mix truth with untruth, nor does it divide the spirit from the flesh, nor did he intend it from the beginning that we should taste death. We brought it upon ourselves, for we are changed and unfit to live in the garden of our joy."

"Still, my husband, it is bitter", replied the woman. "It is not just!"

"Say rather, my wife, that is we who were not just, for we

believed a lie, and through our hearts the lie came into paradise, which we have lost. Yet, see how he loves us still, for he has promised that from our seed shall come another who shall crush the serpent's skull."

Then the man and the woman went together into the shadows, bearing their grief and their lament, their reproach and their hope, within their own flesh.

And the serpent rustled through the thorn bushes, following them, whispering, "The shadows are the light, the shadows are the light, for in the union of good and evil is the fullness of the spectrum."

"He is mercy!" thundered the cherubim. "He is all love! In him there is no darkness!"

But the shadows closed over the backs of the departing ones as they made their way into the barren lands to the east of Eden, and they did not hear the cherubim, for the sound of whispering was loud in their ears.

It was not a heartless punishment, Maurice now saw. This was no cruel blow smashing down on small defenseless creatures, for they had lived as sons of heaven, as gods, before their fall. Powerful was their love, powerful was their union. Powerful was their perfect trust until the moment it was shattered. The choirs of angels wept and sorrowed when the man and the woman fell to the deceiver's art. And so did their Father weep, for he did not cease to be all love. He was no minor deity jealous of his power. He was love, and love would not permit eternal life for creatures who had invited eternal death into their hearts. And so the dying of their flesh was mercy. Seven, eight hundred years he gave them before they returned to dust. And during that time they felt their creaturehood in the height and depth of their beings. From the marrow of their bones to the thoughts of their minds and to the movements of their spirits, they felt weakness. And this weakness was their only strength. For if they had been permitted to live forever with the taste of good and evil on their lips, growing in the strength that is false strength, growing in the knowledge that is unknowledge, that is the engorging of truth and half-truth and untruth, they would have been filled with the spirit of lies, filled and filled with it until there was no more truth, and they would have been filled up entirely with Satan and become Satan. Which is no mercy.

Then Mercy itself took flesh and came among them, for he was love, and he felt everything that they had felt. He was love, and their descendants killed him, and to this day there are many who kill him, and also do they kill his image upon sight, for he is love, and men prefer darkness to light and fear to love.

But there are those who do not, and in their weakness they bear the ancient wound until the final sealing up of all wounds. In meekness and thanksgiving they walk, knowing cold and hunger and thirst and exile, praising God for this great gift. Praising him for his first mercy and for the greater mercy that came after and for the mercy that is yet to come.

Maurice opened his eyes. His heartbeat raced uncontrollably, his face flushed. He felt as if he were choking.

Arrow said something to him, but he could not hear. The whispering was loud in his ears.

The autumn sun was going down in the west, breaking through the pall of overcast, shooting waves of red gold through the darkness toward the earth.

Arrow lifted both of his hands toward Maurice. The old man shrank away.

A beam of light burst through the windshield at that moment, refracted through the dashboard compass, breaking into two beams that struck the boy's hands. The palms were open, the light was red, and for an instant Maurice thought he saw two wounds upon the child's hands.

Shaking himself, he realized that it was an optical illusion.

The boy put a hand on Maurice's shoulder, but it seemed to burn like ice, and the man flinched.

"It's okay", Arrow reassured him. "You don't have to be scared."

Terror and rage surged inside of Maurice, a desperate struggle of conflicting desires—to kill the boy on the spot, to return him to the Institute, to push him from the car, telling him to run, run, don't look back.

Paralyzed, unable to do any of these things, he put his head in his hands. This made it worse, for his mind reeled, swirling with a frothing gurge of hideous and beautiful imagery. Light, darkness, light, darkness, splitting apart, eternally in a state of enmity.

Maurice began to weep. It was a dry, wracking sound that produced no tears. He had shed no tears since the day of a funeral almost seventy years before.

"Are you sad?" the boy asked.

"I was a child once", the old man breathed. "I made beautiful things. I made poems."

"You can make some more", the boy answered, as if that were a simple thing, comforting and encouraging as if he were the adult and Maurice the child.

"You don't know. You don't understand. You don't know the things I've done!" he murmured in a tone of self-loathing.

"My father says you can start over. You can ask it."

"It's too late!"

"No, it's not."

"It is! It is!" He looked at the boy. "I killed . . . I killed your . . ."

Arrow looked down at his hands as if he did not recognize them.

"My father is looking at you", Arrow said wonderingly. "Why is he looking at you?" he asked in a puzzled voice.

"Because . . ."

"My father says, forgive. Why did he say that?"

"There was no time. There was never any time. When the

knowledge began to fill me, I let the poems die. I had no time for them."

"You can make some more. You can."

"A long time ago, the woman who was your father's grandmother taught me to make them. But I had to leave all that", he said miserably. "I let them die. I shouldn't have . . ."

"There is lots of time."

Maurice closed his eyes and laid his head back on the headrest. *"For I who was a child, my tongue's use sleeping, now I have heard you, now in a moment I know what I am for . . ."*

The man groaned and sighed, water seeped from his eyes.

"I awake, and already there are a thousand singers, a thousand songs . . ."

He began to sob in a low, choked voice.

"I don't know if there is any hope for me. But perhaps, somewhere in the universe, maybe somewhere beyond it, my one small act will be noted. It will say that I was not completely evil."

Maurice pulled the remote control from his jacket pocket and pressed a button. The locks on all the car's doors clicked and sprang up.

"I am doing this of my own will", he said. "You have to go, now. Alarm bells are ringing all over the west."

Arrow cocked his head, listening. "I don't hear any bells."

"They are not the kind you can hear with your ears. Warnings are being whispered in every mind that serves my masters. And my own keeper is coming . . ." He paused and seemed to have trouble breathing. "Quickly. If you do not go now, I will not have any will left to continue."

"You want me to go?"

Maurice leaned over and opened Arrow's door.

"You must understand that ninety percent of me is strangling the ten percent that is about to give you your freedom."

Amazed, Arrow looked at the man, unsure of his meaning. He put one leg outside the door.

"Go!"

Arrow stepped outside. Maurice reached into the back seat and pulled something from it. He pushed it into Arrow's hands, saying, "Inside is a gift for you. It's from Father Andrei. It's from your father who is standing on the mountain looking at you."

Arrow stared at the object in his hands. It was his knapsack.

"Run!" Maurice said fiercely and closed the door.

Arrow did not run. He stood on the side of the road and watched the car make a U-turn and drive in the direction from which it had come.

The boy waited for a few minutes, breathing the chilly air, listening to the cries of birds. He looked up at many mountaintops. Then, slowly, he walked toward the Palace of Junque.

* * *

The lights on the gas pumps were off, the venetian blinds on the display windows were shut, the *Closed* sign was hanging in the windowpane of the door. Arrow peered inside the store, but it was too dark in there to see anything. He tried the handle, but it was locked. He rapped on the glass, but Alice didn't come.

He decided to walk around to the back of the building, but he was stopped by the fence that surrounded the junk yard. Because of his many days without food, he was too weak to climb it. He circled the front of the building again and came to the kitchen window on the other side. Nick was in his high chair swatting and rattling chess pieces. A blue jay flew past. When Nick looked up and saw Arrow standing there, he smiled. Then he began to bounce up and down frantically, his mouth making *Awo! Awo!* shapes.

Then Alice appeared beside him in the window. She took one look at Arrow, and her face crumpled. She left the window, and a few seconds later she was outside, on her knees, hugging him, crying, splashing tears all over him, saying crazy things.

She spat out a smoldering cigarette butt, wiped her eyes on her sleeve, and dragged him inside.

Then she sat down in the armchair and pulled him onto her lap, sobbing loudly, uncontrollably, holding him and not letting go.

The lump in the knapsack was beginning to hurt him, so he threw it aside, and it landed on the floor with a thump.

When Alice finally stopped crying, she growled, "Where you been, kid?"

He shook his head, smiling. "I don't know."

That made her start crying all over again. Nick kept bouncing up and down, his little arms flapping as if he were trying to fly, scattering chess pieces, piping, "Awo home! Awo home!" Poody-tat wandered in, scrutinized the scene in a glance, and wandered out again in search of more interesting things to observe.

She held him in her arms, rocking and rocking him, crying, drying her eyes, crying again. When Arrow had had enough of that, he pushed himself upright and said, "Alice, can I have some yogurt and strawberries?"

20

Alice's Misadventure in Wonderland

William Murphy lay in bed listening to the sound of his wife's soft breathing. She was deep in dreamland, probably walking in a sarong through rice paddies, fanning her sweet face with a palm frond.

He was wide awake, staring at the black square of the ceiling in their darkened bedroom on a quiet residential street in suburban Fort George. A patch of cool, soporific moonlight moved slowly across the wall beside the dresser and touched one white, outstretched hand on Patti's crucifix above the mirror. A hand with a nail through it. The furnace cut in, and a few minutes later warm air hummed out of the vent beside the closet door.

It was after midnight, and the sound of traffic had long since ceased. The trick-or-treaters had given up the ghost around nine, and after that he and Patti had watched the *News Journal* on the national network, then gone to bed. A routine day, a normal evening, a pleasant drift into another dreamless sleep.

So why the insomnia? It almost never happened, and when it happened there was always a good reason for it. Always. The night his mother died, the night Tubby cut his first tooth, the night Beth Potter disappeared (thank heavens she'd eventually turned up safe and sound), the night he had too much to drink at the staff ball four years ago (most guys would have gone to sleep for twelve hours—not Buzz Murphy, oh, no, inebriation had the opposite effect on him, such was his luck). He had vowed the next morning never to drink again.

Was he unhappy? No, he was probably the happiest guy in the lower mainland. Was he ill? No, he felt that he could easily get up and jog three or four miles through the deserted streets of nighttime Fort George without undue effort. Was he worried? No, he liked his job, and the house was almost paid off. So what was the matter?

The rhythm of Patti's breathing changed, and he turned his head a little toward her in order to listen. But she was still sleeping. He put his hands behind his head and stretched his legs as far as they would go, felt his toes wiggling off the cliff at the bottom of the bed. Yup, still too tall. No shrinkage yet. He'd always been too tall, except on the basketball court. Needed an Abe Lincoln bed, but where could you buy one of those things in Canada? Patti was five foot one and a half, and you'd need a search party to find her in a bed that size.

Uneasy, uneasy. Why so uneasy?

He watched the shard of moonlight slide across the arm of the body on the crucifix. It was ivory, carved in the Philippines by Patti's great-uncle, an old priest, long dead.

What was bothering him? Probably the OIS brass who had popped into the office early in the afternoon, looking for directions. The guy with the dead-fish eyes. That must be it. There weren't many who could put a chill into Buzz Murphy, but this one sure did. The chill had passed quickly, leaving only a vague disquiet that he had thrown off with Patti's stir-fry supper, a stream of costumed kids at the door, and a half-hour sampling of a paperback called *Dick Tracy in the 21st Century* before lights out. Now the unease was back.

What *was* it about the guy?

The warning about not poking his nose into federal business? The feeling that he was talking with an unidentifiable power source, a nuclear reactor with no red warning lights? That strange, intangible odor when the guy walked out of the detachment office, a scent not registered by the nose but noted

767

somewhere in the subconscious? Like a fish that has rotted a little before the stink is locked into the deep freeze, wrapped in cellophane, just waiting to thaw and spread its misery throughout the household.

Yeah, something like that. Maybe.

Why had OIS been asking about Alice Douglas, of all people? She sure didn't look like your average spy or your neighborhood cutthroat terrorist. She was a bit eccentric, to be sure, but there were plenty of old girls like her in the hills, and gaggles of them in the city. He didn't know much about her, except to say hi when he stopped by her gas station from time to time to put up missing-kid posters. She called him *handsome*. That was nice. Handsome. (*Thanks, Alice*, Buzz smiled.) He'd seen her at the Potters' once, at a political meeting. That was all.

Maybe she knew somebody who knew somebody else, who knew somebody who was crooked or leaking government secrets.

Leaking government secrets in the B.C. bush! Sounds like bathroom humor to me, Buzz chuckled.

It was probably nothing. Maybe the feds were asking the neighbors to keep an eye on the Potters. It probably added some excitement to Alice's day. The guy with the fish eyes would spook her, then he'd go away, and for the rest of her life she'd have a mystery to chew on, and she would like the taste. Though she might feel uneasy about the smell.

Nice cologne the guy had. Nice clothes. Nice big badge— the highest echelon of cop in the country. The nice, big, secret kind. Nice, big, black car with tinted windows and federal plates. (Buzz got a good look at those through the venetian blinds of the office window, but he couldn't remember the numbers now, which was another reason why he'd never get to be an inspector. Not if he hung in for thirty years. He didn't mind. No great loss.)

The moon was moving across the arms and the upper chest. The slice of wound appeared. Patti sucked in a deep breath and stirred. Then her breathing became regular again.

He didn't understand why so many of the staff had unhappy marriages. A few divorces, some sleeping around, soft-porn movies on poker night. Buzz had no use for the first two activities and had only tried the latter once and didn't like it much. He lost twenty-three dollars in loonies and had to push a few sizzling video thoughts out of his head with some extra effort. A youth spent on basketball courts and under cold showers had definitely come in handy. Good training.

The other guys kidded him a lot, said he was Mr. Clean. Mr. Homebody. Murph-the-Smurf, Good Ol' Buzzy, give you the shirt off his back, take night shifts for you, and stand in front of a bullet for you. The strong silent type, they called him, a regular guy, still sporting a 1960s jock buzz-cut. You could see the pink under the short blond bristles on his scalp. Old time Mountie, faithful husky dog by his side, tricked out in an invisible red suit and feltboard hat, sidearm and Sam Browne polished, ready to defend the right. *Maintiens le droit! True patriot love in all thy sons command!*—just like the anthem said. Hey, Buzz, get a horse!

Buzz liked the kidding. And his co-workers liked the way he took it, so good-natured. Even the people he arrested on the street liked him. People he caught in the speed trap liked him. Old ladies with cats up telephone poles liked him. Patti liked him. Tubby liked him. Buzz didn't think too highly of himself, but most everyone else did. Maybe God liked him too, though he wasn't exactly sure about that.

Well, there was Patti. She was a very religious woman. God gave her to him, and that said something, didn't it? Buzz was an only child, baptized Catholic but lapsed for most of his life— *lap-said,* Patti called it. He got more or less serious about religion when he was engaged and took it real seriously for a year or two, but lately he'd got fuzzy around the edges, making his Easter confession, going regularly to Mass, saying a few prayers by rote every morning and night, keeping the Golden Rule, and staying away from all-night video-poker parties. He was in love—permanent-like—and that was more than many a man could hope for in this life. And she was in love with him.

They were both in love with Tubby, and already in love with the baby three months old in Patti's womb, number-two child. Whenever he or she decided to make an appearance, Buzz intended to nickname him or her Chub or Blubber or Miss Pieface, or something else that would prompt Patti to give him a coy smile and a friendly swat on the arm.

Tub's name was, in fact, Ricardo Zumáraga Murphy, which was a mouthful. When he slipped and slid into this world, cocoa-colored and tiny and thin and pucker-faced, with wet jet black hair and little thrashing sticks for arms, with magical fingers and toes, he looked just like a froglet. She'd fattened him up on breast milk soon enough. From tree frog to sumo wrestler in five short months. Behold, Tubby the Tuba.

Buzz laughed. Patti stirred and rolled over on her back. He held his breath and didn't twitch until her night sighing became regular again.

Tired lady, he thought. Sleep, lady.

The moon was washing over the entire corpus now, and the body looked as if it were radiating its own interior light.

Patti came from a big family of Filipinos, all of them with incredible sets of teeth and sparkling eyes, all of them with incongruous Spanish names. Buzz dwelt in the heart of the clan like some cumbersome monolith, a harmless ox that had been adopted as a mascot. They all called him William. They weren't into nicknames the way Canadians were. They sure were a happy crowd. They sure were into Jesus in a big way.

Patti read a lot. She'd brought a library into the house as a kind of dowry. She came from poor farming people on Mindanao, hadn't owned a pair of shoes until she was eighteen years old, but had an uncle who was a village mayor (shot by Marcos' secret police), another uncle who was a bishop (who'd been in prison somewhere in the Philippines but was out now), and an aunt who had visions and who got stigmata every Good Friday. Patti's family didn't like communists, and they didn't like Marcos-style capitalists (Patti said that Marcos' wife had owned over three hundred pairs of shoes before the true Catholics booted them out of office).

Patti's accent wasn't great, but she was very smart. She was a nurse, a real R.N., and aside from her nurse textbooks, clean women's novels, various Bibles and Spanish prayer books, she had thirty or forty paperbacks lying about the house that were downright scary: end-of-the-world stuff. Apparitions of the Virgin Mary, weeping statues, *bleeding* statues, warnings, chastisements, eucharistic miracles, coming world crisis, New World Order, all promising pain, darkness, martyrdom, and an era of peace after the purification of the world.

He'd read one and didn't know what to make of it. There might be something to it, but it sure wasn't what he had signed up for when he became an "ex-lap-said" Catholic.

His left arm had fallen asleep. He carefully withdrew it from behind his head (ouch) and draped the dead limb alongside his thigh. In doing so, he accidentally bumped Patti with it.

"William?" she said in a small voice, rolling over.

"Yeah, hon."

"You okay?"

"Sure, I'm fine."

"How come you not sleeping?"

"Don't know."

She rolled onto her back, rubbing her eyes with the palms of her hands.

"You see him, too?" she asked, yawning.

"Who?"

"The angel."

Buzz looked sideways at her. "Go back to sleep, Patti."

She shook her hair.

"C'mon, sweetie", he said gently, rolling her over on her side. "Back you go. Back to dreamland."

She smiled, resisted, and settled herself where she wanted to be. She kissed him on the cheek. Small women were very good, he noted, at managing large men.

He made a fake snore. "See, I'm already asleep."

She laughed. "No can fool me, William."

Snore.

She sat up against the headboard. "You didn't see him?"

"You were dreaming. Just a dream. Let's get some shut-eye. Ricardo'll be up with the birds."

"He was standing by the foot of the bed, underneath the cross." It was a sleepy voice, calm but alert.

"Who? Tubby?"

She swatted him affectionately. "No, the angel."

"What did he look like? Sparkly wings, tinsel hair, neon halo?"

"He look like a man. Very beautiful man. Eyes like—"

"Did he have a brush cut?"

"No tease me, William. This was real."

"Honey, I was wide awake until the moment you woke up. There weren't any angels in here. You were having a dream."

"He *come* here in a dream. But he was . . . you know, inside of dream and *outside* of dream."

Buzz sat up against the headboard beside her. "Okay, tell me about him. What was his name?"

"I don't know. He didn't say it."

"What was he wearing?"

"White robe, like wool. Gold belt. Sword in his right hand."

"Flowing tresses?"

She gave him a curious look. "No flowers on dresses. He didn't have dresses, just a robe."

"I mean, did he have long golden hair?"

"Short, but longer than you."

Buzz laughed outright. "So, what was he doing here in our bedroom, middle of the night, this guy, this stranger?"

"I think God send him to tell us something."

"And . . . ?"

"He say we going away. Not now—later."

"Later? When later?"

"I don't know. He just say, *I will hide you in the shelter of the rock*."

Buzz mused on that, growing serious. "What do you think he meant?"

She shook her head.

"Anything else?"

"He tell me something about you."

Instantly there flashed through Buzz's mind a series of unpleasant memories: a car he had wrecked when he was seventeen, three lies he had told getting into the Force, a single video-poker party, and the fact that he had trimmed all the fat off his prayer life until it was just a pathetic bone.

"What did he tell you . . . about me?"

"He say you going to do something important to stop the devil in a plan the devil's got. He say you won't know you're doing it. You will think it's little, just nothing. But it will be big. The angel said I should tell you to pray more. Go to confession and Communion more."

Buzz wrinkled his brow. He didn't know what to make of it. Maybe Patti had been feeling he should do all that, and it just leaked out in a dream. Maybe.

Maybe not.

"That's all? Anything else?"

"That's all", she shrugged.

Just like that, he thought, normal as potato pancakes, angels just arrive and depart from our bedroom like it was Grand Central Station.

He slipped down flat and pulled the blanket up over his shoulders.

"So, William, what you think of it?"

He snored.

"William?" she insisted.

"Very interesting, honey", he mumbled. "Now I think we should get ourselves back to sleep."

"Okay", she replied in a small voice.

But as he lay in the dark he could hear her rosary beads clicking for a long time.

* * *

Earlier that night, Father Ron had vested for five o'clock Mass in the sacristy of Saint George's, peering out the window at the children scuttling in twos and threes up and down the streets, ringing doorbells. Most of them were dressed in frightful costumes, devils and witches, ghosts and monsters. He shook his head and prayed for their parents.

He checked his watch. The altar boys were late, and at five minutes after five he proceeded alone to the altar and began the opening prayers of the liturgy. A minute later, two boys ran into the church, dropped pillowcases full of candy on the seat of a front pew, and scampered into the sanctuary, standing at attention beside the altar. They were dressed as Batman and Robin.

Father Ron leaned over and said something to them. They hurried off to the sacristy and returned a minute later, dressed in white albs. Their parents came up to Father Ron while he was unvesting after the closing hymn. They were angry at him for embarrassing the boys. The boys stood by, listening to their parents give Father a piece of their minds. The priest listened patiently, tried to explain the necessity of decorum, proper symbols, and reverence. But they didn't want to hear any of it and huffed out of the room dragging Batman and Robin along with them.

Father Ron sighed.

The doorbell rang as he was scrambling some eggs in the kitchen of the rectory, wondering what he would wear to the All Saints party scheduled for tomorrow, thinking he might dress up as Saint Maximilian Kolbe, a favorite of his. The striped pajamas maybe, the Auschwitz number written in felt pen on a card, pinned to the peejays. Maybe he could borrow somebody's wire-rim spectacles and ask King Balthazar and King Melchior in the storage room to lend him their crowns.

He went to the door, wiping his hands on a dishcloth, expecting to meet more little denizens of the underworld, but was surprised to find Thérèse and Théophane Nguyen standing on the porch.

They looked very worried. Father Ron invited them into the kitchen and offered them coffee. They both shook their heads.

Thérèse fired a round of Vietnamese at him, and he looked at Théophane for a translation.

"My Mum say she saw something pretty bad today. She's really upset."

"What happened, Théo?"

"She say she was taking meals on wheels to the Pottahs up in Steelhead. She had a car accident."

"Oh, no, I'm sorry! Was anyone hurt?"

Thérèse, understanding some of this, fluttered her hand on her son's arm, interrupting.

"Caw, bad caw, Faddah. Ice."

"Oh, I see. The car went out of control? Is it badly damaged?"

"Don't worry about the car, Faddah. That's not the problem. My Mum got stuck on the ice, sideways, block the road, and a big black car stopped. She say it had windows you can't see inside. A man got out and helped her."

"Uh-huh . . . And?"

"My Mum say he a very bad man."

"Bad man, Faddah, bad man!" Thérèse confirmed, nodding intensely.

"Did he bother her?"

Théophane looked uncertain, then consulted his mother in their language.

She shook her head and replied in kind.

"Not like that", Théophane said. "It's hard to describe. I think maybe she bother *him*. He got mad. He swear at her, and he drive away."

Somewhat confused, Father Ron said, "I'm sorry to hear it. That's upsetting. I suppose he was angry because she was blocking the road."

Thérèse and Théophane shook their heads in unison.

Théophane looked agonized. "My English not very good, Faddah, and my Mum talks it so poor. This guy was mad at her, and he say bad words, but that's not the baddest part."

"Tell me."

"My Mum look in his eyes, and she see something."

"What did she see?"

Thérèse babbled, agitated, tears in her eyes. She gestured to her heart, her head, her eyes, and the invisible eyes of the stranger she had met on the road.

"Bad. Kill baby. Kill woman", she cried.

"She says she saw a picture in her mind, Faddah. She say she see inside this man, and he was going to Steelhead to kill the lady who lives up at the gas station."

"What?" Father Ron said slowly. He had known the Nguyens for seven years, ever since they had arrived in town as refugees, boat people. They were among his most fervent parishioners. They didn't have much education, nor were they de-

776

monstrative about their faith, but he knew that Thérèse had some rather unique spiritual gifts.

"You don't mean Alice Douglas, do you?"

They nodded.

It was a bit hard to swallow, but Father Ron recalled a few experiences he had had of the woman's disturbing habit of seeing things that were invisible to most eyes. No gift was perfect, however. Perhaps she had misinterpreted an image that had come to her mind. She was probably shaken up by the near accident, and the fear was coming out in some distorted symbolic form.

"Are you sure?"

"My Mum sure. She say he was going to Steelhead to kill Alice and a baby and a boy with a bow and arrow."

Father Ron blinked and tried to clear his head.

"I think you'd better play that again, Théo."

They told him again.

"Let me get this straight. The man was going to kill them with a bow and arrow?"

The two Vietnamese looked pained.

"No", Théophane replied patiently. "The *boy* had a bow and arrow. The *man* want to kill them . . . Alice, baby, and boy."

"Are you sure this isn't imagination? Alice is a little old to have a baby, and I know for a fact that she doesn't have a boy staying with her."

Father Ron regarded them judiciously. Their intensity, their *certainty,* was disquieting. Their fear was definitely out of character. He didn't know what to think.

"My Mum come home, really scared, tell me, tell my Dad. My Dad say we should call Alice, but Mum say Alice think we crazy peoples. Not believe us. Not call her. Call you."

"Did you call the police?"

"I call them, I tell them, but they not understand it. They say, like you, *im-a-gin-a-tion.*"

"I see."

"We go up there, Faddah? Come now? Talk to Alice?"

"Did your mother say anything else? Was there anything else in what she . . . saw?"

More consultation.

"Mum say the boy has a monkey and the baby has a big head."

Father Ron tried not to smile. "Oh", he said.

"We go there now?" Théophane urged.

"Well, we could, I suppose. But I have a parish council meeting at seven o'clock. Why don't I phone Alice?"

The boy and his mother consulted again, looking anxiously at one another. Their disappointment was obvious, but they thought a phone call was better than nothing.

He found Alice's number in the phone book and dialed. After six rings a gruff voice answered.

"Queenuthuroadcollectibles."

"Alice?"

"Yeah, this is Alice."

"Hi, Alice, this is Father Ron from Saint George's. How are you?"

"Fine, just fine, Revrund. How you doing?"

"Just fine."

"Uh, good. Can I do somethin' for you?"

Father Ron took a deep breath. "Maybe, Alice. Look, I've been thinking about our conversation last spring. Remember, at the Potters'?"

"Yeah, I remember. You still a smoker?"

"Nope."

"Sorry t'hear it. Still drinkin'?"

"Oh, a sip of beer now and then. Listen, something has come up, and well, it's a little unusual."

"Still want me to knit doilies?"

"No, I . . ."

"I could crochet a toilet-paper holder—that's about all I know how to make. I think I got some pink and white in the store."

"Actually, I'm not calling about that."

"'Bout what, then?"

Father Ron heard the distinct sound of a scratching match and a loud exhalation of smoke.

"I . . ."

"Spit it out, Rev. I ain't got all day."

"You're going to think this is very odd, Alice, but do you remember meeting the Nguyens at the Potters' that time?"

"The who?"

"The Vietnamese family, a mother and son."

"Oh yeah, the little lady and her lad."

"That's the ones. Now I know this is going to be a bit hard to understand, but the mother, Thérèse, is, well, unusual—"

"I noticed."

"She has some spiritual gifts, and for some reason I don't understand, she's very worried about you. She says she met a man who she thinks wants to harm you."

"That's goofy! Who in the hell would want to harm me? And how in the heck would *she* know if somebody wanted to, eh? How did she meet the guy anyway? The last time I saw her she had some pretty weird things to say to me that were just plain bananas. A banana split with nuts on top. She's an okay lady, but just between you'n'me, pardner, I think she's got a few screws loose upstairs, if you know what I mean."

It was typical Alice, but Father Ron wondered about the length of her protest, detected a note of apprehension underneath the stream of quaint verbiage. Was it a smoke screen?

"That's a possibility, Alice. I'm not denying that. But I do know that she sees things sometimes—"

"She sees things? So what?"

"So, sometimes they turn out to be real."

There was a long silence after that. Father Ron heard another cigarette being lit. He wanted one too.

"It may be nothing, of course, but I thought I should talk to you about it. Has anyone stopped at the store this afternoon or this evening?"

"Nah, I been closed."

"Anyone suspicious drive by? Anyone in a black car?"

"Nope, not that I could see."

Father Ron eyed Thérèse and Théophane, who were perched on kitchen chairs beside him, listening intensely to his side of the conversation.

"That all, Rev?"

"I guess so. I guess it is", he said, bemused, smiling sheepishly.

"Maybe she saw a spook", Alice offered. "It's Halloween."

"Maybe. She says she saw something."

"That all? Anything else?"

Father Ron turned his back to the Nguyens so they wouldn't see him grinning into the phone. "She said you have a baby and a boy with a bow and arrow. And a monkey."

There was a deafening silence on the other end of the line. Then Alice chortled.

"A monkey? She said I have a monkey?"

"That's right, and a baby with a big head. Which proves your point, I guess."

Alice chortled again. It was a hollow chortle.

Her words came out in a rush: "I ain't got no monkey, Rev. Except maybe a monkey on my back. I gotta cut out the booze one of these days. Maybe your little lady better cut out the hard stuff too. I gotta go now. Bye."

Alice hung up.

It took Father Ron a few seconds to realize that the conversation was over. Then he hung up.

He sat down at the table, shaking his head.

"What she say, Faddah?" Théophane asked.

"She says there's nothing to it. Says no one suspicious drove by, no black cars. She laughed when I mentioned the boy and the baby. So you see it probably means something else."

A council member walked into the kitchen and plunked a box of donuts on the counter. Greetings were exchanged all around.

Father Ron walked Thérèse and Théophane to the door. On the porch steps, he tried to reassure them that the vision, or whatever it was, had probably been something symbolic. Dreams and visions from the Lord were like that, he said. If they prayed about it, the meaning might come clear. By then more council members were arriving, and they swept Father Ron back into the rectory, leaving the Vietnamese standing alone in the parking lot, looking at each other, listening to the excited cries of devils and witches, ghosts and monsters.

* * *

Alice hung up the phone. Then she got the jitters in a big way.

Nick was asleep in his crib, but Arrow was still awake, swinging his slippered feet back and forth, zooming a bunch of matchbox cars around the kitchen table.

She stood by the stove, watching him.

Absorbed in his play, he made engine noises, tire noises, and car crash noises. A little black car screeched to a stop in front of a gray one, just short of collision.

"Arrow, about that man, the one you said dropped you off here, what kind of car was he driving?"

"A black one."

"Tell me more about him. Who was he?"

"I don't know. This morning he took me from that place and—"

"The place with the white walls?"

"Yes. Then he brought me here."

"Was he a nice man?"

781

Arrow thought about that. "He was mad."

"You mean he was mad at you?"

"Yes. First he was nice, and then he was mad, and then he was sad."

"What else did he say?"

"He said a poem."

"Huh? A poem?"

Arrow nodded, his attention wandering back to his cars. He made the gray car spin in a circle.

"Then a little lady got out of her car", Arrow said distractedly.

"A little lady, eh? Then what?"

"They talked."

"What did they say?"

"I couldn't hear it."

"That's all? Nothing else happened?"

"I saw my father standing on a mountaintop. He was looking at me."

Alice squinted at him, lighting up a cigarette.

"Then what?"

"He gave me my knapsack and told me to go."

"He wasn't mean to you? He didn't try to hurt you?"

Arrow looked up at her, his eyes clouding over. "He said he would, but then he didn't. He said there was something for me from Andrei, and from my father, in the knapsack."

Slowly, as if recalling a fading dream, he looked at the empty armchair. The knapsack lay beside it, unopened, where he had dropped it when Alice was rocking him.

He got up and went over to it. Alice watched him untie the drawstrings slowly and carefully. Arrow pulled one of his stuffed animals out of it.

"Curious George!" he said with a smile of delight. He hugged the monkey to his chest.

"Leo!" he cried. Followed by, "Freddy-the-Teddy!"

Alice would have enjoyed it if she hadn't been fending off the jitters. Since last night when she had found Donnie's Bible, she had been doing a lot of reading in it and a lot of thinking. Despite what she had said to the Catholic priest about bananas with nuts on top, she had begun to wonder if there wasn't a heck of a lot more going on in the world than she had suspected. One big whopper of a mystery story it was, and a whole bunch of the heroes in the story sure seemed to go around saying things like the little lady said. And if that little lady was right, then maybe she and the boys had been in some kind of danger from the man in the black car (wasn't that just like a cheap thriller to put the bad guy in a black car!). But the bad guy had dropped the kid off and said, "Run, Arrow, run, and don't look back!" Just like Bambi.

Was he bad or good? Maybe he was like the weird critters in Wonderland who changed into other things whenever you looked at them too closely. Through the looking glass or what!

On the other hand, maybe the bad guy *had* been thinking of bumping off her and the boys but changed his mind at the last moment.

Then it struck her that if he could change his mind one way, he could also change it back again. That brought the jitters on again. She went to the booze cupboard and poured herself a small one, very small, just enough to take the edge off.

Arrow reached into the bottom of the bag.

"Look, Alice!"

"What the heck is that thing?" she said, coming over.

"I don't know."

She took it from his hands. It was heavy, old, dark, pitted, and chipped. It was a stone cross of some kind. It had some rusty stains on it and some letters scratched on the wheel around the crossbar— V E R I T A S.

"I don't get it", Alice said, handing it back.

"My father sent this to me", Arrow said in a low voice. Eyes wide, mouth open, he pressed it to his chest and held it without saying anything more.

He started yawning. She told him to brush his teeth and get into his pajamas. When he was snug in bed with the three teddies packed in around him, she sat down beside him. She spotted a big lump under his pillow, pulled the cross out of there, and put it on the bedside table.

"It's safe and sound, kid. It'll be waiting for you in the morning."

"Okay."

Looking over her shoulder to make sure no one was listening, she said, uncomfortably, "Want me to say a prayer?"

"Okay."

She folded her hands and bowed her head, the only thing she could remember from Sunday School.

"Now I lay me down t'sleep, and I pray the Lord my soul t'keep. If I should . . . if I should . . . well, if I don't feel too good before I wake, I just pray the Lord my soul t'keep."

Arrow was watching her with a steady gaze.

"How was that?" she asked.

"Good."

He rolled over onto his side, closed his eyes, sighed, and was instantly asleep.

She checked Nick, wiped away some drool, turned off the light, and went out, closing the door behind her.

The jitters were gone, and she felt better than she had for weeks, felt that something had happened that she could never in a million years understand, and the whole mess had somehow turned out all right. She wasn't on the chain gang, Beth was back in the bosom of her family, Arrow was home, and no bad guys had barged in firing their irons off, pumping lead into anything that moved.

She considered phoning Beth to tell her that Arrow was back

but decided that the Potters were probably still mad at her; they hadn't come by to see her since Ted told her to stop phoning, hadn't bought any gas, just sent a check in the mail to pay off the last of their debt, no note, no nothing.

Poody-tat wandered in and began scratching the arm of the chair. She reached down and dragged him up for lap duty. He didn't fight very hard, eventually got the point, and curled into a nice hot ball of orange and white *purrrr* in her lap.

Alice looked around her kitchen, feeling great affection for it. The room was a mess, but hey, it was home. The fire snapped in a familiar, soothing way. The tea kettle steamed softly on the back burner. The geraniums needed watering. The dang sink tap was dripping again, but that was kind of homey too.

She picked up Donnie's Bible and began to read. Funny how the thing just kept you interested, after you got used to the antique lingo. A thriller that never quite ended, always a new chapter, hundreds of stories inside the biggest mystery story of them all.

It was a long night. Alice didn't feel much like sleeping. There was a lot to think about. A lot to plan. She needed to sell the Palace and find a quieter place to live until things settled down. The man in the black car had gone away, maybe forever, but it had been a close call. Time to move on. Maybe she could give the hens and goats to the Potters, sort of in compensation for all the trouble she'd caused them. Maybe she could try her hand at driving again, buy a car, go east. Find another place where nobody knew her. No one in this world was missing Nick, and pretty soon Arrow would start stretching, his face changing, and before you knew it, he'd be just another teenager no one would look at twice. They'd go far away. Far, far away. Maybe they'd go to Saint John's first, catch up on old times with Kurly, then up into Labrador or Québec, or down to some nice bay on the coast of New Brunswick. There must be places there where you could rent a house on the ocean, go for boat rides, scratch the dirt a little and grow marigolds and tomatoes, and not have to explain to some official every motherlovin' thing you did. No more hiding, no more cheating, no more jitters. She'd get old, of course, but she was sure she could find some good people who'd look after Nick. Maybe Arrow would find a nice girl and get married, and he could look after Nick. Then she'd grow old disgracefully, the way she'd always planned, and maybe some day she'd check into an old folks' home (not that she needed it), read some more cliff-hangers, catch lung cancer or Alzheimer's (just like she always knew she would), and die happy.

Sounded pretty good.

She'd phone the real estate agent next week, maybe. Winter wasn't the greatest time to put your place on the market. No need to rush, but soon. Soon.

She dozed for a while, and when she woke up, Poody-tat was nowhere in sight. The Bible was open on her lap. She put on her owl-rim reading glasses.

Isaiah something.

> Woe to those who call evil good, and good evil,
> who change darkness into light, and light into darkness,
> who change bitter into sweet, and sweet into bitter!
> Woe to those who are wise in their own sight,
> and prudent in their own esteem!
> Woe to the champions at wine drinking,
> the valiant at mixing strong drink!
> To those who acquit the guilty for bribes,
> and deprive the just man of his rights!

Good stuff, thought Alice. Even back in the old days the bad cowboys had black hats, and the good cowboys had white ones. The part about champion drinkers applied to her, all right, but she was just about finished with booze. Soon, maybe when she and the boys were digging clams in the east, she wouldn't need to touch a drop again. Ever! The other part—the dark into light and the bitter into sweet—no way, that wasn't for her! Her hat had a few smudges and dents, no doubt about it, but it was basic white. Just let the bad hats try their tricks on her, and see what happens! Woe to them!

Still, Alice couldn't sleep. The stabs in her chest were back. Murdo the King of the Geriatrics told her last year that they were caused by tension. Muscle spasms. Her arteries were in tip-top shape, cholesterol within the safety range, healthy as an old nanny goat.

She was worried. That was all, just worried. Why shouldn't she be uptight? There might be a long way to go before she and the boys could rest easy—weeks, maybe months. If the guy in the black car had a change of heart, he might show up again looking for Arrow.

Alice checked her wristwatch. It was 1:30 A.M. She got up and poured herself another whiskey and drank it. The pain in her chest went away. She went out into the store, and in the hardware section she found a few packages of deadbolt locks, a hammer, and a screwdriver.

It took her a half hour to get the bolts onto the front door, the inner door to her living quarters, and the woodshed door in the kitchen. She felt silly doing it, knew she was just being a nervous Nelly, but thought it wouldn't hurt to take a few pre-cautions. As an afterthought, she went back to the store and pushed and jiggled the jukebox across the floor (thanking her lucky stars it had wheels), and shoved it tight against the front door. Just let them try anything! Woe to them!

Anybody who wanted to break in could smash the display windows, she supposed, but there'd be one hell of a noise if they tried it. She and the boys would have plenty of time to get out the back door, through the maze of the junkyard, and into the woods.

Trixie Belden and the Blue Scarf!

That made Alice sad for a moment, because she wasn't sure if Bethie would be any too eager to drive down looking for a scarf on a tree, not after what she'd been through. Not after what Alice had put her through.

Besides, she reminded herself, the Potters had just put a *For Sale* sign up by their gate. Harry Bird had told her.

Alice went behind the counter and opened the oak cupboard beneath the cash register. There it was, Donnie's double-barrel shotgun, dusty as a crap-shooter's Bible, never been used, the one he kept handy for thieves. Poor Donnie, the only bandit he ever faced was a tumor on the pancreas, and it got him in the end.

Alice levered two shells into the chambers and snapped the barrels shut.

Annie Oakley shoots it out with the Mind Cops of the Eighth Dimension! Or was it Calamity Jane?

Alice laughed.

Throw down your weapon, lady, it's the G-Men!

She laughed harder, guffawing, the echoes rebounding off the walls. The stuffed birds, beavers, and the single mountain lion stared at her, shocked out of their skulls.

She lit a cigarette, sucked hard on it, squinted, and aimed the shotgun at the door.

"Kablam!" she whispered.

That was fun.

Then, seeing the missile hanging from the ceiling in the army surplus section, she had an idea. The eight-foot-long gray and white bomb didn't contain any gunpowder or nuclear material or anything like that, but it just might give somebody a fright. She rolled a shopping basket across the floor, positioned it under the missile, unhooked the pulley rope, and lowered the missile onto the top of the cart. Rolling the whole works back into the center aisle, she wheeled it clockwise, nose cone facing the front door.

Just let those pointy-headed intellectuals and crime busters try to get at her and the boys. Just let them try! Woe to them!

Alice laughed again, picked up the shotgun, and took it to bed.

* * *

788

The morning light was splintering through the shades of her bedroom window when she awoke. The loud banging on the front door jerked her upright in bed, and she grabbed the shotgun that was leaning against the side table.

She crept stealthily through the kitchen, gun in arm, pulled the bolt of the door to the store, and opened it a crack.

Two shadows were silhouetted against the glass. Awful short shadows for G-Men.

Rap-rap-rap-rap-rap!

"Anybody home, Missus?" came a teenager's voice. Then babbling in a foreign language.

It was the little gal and her kid.

Alice carefully leaned the gun against the wall by the front door, pushed the jukebox away, and opened the door six inches wide.

The boy spoke first. "Morning, Missus. We come to visit you. We come in?"

"Uh, nah, I'm sorry, I ain't open yet. Gas pumps'll be turned on at nine."

"We not need gas, Missus."

"Yeah, well, my apologies, but if I start openin' up for one, I'll have t'start openin' up for everyone, all hours of the day or night."

Alice tried to close the door, but the boy's hand resisted it. That irritated Alice plenty.

"Now, don't give me no trouble!" she growled.

"Please, Alice, me and my Mum need to talk with you. Bad man . . ."

"Yeah, yeah, bad man in a black car. Ronnie told me about you two gettin' your shirts in a knot over me. Now, don't you be worryin' your little heads about nothin'."

"It not nothing", the boy insisted. His mother began babbling, a terrible anxiety written across her face. She stepped in front of her son and pushed a glass pyrex dish toward the crack. The dish was covered with aluminum foil. Alice smelled hot food.

"Lady. Supper for you, baby, boy", she said.

Alice quickly donned her nastiest mask. "I don't know what yer talkin about!" she snarled.

"Please, Missus", the boy pleaded. "My Mum not crazy."

Alice relented and eased the door open another six inches. "We come in?"

These people sure have no qualms about wheedling! Alice thought to herself. *Pushy, pushy, pushy!*

"Nah, you can't come in. Look, I don't want to hurt your feelings, but it's not a good time for me to have company."

The boy and his mother looked at each other.

"Careful!" the woman said (she pronounced it *cayofoo*). "Bad mans come. You run. You run."

The woman pushed the dish through the door, and before she realized it, Alice was balancing it in both hands. Instantly, she dropped the nasty-mask and put on a pleased-as-punch-neighbor-mask. "Well, hey, that's real nice of you people. Why don't you come by the place tomorrow, and I'll give you the dish back. But, like I said, right now it's not a good time to have anybody in. Hope you understand."

The two Vietnamese nodded that they understood, but Alice could see they weren't any too happy about it.

"My boy stay here! Watch out bad mans!" the woman said. "He strong. Fight hard!"

Alice grinned. "Gee whillikers, thanks a million. But I'm okay, and no bad mans is gonna get in here."

Alice opened the door wider and pointed to the shotgun.

The boy and his mother looked at it and nodded solemnly.

"Okay, Missus", Théophane said reluctantly. Looking deflated, they went down the porch steps to their car.

"You can come back some time", Alice called after them. "Hey, I'll fix you somethin' nice for supper. I'll call you." But it was a lie. She had no intention of calling them.

She closed the door and locked up, shot the deadbolt, and

rolled the jukebox back in front of the door as an added precaution. It tilted slightly, and she heard an errant loonie go tinkling down into its innards. The machine suddenly lit up its pink, green, and blue neon (giving Alice a fright), flipped a single 45 rpm onto the wheel, and began to play something called *I Can't Get No Sat-is-fac-tion.*

Alice said a bad word. It sounded to her as if the *bad mans* were already right inside her store, singing a dirty song, sounding like shrieking sex-starved toads, or drunk warlocks—maybe more like howling wolverines, befouling any caches they could rip apart and rob.

She gave the machine a good kick, then yanked the extension cord out of its socket.

Back in the kitchen, she put the pyrex dish on the back burner of the stove, pokered around in the firebox until she found a mound of live coals, and threw some kindling onto it. The dish was faintly warm. Whatever was in it smelled good, meaty and spicy. Not exactly your Great American Breakfast, but it would save her the trouble of making a pot of slow-oats porridge. There were bits of strange-looking herbs in it and slices of something that looked like—she peered and sniffed—like squid guts. She spooned up a ladleful and sipped from it.

Gag! She spewed it out. It was hotter than pure hell. Not the temperature, because that was only lukewarm, but some kind of liquid fire those orientals liked to season their grub with. Unfit for human consumption.

Carrying the dish, she went out the woodshed door to the back lot and threw the whole mess into the chicken run. The Harcos and the Rhode Island Reds went for it with a vengeance, but the fastidious banties shied daintily away. Alice wondered if her fried eggs would start tasting like red hot chili peppers in a day or so. *Always* look a gift horse in the mouth! she admonished herself.

After she fed Arrow and Nick their plain old gruel, she penned a note on a sheet of paper and Scotch-taped it face out on the front door: *Closed Till Further Notice.*

There were a few gas pump dings later in the morning, but eventually whoever they were went away. The phone rang once, but it was just a high-pressure light bulb salesman. No thanks, said Alice. The guy wouldn't take no for an answer, so she hung up on him.

Someone else banged on the door at four-thirty. Alice ignored the noise, and whoever it was went away.

The phone rang again after the boys were in bed. She hesitated before answering but decided it would look better if she pretended life was going on as usual inside the Palace.

It was the Vietnamese kid, wanting to know if she was all right, asking if anyone had driven by, if anyone peculiar had come knocking on the door, and how she had enjoyed the stew.

"Oh, hey", Alice said enthusiastically. "That stuff was real popular around here. Thanks a million!"

"We stop by tonight to get dish?"

"Nah. I'll get it back to you someday."

"We stop by tomorrow?"

"You in a hurry?"

"Yes, Missus, we need dish back real bad. Got to take meals on wheels to Pottah family, on the road far after your place."

"Oh, yeah." Alice imagined Ted sneaking out to his barn to throw the bowl of lava to his pigs.

She laughed.

"Okay, you can drop by tomorrow morning to get the dish. Hey, I don't want you thinking I don't appreciate it. It was real nice of you."

"Yes, Missus. God bless you, Missus."

"Yeah, you too, kid."

There was no need for the shotgun that night.

The Vietnamese rapped on the front door at eight o'clock the next morning, asking for their dish, asking if Alice had heard anything funny, seen any strangers.

"Nothing", she told them. "Big fat zero. Now, I think you guys should just relax. Everything's fine."

"How is baby and boy with an arrow?" Théophane asked earnestly.

"Say again?" Alice replied, playing it slow and easy.

"Baby. Boy. You", the little woman replied.

Alice opened her mouth, trying to formulate a lie, but for the life of her she just couldn't do it. Not to those two clean faces.

"Baby? Boy?" she mumbled, unable to meet their eyes. "I . . . ain't never been married." Not exactly a lie, she told herself. It was just evasive action.

"Cayofoo!" the woman said as she went down the steps, her son following.

"Bye-bye, Missus", he said over his shoulder. "If you got trouble you phone us, okay? Nguyen in phone book." He spelled it out for her. Alice bestowed her grandest fake grin and waved good-bye.

The next day was much the same.

And the next.

* * *

Corporal Buzz Murphy was feeling great. He had gone to confession and Mass at Saint George's on his way to work. After confession he felt as if he had taken a shower; after Communion, just as if he had eaten a wonderful meal.

Kneeling in the pew with all the mothers and toddlers and retired folks, he had felt a little out of place, but it didn't matter really. The feeling inside of him was so warm and peaceful. Like floating. No words or pictures in his head. No prayers. Just that quiet hush, the way you felt when you were seventeen, sitting exhausted and elated in the locker room after a game, the game

793

you had won because you broke the tie with a super slam-dunk in the final thirty seconds of play.

Empty and full. Happy was too small a word for it.

He spent the first half hour on duty whistling to himself, straightening up the office desk, cracking jokes with the two new guys, Leblanc and McConnell, until they went out on patrol, one to the speed trap east of town and the other to check out a jimmied lock at the hotel. Routine stuff.

Shortly after nine, two plainclothes cops walked into the office and flashed their badges at him: OIS.

They were in their late thirties, clean-cut, nice suits, pleasant enough if you ignored the eyes—deadfish eyes, just like the big brass who had dropped by on Halloween night.

"Good morning, corporal", one of them said.

Buzz nodded. "What can I do for you fellows?" he asked nonchalantly.

"We're investigating a violation of federal security regulations and have reason to believe that a suspect in the case is living in this region."

"Wow, that's bad stuff." Buzz raised his eyebrows. "Any idea who it might be?"

"We're not sure, but quite a few trails lead to Fort George. We have pretty good indications that a member of our bureau has been involved in it and has contacts here. Fort George seems to be a crossroads for the traffic of clandestine activities."

"Oh, no", Buzz replied, looking worried. "That's bad news. You mean secret stuff?"

The two visitors nodded slowly.

"Any clues as to who they are?" Buzz asked.

"No on-site leads. Our major trail begins in the head office, but it ends here. We thought local R.C.M.P. might be able to help us find the connection to the organization."

"Sure, fellows, we'll do everything we can. But frankly, I don't know where even to begin to suggest—"

"Has there been any individual from OIS, or pretending to be a member of the agency, inquiring at this office during the past two weeks?"

The visitors fixed Buzz with their dead-fish gazes. Buzz leaned his elbows on the desk, frowning in deep thought. The last scraps of his peaceful floating feeling departed. He began to catch a faint whiff of something smelly in the freezer. He thought hard and fast. The big brass had warned him: Not a word of his presence was to leak out of the office—actually, out of Buzz's mouth. Which was pretty strange, now that he thought about it. All the law enforcement agencies were on the same side, weren't they?

On the other hand, maybe this was an OIS security check. Maybe the big fish had sent these two flunkies to test Buzz's reliability. Was this a no-win game or a win-win game?

Buzz rubbed his face. He'd taken an oath a few years back. And if the big fish *had* gone rotten, the best way to remain faithful to that oath, to maintain the right, was to tell these guys what he knew. He certainly hadn't made any oaths to the big fish.

"Yeah", he replied slowly, as if trying to recall a vague memory. "There was a guy from your office came in here about a week ago. Halloween night, if I recall. Said he was tracking down the same stuff you guys are onto."

"Did he tell you his name?"

"No, but he flashed his badge, same kind of badge you're carrying."

"What was he looking for?"

"Well, he didn't stay long, just a couple of minutes. Wanted to know if we knew anybody named Queen of Junk."

The two agents looked at each other. Signals passed between them. Buzz began to feel very uneasy when they did that but didn't know why.

"Queen of Junk?" one repeated.

"Uh-huh", Buzz replied. "An old lady name of Alice Douglas, who lives out at Steelhead, north of town."

"Did he say why he wanted to locate her?"

"No", Buzz shook his head. "Not a word. He just said it was a federal matter and strictly confidential."

"I see. That's all he said?"

"Yes."

"And that's all you were able to tell him?"

Buzz nodded. "What's it all about, fellahs?"

One of the two men gave Buzz a very serious look and replied: "Like the man said, it's confidential. Now, I will ask you to keep our conversation strictly between ourselves."

"Do you understand?" said the other agent. "I mean *strictly*. National security is depending on this."

"Okay, guys. I understand. Don't give it another thought."

The agents did not acknowledge this. They walked to a wall map of the district and located Steelhead on it.

"Show us where the woman lives, corporal."

Buzz tapped the spot with his forefinger. "Sure beats all", he said, shaking his head. "Alice M. Douglas, of all people. She's kind of an oddball, but I can't imagine her being involved in anything like that. She doesn't seem like the kind of person to—"

"They never do", one agent cut him off.

"Deep cover", said the other.

Then they walked out without saying good-bye.

One of the new corporals, McConnell, came in the front door a minute later. "Who were those guys, Buzz?"

"Government", Buzz said uncomfortably.

"They looked like spooks to me. What did they want?"

Buzz shrugged, his transparent face revealing everything.

"Can't tell me, eh? Okay, I get the picture."

McConnell studied Buzz for a moment, then said something that made him look up. "Lot of funny things going on these days, aren't there, Murph?"

Buzz squirmed. "What do you mean?"

"I saw some things up north before I was transferred", McConnell replied cryptically.

"What kind of things?"

"Can't really say." McConnell paused. "Nothing you could put your finger on. It's just that people have a way of disappearing lately."

That made Buzz really nervous. He remembered the Beth Potter case and the look of terror in her husband's eyes as he stood in this very office twisting his green cap in his hands. Remembered suddenly that the Potters lived in Steelhead and that Alice Douglas lived there too.

A call came in just then, a 911 reporting a car crash on the bridge. McConnell hoofed it out to his patrol car and peeled out of the parking lot. Buzz called the hospital ambulance number, then radioed Leblanc and told him to get over to the bridge.

He sat down at his desk and brooded. He didn't feel right. Communion was a long time ago. The peace was totally gone. Those two OIS guys had blasted it out of him with their eyes and their reasonable voices.

Not knowing why he did it, he picked up the phone book, found the number of Queen of the Road Collectibles, and dialed the number.

"Alice here", the old lady's voice answered.

"Hi, Miss Douglas. This is Corporal Murphy at the R.C.M.P. in Fort George. You remember me?"

"Sure I remember you. How you doin', handsome?"

"Just great. Look, you're gonna think I've gone squirrelly, but something strange has just happened, and . . ."

"And . . . ?"

Buzz hemmed and hawed, rubbing his face, wondering if he was making the biggest mistake of his life.

"Spit it out, buddy. Something strange just happened. Want to tell me about it?"

Buzz saw Tubby rolling around the living-room rug, giggling at the homemade teddy his grandmother had made for him, saw Patti clicking her rosary beads, saw himself slam-dunking, saw Father Ron lifting the Eucharist high over the altar like a miniature sun.

He cleared his throat. "Yeah. Two guys just walked out of here about five minutes ago. They're on their way to your place."

Dead silence.

"Are you there, Miss Douglas?"

"I'm here", she said slowly.

"I didn't like the feel of those guys."

"What kind of guys were they?" she asked, her voice small and afraid.

"They're government guys", Buzz said slowly. "Top class of cop. I don't know why they want to talk to you, but I just thought you might want to be prepared."

More dead air.

"Look, I don't believe you're involved in anything illegal. And this is the stupidest thing a cop like me could ever do, calling you like this, but something doesn't smell right. I just wanted you to know."

"You just wanted me to know", she mumbled.

"And I'd appreciate it if you don't say anything to them about me calling you."

"I won't." Her voice was shaky. He could barely hear her.

She hung up.

Buzz exhaled loudly, sat up straight, swivelled the chair around to face the window, and for a minute or two felt pretty shaky himself. What if she cracked? What if she mentioned his name? Maybe he had just destroyed his career in a single stroke. As he stared out at the cloud cover hanging over Fort George, he thought he saw a white shape separate itself from the gray mass, a smaller cloud or a fracture of light, moving faster than it should, heading north to Steelhead like an angel with out-stretched sword. The wind blew it apart as it rocketed away, but the radiance remained suspended in the sky for a split second.

The peace of Communion returned. He saw Patti and Tubby again, and a rock, and shelter in the rock.

"Last thirty seconds of the game, score tied, one slam-dunk", he said to himself.

* * *

The two OIS agents drove without haste to Steelhead.

"How much farther?" the driver asked.

His companion checked the road map. "Ten minutes. We got 'em."

"Yes, we've got them. No more leaks."

"What a break! The world is a safer place with dumb cops like that looking after things."

They chuckled.

"Minor troubles in the realm", the driver said. "*Strictly* minor."

"Why did he do it, Wade?"

"Why did who do what?"

"Maurice."

"Oh, Morris."

"Why did he let them run in the first place?"

"Don't ask me, Bryce. I always thought it was a mistake, him handling a case from his own hometown. There are always too many ties that bind. You know—like a doctor operating on a member of his family. It never works."

"He blew it. He blew it big."

"Not so big. We caught some of them, and we're about to do a little damage control that should tidy things up quite nicely."

"I still don't get it. He was one of the higher-ups. He was going higher. He was the boss. So why did he crack?"

Wade shook his head grimly. "I don't know."

"He talked in the end."

"They always do."

"Blew his deep cover."

"Cover? No, I don't think it was anything like that. He wasn't working for them. It was just a moment of . . . weakness."

"Nostalgia, maybe", Bryce suggested.

"Something like that."

"It cost him in the end."

"It cost him a lot."

"You'd think a guy that high up would know his car was pinned. The chip reading shows a wild goose chase after he arrived at Fort George. The graph says he circled up and down all the back roads for an hour or two. Do you think he was laying false trails?"

"Absolutely. That's exactly what he was doing."

"It doesn't make sense after that. He leaves an electronic trail a mile wide, drops the staff car in a rental lot, uses his personal card to rent a car, and four hours later he's climbing onto a commercial flight in Seattle with two tickets, one for himself and one for the boy. Only problem is, the boy isn't on the plane. Then he arrives in Dallas, where we pick up his paper trail, and we nab him in the terminal in Mexico City, just as he's buying two tickets for Buenos Aires. I mean, really, how could he be so stupid?"

"He was buying time", Wade said irritably.

"He didn't buy much for himself."

"He was buying time for the kid."

"But why?"

"I don't know why. It doesn't matter why. He blew it. Right now that kid is sitting in Steelhead with the old woman. By the end of the day, she and the kid are history. Morris is history. This whole scene is history. It never happened."

The two agents mused on that in silence. They passed a sign:

Get Everything You Want at Queen of the Road Collectibles
We buy junque. We sell antiques.
Alice M. Douglas, prop.
3 Km ahead

"We'll add them to the collection", said the driver.

"I still don't get it, Wade. He had it all, but he threw it away. For what?"

Wade was beginning to find the other agent's questions tedious and did not respond.

"I mean, he must have known he couldn't get far. He knew, he knew."

"Yes, he knew. That came out in the interrogation."

Bryce shuddered. "The medical people know their stuff."

"Yes, they know their stuff."

"It took them two days. Did they get it all?"

"Oh, yes, they got it all. I was there. Morris held nothing back. Nothing."

"I wouldn't say *nothing*. He didn't tell them where the kid was, did he?"

Wade ignored that.

"Did he?"

"He would have. But someone went too far. They're not always careful."

Another sign:

Slow!
Province of British Columbia
Ministry of Highways
Building a Better Tomorrow

"We're building a better tomorrow", Wade said dryly.

"Morris wasted himself for nothing."

"He failed in the end. We haven't lost a thing. And we've learned something important too."

"What's that?"

"We've learned that no one is indispensable."

"Not even us?"

"No one. Not even us."

* * *

Father Ron was making himself a breakfast of toast and coffee. He didn't know why, but the craving for tobacco had returned with a vengeance. Moreover, he was feeling despondent and irritable, prophecy doubts were stinging like a swarm of mosquitoes, and for the first time in months he longed for a "spiritual" conversation with his imaginary girlfriend.

He had thought often about what the archbishop had said concerning the "tabernacle of the heart", or the "heart of the soul". Since that conversation he had been faithful to his daily hour of adoration, and there had even been some moments when he felt the Presence interiorly. It was a quiet feeling, low key, as if time were slipping away and everything was suspended in perfect stillness. Like a small glowing ember of light and warmth. But he wasn't able to make it come whenever he wanted, and he certainly didn't know the first thing about constructing the interior tabernacle. Of course, that was exactly what the archbishop had told him: no one could build it, no one could make it a success. Only God could do it.

Even so, he was troubled that he had made so little progress in this regard, especially since the temptations seemed to be returning with renewed force. Why they should do so now, and all at once, was a total puzzle. What was wrong? His health was fine. He was in the state of grace. He hadn't felt so alive in years. He had every good reason to be happy, because the archdiocese was waking up, his parish was scratching itself and smelling the coffee, the daily Mass crowd was growing steadily in numbers. Even a young R.C.M.P. corporal had attended this morning, after making a good confession.

Maybe he was a bit out of sorts because of the dream he had had the night before. In it he was walking through a devastated garden. It had not been weeded, fertilized, or watered. Huge deformed sunflowers bent and twisted this way and that, covered with undeveloped seeds and rot. He was saddened by this until he parted a wall of choking weeds and found hidden behind them clumps of rose bushes with very large buds on the verge of blooming. The sight heartened him greatly. He was standing there loving them, waiting for them to burst open into full color, when he heard a sinister growl that came out of nowhere, like a stalking wolf, and he awoke in terror.

Creepy, but just a dream. The symbolism was obvious—a picture of the Church but, more important, the Church that was just about to be born. There was a wolf in the garden, of course, but that was to be expected. No psychoanalysis needed for that one. Crystal clear.

Father Ron sighed. Understanding the dream didn't help much, didn't cheer him. Time to take up jogging again, he said to himself, time to get those endorphins, or endomuffins or whatever they called them, pumping through his veins.

To distract himself, he switched on the kitchen radio. Sipping from his coffee cup and munching toast and blueberry jam, he listened, not really caring what the program was.

It seemed to be some kind of special report that was already under way.

A spokesman for a group of Nobel Prize-winning scientists announced that the human population of the earth had reached critical mass and must be reduced by 25 to 30 percent within the coming decade if the ecological balance of the planet (which was already radically destabilized) was to be restored. If it was not soon restored, they maintained, the ecology would collapse in on itself, destroying everyone.

Hand in hand with the need to integrate global policy on ecology was the need to develop a consensus on world "governance". The several bombings of federal facilities in America, and two similar events in Canada during the previous week, had ignited a massive citizens' reaction, demanding increased authority for international cooperation in controlling terrorism. It was expected that the Omnibus Anti-Terrorist Bill would be passed in Parliament next week.

The director of the Canadian Association for the Club of Rome made a speech before an international gathering of energy and finance ministers of the G-7 nations and the European Union. In an impassioned address, he described the "synergy" of crises that were converging at this very moment: global overpopulation, the decline of arable land, the increase of pollutants being pumped into the atmosphere, the looming greenhouse effect, dissipation of the ozone layer, acid rain, declining mineral and fossil fuel resources, loss of natural germ plasm in the wilds, and more. He exhorted the ministers to use every effort to speed the integration of energy and finance infrastructures, to ensure the most efficient "reconfiguration" of consumption and civil order in the Western world. The emerging models of economy, he said, were the best hope for mankind as it approached the twenty-first century. There would be opposition, he warned, but the public needed to understand that opposition would come mainly from right-wing reactionary groups, whose motives were greed, and from religious fundamentalists, who were victims of paranoia. Much of the public unease about the new models would be dispelled by the overwhelming success of the pilot program in the Ontario city of Guelph. Plans were underway to expand the experimental program to six other Canadian cities within the next three months

"The time is now", he concluded. "All responsible leaders must make a virtue and a powerful benevolent force out of the need to control the rate of consumption of energy. The key is education—education of the young generation through every stage of the school system and media education of the public regarding the damage caused by the forces of the *problématique*, the old order of nation-states and religions."

The World Congress of Religions, meeting the day before in San Francisco under the auspices of the United Nations Organization, had issued a "global manifesto" for the bringing together of all world religions, with a view to forging a global spirituality that would assist "humankind" in its quest for world unity. A committee of American and Canadian bishops voted to become full members of the Congress, over Vatican protests, voicing their dissatisfaction with Vatican interference in the particular churches of North America.

Father Ron listened to the rest, staring at the tabletop, the coffee in his cup growing cold. When it was over, it was time for the ten o'clock news. He retained none of the news items, noting only that they were of a piece with the special report. His ears pricked up during the local news, when it was announced that the archdiocese of Vancouver had lost a defamation of character suit brought against it by a doctor of a Catholic hospital in the city. The archdiocese had been instructed by the court to pay the doctor two million dollars. In other news, the Provincial government had ordered Catholic hospitals in the province to establish women's health clinics on their premises. If they refused to comply, all public funding would be withdrawn. The doctor, apparently a champion of human rights, was quoted at length, praising the move. The archbishop was allowed one and a half sentences in the interview, the quote garbled and inconsequential.

Father Ron turned off the radio.

Heavy-footed, he trudged down the hall to the church entrance and went in. The nave was hot and stuffy, airless, thick with the smell of burning wax. He opened two side windows to get a breeze wafting across the altar. He felt sick at heart. He didn't feel much like praying. Nevertheless, he knelt in front of the tabernacle, bowed his head, and closed his eyes.

He reminded himself of what the archbishop had said about trust, about the sanctuary of the heart. But his emotions fought hand-to-hand combat with each other. He knew that the media were reshaping people's opinions, distorting by selection, poisoning minds by inference and impression. Yesterday he had read a report that had come through the Internet about a group of three hundred scientists who had declared the ecological crisis to be a fabricated political event manufactured by violating established principles of scientific method. Yes, there was widespread eco-damage, and it needed to be cleaned up. But the hysteria was vastly disproportionate to the objective situation. The emissions from a single volcanic eruption, they said, pumped far more debris into the atmosphere than all the industrial pollutants in human history combined.

Why wasn't that reported? Father Ron asked angrily. On and on he argued with the lies he had just heard on the news, refuting them all, one after another. Yet he felt his confidence shaken. Maybe the world-shapers had already won. They controlled just about everything now. Was there any use in fighting them? He knew that his dark mood was a temptation, knew the pattern, yet remained unable to resist the downcast feeling, the doubting. He wondered if all his religious activity was in fact a product of the ego, self-will, imagination, at best a fanciful dream of a fair haven, a heavenly city that could never connect to the realities of the world.

Enraged, frustrated, he prayed, "Where are you, my Lord? Why have the voices stopped? Was it all inside me? Was it only chemical surges in my brain?"

He was empty, and sad, and frightened.

Then the voice spoke interiorly: *They shall know that a prophet has been among them!*

Father Ron opened his eyes and glanced at the tabernacle.

"It's just my mind", he argued. "That was just an image I have of myself. Ronnie the prophet, Road Warrior Eschatologist!"

He laughed bitterly. Maybe the liberals were right. Maybe everything, good-bad, left-right, was in the head. Maybe he'd been fooling himself. Maybe the best he could hope for was to get his flock through these dark years with the least amount of trouble. Help them to be happy, contented, raise their kids, die in peace.

They shall know that a prophet has been among them! the voice came again.

Father Ron felt like crying. Him? A prophet?

A small bird flew in the window, rising and falling and rising as it crossed the sanctuary. It landed on the lectern and just sat there, looking at him.

He got up off his knees and went over to the lectern. The bird—a sparrow, he thought—did not fly away. Amazed, he scooped it up in his hands, took it gently to the window, trying not to squeeze its fragile bones, and set it free. It flew off, leaving a trail of song behind it.

They shall know that a prophet has been among them!

Father Ron, still wondering and confused, went back to the lectern intending to make sure the bird hadn't left any droppings on the lectionary. There were no little mementos, he was glad to see.

He stood there, shaking his head, surprised by the incident, but still largely despondent. He looked at the lectionary, which was closed. Then he saw his personal Bible beside it—open.

That was strange. It hadn't been there this morning. After Mass he had cleaned up, leaving everything in order for tomorrow's liturgy.

Feeling an overwhelming inner prompting, he glanced down at the text. The first line he saw was something from Ezekiel—Ezekiel 2.

"—for they shall know that a prophet has been among them—"

He took a step back, stared at the Bible, turned around and stared at the tabernacle, then back at the Bible.

Speechless, he pondered it, wonder and gratitude swelling within him.

He knelt down again and now was able to pray with renewed strength. The river surged up from the hidden spring and filled him. An anointing like warm, flowing oil spread through his mind and heart and limbs. When it faded to a soft undercurrent, he wanted to remain there forever, resting in absolute tranquillity, timelessness, and joy.

But the voice spoke again. One word: *Alice.*

Father Ron shook his head as if to clear his mind of the irrational thought.

Go to Alice!

"Alice? Why Alice?"

Now!

Standing up, Father Ron patted his pants pocket and felt the lump of his key chain. It jangled as he hit it. Then, moving purposefully, he went to the parking lot and got into his car.

* * *

Alice hung up the phone.

Two guys, top class of cop, don't like the feel of those guys. They want to see you. On their way to your place.

Oh geeeez! Baaaad news!

It was so baaaad that she couldn't even be bothered having the jitters.

Her heart started hammering, palpitating, skipping beats, giving her two or three sharp stabs. She thumped her chest with her right fist, opened her cigarette pack with shaking fingers, spilled a few across the kitchen counter, picked up one, and lit it.

"What am I gonna do?" she wailed.

Arrow and Nick stopped playing and looked up at her curiously.

"Oh, geez, oh, lordy!" she said in a lower voice.

Alice went to the booze cupboard and poured herself a

drink, filling the tumbler to the top, warm, no ice, no mix. She drank a quarter of it. The stab wound eased a little.

They left five minutes ago. Take them twenty minutes unless they're breaking all speed limits. Be here in fifteen, maybe less.

She gulped the whiskey down to half-empty.

"Arrow", she barked. "C'mere!"

Arrow put his toy cars carefully onto the floor and walked over to her, cocking his head, wondering what was going on.

Alice hadn't had breakfast yet, and the alcohol was hitting her bloodstream. Swaying a little, she said, "Bad man's comin', kid. Black beetles flyin' in at twelve o'clock high. We gotta make you scarce." She flicked her eyes at Nick. "Gotta hide Nick too. Come on, we don't have much time."

She pulled Nick out of his high chair and carried him into the bedroom. Arrow followed.

She laid Nick down on Arrow's bed, tore the mattress and blankets out of the crib, and shoved them under the bed. Then she told Arrow to get under the bed too, pronto. Pokerfaced, he obeyed. Feeling her bad hip trying to rip, she pulled Nick into her arms and slid him under the bed.

"Make him comfy, Arrow. You two guys just lie under there and don't make a sound, okay?"

"Okay, Alice."

"Nick, you be a good boy and go to sleep, okay?"

"Seep, Awis, seep."

"There's the good laddies. Now some of those bad hats is gonna poke around for a few minutes, but there's nothin' here that proves a dang thing. They'll go away. And we're gonna go away too. Soon, real soon. This is the last time you'll have to worry about any funny business. I promise."

Arrow and Nick did not reply.

She pushed her old wrinkled face under the bed and hissed, finger to mouth, "Now, not a word, you two! Understand? Not a peep!"

The boys nodded in unison. Nick smiled at her. Arrow's eyes were large and somber.

She flipped the blankets down, covering the gap. Then, rushing about the room, she gathered up anything that looked boyish—heaps of kids' clothes, toys, teddies, Arrow's knapsack, Nick's bottle—and flung it all under the foot of the bed. She straightened the sheets, turned out the light, and closed the door. In the kitchen she kicked the toy cars behind the kindling box, dragged Nick's high chair to the back door, and pushed it out into the woodshed. She closed that door, shot the bolt. Taking her whiskey glass along for the ride, she went out front into the store, closing and locking the door to the living quarters behind her. She sat down on the stool behind the counter, trying to catch her breath, trying to calm the damn shaking in her hands.

The shotgun leaned against the inside of the counter, just by her right knee. The jukebox was tight against the door. Staring at it, she realized suddenly that it was too obvious, a dead giveaway, the kind of stupid thing an old lady would do to build a makeshift fortress. And why would you build a fortress on a quiet, ordinary morning in a nice, safe country if you didn't have something awful embarrassing to hide? She heaved the jukebox sideways, and then her bad hip did tear, and she yelped in pain. Ignoring it, she wheeled the machine back to its corner by the front window. She plugged it in; instantly it lit up, neon flashing, needle swinging on the platter, the drugged warlocks and the sex-starved toads growling in chorus. *"I can't get no sa-tis-fac-tion; I can't get no sa-tis-fac-tion . . ."*

She swore and kicked the plug out of the wall socket, the music grinding down to a grunt.

Huffing and puffing, Alice limped back to the counter, banged the NO SALE sign on the cash register, and sat down.

"Circle the wagons, boys. Calamity Jane is here!" she muttered, forcing a laugh. It came out hollow, scared.

"Alice's last stand!" she shouted, baring her dentures. "Bring on your G-Men, bring on your black beetles! Alice is armed and dangerous!"

Then it got terribly quiet in the room. The only noise was the unsteady rasp of her breathing, the drumming of her heart.

Whew! I'm ready for anything now. That probably took five minutes, she told herself, checking her wristwatch. *They'll be here in another five minutes, give or take a few.*

Alice drank the tumbler down to three-quarters empty. Lit a cigarette, crossed her legs (that hurt), straightened her red hair, flipped the bobbley-bangley earrings so the little parrots swung. Lit another cigarette. Opened a copy of *Teen Romance*, August 1964, and tried to concentrate on a short piece about a saucy dreamboat gal and a cute dreamboat guy, who were, she thought, probably fat, graying car salesmen in Los Angeles by now.

Three minutes later she heard the sound of tires crunching gravel on the other side of the display windows. There was a faint rumble as an engine was killed. Then silence.

Alice put a hand to her throat and held her breath.

"This is it, God", she prayed silently. "It's either you or the meat box. Who wins? I'm bettin' on *you*. You done pretty good so far, but we need somethin' special for this one."

She began to breathe again.

"I'm countin' on you, now", she scolded. "Let's send these guys packin'. And if we can't do that, let's just save the boys. You can do what you want with me, send me to the slammer if you like, but just see that Arrow and Nick make it."

Silence.

"A deal?"

Two shadows appeared in the front-door window. The lock rattled.

"I said, is it a deal?"

Alice wasn't sure she heard any answers, but she got a feeling

811

way down inside herself, somewhere behind the stab wounds, deep in the storage room of memory, somewhere inside the jumble of dusty boxes and rusty cans that contained her sleepless nights and baby bottles and secret sobs, a dead soldier, a dead niece, a dead brother, the dirt and drink and loss, and all the mystery stories like Russian stacking dolls inside the one great mystery story of life—somewhere buried beneath the whole sad mess of her many, many failures as a human being— yes, somewhere down there a simple word was spoken in reply. She could hardly hear it, and what it said she couldn't begin to guess, because the shadows were banging on the door.

She reached down and flicked the safety on the shotgun. Up for shoot, down for no shoot. She left it up.

"Just in case", she said in a stage whisper.

"Miss Douglas?" one of the shadows called, pressing his face to the opaque glass.

Alice held her breath.

"Miss Douglas, this is the police. Would you open the door, please?"

A big shoulder leaned against the door and pushed. It creaked, but the deadbolt held firm.

"Open up," said the other shadow, "or we'll have to enter by force."

"Go away!" Alice shouted. "I'm closed."

Bang-bang, rattle-rattle.

"Open up!"

"I said I'm closed. Now git your butts outa here, or I'll call the cops."

"We *are* the cops. Now open this door."

"How do I know you're the cops? There's been a lot of robberies lately."

"Unless you open up right now, lady, you're going to be in a lot of trouble."

"I said beat it. You're crooks!"

The two shadows consulted. Then one stood to the side, and the other lifted its arm.

There was a tremendous explosion, and the handle of the door blew off, scattering wood chips and scraps of metal across the hardwood floor. Alice ducked down behind the counter and held the shotgun against her chest.

Two more loud explosions followed; the deadbolt sailed all twenty feet from the door to the counter, and flew over Alice's head. The front door banged wide open, the glass shattering out of it.

Alice stood up and aimed the barrel of the gun in the direction of the door. Two men stood in the opening, stopped in their tracks.

"Drop it!" she roared.

One of the agents raised his gun at her. Alice pulled a trigger, there was a furious *kablam*, blue smoke, and the wall to the right of the gun-toter disintegrated. His hand was stung by stray shot. He yowled, dropped the gun, and danced around holding his blood-spattered hand. The other dropped to the floor and rolled. Disoriented by the unexpected shock of the gun-blast, he fumbled in his jacket. This gave Alice three precious seconds to hunker down behind the counter and lever another shell into the empty chamber. She popped up and aimed the gun.

"Freeze!" she barked. "Take that hand outa your jacket!"

The agent obeyed.

"Stand up!"

He stood up.

"Back yourselves outa here, the both of you", Alice snapped.

"Now, Miss", said Wade, edging toward the counter. "Please don't do anything foolish. Just give me the gun."

Alice aimed at the floor beside him and pulled one of the triggers. *Kablam!* A smoking hole appeared in the floor a few inches from his shoes. Stunned, crouched into a defensive position, he stared at the hole, then up at her.

"That's called an Alice M. Douglas Special, bud, and if you don't get out of my place this minute, there's gonna be one of them holes in your guts!"

The man stood upright. "Hold on just a moment", he said, flashing her a scarecrow smile, reaching inside his jacket, under his arm.

"I toldya before, keep that hand outa your jacket. I can't get both of you, but one of you is gonna die unless you back off."

The man withdrew his hand from his jacket and shuffled backward toward the door, arms raised.

Alice felt a rush of pleasure. Just like the movies.

Bryce spread his arms wide. "We *are* police, Ma'am."

"You don't look it. Where's your uniforms?"

"We . . . we're special agents. Federal government."

"Ha! Show me your badges then, real slow. One false move, and there's gonna be blood all over this floor."

Both men gingerly extracted leather wallets from their side pockets, flipped them open, and held them up.

"You're too far away. I can't see proper. Looks like fake to me."

"They're real, Ma'am. OIS", said Wade.

"OIS? What the hell is OIS? Never heard of it. Over in the toy section I got a dozen plastic police badges. Cost ninety-five cents each. You can't fool me."

The two men eyeballed each other. Imperceptibly they moved apart.

"Don't move!" Alice growled. "Stay together. I know you're thieves and sneaks. I know you just want my money. I got a right to protect what's mine. You blew a hole in my door, and I'm gonna blow holes in you."

Wade moved slowly forward a step at a time, talking to her in a calm voice.

"This is really inappropriate behavior, Miss. If you'll just give us a chance to expl—"

"Bottle the act, pal. I heard about guys like you, tricking old people, robbing pension checks. All my life I been horn-swoggled, insulted, injured, and generally not treated very nice by People Who Should Know Better. And I ain't standing for it any more!"

Alice came around from behind the counter, aiming the barrel at the agent's chest. He stopped. He was now ten feet away, just in front of the nose cone of the missile. He might try to jump her, but he'd be dead on arrival.

"Back up", she commanded. "I shoot to kill."

"Wade, she means it", said the other agent.

Wade backed up.

"Right out the door, Wade", said Alice with a cruel grin. As he withdrew, she inched forward until she was standing behind the tail fins of the missile.

"Outside, G-Men!" she snarled sarcastically.

That was a mistake.

Both men halted, looked at each other, and turned around.

"You're a good actress, Miss Douglas", Wade said, smiling.

"I ain't acting", Alice snorted nervously, training the sight on his chest.

"You know why we're here", said Wade, taking a step forward. "You have the boy in there. You wouldn't want to kill anyone over a thing like that, would you?"

"Boy? What boy? I ain't never been married", Alice stammered. "Stand back, or I'll cream you!"

"No, you won't", Wade said evenly. "Give me the gun." He stepped closer.

Alice reached down under the missile, fumbled blindly, keeping her eyes on the agents.

"I'm a crazy woman", she said. "I'm ready to die. I ain't scared. And if I take two of you with me, I'll be pleased as punch. See this missile, here. It's loaded."

Bryce, standing uneasily by the door, grinned crookedly, "You have an A-bomb there?"

"No, but I packed it full of enough TNT to blow this palace sky high. I rigged a timer on it too."

Alice flicked a switch under the missile, setting off a faint *rat-a-tat-tat* sound and a tiny flashing red light.

"You got thirty seconds!" she warned. "I'm nuttier than a fruitcake, and I'm ready to die."

The men stared at her, their smiles fading.

"She's bluffing, Bryce."

"I know," Bryce replied uncertainly, staring at the nose cone. "But . . ."

"Twenty seconds, fellahs."

"Come on, let's not chance it, Wade."

"Get out of my place of business right now!" Alice shouted.

"Come on, she *is* nuttier than a fruitcake. We'll radio for a response team."

Wade shook his head. He walked around the head of the nose cone, holding his hand out to Alice.

"Fifteen seconds", she warned him. "This timer thing can't be shut off. You boys better run!"

Wade was now three feet away, locking Alice's eyes with his stare. Alice knew she couldn't kill anybody, not even a guy with cobra eyes. She aimed the gun at his kneecaps and pulled the trigger.

Nothing happened. She looked down. Somehow the safety catch had fallen down to no shoot.

Wade leaped forward and grabbed the barrel of the gun, yanking it from Alice's trembling hands. Alice wailed; tears sprang to her eyes.

Wade reached under the missile, fumbling for the timer mechanism. He pulled it out.

"Here's your doomsday weapon", he yelled to Bryce. But his partner was nowhere in sight. "Get in here, you idiot!"

Bryce sidled in the front door. Wade held out the timer for him to see.

"What's that?" Bryce asked, puzzled.

"It's a rabbit, dummy. A toy rabbit." The little raps of the drum died, the bunny nose flashed red one last time and winked out.

"All right, where is he?" Wade demanded.

"Where's who?" Alice asked innocently.

"The boy."

"What boy?"

"Arrow Delaney."

Alice shrugged, "Like I said, I ain't never been married."

Alice backed up to the door to her living quarters. Wade grabbed her arm and twisted it behind her back, pulling her away from the door. Bryce rattled the handle.

"Where's the key?" Wade said in a low voice.

"Dunno", Alice mumbled.

"I said, where's the key?" He gave Alice's arm a sharp jerk upward, and she shrieked in pain.

They found her key ring in her sweater pocket and unlocked the door. Pushing Alice ahead of them into the kitchen, they looked left and right. Wade held Alice tightly by the arm while the agent with the bleeding hand checked the other rooms. Alice closed her eyes and prayed, *A deal's a deal.*

Bryce returned, scowling. "Nothing. Not a sign."

"Where is he?" Wade gave Alice's arm another sharp wrench upward.

"I dunno! I dunno!"

Wade pushed Alice into her armchair, gave her a look full of hate, and turned to his partner.

"You checked everything?"

"Everything. There are some toys and kid's clothes under a bed. He was here all right."

Both men stared at Alice. Alice checked her fingernails, tousled her hair, and tried to look unconcerned.

"How long ago did he leave, lady?"

"No idea. Can I, uh, have a smoke?"

"You can have a smoke when we find him." Turning to Bryce, he said, "Check the back."

Bryce went out through the woodshed door. In the corner of her eye, Alice saw a slice of red on the door stoop. She leaned forward. Curious George. Beside him Freddy-the-Teddy, and beyond him, Leo.

Bryce returned a minute later, looking supremely irritated. "You won't believe what I found out there. A junk heap to end all junk heaps. It'll take three hours to check through all that stuff."

"All right", Wade replied. "Radio the response unit, get a bird and a team here as fast as you can, surround the perimeter, and start going through it with a fine-tooth comb."

Wade sat down on a kitchen chair, facing Alice, his eyes hard and brilliant as anthracite, exhaling loudly through his nostrils.

"You might as well tell us everything", he said in an ominously quiet voice. "We'll know it all in the end. We always do."

"That so?" Alice answered, unconcerned.

She looked away, studied the blue jays at the feeder, listened to the fire crackling in the stove, tried to imagine what it would have been like going for boat rides, walking the boys on a sunny beach, digging clams.

Not long after, a hum and a zing went over the roof, and a squad of men dressed in black jumpsuits ran past the window. Wade and the other agent took Alice out through the ruined front doorway, threw her into a black car, and drove away.

21

The Camp of the Saints

Contrary to her expectations, Alice M. Douglas did not succumb to Alzheimer's disease, nor did she die of her long-anticipated lung cancer. Five minutes down the road to Fort George, sitting beside the agent in the back seat, she felt a whopper of a pain in her chest. Everything in the car sort of faded out slowly, and a great big guy with a sword faded in, standing there with a troop of no-nonsense, really good-lookin' pals, fully armed. They were all smiling at her like she'd won the lottery.

Then the mother of all pains went off in her chest, she groaned, and her head fell sideways. The two agents thought she had fainted or fallen asleep, and only upon their arrival in Vancouver did they realize that she had slipped through their fingers forever.

Father Ron, racing toward Steelhead, saw the vehicle going in the other direction and noted in passing that it was big, modern, and black, its windows tinted so darkly he couldn't see inside.

A hundred yards before the Palace of Junque, he spotted a black helicopter parked beyond the gas pumps and a man in a black suit unrolling a yellow ribbon waist-high around the perimeter of the property. He eased to a stop as close as the ribbon would allow and rolled down the passenger side of the window.

The man in black gave him a neutral look and waved him away.

"Anything wrong?" Father Ron asked.

"Criminal investigation, sir. Move along, please."

Father Ron rolled up the window and drove a few hundred yards farther along the road and around the bend in the hill. Out of sight, he pulled over to the shoulder and let the car sit idling.

He was too late. Something had happened to Alice. Who were these guys in black? They weren't regular police.

He put the car into second gear, did a U-turn, and drove back the way he had come, observing the front lot of the Palace from the corner of his eye as he passed. Not knowing where he was going, he took the first left, turning onto a dirt road that led to the mountains beyond Stave Lake. He kept the speed down to fifteen miles an hour so he wouldn't spin off into the ravines that bordered the road.

He tried to think, but no thoughts materialized. He tried to pray, but no voices spoke to him.

"What next?" he asked himself.

He had just decided to turn around and go back to Fort George when he spotted something moving through the trees on his left, a shadow that flitted through the thick cedars on the high embankment.

Deer, he thought.

Then the shadow broke through the edge of the forest for a second and darted back into it.

A child!

What was a child doing so far out in the woods, alone, on a school day, running nowhere? Braking the car, he got out and called to the retreating form, which instantly disappeared into the forest.

"Hey!" he yelled. "Hello there! You need a ride?"

He closed the car door and walked across the road to the embankment, climbed up, and stood at the edge of the woods, trying to see where the kid had gone. He strolled along, peering between the trees, until he came to an old deer path and spotted a distant form running down it—running slowly, bent over, carrying a heavy load on its back.

Father Ron broke into a sprint and a minute later was thumping only ten yards behind—it was a boy, chugging under full steam, his breathing audible even at that distance, a mixture of gasps and cries of fear. When the boy glanced over his shoulder and saw Father Ron gaining, he veered off into the woods and began scrambling over fallen trees, gasping loudly now, zigging and zagging through the giant trunks, going deeper into the damp shadows.

"Whoa, buddy! Hold on a minute. Stop!"

The boy doubled his efforts to escape. The gasps were now loud cries, and Father Ron thought he heard the words *black* and *beetles*.

The boy tripped and fell into a hummock of moss that covered a rotten stump. The stump disintegrated, and the boy fell forward on his face into the debris. He lay there sobbing under a huge backpack, an aluminum-frame army-surplus affair.

Father Ron came to a full stop, hands on his waist, huffing and puffing.

"Hey, there, son, nobody's going to hurt you."

The boy buried his face in his hands and screamed, trailing off into the most miserable wails Father Ron had ever heard. The sound seemed to echo throughout the woods, as if it were two voices, two cries, two separate bursts of pain and terror. Then a hole opened in the backpack and a tiny hand popped out, pushing the flap aside an inch or so, revealing two beautiful eyes that were spilling tears.

"What on earth . . . ?" Father Ron exclaimed, squatting down. He pulled back the flap of the knapsack, and his mouth dropped open.

"Good Lord!"

It was by far the strangest thing he had ever seen: An absolutely terrified eight- or nine-year-old, with a Miraculous Medal dangling from his neck, crying his eyes out, and on his back what looked like a baby—one heck of a weird baby—crying too.

Father Ron shook his head, trying to take it all in.

Later, whenever he recalled that day, he could not explain what happened next. The wind blew in, mild and gentle on that chilly wet day, and a flock of small birds twittered as they dipped and scattered through the swaying branches above his head. Time seemed to stop entirely, or melted, or simply slackened its course. Stillness engulfed everything, the braided strands of the two children's cries went up, up, up into the overcast above the forest crown and were greeted by a burst of light brighter than the sun, which broke through and filled the forest with a wave of silver that was as warm as scented oil. It lasted only a moment, if indeed moments still existed in that state which is the cessation of time, which is the eternal present. As he floated in it, he began to wonder if the two children were connected to what had happened at Alice's place.

As if unfolding a map composed of many invisible dimensions, as if he were struggling to read the secret shape of the world, to know the form of it and the meaning of it for the first time, he saw the movements of principalities and powers, governments and dominions, armies of angels, dark and light, with no neutral ground between them; armies of human beings, dark and light, and many in between, who struggled for a neutral ground that would ever evade them as they merged and fragmented, congealed into groups, and scattered into the manifold quadrants of the world, seeking sanctuary.

He understood, then, the Father's will: that he must take this small flock composed of two inexplicable boys to a place of refuge. But why? Who were they? Where would he take them? He did not know. How? He did not know that either. That he must do it was certain.

The silver light faded, casting the forest back into its perpetual gloom. He looked up at a gap in the trees and saw two tiny, soundless helicopters shoot across it in the direction of Steelhead.

"Come on, lad", he said, patting the runner's head. "There's nothing to be afraid of. I won't hurt you."

The boy quivered and cried harder.

Father Ron touched the boy's medal. "Do you know who this lady is?"

Arrow nodded, choking back his cries.

"She sent me to help you", the priest said.

Father Ron pulled a chain out from behind his Roman collar and showed the boy a medal that dangled from it.

"See, I've got one too. She's my mother."

The boy stopped crying. "Are you Jesus?" he asked, looking up curiously.

"Actually, no. But Jesus is the man I work for. That's not the best way to put it—he's the King, but he's also my friend. You know who he is, don't you?"

"He killed the giants."

"Uh, yes, something like that."

"Is the lady going to kill the giants?"

"Hey, now, that's a heavy theological question for a guy like you! Let's just say she's going to kill snakes. She doesn't like snakes, especially the ones that try to bite children. She loves you, and she loves your friend here, too."

"Too", said a little voice from the knapsack.

"Come on, stand up now. We've got a long way to go."

* * *

The boys were wet and cold, dirty with moss and wood chips, muddied by tears. Father Ron tucked them into the back seat of his car under a blanket and turned the heater on high. They sat huddled together, watching him, their eyes almost dry. The boy wiped the baby's face with his jacket sleeve.

The boy looked vaguely familiar. Then Father Ron's memory kicked in, and he realized this was the lad Beth Potter had taken to the hospital. Suddenly, a vast, multi-tiered landscape opened up before him, a topographical chart of the spirit, transparent, readable. In a moment, he understood their precise position.

"What's your name, son?"

"Arrow", the boy mumbled.

Arrow? thought Father Ron.

"And what's the baby's name?"

"Nick."

That was better, a real name.

"Nick's twenty-two and a half years old", the boy added solemnly.

"Uh, okay. Now where should I take you, Nick and Arrow?"

"I don't know."

"Where is your home?"

"Alice's."

Father Ron digested the response, putting together yet another corner of the puzzle: Théophane, Thérèse, a bow and arrow, a baby—and *bad man, kill baby, kill woman!*

"I'm afraid we can't go back to Alice's just yet", he said.

"Black beetles. Guns. Loud", the boy said, his eyes filling up again.

"It scared you, didn't it? Don't worry, we won't go back there. Do you have a family? Can I take you to them?"

Arrow shook his head, then stopped in mid-shake and looked up as if an idea had struck him.

"My great-grandpa."

Father Ron nodded. "Okay, I'll take you to him. Where does he live?"

"I don't know."

"Are you sure? Can you tell me anything more? Anything at all that would help us find him?"

"Mountains. Tyler. Zöe."

"Mountains? Yes, but which mountains?"

"Horse. Fly."

"Are there horses there? And flies?"

"Horse! Fly!" Arrow repeated, his mind struggling to remember something.

"Do we have to fly to get there? Whitehorse? Is your great-grandfather in the Yukon?"

Arrow shook his head.

"Stam-peed."

Father Ron glanced at the sky anxiously. "Anything else?"

"William."

"William? Is that your great-grandpa's name?"

"No, his name's Thaddaeus." Arrow paused. "William has a lake", he added.

Then the connections began to snap into place, and Father Ron understood.

"Williams Lake!"

Arrow nodded. The priest opened a road map of the province and found the town of Williams Lake in the central highlands, situated between the Chilcotin and the Cariboo. One inch to the northeast there was a tiny dot with the word *Horsefly* beside it.

He closed the map, put the car into gear, and drove on.

* * *

He chose the old Fraser highway, praying throughout the two-hour journey to the head of the canyon that no one would stop the car. It was too early, he supposed, for roadblocks to be thrown up on every back lane of the province. But it wouldn't take the police long.

As they drove north, the story came out of the boy in bits and pieces. Father Ron found much of it confusing, but it gradually solidified into a coherent form in his mind, to the extent that the sense of purpose and peace he had felt in the forest was replaced by outrage and not a few moments of genuine terror. He had known the country was in bad shape, but not this bad.

825

Near the town of Lytton, he pulled into a deserted rest stop that had a phone booth. He dialed the number of Saint George's and got the answering machine. The parish accountant would arrive at the office at one o'clock; seeing that Father Ron was not there, she would probably check the machine.

After the beep, he left a message explaining that he had been called away on an emergency and probably wouldn't return until the following day. Would she please contact one of the priests at the neighboring parishes and ask him to fill in for the Mass scheduled for tomorrow morning?

At Lytton he pulled into the drive-thru of a hamburger joint and ordered bags full of lunch for himself and the boys (who were lying under the blanket). When they were safely beyond town, Arrow pulled Nick upright again and began to push bits of bun into Nick's mouth. Father Ron turned northwest onto Highway 12 and drove toward Lilooet. At Lilooet he turned onto 99 northeast, and at the little village of Pavilion he rerouted onto a gravel-topped road that connected twenty-five miles farther on with Highway 97 north.

Two hours later, the rusty blue Volvo cruised past the Stampede Motel and a minute later turned onto a narrow paved road that wound up into the eastern hills. Forty-five minutes after that, the car slowed as it broke through the wall of forest and emerged into the village of Horsefly, British Columbia. On the outskirts he found a dilapidated general store with an antique gas pump out front and a block of six motel rooms crumbling into quiet decrepitude out back. An incongruously large sign on the roof proclaimed:

HORSEFLY HILTON
GOLDEN GATE TO THE CARIBOOS

Before going in, Father Ron removed his Roman collar and zipped his tan jacket tight around his throat. In the general store *cum* motel office, an old woman, pleasant but uninterested, dressed in housedress and slippers, came out from behind a post office wicket and lifted a green visor off her brow, the better to see him with. She took thirty dollars from him, slammed a key onto the counter, and said, "Room five. Turn the 'lectric heater on when you go in. I'll turn on the water from here. Just you and the missuz stayin'?"

"Uh, no. Just me and the boys."

"You need supper?"

"No, thanks, Ma'am. But I could use some bread and milk, cheese if you have it, some cookies, and a pack of Players Filter."

It was an old-fashioned country store, the kind where proprietors weren't keen on self-service. All the merchandise was behind the wall-to-wall counter. She fetched the various items with a shuffling gate, grunting as she climbed a rolling stepladder, sighing as she descended.

"What kind of cookies you want? I got macaroons, ginger snaps, and digestive biscuits."

"One bag of each, please."

She stacked everything on the counter and started adding it up on a pad of paper, licking the pencil point after noting each item.

"On second thought, you might as well forget the cigarettes", Father Ron said uncomfortably.

She glanced up at him and frowned. "Change your mind?"

"Yeah, been trying to give it up."

"I got chewin' tobacco. Sometimes that helps. Want some?"

"No, thanks. I'd better go cold turkey."

She smiled at him and asked for $18.45.

He drove the Volvo around back to the motel annex and parked in front of a door with a poorly painted number five on its chipped red enamel. He unlocked, went in, flicked the light switch, and turned on the heater. The room smelled of cigarette smoke and old beer but otherwise was clean. He put the grocery bags on one of the sagging double beds. He went back out to the car and brought the boys inside, laying Nick down on the other bed. The boys watched his every move, saying nothing.

He closed the door and locked it.

Father Ron put together a makeshift meal and handed it to Nick and Arrow. Nick bounced up and down, then tried to cram a cheese sandwich into his mouth. The sandwich wouldn't go in, sideways or otherwise, and stayed wedged at the opening. Nick whimpered. Arrow pulled the wad of food out of Nick's mouth.

"He doesn't know how to eat", Arrow explained. He put an arm around Nick's shoulders and with his free hand began to push small bits of bread and cheese inside the open mouth. That was followed by many small sips of milk administered by Arrow from a paper cup. When the meal was finished, the boy informed the priest, "Nick needs a change."

"A change? Some cookies maybe?"

"He stinks", Arrow explained, pointing at Nick's pants.

Father Ron balked at that but decided he didn't have many options. "You stay with him", he said to Arrow. "I'll be right back."

He walked across the lot to the store and went inside. The old woman was bent over a tabloid newspaper, reading it with devotion. She looked up sharply and said, "Everything okay?"

"Everything's fine", he assured her. "I forgot to get some diapers."

"I got disposables. Small, medium, or large?"

"Large, please."

While he was rifling through his wallet, she fixed inquisitive eyes on him and said, "Single dad?"

"Uh-huh", he nodded. "Single dad."

"That's too bad", she replied, taking his money and giving him change. "Want a wake-up call in the morning?"

"No, thanks. We'll be up pretty early and gone."

"Where you going to?"

"Oh, just seeing the country."

"Not a great time of year to see this country. Sure must be tough doin' it with kids taggin' along."

"Not so bad. They're good boys."

"Lookin' for anything in particular?"

"Well, now that you mention it, I am. I'm looking for a man. I want to drop something off for him."

"What's his name?"

"Thaddaeus."

"First name or last?"

"I'm not sure."

She shook her head. "Don't know anybody by that name. Know where he lives?"

"Somewhere in the Cariboo country, I think. How far is it to the nearest town?"

"Williams Lake is about an hour back thataway. The next place is Likely to the north and Black Creek to the east, but hardly anybody goes on those roads."

"Who lives back there?"

"A few homesteaders and ranchers, couple of guys with logging operations, a bush camp or two for fallers and buckers, and some Indians."

"Is there a Catholic church near here?"

She looked at him curiously. "Not around here. There's one on the reserve somewhere up by the Spectacle Lakes, east of the provincial park. I never been there, hardly anybody goes there. Thirty or forty miles thataway." She jigged her thumb in the direction of a side window. "It's a bad road at the best of times, banged up by them damn logging trucks. It's a killer, especially when we get an early snow. Your friend an Indian?"

"I don't know."

"You a Catholic?"

He nodded, feeling uneasy.

The old woman shrugged. "I used t'be a Catholic, long time ago."

She launched into a tangent of musing and remembrance, opinion and prejudice, which made Father Ron squirm. At another time and another place, he might have tried to insert some helpful insight into the stream of her convictions, but he remembered Nick's predicament.

"Well, I better get back to the boys", he interrupted. "Thanks for the advice. Have a good night, Ma'am."

"You too", she replied, still looking inward at the tabloid of her memories.

Back in the room, Father Ron girded his emotional loins and unwrapped Nick. It wasn't a pretty picture. He went into the bathroom and turned on the sink tap; rusty water came shooting out, then ran clear. He soaked a washcloth and returned with it to clean up Nick. As he worked away, Arrow came over, knelt down beside the bed, and put his face close to Nick's.

"Nicolo Piccolo!" he said tentatively.

Nick's arms flew up like a happy bird's.

"Wok-wok, Awo!"

"Nicolo Piccolo wok-wok!" Arrow answered, smiling.

Burbling laughter erupted. Busily scrubbing, Father Ron smiled to himself, thinking that they were amazingly resilient, considering what they had been through.

"Dumpster boy, jumpster boy!" Arrow sang.

"Play, Awo, play!" Nick sang back.

Arrow bounced the mattress up and down with both hands. Nick's laughter pealed through the room.

"Whoa, hold on there, pardner," Father Ron grinned. "Wait till I get this diaper on him."

When Nick was clean, dry, and snug at last, Father Ron bundled him in a big bath towel and tucked him under the covers of the bed farthest from the door. Nick yawned and closed his eyes.

Arrow was yawning too, probably worn out from his big run through the forest. Father Ron told him to get ready for bed. There were no pajamas available, so Arrow snuggled fully dressed under the covers beside Nick. Instantly, he curled into a semi-fetal position and closed his eyes. Father Ron made the sign of the cross over the boys, turned off the harsh overhead light (a naked 150-watt bulb), and switched on a small lamp on the table beside his bed. He lay down, stretched out, and pulled a rosary from his pocket.

The boys were sound asleep by the time he finished the Sorrowful Mysteries. He prayed the Glorious Mysteries, and when they were completed, he felt an indescribable longing for his breviary.

He turned out the light, replayed the day in his mind, shaking his head in disbelief. It was a long, long time since he had eaten that piece of toast with blueberry jam, way back a thousand years ago before a sparrow had flown in to mess up his schedule. If someone had suggested to him this morning that by 9 P.M. this evening he would be three hundred miles from home, deep in the bush, in a run-down motel, guarding a nine-year-old fugitive from justice and one very strange baby, looking for someone he didn't know and trying to find a place he wouldn't recognize if he drove right through it, he would have said he was out of his mind. Yet here he was, afloat in total unknowing. Total irrationality. And quite possibly total insanity!

Oh boy! he thought. *First it's fires in the parking lot, then it's playing John the Baptist, and now this. What on earth am I going to tell His Grace?*

* * *

The stars were still bright when he woke up, but the eastern sky over the Cariboo range was gray. After a breakfast of cookies, cheese, and milk (and the martyrdom of another diaper change), Father Ron loaded the boys into the car and drove

831

away down the road, travelling vaguely north. A mile from town the pavement ended, gravel took over, the road narrowed, and he felt the car begin to rattle and slide under the grip of his hands. It took some getting used to, but the Volvo steadied as he prayed his morning office. He substituted for the absent breviary readings Scripture passages he had memorized over the years—the lilies of the field, not a sparrow falls from heaven that your Father does not see, Psalm 121, I will lift up my eyes to the mountains from whence comes my help—and a list of urgent petitions.

"You've got to help me, Lord. I'm flying blind. I don't know the way. Where are we going?"

There was one near disaster when an empty logging truck barrelled around a corner and nearly collided with the Volvo. Father Ron jerked the wheel to the right, the logger careened to the left, and they screeched past each other safely, leaving only a few chips of rust on the road.

North. That was all he knew. They were going north, and some inner compass told him he was heading in the right direction.

At sunrise the road was still hard with night frost, the surface corrugated like washboard, punctuated with many potholes that guaranteed the poor old car would never be the same. The sun began to thaw the road eventually, and the surface became slick with a thin coating of mud. He slowed to a crawl and proceeded at that speed for just under an hour.

"Show me, Lord. Speak to me. Lead, kindly light, amid encircling gloom, for it is night and I am far from home."

The actual night was now completely dissipated by the winter sun, but he felt the awful weight of the invisible night that still gripped the land, the spiritual darkness that was seeping into every settlement and habitation of mankind.

Soon, said an interior voice.

Five minutes later an intersection sign appeared on the right.

A sideways T, tilting on its rotting pole, riddled with hunters' pot shots.

This is the way you shall go.

"Okay", Father Ron exhaled, raising his brows dubiously. He turned onto a one-lane dirt road that pierced a thick jack pine forest and threaded its way toward the Cariboo mountains. Slowing to ten miles per hour, he prayed that he would meet no traffic coming from the opposite direction, because if he did, it would mean a head-on collision. Swamp and muskeg bracketed the road on both sides.

No other vehicles appeared. An hour and a half later, the forest began to thin, the road widened slightly and approached a clearing. The trees were little more than poles here, dark, gray, brittle, covered in scraggy moss. Beyond the clearing Father Ron saw wide stretches of natural meadow that rose in tiers to the foothills of the Cariboos. The range was much closer now, a massive wall, the peaks above the black treeline covered with snow. Ravens beat their wings through the sky above the clearing. Father Ron braked the car and saw in the distance a cluster of a dozen shanties and log cabins, from which rose the spire of a clapboard church. A muddy rutted lane joined the road at that point, and he turned onto it, heading toward the church. The car bounced through a field of wild grass and leafless birch saplings, arriving eventually, much to the driver's relief, in the center of the ragged village.

Father Ron opened the car door and got out, looking around, feeling somewhat dismayed. If Thaddaeus lived here, he thought, there certainly wasn't any evidence of it. The windows of some of the cabins were broken, and no smoke came from any of the chimneys. The church was badly in need of repair, the paint peeling, the lattice in the bell tower missing slats, the front steps broken, one of the windows covered with a plastic sheet.

He turned in a full circle, taking it all in. The air was cold but

833

sweet, the wind making the surrounding forest sway and creak. Ravens cawed. A brown hare bolted across the clearing.

Cupping his hands around his mouth, Father Ron shouted, "Hello! Anyone here?"

The sound of his own voice startled him, the rustling in the grass was the only reply.

He climbed the rickety steps of the church and tried the door. It was locked. A sign nailed to the wall beside the door declared:

Saint Philomena's Parish
Jackfish Lake Reserve
Mass 11:00 A.M. Sundays

It was a very old sign. He walked around the side of the building and found a picket fence that had long ago been painted white but was now a blistered gray. Most of the fence had fallen down, and saplings were growing up through it. There were more than a hundred crosses in the graveyard, all of them made of wood, tilting at odd angles, bearing lichen, inscribed with names that were quaint and biblical. There were faded plastic flowers scattered throughout, and at the foot of some crosses were empty pickle jars containing the burned-out stubs of candles.

His heart gave a painful leap when he saw scattered across a grave several bones that were covered with sinew and scraps of red meat. Then he realized, after a moment's consideration, that they were too large for human bones and must be the remains of moose or caribou.

Father Ron left the cemetery and returned to the car. He got into the front seat and turned to Arrow.

"There's no one here. I guess we move on."

He was about to turn the key in the ignition when Arrow pointed out the side window and said, "A man."

The man was standing beside the front steps of the church, looking at them. His face was not old, but neither was it young.

834

His receding hair was silver, cropped short, and his beard was gray, down to his mid-chest. He wore brown overalls and a striped shirt. The eyes behind his wire-rim spectacles were shining, blue, solemn.

Father Ron stepped out of the car.

"Hi", he said, raising his right hand in a wave. "I didn't see you there. We thought nobody was home."

The man smiled gently and nodded.

"Uh, I'm not even sure where we are. It's not on the map."

The man smiled again and shook his head.

"Maybe you can help us."

"How can I help you?" the man said in a quiet voice, speaking for the first time. The voice was like a deep lake, unriffled by a breeze.

"I'm looking for a man named Thaddaeus."

The man nodded again. "I know Thaddaeus", he said with a simplicity that begged no questions.

Father Ron blinked, not sure if he had heard correctly, struggled to think of a response, then said, "Oh! You know him! That's great!"

"Why don't you come inside?" the man said.

Not knowing what else to say, Father Ron blurted, "Okay."

He opened the car doors for the boys, wondering why he felt at a loss for words, knowing that ordinary conversation would be superfluous.

Arrow jumped out and stared at the man. Father Ron pulled Nick out and held him in his arms.

Nick grinned at the man and flapped his arms like a bird. The man smiled at him.

"Well, I guess I should introduce myself, shouldn't I? My name's Ron. This is Nick, and this is Arrow. He's Thaddaeus' great-grandson."

Ron held out his hand, and the man shook it. The grip was like the look in the eyes—strong, unhurried, gentle.

"And you are . . . ?" Father Ron prompted.

"You can call me Raymond."

Raymond turned and led them around to the back of the church. He opened a door in a lean-to addition and went in; Ron and the boys followed him inside. The room was small, roughly eight feet by ten, containing a cot, wood stove, a wood-box, a sideboard with jug and basin, a plank table and four rickety chairs, a doorless cupboard, and a sink counter with a water pump jutting out of it. A single window with small, dusty panes allowed some light to penetrate.

"Are you the parish priest?" Father Ron asked.

"No", the man shook his head, offering no explanation.

"Oh, you're the caretaker, then?"

The man considered the question, then nodded, "Yes."

"Is the church closed?"

"No", Raymond replied slowly. "A priest from Williams Lake comes out to say Mass on Sunday mornings."

"Where are all the people?"

"They have moved away. Some to the mountains, others to places far from here, a few have gone deeper into the forest."

"Oh, that's too bad. It must have been a pretty place once. Who attends Mass now?"

"The remnant scattered throughout these hills. Many of them walk a great distance."

Hearing the word *remnant*, Father Ron looked at the man more closely. That was an unusual word to come from the mouth of a simple soul living in a primitive area such as this.

"You're a priest", Father Ron whispered.

The man nodded. "And you also are a priest."

"Yes. How did you know?"

"Tell me first, how did you know that I am a priest?"

Father Ron hesitated. "I'm not sure. I don't even know why I said that."

Raymond smiled. "Our priesthood is written in the heart

and in the soul. The sign of our Savior is upon your fore-head."

Feeling more puzzled by the minute, Father Ron shifted Nick to his left knee.

Raymond stood up and went to the stove. He opened the firebox, put some kindling into it, and lit a match under the kindling. Soon it was crackling, and warmth began to fill the room.

"You have travelled far. You are hungry. I have bread. I will make tea."

Raymond jogged the handle of the pump, and a stream of clear water gushed out of the nozzle, filling a dented nickel-plated kettle. When it was full, he put it on the top of the stove. Then he brought a loaf of bread from the cupboard and put it before them on the table.

Father Ron gave Nick to Arrow and went back outside to the car, returning a minute later with the bag of groceries. When he came into the room, he was surprised to see Nick cuddling in Raymond's arms and Arrow leaning against him with his arms around the man's waist.

The stillness in the room was awesome, the look of love with which Raymond regarded the boys was even more so.

Wondering if he had stumbled into another dimension, Father Ron unpacked the bag slowly, feeling confused, question-ing, but completely unable to formulate a question.

Raymond put Nick into Father Ron's arms and made the sign of the cross over the meal, murmuring foreign words with his eyes closed.

"Please, eat", he said at last. The visitors sat down and obeyed.

"Aren't you hungry?" Arrow asked Raymond, when he no-ticed that the man did not join them. Raymond shook his head, smiling. He sat down on the fourth chair and seemed content merely to watch them.

Arrow tried to push bits of ginger snap into Nick's mouth,

but Nick didn't like the taste. He spat it out. Arrow pushed a bit of coconut macaroon into his mouth, and Nick liked it very much.

Raymond and Father Ron laughed. Raymond's laugh was like his eyes and his voice.

Sipping from a mug of tea, Father Ron said, "You say you know Thaddaeus?"

Raymond nodded.

"Where is he?"

Raymond tilted his head slightly and replied, "In the camp of the saints."

"Huh? Where?"

"Soon I will take these children to him."

Father Ron said simply, "Oh."

"You must return to your flock, my brother. You have borne many wounds for the Lord, and you will bear more for him."

"I can't just leave the boys! How will I know they're . . . safe?"

"They will be safe."

"Will I ever see them again?"

"Perhaps. You will return here one day, bringing with you a flock."

"What flock?"

"The flock may be small, or it may be great. Man is free, for such is the Father's will. So he has made us, and so we remain. Much will depend on prayer. Much will depend on how well they listen to you. The voice of the Holy Spirit is strong, but he does not force. The hand of the Mother is gentle, but she does not demand. She asks. We choose."

After the meal, Raymond stood up and opened a door leading into the church. It was dark inside, but it did not seem cold. A candle flickered in a vigil lamp beside the tabernacle.

Raymond knelt and bowed to the Presence. His head touched the floor and remained in that position for many minutes. Father Ron knelt beside him, holding Nick in his arms. Nick rested against his chest, very still, very quiet. Arrow stood beside them, his hand on Father Ron's shoulder.

After what seemed an eternity, Raymond stood upright and turned to Father Ron. He placed both of his hands on the young priest's head and prayed for a time. Then, opening his eyes, he said:

"Son of man, you have seen the bones of the whole House of God. They have been saying, 'All hope is lost, our life is dried up, and we are cut off.' Therefore you must say to them, 'O my people, I will open your graves and have you rise from them, and bring you back to your own true home. Thus you will know that it is the Lord who saves you. I will do it. I have promised, and I will do it.' "

A light flowed through Father Ron, and he felt washed in it, rested in it, sighing from the depths of his soul.

"The river of life that is within you shall be as a tiny stream that grows as it flows to the sea. It shall swell in the singing, until it is a river of immense breadth and depth and power. Many are the tribulations that are coming upon my people, and you must comfort them. Be not afraid. The Light of the world is with you, the rider and the chariot are with you. Ezekiel, your father, is with you, and the Mother of the Church is with you until the final consummation."

Raymond closed his eyes, stepped back, and turned toward the tabernacle. He knelt, prostrated himself, and remained there without moving.

The rivulet swelled in Father Ron's throat, became a mighty river, flowed outward soundlessly, and though it was without word or visible form, it was broad and deep, and the strength of it grew in the singing.

When he opened his eyes, Nick was asleep in his arms, Arrow, also asleep, was lying on the floor of the sanctuary. Father Raymond stood before Father Ron, looking into his eyes.

"Go now, and strengthen the things that remain."

As if in a dream, Father Ron traced the sign of the cross on Nick's forehead and handed him to Raymond. Then he blessed Arrow. He left the church without another word, got into his car, and drove away. The journey to the coast passed as if it were the blink of an eye, or the pause between the beats of a heart. He arrived at Saint George's just in time for evening Benediction. That night the church was full.

*　*　*

After Father Ron left Jackfish Reserve, Father Raymond woke up the boys and returned with them to the lean-to rectory. He put Nick into the backpack and lifted it onto his back, tying the straps firmly about his waist. Then he extended his right hand toward Arrow. The boy looked at it, then took it in his own hand.

"Come, we are going now", the man said.

"Where are we going?"

"To meet Thaddaeus."

Side by side they walked across the clearing behind the church and went into a stand of black spruce. Though the day was cold, no snow had yet fallen from the overcast sky. The going was easy, the undergrowth was sparse, the moss soft and thick, and their feet left no prints. Minutes later they came to a deer path that cut through the forest, winding leisurely toward the mountains. They turned onto it and followed.

They walked without haste for an hour. Each time Arrow looked up to the peaks of the looming massif, he was surprised to see that it did not appear much closer. They halted at midday, and Raymond gave the boys bread and water. The meal was austere but seemed to satisfy them. The man ate nothing. While Arrow was chewing his third slice of bread, he wrinkled his brow and said, "I forgot."

"What did you forget?" Raymond asked.

Arrow rummaged in a big side pocket of the backpack and removed a stone object. He held it up for the man to see.

"My father sent this to me", he explained.

"Your father loves you", Raymond replied with a note of sadness.

"I saw my father standing on a mountain. Are we going to his mountain?"

"No, that was another mountain."

"Will I see my father?"

"Your father sees you."

"Is he looking at me?"

"Yes, he is looking at you."

"Oh", said Arrow, putting the stone cross back into the pocket.

They walked on. In midafternoon the deer path branched into another trail that skirted a small, round lake. Arrow looked across the water and saw that the mountains were now very close. The sun broke through the clouds, illuminating the snow-covered peaks. On the far side of the lake, the path entered a stand of thick cedars that crowded close together. The sound of water running somewhere behind the veil of the trees increased steadily, and in the deeper shadows the air was colder. The noise grew into a sound like rushing wind, and when the path turned around a large boulder, the source became visible. A narrow brook ran along the base of the mountain, babbling content-edly in a persistent flow that had worn a channel into the gran-ite. Arrow crouched on the stone outcropping of its banks for a few minutes, watching golden minnows dart this way and that.

Raymond led the way across a fallen log, and after that the path began to climb steeply into the foothills. The path was a deep groove in the soil now, covered with pine needles that ra-diated a wonderful incense under the beating rays of the sun. Arrow looked back and saw in the distance, far below, the tiny church and its cabins. Beyond the clearing the forest spread like a vast sea, flowing in waves over the bones of the earth toward the horizon. In the west there were more mountains, though they were tawny brown and not so high as the Cariboos. In the south, there was yet another wall of peaks, dwindling into infinity.

The sun was scattering the last of the clouds. It was falling in a tangent across the wide blue space between south and west. Eagles cried high above, circling in updrafts. Ravens beat their slow, silken wings and plunged from the tops of dead tamarisks into precipitous gorges. The path was steeper now, and it began to zig and zag across the face of the incline, passing through copses of stripped birch, then through conifer stands, no longer the tall, thin lodgepole pines of the valley bottom, but the bluer green of the heights, dwarf spruce and balsam that seemed to grow shorter as they climbed.

The path crossed another brook, fast, rampant, noisy with its laughter, singing loudly, shooting spray from small rapids, cascading down from unseen sources above. Arrow was forced to stretch his legs wide to hop from one stepping stone to the next. Raymond held his hand, and together they made it safely across. On the other side, the path, which was now surfaced with fine buff-colored gravel, veered sharply to the left, shooting straight up into a field of tumbled granite and mixed evergreen stands. The cries of small rock mammals, picas, squirrels, and marmots, greeted them. Jays and chickadees competed for attention.

They climbed for another hour, stopping only for a short rest late in afternoon. As he fed Nick small bits of macaroon, Arrow remarked that they must be very high on the mountain by now. Raymond told him that they were not yet halfway to the peak. Arrow's legs were aching, and his chest hurt from the thin, cold air.

"We will not climb all the way. Your journey is almost complete."

"How far do we go now?"

"Not far", Raymond smiled down at him.

Once again they climbed. Arrow lagged behind, gasping, trying not to complain, permitting himself only small groans. From time to time Raymond stopped and waited for him to catch up, giving the boy a smile of encouragement. Arrow opened the flap of the backpack to check on Nick and saw that he was sleeping, his breath whistling peacefully in and out.

The path ended abruptly at the face of a cliff. Raymond turned to Arrow and put both of his hands on the boy's shoulders.

"Now you must go on alone", he said

Arrow looked up at the rock face. He stepped back.

"It's too high!" he cried.

"He shall hide you in the shadow of the rock", Raymond answered.

"It's too high! It's too high!"

"You will go through, my son."

"I can't!" Arrow's lips trembled, and tears brimmed in his eyes.

"You can", the man said. "Look, I will show you."

He led the way along the base of the cliff to a clump of fir trees. A shallow stream gushed from between their roots and tumbled away down the mountain.

Raymond pulled one of the trees aside.

"You see?"

Behind the trees there was a fissure in the rock about three feet wide and four feet high. The stream poured from it.

"To see a thing from the outside is to see a part that is not the whole", Raymond said. "To see it from the inside and from above is to know its purpose."

Arrow did not understand what he meant.

"I must leave you now. You will go through. Then you will go up."

"I can't. I can't!"

"You can."

"Take me with you!" the boy cried.

"I must go back."

"Why? Why?"

"There are others who do not know the way. I must show them."

Raymond removed the backpack and put it onto Arrow's shoulders.

"You must take your little brother with you."

Arrow burst into tears.

"Nick needs you. You will go together."

"I can't. There're no grown-ups."

"Trust, little boy. Trust. Go through the cleft of the rock, and you will see."

Arrow turned and looked into the yawning stone mouth.

He stepped into the water and took a pace toward the entrance. He looked back and saw Raymond blessing him with the sign of the cross. Swallowing hard, Arrow turned again and, bending low, entered the shadow of the rock. Feeling a moment of terror, he looked back, but Raymond was gone.

"Awo?" Nick piped.

"It's okay, Nick. It's okay."

The water swirling around his ankles was freezing. The roar of the current echoing off the walls deafened him. Trying not to cry, closing his eyes, he inched forward, spreading his arms wide so that his fingers played along the surface of the walls. Step after step, fighting the agony in his feet, resisting the impulse to scream, he moved upstream.

A minute later a gust of warm air blew across his face, and a shaft of sunlight fell on him. He opened his eyes. He straightened his body upright. He was standing in a deep gully, surrounded by massive slabs of granite that towered on all sides. Dark green conifers surrounded the upper rim of the bowl. The gully floor was about twenty feet wide, carpeted with moss, sweeping upward to the far end, where the stream fell from a crest, spilling into the gully in a slender waterfall. A footpath composed of flat stones ascended like steps beside it.

Arrow looked down at his feet. He was still standing in mid-stream, the water flowing around his ankles, but it no longer felt as cold as it had inside the cliff. He sloshed upstream until the footpath began. He stepped from the water and climbed slowly from stone to stone.

He was exhausted as he neared the top. His legs and back ached. Nick's weight had become almost unbearable. When he heaved himself over the final step, he was too tired to look at what lay beyond. He fell down onto his side and rested on a bed of green grass, eyes closed, breathing hard.

"Awo?"

"Sorry, Nick", Arrow said, sitting up. "I didn't mean to squash you."

He jiggled himself out of the straps, pulled Nick from the backpack, and held him in his lap. Together the two boys looked out over the land beyond the cleft in the rock.

Though it was early winter, and high in the mountains, the little valley that lay before them was green. Stands of blue spruce trees were interspersed with natural meadows. A warm breeze lifted the wisps of Nick's mousy hair. Nick bounced and flapped his wings.

"Play, Awo, play!"

Arrow hardly heard him. He stared at the valley as if it were not real. Sheep dotted the meadows. Above a skirt of forest the dazzling white peaks soared, close and mighty, encompassing the valley on all sides.

"Wok-wok, Awo?"

"Okay, Nick, we go wok-wok."

Arrow stood. He saw that the stream he had just ascended had its source in a small glacier-fed pond. On its far side, a second stream drained into the valley, winding through it like a thread of silver. Abandoning the backpack, Arrow carried Nick in his arms around the pond and, when he came to the far stream, went down the grassy slope following its course. Small flowers dotted the meadows, purple heather, white alpine avens, and tufts of arctic cotton.

Arrow could not understand why it was summer. Why was the air warm? He stepped into the stream. Why was the water no longer freezing?

Then he jumped up and down in it, its crystal spray beading Nick and him to their waists.

Nick played his flute, and Arrow produced a small, perplexed chuckle.

"Jump, Awo, jump!"

Arrow jumped. Splash!

"Jumpster-dumpster, Nick!"

Splash, splash, splash! He hopped and skipped downstream, the pent-up laughter deep inside the ocean beds of his heart agitating and rising, erupting finally from his lips. He laughed in childish delight, tears streaming down his face, pain and joy intermingled, relief and hope flooding his eyes.

It was water! Sweet, warm water!

It was like holding the wheel of the *Osprey!*

It was like plunging into a pool where red fish swim and pebbles laugh!

It was sea shells on mountaintops and cities under oceans!

It was water above and water below—fish water and star water!

It was Jesus water!

He sloshed to the bank of the stream and plunked down on the grass, leaving his feet dangling in the shallows. He rested there for a time, he and Nick smiling at each other. Long shadows moved across the side of the valley.

Sheep bells *ting-tanged* faintly in the distance. Arrow whipped his head in their direction. The sound came from beyond a stand of yellow-leafed poplar farther downstream. Arrow stood and walked cautiously toward it, Nick in his arms.

"Shhh, Nick, shhh!"

"Shhh, Awo."

Low voices could be heard through the trees, mingled with *ting-tanging* sheep bells. Arrow crouched down behind some blueberry bushes and parted the branches.

A man and a woman were there, looking away, watching a flock of thirty or forty sheep that were nibbling grass in a dip of the meadow. The man was seated on a rock, reading aloud from a book. The woman stood beside him, her arms folded, listening.

Arrow crept closer.

The man was neither young nor old. The woman had long brown hair. She was young.

Fragments of words drifted into the copse where Arrow and Nick hid.

"And when the thousand years are ended", the man said, hunching over the book, rocking slightly.

Arrow crept closer, inching forward on his knees, trying not to crackle the twigs of the bushes. The man's voice was slow and faltering, as if he did not know how to read very well.

"And when the thousand years are ended, Satan will be loosed from his prison and will come out to deceive the nations which are at the ends of the four corners of the earth, that is, Gog and Magog, to gather them for battle. Their number is like the sand of the sea."

The woman knelt down beside the man and flipped a page for him.

"And they marched up over the broad earth", the man went on, "and surrounded the camp of the saints and the beloved city; but fire came down from heaven and consumed them, and the devil who had deceived them was thrown into the lake of fire and brimstone where the beast and the false prophet were, and they will be tormented day and night for ever and ever."

The man shook his head.

"What are you thinking, Joseph?" the woman asked.

"I am thinking a worrisome thing. I am thinking, will we too be surrounded? Will they find us?"

"We are hidden under the two hearts. Have you not felt the grace of this haven?"

"Yes. But will it last until the end of things?"

"No one knows the day or the hour, nor have any unlocked the mystery of the times, for such is the Father's will. Even among the beloved there are differing views. Some say a thousand years until the very end, others say three and a half years, some search the skies daily."

"Yet he is near."

The woman placed a hand on the man's shoulder, reached over to the book, and flipped the pages.

"Read this", she said.

"When the dragon saw that it had been thrown down to earth, it pursued the woman who had given birth to the male child. But the woman was given two wings of the great eagle, so that she could fly to her place in the desert, where, far from the serpent, she was taken care of for a year, two years, and a half year."

"Be at peace, Joseph", said the woman. "For just as the Woman of Revelation is taken care of, so will we be protected."

"Many will suffer", the man said sadly.

"Yes, many will bear witness with their blood. But some will die in peace before the worst of the calamities, and others will be hidden in the shelter of the rock."

Arrow closed the branches, but a twig slipped from his hands and brushed Nick's cheek. Startled, Nick jumped and piped loudly, "Awo!"

The man and the woman turned around and stared at the copse of trees.

Arrow crouched low.

The woman stood up.

She walked to the edge of the trees. "It's all right. You can come out."

Arrow stood up with Nick in his arms.

The woman looked at them with great love. Her face was dark brown. Her dress was pale blue, threadbare, and patched.

"Come out", she said. "You have nothing to fear."

Trembling, Arrow carried Nick out of the trees and stopped at the edge of the meadow. The man got up from his rock and walked toward them. He came up beside the woman and looked down at the boys, measuring them with his eyes.

"This is Joseph", the woman said. "I am Kateri."

She touched Nick's cheek with her hand. "Who are you?"

"His name's Nick", Arrow answered.

"Welcome, Nick."

Nick bounced up and down, grinning, eyes flashing.

"And who are you?" the woman asked, gazing at Arrow.

"My name's Arrow", he mumbled.

The woman looked deep into his eyes. "No," she said gently, "your name is Aaron."

* * *

The man gazed at the sky and said, "The sun is setting. I'd better get the sheep into the paddock." Kateri nodded and reached for Nick. Nick leaned forward, offering his tiny hands, and let himself be taken into her arms.

Joseph went on ahead, walking a wide circle around the sheep, whistling to them. The sheep looked up, shook their bells, and began to flock together as they ambled down the bowl of the meadow.

The valley bent in the middle, exposing the eastern slopes to the last of the light. On the lee side of the bend, they entered a thick stand of spruce. A narrow trail began here; cut into the sod by the countless feet of sheep and men, it wound through the trees toward the edge of the western wall of the valley. High cliffs rose up to the snow fields, which glowed mauve and blue above the timberline. Farther on, the trail petered out in a clearing. Tucked inside the surrounding trees were many small cabins, some made of logs, others of stone. Smoke came from their chimneys. Amber light spilled from windows and open doorways. Children played in the yards. In the heart of the village was a stone church, and the sound of singing came from it.

In front of a hut, an old man was chopping firewood. Two youths were stacking the split wood. The old man wore a checkered bush jacket. On his head sat a peaked wool cap; pinned to his chest was a red badge shaped like a heart. When he saw Joseph and Kateri approaching with two little boys, he straightened, leaned the axe on the chopping block, and looked at them curiously. He was a very short man, and his face was so brown it was almost black. The teenage boy beside him was taller, about thirteen years old, unkempt blond hair shooting out from under his tuque. The other child, a girl of about eleven years, was winded and ruddy-cheeked from exertion, gold braids falling over her shoulders.

As the little boys approached, the old native man stared hard, and his eyes narrowed with emotion, for the face of the walking boy was the face of Nathaniel Delaney.

In this way was Aaron Nathaniel, an arrow in the bow of the Lord, gathered in among them, and was known, and was finally home.

Epilogue

AND SO, children, we come to the part of the tale in which you live. There are so many things to say about those times, but your parents can tell you much of it.

After the darkness, there came light. After the desolation, there came fruitfulness. The Church leapt out of the tomb, as she has done from the beginning. In the year after the darkness, more priests wandered out of the desert, bringing with them their burned companions. The remnant, they called themselves. A bishop came in the fourth year, wearing a tattered woolen robe, carrying a crudely carved shepherd's staff. When he found us, he burst into tears, fell to the ground, and kissed it, thanking God for giving him a flock. He now lives in Corpus Christi, a village forty-five miles to the southwest, which is the seat of his diocese. He will return on the Feast of Divine Mercy for confirmations. He has been given a horse but prefers to walk, saying that he likes to remember the time he found us, for he had wandered alone in the burned lands before that day, believing everything had been destroyed.

Our village is called Sursum Corda—Lift Up Your Hearts. The light is always with us. The radiant light of the Presence. The heart of the Mother is also with us. The earth has been cleansed of demons, and we have been freed to be what we were intended to be. The scorched earth was enriched by the burning and produces three crops a year. The seasons have changed, and the path of the sun. The winters are now warmer.

Rarely have we seen snow, and then only for a day or two; it is swiftly gone, leaving its gift of delight.

Kateri and Joseph were with us for many years. They were the mother and the father of the people. In the later years they moved slowly about the village with the assistance of walking sticks. They rose early each morning, hours before dawn, to kneel in adoration in the church; they spent much of each day there. With patient care they tended their vegetables and flowers and the flocks of children who were soon born to us. Joseph died of pneumonia last spring, and he too is missed, icon of the Father that he was for us. He is buried beside my great-grandfather, Thaddaeus Tobac.

My sister, Zöe, is a grandmother and lives with her husband in a village seventeen miles to the north. I visit her often. She has told me many fine things about my father. I have told her the good things about our mother. Her community is called God Prepares. My brother, Tyler, is a priest and is an assistant to the bishop. It is thought by many that the Holy Spirit will choose him to be the next shepherd of the flock when the bishop dies.

Nicolo Piccolo was with us for a few years during the period when we built the village on the mountain. He was ever a joy to us, filled with wisdom and grace. Many a heart did he raise with his love and his need for love. When he died in his thirty-third year, all the people grieved—and rejoiced. We raised a white stone over his grave, and from the day of his burial many healings took place at the site of his resting place. We never learned anything about his origins, his parents, his name—nothing. He was always Nicolo Piccolo to us, for his heart was like a high and beautiful instrument, a reed of God, infecting us with his peculiar joy. You, the young, did not know him, and yet you know him, for he has left his mark on each of us. He is called Nicholas in the annals of the kingdom.

Each year on his feast day, I go out to the cliffs that overlook the desert and watch the sun rise. I sit with my legs hanging over the abyss, and I raise my arms to heaven. I thank the Lord for sending us such a one as he. I talk with my old friend, though, of course, I hear no reply. I see him in the dart of swallows that are nesting in the cleft of the rock and in the waves of gold that pour over the horizon, and I hear him in the wind. I recall how he used to raise his small, deformed arms to me.

"Lift me up, Aaron", he would say in his piping voice. "Hold me, Aaron."

Each year I celebrate a private dialogue in my memory; the fragments unite, and I am there again in the Palace of Junque.

"Dumpster boy, jumpster boy", I cry, hearing his burbling laughter in reply.

"Guh bluh, Awo!" he says, making me smile at the landscape of disaster.

I recall the exact words but revise our conversations, saying to him the things I would have said had I known the full measure of him.

"I love you, Nicolo. I love you."

"Play, Aaron, play!" he shouts in his wise baby voice.

"Teach us joy, teach us joy!" I reply.

And then, I feel myself lifted: he the parent and I the deformed child. He raises me up out of the rusty shopping cart of my self, and I am held.

What can I tell you about the dark years? What can I say that would be of use to you? I have told you my story. That is the way it was. In those days we could not see the true shape of things, for we were covered by the great shadow that lay over the end of time. We had delayed our battle with it, century after century. When it came at last, we did not recognize it, for we were inside it.

The shadow has now passed. The eclipse of the sun is finished. We have lived through the end of things and come to a new beginning. There, beyond the islands of green, in the burned lands that are still sleeping, the crocus and the jonquil are returning. Soon the villages and the fields will spread and unite. Time passes so swiftly. Memory fades. Man falls into disremembering. You did not see what we saw. You do not understand when we speak of it.

Do not forget, children. Do not forget.

Author's Afterword

A novel is an imaginative rendering of the world in a form that attempts to make the dizzying complexities of life more intelligible. The novelist selects from the rampant undergrowth of details that compose the texture of everyday life, that crowd our minds and can easily blur our vision. If he selects well, he enables his reader to focus and thus to see more clearly the shape of reality—as one of my characters says, "seeing the form".

When the subject matter is apocalyptic, the risks are high, for the genre is charged with emotional and ideological conflict. Who among us does not bring to such a tale his intuitions and denials, his fears and hopes? It is important to remember in this regard that a truly Catholic "end-times" novel does not so much attempt to predict the future as it strives to raise the essential questions that must be asked by every generation. Thus, it is not my intention to leave the reader with a neat package; it is rather my hope that the reader will take away from this book a heightened sense of awareness and a number of urgent questions: Are we living in the decisive moment of history? How dire is our situation? Have we exaggerated, or have we underestimated, the seriousness of the present crisis? Do we live in pessimistic dread, or facile optimism, or a Christian realism founded on hope?

We are familiar with the widespread undermining of moral absolutes in law and politics, the many attempts to compromise the Church from within and without, and the media mesmerism that captivates the minds of so many people. These I have woven into *Eclipse of the Sun* as part of the "ordinary" background noise that saturates our lives. Regarding more specific developments, several of the ominous events reenacted in the novel have already occurred: the State's abduction of children from healthy families, the paraliturgy in an unnamed diocese, the exhibition of blasphemous art works in public galleries, media blackout of news, globalist conferences at which the forced elimination of a portion of mankind is discussed as a reasonable option, the meeting in Calgary regarding concentration camps on our own soil, and numerous other details—details that would have been unthinkable when I was a youth but that have risen around us so gradually that we have come to think of them as normal.

Although they compose a significant part of the fabric of the current social situation, we do not yet know if they are symptomatic of a larger and possibly terminal illness. Only by hindsight will we be able to know how serious a threat they posed to the right order of society, to our freedoms and responsibilities. If this literary speculation is proved wrong, there will be no one happier about it than I. If it is proved right, there will be no history to recount what happened, to tell us who we were and what we might have been.

Michael O'Brien
Feast of the Archangels
September 29, 1997

Other novels in the *Children of the Last Days* series:

A Cry of Stone *
Strangers and Sojourners
Plague Journal *
Eclipse of the Sun
Sophia House *
Father Elijah

* Asterisks indicate titles that are forthcoming.